THE
PENGUIN BOOK
OF GAY SHORT
STORIES

THE

PENGUIN BOOK

OF GAY SHORT

STORIES

~ ~ ~ ~ ~ ~ ~

Edited by
David Leavitt and Mark Mitchell

INTRODUCTION BY
DAVID LEAVITT

VIKING

VIKING
Published by the Penguin Group
Penguin Books USA Inc., 375 Hudson Street, New York, New York 10014, U.S.A.
Penguin Books Ltd, 27 Wrights Lane, London W8 5TZ, England
Penguin Books Australia Ltd, Ringwood, Victoria, Australia
Penguin Books Canada Ltd, 10 Alcorn Avenue, Toronto, Ontario, Canada M4V 3B2
Penguin Books (N.Z.) Ltd, 182-190 Wairau Road, Auckland 10, New Zealand

Penguin Books Ltd, Registered Offices:
Harmondsworth, Middlesex, England

First published in 1994 by Viking Penguin,
a division of Penguin Books USA Inc.

3 5 7 9 10 8 6 4 2

Copyright © David Leavitt and Mark Mitchell, 1994
Copyright © David Leavitt, 1994
Copyright © James Kirkup, 1994
Copyright © Larry Kramer, 1994
Copyright © David Plante, 1994
Copyright © Michael Cunningham, 1994
Copyright © Neil Bartlett, 1994
Copyright © Gary Glickman, 1994
Copyright © Christopher Coe, 1994
Copyright © Gerry Albarelli, 1994
All rights reserved

Pages 653–655 constitute an extension of this copyright page.

LIBRARY OF CONGRESS CATALOGING IN PUBLICATION DATA
Penguin book of gay short stories / edited by David Leavitt and Mark
Mitchell : with an introduction by David Leavitt.
p.   cm.
ISBN 0–670–85468–9
1. Gay men—Fiction. 2. Short stories, English. 3. Short
stories, American. 4. English fiction. 5. American fiction.
I. Leavitt, David. II. Mitchell, Mark.
PR1309.H57P46   1994
823'.010806642—dc20   93-1390

Printed in the United States of America
Set in Bembo   Designed by Brian Mulligan

To the heroes of the AIDS wars,
the fallen and the fighting

Acknowledgments

Several friends contributed to the construction of this anthology. Frances Kiernan pointed us to two stories—William Trevor's "Torridge" and Ann Beattie's "The Cinderella Waltz" —that we might otherwise have overlooked. At Penguin Books, Beena Kamlani, Tony Lacey, Ravi Mirchandani, and Dawn Seferian shepherded the book through its many phases of production and offered valuable editorial advice.

Finally, Michael Milley, our unfailingly congenial assistant on the project, deserves particular thanks not only for his acumen at negotiating permissions but for his extraordinary perceptiveness as a reader.

Contents

xii ~ Contents

Introduction

I

The first novel I ever read about gay men was called *The Lord Won't Mind.* I was sixteen at the time—1977—a high school junior growing up thirty miles south of San Francisco, in what was just becoming Silicon Valley. Palo Alto had a wonderful left-of-center bookstore in those days, which actually maintained a gay section—just a few shelves, yet I knew their contents by heart. *The Lord Won't Mind,* by Gordon Merrick, caught my attention because its cover, on which two radiantly handsome blond men stared longingly into each other's eyes, suggested what seemed to me a promising combination of erotic heat and practical information. So I bought the book, slipping the copy I'd chosen between two innocuous magazines in case I ran into someone I knew on the trip from the gay section to the cash register. What I feared, peculiarly, was being obliged to confess an identity to which my libido had already made an unwavering commitment. No one saw me, however. Now I wish someone had.

Today, *The Lord Won't Mind* is out of print. Turning up a copy took me ages, but I finally found one. The story concerns Charlie, just out of Princeton, and Peter, just about to start Princeton, who are brought together by a wealthy woman of large gestures called C. B. Both are blond, rock-hard, stunningly handsome. In the first chapter Charlie seduces Peter by parading in front of him in only a towel, then suggesting that Peter undress so that they can compare their bodies in order to deduce whether they might share clothes. This titillating striptease leads, of course, to the inevitable dropping of drawers, the revelation of male members "extended to [their] fullest limits before actual erection, prodigious but blameless." The words "cock," "fuck," "suck," are never used; Merrick's pornography is insistently polite, even highbrow—just like his Princetonian protagonists. "Before the staggering fact of Peter at last revealed," Merrick writes, "Charlie thought for an instant that he had been surpassed. A quick glance for comparison reassured him. It was more slender than his and an inch or two shorter, just the way Charlie would have wished it, but without threatening his supremacy."

What was my reaction to all this? Hot arousal, most certainly. And in the aftermath of hot arousal, bewilderment. Finally, after judicious effort, I had located a work of fiction that described the "first time" experience I suspected (hoped) I would someday have. And yet this tale of bronzed gods with erections the size of tennis ball cans disturbed me as well. Was sex between men, I wondered, the exclusive property of the beautiful, the muscular, the superhuman?

Of course I didn't know anything then about the history of the way gay men have been portrayed, both in literature and in film: the history of the lisping twit and the oleaginous villain. Nor did I understand how Merrick and other homosexual writers of the early seventies, energized by Stonewall and the evolving gay liberation movement, might have found this sort of glorification of the male body both invigorating and celebratory. Growing up near San Francisco, I knew nothing of what was going on *in* San Francisco. I knew only that I longed to read a novel in which the gay characters were neither reduced to a subhuman nor elevated to a superhuman level. Instead I wanted to read a novel that told something like the truth.

Dancer from the Dance, by Andrew Holleran, was the second novel about gay men I read. This was a serious work of literature, even though it had a racy cover. The novel followed the progress of a beautiful young man named Malone as he explores the neon-lit underworld of gay Manhattan in the late seventies: a decadent, sex-soaked, drunken, clothes-conscious orgy of a culture. The story is told in a voice that is literate, thoughtful, occasionally gothic, with distinct Southern twangs. (The ghosts of Tennessee Williams and Truman Capote hover in the white space.) It horrified me in ways the cartoon porn-boys in *The Lord Won't Mind* never could have. Here is a scene that exemplifies why.

An old queen called Sutherland is leading an innocent boy—an ephebe—on a sort of tour of the gay underworld. (Remember the song "Disco Inferno"?) The boy sees a man with whom he falls instantly in love. "Who is that?" he asks.

"His name is Alan Solis, he has *huge* balls and does public relations work for Pan Am. . . . I used to be in love with Alan Solis, when I came to New York. I was so in love with him . . . that when he used the bathroom on the train to Sayville, I used to go in right after him and lock the door, just to smell his farts! To simply breathe the gas of his very bowels!"

"You know," said the boy, bending over as if in pain, his eyes on Alan Solis with all the intensity of a mongoose regarding a snake, "if I can only find a flaw. If I can find a flaw in someone, then it's not so bad, you know? But that boy seems to be perfect!" he said. "Oh, God, it's terrible!" And he put a hand to his forehead, stricken by that deadliest of forces, Beauty.

"A flaw, a flaw," said Sutherland, dropping his ash into the ashtray on his left, "I understand perfectly."

"If I can just see a flaw, then it's not so hopeless and depressing," said the boy, his face screwed up in agony, even though Solis, talking to a short, muscular Italian whom he wanted to take home that night, was completely oblivious to this adoring fan whose body was far too thin to interest him.

"I've got it," said Sutherland, who turned to his companion now. "I remember a flaw. His chest," he said, "his chest is so hairy that one can't really see the deep, chiseled indentation between the breasts. Will that do, darling?"

The boy gnawed on his lip and considered.

"I'm afraid it will have to. There isn't a thing else wrong with the man, other than the fact that he knows it."

Chilly perfection. Inaccessibility. Disinterest. Were the only choices for gay men, I wondered, either to exude or suffer from these unpleasant qualities? There is irony in Holleran's vision, of course, but I wasn't wise to it then; it didn't occur to me that he might, in some subtle way, have been mocking the exclusive mating rituals that characterized gay male life in American urban centers in the seventies. (It is easier than one might think to mock and romanticize simultaneously.) Instead I saw only, and with a kind of ashen horror, my future, or what I feared my future was going to amount to: relegation to some marginal role in a world where supermen possessed of almost blinding physical perfection preen, parade, ignore, dismiss. Seventies gay male culture did not have very much patience for the ugly man, the old man, the man with a small dick or a potbelly or no hair on his head. (It has only slightly more these days.) According to *Dancer from the Dance* and *The Lord Won't Mind,* only the most exceptionally beautiful among gay men were entitled to erotic fulfillment. The rest of us, it seemed, had no choice but to salivate in the wings, or at best, try and buy our way in.

A tendency to romanticize rejection—to romanticize the very farts deposited into the air by the object of idealization—characterizes Robert Ferro's *The Family of Max Desir* as well. (This book I read considerably later, when I had just graduated from college.) Here the author's obsession with the physical beauty of his hero—even his name suggests what he is the object of—overwhelms the eponymous family: the novel would be better titled *Desiring Max Desir.* For instance, in a long flashback, Ferro recalls Max's arrest in Florence after he makes a pass at a plainclothes policeman. Max ends up in jail, where he meets Nick Flynn, who becomes his lover. As in *The Lord Won't Mind,* their budding relationship is helped along by a rich, theatrically self-dramatizing woman, this time an Italian named Lydia. Older men constantly fall for one or another of the pair; indeed, their beauty is such that at one point it quite literally kills an elderly monsignor who loves "angels as they appeared in the form of young boys":

It had been his heart, concerning which this was the last of several incidents, but it seemed at the time, to Nick and Max, to be *them.* What strains had they put on the old man's failing health? Not that they had ever spent a moment alone with him, or thought of it. But it was death at close range, the first for either of them. And it seemed, like so much in their lives—as for instance their meeting in prison—to have some larger meaning. This impression was further developed a few weeks later when the host of a similar weekend house party, at which Lydia was not a guest, just as suddenly dropped dead, this time not actually in their presence but very soon after leaving it.

Talk about looks that kill! But as the novel progresses, the dreamlike tone of the Italian section gives way to a grittier American realism; more important, Ferro finally gets down to the subject at hand, namely Max's relationship with his father, John, particularly after his mother, Marie, has died. Nonetheless Max's erotic obsessiveness routinely intrudes on the family drama that is the novel's ostensible centerpiece, as in this scene, in which Max and his father fly to Vermont to supervise the construction of Marie's tombstone:

> They drove to the airport, left the car in the lot, and had breakfast after checking in. A man behind the counter in the coffee shop was one of the most beautiful Max had ever seen. It was implausible that such a being had not conquered films, Seventh Avenue, or the Sultan of Oman, but was instead breaking eggs at La Guardia Marine. John did not notice. The man smiled back at Max. His was a body reserved for the transubstantiation of visiting angels, with the same perfect evenness, proportion and symmetry found in the beautiful face. . . . While Max ate his breakfast John read the paper. The counterman had arranged the bacon on Max's plate in the shape of a question mark.

Unlike *Dancer from the Dance, The Family of Max Desir* isn't *about* its hero's (or its author's) obsession with male beauty. Instead it's that rarity: a novel in which a gay man plays an integral role in the unfolding drama of family life. But the obsession with male beauty *is* a constant and intrusive element here. What I found myself longing for, as I read the book, was a gay literature that, rather than fawning over angels made flesh, transformed homosexual experience into human drama; a gay literature that was literature first and gay second. Yes, writers might constantly be distracted by the sight of pretty boys behind breakfast counters; they could afford to be distracted; a work of literature cannot.

I had a conversation with a twenty-one-year-old friend of mine recently. When I told him I was planning to take on some sacred cows in this essay—most notably *Dancer from the Dance*—his response was swift and unhesitant: "Thank God someone's doing it," he said; "it's the first gay book most young American gay men read, and I can't think of another that's done as much damage." Damage is the key here: the voyeuristic fixation with beauty that powers the novel (and undermines *The*

Family of Max Desir) compels younger gay men who don't know better to wonder if that's all there is to the business of being gay, a question to which the answer is a resounding no (a no echoed by any number of lesser-known novels and stories). For contrary to popular opinion, most gay men *do* want more from their lives than a few decades spent panting after unattainable perfection; indeed, most want relationships based on spiritual as well as physical attraction, which grow more solid as the years go on. *Dancer from the Dance* romanticized—even exalted—what is to many of us the dreariest aspect of gay experience. (It is curious that its publication so vastly overshadowed the almost simultaneous appearance of Larry Kramer's *Faggots,* a novel that savagely satirized, even condemned, the very bars and discos, Fire Island beaches and popper-hazed back rooms, about which Holleran writes so lushly. Holleran exults in the romance of dark, smoky rooms; Kramer rudely shuts off the disco music, switches on the lights, and forces us to see things as they are.)

In those days, the gay section at the bookstore in Palo Alto didn't stock many books, and in retrospect, it's to the credit of that sadly defunct place that a gay section existed at all. I had little right to complain; in terms of liberal tolerance, northern California in the late seventies was paradise. Still, even the luckiest young gay men and lesbians are isolated; even in places where people tell you it's okay to be gay, you have to tell *them* you're gay first, and that's never easy. Unlike our heterosexual counterparts, for whom history, rituals of courtship, models for behavior, and codes of decorum are handed out daily in the classroom, we must seek out, furtively, some sense of our connection to official history, not to mention some sense of our own history, which by definition is discontinuous, a series of stops and starts that begins again each time a young gay man or lesbian sneaks his or her way to the gay section at a bookstore—if indeed there is a gay section; if indeed there is a bookstore. Well, in my case there was. And what was in it? *The Lord Won't Mind* and its endless interminable sequels. *The Front Runner* by Patricia Nell Warren. John Rechy's *The Sexual Outlaw* with its seedy "street" ambience and awkward neologisms ("youngman" as one word). *Dancer from the Dance.* What wasn't in it that should have been? For starters, *The Folded Leaf,* William Maxwell's seminal tale of love between teenage boys, published in the late forties. J. R. Ackerley's agonizingly honest autobiography, *My Father and Myself;* Sanford Friedman's *Totempole;* perhaps some of Forster's posthumously published gay stories. I knew about none of these books back then. I didn't even know about them in 1984, when in direct response to the dearth of decent gay literature that characterized my adolescence I started my own first novel, *The Lost Language of Cranes.* It took the intervention of my agent to point me toward *The Folded Leaf.* It took years more to dig out the other books I could have read when I was sixteen, instead of *The Lord Won't Mind* and *Dancer from the Dance.* Not that these books prettified or idealized gay experience—we are talking about nothing so simple as "positive role models"; but they told the truth. The men who inhabited them were recognizably human. And the impulse that fueled their creation was not the impulse to glorify or romanticize; it was the impulse to articulate the process by which gay men, in the words of E. M. Forster, go about "the prosecution of daily life."

One characteristic of most pre-eighties gay literature was the assumption that an irrevocable gulf existed between "them" and "us," the heterosexual and homosexual realms. Before *The Family of Max Desir,* few works of literature about gay men allowed for any nonhostile communication between the two. The gay underworld portrayed in Rechy's *City of Night* and *The Sexual Outlaw* or in films like *Nighthawks* and *Taxi zum Klo* existed as a kind of parallel universe with the straight world, a shadowland, if you will, where gay men by night led secret lives. Crucially, in these works night brought on the transformation not only of the men but of the world itself; a park where by day children played innocently becomes by night the scene of Bacchic frenzies. Few novels portrayed the option of freeing oneself from this double life; indeed, one of the only ones that did, *The Seraglio,* written in 1954 by the esteemed poet James Merrill, offered a protagonist who achieves liberation by means of an act of extraordinary violence: he slices off his own penis. Afterward, quite literally "cut off" from the heterosexual imperative his wealthy parents have demanded he obey, our hero reemerges a happy, bookish intellectual living in a brownstone in *louche* Greenwich Village. But at what cost?

Dancer from the Dance is an historic novel because its protagonists had freed themselves from the tyranny of this double life; they were made to suffer much more by each other than by heterosexual agents of oppression. The gay underworld thus gave way to the gay ghetto, where men held hands and kissed in public and dared the "public" to say a word about it. And at the time of its publication, all over the country, gay men

were urging each other to "come out of the closet," a misleading metaphor, since in those days coming out by definition seemed to require
vacating not only the closet but the house itself. To come out was not
merely to announce oneself, it was to change one's way of dressing, speaking, thinking; in many cases it required a literal relocation, to San Francisco's Castro district or New York's Greenwich Village or, in the
summer, to Fire Island, Provincetown, Key West. These neighborhoods
became meccas for gay men eager to live free, though not always un-
troubled by the knowledge that in joining their fellow "tribesmen" they
were, in effect, accepting residency in a realm that was separate and only
perhaps equal: a realm of bars and pornographic card shops and more bars
and more pornographic card shops. As Susan Sontag has succinctly put
it, in the 1970s "many male homosexuals reconstituted themselves as
something like an ethnic group, one whose distinctive folkloric custom
was sexual voracity, and the institutions of urban homosexual life became
a sexual delivery system of unprecedented speed, efficiency, and volume."
AIDS wasn't the only fallout; as Larry Kramer's prophetic novel *Faggots*
suggests, such a life-style can destroy souls as well as T-cells.

I remember, in the early eighties, standing on the brink of coming
out and being deterred not by fear of retribution so much as by fear of
the culture into which coming out seemed inevitably destined to thrust
me. Yes, I wanted to be openly gay; even so, my few forays into gay
New York left me shaken. This wasn't the world I wanted to live in,
and I saw no advertised alternatives. More important, I flinched at the
notion that coming out somehow meant that I would have not only to
reimagine myself totally but to cut off my ties to my family, my heterosexual friends—indeed, the totality of the world I'd grown up in. To do
so, it seemed to me, was to risk doing myself real psychic violence. Yes,
I was gay, but I was also Jewish, a Leavitt, a writer: so many other things!
Why should my sexual identity subsume all my other identities? I wondered. And then I saw the answer: because the world, the "straight"
world, the "normal" world, upon learning I was gay, would see me only
as gay; because ghettos are invented not by the people who live in them
but by the people who don't live in them. A new level of liberation
needed to be achieved, I decided then: one that would allow gay men
and lesbians to celebrate their identities without having to move into a
gulag.

II

What makes a "gay story" gay? This is a more complicated question than it may at first sound. Traditionally, anthologies of so-called gay fiction have collected stories by gay male writers writing about the lives of gay men. On the other hand, numerous gay male writers, both contemporary and historic, have written fiction that at least explicitly has nothing to do with the gay experience, even though it may exhibit a "gay sensibility" or "gay style" (two more problematic terms). Conversely, heterosexual writers sometimes write pieces of fiction that deal eloquently with the experience of gay men. What about them? And what about the thornier question of fiction by lesbians? The majority of gay anthologists have not only left lesbian work out entirely; they haven't even seen fit to apologize for the exclusion, which simply proves that sexism is as alive and well in the gay community as it is in the heterosexual community. On the other hand, limits must be agreed upon if an anthology is not to become so enormous as to defy publication. Some rules—arbitrary though they may be—must be set down.

For the purposes of this anthology, then, a gay story has been defined as one that illuminates the experience of love between men, explores the nature of homosexual identity, or investigates the kinds of relationships gay men have with each other, with their friends, and with their families. The sexuality of the author, according to this definition, is finally irrelevant, although obviously more gay men write about these topics than heterosexual men or women. The anthology limits itself to twentieth-century fiction written originally in English, simply because not imposing some sort of restriction would necessitate multiple volumes. (And indeed, a second anthology, of international gay writing, is currently in the works.) Lesbian fiction gets its own anthology: *The Penguin Book of Lesbian Short Stories,* edited by Margaret Reynolds. Finally, excerpts from longer narratives have been avoided wherever possible; there are only a very few in this anthology. The rest of the pieces are self-contained, autonomous works, most of which fit comfortably within the rubric of the traditional short story.

The anthology begins with a brief narrative of adolescent love, D. H. Lawrence's "A Poem of Friendship," published in 1911, and ends with a brief narrative of adolescent love, A. M. Homes's "The Whiz Kids," published in 1991. Comparing these two stories tells us a lot about how the lives of gay men have—and haven't—changed over the course of eighty years. In "A Poem of Friendship," for instance, the narrator and his beloved friend, George, swim and frolic, then dry off together:

He saw I had forgotten to continue my rubbing, and laughing he took hold of me and began to rub me briskly, as if I were a child, or rather, a woman he loved and did not fear. I left myself quite limply in his hands, and to get a better grip of me, he put his arm round me and pressed me against him, and the sweetness of the touch of our naked bodies one against the other was superb. It satisfied in some measure the vague, indecipherable yearning of my soul; and it was the same with him. When he had rubbed me all warm, he let me go, and we looked at each other with eyes of still laughter, and our love was perfect for a moment, more perfect than any love I have known since, either for man or woman.

Likewise, in "The Whiz Kids," the narrator and his friend (unnamed) take a bath together:

In the big bathtub in my parents' bedroom, he ran his tongue along my side, up into my armpits, tugging the hair with his teeth. "We're like married," he said, licking my nipples.

I spit at him. A foamy blob landed on his bare chest. He smiled, grabbed both my arms, and held them down.

He slid his face down toward my stomach, dipped it under the water, and put his mouth over my cock.

My mother knocked on the bathroom door. "I have to get ready. Your father and I are leaving in twenty minutes."

. . . Later, in the den, picking his nose, examining the results on his finger, slipping his finger into his mouth with a smack and a pop, he explained that as long as we never slept with anyone else, we could do whatever we wanted. "Sex kills," he said, "but this," he said, "this is the one time, the only time, the chance of a life time." He ground his front teeth on the booger.

The changes aren't only in the vernacular. In comparison to Lawrence, Homes's narration of "The Whiz Kids" is shockingly direct, even pornographic. There's no apologizing here, no prettying up for the sake of the uninitiated or faint of heart. More crucially, by 1991 AIDS has entered the picture. These sophisticated boys know that what they're experiencing together—sex free of complication, not to mention the threat of death—is something they can never again experience in their lives.

Still, both these stories are about first love and, as such, heart-stopping in their sweetness. In both, erotic discovery germinates in the fertile innocence of water, under the watchful eye of parents who would never suspect such ideas to be entering their sons' heads. In the watering hole or the warm, soapy rinse of the womblike tub, among rubber ducks and bubble bath and towels and other children, desire discovers itself, boys discover each other. That Homes is a woman only adds to our sense of simultaneous mystification and delight.

In between these two stories there is every imaginable kind of gay story, written by every imaginable kind of writer. Some are already famous—Isherwood's "Sally Bowles," Allan Gurganus's "Adult Art." Then there are the surprises. Noël Coward? you may ask. My coeditor on this project, Mark Mitchell, turned up that one, an elegant and moving story about a gay man who has spent most of his life shepherding a group of showgirls around the world, and a joyous discovery for many reasons, not least of which is its portrayal of gay men in long-term relationships —something rare in those days. By contrast, J. R. Ackerley's "My Father and Myself" (excerpted here) features the author's rigorously honest appraisal of, among other things, his own unfortunate tendency toward "sexual incontinence," as well as speculation that a sailor lover might have left him because Ackerley attempted to perpetrate upon him an act of sexual congress considered in those days and in that place shocking, even though it has become in these days and this place utterly commonplace. (This is, incidentally, one of several works included here that challenge the traditional definition of "fiction": while neither novel nor story, "My Father and Myself" reimagines—rather than reports—experience; as such, it is fiction, to our view.) William Trevor's "Torridge" is another surprise, primarily because its author, while generally recognized as a contemporary master of the short story, is not remotely gay. Still, he has crafted an incendiary tale about hypocrisy at an English boys' school, a story that articulates more forcefully and effectively than any I can name the anger so many British gay men often feel toward those institutions that silently encourage homosexual behavior while simultaneously condemning homosexual identity.

There are, in these stories, gay parents (Ann Beattie's "The Cinderella Waltz"), as well as gay children (Peter Cameron's "Jump or Dive," Christopher Coe's "Gentlemen Can Wash Their Hands in the Gents' "). The discoveries of the young (David Plante's "The Princess from Africa," William Maxwell's "The Folded Leaf," Richard McCann's "My Mother's Clothes") elbow the consolations of the middle-aged and old (Edmund White's "Reprise," John Cheever's "Falconer," Larry Kramer's "Mrs. Tefillin"). And the tragedy of AIDS is evoked in all its splendor and terror by writers as diverse as Michael Cunningham, Dennis McFarland, the late Allen Barnett, and the New Zealand writer Peter Wells. As a subcategory, these stories constitute, it seems to me, the best collection of AIDS literature yet written. It is hard to emerge from Barnett's Fire Island unshaken, just as it is impossible to forget the erotic games played by the men in Stephen Greco's "Good with Words," for whom the threat of HIV infection turns out to be the source of surprising arousal. Nothing easy here, nothing status quo or correct; most defiantly not the usual suspects. While most of these stories, moreover, are conventional in form, they are far from conventional in content. The traditional gay male distractions are avoided here; these writers have their fingers too firmly on the pulse of experience to waste time with any of that.

It's become common, over the last twenty years, for American gay people to think of themselves as constituting an ethnic group, a "tribe" (to borrow the language of the seventies) or a "queer nation" (to borrow the language of the eighties). Such thinking has transformed what was a sundry assortment of isolated, secretive individuals into a community capable of wielding real power, even in presidential elections. To envision homosexuality, however, as an ethnic identity is to risk forgetting that sexuality is an extremely individualistic business; that each gay man and lesbian is gay or lesbian in his or her own way. Literature confronts the perversity of individual experience. Its role has never been to promote or prescribe particular ways of being but rather to expose the fine tension that exists between the way people actually are and the way the culture they live in would have them be. Recognizing that nothing is actually wrong with us is an important and difficult step for gay men and lesbians, and one with which the complicated process of self-definition becomes irrevocably tangled. As long as the society we live in despises us as a group, we *are* a group, whether we like it or not.

Many people ask me if I consider myself a "gay writer." My answer is that the question is irrelevant; as long as the culture I live in considers me a gay writer—and it considers every writer who tackles gay subject matter a gay writer—I'm stuck with the title. My sexual identity will subsume all other aspects of my identity—I might be a "gay Jewish writer," never a "Jewish gay writer"—no matter how loudly I protest. The same people also ask, with annoying frequency, why I always write about gay characters, which I don't. Well, I answer, if I were John Updike, would you ask, "Mr. Updike, why do you always write about *heterosexual* characters?" They cough and get nervous. Because heterosexuality is the norm, writers have permission to explore its nuances without raising any eyebrows. To write about gay characters, by contrast, is always, necessarily, to make some sort of "statement" about the fact of being gay. Stories in which a character's homosexuality is, as it were, "beside the point" confuse us: why bring it up? asks the writing teacher in our heads. Similarly, reviewers complain about books in which too many characters are gay. (Does anyone complain about too many characters in *Rabbit, Run* being straight?) The problem is that this kind of thinking gets into our heads; we begin to believe that the sexuality of our characters really does define them. Which may be why E. M. Forster, at the height of his career, chose to give up publishing fiction. On the one hand he longed to write stories and novels about homosexual experience. Wouldn't doing so, however, have reduced the illustrious author of *A Passage to India,* at least in the eyes of the public, to a kind of literary sideshow freak—the male Radclyffe Hall? Lucky for us, he continued writing; but his gay stories—one of which is included here—were not published until after his death.

These are stories that present the problem of sexual identity in all its individualistic complexity, while at the same time exploring the dilemma of living as part of a minority, in which what distinguishes each member isn't anything so explicit as eye shape or skin color but rather a sexual tendency that becomes visible only when we (or someone else) choose to call attention to it. At the same time, like all good works of literature, they do not attempt to answer questions so much as to amplify, convolute, elaborate them; their purpose is not to solve a mystery but to illuminate its parameters. Finally, they resist mightily the impulse to reduce gay experience to a set of clichés: what we as individuals are supposed to be as opposed to what we are. One hopes a reader will reach the last page having learned a few things, chief among them just how much of a mistake it is to draw conclusions about other people's lives.

That non-gay writers have agreed to be included in an anthology with a title like this surprises me and does my heart good. I'm reminded of a performance I saw a few years back by the artist Holly Hughes. This was during the frightening days when the American right wing, led by Senator Jesse Helms, was attempting to use the National Endowment for the Arts as a weapon in its never-ending battle against sexual self-expression. A diverse group of writers, singers, and performers—myself and Hughes among them—had gotten together to raise money for Harvey Gantt, the senatorial candidate opposing Helms. Hughes was announced, but she did not appear; instead a young man and woman strode onto the stage, identified themselves as "a fag" and "a dyke," and informally polled the audience. Would everyone who was gay please stand up? the young woman asked. Nervously, about a quarter of us did so. And now, the young man said, would everyone who does not consider him or herself to be gay but *has* slept with a member of the same sex stand up? A few more people stood, reluctantly. We were then instructed to sit down again. Now the young man and woman reminded us about what had happened in Denmark during World War II; how the king of Denmark, hearing that his Jewish subjects would be compelled to wear yellow stars, himself donned a yellow star; how indeed most Danes wore yellow stars, so that the Jews could not be distinguished from the non-Jews. Presumably everyone in the audience—given the evening's purpose—must have caught the allusion; I can't believe they failed to. And now, the young woman said, remembering what happened in Denmark, I ask you again: would all of you in the audience who are gay stand up?

About three quarters of the people there did. As for the others, they remained in their seats, eyes grim and steadfast, clutching their armrests as if for dear life.

THE

PENGUIN BOOK

OF GAY SHORT

STORIES

~ *D. H. Lawrence* ~

A
Poem of
Friendship

The magnificent promise of spring was broken before the May-blossom was fully out. All through the beloved month the wind rushed in upon us from the north and northeast, bringing the rain fierce and heavy. The tender-budded trees shuddered and moaned; when the wind was dry, the young leaves flapped limp. The grass and corn grew lush, but the light of the dandelions was quite extinguished, and it seemed that only a long time back had we made merry before the broad glare of these flowers. The bluebells lingered and lingered; they fringed the fields for weeks like purple fringe of mourning. The pink campions came out, only to hang heavy with rain; hawthorn buds remained tight and hard as pearls, shrinking into the brilliant green foliage; the forget-me-nots, the poor pleiades of the wood, were ragged weeds. Often at the end of the day, the sky opened, and stately clouds hung over the horizon infinitely far away, glowing, through the yellow distance, with an amber lustre. They never came any nearer, always they remained far off, looking calmly and majestically over the shivering earth, then, saddened, fearing their radiance might be dimmed, they drew away, and sank out of sight. Some-

---

D. H. LAWRENCE will probably be best remembered for such novels as Women in Love, The Rainbow, *and* Sons and Lovers. *"A Poem of Friendship" is from Lawrence's first book,* The White Peacock. *Readers interested in further examples of homoeroticism in Lawrence's work should have a look at his story "The Prussian Soldier."*

times, towards sunset, a great shield stretched dark from the west to the zenith, tangling the light along its edges. As the canopy rose higher, it broke, dispersed, and the sky was primrose coloured, high and pale above the crystal moon. Then the cattle crouched among the gorse, distressed by the cold, while the long-billed snipe flickered round high overhead, round and round in great circles, seeming to carry a serpent from its throat, and crying a tragedy, more painful than the poignant lamentations and protests of the peewits. Following these evenings came mornings cold and grey.

Such a morning I went up to George, on the top fallow. His father was out with the milk—he was alone; as I came up the hill I could see him standing in the cart, scattering manure over the bare red fields; I could hear his voice calling now and then to the mare, and the creak and clank of the cart as it moved on. Starlings and smart wagtails were running briskly over the clods, and many little birds flashed, fluttered, hopped here and there. The lapwings wheeled and cried as ever between the low clouds and the earth, and some ran beautifully among the furrows, too graceful and glistening for the rough field.

I took a fork and scattered the manure along the hollows, and thus we worked, with a wide field between us, yet very near in the sense of intimacy. I watched him through the wheeling peewits, as the low clouds went stealthily overhead. Beneath us, the spires of the poplars in the spinney were warm gold, as if the blood shone through. Further gleamed the grey water, and below it the red roofs. Nethermere was half hidden, and far away. There was nothing in this grey, lonely world but the peewits swinging and crying, and George swinging silently at his work. The movement of active life held all my attention, and when I looked up, it was to see the motion of his limbs and his head, the rise and fall of his rhythmic body, and the rise and fall of the slow waving peewits. After a while, when the cart was empty, he took a fork and came towards me, working at my task.

It began to rain, so he brought a sack from the cart, and we crushed ourselves under the thick hedge. We sat close together and watched the rain fall like a grey striped curtain before us, hiding the valley; we watched it trickle in dark streams off the mare's back, as she stood dejectedly; we listened to the swish of the drops falling all about; we felt the chill of the rain, and drew ourselves together in silence. He smoked his pipe, and I lit a cigarette. The rain continued; all the little pebbles and the red earth glistened in the grey gloom. We sat together, speaking occasionally. It was at these times we formed the almost passionate attachment which later years slowly wore away.

When the rain was over, we filled our buckets with potatoes, and went along the wet furrows, sticking the spritted tubers in the cold ground. Being sandy, the field dried quickly. About twelve o'clock, when nearly all the potatoes were set, he left me and, fetching up Bob from the far hedge-side, harnessed the mare and him to the ridger, to cover the potatoes. The sharp light plough turned the soil in a fine furrow over the potatoes; hosts of little birds fluttered, settled, bounded off again after the plough. He called to the horses, and they came downhill, the white stars on the two brown noses nodding up and down, George striding firm and heavy behind. They came down upon me; at a call the horses turned, shifting awkwardly sideways; he flung himself against the plough and, leaning well in, brought it round with a sweep: a click, and they are off uphill again. There is a great rustle as the birds sweep round after him and follow up the new-turned furrow. Untackling the horses when the rows were all covered, we tramped behind them down the wet hillside to dinner.

I kicked through the drenched grass, crushing the withered cowslips under my clogs, avoiding the purple orchids that were stunted with harsh upbringing but magnificent in their powerful colouring, crushing the pallid lady smocks, the washed-out wild gillivers. I became conscious of something near my feet, something little and dark, moving indefinitely. I had found again the larkie's nest. I perceived the yellow beaks, the bulging eyelids of two tiny larks, and the blue lines of their wing quills. The indefinite movement was the swift rise and fall of the brown fledged backs, over which waved long strands of fine down. The two little specks of birds lay side by side, beak to beak, their tiny bodies rising and falling in quick unison. I gently put down my fingers to touch them; they were warm; gratifying to find them warm, in the midst of so much cold and wet. I became curiously absorbed in them, as an eddy of wind stirred the strands of down. When one fledgling moved uneasily, shifting his soft ball, I was quite excited; but he nestled down again, with his head close to his brother's. In my heart of hearts, I longed for someone to nestle against, someone who would come between me and the coldness and wetness of the surroundings. I envied the two little miracles exposed to any tread, yet so serene. It seemed as if I were always wandering, looking for something which they had found even before the light broke into their shell. I was cold; the lilacs in the mill garden looked blue and perished. I ran with my heavy clogs and my heart heavy with vague longing, down to the mill, while the wind blanched the sycamores, and pushed the sullen pines rudely, for the pines were sulking because their million creamy sprites could not fly wet-winged. The horse-chestnuts bravely kept their white candles erect in the socket of every bough, though no sun came to light them. Drearily a cold swan swept up the water, trailing its black feet, clacking its great hollow wings, rocking the frightened water hens, and insulting the staid black-necked geese. What did I want that I turned thus from one thing to another?

~ ~ ~

At the end of June the weather became fine again. Hay harvest was to begin as soon as it settled. There were only two fields to be mown this year, to provide just enough stuff to last until the spring. As my vacation had begun, I decided I would help, and that we three, the father, George, and I, would get in the hay without hired assistance.

I rose the first morning very early, before the sun was well up. The clear sound of challenging cocks could be heard along the valley. In the bottoms, over the water and over the lush wet grass, the night mist still stood white and substantial. As I passed along the edge of the meadow the cow-parsnip was as tall as I, frothing up to the top of the hedge, putting the faded hawthorn to a wan blush. Little, early birds—I had not heard the lark—fluttered in and out of the foamy meadow-sea, plunging under the surf of flowers washed high in one corner, swinging out again, dashing past the crimson sorrel cresset. Under the froth of flowers were the purple vetch-clumps, yellow milk vetches, and the scattered pink of the wood-betony, and the floating stars of marguerites. There was a weight of honeysuckle on the hedges, where pink roses were waking up for their broad-spread flight through the day.

Morning silvered the swaths of the far meadow, and swept in smooth, brilliant curves round the stones of the brook; morning ran in my veins; morning chased the silver, darting fish out of the depth, and I, who saw them, snapped my fingers at them, driving them back.

I heard Trip barking, so I ran towards the pond. The punt was at the island, where from behind the bushes I could hear George whistling. I called to him, and he came to the water's edge half dressed.

"Fetch a towel," he called, "and come on."

I was back in a few moments, and there stood my Charon fluttering in the cool air. One good push sent us to the islet. I made haste to undress, for he was ready for the water, Trip dancing round, barking with excitement at his new appearance.

"He wonders what's happened to me," he said, laughing, pushing the dog playfully away with his bare foot. Trip bounded back, and came leaping up, licking him with little caressing licks. He began to play with the dog, and directly they were rolling on the fine turf, the laughing, expostulating, naked man and the excited dog, who thrust his great head onto the man's face, licking, and, when flung away, rushed forward again, snapping playfully at the naked arms and breasts. At last George lay back, laughing and panting, holding Trip by the two forefeet, which were planted on his breast, while the dog, also panting, reached forward his head for a flickering lick at the throat pressed back on the grass, and the mouth thrown back out of reach. When the man had thus lain still for a few moments, and the dog was just laying his head against his master's neck to rest too, I called, and George jumped up, and plunged into the pond with me, Trip after us.

The water was icily cold, and for a moment deprived me of my senses. When I began to swim, soon the water was buoyant, and I was sensible of nothing but the vigorous poetry of action. I saw George swimming on his back laughing at me, and in an instant I had flung myself like an impulse after him. The laughing face vanished as he swung over and fled, and I pursued the dark head and the ruddy neck. Trip, the wretch, came paddling towards me, interrupting me; then, all bewildered with excitement, he scudded to the bank. I chuckled to myself as I saw him run along, then plunge in and go plodding to George. I was gaining. He tried to drive off the dog, and I gained rapidly. As I came up to him and caught him, with my hand on his shoulder, there came a laughter from the bank. It was Emily.

I trod the water and threw handfuls of spray at her. She laughed and blushed. Then Trip waded out to her, and she fled swiftly from his shower-bath. George was floating just beside me, looking up and laughing.

We stood and looked at each other as we rubbed ourselves dry. He was well proportioned, and naturally of handsome physique, heavily limbed. He laughed at me, telling me I was like one of Aubrey Beardsley's long, lean ugly fellows. I referred him to many classic examples of slenderness, declaring myself more exquisite than his grossness, which amused him.

But I had to give in, and bow to him, and he took on an indulgent, gentle manner. I laughed and submitted. For he knew how I admired the noble, white fruitfulness of his form. As I watched him, he stood in white relief against the mass of green. He polished his arm, holding it out straight and solid; he rubbed his hair into curls, while I watched the deep muscles of his shoulders and the bands standing out in his neck as he held it firm; I remembered the story of Annable.

He saw I had forgotten to continue my rubbing, and laughing he took hold of me and began to rub me briskly, as if I were a child, or rather, a woman he loved and did not fear. I left myself quite limply in his hands, and to get a better grip of me, he put his arm round me and pressed me against him, and the sweetness of the touch of our naked bodies one against the other was superb. It satisfied in some measure the vague, indecipherable yearning of my soul; and it was the same with him. When he had rubbed me all warm, he let me go, and we looked at each other with eyes of still laughter, and our love was perfect for a moment, more perfect than any love I have known since, either for man or woman.

We went together down to the fields, he to mow the island of grass he had left standing the previous evening, I to sharpen the machine knife, to mow out the hedge-bottoms with the scythe, and to rake the swaths from the way of the machine when the unmown grass was reduced to a triangle. The cool, moist fragrance of the morning, the intentional stillness of everything, of the tall bluish trees, of the wet, frank flowers, of the trustful moths folded and unfolded in the fallen swaths, was a perfect medium of sympathy. The horses moved with a still dignity, obeying his commands. When they were harnessed, and the machine oiled, still he was looking loth to mar the perfect morning, but stood looking down the valley.

"I shan't mow these fields any more," he said, and the fallen, silvered swaths flickered back his regret, and the faint scent of the limes was wistful. So much of the field was cut, so much remained to cut; then it was ended. This year the elder flowers were widespread over the corner bushes, and the pink roses fluttered high above the hedge. There were the same flowers in the grass as we had known many years; we should not know them any more.

"But merely to have mown them is worth having lived for," he said, looking at me.

We felt the warmth of the sun trickling through the morning's mist of coolness.

"You see that sycamore," he said, "that bushy one beyond the big willow? I remember when father broke off the leading shoot because he wanted a fine straight stick, I can remember I felt sorry. It was running up so straight, with such a fine balance of leaves—you know how a young strong sycamore looks about nine feet high—it seemed a cruelty. When you are gone, and we are left from here, I shall feel like that, as if my leading shoot were broken off. You see, the tree is spoiled. Yet how it went on growing. I believe I shall grow faster. I can remember the bright red stalks of the leaves as he broke them off from the bough."

He smiled at me, half proud of his speech. Then he swung into the seat of the machine, having attended to the horses' heads. He lifted the knife.

"Good-bye," he said, smiling whimsically back at me. The machine started. The bed of the knife fell, and the grass shivered and dropped over. I watched the heads of the daisies and the splendid lines of the cocksfool grass quiver, shake against the crimson burnet, and drop over. The machine went singing down the field, leaving a track of smooth, velvet green in the way of the swath-board. The flowers in the wall of uncut grass waited unmoved, as the days wait for us. The sun caught in the up-licking scarlet sorrel flames, the butterflies woke, and I could hear the fine ring of his "Whoa!" from the far corner. Then he turned, and I could see only the tossing ears of the horses, and the white of his shoulder, as they moved along the wall of the high grass on the hill slope. I sat down under the elm, to file the sections of the knife. Always as he rode he watched the falling swath, only occasionally calling the horses into line. It was his voice which rang the morning awake. When we were at work we hardly noticed one another. Yet his mother had said:

"George is so glad when you're in the field—he doesn't care how long the day is."

Later, when the morning was hot, and the honeysuckle had ceased to breathe, and all the other scents were moving in the air about us, when all the field was down, when I had seen the last trembling ecstasy of the harebells, trembling to fall; when the thick clump of purple vetch had sunk; when the green swaths were settling, and the silver swaths were glistening and glittering as the sun came along them, in the hot ripe morning we worked together turning the hay, tipping over the yesterday's swaths with our forks, and bringing yesterday's fresh, hidden flowers into the death of sunlight.

It was then that we talked of the past, and speculated on the future. As the day grew older, and less wistful, we forgot everything, and worked on, singing, and sometimes I would recite him verses as we went, and sometimes I would tell him about books. Life was full of glamour for us both.

~ *E. M. Forster* ~

Arthur
Snatchfold

1

Conway (Sir Richard Conway) woke early, and went to the window to have a look at the Trevor Donaldsons' garden. Too green. A flight of mossy steps led up from the drive to a turfed amphitheatre. This contained a number of trees of the lead-pencil persuasion, and a number of flower-beds, profuse with herbaceous promises which would certainly not be fulfilled that weekend. The summer was heavy-leaved and at a moment between flowerings, and the gardener, though evidently expensive, had been caught bending. Bounding the amphitheatre was a high yew hedge, an imposing background had there been any foreground, and behind the hedge a heavy wood shut the sky out. Of course what was wanted was colour. Delphinium, salvia, red-hot-poker, zinnias, tobacco-plant, anything. Leaning out of the baronial casement, Conway consid-

---

E. M. FORSTER is considered by many to be among the century's greatest English writers. His novels include Where Angels Fear to Tread, The Longest Journey, A Room with a View, Howards End, *and the posthumously published* Maurice. *Shortly after the appearance of his last and most successful novel,* A Passage to India, *Forster made the decision no longer to publish fiction, since he felt he could not in good conscience write any more novels that took place in a heterosexual milieu. As he observed in his diary late in life, "I should have been a more famous writer if I had written or rather published more, but sex has prevented the latter." For the next forty-five years—half his life—Forster's literary output consisted chiefly of essays, memoirs, and biographies; in addition, he wrote many short stories on homosexual themes—among them "Arthur Snatchfold"—none of which saw publication until after his death in 1970.*

ered this, while he waited for his tea. He was not an artist, nor a philosopher, but he liked exercising his mind when he had nothing else to do, as on this Sunday morning, this country morning, with so much ahead to be eaten, and so little to be said.

The visit, like the view, threatened monotony. Dinner had been dull. His own spruce grey head, gleaming in the mirrors, really seemed the brightest object about. Trevor Donaldson's head was mangy, Mrs. Donaldson's combed up into bastions of iron. He did not get unduly fussed at the prospect of boredom. He was a man of experience with plenty of resources and plenty of armour, and he was a decent human being too. The Donaldsons were his inferiors—they had not travelled or read or gone in for sport or love, they were merely his business allies, linked to him by a common interest in aluminium. Still, he must try to make things nice, since they had been so good as to invite him down. "But it's not so easy to make things nice for us business people," he reflected, as he listened to the chonk of a blackbird, the clink of a milk-can, and the distant self-communings of an electric pump. "We're not stupid or uncultivated, we can use our minds when required, we can go to concerts when we're not too tired, we've invested—even Trevor Donaldson has —in the sense of humour. But I'm afraid we don't get much pleasure out of it all. No. Pleasure's been left out of our packet." Business occupied him increasingly since his wife's death. He brought an active mind to bear on it, and was quickly becoming rich.

He looked at the dull costly garden. It improved. A man had come into it from the back of the yew hedge. He had on a canary-coloured shirt, and the effect was exactly right. The whole scene blazed. *That* was what the place wanted—not a flower-bed, but a man, who advanced with a confident tread down the amphitheatre, and as he came nearer Conway saw that besides being proper to the colour scheme he was a very proper youth. His shoulders were broad, his face sensuous and open, his eyes, screwed up against the light, promised good temper. One arm shot out at an angle, the other supported a milk-can. "Good morning, nice morning," he called, and he sounded happy.

"Good morning, nice morning," he called back. The man continued at a steady pace, turned left, and disappeared in the direction of the servants' entrance, where an outburst of laughter welcomed him.

Conway hoped he might return by the same route, and waited. "That is a nice-looking fellow, I do like the way he holds himself, and probably no nonsense about him," he thought. But the vision had departed, the sunlight stopped, the garden turned stodgy and green again, and the maid came in with his tea. She said, "I'm sorry to be late, we were waiting for the milk, sir." The man had not called him sir, and the omission flattered him. "Good morning, sir" would have been the more natural salutation to an elderly stranger, a wealthy customer's guest. But the vigorous voice had shouted "Good morning, nice morning," as if they were equals.

Where had he gone off to now, he and his voice? To finish his round, welcomed at house after house, and then for a bathe perhaps, his shirt golden on the grass beside him. Ruddy brown to the waist he would show now. . . . What was his name? Was he a local? Sir Richard put these questions to himself as he dressed, but not vehemently. He was not a sentimentalist, there was no danger of him being shattered for the day. He would have liked to meet the vision again, and spend the whole of Sunday with it, giving it a slap-up lunch at the hotel, hiring a car, which they would drive alternately, treating it to the pictures in the neighbouring town, and returning with it, after one drink too much, through dusky lanes. But that was sheer nonsense, even if the vision had been agreeable to the programme. He staying with the Trevor Donaldsons; and he must not repay their hospitality by moping. Dressed in a cheerful grey, he ran downstairs to the breakfast-room. Mrs. Donaldson was already there, and she asked him how his daughters were getting on at their school.

Then his host followed, rubbing his hands together, and saying "Aha, aha!" and when they had eaten they went into the other garden, the one which sloped towards the water, and started talking business. They had not intended to do this, but there was also of their company a Mr. Clifford Clarke, and when Trevor Donaldson, Clifford Clarke, and Richard Conway got together, it was impossible that aluminium should escape. Their voices deepened, their heads nodded or shook as they recalled vast sums that had been lost through unsound investments or misapplied advice. Conway found himself the most intelligent of the three, the quickest at taking a point, the strongest at following an argument. The moments passed, the blackbird chonk-chonked unheeded, unnoticed was the failure of the gardener to produce anything but tightly furled geraniums, unnoticed the ladies on the lawn, who wanted to get some golf. At last the hostess called, "Trevor! Is this a holiday or isn't it?" and they stopped, feeling rather ashamed. The cars came round, and soon they were five miles away, on the course, taking their turn in a queue of fellow merry-makers. Conway was good at golf, and got what excitement he could from it, but as soon as the ball flew off he was aware of a slight sinking feeling. This occupied them till lunch. After coffee they walked down to the water, and played with the dogs—Mrs. Donaldson bred Sealyhams. Several neighbours came to tea, and now the animation rested with Donaldson, for he fancied himself as a country magnate, and wanted to show how well he was settling into the part. There was a good deal of talk about local conditions, women's institutes, education through discipline, and poaching. Conway found all this quite nonsensical and unreal. People who are not feudal should not play at feudalism, and all magistrates (this he said aloud) ought to be trained and ought to be paid. Since he was well-bred, he said it in a form which did not give offence. Thus the day wore away, and they filled in the interval before dinner by driving to see a ruined monastery. What on earth had they got to do with a monastery? Nothing at all. Nothing at all. He caught sight of Clifford Clarke looking mournfully at a rose-window, and he got the feeling that they were all of them looking for something which was not there, that there was an empty chair at the table, a card missing from the bridge-pack, a ball lost in the gorse, a stitch dropped in the shirt; that the chief guest had not come. On their way out they passed through the village, on their way back past a cinema, which was giving a Wild West stunt. They returned through darkling lanes. They did not say, "Thank you! What a delightful day!" That would be saved up for tomorrow morning, and for the final gratitude of departure. Every word would be needed then. "I *have* enjoyed myself, *I have*, absolutely marvellous!" the women would chant, and the men would grunt, as if moved beyond words, and the host and hostess would cry, "Oh but come again, then, come again." Into the void the little unmemorable visit would fall, like a leaf it would fall upon similar leaves, but Conway wondered whether it hadn't been, so to speak, specially negative, out of the way unflowering, whether a champion, one bare arm at an angle, hadn't carried away to the servants' quarters some refreshment which was badly needed in the smoking-room.

"Well, perhaps we shall see, we may yet find out," he thought, as he went up to bed, carrying with him his raincoat.

For he was not one to give in and grumble. He believed in pleasure; he had a free mind and an active body, and he knew that pleasure cannot be won without courage and coolness. The Donaldsons were all very well, but they were not the whole of his life. His daughters were all very well, but the same held good of them. The female sex was all very well and he was addicted to it, but permitted himself an occasional deviation. He set his alarm watch for an hour slightly earlier than the hour at which he had woken in the morning, and he put it under his pillow, and he fell asleep looking quite young.

Seven o'clock tinkled. He glanced into the passage, then put on his raincoat and thick slippers, and went to the window.

It was a silent sunless morning, and seemed earlier than it actually was. The green of the garden and of the trees was filmed with grey, as if it wanted wiping. Presently the electric pump started. He looked at his watch again, slipped down the stairs, out of the house, across the amphitheatre, and through the yew hedge. He did not run, in case he was seen and had to explain. He moved at the maximum pace possible for a gentleman, known to be an original, who fancies an early stroll in his pyjamas. "I thought I'd have a look at your formal garden, there wouldn't have been time after breakfast" would have been the line. He had of course looked at it the day before, also at the wood. The wood lay before him now, and the sun was just tipping into it. There were two paths through the bracken, a broad and a narrow. He waited until he heard the milk-can approaching down the narrow path. Then he moved quickly, and they met, well out of sight of the Donaldsonian demesne.

"Hullo!" he called in his easy out-of-doors voice; he had several voices, and knew by instinct which was wanted.

"Hullo! Somebody's out early!"

"You're early yourself."

"Me? Whor'd the milk be if I worn't?" The milkman grinned, throwing his head back and coming to a standstill. Seen at close quarters he was coarse, very much of the people and of the thick-fingered earth; a hundred years ago his type was trodden into the mud, now it burst and flowered and didn't care a damn.

"You're the morning delivery, eh?"

"Looks like it." He evidently proposed to be facetious—the clumsy fun which can be so delightful when it falls from the proper lips. "I'm not the evening delivery anyway, and I'm not the butcher nor the grocer, nor'm I the coals."

"Live around here?"

"Maybe. Maybe I don't. Maybe I flop about in them planes."

"You live around here, I bet."

"What if I do?"

"If you do you do. And if I don't I don't."

This fatuous retort was a success, and was greeted with doubled-up laughter. "If you don't you don't! Ho, you're a funny one! There's a thing to say! If you don't you don't! Walking about in yer night things too, you'll ketch a cold, you will, that'll be the end of you! Stopping back in the 'otel, I suppose?"

"No. Donaldson's. You saw me there yesterday."

"Oh, Donaldson's, that's it. You was the old granfa' at the upstairs window."

"Old granfa' indeed . . . I'll granfa' you," and he tweaked at the impudent nose. It dodged; it seemed used to this sort of thing. There was probably nothing the lad wouldn't consent to if properly handled, partly out of mischief, partly to oblige. "Oh, by the way . . . ," and he felt the shirt as if interested in the quality of its material. "What was I going to say?" and he gave the zip at the throat a downward pull. Much slid into view. "Oh, I know—when's this round of yours over?"

" 'Bout eleven. Why?"

"Why not?"

" 'Bout eleven *at night*. Ha ha. Got yer there. Eleven at night. What you want to arst all them questions for? We're strangers, aren't we?"

"How old are you?"

"Ninety, same as yourself."

"What's your address?"

"There you go on! Hi! I like that. Arstin questions after I tell you No."

"Got a girl? Ever heard of a pint? Ever heard of two?"

"Go on. Get out." But he suffered his forearm to be worked between massaging fingers, and he set down his milk-can. He was amused. He was charmed. He was hooked, and a touch would land him.

"You look like a boy who looks all right," the elder man breathed.

"Oh, *stop* it. . . . All right, I'll go with you."

Conway was entranced. Thus, exactly thus, should the smaller pleasures of life be approached. They understood one another with a precision impossible for lovers. He laid his face on the warm skin over the clavicle, hands nudged him behind, and presently the sensation for which he had planned so cleverly was over. It was part of the past. It had fallen like a flower upon similar flowers.

He heard "You all right?" It was over there too, part of a different past. They were lying deeper in the wood, where the fern was highest. He did not reply, for it was pleasant to lie stretched thus and to gaze up through bracken fronds at the distant treetops and the pale blue sky, and feel the exquisite pleasure fade.

"That was what you wanted, wasn't it?" Propped on his elbows, the young man looked down anxiously. All his roughness and pertness had gone, and he only wanted to know whether he had been a success.

"Yes . . . Lovely."

"Lovely? You say lovely?" He beamed, prodding gently with his stomach.

"Nice boy, nice shirt, nice everything."

"That a fact?"

Conway guessed that he was vain, the better sort often are, and laid on the flattery thick to please him, praised his comeliness, his thrusting thrashing strength; there was plenty to praise. He liked to do this and to see the broad face grinning and feel the heavy body on him. There was no cynicism in the flattery, he was genuinely admiring and gratified.

"So you enjoyed that?"

"Who wouldn't?"

"Pity you didn't tell me yesterday."

"I didn't know how to."

"I'd a met you down where I have my swim. You could 'elped me strip, you'd like that. Still, we mustn't grumble." He gave Conway a hand and pulled him up, and brushed and tidied the raincoat like an old friend. "We could get seven years for this, couldn't we?"

"Not seven years, still we'd get something nasty. Madness, isn't it? What can it matter to anyone else if you and I don't mind?"

"Oh, I suppose they've to occupy themselves with somethink or other," and he took up the milk-can to go on.

"Half a minute, boy—do take this and get yourself some trifle with it." He produced a note which he had brought on the chance.

"I didn't do it fer that."

"I know you didn't."

"Naow, we was each as bad as the other. . . . Naow . . . keep yer money."

"I'd be pleased if you would take it. I expect I'm better off than you and it might come in useful. To take out your girl, say, or towards your next new suit. However, please yourself, of course."

"Can you honestly afford it?"

"Honestly."

"Well, I'll find a way to spend it, no doubt. People don't always behave as nice as you, you know."

Conway could have returned the compliment. The affair had been trivial and crude, and yet they both had behaved perfectly. They would never meet again, and they did not exchange names. After a hearty hand-shake, the young man swung away down the path, the sunlight and the shadow rushing over his back. He did not turn round, but his arm, jerking sideways to balance him, waved an acceptable farewell. The green flowed over his brightness, the path bent, he disappeared. Back he went to his own life, and through the quiet of the morning his laugh could be heard as he whooped at the maids.

Conway waited for a few moments, as arranged, and then he went back too. His luck held. He met no one, either in the amphitheatre garden or on the stairs, and after he had been in his room for a minute the maid arrived with his early tea. "I'm sorry the milk was late again, sir," she said. He enjoyed it, bathed and shaved and dressed himself for town. It was the figure of a superior city-man which was reflected in the mirror as he tripped downstairs. The car came round after breakfast to take him to the station, and he was completely sincere when he told the Trevor Donaldsons that he had had an out-of-the-way pleasant weekend. They believed him, and their faces grew brighter. "Come again, then, come by all means again," they cried as he slid off. In the train he read the papers rather less than usual and smiled to himself rather more. It was so pleasant to have been completely right over a stranger, even down to little details like the texture of the skin. It flattered his vanity. It increased his sense of power.

2

He did not see Trevor Donaldson again for some weeks. Then they met in London at his club, for a business talk and a spot of lunch. Circumstances which they could not control had rendered them less friendly. Owing to regrouping in the financial world, their interests were now opposed, and if one of them stood to make money out of aluminium, the other stood to lose. So the talk had been cautious. Donaldson, the weaker man, felt tired and worried after it. He had not, to his knowledge, made a mistake, but he might have slipped unwittingly, and be poorer, and have to give up his county estate. He looked at his host with hostility and wished he could harm him. Sir Richard was aware of this, but felt no hostility in return. For one thing, he was going to win; for another, hating never interested him. This was probably the last occasion on which they would foregather socially; but he exercised his usual charm. He wanted, too, to find out during lunch how far Donaldson was aware of his own danger. Clifford Clarke (who was allied with him) had failed to do this.

After adjourning to the cloakroom and washing their hands at adjacent basins, they sat opposite each other at a little table. Down the long room sat other pairs of elderly men, eating, drinking, talking quietly, instructing the waiters. Inquiries were exchanged about Mrs. Donaldson and the young Miss Conways, and there were some humorous references to golf. Then Donaldson said, with a change in his voice: "Golf's all you say, and the great advantage of it in these days is that you get it practically anywhere. I used to think our course was good, for a little country course, but it is far below the average. This is somewhat of a disappointment to us both, since we settled down there specially for the golf. The fact is, the country is not at all what it seems when first you go there."

"So I've always heard."

"My wife likes it, of course, she has her Sealyhams, she has her flowers, she has her local charities—though in these days one's not supposed to speak of 'charity.' I don't know why. I should have thought it was a good word, charity. She runs the Women's Institute, so far as it consents to be run, but Conway, Conway, you'd never believe how offhand the village women are in these days. They don't elect Mrs. Donaldson president yearly as a matter of course. She takes turn and turn with cottagers."

"Oh, that's the spirit of the age, of course. One's always running into it in some form or other. For instance, I don't get nearly the deference I did from my clerks."

"But better work from them, no doubt," said Donaldson gloomily.

"No. But probably they're better men."

"Well, perhaps the ladies at the Women's Institute are becoming better women. But my wife doubts it. Of course our village is particularly unfortunate, owing to that deplorable hotel. It has had such a bad influence. We had an extraordinary case before us on the Bench recently, connected with it."

"That hotel did look too flash—it would attract the wrong crowd."

"I've also had bother bother bother with the Rural District Council over the removal of tins, and another bother—a really maddening one—over a right of way through the church meadows. That almost made me lose my patience. And I really sometimes wonder whether I've been sensible in digging myself in in the country, and trying to make myself useful in local affairs. There is no gratitude. There is no warmth of welcome."

"I quite believe it, Donaldson, and I know I'd never have a country place myself, even if the scenery is as pleasant as yours is, and even if I could afford it. I make do with a service flat in town, and I retain a small furnished cottage for my girls' holidays, and when they leave school I shall partly take them and partly send them abroad. I don't believe in undiluted England, nice as are sometimes the English. Shall we go up and have coffee?"

He ran up the staircase briskly, for he had found out what he wanted to know: Donaldson was feeling poor. He stuck him in a low leathern armchair, and had a look at him as he closed his eyes. That was it: he felt he couldn't afford his "little place," and was running it down, so that no one should be surprised when he gave it up. Meanwhile, there was one point in the conversation it amused him to take up now that business was finished with: the reference to that "extraordinary case" connected with the local hotel.

Donaldson opened his eyes when asked, and they had gone prawn-like. "Oh, that was a case, it was a really really," he said. "I knew such things existed, of course, but I assumed in my innocence they were confined to Piccadilly. However, it has all been traced back to the hotel, the proprietress has had a thorough fright, and I don't think there will be any trouble in the future. Indecency between males."

"Oh, good Lord!" said Sir Richard coolly. "Black or white?"

"White, please, it's an awful nuisance, but I can't take black coffee now, although I greatly prefer it. You see, some of the hotel guests— there was a bar, and some of the villagers used to go in there after cricket because they thought it smarter than that charming old thatched pub by the church—you remember that old thatched pub. Villagers are terrific snobs, that's one of the disappointing discoveries one makes. The bar got a bad reputation of a certain type, especially at week-ends, someone complained to the police, a watch was set, and the result was this quite extraordinary case. . . . Really, really, I wouldn't have believed it. A *little* milk, please, Conway, if I may, just a little; I'm not allowed to take my coffee black."

"So sorry. Have a liqueur."

"No, no thanks, I'm not allowed that, even, especially after lunch."

"Come on, do—I will if you will. Waiter, can we have two double cognacs?"

"He hasn't heard you. Don't bother."

Conway had not wanted the waiter to hear him, he had wanted an excuse to be out of the room and have a minute alone. He was suddenly worried in case that milkman had got into a scrape. He had scarcely thought about him since—he had a very full life, and it included an intrigue with a cultivated woman, which was gradually ripening—but nobody could have been more decent and honest, or more physically attractive in a particular way. It had been a charming little adventure, and a remarkably lively one. And their parting had been perfect. Wretched if the lad had come to grief! Enough to make one cry. He offered up a sort of prayer, ordered the cognacs, and rejoined Donaldson with his usual briskness. He put on the Renaissance armour that suited him so well, and "How did the hotel case end?" he asked.

"We committed him for trial."

"Oh! As bad as that?"

"Well, we thought so. Actually a gang of about half a dozen were involved, but we only caught one of them. His mother, if you please, is president of the Women's Institute, and hasn't had the decency to resign! I tell you, Conway, these people aren't the same flesh and blood as oneself. One pretends they are, but they aren't. And what with this disillusionment, and what with the right of way, I've a good mind to clear out next year, and leave the so-called country to stew in its own juice. It's utterly corrupt. This man made an awfully bad impression on the Bench, and we didn't feel that six months, which is the maximum we were allowed to impose, was adequate to the offence. And it was all so revoltingly commercial—his only motive was money."

Conway felt relieved; it couldn't be his own friend, for anyone less grasping . . .

"And another unpleasant feature—at least for me—is that he had the habit of taking his clients into my grounds."

"How most vexatious for you!"

"It suited his convenience, and of what else should he think? I have a little wood—you didn't see it—which stretches up to the hotel, so he could easily bring people in. A path my wife was particularly fond of— a mass of bluebells in springtime—it was there they were caught. You may well imagine this has helped to put me off the place."

"Who caught them?" he asked, holding his glass up to the light; their cognacs had arrived.

"Our local bobby. For we do possess that extraordinary rarity, a policeman who keeps his eyes open. He sometimes commits errors of judgement—he did on this occasion—but he's certainly observant, and as he was coming down one of the other paths, a public one, he saw a bright yellow shirt through the bracken—upsa! Take care!"

"Upsa!" were some drops of brandy, which Conway had spilt. Alas, alas, there could be no doubt about it. He felt deeply distressed, and rather guilty. The young man must have decided after their successful encounter to use the wood as a rendezvous. It was a cruel stupid world, and he was countenancing it more than he should. Wretched, wretched, to think of that good-tempered, harmless chap being bruised and ruined . . . the whole thing so unnecessary . . . betrayed by the shirt he was so proud of. Conway was not often moved, but this time he felt much regret and compassion.

"Well, he recognized that shirt at once. He had particular reasons for keeping a watch on its wearer. And he got him, he got him. But he lost the other man. He didn't charge them straight away, as he ought to have done. I think he was genuinely startled and could scarcely believe his eyes. For one thing, it was so early in the morning—barely seven o'clock."

"A strange hour!" said Conway, and put his glass down, and folded his hands on his knee.

"He caught sight of them as they were getting up after committing the indecency, also he saw money pass, but instead of rushing in there and then he made an elaborate and totally unnecessary plan for interrupting the youth on the further side of my house, and of course he could have got him any time, any time. A stupid error of judgement. A great pity. He never arrested him until 7:45."

"Was there then sufficient evidence for an arrest?"

"There was abundant evidence of a medical character, if you follow me—what a case, oh, what a case! Also there was the money on him, which clinched his guilt."

"Mayn't the money have been in connection with his round?"

"No. It was a note, and he only had small change in connection with his round. We established that from his employer. But however did you guess he was on a round?"

"You told me," said Conway, who never became flustered when he made a slip. "You mentioned that he had a milk round and that the mother was connected with some local organization which Mrs. Donaldson takes an interest in."

"Yes, yes, the Women's Institute. Well, having fixed all that up, our policeman then went on to the hotel, but it was far too late by that time, some of the guests were breakfasting, others had left, he couldn't go round cross-questioning everyone, and no one corresponded to the description of the person whom he saw being hauled up out of the fern."

"What was the description?"

"An old man in pyjamas and a mackintosh. Our Chairman was awfully anxious to get hold of him—oh, you remember our Chairman, Ernest Dray, you met him at my little place. He's determined to stamp this sort of thing out, once and for all. Hullo, it's past three, I must be getting back to my grindstone. Many thanks for lunch. I don't know why I've discoursed on this somewhat unsavoury topic. I'd have done better to consult you about the right of way."

"You must another time. I did look up the subject once."

"How about a spot of lunch with me this day week?" said Donaldson, remembering their business feud, and becoming uneasily jolly.

"This day week? Now can I? No, I can't. I've promised this day week to go and see my little girls. Not that they're little any longer. Time flies, doesn't it? We're none of us younger."

"Sad but true," said Donaldson, heaving himself out of the deep leather chair. Similar chairs, empty or filled with similar men, receded down the room, and far away a small fire smoked under a heavy mantelpiece. "But aren't you going to drink your cognac? It's excellent cognac."

"I suddenly took against it—I do indulge in caprices." Getting up, he felt faint; the blood rushed to his head and he thought he was going to fall. "Tell me," he said, taking his enemy's arm and conducting him to the door, "this old man in the mackintosh—how was it the fellow you caught never put you on his track?"

"He tried to."

"Oh, did he?"

"Yes indeed, and he was all the more anxious to do so, because we made it clear that he would be let off if he helped us to make the major arrest. But all he could say was what we knew already—that it was someone from the hotel."

"Oh, he said that, did he? From the hotel."

"Said it again and again. Scarcely said anything else, indeed almost went into a sort of fit. There he stood with his head thrown back and his eyes shut, barking at us. 'Th'otel. Keep to th'otel. I tell you he come from th'otel.' We advised him not to get so excited, whereupon he became insolent, which did him no good with Ernest Dray, as you may well imagine, and called the Bench a row of interfering bastards. He was instantly removed from the court, and as he went he shouted back at us —you'll never credit this—that if he and the old grandfather didn't mind it why should anyone else. We talked the case over carefully and came to the conclusion it must go to Assizes."

"What was his name?"

"But we don't know, I tell you, we never caught him."

"I mean the name of the one you did catch, the village boy."

"Arthur Snatchfold."

They had reached the top of the club staircase. Conway saw the reflection of his face once more in a mirror, and it was the face of an old man. He pushed Trevor Donaldson off abruptly, and went back to sit down by his liqueur-glass. He was safe, safe, he could go forward with his career as planned. But waves of shame came over him. Oh for prayer!—but whom had he to pray to, and what about? He saw that little things can turn into great ones, and he did not want greatness. He was not up to it. For a moment he considered giving himself up and standing his trial; however, what possible good would that do? He would ruin himself and his daughters, he would delight his enemies, and he would not save his saviour. He recalled his clever manoeuvres for a little fun, and the good-humoured response, the mischievous face, the obliging body. It had all seemed so trivial. Taking a notebook from his pocket, he wrote down the name of his lover, yes, his lover who was going to prison to save him, in order that he might not forget it. Arthur Snatchfold. He had only heard the name once, and he would never hear it again.

~ *Christopher Isherwood* ~

Sally
Bowles

One afternoon, early in October, I was invited to black coffee at Fritz Wendel's flat. Fritz always invited you to "black coffee," with emphasis on the black. He was very proud of his coffee. People used to say that it was the strongest in Berlin.

Fritz himself was dressed in his usual coffee-party costume—a very thick white yachting sweater and very light blue flannel trousers. He greeted me with his full-lipped, luscious smile:

" 'lo, Chris!"

"Hullo, Fritz. How are you?"

"Fine." He bent over the coffee-machine, his sleek black hair un-plastering itself from his scalp and falling in richly scented locks over his eyes. "This darn thing doesn't go," he added.

"How's business?" I asked.

"Lousy and terrible." Fritz grinned richly. "Or I pull off a new deal in the next month or I go as a gigolo."

CHRISTOPHER ISHERWOOD was born in England in 1904 and spent most of his youth as an expatriate, chiefly in Berlin. After the Second World War he moved to California, where he lived until his death in 1986. He was the author of many extraordinary works of fiction, among them Goodbye to Berlin, Mr. Norris Changes Trains, Prater Violet, Down There on a Visit, *and* A Single Man, *as well as the revisionist autobiography* Christopher and His Kind.

"*Either* . . . or . . . ," I corrected, from force of professional habit.

"I'm speaking a lousy English just now," drawled Fritz, with great self-satisfaction. "Sally says maybe she'll give me a few lessons."

"Who's Sally?"

"Why, I forgot. You don't know Sally. Too bad of me. Eventually she's coming around here this afternoon."

"Is she nice?"

Fritz rolled his naughty black eyes, handing me a rum-moistened cigarette from his patent tin.

"*Mar*-vellous!" he drawled. "Eventually I believe I'm getting crazy about her."

"And who is she? What does she do?"

"She's an English girl, an actress: sings at the Lady Windermere—hot stuff, believe me!"

"That doesn't sound much like an English girl, I must say."

"Eventually she's got a bit of French in her. Her mother was French."

A few minutes later, Sally herself arrived.

"Am I terribly late, Fritz darling?"

"Only half of an hour, I suppose," Fritz drawled, beaming with proprietary pleasure. "May I introduce Mr. Isherwood—Miss Bowles? Mr. Isherwood is commonly known as Chris."

"I'm not," I said. "Fritz is about the only person who's ever called me Chris in my life."

Sally laughed. She was dressed in black silk, with a small cape over her shoulders and a little cap like a page-boy's stuck jauntily on one side of her head.

"Do you mind if I use your telephone, sweet?"

"Sure. Go right ahead." Fritz caught my eye. "Come into the other room, Chris. I want to show you something." He was evidently longing to hear my first impressions of Sally, his new acquisition.

"For heaven's sake, don't leave me alone with this man!" she exclaimed. "Or he'll seduce me down the telephone. He's most terribly passionate."

As she dialled the number, I noticed that her fingernails were painted emerald green, a colour unfortunately chosen, for it called attention to her hands, which were much stained by cigarette-smoking and as dirty as a little girl's. She was dark enough to be Fritz's sister. Her face was long and thin, powdered dead white. She had very large brown eyes which should have been darker, to match her hair and the pencil she used for her eyebrows.

"Hilloo," she cooed, pursing her brilliant cherry lips as though she were going to kiss the mouthpiece. "Ist dass Du, mein Liebling?" Her mouth opened in a fatuously sweet smile. Fritz and I sat watching her, like a performance at the theatre. "Was wollen wir machen, Morgen Abend? Oh, wie wunderbar. . . . Nein, nein, ich werde bleiben Heute Abend zu Hause. Ja, ja, ich werde wirklich bleiben zu Hause. . . . Auf Wiedersehen, mein Liebling. . . ."

She hung up the receiver and turned to us triumphantly.

"That's the man I slept with last night," she announced. "He makes love marvellously. He's an absolute genius at business and he's terribly rich—" She came and sat down on the sofa beside Fritz, sinking back into the cushions with a sigh. "Give me some coffee, will you, darling? I'm simply dying of thirst."

And soon we were on to Fritz's favourite topic: he pronounced it *larve*.

"On the average," he told us, "I'm having a big affair every two years."

"And how long is it since you had your last?" Sally asked.

"Exactly one year and eleven months!" Fritz gave her his naughtiest glance.

"How marvellous!" Sally puckered up her nose and laughed a silvery little stage-laugh: "*Doo* tell me—what was the last one like?"

This, of course, started Fritz off on a complete autobiography. We had the story of his seduction in Paris, details of a holiday flirtation at Las Palmas, the four chief New York romances, a disappointment in Chicago and a conquest in Boston; then back to Paris for a little recreation, a very beautiful episode in Vienna, to London to be consoled, and, finally, Berlin.

"You know, Fritz darling," said Sally, puckering up her nose at me, "*I* believe the trouble with you is that you've never really found the right woman."

"Maybe that's true—" Fritz took this idea very seriously. His black eyes became liquid and sentimental. "Maybe I'm still looking for my ideal. . . ."

"But you'll find her one day, I'm absolutely certain you will." Sally included me, with a glance, in the game of laughing at Fritz.

"You think so?" Fritz grinned lusciously, sparkling at her.

"Don't *you* think so?" Sally appealed to me.

"I'm sure I don't know," I said. "Because I've never been able to discover what Fritz's ideal is."

For some reason, this seemed to please Fritz. He took it as a kind of testimonial. "And Chris knows me pretty well," he chimed in. "If Chris doesn't know, well, I guess no one does."

Then it was time for Sally to go.

"I'm supposed to meet a man at the Adlon at five," she explained. "And it's six already! Never mind, it'll do the old swine good to wait. He wants me to be his mistress, but I've told him I'm damned if I will till he's paid all my debts. Why are men always such beasts?" Opening her bag, she rapidly retouched her lips and eyebrows: "Oh, by the way, Fritz darling, could you be a perfect angel and lend me ten marks? I haven't got a bean for a taxi."

"Why sure!" Fritz put his hand into his pocket and paid up without hesitation, like a hero.

Sally turned to me: "I say, will you come and have tea with me sometime? Give me your telephone number. I'll ring you up."

I suppose, I thought, she imagines I've got cash. Well, this will be a lesson to her, once for all. I wrote my number in her tiny leather book. Fritz saw her out.

"Well!" He came bounding back into the room and gleefully shut the door. "What do you think of her, Chris? Didn't I tell you she was a good-looker?"

"You did indeed!"

"I'm getting crazier about her each time I see her!" With a sigh of pleasure, he helped himself to a cigarette. "More coffee, Chris?"

"No, thank you very much."

"You know, Chris, I think she took a fancy to you, too!"

"Oh, rot!"

"Honestly, I do!" Fritz seemed pleased. "Eventually I guess we'll be seeing a lot of her from now on!"

When I got back to Frl. Schroeder's, I felt so giddy that I had to lie down for half an hour on my bed. Fritz's black coffee was as poisonous as ever.

~ ~ ~

A few days later, he took me to hear Sally sing.

The Lady Windermere (which now, I hear, no longer exists) was an arty "informal" bar, just off the Tauentzienstrasse, which the proprietor had evidently tried to make look as much as possible like Montparnasse. The walls were covered with sketches on menu-cards, caricatures, and signed theatrical photographs. ("To the one and only Lady Windermere." "To Johnny, with all my heart.") The Fan itself, four times life size, was displayed above the bar. There was a big piano on a platform in the middle of the room.

I was curious to see how Sally would behave. I had imagined her, for some reason, rather nervous, but she wasn't, in the least. She had a surprisingly deep, husky voice. She sang badly, without any expression, her hands hanging down at her sides—yet her performance was, in its own way, effective because of her startling appearance and her air of not caring a curse what people thought of her. Her arms hanging carelessly limp, and a take-it-or-leave-it grin on her face, she sang:

Now I know why Mother
Told me to be true;
She meant me for someone
Exactly like you.

There was quite a lot of applause. The pianist, a handsome young man with blond wavy hair, stood up and solemnly kissed Sally's hand. Then she sang two more songs, one in French and the other in German. These weren't so well received.

After the singing, there was a good deal more hand-kissing and a general movement towards the bar. Sally seemed to know everybody in the place. She called them all Thou and Darling. For a would-be demimondaine, she seemed to have surprisingly little business sense or tact. She wasted a lot of time making advances to an elderly gentleman who would obviously have preferred a chat with the barman. Later, we all got rather drunk. Then Sally had to go off to an appointment, and the manager came and sat at our table. He and Fritz talked English Peerage. Fritz was in his element. I decided, as so often before, never to visit a place of this sort again.

～　～　～

Then Sally rang up, as she had promised, to invite me to tea.

She lived a long way down the Kurfürstendamm, on the last dreary stretch which rises to Halensee. I was shown into a big gloomy half-furnished room by a fat untidy landlady with a pouchy sagging jowl like a toad. There was a broken-down sofa in one corner and a faded picture of an eighteenth-century battle, with the wounded reclining on their elbows in graceful attitudes, admiring the prancings of Frederick the Great's horse.

"Oh, hullo, Chris darling!" cried Sally from the doorway. "How sweet of you to come! I was feeling most terribly lonely. I've been crying on Frau Karpf's chest. Nicht wahr, Frau Karpf?" She appealed to the toad landlady: "Ich habe geweint auf Dein Brust." Frau Karpf shook her bosom in a toad-like chuckle.

"Would you rather have coffee, Chris, or tea?" Sally continued. "You can have either. Only I don't recommend the tea much. I don't know what Frau Karpf does to it; I think she empties all the kitchen slops together into a jug and boils them up with the tea-leaves."

"I'll have coffee, then."

"Frau Karpf, Leibling, willst Du sein ein Engel und bring zwei Tassen von Kaffee?" Sally's German was not merely incorrect; it was all her own. She pronounced every word in a mincing, specially "foreign" manner. You could tell that she was speaking a foreign language from her expression alone. "Chris darling, will you be an angel and draw the curtains?"

I did so, although it was still quite light outside. Sally, meanwhile, had switched on the table-lamp. As I turned from the window, she curled herself up delicately on the sofa like a cat and, opening her bag, felt for a cigarette. But hardly was the pose complete before she'd jumped to her feet again.

"Would you like a Prairie Oyster?" She produced glasses, eggs, and a bottle of Worcester sauce from the boot-cupboard under the dismantled washstand. "I practically live on them." Dexterously, she broke the eggs into the glasses, added the sauce, and stirred up the mixture with the end of a fountain-pen: "They're about all I can afford." She was back on the sofa again, daintily curled up.

She was wearing the same black dress today, but without the cape. Instead, she had a little white collar and white cuffs. They produced a kind of theatrically chaste effect, like a nun in grand opera. "What are you laughing at, Chris?" she asked.

"I don't know," I said. But still I couldn't stop grinning. There was, at that moment, something so extraordinarily comic in Sally's appearance. She was really beautiful, with her little dark head, big eyes, and finely arched nose—and so absurdly conscious of all these features. There she lay, as complacently feminine as a turtle-dove, with her poised self-conscious head and daintily arranged hands.

"Chris, you swine, do tell me why you're laughing?"

"I really haven't the faintest idea."

At this, she began to laugh too: "You are mad, you know!"

"Have you been here long?" I asked, looking round the large gloomy room.

"Ever since I arrived in Berlin. Let's see—that was about two months ago."

I asked what had made her decide to come out to Germany at all. Had she come alone? No, she'd come with a girl friend. An actress. Older than Sally. The girl had been to Berlin before. She'd told Sally that they'd certainly be able to get work with the Ufa. So Sally borrowed ten pounds from a nice old gentleman and joined her.

She hadn't told her parents anything about it until the two of them had actually arrived in Germany. "I wish you'd met Diana. She was the most marvellous gold-digger you can imagine. She'd get hold of men anywhere—it didn't matter whether she could speak their language or not. She made me nearly die of laughing. I absolutely adored her."

But when they'd been together in Berlin three weeks and no job had appeared, Diana had got hold of a banker, who'd taken her off with him to Paris.

"And left you here alone? I must say I think that was pretty rotten of her."

"Oh, I don't know. . . . Everyone's got to look after themselves. I expect, in her place, I'd have done the same."

"I bet you wouldn't!"

"Anyhow, I'm all right. I can always get along alone."

"How old are you, Sally?"

"Nineteen."

"Good God! And I thought you were about twenty-five!"

"I know. Everyone does."

Frau Karpf came shuffling in with two cups of coffee on a tarnished metal tray.

"Oh, Frau Karpf, Leibling, wie wunderbar von Dich!"

"Whatever makes you stay in this house?" I asked, when the landlady had gone out. "I'm sure you could get a much nicer room than this."

"Yes, I know I could."

"Well then, why don't you?"

"Oh, I don't know. I'm lazy, I suppose."

"What do you have to pay here?"

"Eighty marks a month."

"With breakfast included?"

"No—I don't think so."

"You don't *think* so?" I exclaimed severely. "But surely you must know for certain?"

Sally took this meekly. "Yes, it's stupid of me, I suppose. But, you see, I just give the old girl money when I've got some. So it's rather difficult to reckon it all up exactly."

"But, good heavens, Sally—I only pay fifty a month for my room, with breakfast, and it's ever so much nicer than this one!"

Sally nodded, but continued apologetically: "And another thing is, you see, Christopher darling, I don't quite know what Frau Karpf would do if I were to leave her. I'm sure she'd never get another lodger. Nobody else would be able to stand her face and her smell and everything. As it is, she owes three months' rent. They'd turn her out at once if they knew she hadn't any lodgers: and if they do that, she says she'll commit suicide."

"All the same, I don't see why you should sacrifice yourself for her."

"I'm not sacrificing myself, really. I quite like being here, you know. Frau Karpf and I understand each other. She's more or less what I'll be in thirty years' time. A respectable sort of landlady would probably turn me out after a week."

"My landlady wouldn't turn you out."

Sally smiled vaguely, screwing up her nose. "How do you like the coffee, Chris darling?"

"I prefer it to Fritz's," I said evasively.

Sally laughed. "Isn't Fritz marvellous? I adore him. I adore the way he says, 'I give a damn.' "

" 'Hell, I give a damn.' " I tried to imitate Fritz. We both laughed. Sally lit another cigarette: she smoked the whole time. I noticed how old her hands looked in the lamplight. They were nervous, veined and very thin—the hands of a middle-aged woman. The green fingernails seemed not to belong to them at all; to have settled on them by chance—like hard, bright, ugly little beetles. "It's a funny thing," she added meditatively. "Fritz and I have never slept together, you know." She paused, asked with interest: "Did you think we had?"

"Well, yes—I suppose I did."

"We haven't. Not once . . ." She yawned. "And now I don't suppose we ever shall."

We smoked for some minutes in silence. Then Sally began to tell me about her family. She was the daughter of a Lancashire mill-owner. Her mother was a Miss Bowles, an heiress with an estate, and so, when she and Mr. Jackson were married, they joined their names together: "Daddy's a terrible snob, although he pretends not to be. My real name's Jackson-Bowles; but, of course, I can't possibly call myself that on the stage. People would think I was crazy."

"I thought Fritz told me your mother was French?"

"No, of course not!" Sally seemed quite annoyed. "Fritz is an idiot. He's always inventing things."

Sally had one sister, named Betty. "She's an absolute angel. I adore her. She's seventeen, but she's still most terribly innocent. Mummy's bringing her up to be very county. Betty would nearly die if she knew what an old whore I am. She knows absolutely nothing whatever about men."

"But why aren't you county too, Sally?"

"I don't know. I suppose that's Daddy's side of the family coming out. You'd love Daddy. He doesn't care a damn for anyone. He's the most marvellous business man. And about once a month he gets absolutely dead tight and horrifies all Mummy's smart friends. It was he who said I could go to London and learn acting."

"You must have left school very young?"

"Yes. I couldn't bear school. I got myself expelled."

"However did you do that?"

"I told the headmistress I was going to have a baby."

"Oh, rot, Sally, you didn't!"

"I did, honestly! There was the most terrible commotion. They got a doctor to examine me, and sent for my parents. When they found out there was nothing the matter, they were most frightfully disappointed. The headmistress said that a girl who could even think of anything so disgusting couldn't possibly be allowed to stay on and corrupt the other girls. So I got my own way. And then I pestered Daddy till he said I might go to London."

Sally had settled down in London, at a hostel, with other girl students. There, in spite of supervision, she had managed to spend large portions of the night at young men's flats. "The first man who seduced me had no idea I was a virgin until I told him afterwards. He was marvellous. I adored him. He was an absolute genius at comedy parts. He's sure to be terribly famous, one day."

After a time, Sally had got crowd-work in films, and finally a small part in a touring company. Then she had met Diana.

"And how much longer shall you stay in Berlin?" I asked.

"Heaven knows. This job at the Lady Windermere only lasts another week. I got it through a man I met at the Eden Bar. But he's gone off to Vienna now. I must ring up the Ufa people again, I suppose. And then there's an awful old Jew who takes me out sometimes. He's always promising to get me a contract; but he only wants to sleep with me, the old swine. I think the men in this country are awful. They've none of them got any money, and they expect you to let them seduce you if they give you a box of chocolates."

"How on earth are you going to manage when this job comes to an end?"

"Oh well, I get a small allowance from home, you know. Not that that'll last much longer. Mummy's already threatened to stop it if I don't come back to England soon. . . . Of course, they think I'm here with a girl friend. If Mummy knew I was on my own, she'd simply pass right out. Anyhow, I'll get enough to support myself somehow, soon. I loathe taking money from them. Daddy's business is in a frightfully bad way now, from the slump."

"I say, Sally—if you ever really get into a mess I wish you'd let me know."

Sally laughed. "That's terribly sweet of you, Chris. But I don't sponge on my friends."

"Isn't Fritz your friend?" It had jumped out of my mouth. But Sally didn't seem to mind a bit.

"Oh yes, I'm awfully fond of Fritz, of course. But he's got pots of cash. Somehow, when people have cash, you feel differently about them—I don't know why."

"And how do you know I haven't got pots of cash too?"

"You?" Sally burst out laughing. "Why, I knew you were hard-up the first moment I set eyes on you!"

~ ~ ~

The afternoon Sally came to tea with me, Frl. Schroeder was beside herself with excitement. She put on her best dress for the occasion and waved her hair. When the door-bell rang, she threw open the door with a flourish: "Herr Issyvoo," she announced, winking knowingly at me and speaking very loud, "there's a lady to see you!"

I then formally introduced Sally and Frl. Schroeder to each other. Frl. Schroeder was overflowing with politeness: she addressed Sally repeatedly as "Gnädiges Fräulein." Sally, with her page-boy cap stuck over one ear, laughed her silvery laugh and sat down elegantly on the sofa. Frl. Schroeder hovered about her in unfeigned admiration and amazement. She had evidently never seen anyone like Sally before. When she brought in the tea there were, in place of the usual little chunks of pale unappetising pastry, a plateful of jam tarts arranged in the shape of a star. I noticed also that Frl. Schroeder had provided us with two tiny paper serviettes, perforated at the edges to resemble lace. (When, later, I complimented her on these preparations, she told me that she had always used the serviettes when the Herr Rittmeister had had his fiancée to tea. "Oh, yes, Herr Issyvoo. You can depend on me! I know what pleases a young lady!")

"Do you mind if I lie down on your sofa, darling?" Sally asked, as soon as we were alone.

"No, of course not."

Sally pulled off her cap, swung her little velvet shoes up onto the sofa, opened her bag, and began powdering. "I'm most terribly tired. I didn't sleep a wink last night. I've got a marvellous new lover."

I began to put out the tea. Sally gave me a sidelong glance.

"Do I shock you when I talk like that, Christopher darling?"

"Not in the least."

"But you don't like it?"

"It's no business of mine." I handed her the tea-glass.

"Oh, for God's sake," cried Sally, "don't start being English! Of course it's your business what you think!"

"Well then, if you want to know, it rather bores me."

This annoyed her even more than I had intended. Her tone changed: she said coldly, "I thought you'd understand." She sighed. "But I forgot—you're a man."

"I'm sorry, Sally. I can't help being a man, of course. . . . But please don't be angry with me. I only meant that when you talk like that it's really just nervousness. You're naturally rather shy with strangers, I think: so you've got into this trick of trying to bounce them into approving or disapproving of you, violently. I know, because I try it myself sometimes. . . . Only I wish you wouldn't try it on me, because it just doesn't work and it only makes me feel embarrassed. If you go to bed with every single man in Berlin and come and tell me about it each time, you still won't convince me that you're *La Dame aux Camélias*—because really and truly, you know, you aren't."

"No . . . I suppose I'm not." Sally's voice was carefully impersonal. She was beginning to enjoy this conversation. I had succeeded in flattering her in some new way. "Then what *am* I, exactly, Christopher darling?"

"You're the daughter of Mr. and Mrs. Jackson-Bowles."

Sally sipped her tea. "Yes . . . I think I see what you mean. . . . Perhaps you're right. . . . Then you think I ought to give up having lovers altogether?"

"Certainly I don't. As long as you're sure you're really enjoying yourself."

"Of course," said Sally gravely, after a pause, "I'd never let love interfere with my work. Work comes before everything. . . . But I don't believe that a woman can be a great actress who hasn't had any love-affairs—" She broke off suddenly: "What are you laughing at, Chris?"

"I'm not laughing."

"You're always laughing at me. Do you think I'm the most ghastly idiot?"

"No, Sally. I don't think you're an idiot at all. It's quite true, I *was* laughing. People I like often make me want to laugh at them. I don't know why."

"Then you do like me, Christopher darling?"

"Yes, of course I like you, Sally. What did you think?"

"But you're not in love with me, are you?"

"No. I'm not in love with you."

"I'm awfully glad; I've wanted you to like me ever since we first met. But I'm glad you're not in love with me, because, somehow, I couldn't possibly be in love with you—so, if you had been, everything would have been spoilt."

"Well then, that's very lucky, isn't it?"

"Yes, very . . ." Sally hesitated. "There's something I want to confess to you, Chris darling. . . . I'm not sure if you'll understand or not."

"Remember, I'm only a man, Sally."

Sally laughed. "It's the most idiotic little thing. But somehow, I'd hate it if you found out without my telling you. . . . You know, the other day, you said Fritz had told you my mother was French?"

"Yes, I remember."

"And I said he must have invented it? Well, he hadn't. . . . You see, I'd told him she was."

"But why on earth did you do that?"

We both began to laugh. "Goodness knows," said Sally. "I suppose I wanted to impress him."

"But what is there impressive in having a French mother?"

"I'm a bit mad like that sometimes, Chris. You must be patient with me."

"All right, Sally, I'll be patient."

"And you'll swear on your honour not to tell Fritz?"

"I swear."

"If you do, you swine," exclaimed Sally, laughing and picking up the paper-knife dagger from my writing-table, "I'll cut your throat!"

Afterwards, I asked Frl. Schroeder what she'd thought of Sally. She was in raptures: "Like a picture, Herr Issyvoo! And so elegant: such beautiful hands and feet! One can see that she belongs to the very best society. . . . You know, Herr Issyvoo, I should never have expected you to have a lady friend like that! You always seem so quiet. . . ."

"Ah, well, Frl. Schroeder, it's often the quiet ones—"

She went off into her little scream of laughter, swaying backwards and forwards on her short legs.

"Quite right, Herr Issyvoo! Quite right!"

～ ～ ～

On New Year's Eve, Sally came to live at Frl. Schroeder's.

It had all been arranged at the last moment. Sally, her suspicions sharpened by my repeated warnings, had caught out Frau Karpf in a particularly gross and clumsy piece of swindling. So she had hardened her heart and given notice. She was to have Frl. Kost's old room. Frl. Schroeder was, of course, enchanted.

We all had our Sylvester Abend dinner at home: Frl. Schroeder, Frl. Mayr, Sally, Bobby, a mixer colleague from the Troika, and myself. It was a great success. Bobby, already restored to favour, flirted daringly with Frl. Schroeder. Frl. Mayr and Sally, talking as one great artiste to another, discussed the possibilities of music-hall work in England. Sally told some really startling lies, which she obviously for the moment half-believed, about how she'd appeared at the Palladium and the London Coliseum. Frl. Mayr capped them with a story of how she'd been drawn through the streets of Munich in a carriage by excited students. From this point it did not take Sally long to persuade Frl. Mayr to sing "Sennerin Abschied von der Alm," which, after claret cup and a bottle of very inexpensive cognac, so exactly suited my mood that I shed a few tears. We all joined in the repeats and the final, ear-splitting *Juch-he!* Then Sally sang "I've Got Those Little Boy Blues" with so much expression that Bobby's mixer colleague, taking it personally, seized her round the waist and had to be restrained by Bobby, who reminded him firmly that it was time to be getting along to business.

Sally and I went with them to the Troika, where we met Fritz. With him was Klaus Linke, the young pianist who used to accompany Sally when she sang at the Lady Windermere. Later, Fritz and I went off alone. Fritz seemed rather depressed: he wouldn't tell me why. Some girls did classical figure-tableaux behind gauze. And then there was a big dancing-hall with telephones on the tables. We had the usual kind of conversations: "Pardon me, Madame, I feel sure from your voice that you're a fascinating little blonde with long black eyelashes—just my type. How did I know? Aha, that's my secret! Yes—quite right: I'm tall, dark, broad-shouldered, military appearance, and the tiniest little moustache. . . . You don't believe me? Then come and see for yourself!" The couples were dancing with hands on each other's hips, yelling in each other's faces, streaming with sweat. An orchestra in Bavarian costume whooped and drank and perspired beer. The place stank like a zoo. After this, I think I strayed off alone and wandered for hours and hours through a jungle of paper streamers. Next morning, when I woke, the bed was full of them.

I had been up and dressed for some time when Sally returned home. She came straight into my room, looking tired but very pleased with herself.

"Hullo, darling! What time is it?"

"Nearly lunch-time."

"I say, is it really? How marvellous! I'm practically starving. I've had nothing for breakfast but a cup of coffee. . . ." She paused expectantly, waiting for my next question.

"Where have you been?" I asked.

"But, darling." Sally opened her eyes very wide in affected surprise. "I thought you knew!"

"I haven't the least idea."

"Nonsense!"

"Really I haven't, Sally."

"Oh, Christopher darling, how can you be such a liar! Why, it was obvious that you'd planned the whole thing! The way you got rid of Fritz—he looked so cross! Klaus and I nearly died of laughing."

All the same, she wasn't quite at her ease. For the first time, I saw her blush.

"Have you got a cigarette, Chris?"

I gave her one and lit the match. She blew out a long cloud of smoke and walked slowly to the window.

"I'm most terribly in love with him."

She turned, frowning slightly; crossed to the sofa and curled herself up carefully, arranging her hands and feet. "At least, I think I am," she added.

I allowed a respectful pause to elapse before asking: "And is Klaus in love with you?"

"He absolutely adores me." Sally was very serious indeed. She smoked for several minutes: "He says he fell in love with me the first time we met, at the Lady Windermere. But as long as we were working together, he didn't dare to say anything. He was afraid it might put me off my singing. . . . He says that, before he met me, he'd no idea what a marvellously beautiful thing a woman's body is. He's only had about three women before, in his life. . . ."

I lit a cigarette.

"Of course, Chris, I don't suppose you really understand. . . . It's awfully hard to explain. . . ."

"I'm sure it is."

"I'm seeing him again at four o'clock." Sally's tone was slightly defiant.

"In that case, you'd better get some sleep. I'll ask Frl. Schroeder to scramble you some eggs; or I'll do them myself if she's still too drunk. You get into bed. You can eat them there."

"Thanks, Chris darling. You are an angel." Sally yawned. "What on earth I should do without you, I don't know."

~ ~ ~

After this, Sally and Klaus saw each other every day. They generally met at our house; and, once, Klaus stayed the whole night. Frl. Schroeder didn't say much to me about it, but I could see that she was rather shocked. Not that she disapproved of Klaus: she thought him very attractive. But she regarded Sally as my property, and it shocked her to see me standing so tamely to one side. I am sure, however, that if I hadn't known about the affair, and if Sally had really been deceiving me, Frl. Schroeder would have assisted at the conspiracy with the greatest relish.

Meanwhile, Klaus and I were a little shy of each other. When we happened to meet on the stairs, we bowed coldly, like enemies.

~ ~ ~

About the middle of January, Klaus left suddenly, for England. Quite unexpectedly he had got the offer of a very good job, synchronizing music for the films. The afternoon he came to say good-bye there was a positively surgical atmosphere in the flat, as though Sally were undergoing a dangerous operation. Frl. Schroeder and Frl. Mayr sat in the living-room and laid cards. The results, Frl. Schroeder later assured me, couldn't have been better. The eight of clubs had appeared three times in a favourable conjunction.

~ ~ ~

Sally spent the whole of the next day curled up on the sofa in her room, with pencil and paper on her lap. She was writing poems. She wouldn't let me see them. She smoked cigarette after cigarette, and mixed Prairie Oysters, but refused to eat more than a few mouthfuls of Frl. Schroeder's omelette.

"Can't I bring you something in, Sally?"

"No, thanks, Chris darling. I just don't want to eat anything at all. I feel all marvellous and ethereal, as if I was a kind of most wonderful saint, or something. You've no idea how glorious it feels. . . . Have a chocolate, darling? Klaus gave me three boxes. If I eat any more, I shall be sick."

"Thank you."

"I don't suppose I shall ever marry him. It would ruin our careers. You see, Christopher, he adores me so terribly that it wouldn't be good for him to always have me hanging about."

"You might marry after you're both famous."

Sally considered this.

"No. . . . That would spoil everything. We should be trying all the time to live up to our old selves, if you know what I mean. And we should both be different. . . . He was so marvellously primitive: just like a faun. He made me feel like a most marvellous nymph, or something, miles away from anywhere, in the middle of the forest."

~ ~ ~

The first letter from Klaus duly arrived. We had all been anxiously awaiting it; and Frl. Schroeder woke me up specially early to tell me that it had come. Perhaps she was afraid that she would never get a chance of reading it herself and relied on me to tell her the contents. If so, her fears were groundless. Sally not only showed the letter to Frl. Schroeder, Frl. Mayr, Bobby, and myself, she even read selections from it aloud in the presence of the porter's wife, who had come up to collect the rent.

From the first, the letter left a nasty taste in my mouth. Its whole tone was egotistical and a bit patronizing. Klaus didn't like London, he said. He felt lonely there. The food disagreed with him. And the people at the studio treated him with lack of consideration. He wished Sally were with him: she could have helped him in many ways. However, now that he was in England, he would try to make the best of it. He would work hard and earn money; and Sally was to work hard too. Work would cheer her up and keep her from getting depressed. At the end of the letter came various endearments, rather too slickly applied. Reading them, one felt: he's written this kind of thing several times before.

Sally was delighted, however. Klaus's exhortation made such an impression upon her that she at once rang up several film companies, a theatrical agency, and half a dozen of her "business" acquaintances. Nothing definite came of all this, it is true; but she remained very optimistic throughout the next twenty-four hours—even her dreams, she told me, had been full of contracts and four-figure cheques. "It's the most marvellous feeling, Chris. I know I'm going right ahead now and going to become the most wonderful actress in the world."

∼   ∼   ∼

One morning, about a week after this, I went into Sally's room and found her holding a letter in her hand. I recognized Klaus's handwriting at once.

"Good morning, Chris darling."

"Good morning, Sally."

"How did you sleep?" Her tone was unnaturally bright and chatty.

"All right, thanks. How did you?"

"Fairly all right. . . . Filthy weather, isn't it?"

"Yes." I walked over to the window to look. It was.

Sally smiled conversationally. "Do you know what this swine's gone and done?"

"What swine?" I wasn't going to be caught out.

"Oh, Chris! For God's sake, don't be so dense!"

"I'm very sorry. I'm afraid I'm a bit slow in the uptake this morning."

"I can't be bothered to explain, darling." Sally held out the letter. "Here, read this, will you? Of all the blasted impudence! Read it aloud. I want to hear how it sounds."

"Mein liebes, armes Kind," the letter began. Klaus called Sally his poor dear child because, as he explained, he was afraid that what he had to tell her would make her terribly unhappy. Nevertheless, he must say it: he must tell her that he had come to a decision. She mustn't imagine that this had been easy for him: it had been very difficult and painful. All the same, he knew he was right. In a word, they must part.

"I see now," wrote Klaus, "that I behaved very selfishly. I thought only of my own pleasure. But now I realize that I must have had a bad influence on you. My dear little girl, you have adored me too much. If we should continue to be together, you would soon have no will and no mind of your own." Klaus went on to advise Sally to live for her work. "Work is the only thing which matters, as I myself have found." He was very much concerned that Sally shouldn't upset herself unduly: "You must be brave, Sally, my poor darling child."

Right at the end of the letter, it all came out:

"I was invited a few nights ago to a party at the house of Lady Klein, a leader of the English aristocracy. I met there a very beautiful and intelligent young English girl named Miss Gore-Eckersley. She is related to an English lord whose name I couldn't quite hear—you will probably know which one I mean. We have met twice since then and had wonderful conversations about many things. I do not think I have ever met a girl who could understand my mind so well as she does—"

"That's a new one on me," broke in Sally bitterly, with a short laugh. "I never suspected the boy of having a mind at all."

At this moment we were interrupted by Frl. Schroeder, who had come, sniffing secrets, to ask if Sally would like a bath. I left them together to make the most of the occasion.

"I can't be angry with the fool," said Sally, later in the day, pacing up and down the room and furiously smoking. "I just feel sorry for him in a motherly sort of way. But what on earth'll happen to *his* work, if he chucks himself at these women's heads, I can't imagine."

She made another turn of the room.

"I think if he'd been having a proper affair with another woman, and had only told me about it after it'd been going on for a long time, I'd have minded more. But this girl! Why, I don't suppose she's even his mistress."

"Obviously not," I agreed. "I say, shall we have a Prairie Oyster?"

"How marvellous you are, Chris! You always think of just the right thing. I wish I could fall in love with you. Klaus isn't worth your little finger."

"I know he isn't."

"The blasted cheek," exclaimed Sally, gulping the Worcester sauce and licking her upper lip, "of his saying I adored him! . . . The worst of it is, I did!"

That evening I went into her room and found her with pen and paper before her.

"I've written about a million letters to him and torn them all up."

"It's no good, Sally. Let's go to the cinema."

"Right you are, Chris darling." Sally wiped her eyes with the corner of her tiny handkerchief. "It's no use bothering, is it?"

"Not a bit of use."

"And now I jolly well *will* be a great actress—just to show him!"

"That's the spirit!"

We went to a little cinema in the Bülowstrasse, where they were showing a film about a girl who sacrificed her stage career for the sake of a Great Love, Home, and Children. We laughed so much that we had to leave before the end.

"I feel ever so much better now," said Sally, as we were coming away.

"I'm glad."

"Perhaps, after all, I can't have been properly in love with him. . . . What do you think?"

"It's rather difficult for me to say."

"I've often thought I was in love with a man, and then I found I wasn't. But this time"—Sally's voice was regretful—"I really did feel *sure* of it. . . . And now, somehow, everything seems to have got a bit confused. . . ."

"Perhaps you're suffering from shock," I suggested.

Sally was very pleased with this idea: "Do you know, I expect I am! . . . You know, Chris, you do understand women most marvellously: better than any man I've ever met. . . . I'm sure that some day you'll write the most marvellous novel, which'll sell simply millions of copies."

"Thank you for believing in me, Sally!"

"Do you believe in me too, Chris?"

"Of course I do."

"No, but honestly?"

"Well . . . I'm quite certain you'll make a terrific success at something—only I'm not sure what it'll be. . . . I mean, there's so many things you could do if you tried, aren't there?"

"I suppose there are." Sally became thoughtful. "At least, sometimes I feel like that. . . . And sometimes I feel I'm no damn use at anything. . . . Why, I can't even keep a man faithful to me for the inside of a month."

"Oh, Sally, don't let's start all that again!"

"All right, Chris—we won't start all that. Let's go and have a drink."

～　～　～

During the weeks that followed, Sally and I were together most of the day. Curled up on the sofa in the big dingy room, she smoked, drank

Prairie Oysters, talked endlessly of the future. When the weather was fine, and I hadn't any lessons to give, we strolled as far as the Wittenbergplatz and sat on a bench in the sunshine, discussing the people who went past. Everybody stared at Sally, in her canary yellow beret and shabby fur coat, like the skin of a mangy old dog.

"I wonder," she was fond of remarking, "what they'd say if they knew that we two old tramps were going to be the most marvellous novelist and the greatest actress in the world."

"They'd probably be very much surprised."

"I expect we shall look back on this time when we're driving about in our Mercedes, and think: After all, it wasn't such bad fun!"

"It wouldn't be such bad fun if we had that Mercedes now."

We talked continually about wealth, fame, huge contracts for Sally, record-breaking sales for the novels I should one day write. "I think," said Sally, "it must be marvellous to be a novelist. You're frightfully dreamy and unpractical and unbusinesslike, and people imagine they can fairly swindle you as much as they want—and then you sit down and write a book about them which fairly shows them what swine they all are, and it's the most terrific success and you make pots of money."

"I expect the trouble with me is that I'm not quite dreamy enough. . . ."

". . . if only I could get a really rich man as my lover. Let's see . . . I shouldn't want more than three thousand a year, and a flat and a decent car. I'd do anything, just now, to get rich. If you're rich you can afford to stand out for a really good contract; you don't have to snap up the first offer you get. . . . Of course, I'd be absolutely faithful to the man who kept me—"

Sally said things like this very seriously and evidently believed she meant them. She was in a curious state of mind, restless and nervy. Often she flew into a temper for no special reason. She talked incessantly about getting work, but made no effort to do so. Her allowance hadn't been stopped, so far, however, and we were living very cheaply, since Sally no longer cared to go out in the evenings or to see other people at all. Once, Fritz came to tea. I left them alone together afterwards to go and write a letter. When I came back Fritz had gone and Sally was in tears.

"That man *bores* me so!" she sobbed. "I hate him! I should like to kill him!"

But in a few minutes she was quite calm again. I started to mix the inevitable Prairie Oyster. Sally, curled up on the sofa, was thoughtfully smoking.

"I wonder," she said suddenly, "if I'm going to have a baby."

"Good God!" I nearly dropped the glass. "Do you really think you are?"

"I don't know. With me it's so difficult to tell: I'm so irregular. . . . I've felt sick sometimes. It's probably something I've eaten. . . ."

"But hadn't you better see a doctor?"

"Oh, I suppose so." Sally yawned listlessly. "There's no hurry."

"Of course there's a hurry! You'll go and see a doctor tomorrow!"

"Look here, Chris, who the hell do you think you're ordering about? I wish now I hadn't said anything about it at all!" Sally was on the point of bursting into tears again.

"Oh, all right! All right!" I hastily tried to calm her. "Do just what you like. It's no business of mine."

"Sorry, darling. I didn't mean to be snappy. I'll see how I feel in the morning. Perhaps I will go and see that doctor, after all."

But of course, she didn't. Next day, indeed, she seemed much brighter. "Let's go out this evening, Chris. I'm getting sick of this room. Let's go and see some life!"

"Right you are, Sally. Where would you like to go?"

"Let's go to the Troika and talk to that old idiot Bobby. Perhaps he'll stand us a drink—you never know!"

Bobby didn't stand us any drinks; but Sally's suggestion proved to have been a good one, nevertheless. For it was while sitting at the bar of the Troika that we first got into conversation with Clive.

~   ~   ~

From that moment onwards we were with him almost continuously; either separately or together. I never once saw him sober. Clive told us that he drank half a bottle of whisky before breakfast, and I had no reason to disbelieve him. He often began to explain to us why he drank so much—it was because he was very unhappy. But why he was so unhappy I never found out, because Sally always interrupted to say that it was time to be going out or moving on to the next place or smoking a cigarette or having another glass of whisky. She was drinking nearly as much whisky as Clive himself. It never seemed to make her really drunk, but sometimes her eyes looked awful, as though they had been boiled. Every day the layer of make-up on her face seemed to get thicker.

Clive was a very big man, good-looking in a heavy Roman way, and just beginning to get fat. He had about him that sad, American air of vagueness which is always attractive; doubly attractive in one who possessed so much money. He was vague, wistful, a bit lost: dimly anxious to have a good time and uncertain how to set about getting it. He seemed never to be quite sure whether he was really enjoying himself, whether what we were doing was *really* fun. He had constantly to be reassured. *Was* this the genuine article? *Was* this the real guaranteed height of a Good Time? It was? Yes, yes, of course—it was marvellous! It was great! Ha, ha, ha! His big school-boyish laugh rolled out, re-echoed, became rather forced, and died away abruptly on that puzzled note of enquiry. He couldn't venture a step without our support. Yet, even as he appealed to us, I thought I could sometimes detect odd sly flashes of sarcasm. What did he really think of us?

Every morning, Clive sent round a hired car to fetch us to the hotel where he was staying. The chauffeur always brought with him a wonderful bouquet of flowers, ordered from the most expensive flower-shop in the Linden. One morning I had a lesson to give and arranged with Sally to join them later. On arriving at the hotel, I found that Clive and Sally had left early to fly to Dresden. There was a note from Clive, apologizing profusely and inviting me to lunch at the hotel restaurant, by myself, as his guest. But I didn't. I was afraid of that look in the head waiter's eye. In the evening, when Clive and Sally returned, Clive had brought me a present: it was a parcel of six silk shirts. "He wanted to get you a gold cigarette case," Sally whispered in my ear, "but I told him shirts would be better. Yours are in such a state. . . . Besides, we've got to go slow at present. We don't want him to think we're gold-diggers. . . ."

I accepted them gratefully. What else could I do? Clive had corrupted us utterly. It was understood that he was going to put up the money to launch Sally upon a stage career. He often spoke of this, in a thoroughly nice way, as though it were a very trivial matter, to be settled, without fuss, between friends. But no sooner had he touched on the subject than his attention seemed to wander off again—his thoughts were as easily distracted as those of a child. Sometimes Sally was very hard put to it, I could see, to hide her impatience. "Just leave us alone for a bit now, darling," she would whisper to me. "Clive and I are going to talk business." But however tactfully Sally tried to bring him to the point, she never quite succeeded. When I rejoined them, half an hour later, I would find Clive smiling and sipping his whisky; and Sally also smiling, to conceal her extreme irritation.

"I adore him," Sally told me, repeatedly and very solemnly, whenever we were alone together. She was intensely earnest in believing this. It was like a dogma in a newly adopted religious creed: Sally adores Clive. It is a very solemn undertaking to adore a millionaire. Sally's features began to assume, with increasing frequency, the rapt expression of the theatrical nun. And indeed, when Clive, with his charming vagueness, gave a particularly flagrant professional beggar a twenty-mark note, we would exchange glances of genuine awe. The waste of so much good money affected us both like something inspired, a kind of miracle.

~ ~ ~

There came an afternoon when Clive seemed more nearly sober than usual. He began to make plans. In a few days we were all three of us to leave Berlin, for good. The Orient Express would take us to Athens. Thence, we should fly to Egypt. From Egypt to Marseilles. From Marseilles, by boat to South America. Then Tahiti. Singapore. Japan. Clive pronounced the names as though they had been stations on the Wannsee railway, quite as a matter of course: he had been there already. He knew it all. His matter-of-fact boredom gradually infused reality into the preposterous conversation. After all, he could do it. I began seriously to believe that he meant to do it. With a mere gesture of his wealth, he could alter the whole course of our lives.

What would become of us? Once started, we should never go back. We could never leave him. Sally, of course, he would marry. I should occupy an ill-defined position: a kind of private secretary without duties. With a flash of vision, I saw myself ten years hence, in flannels and black and white shoes, gone heavier round the jowl and a bit glassy, pouring out a drink in the lounge of a Californian hotel.

"Come and cast an eye at the funeral," Clive was saying.

"What funeral, darling?" Sally asked, patiently. This was a new kind of interruption.

"Why, say, haven't you noticed it?" Clive laughed. "It's a most elegant funeral. It's been going past for the last hour."

We all three went out onto the balcony of Clive's room. Sure enough, the street below was full of people. They were burying Hermann Müller. Ranks of pale steadfast clerks, government officials, trade union secretaries—the whole drab weary pageant of Prussian Social Democracy—trudged past under their banners towards the silhouetted arches of the Brandenburger Tor, from which the long black streamers stirred slowly in an evening breeze.

"Say, who was this guy, anyway?" asked Clive, looking down. "I guess he must have been a big swell?"

"God knows," Sally answered, yawning. "Look, Clive darling, isn't it a marvellous sunset?"

She was quite right. We had nothing to do with those Germans down there, marching, or with the dead man in the coffin, or with the words on the banners. In a few days, I thought, we shall have forfeited all kinship with ninety-nine per cent of the population of the world, with the men and women who earn their living, who insure their lives, who are anxious about the future of their children. Perhaps in the Middle Ages people felt like this, when they believed themselves to have sold their souls to the Devil. It was a curious, exhilarating, not unpleasant sensation: but, at the same time, I felt slightly scared. Yes, I said to myself, I've done it, now. I am lost.

~ ~ ~

Next morning, we arrived at the hotel at the usual time. The porter eyed us, I thought, rather queerly.

"Whom did you wish to see, Madam?"

The question seemed so extraordinary that we both laughed.

"Why, number 365, of course," Sally answered. "Who did you think? Don't you know us by this time?"

"I'm afraid you can't do that, Madam. The gentleman in 365 left early this morning."

"Left? You mean he's gone out for the day? That's funny! What time will he be back?"

"He didn't say anything about coming back, Madam. He was travelling to Budapest."

As we stood there goggling at him, a waiter hurried up with a note.

"Dear Sally and Chris," it said, "I can't stick this darned town any longer, so am off. Hoping to see you sometime, Clive.

"(These are in case I forgot anything.)"

In the envelope were three hundred-mark notes. These, the fading flowers, Sally's four pairs of shoes and two hats (bought in Dresden), and my six shirts were our total assets from Clive's visit. At first, Sally was very angry. Then we both began to laugh.

"Well, Chris, I'm afraid we're not much use as gold-diggers, are we, darling?"

We spent most of the day discussing whether Clive's departure was a premeditated trick. I was inclined to think it wasn't. I imagined him leaving every new town and every new set of acquaintances in much the same sort of way. I sympathized with him, a good deal.

Then came the question of what was to be done with the money. Sally decided to put by two hundred and fifty marks for some new clothes: fifty marks we would blow that evening.

But blowing the fifty marks wasn't as much fun as we'd imagined it would be. Sally felt ill and couldn't eat the wonderful dinner we'd ordered. We were both depressed.

"You know, Chris, I'm beginning to think that men are always going to leave me. The more I think about it, the more men I remember who have. It's ghastly, really."

"I'll never leave you, Sally."

"Won't you, darling? . . . But seriously, I believe I'm a sort of Ideal Woman, if you know what I mean. I'm the sort of woman who can take men away from their wives, but I could never keep anybody for long. And that's because I'm the type which every man imagines he wants, until he gets me; and then he finds he doesn't really, after all."

"Well, you'd rather be that than the Ugly Duckling with the Heart of Gold, wouldn't you?"

". . . I could kick myself, the way I behaved to Clive. I ought never to have bothered him about money, the way I did. I expect he thought I was just a common little whore, like all the others. And I really did adore him—in a way. . . . If I'd married him, I'd have made a man out of him. I'd have got him to give up drinking."

"You set him such a good example."

We both laughed.

"The old swine might at least have left me with a decent cheque."

"Never mind, darling. There's more where he came from."

"I don't care," said Sally. "I'm sick of being a whore. I'll never look at a man with money again."

~ ~ ~

Next morning, Sally felt very ill. We both put it down to the drink. She stayed in bed the whole morning and when she got up she fainted. I wanted her to see a doctor straight away, but she wouldn't. About tea-time, she fainted again and looked so bad afterwards that Frl. Schroeder and I sent for a doctor without consulting her at all.

The doctor, when he arrived, stayed a long time. Frl. Schroeder and I sat waiting in the living-room to hear his diagnosis. But, very much to our surprise, he left the flat suddenly, in a great hurry, without even looking in to wish us good afternoon. I went at once to Sally's room. Sally was sitting up in bed, with a rather fixed grin on her face.

"Well, Christopher darling, I've been made an April Fool of."

"What do you mean?"

"He says I'm going to have a baby." Sally tried to laugh.

"Oh my God!"

"Don't look so scared, darling! I've been more or less expecting it, you know."

"It's Klaus's, I suppose?"

"Yes."

"And what are you going to do about it?"

"Not have it, of course." Sally reached for a cigarette. I sat stupidly staring at my shoes.

"Will the doctor . . . ?"

"No, he won't. I asked him straight out. He was terribly shocked. I said: 'My dear man, what do you imagine would happen to the unfortunate child if it was born? Do I look as if I'd make a good mother?'"

"And what did he say to that?"

"He seemed to think it was quite beside the point. The only thing which matters to him is his professional reputation."

"Well then, we've got to find someone without a professional reputation, that's all."

"I should think," said Sally, "we'd better ask Frl. Schroeder."

So Frl. Schroeder was consulted. She took it very well: she was alarmed but extremely practical. Yes, she knew of somebody. A friend of a friend's friend had once had difficulties. And the doctor was a fully qualified man, very clever indeed. The only trouble was, he might be rather expensive.

"Thank goodness," Sally interjected, "we haven't spent all that swine Clive's money!"

"I must say, I think Klaus ought—"

"Look here, Chris. Let me tell you this once for all: if I catch you writing to Klaus about this business, I'll never forgive you and I'll never speak to you again!"

"Oh, very well . . . Of course I won't. It was just a suggestion, that's all."

I didn't like the doctor. He kept stroking and pinching Sally's arm and pawing her hand. However, he seemed the right man for the job. Sally was to go into his private nursing-home as soon as there was a vacancy for her. Everything was perfectly official and above-board. In a few polished sentences, the dapper little doctor dispelled the least whiff of sinister illegality. Sally's state of health, he explained, made it quite impossible for her to undergo the risks of childbirth: there would be a certificate to that effect. Needless to say, the certificate would cost a lot of money. So would the nursing-home and so would the operation itself. The doctor wanted two hundred and fifty marks down before he would make any arrangements at all. In the end, we beat him down to two hundred. Sally wanted the extra fifty, she explained to me later, to get some new nightdresses.

~ ~ ~

At last, it was spring. The cafés were putting up wooden platforms on the pavement and the ice-cream shops were opening, with their rainbow-wheels. We drove to the nursing-home in an open taxi. Because of the lovely weather, Sally was in better spirits than I had seen her in for weeks. But Frl. Schroeder, though she bravely tried to smile, was on the verge of tears. "The doctor isn't a Jew, I hope?" Frl. Mayr asked me sternly. "Don't you let one of those filthy Jews touch her. They always try to get a job of that kind, the beasts!"

Sally had a nice room, clean and cheerful, with a balcony. I called there again in the evening. Lying in bed without her make-up, she looked years younger, like a little girl.

"Hullo, darling. . . . They haven't killed me yet, you see. But they've been doing their best to. . . . Isn't this a funny place? . . . I wish that pig Klaus could see me. . . . This is what comes of not understanding his *mind*. . . ."

She was a bit feverish and laughed a great deal. One of the nurses came in for a moment, as if looking for something, and went out again almost immediately.

"She was dying to get a peep at you," Sally explained. "You see, I told her you were the father. You don't mind, do you, darling . . . ?"

"Not at all. It's a compliment."

"It makes everything so much simpler. Otherwise, if there's no one, they think it so odd. And I don't care for being sort of looked down on and pitied as the poor betrayed girl who gets abandoned by her lover. It isn't particularly flattering for me, is it? So I told her we were most terribly in love but fearfully hard up, so that we couldn't afford to marry, and how we dreamed of the time when we'd both be rich and famous and then we'd have a family of ten, just to make up for this one. The nurse was awfully touched, poor girl. In fact, she wept. Tonight, when she's on duty, she's going to show me pictures of *her* young man. Isn't it sweet?"

~ ~ ~

Next day, Frl. Schroeder and I went round to the nursing-home together. We found Sally lying flat, with the bedclothes up to her chin.

"Oh, hullo, you two! Won't you sit down? What time is it?" She turned uneasily in bed and rubbed her eyes: "Where did all these flowers come from?"

"We brought them."

"How marvellous of you!" Sally smiled vacantly. "Sorry to be such a fool today. . . . It's this bloody chloroform. . . . My head's full of it."

We only stayed a few minutes. On the way home Frl. Schroeder was terribly upset. "Will you believe it, Herr Issyvoo, I couldn't take it more to heart if it was my own daughter? Why, when I see the poor child suffering like that, I'd rather it was myself lying there in her place—I would indeed!"

Next day Sally was much better. We all went to visit her: Frl. Schroeder, Frl. Mayr, Bobby, and Fritz. Fritz, of course, hadn't the faintest idea what had really happened. Sally, he had been told, was being operated upon for a small internal ulcer. As always is the way with people when they aren't in the know, he made all kinds of unintentional and startlingly apt references to storks, gooseberry-bushes, perambulators, and babies generally; and even recounted a special new item of scandal about a well-known Berlin society lady who was said to have undergone a recent illegal operation. Sally and I avoided each other's eyes.

~ ~ ~

On the evening of the next day, I visited her at the nursing-home for the last time. She was to leave in the morning. She was alone and we sat together on the balcony. She seemed more or less all right now and could walk about the room.

"I told the sister I didn't want to see anybody today except you." Sally yawned languidly. "People make me feel so tired."

"Would you rather I went away too?"

"Oh no," said Sally, without much enthusiasm. "If you go, one of the nurses will only come in and begin to chatter; and if I'm not lively and bright with her, they'll say I have to stay in this hellish place a couple of extra days, and I couldn't stand that."

She stared out moodily over the quiet street.

"You know, Chris, in some ways I wish I'd had that kid. . . . It would have been rather marvellous to have had it. The last day or two, I've been sort of feeling what it would be like to be a mother. Do you know, last night, I sat here for a long time by myself and held this cushion in my arms and imagined it was my baby? And I felt a most marvellous sort of shut-off feeling from all the rest of the world. I imagined how it'd grow up and how I'd work for it, and how, after I'd put it to bed at nights, I'd go out and make love to filthy old men to get money to pay for its food and clothes. . . . It's all very well for you to grin like that, Chris . . . I did really!"

"Well, why don't you marry and have one?"

"I don't know. . . . I feel as if I'd lost faith in men. I just haven't any use for them at all. . . . Even you, Christopher, if you were to go out into the street now and be run over by a taxi . . . I should be sorry in a way, of course, but I shouldn't really *care* a damn."

"Thank you, Sally."

We both laughed.

"I didn't mean that, of course, darling—at least, not personally. You mustn't mind what I say while I'm like this. I get all sorts of crazy ideas into my head. Having babies makes you feel awfully primitive, like a sort of wild animal or something, defending its young. Only the trouble is, I haven't any young to defend. . . . I expect that's what makes me so frightfully bad-tempered to everybody just now.''

~ ~ ~

It was partly as the result of this conversation that I suddenly decided, that evening, to cancel all my lessons, leave Berlin as soon as possible, go to some place on the Baltic, and try to start working. Since Christmas, I had hardly written a word.

Sally, when I told her my idea, was rather relieved, I think. We both needed a change. We talked vaguely of her joining me later; but, even then, I felt that she wouldn't. Her plans were very uncertain. Later, she might go to Paris, or to the Alps, or to the South of France, she said—if she could get the cash. "But probably," she added, "I shall just stay on here. I should be quite happy. I seem to have got sort of used to this place.''

~ ~ ~

I returned to Berlin towards the middle of July.

All this time I had heard nothing of Sally, beyond half a dozen post-cards, exchanged during the first month of my absence. I wasn't much surprised to find she'd left her room in our flat.

"Of course, I quite understand her going. I couldn't make her as comfortable as she'd the right to expect; especially as we haven't any running water in the bedrooms." Poor Frl. Schroeder's eyes had filled with tears. "But it was a terrible disappointment to me, all the same. . . . Frl. Bowles behaved very handsomely, I can't complain about that. She insisted on paying for her room until the end of July. I was entitled to the money, of course, because she didn't give notice until the twenty-first—but I'd never have mentioned it. . . . She was such a charming young lady—"

"Have you got her address?"

"Oh yes, and the telephone number. You'll be ringing her up, of course. She'll be delighted to see you. . . . The other gentlemen came and went, but you were her real friend, Herr Issyvoo. You know, I always used to hope that you two would get married. You'd have made an ideal couple. You always had such a good steady influence on her, and she used to brighten you up a bit when you got too deep in your books and studies. . . . Oh yes, Herr Issyvoo, you may laugh—but you never can tell! Perhaps it isn't too late yet!"

～　～　～

Next morning, Frl. Schroeder woke me in great excitement.

"Herr Issyvoo, what do you think! They've shut the Darmstädter und National! There'll be thousands ruined, I shouldn't wonder! The milkman says we'll have civil war in a fortnight! Whatever do you say to that!"

As soon as I'd got dressed, I went down into the street. Sure enough, there was a crowd outside the branch bank on the Nollendorfplatz corner, a lot of men with leather satchels and women with stringbags—women like Frl. Schroeder herself. The iron lattices were drawn down over the bank windows. Most of the people were staring intently and rather stupidly at the locked door. In the middle of the door was fixed a small notice, beautifully printed in Gothic type, like a page from a classic author. The notice said that the Reichspresident had guaranteed the deposits. Everything was quite all right. Only the bank wasn't going to open.

A little boy was playing with a hoop amongst the crowd. The hoop ran against a woman's legs. She flew out at him at once: "Du, sei bloss nicht so frech! Cheeky little brat! What do you want here!" Another woman joined in, attacking the scared boy: "Get out! You can't understand it, can you?" And another asked, in furious sarcasm: "Have you got your money in the bank too, perhaps?" The boy fled before their pent-up, exploding rage.

In the afternoon it was very hot. The details of the new emergency decrees were in the early evening papers—terse, governmentally inspired. One alarmist headline stood out boldly, barred with blood-red ink: "Everything Collapses!" A Nazi journalist reminded his readers that to-morrow, the fourteenth of July, was a day of national rejoicing in France; and doubtless, he added, the French would rejoice with especial fervour this year, at the prospect of Germany's downfall. Going into an outfitter's, I bought myself a pair of ready-made flannel trousers for twelve marks fifty—a gesture of confidence by England. Then I got into the Underground to go and visit Sally.

She was living in a block of three-room flats, designed as an artists' colony, not far from the Breitenbachplatz. When I rang the bell, she opened the door to me herself.

"Hilloo, Chris, you old swine!"

"Hullo, Sally darling!"

"How are you? . . . Be careful, darling, you'll make me untidy. I've got to go out in a few minutes."

I had never seen her all in white before. It suited her. But her face looked thinner and older. Her hair was cut in a new way and beautifully waved.

"You're very smart," I said.

"Am I?" Sally smiled her pleased, dreamy, self-conscious smile. I followed her into the sitting-room of the flat. One wall was entirely window. There was some cherry-coloured wooden furniture and a very low divan with gaudy fringed cushions. A fluffy white miniature dog jumped to its feet and yapped. Sally picked it up and went through the gestures of kissing it, just not touching it with her lips.

"Freddi, mein Liebling, Du bist *soo* süss!"

"Yours?" I asked, noticing the improvement in her German accent.

"No. He belongs to Gerda, the girl I share this flat with."

"Have you known her long?"

"Only a week or two."

"What's she like?"

"Not bad. As stingy as hell. I have to pay for practically everything."

"It's nice here."

"Do you think so? Yes, I suppose it's all right. Better than that hole in the Nollendorfstrasse, anyhow."

"What made you leave? Did you and Frl. Schroeder have a row?"

"No, not exactly. Only I got so sick of hearing her talk. She nearly talked my head off. She's an awful old bore, really."

"She's very fond of you."

Sally shrugged her shoulders with a slight impatient listless movement. Throughout this conversation, I noticed that she avoided my eyes. There was a long pause. I felt puzzled and vaguely embarrassed. I began to wonder how soon I could make an excuse to go.

Then the telephone bell rang. Sally yawned, pulled the instrument across onto her lap.

"Hilloo, who's there? Yes, it's me. . . . No. . . . No. . . . I've really no idea. . . . *Really* I haven't! I'm to guess?" Her nose wrinkled. "Is it Erwin? No? Paul? No? Wait a minute. . . . Let me see. . . ."

"And now, darling, I must fly!" cried Sally, when, at last, the conversation was over. "I'm about two hours late already!"

"Got a new boy friend?"

But Sally ignored my grin. She lit a cigarette with a faint expression of distaste.

"I've got to see a man on business," she said briefly.

"And when shall we meet again?"

"I'll have to see, darling. . . . I've got such a lot on, just at present. . . . I shall be out in the country all day tomorrow, and probably the day after. . . . I'll let you know. . . . I may be going to Frankfurt quite soon."

"Have you got a job there?"

"No. Not exactly." Sally's voice was brief, dismissing this subject. "I've decided not to try for any film work until the autumn, anyhow. I shall take a thorough rest."

"You seem to have made a lot of new friends."

Again, Sally's manner became vague, carefully casual.

"Yes, I suppose I have. . . . It's probably a reaction from all those months at Frl. Schroeder's, when I never saw a soul."

"Well." I couldn't resist a malicious grin. "I hope for your sake that none of your new friends have got their money in the Darmstädter und National."

"Why?" She was interested at once. "What's the matter with it?"

"Do you really mean to say you haven't heard?"

"Of course not. I never read the papers, and I haven't been out today, yet."

I told her the news of the crisis. At the end of it, she was looking quite scared.

"But why on earth," she exclaimed impatiently, "didn't you tell me all this before? It may be serious."

"I'm sorry, Sally. I took it for granted that you'd know already . . . especially as you seem to be moving in financial circles, nowadays."

But she ignored this little dig. She was frowning, deep in her own thoughts.

"If it was *very* serious, Leo would have rung up and told me . . . ," she murmured at length. And this reflection appeared to ease her mind considerably.

We walked out together to the corner of the street, where Sally picked up a taxi.

"It's an awful nuisance living so far off," she said. "I'm probably going to get a car soon."

"By the way," she added just as we were parting, "what was it like on Ruegen?"

"I bathed a lot."

"Well, good-bye, darling. I'll see you sometime."

"Good-bye, Sally. Enjoy yourself."

~ ~ ~

About a week after this, Sally rang me up.

"Can you come round at once, Chris? It's very important. I want you to do me a favour."

This time, also, I found Sally alone in the flat.

"Do you want to earn some money, darling?" she greeted me.

"Of course."

"Splendid! You see, it's like this. . . ." She was in a fluffy pink dressing-wrap and inclined to be breathless. "There's a man I know who's starting a magazine. It's going to be most terribly highbrow and artistic, with lots of marvellous modern photographs, ink-pots and girls' heads upside down—you know the sort of thing. . . . The point is, each number is going to take a special country and kind of review it, with articles about the manners and customs, and all that. . . . Well, the first country they're going to do is England, and they want me to write an article on the English Girl. . . . Of course, I haven't the foggiest idea what to say, so what I thought was: you could write the article in my name and get the money—I only want not to disoblige this man who's editing the paper, because he may be terribly useful to me in other ways, later on. . . ."

"All right, I'll try."

"Oh, marvellous!"

"How soon do you want it done?"

"You see, darling, that's the whole point. I must have it at once. . . . Otherwise it's no earthly use, because I promised it four days ago and I simply must give it him this evening. . . . It needn't be very long. About five hundred words."

"Well, I'll do my best. . . ."

"Good. That's wonderful. . . . Sit down wherever you like. Here's some paper. You've got a pen? Oh, and here's a dictionary, in case there's a word you can't spell. . . . I'll just be having my bath."

When, three quarters of an hour later, Sally came in, dressed for the day, I had finished. Frankly, I was rather pleased with my effort.

She read it through carefully, a slow frown gathering between her beautifully pencilled eyebrows. When she had finished, she laid down the manuscript with a sigh.

"I'm sorry, Chris. It won't do at all."

"Won't do?" I was genuinely taken aback.

"Of course, I dare say it's very good from a literary point of view, and all that. . . ."

"Well then, what's wrong with it?"

"It's not nearly snappy enough." Sally was quite final. "It's not the kind of thing this man wants, at all."

I shrugged my shoulders. "I'm sorry, Sally. I did my best. But journalism isn't really in my line, you know."

There was a resentful pause. My vanity was piqued.

"My goodness, I know who'll do it for me if I ask him!" cried Sally, suddenly jumping up. "Why on earth didn't I think of him before?" She grabbed the telephone and dialled a number: "Oh, hilloo, Kurt darling. . . ."

In three minutes, she had explained all about the article. Replacing the receiver on its stand, she announced triumphantly: "That's marvellous! He's going to do it at once. . . ." She paused impressively and added: "That was Kurt Rosenthal."

"Who's he?"

"You've never heard of him?" This annoyed Sally; she pretended to be immensely surprised. "I thought you took an interest in the cinema. He's miles the best young scenario writer. He earns pots of money. He's only doing this as a favour to me, of course. . . . He says he'll dictate it to his secretary while he's shaving and then send it straight round to the editor's flat. . . . He's marvellous!"

"Are you sure it'll be what the editor wants, this time?"

"Of course it will! Kurt's an absolute genius. He can do anything. Just now, he's writing a novel in his spare time. He's so fearfully busy, he can only dictate it while he's having breakfast. He showed me the first few chapters, the other day. Honestly, I think it's easily the best novel I've ever read."

"Indeed?"

"That's the sort of writer I admire," Sally continued. She was careful to avoid my eye. "He's terribly ambitious and he works the whole time; and he can write anything—anything you like: scenarios, novels, plays, poetry, advertisements. . . . He's not a bit stuck-up about it either. Not like these young men who, because they've written one book, start talking about Art and imagining they're the most wonderful authors in the world. . . . They make me sick. . . ."

Irritated as I was with her, I couldn't help laughing.

"Since when have you disapproved of me so violently, Sally?"

"I don't disapprove of you"—but she couldn't look me in the face—"not exactly."

"I merely make you sick?"

"I don't know what it is. . . . You seem to have changed, somehow. . . ."

"How have I changed?"

"It's difficult to explain. . . . You don't seem to have any energy or want to get anywhere. You're so dilettante. It annoys me."

"I'm sorry." But my would-be facetious tone sounded rather forced. Sally frowned down at her tiny black shoes.

"You must remember I'm a woman, Christopher. All women like men to be strong and decided and following out their careers. A woman wants to be motherly to a man and protect his weak side, but he must have a strong side too, which she can respect. . . . If you ever care for a woman, I don't advise you to let her see that you've got no ambition. Otherwise she'll get to despise you."

"Yes, I see. . . . And that's the principle on which you choose your friends—your *new* friends?"

She flared up at this.

"It's very easy for you to sneer at my friends for having good business heads. If they've got money, it's because they've worked for it. . . . I suppose you consider yourself better than they are?"

"Yes, Sally, since you ask me—if they're at all as I imagine them, I do."

"There you go, Christopher! That's typical of you. That's what annoys me about you: you're conceited and lazy. If you say things like that, you ought to be able to prove them."

"How does one prove that one's better than somebody else? Besides, that's not what I said. I said I considered myself better—it's simply a matter of taste."

Sally made no reply. She lit a cigarette, slightly frowning.

"You say I seem to have changed," I continued. "To be quite frank, I've been thinking the same thing about *you*."

Sally didn't seem surprised. "Have you, Christopher? Perhaps you're right. I don't know. . . . Or perhaps we've neither of us changed. Perhaps we're just seeing each other as we really are. We're awfully different in lots of ways, you know."

"Yes, I've noticed that."

"I think," said Sally, smoking meditatively, her eyes on her shoes, "that we may have sort of outgrown each other a bit."

"Perhaps we have. . . ." I smiled: Sally's real meaning was so obvious. "At any rate, we needn't quarrel about it, need we?"

"Of course not, darling."

There was a pause. Then I said that I must be going. We were both rather embarrassed now, and extra polite.

"Are you certain you won't have a cup of coffee?"

"No, thanks awfully."

"Have some tea? It's specially good. I got it as a present."

"No, thanks very much indeed, Sally. I really must be getting along."

"Must you?" She sounded, after all, rather relieved. "Be sure and ring me up some time soon, won't you?"

"Yes, rather."

~ ~ ~

It wasn't until I had actually left the house and was walking quickly away up the street that I realized how angry and ashamed I felt. What an utter little bitch she is, I thought. After all, I told myself, it's only what I've always known she was like—right from the start. No, that wasn't true: I hadn't known it. I'd flattered myself—why not be frank about it?—that she was fond of me. Well, I'd been wrong, it seemed; but could I blame her for that? Yet I did blame her, I was furious with her; nothing would have pleased me more, at that moment, than to see her soundly whipped. Indeed, I was so absurdly upset that I began to wonder whether I hadn't, all this time, in my own peculiar way, been in love with Sally myself.

But no, it wasn't love either—it was worse. It was the cheapest, most childish kind of wounded vanity. Not that I cared a curse what she thought of my article—well, just a little, perhaps, but only a very little; my literary self-conceit was proof against anything *she* could say—it was her criticism of myself. The awful sexual flair women have for taking the stuffing out of a man! It was no use telling myself that Sally had the vocabulary and mentality of a twelve-year-old schoolgirl, that she was altogether comic and preposterous; it was no use—I only knew that I'd been somehow made to feel a sham. Wasn't I a bit of a sham anyway—though not for her ridiculous reasons—with my arty talk to lady pupils and my newly acquired parlour-socialism? Yes, I was. But she knew nothing about that. I could quite easily have impressed her. That was the most humiliating part of the whole business; I had mismanaged our interview from the very beginning. I had blushed and squabbled, instead of being wonderful, convincing, superior, fatherly, mature. I had tried to compete with her beastly little Kurt on his own ground; just the very thing, of course, which Sally had wanted and expected me to do! After all these months, I had made the one really fatal mistake—I had let her see that I was not only incompetent but jealous. Yes, vulgarly jealous. I could have kicked myself. The mere thought made me prickly with shame from head to foot.

Well, the mischief was done, now. There was only one thing for it, and that was to forget the whole affair. And of course it would be impossible for me ever to see Sally again.

~   ~   ~

It must have been about ten days after this that I was visited, one morning, by a small pale dark-haired young man who spoke American fluently with a slight foreign accent. His name, he told me, was George P. Sandars. He had seen my English-teaching advertisement in the *B.Z. am Mittag*.

"When would you like to begin?" I asked him.

But the young man shook his head hastily. Oh no, he hadn't come to take lessons, at all. Rather disappointed, I waited politely for him to explain the reason of his visit. He seemed in no hurry to do this. Instead, he accepted a cigarette, sat down, and began to talk chattily about the States. Had I ever been to Chicago? No? Well, had I heard of James L. Schraube? I hadn't? The young man uttered a faint sigh. He had the air of being very patient with me, and with the world in general. He had evidently been over the same ground with a good many other people already. James L. Schraube, he explained, was a very big man in Chicago: he owned a whole chain of restaurants and several cinemas. He had two large country houses and a yacht on Lake Michigan. And he possessed no less than four cars. By this time, I was beginning to drum with my fingers on the table. A pained expression passed over the young man's face. He excused himself for taking up my valuable time; he had only told me about Mr. Schraube, he said, because he thought I might be interested—his tone implied a gentle rebuke—and because Mr. Schraube, had I known him, would certainly have vouched for his friend Sandars's respectability. However . . . it couldn't be helped . . . well, would I lend him two hundred marks? He needed the money in order to start a business; it was a unique opportunity, which he would miss altogether if he didn't find the money before tomorrow morning. He would pay me back within three days. If I gave him the money now he would return that same evening with papers to prove that the whole thing was perfectly genuine.

No? Ah well . . . He didn't seem unduly surprised. He rose to go at once, like a business man who has wasted a valuable twenty minutes on a prospective customer: the loss, he contrived politely to imply, was mine, not his. Already at the door, he paused for a moment: Did I happen, by any chance, to know some film actresses? He was travelling, as a sideline, in a new kind of face-cream specially invented to keep the skin from getting dried up by the studio lights. It was being used by all the Hollywood stars already, but in Europe it was still quite unknown. If he could find half a dozen actresses to use and recommend it, they should have free sample jars and permanent supplies at half-price.

After a moment's hesitation, I gave him Sally's address. I don't know quite why I did it. Partly, of course, to get rid of the young man, who showed signs of wishing to sit down again and continue our conversation. Partly, perhaps, out of malice. It would do Sally no harm to have to put up with his chatter for an hour or two: she had told me that she liked men with ambition. Perhaps she would even get a jar of the face-cream —if it existed at all. And if he touched her for the two hundred marks —well, that wouldn't matter so very much either. He couldn't deceive a baby.

"But whatever you do," I warned him, "don't say that I sent you." He agreed to this at once, with a slight smile. He must have had his own explanation of my request, for he didn't appear to find it in the least strange. He raised his hat politely as he went downstairs. By the next morning, I had forgotten about his visit altogether.

~ ~ ~

A few days later, Sally herself rang me up. I had been called away in the middle of a lesson to answer the telephone and was very ungracious.

"Oh, is that you, Christopher darling?"

"Yes. It's me."

"I say, can you come round and see me at once?"

"No."

"Oh. . . ." My refusal evidently gave Sally a shock. There was a little pause, then she continued, in a tone of unwonted humility: "I suppose you're most terribly busy?"

"Yes. I am."

"Well . . . would you mind frightfully if I came round to see you?"

"What about?"

"Darling"—Sally sounded positively desperate—"I can't possibly explain to you over the telephone. . . . It's something really serious."

"Oh, I see"—I tried to make this as nasty as possible—"another magazine article, I suppose?"

Nevertheless, as soon as I'd said it, we both had to laugh.

"Chris, you are a brute!" Sally tinkled gaily along the wire, then checked herself abruptly. "No, darling—this time I promise you: it's most terribly serious, really and truly it is." She paused; then impressively added: "And you're the only person who can possibly help."

"Oh, all right. . . ." I was more than half melted already. "Come in an hour."

~ ~ ~

"Well, darling, I'll begin at the very beginning, shall I? . . . Yesterday morning, a man rang me up and asked if he could come round and see me. He said it was on very important business; and as he seemed to know my name and everything, of course I said: Yes, certainly, come at once. . . . So he came. He told me his name was Rakowski—Paul Rakowski —and that he was a European agent of Metro-Goldwyn-Mayer and that he'd come to make me an offer. He said they were looking out for an English actress who spoke German to act in a comedy film they were going to shoot on the Italian Riviera. He was most frightfully convincing about it all; he told me who the director was and the camera-man and the art-director and who'd written the script. Naturally, I hadn't heard of any of them before. But that didn't seem so surprising: in fact, it really made it sound much more real, because most people would have chosen one of the names you see in the newspapers. . . . Anyhow, he said that, now he'd seen me, he was sure I'd be just the person for the part, and he could practically promise it to me, as long as the test was all right . . . so of course I was simply thrilled and I asked when the test would be and he said not for a day or two, as he had to make arrangements with the Ufa people. . . . So then we began to talk about Hollywood and he told me all kinds of stories—I suppose they *could* have been things he'd read in fan magazines, but somehow I'm pretty sure they weren't—and then he told me how they make sound-effects and how they do the trick-work; he was really most awfully interesting and he certainly must have been inside a great many studios. . . . Anyhow, when we'd finished talking about Hollywood, he started to tell me about the rest of America and the people he knew, and about the gangsters and about New York. He said he'd only just arrived from there and all his luggage was still in the customs at Hamburg. As a matter of fact, I *had* been thinking to myself that it seemed rather queer he was so shabbily dressed; but after he said that, of course, I thought it was quite natural. . . . Well—now you must promise not to laugh at this part of the story, Chris, or I simply shan't be able to tell you—presently he started making the most passionate love to me. At first I was rather angry with him, for sort of mixing business with pleasure; but then, after a bit, I didn't mind so much: he was quite attractive, in a Russian kind of way. . . . And the end of it was, he invited me to have dinner with him; so we went to Horcher's and had one of the most marvellous dinners I've ever had in my life (that's one consolation); only, when the bill came, he said: 'Oh, by the way, darling, could you lend me three hundred marks until tomorrow? I've only got dollar bills on me, and I'll have to get them changed at the bank.' So, of course, I gave them to him: as bad luck would have it, I had quite a lot of money on me, that evening. . . . And then he said: 'Let's have a bottle of champagne to celebrate your film contract.' So I agreed, and I suppose by that time I must have been pretty tight, because when he asked me to spend the night with him, I said Yes. We went to one of those little hotels in the Augsburgerstrasse—I forget its name, but I can find it again, easily.

. . . It was the most ghastly hole. . . . Anyhow, I don't remember much more about what happened that evening. It was early this morning that I started to think about things properly, while he was still asleep; and I began to wonder if everything was really quite all right. . . . I hadn't noticed his underclothes before: they gave me a bit of a shock. You'd expect an important film man to wear silk next to his skin, wouldn't you? Well, his were the most extraordinary kind of stuff like camel-hair or something; they looked as if they might have belonged to John the Baptist. And then he had a regular Woolworth's tin clip for his tie. It wasn't so much that his things were shabby; but you could see they'd never been any good, even when they were new. . . . I was just making up my mind to get out of bed and take a look inside his pockets, when he woke up and it was too late. So we ordered breakfast. . . . I don't know if he thought I was madly in love with him by this time and wouldn't notice, or whether he just couldn't be bothered to go on pretending, but this morning he was like a completely different person—just a common little guttersnipe. He ate his jam off the blade of his knife, and of course most of it went onto the sheets. And he sucked the insides out of the eggs with a most terrific squelching noise. I couldn't help laughing at him, and that made him quite cross. . . . Then he said: 'I must have beer!' Well, I said, all right; ring down to the office and ask for some. To tell you the truth, I was beginning to be a bit frightened of him. He'd started to scowl in the most cavemannish way: I felt sure he must be mad. So I thought I'd humour him as much as I could. . . . Anyhow, he seemed to think I'd made quite a good suggestion, and he picked up the telephone and had a long conversation and got awfully angry, because he said they refused to send beer up to the rooms. I realize now that he must have been holding the hook all the time and just acting; but he did it most awfully well, and anyhow I was much too scared to notice things much. I thought he'd probably start murdering me because he couldn't get his beer. . . . However, he took it quite quietly. He said he must get dressed and go downstairs and fetch it himself. All right, I said. . . . Well, I waited and waited and he didn't come back. So at last I rang the bell and asked the maid if she'd seen him go out. And she said: 'Oh yes, the gentleman paid the bill and went away about an hour ago. . . . He said you weren't to be disturbed.' I was so surprised, I just said: 'Oh, right, thanks. . . .' The funny thing was, I'd so absolutely made up my mind by this time that he was a loony that I'd stopped suspecting him of being a swindler. Perhaps that was what he wanted. . . . Anyhow, he wasn't such a loony, after all, because, when I looked in my bag, I found he'd helped himself to all the rest of my money, as well as the change from the three hundred marks I'd lent him the night before. . . . What really annoys me about the whole business is that I bet he thinks I'll be ashamed to go to the police. Well, I'll just show him he's wrong—"

"I say, Sally, what exactly did this young man look like?"

"He was about your height. Pale. Dark. You could tell he wasn't a born American; he spoke with a foreign accent—"

"Can you remember if he mentioned a man named Schraube, who lives in Chicago?"

"Let's see. . . . Yes, of course he did! He talked about him a lot. . . . But, Chris, how on earth did you know?"

"Well, it's like this. . . . Look here, Sally, I've got a most awful confession to make to you. . . . I don't know if you'll ever forgive me. . . ."

～ ～ ～

We went to the Alexanderplatz that same afternoon.

The interview was even more embarrassing than I had expected. For myself at any rate. Sally, if she felt uncomfortable, did not show it by so much as the movement of an eyelid. She detailed the facts of the case to the two bespectacled police officials with such brisk bright matter-of-factness that one might have supposed she had come to complain about a strayed lapdog or an umbrella lost in a bus. The two officials—both obviously fathers of families—were at first inclined to be shocked. They dipped their pens excessively in the violet ink, made nervous inhibited circular movements with their elbows, before beginning to write, and were very curt and gruff.

"Now about this hotel," said the elder of them sternly: "I suppose you knew, before going there, that it was an hotel of a certain kind?"

"Well, you didn't expect us to go the Bristol, did you?" Sally's tone was very mild and reasonable: "They wouldn't have let us in there without luggage, anyway."

"Ah, so you had no luggage?" The younger one pounced upon this fact triumphantly, as of supreme importance. His violet copperplate police-hand began to travel steadily across a ruled sheet of foolscap paper. Deeply inspired by his theme, he paid not the slightest attention to Sally's retort:

"I don't usually pack a suitcase when a man asks me out to dinner."

The elder one caught the point, however, at once:

"So it wasn't till you were at the restaurant that this young man invited you to—er—accompany him to the hotel?"

"It wasn't till after dinner."

"My dear young lady"—the elder one sat back in his chair, very much the sarcastic father—"may I enquire whether it is your usual custom to accept invitations of this kind from perfect strangers?"

Sally smiled sweetly. She was innocence and candour itself:

"But, you see, Herr Kommissar, he wasn't a perfect stranger. He was my fiancé."

That made both of them sit up with a jerk. The younger one even made a small blot in the middle of his virgin page—the only blot, perhaps, to be found in all the spotless dossiers of the Polizeipräsidium.

"You mean to tell me, Frl. Bowles"—but in spite of his gruffness, there was already a gleam in the elder one's eye—"you mean to tell me that you became engaged to this man when you'd only known him a single afternoon?"

"Certainly."

"Isn't that—well, rather unusual?"

"I suppose it is," Sally seriously agreed. "But nowadays, you know, a girl can't afford to keep a man waiting. If he asks her once and she refuses him, he may try somebody else. It's all these surplus women—"

At this, the elder official frankly exploded. Pushing back his chair, he laughed himself quite purple in the face. It was nearly a minute before he could speak at all. The young one was much more decorous; he produced a large handkerchief and pretended to blow his nose. But the nose-blowing developed into a kind of sneeze which became a guffaw; and soon he too had abandoned all attempt to take Sally seriously. The rest of the interview was conducted with comic-opera informality, accompanied by ponderous essays in gallantry. The elder official, particularly, became quite daring; I think they were both sorry that I was present. They wanted her to themselves.

"Now don't you worry, Frl. Bowles," they told her, patting her hand at parting. "We'll find him for you, if we have to turn Berlin inside out to do it!"

~ ~ ~

"Well!" I exclaimed admiringly, as soon as we were out of earshot. "You do know how to handle them, I must say!"

Sally smiled dreamily: she was feeling very pleased with herself. "How do you mean, exactly, darling?"

"You know as well as I do—getting them to laugh like that: telling them he was your fiancé! It was really inspired!"

But Sally didn't laugh. Instead, she coloured a little, looking down at her feet. A comically guilty, childish expression came over her face.

"You see, Chris, it happened to be quite true—"

"True!"

"Yes, darling." Now, for the first time, Sally was really embarrassed; she began speaking very fast: "I simply couldn't tell you this morning—after everything that's happened, it would have sounded too idiotic for words. . . . He asked me to marry him while we were at the restaurant, and I said Yes. . . . You see, I thought that, being in films, he was probably quite used to quick engagements like that: after all, in Hollywood, it's quite the usual thing. . . . And, as he was an American, I thought we could get divorced again easily, any time we wanted to. . . . And it would have been a good thing for my career—I mean, if he'd been genuine—wouldn't it? . . . We were to have got married today, if it could have been managed. . . . It seems funny to think of now—"

"But, Sally!" I stood still. I gaped at her. I had to laugh. "Well, really . . . You know, you're the most extraordinary creature I ever met in my life!"

Sally giggled a little, like a naughty child which has unintentionally succeeded in amusing the grown-ups.

"I always told you I was a bit mad, didn't I? Now perhaps you'll believe it. . . ."

~ ~ ~

It was more than a week before the police could give us any news. Then, one morning, two detectives called to see me. A young man answering to our description had been traced and was under observation. The police knew his address, but wanted me to identify him before making the arrest. Would I come round with them at once to a snack-bar in the Kleist-strasse? He was to be seen there, about this time, almost every day. I should be able to point him out to them in the crowd and leave again at once, without any fuss or unpleasantness.

I didn't like the idea much, but there was no getting out of it now. The snack-bar, when we arrived, was crowded, for this was the lunch-hour. I caught sight of the young man almost immediately: he was stand-ing at the counter, by the tea-urn, cup in hand. Seen thus, alone and off his guard, he seemed rather pathetic: he looked shabbier and far younger—a mere boy. I very nearly said: "He isn't here." But what would have been the use? They'd have got him, anyway. "Yes, that's him," I told the detectives. "Over there." They nodded. I turned and hurried away down the street, feeling guilty and telling myself: I'll never help the police again.

~ ~ ~

A few days later, Sally came round to tell me the rest of the story: "I had to see him, of course. . . . I felt an awful brute; he looked so wretched. All he said was: 'I thought you were my friend.' I'd have told him he could keep the money, but he'd spent it all, anyway. . . . The police said he really had been to the States, but he isn't American; he's a Pole. . . . He won't be prosecuted, that's one comfort. The doctor's seen him and he's going to be sent to a home. I hope they treat him decently there. . . ."

"So he was a loony, after all?"

"I suppose so. A sort of mild one. . . ." Sally smiled. "Not very flattering to me, is it? Oh, and Chris, do you know how old he was? You'd never guess!"

"Round about twenty, I should think."

"Sixteen!"

"Oh, rot!"

"Yes, honestly. . . . The case would have to have been tried in the Children's Court!"

We both laughed. "You know, Sally," I said, "what I really like about you is that you're so awfully easy to take in. People who never get taken in are so dreary."

"So you still like me, Chris darling?"

"Yes, Sally. I still like you."

"I was afraid you'd be angry with me—about the other day."

"I was. Very."

"But you're not now?"

"No . . . I don't think so."

"It's no good my trying to apologize, or explain, or anything. . . . I get like that, sometimes. . . . I expect you understand, don't you, Chris?"

"Yes," I said. "I expect I do."

~ ~ ~

I have never seen her since. About a fortnight later, just when I was thinking I ought really to ring her up, I got a post-card from Paris: "Arrived here last night. Will write properly tomorrow. Heaps of love." No letter followed. A month after this, another post-card arrived, from Rome, giving no address: "Am writing in a day or two," it said. That was six years ago.

So now I am writing to her.

When you read this, Sally—if you ever do—please accept it as a tribute, the sincerest I can pay, to yourself and to our friendship.

And send me another post-card.

~ *Noël Coward* ~

Me and
the Girls

Tuesday

I like looking at mountains because they keep changing, if you know what I mean; not only the colours change at different times of the day but the shapes seem to alter too. I see them first when I wake up in the morning and Sister Dominique pulls up the blind. She's a dear old camp and makes clicking noises with her teeth. The blind rattles up and there they are—the mountains I mean. There was fresh snow on them this morning, that is on the highest peaks, and they looked very near in the clear air, blue and pink as if someone had painted them, rather like those pictures you see in frame shops in the King's Road, bright and a bit common but pretty.

Today was the day when they all came in: Dr. Pierre and Sister Françoise and the other professor, with the blue chin and a gleam in his eye, quite a dish really he is, hairy wrists but lovely long slim hands. He was the one who actually did the operation. I could go for him in a big way if I was well enough, but I'm not and that's that, nor am I likely to be for a long time. It's going to be a slow business. Dr. Pierre explained it

No doubt the forthright and reflective "Me and the Girls" will come as a great surprise to readers familiar only with Sir NOËL COWARD's theatrical writing and song writing. A celebrated actor as well as lyricist and playwright, he is probably best remembered for such famous comedies as Private Lives, Design for Living, *and* Blithe Spirit, *and was lampooned in the 1930s comedy* The Man Who Came to Dinner. *"Me and the Girls" complicates our received ideas about this man known primarily for his wit and urbane sophistication.*

carefully and very very gently, not at all like his usual manner which is apt to be a bit offish. While I was listening to him I looked at the professor's face: he was staring out at the mountains and I thought he looked sad. Sister Françoise and Sister Dominique stood quite still except that Sister Françoise was fiddling with her rosary. I got the message all right but I didn't let on that I did. They think I'm going to die and as they've had a good dekko inside me and I haven't, they probably know. I've thought of all this before of course, before the operation, actually long before when I was in the other hospital. I don't know yet how I feel about it quite, but then I've had a bit of a bashing about and I'm tired. It's not going to matter to anyone but me anyway and I suppose when it does happen I shan't care, what with being dopey and one thing and another. The girls will be sorry, especially Mavis, but she'll get over it. Ronnie will have a crying jag and get pissed and wish he'd been a bit nicer, but that won't last long either. I know him too well. Poor old Ron. I expect there were faults on both sides, there always are, but he was a little shit and no two ways about it. Still I brought it all on myself so I mustn't complain. It all seems far away now anyhow. Nothing seems very near except the mountains and they look as if they wanted to move into the room.

When they had all filed out and left me alone Sister D. came back because she'd forgotten my temperature chart and wanted to fill it in or something, at least that was what she said, but she didn't fool me: what she really came back for was to see if I was all right. She did a lot of teeth clicking and fussed about with my pillows and when she'd finally buggered off I gave way a bit and had a good cry, then I dropped off and had a snooze and woke up feeling quite spry. Maybe the whole thing's in my imagination anyhow. You never know really do you?—I mean when you're weak and kind of low generally you have all sorts of thoughts that you wouldn't have if you were up and about. All the same there *was* something in the way Dr. Pierre talked. The professor squeezed my hand when he left and smiled but his eyes still looked sad. It must be funny to be a doctor and always be coping with ill people and cheering them up even if you have to tell them a few lies while you're at it. Not that he said much. He just stood there most of the time like I said, looking at the mountains.

This is quite a nice room as hospital rooms go. There is a chintzy armchair for visitors and the walls are off-white so as not to be too glarey.

Rather like the flat in the rue Brochet, which Ronnie and I did over just after we'd first met. If you mix a tiny bit of pink with the white it takes the coldness out of it but you have to be careful that it doesn't go streaky. I can hardly believe that all that was only three years ago, it seems like a lifetime.

All the girls sent me flowers except Mavis and she sent me a bottle of Mitsouko toilet water which is better than flowers really because it lasts longer and it's nice to dab on at night when you wake up feeling hot and sweaty. She said she'd pop in and see me this afternoon just for a few minutes to tell me how the act's getting on. I expect it's a bit of a shambles really without me there to bound on and off and keep it on the tracks. They've had to change the running-order. Mavis does her single now right after the parasol dance so as to give the others time to get into their kimonos for the Japanese number. I must remember to ask her about Sally. She was overdue when I left and that's ten days ago. She's a silly little cow that girl if ever there was one, always getting carried away and losing her head. A couple of drinks and she's gone. Well if she's clicked again she'll just have to get on with it and maybe it'll teach her to be more careful in the future. I expect it was that Hungarian but she swears it wasn't. Anyway Mavis will know what to do, Mavis always knows what to do except when she gets what she calls "emotionally disturbed," then she's hell. She ought to get out of the act and marry somebody and settle down and have children, she's still pretty but it won't last and she'll never be a star if she lives to be a hundred, she just hasn't got that extra something. Her dancing's okay and she can put over a number all right but that dear little *je ne sais quoi* just isn't there poor bitch and it's no good pretending it is. I know it's me that stands in her way up to a point but I can't do anything about it. She knows all about me. I've explained everything until I'm blue in the face but it doesn't make any difference. She's got this "thing" about me not really being queer but only having caught it like a bad habit. Would you mind! Of course I should never have gone to bed with her in the first place. That sparked off the whole business. Poor old Mavis. These girls really do drive me round the bend sometimes. I will say one thing though, they *do* behave like ladies, out-wardly at least. I've never let them get off a plane or a train without lipstick and the proper clothes and shoes. None of those pony-tails and tatty slacks for George Banks Esq.: not on your Nelly. My girls have got to look dignified whether they like it or not. To do them justice they generally do. There have been one or two slip-ups, like that awful Maureen. She was a slut from the word go. I was forever after her about one thing or another. She always tried to dodge shaving under the arms because some silly bitch had told her that the men liked it. Imagine! I told her that that lark went out when the Moulin Rouge first opened in eighteen-whatever-it-was but as she'd never heard of the Moulin Rouge anyway it didn't make much impression on her. At any rate she finally got mumps in Brussels and had to be sent home and I was glad to see the last of her. This lot are very good on the whole. Apart from Mavis there's Sally, blond and rather bouncy; Irma, skin a bit sluggish but comes up a treat under the lights; Lily-May, the best dancer of the lot but calves a bit on the heavy side; and Beryl and Sylvia Martin. They're our twins and they're planning to work up a sister act later on. They're both quite pretty but that ole debbil talent has failed to touch either of them with his fairy wings so I shouldn't think the sister act will get much further than the Poland Rehearsal Rooms. The whole show closes here next Saturday week then God knows what will happen. I wrote off to Ted before my operation telling him that the act would have to be disbanded and asking him what he could do for them, but you know what agents are, all talk and no do as a rule. Still he's not a bad little sod taken by and large so we shall see.

Wednesday

Mavis came yesterday afternoon as promised. I didn't feel up to talking for long but I did my best. She started off all right, a bit overcheerful and taking the "Don't worry everything's going to be all right" line, but I could see she was in a bit of a state and trying not to show it. I don't know if she'd been talking to any of the sisters or whether they'd told her anything or not. I don't suppose they did, and her French isn't very good anyhow. She said the act was going as well as could be expected and that Monsieur Philippe had come backstage last night and been quite nice. She also asked if I'd like her to write to Ronnie and tell him about me being ill but I jumped on that double-quick pronto. It's awful when women get too understanding. I don't want her writing to Ronnie any more than I want Ronnie writing to me. He's got his ghastly Algerian *and* the flat so he can bloody well get on with it. I don't mind any more anyway. I did at first of course, I couldn't help myself, it wasn't the Algerian so much, it was all the lies and scenes. Fortunately I was rehearsing all through that month and had a lot to keep my mind occupied. It was bad I must admit but not so bad that it couldn't have been worse. No more being in love for me thank you very much. Not that I expect I shall have much chance. But if I do get out of this place all alive-o there's going to be no more of that caper. I've had it, once and for all. Sex is all very well in its way and I'm all for it but the next time I begin to feel that old black magic that I know so well I'll streak off like a bloody greyhound.

When Mavis had gone Sister Clothilde brought me my tea. Sister Clothilde's usually on in the afternoons. She's small and tubby and has a bit of a guttural accent having been born in Alsace-Lorraine; she also has bright bright red cheeks which look as if someone had pinched them hard just before she came into the room. She must have been quite pretty in a dumpy way when she was a girl before she took the veil or whatever it is you have to take before you give yourself to Jesus. She has quite a knowing look in her eye too as though she wasn't quite so far away from the wicked world as she pretended to be. She brought me a madeleine with my tea but it was a bit dry. When she'd gone and I'd had the tea and half the madeleine I settled back against the pillows and relaxed. It's surprising what funny things pop into your mind when you're lying snug in bed and feeling a bit drowsy. I started to try to remember everything I could from the very beginning like playing a game, but I couldn't keep dead on the beam: I'd suddenly jump from something that happened fifteen years ago to something that happened two weeks back. That was when the pain had begun to get pretty bad and Monsieur Philippe came into the dressing-room with Dr. Pierre and there was I writhing about with nothing but a jock-strap on and sweating like a pig. That wasn't so good that bit because I didn't know what was going to happen to me and I felt frightened. I don't feel frightened now, just a bit numb as though some part of me was hypnotised. I suppose that's the result of having had the operation. My inside must be a bit startled at all that's gone on and I expect the shock has made my mind tired. When I try to think clearly and remember things, I don't seem able to hold on to any subject for long. The thing is to give up to the tiredness and not worry. They're all very kind, the sisters and the doctors, even the maid who does the room every morning gives me a cheery smile as if she wanted to let me know she was on my side. She's a swarthy type with rather projecting eyes like a pug. I bet she'll finish up as a concierge with those regulation black stockings and a market-basket. There's a male orderly who pops in and out from time to time and very sprightly he is too, you'd think he was about to take off any minute. He's the one who shaved me before the operation and that was a carry-on if ever there was one. I wasn't in any pain because they'd given me an injection but woozy as I was I managed to make a few jokes. When he pushed my old man aside almost caressingly with his hand I said *"Pas ce soir Josephine, demain peutêtre"* and he giggled. It can't be much fun being an orderly in a hospital and have to shave people's privates and give them enemas and sit them on bed-pans from morning till night, but I suppose they must find it interesting otherwise they'd choose some other profession. When he'd finished he gave my packet a friendly little pat and said, *"Vive le sport." Would* you mind! Now whenever he comes in he winks at me as though we shared a secret and I have a sort of feeling he's dead right. I suppose if I didn't feel so weak and seedy I'd encourage him a bit just for the hell of it. Perhaps when I'm a little stronger I'll ask him to give me a massage or something just to see what happens—as if I didn't know! On the other hand of course if what I suspect is true, I shan't get strong again so the question won't come up. Actually he reminds me a bit of Peter when we first met at Miss Llewellyn's Dancing Academy, stocky and fair with short legs and a high colour. Peter was the one that did the pas de deux from *Giselle* with Coralie Hancock and dropped her on her head during one of the lifts and she had concussion and had to go to St. George's Hospital. It's strange to think of those early days. I can see myself now getting off the bus at Marble Arch with my ballet shoes in that tatty old bag of Aunt Isobel's. I had to walk down Edgware Road and then turn to the left and the dancing academy was down some steps under a public house called the Swan. There was a mirror all along one wall with a *barre* in front of it and Miss Adler used to thump away at the upright while we did our bends and kicks and positions. Miss Llewellyn was a character and no mistake. She had frizzed-up fair hair, very black at the parting; a heavy stage make-up with a beauty spot under her left eye if you please and a black velvet band around her neck. She always wore this rain or shine. Peter said it was to hide the scar where someone had tried to cut her throat. She wasn't a bad old tart really and she did get me my first job, in a Christmas play called *Mr. Birdie*. I did an audition for it at the Garrick Theatre. Lots of other kids had been sent for and there we were all huddled at the side of the stage in practice clothes waiting to be called out. When my turn came I pranced on, followed by Miss Adler, who made a beeline for the piano, which sounded as if someone had dropped a lot of tin ashtrays inside it, you know, one of those diabolical old uprights that you only get at auditions. Anyhow I sang "I Hear You Calling Me"—it was before the poor darlings dropped so I was still a soprano—and then I did the standard sailor's hornpipe as taught at the academy, a lot of hopping about and hauling at imaginary ropes and finishing with a few quick turns and a leap off. Mr. Alec Sanderson, who was producing *Mr. Birdie,* then sent for me to go and speak to him in the stalls. Miss Adler came with me and he told me I could play the heroine's little brother in the first act, a gnome in the second, and a frog in the third, and that he'd arrange the business side with Miss Llewellyn. Miss Adler and I fairly flew out into Charing Cross Road and on wings of song to Lyon's Corner House where she stood me tea and we had an éclair each. I really can't think about *Mr. Birdie* without laughing and when I laugh it hurts my stitches. It really was a fair bugger, whimsical as all get-out. Mr. Birdie, played by Mr. Sanderson himself, was a lovable old professor who suddenly inherited a family of merry little kiddos of which I was one. We were all jolly and ever so mischievous in act one and then we all went to sleep in a magic garden and became elves and gnomes and what have you for acts two and three. Some of us have remained fairies to this day. The music was by Oliver Bakewell, a ripsnorting old queen who used to pinch our bottoms when we were standing round the piano learning his gruesome little songs. Years later when I knew what was what I reminded him of this and he whinnied like a horse.

Those were the days all right, days of glory for child actors. I think the boys had a better time than the girls on account of not being so well protected. I shall never forget those jovial wet-handed clergymen queueing up outside the stage-door to take us out to tea and stroke our knees under the table. Bobby Clews and I used to have bets as to how much we could get without going too far. I once got a box of Fuller's soft-centres and a gramophone record of *Casse Noisette* for no more than a quick grope in a taxi. After my voice broke I got pleurisy and a touch of TB and had to be sent to a sanatorium near Buxton. I was cured and sent home to Auntie Iso after six months but it gave me a fright I can tell you. I was miserable for the first few weeks and cried my eyes out, but I got used to it and quite enjoyed the last part when I was moved into a small room at the top of the house with a boy called Digby Lawson. He was two years older than me, round about seventeen and a half. He died a short time later and I really wasn't surprised. It's a miracle that I'm alive to tell the tale, but I must say we had a lot of laughs.

It wasn't until I was nineteen that I got into the chorus at the Palladium and that's where I really learnt my job. I was there two and a half years in all and during the second year I was given the understudy of Jackie Foal. He was a sensational dancer and I've never worked so hard in my life. I only went on for him three times but one of the times was for a whole week and it was a thrill I can tell you when I got over the panic. One night I got round Mr. Lewis to let me have the house seats for Aunt Iso and Emma, who's her sort of maid-companion, and they dressed themselves up to the nines and had a ball. Emma wore her best black with a bead necklace she borrowed from Clara two doors down and Auntie Iso looked as though she were ready for tiara night at the opera: a full evening dress made of crimson taffeta with a sort of lace overskirt of the same colour; a dramatic headdress that looked like a coronet with pince-nez attached and the Chinese coat Uncle Fred had brought her years ago when he was in the merchant navy. I took them both out to supper afterwards at Giovanni's in Greek Street. He runs the restaurant with a boy friend of his, a sulky-looking little sod as a rule but he played up that night and both he and Giovanni laid on the full VIP treatment, cocktails on the house, a bunch of flowers for the old girls, and a lot of hand kissing. It all knocked me back a few quid but it was worth it to see how they enjoyed themselves. They both got a bit pissed on Chianti and Emma laughed so much that her upper plate fell into the zabaglione and she had to fish it out with a spoon. Actually it wasn't long after that that Auntie Iso died and Emma went off to live with her sister in Lowestoft. I hated it when Auntie Iso died and even now after all these years it still upsets me to think of it. After all she was all I'd got in the way of relations and she'd brought me up and looked after me ever since I was five. After she'd gone I shared a flat with Bunny Granger for a bit in Longacre which was better than nothing but I'd rather have been on my own. Bunny was all right in his way; he came to the funeral with me and did his best to cheer me up but he didn't stay the course very long really if you know what I mean and that flat was a shambles, it really was. Nobody minds fun and games within reason but you can have too much of a good thing. There was hardly a night he didn't bring someone or other home and one night if you please I nipped out of my room to go to the bathroom which was up one flight and there was a policeman scuffling back into his uniform. I nearly had a fit but actually he turned out to be quite nice. Anyway I didn't stay with Bunny long because I met Harry and that was that. Harry was the first time it ever happened to me seriously. Of course I'd hopped in and out of bed with people every now and again and never thought about it much one way or another. I never was one to go off into a great production about being queer and work myself up into a state like some people I know. I can't think why they waste their time. I mean it just doesn't make sense does it? You're born either hetero, bi, or homo and whichever way it goes there you are stuck with it. Mind you people are getting a good deal more hep about it than they used to be but the laws still exist that make it a crime and poor bastards still get hauled off to the clink just for doing what comes naturally as the song says. Of course this is what upsets some of the old magistrates more than anything, the fact that it *is* as natural as any other way of having sex, leaving aside the strange ones who get excited over old boots or used knickers or having themselves walloped with straps. Even so I don't see that it's anybody's business but your own what you do with your old man providing that you don't make a beeline for the dear little kiddies, not, I am here to tell you, that quite a lot of the aforesaid dear little kiddies don't enjoy it tip-top. I was one myself and I know. But I digress as the bride said when she got up in the middle of her honeymoon night and baked a cake. That's what I mean really about the brain not hanging on to one thing when you're tired. It keeps wandering off. I was trying to put down about Harry and what I felt about it and got side-tracked. All right—all right—let's concentrate on Harry-boy and remember what he looked like and not only what he looked like, but him, him himself. To begin with he was inclined to be moody and when we first moved into the maisonette in Swiss Cottage together he was always fussing about whether Mrs. Fingal suspected anything or not, but as I kept explaining to him, Mrs. Fingal wouldn't have minded if we poked Chinese mice providing that we paid the rent regularly and didn't make a noise after twelve o'clock at night. As a matter of fact she was quite a nice old bag and I don't think nor ever did think that she suspected for a moment, she bloody well knew. I don't mean to say that she thought about it much or went on about it to herself. She just accepted the situation and minded her own business and if a few more people I know had as much sense the world would be a far happier place. Anyway, Harry-boy got over being worried about her or about himself and about us after a few months and we settled down, loved each other good and true for two and a half years until the accident happened and he was killed. I'm not going to think about that because even now it still makes me feel sick and want to cry my heart out. I always hated that fucking motor bike anyhow but he was mad for it, forever tinkering with it and rubbing it down with oily rags and fiddling about with its engine. But that was part of his character really. He loved machinery and engineering and football matches and all the things I didn't give a bugger about. We hadn't a thing in common actually except the one thing you can't explain. He wasn't even all that good-looking now I come to think of it. His eyes were nice but his face wasn't anything out of the ordinary: his body was wonderful, a bit thick-set but he was very proud of it and never stopped doing exercises and keeping himself fit. He never cared what the maisonette looked like and once when I'd bought a whole new set of loose covers for the divan bed and the two armchairs, he never even noticed until I pointed them out to him. He used to laugh at me too and send me up rotten when I fussed about the place and tried to keep things tidy. But he loved me. That's the shining thing I like to remember. He loved me more than anyone has ever loved me before or since. He used to have affairs with girls every now and again, just to keep his hand in, as he used to say. I got upset about this at first and made a few scenes but he wouldn't stand for any of that nonsense and let me know it in no uncertain terms. He loved me true did Harry-boy and I loved him true, and if the happiness we gave each other was wicked and wrong in the eyes of the Law and the Church and God Almighty, then the Law and the Church and God Almighty can go dig a hole and fall down it.

Thursday

I had a bad night and at about two in the morning Sister Jeanne-Marie gave me a pill and I got off to sleep all right and didn't wake until seven. I couldn't see the mountains at all because the clouds had come down and wiped them away. My friend the orderly came in at eight o'clock and gave me an enema on account of I hadn't been since the day before yesterday and then only a few goat's balls. He was very cheery and kiss-me-arse and kept on saying *"Soyez courageux"* and *"Tenez le"* until I could have throttled him. After it was all over he gave me a bath and soaped me and then, when he was drying me, I suddenly felt sort of weak and despairing and burst into tears. He at once stopped being happy-chappy and good-time-Charlie and put both his arms round me tight. He'd taken his white coat off to bathe me and he had a stringy kind of vest and I could feel the hairs on his chest against my face while he held me. Presently he sat down on the loo seat and took me onto his lap as though I were a child. I went on crying for a bit and he let me get on with it without saying a word or trying to cheer me up. He just patted me occasionally with the hand that wasn't holding me and kept quite still. After a while the tears stopped and I got hold of myself. He dabbed my face gently with a damp towel, slipped me into my pyjama jacket, carried me along the passage, and put me back into bed. It was already made, cool and fresh, and the flowers the girls had sent me had been brought back in their vases and put about the room. I leant back against the pillows and closed my eyes because I was feeling fairly whacked, what with the enema and the crying-jag and one thing and another. When I opened them he had gone.

I dozed on and off most of the morning and in the afternoon Sally came to see me. She brought me last week's *Tatler* and this week's *Paris Match,* which was full of Brigitte Bardot as usual. If you ask me, what that poor girl needs is less publicity and more discipline. Sally was wearing her beige two-piece with a camp little red hat. She looked very pretty and was in high spirits having come on after all nearly ten days late. She said the Hungarian had come to the show the night before last and given her a bottle of Bellodgia. I asked her if she'd been to bed with him again and she giggled and said, "Of course not, for obvious reasons." Then I asked her if she really had a "thing" about him and she giggled some more and said that in a way she had because he was so aristocratic and had lovely muscular legs but that it wasn't serious and that anyhow he was going back to his wife in Vienna. She said he went into quite an act about this and swore that she would be forever in his heart but that she didn't believe a word of it. I told her that she'd better be more careful in the future and see to it that another time she got more out of a love affair than a near miss and a bottle of Bellodgia. She's a nice enough kid really, our Sally, but she just doesn't think or reason things out. I asked her what she was going to do when the act folds on Saturday week and she said she wasn't sure but she'd put a phone call through to London to a friend of hers who thinks he can get some modelling for her, to fill in for the time being. She said that all the girls sent me their love and that one or other of them was coming to see me every day, but Mavis had told them not more than one at a time and not to stay long at that. Good old Mavis. Bossy to the last.

Sally had brought me a packet of mentholated filter-tip cigarettes and when she'd gone I smoked one just for a treat and it made me quite dizzy because I've not been smoking at all for the last few days, I somehow didn't feel like it. During the dizziness the late afternoon sun came out and suddenly there were the mountains again, wobbling a bit but as good as new. I suppose I've always had a "thing" about mountains ever since I first saw any, which was a great many too many years ago as the crow flies and I'd just got my first "girl" act together and we had a booking on the ever so gay continent. Actually it was in Zurich in a scruffy little dive called Die Kleine Maus or something. There were only four girls and me and we shared a second-class compartment on the night train from Paris. I remember we all got nicely thank you on a bottle of red wine I bought at the station buffet and when we woke up from our communal coma in the early hours of the morning there were the mountains with the first glow of sunrise on them and everyone did a lot of ooh-ing and aah-ing and I felt as though suddenly something wonderful had happened to me. We all took it in turns to dart down the corridor to the lav and when we'd furbished ourselves up and I'd shaved and the girls had put some slap on, we staggered along to the restaurant car and had large bowls of coffee and croissants with butter and jam. The mountains were brighter then, parading past the wide windows and covered in snow, and I wished we weren't going to a large city but could stay off for a few days and wander about and look at the waterfalls. However we *did* go to a large city and when we got there we laid a great big gorgeous egg and nobody came to see us after the first performance. It was a dank little room we had to perform in with a stage at one end, then a lot of tables and then a bar with a looking-glass behind it so we could see our reflections, which wasn't any too encouraging I can tell you. A handful of square-looking Swiss gentlemen used to sit at the tables with their girl friends and they were so busy doing footy-footy and gropey-gropey that they never paid any attention to us at all. We might just as well not have been there. One night we finished the Punch and Judy number without a hand except from one oaf in the corner on the right, and he was only calling the waiter. There were generally a few poufs clustered round the bar hissing at each other like snakes, apart from them that was it. The manager came round after the third performance and told us we'd have to finish at the end of the week. He was lovely he was, bright red in the face and shaped like a pear. I had a grand upper and downer with him because we'd been engaged on a two weeks' contract. His English wasn't up to much and in those days I couldn't speak a word of German or French so the scene didn't exactly flow. There was a lot of arm waving and banging on the dressing-table and the girls sat round giggling, but I finally made him agree to pay us half our next week's salary as compensation. The next morning I had another upper and downer with Monsieur Huber, who was the man who had booked the act through Ted Bentley, my agent in London. Monsieur Huber was small and sharp as a needle, with a slight cast in his eye like Norma Shearer only not so pretty. As a matter of fact he wasn't so bad. At least he took our part and called up the red pear and there was a lot of palava in Switzer-Deutsch which to my mind is not a pretty language at all and sounds as if you'd got a nasty bit of phlegm in your throat and were trying to get rid of it. At any rate the upshot of the whole business was that he, Monsieur Huber, finally got us another booking in a small casino on the Swiss side of Lake Lugano and we all drove there in a bus on the Sunday and opened on the Monday night without a band call or even a dress rehearsal. I can't truthfully say that we tore the place up but we didn't do badly, anyway we stayed there for the two weeks we'd been booked for. We lived in a pension, if you'll excuse the expression, up a steep hill at the back of the town which was run by a false-blond Italian lady who looked like an all-in wrestler in drag. She wasn't a bad sort and we weren't worried by the other boarders on account of there weren't any. The girls shared two rooms on the first floor and I had a sort of attic at the top like *La Bohème,* which had a view, between houses, of the lake and the mountains. I used to watch them, the mountains, sticking up out of the mist in the early mornings, rather like these I'm looking at now. Madame Corelli, the all-in wrestler, took quite a fancy to us and came to see the show several times with her lover, who was a friend of the man who ran the casino. I wish you could have seen the lover. He was thick and short and bald as a coot and liked wearing very tight trousers to prove he had an enormous packet which indeed he had: it looked like an entire Rockingham tea service, milk jug and all. His name was Guido Mezzoni and he could speak a little English because he'd been a waiter in Soho in the dear dead days before the war. He asked us all to his place one night after the show and put on a chef's hat and made spaghetti Bolognese and we all got high as kites on vino rosso and a good time was had by *tutti* until just before we were about to leave when he takes Babs Mortimer, our youngest, into the bathroom, where she wanted to go and instead of leaving her alone to have her Jimmy Riddle in peace and quiet, he whisked her inside, locked the door, and showed her all he'd got. Of course the silly little cow lost her head and screamed bloody murder whereupon Madame Corelli went charging down the passage baying like a bloodhound. That was a nice ending to a jolly evening I must say. Nice clean fun and no questions asked. You've never heard such a carry-on. After a lot of banging on the bathroom door and screaming he finally opened it and Babs came flying into the room in hysterics and I had to give her a sharp slap in the face to quiet her, meanwhile the noise from the passage sounded as though the Mau Maus had got in. We all had another swig all round at the vino while the battle was going on and I couldn't make up my mind whether to grab all the girls and bugger off home or wait and see what happened, then I remembered that Madame Corelli had the front-door key anyhow so there wouldn't be much point in going back and just sitting on the kerb. Presently the row subsided a bit and poor old Guido came back into the room looking very hang-dog with a nasty red scratch all down one side of his face. Madame followed him wearing what they call in novels a "set expression" which means that her mouth was in a straight line and her eyes looked like black beads. We all stood about and looked at each other for a minute or two because nobody could think of anything to say. Finally Madame hissed something to Guido in Italian and he went up miserably to Babs and said, "I am sawry, so sawry, and I wish beg your pardon." Babs shot me a look and I nodded irritably and she said "Granted I'm sure" in a very grand voice and minced over to look out of the window which was fairly silly because it looked out on a warehouse and it was pitch dark anyway. Madame Corelli then took charge of the situation. Her English wasn't any too hot at the best of times and now that she was in the grip of strong emotion it was more dodgy than ever, however she made a long speech most of which I couldn't understand a word of, and gave me the key of the front door, from which I gathered that she was going to stay with Guido and that we were expected to get the hell out and leave them to it. I took the key, thanked Guido for the evening, and off we went. It was a long drag up the hill and there was no taxi in sight at that time of the morning so we had to hoof it. When we got to the house the dawn was coming up over the lake. I stopped to look at it for a moment, the air was fresh and cool and behind the mountains the sky was pale green and pink and yellow like a Neapolitan ice, but the girls were grumbling about being tired and their feet hurting so we all went in and went to bed.

The next day I had a little set-to with Babs because I thought it was necessary. I took her down to a café on the lake front and gave her an iced coffee and explained a few of the facts of life to her. Among other things I told her that you can't go through life shrieking and making scenes just because somebody makes a pass at you. There are always ways of getting out of a situation like that without going off into the second act of *Tosca*. In any case Guido hadn't really made a pass at her at all, he was obviously the type who's overproud of his great big gorgeous how-do-you-do and can't resist showing it to people. If he'd grabbed her and tried to rape her it would have been different, but all the poor little sod wanted was a little honest appreciation and probably if she'd just said something ordinary like "Fancy" or "What a whopper!" he wouldn't have wanted to go any further and all would have ended happily. She listened to me rather sullenly and mumbled something about it having been a shock and that she wasn't used to that sort of thing, having been brought up like a lady, to which I replied that having been brought up like a lady was no help in cabaret and that if she was all that refined she shouldn't have shoved her delicate nose into show business in the first place. Really these girls make me tired sometimes. They prance about in bikinis showing practically all they've got and then get hoity-toity when anyone makes a little pounce. What's so silly about it really is that that very thing is what they want more than anything only they won't admit it. Anyway she had another iced coffee and got off her high horse and confessed, to my great relief, that she wasn't a virgin and had had several love affairs only none of them had led to anything. I told her that it was lucky for her that they hadn't and that if at any time she got herself into trouble of any sort she was to come straight to me. After that little fireside chat we became quite good friends and when she left the act, which was about three months later, I missed her a lot. She finally got into the chorus of a musical at the Coliseum and then got married. I sometimes get a post-card from her but not very often. She must be quite middle-aged now. Good old Babs.

The other three were not so pretty as Babs but they danced better. Moira Finch was the eldest, about twenty-six, then there were Doreen March and Elsie Pendleton. Moira was tall and dark with nice legs and no tits to speak of. Doreen was mousey, mouse-coloured hair, mouse-coloured eyes, and a mouse-coloured character, she also had a squeaky voice just to make the whole thing flawless. I must say one thing for her though, she *could* dance. Her kicks were wonderful, straight up with both legs and no faking, and her turns were quick as lightning. Elsie was the sexiest of the bunch, rather pallid and languorous with the sort of skin that takes make-up a treat and looks terrible without it. They were none of them very interesting really, but they were my first lot and I can remember them kindly on the whole. We were together on and off for nearly a year and played different dance-halls and casinos all over Italy, Spain, Switzerland, and France. I learnt a lot during that tour and managed to pick up enough of the various languages to make myself understood. Nothing much happened over and above a few rows. Elsie got herself pregnant in Lyons, where we were appearing in a sort of nightclub-cum-knocking shop called Le Perroquet Vert. A lot of moaning and wailing went on but fortunately the old tart who ran the joint knew a character who could do the old crochet-hook routine and so she and I took Elsie along to see him and waited in a sitting-room with a large chandelier, a table with a knitted peacock-blue cloth on it, and a clanking old clock on the mantelpiece set between two pink china swans, the neck of one of them was broken and the head had been stuck on again crooked. After quite a long while during which Violette whatever-her-name-was told me a long saga about how she'd first been seduced at the age of thirteen by an uncle by marriage, Elsie came back with the doctor. He was a nasty piece of work if ever I saw one. He wore a greasy alpaca jacket with suspicious-looking stains on it and his eyes seemed to be struggling to get at each other over one of the biggest bonks since Cyrano de Bergerac. Anyway I paid him what he wanted, which was a bloody sight more than I could afford, and we took Elsie back to the hotel in a taxi and put her to bed. She looked pale and a bit tearful but I suppose that was only to be expected. Violette said she'd better not dance that night so as to give her inside time to settle down after having been prodded about and so I had to cut the pony quartette which couldn't be done as a trio and sing "The Darktown Strutters' Ball" with a faked-up dance routine that I invented as I went along. Nobody seemed to care anyway.

When we finally got back to London I broke up the act and shopped around to see if I could get a job on my own. I had one or two chorus offers but I turned them down. A small part, yes, even if it was only a few lines, but not the chorus again. I had a long talk with Ted Bentley and he advised me to scratch another act together, this time with better material. I must say he really did his best to help and we finally fetched up with quite a production. There was a lot of argle-bargle about how the act should be billed and we finally decided on "Georgie Banks and His Six Bombshells." Finding the six bombshells wasn't quite so easy. We auditioned hundreds of girls of all sorts and kinds until at long last we settled on what we thought were the best six with an extra one as a standby. In all fairness I must admit they were a bright little lot, all good dancers and pretty snappy to look at. Avice Bennet was the eldest, about twenty-seven, with enormous eyes and a treacherous little gold filling which only showed when she laughed. Then there was Sue Mortlock, the sort of bouncy little blonde that the tired businessmen are supposed to go for. Jill Kenny came next on the scroll of honour, she was a real smasher, Irish with black hair and violet blue eyes and a temper of a fiend. Ivy Baker was a redhead, just for those who like that sort of thing, she ponged a bit when she got overheated like so many redheads do and I was always after her with the Odorono, but she was a good worker and her quick spins were sensational. Gloria Day was the languid, sensuous type, there always has to be one of those, big charlies and hair like kapok, but she could move when she had to. (Her real name was Betty Mott but her dear old white-headed mum who was an ex–Tiller girl thought Gloria Day would look better on the bills.) The last, but by no means the least, was Bonny Macintyre, if you please. She was the personality kid of the whole troupe, not exactly pretty but cute—God help us all—and so vivacious that you wanted to strangle her, however she was good for eccentric numbers and the audiences always liked her. The standby, Myrtle Kennedy, was a bit horsey to look at but thoroughly efficient and capable of going on for anyone which after all was what she was engaged for. This was the little lot that I traipsed around the great big glorious world with for several years on and off, four and a half to be exact. Oh dear! On looking back I can hardly believe it. I can hardly believe that *Io stesso—Io mismo—Je, moi-même, Il signore*—El señor—Monsieur George Banks Esq. lying here rotting in a hospital bed really went through all that I did go through with that merry little bunch of egomaniacs. I suppose I enjoyed quite a lot of it but I'm here to say I wouldn't take it on again, not for all the rice in Ram Singh's Indian restaurant in the Brompton Road.

Friday

The loveliest things happen to yours truly and no mistake. I'm starting a bedsore! Isn't that sweet? Dr. Pierre came in to see me this morning and he and Sister Dominique put some ointment and lint on my fanny and here I am sitting up on a hot little rubber ring and feeling I ought to bow to people like royalty.

There was quite a to-do in the middle of the night because somebody died in number eleven, which is two doors down the passage. I wouldn't have known anything about it except that I happened to be awake and having a cup of Ovaltine and heard a lot of murmuring and sobbing going on outside the door. It was an Italian man who died and the murmuring and sobbing was being done by his relatives. Latins aren't exactly tight-lipped when it comes to grief or pain are they? I mean they really let go and no holds barred. You've never heard such a commotion. It kind of depressed me all the same, not that it was all that sad. According to Sister Jeanne-Marie the man who died was very old indeed and a disagreeable old bastard into the bargain, but it started me off thinking about dying myself and wondering what it would feel like, if it feels like anything at all. Of course death's got to come sometime or other so it's no use getting morbid about it but I can't quite imagine not being here any more. It's funny to think there's going to be a last time for everything; the last time I shall go to the loo, the last time I shall eat a four-minute egg, the last time I shall arrive in Paris in the early morning and see waiters in shirt-sleeves setting up the tables outside cafés, the last time I shall ever feel anybody's arms round me. I suppose I can count myself lucky in a way not to have anybody too close to worry about. At least when it happens I shall be on my own with no red-eyed loved ones clustered round the bed and carrying on alarming. I sometimes wish I was deeply religious and could believe that the moment I conked out I should be whisked off to some lovely place where all the people I'd been fond of and who had died would be waiting for me, but as a matter of fact this sort of wishing doesn't last very long. I suppose I'd like to see Auntie Iso again and Harry-boy but I'm not dead sure. I've got sort of used to being without them and they might have changed or I might have changed and it wouldn't be the same. After all nothing stays the same in life does it? And I can't help feeling that it's a bit silly to expect that everything's going to be absolutely perfect in the after-life, always providing that there is such a thing. Some people of course are plumb certain of this and make their plans accordingly, but I haven't got any plans to make and I never have had for the matter of that, anyway not those sort of plans. Perhaps there is something lacking in me. Perhaps this is one of the reasons I've never quite made the grade, in my career I mean. Not that I've done badly, far from it. I've worked hard and had fun and enjoyed myself most of the time and you can't ask much more than that can you? But I never really got to the top and became a great big glamorous star which after all is what I started out to be. I'm not such a clot as not to realise that I missed out somewhere along the line. Then comes the question of whether I should have had such a good time if I *had* pulled it off and been up there in lights. You never really know do you? And I'm buggered if I'm going to sit here on my rubber ring sobbing my heart out about what might have been. To hell with what might have been. What *has* been is quite enough for me, and what *will* be will have to be coped with when the time comes.

Another scrumptious thing happened to me today which was more upsetting than the bedsore and it was all Mavis's fault and if I had the strength I'd wallop the shit out of her. Just after I'd had my tea there was a knock on the door and in came Ronnie! He looked very pale and was wearing a new camel-hair overcoat and needed a hair-cut. He stood still for a moment in the doorway and then came over and kissed me and I could tell from his breath that he'd had a snifter round the corner to fortify himself before coming in. He had a bunch of roses in his hand and the paper they were wrapped in looked crinkled and crushed as though he'd been holding them too tightly. I was so taken by surprise that I couldn't think of anything to say for a minute then I pulled myself to-gether and told him to drag the chintz armchair nearer the bed and sit

down. He did what I told him after laying the flowers down very carefully
on the bed-table as though they were breakable and said, in an uncertain
voice, "Surprise—surprise!" I said "It certainly is" a little more sharply
than I meant to and then suddenly I felt as if I was going to cry, which
was plain silly when you come to analyse it because I don't love him any
more, not really, anyhow not like I used to at first. Fortunately at this
moment Sister Françoise came in and asked if Ronnie would like a cup
of tea and when he said he didn't want anything at all thank you she
frigged about with my pillows for a moment and then took the roses and
went off to find a vase for them. This gave me time to get over being
emotional and I was grateful for it I can tell you. After that we began to
talk more or less naturally. I asked after the Algerian and Ronnie looked
sheepish and said he wasn't with him any more, then he told me about
the flat and having to have the bathroom repainted because the steam
from the geyser had made the walls peel. We went on talking about this
and that and all the time the feeling of emptiness seemed to grow between
us. I don't know if he felt this as strongly as I did, the words came
tumbling out easily enough and he even told me a funny story that somebody had told him about a nun and a parrot and we both laughed. Then
suddenly we both seemed to realise at the same moment that it wasn't
any good going on like that. He stood up and I held out my arms to him
and he buried his head on my chest and started to cry. He was clutching
my left hand tightly so I stroked his hair with my right hand and cried
too and hoped to Christ Sister Françoise wouldn't come flouncing in
again with the roses. When we'd recovered from this little scene he blew
his nose and went over to the window and there wasn't any more strain.
He stayed over an hour and said he'd come and see me again next weekend. He couldn't make it before because he was starting rehearsals for a
French TV show in which he had a small part of an English sailor. I told
him he'd better have a hair-cut before he began squeezing himself into a
Tiddley suit and he laughed and said he'd meant to have it done ages ago
but somehow or other something always seemed to get in the way. He
left at about five-thirty because he was going to have a drink with Mavis
at the L'Éscale and then catch the seven forty-five back to Paris. When
he'd gone I felt somehow more alone than I had felt before he came so
I had another of Sally's mentholated cigarettes just to make me nonchalant
but it didn't really. Him coming in like that so unexpectedly had given
me a shock and it was no good pretending it hadn't. I wriggled myself

into a more comfortable position on the rubber ring, looked out at the view, and tried to get me and Ronnie and everything straight in my mind but it wasn't any use because suddenly seeing him again had started up a whole lot of feelings that I thought weren't there any more. I cursed Mavis of course for being so bloody bossy and interfering and yet in a way I was glad she had been. The sly little bitch had kept her promise not to write to him but had telephoned instead. I suppose it was nice of her really considering that she'd been jealous as hell of him in the past and really hated his guts. You'd have thought that from her point of view it would have been better to let sleeping dogs lie. She obviously thought that deep down inside I wanted to see him in spite of the way I'd carried on about him and the Algerian and sworn I never wanted to clap eyes on him again. After all she *had* been with me all through the bad time and I *had* let my hair down and told her much more than I should have. I don't believe as a rule in taking women too much into your confidence about that sort of thing. It isn't exactly that they're not to be trusted but it's hard for them to understand really, however much they try, and it's more difficult still if they happen to have a "thing" about you into the bargain. I never pretended to be in love with Mavis. I went to bed with her every now and again mainly because she wanted me to and because it's always a good thing to lay one member of the troupe on account of it stops the others gabbing too much and sending you up rotten. I leant back against the pillows which had slipped down a bit like they always do and stared out across the lake at the evening light on the mountains and for the first time I found myself hating them and wishing they weren't there standing between me and Paris and the flat and Ronnie and the way I used to live when I was up and about. I pictured Mavis and Ronnie sitting at L'Éscale and discussing whether I was going to die or not and her asking him how he thought I looked and him asking her what the doctor had said and then of course I got myself as low as a snake's arse and started getting weepy again and wished to Christ I *could* die, nice and comfortably in my sleep, and have done with it.

I must have dropped off because the next thing I knew was Sister Françoise clattering in with my supper tray and the glow had gone from the fucking mountains and the lights were out on the other side of the lake and one more day was over.

Saturday

Georgie Banks and His Six Bombshells I am here to tell you began their merry career together by opening a brand-new night-spot in Montevideo which is in Uruguay or Paraguay or one of the guays and not very attractive whichever it is. The name of the joint was La Cumparsita and it smelt of fresh paint and piddle on account of the lavatories not working properly. We'd had one hell of a voyage tourist class in a so-called luxury liner which finished up in a blaze of misery with a jolly ship's concert in the first-class lounge. We did our act in its entirety with me flashing on and off every few minutes in my new silver lamé tail suit, which split across the bottom in the middle of "Embraceable You." The girls were nervous and Jill Kenny caught her foot in the hem of her skirt in the Edwardian quartette and fell arse over apple-cart into a tub of azaleas which the purser had been watering with his own fair hands for weeks. She let out a stream of four-letter words in a strong Irish brogue and the first-class passengers left in droves. The purser made a speech at the end thanking us all very much indeed but it didn't exactly ring with sincerity. Anyhow our opening at La Cumparsita went better and we got a rave notice in one local paper and a stinker in the other which sort of levelled things out. The Latin-Americanos were very friendly on the whole if a bit lecherous and the girls had quite a struggle not to be laid every night rain or shine. Bonny Macintyre, vivacious to the last, was the first to get herself pregnant. This fascinating piece of news was broken to me two weeks after we'd left Montevideo and moved on to Buenos Aires. Fortunately I was able to get her fixed up all right but it took a few days to find the right doctor to do it and those few days were a proper nightmare. She never stopped weeping and wailing and saying it was all my fault for not seeing that she was sufficiently protected. *Would* you mind! When it was all over bar the shouting she got cuter than ever and a bit cocky into the bargain and I knew then and there that out of the whole lot our Bonny was the only one who was going to cause me the most trouble, and baby was I right! The others behaved fairly well taken by and large. Jill was a bit of a trouble-maker and liable to get pissed unless carefully watched. Ivy Baker got herself into a brawl with one of the local tarts when we were working in the Casino at Vina del Mar. The tart accused her of giving the come-on to her boy friend and slapped her in the face in the ladies' john, but she got as good as she gave. Ivy wasn't a redhead for nothing. The manager came and complained to me but I told him to stuff it and the whole thing died away like a summer breeze.

On looking back on that first year with the bombshells I find it difficult to remember clearly, out of all the scenes and dramas and carry-ons, what happened where and who did what to who. It's all become a bit of a jumble in my mind like one of those montages you see in films when people jump from place to place very quickly and there are shots of pages flying off a calendar. This is not to be surprised at really because we did cover a lot of territory. It took us over seven months to squeeze Latin America dry and then we got a tour booked through Australia and New Zealand. By this time all the costumes looked as though we'd been to bed in them for years and so they had to be redone. We had a lay-off for a week in Panama City and we shopped around for materials in the blazing heat and then went to work with our needles and thread. Avice was the best at this lark. I know I nearly went blind sewing sequins onto a velvet bodice for Sue Mortlock, who had to do a single while we were all changing for "The Darktown Strutters' Ball" which we had to do in home-made masks because there wasn't any time to black up.

The voyage from Panama City to western Australia was wonderful. The ship was quite small, a sort of freighter, but we had nice cabins and the food wasn't bad. It was the first time we'd had a real rest for months and we stopped off at various islands in the South Seas and bathed in coral lagoons and got ourselves tanned to a crisp all except poor Ivy, who got blistered and had to be put to bed with poultices of soda-bicarb plastered all over her. She ran a temperature poor bitch and her skin peeled off her like tissue-paper. All the girls behaved well nearly all the time and there were hardly any rows. There was a slight drama when Bonny was found naked in one of the lifeboats with the chief engineer. It would have been all right if only it hadn't been the captain who found them. The captain was half Norwegian and very religious and he sent for me to his cabin and thumped the table and said I ought to be ashamed of myself for traipsing round the world with a lot of harlots. I explained as patiently as I could that my girls were not harlots but professional artistes and that in any case I was not responsible for their private goings-on and I added that harlots were bloody well paid for what they did in the hay whereas all Bonny got out of the chief engineer was a native necklace made of red seeds and a couple of conch shells which were too big to pack. After a while he calmed down and we had two beers sitting side by side on his bunk. When he'd knocked back his second one he rested his hand a little too casually on my thigh and I thought to myself: 'Allo 'allo! Religious or not religious we now know where we are! From then on we lived happily ever after as you might say. It all got a bit boring but anything for a quiet life.

The Australian tour believe it or not was a wow, particularly in Sydney, where we were booked for four weeks and had to stay, by popular demand, for another two. It was in Sydney that Gloria Day fell in love with a life-guard she met on the beach, really in love too, not just an in and out and thank you very much. I must say I saw her point because he had a body like a Greek god. Unfortunately he also had a wife and two bouncing little kiddies tucked away somewhere in the bush and so there was no future in it for poor Gloria, and when we went away finally there was a lot of wailing and gnashing of teeth and threats of suicide. I gave her hell about this and reeled off a lot of fancy phrases like life being the most precious gift and time being a great healer etc., etc., and by the time we'd got to Singapore, which was our next date, she'd forgotten all about him and was working herself up into a state about the ship's doctor, who apart from being an alcoholic was quite attractive in a battered sort of way.

It was on that particular hop that things came to a head between me and Avice. We'd been in and out of bed together on and off for quite a long while but more as a sort of convenience than anything else. Then suddenly she took it into her head that I was the one great big gorgeous love of her life and that she couldn't live without me and that when we got back home to England we'd get married and have children and life would blossom like a rose. Now this was all cock and I told her so. In the first place I had explained, not in detail but generally, what I was really like and that although I liked girls as girls and found them lovely to be with they didn't really send me physically, anyway not enough to think of hitching myself up forever. Then of course there was a big dramatic scene during which she trotted out all the old arguments about me not really being like that at all and that once I'd persevered and got myself into the habit of sleeping with her regularly I'd never want to do the other thing again. After that snappy little conversation I need hardly say that there was a slight strain between us for the rest of the tour. Poor old Avice. I still hear from her occasionally. She finally married an electrician and went to Canada. She sent me a snapshot of herself and her family about a year ago. I could hardly recognise her. She looked as though she'd been blown up with a bicycle pump.

After Singapore we played various joints in Burma and Siam and one in Sumatra which was a bugger. It was there that Myrtle Kennedy, the standby, got amoebic dysentery and had to be left behind in a Dutch hospital where she stayed for nearly four weeks. She ultimately rejoined us in Bombay looking very thin and more like a horse than ever.

Bonny Macintyre's big moment came in Calcutta. She'd been getting more and more cock-a-hoop and pleased with herself mainly I think because her balloon dance always went better than anything else. It was our one unfailing show-stopper and even when there was hardly anyone in front she always got the biggest hand of the evening with it. In Calcutta she started ritzing the other girls and complaining about her hotel accommodation and asking for new dresses. She also had a brawl in the dressing-room with Jill and bashed her on the head so hard with her hair-brush that the poor kid had concussion and had to miss two performances. This was when I stepped in and gave our Bonny a proper walloping. I don't usually approve of hitting women but this was one of those times when it had to be done. She shrieked bloody murder and all the waiters in the joint came crowding into the room to see what was going on. The next day all was calm again, or outwardly so at least. That night however when I arrived at the club in time to put my slap on I was met by Avice wearing her tragedy queen expression. She went off into a long rigmarole which I couldn't help feeling she was enjoying a good deal more than she pretended to. There was always a certain self-righteous streak in Avice. Anyway what had happened was that Bonny had bolted with a Parsee radio announcer who she'd been going with for the last ten days. She'd left me a nasty little note which she had put into Avice's box in the hotel explaining that she was never coming back again because I wasn't a gentleman and that she'd cabled home to her mother in High Wycombe to say she was going to be married. She didn't say where she and the Parsee had bolted to and so that was that. There really wasn't anything to be done. I knew she couldn't possibly leave India because I'd got her passport—one of the first rules of travelling around with a bunch of female artistes is to hang on to their passports—however we were all due to leave India in a few weeks' time and I couldn't see myself setting off to search the entire bloody continent for Bonny Macintyre. Nor could I very well leave her behind. I was after all responsible for her. It was a fair bitch of a situation I can tell you. Anyhow there I was stuck with it and the first thing to do was to get the show reorganised for that night's performance. I sent Avice hareing off to get Sue into the balloon dance dress; sent for the band leader to tell him we were altering the running order; told Myrtle to be ready to go on in all the concerted numbers. I then did a thing I never never do before a performance. I had myself a zonking great whisky and soda and pranced out gallantly onto the dance floor ready to face with a stiff upper lip whatever further blows destiny had in store for me.

The next week was terrible. No word from Bonny and frantic cables arriving every day from her old mum. Avice I must say was a Rock of Gibraltar. She kept her head and came with me to the broadcasting station where we tried to trace the Parsee. We interviewed lots of little hairy men with green faces and high sibilant voices and finally discovered that Bonny's fiancé—to coin a phrase—had been given two weeks off to go up to the hills on account of he'd had a bad cough. Nobody seemed to know or care what part of the hills he'd gone to. We sat about for a further few days worrying ourselves silly and wondering what to do. Our closing date was drawing nearer and we had all been booked tourist class on a homeward-bound P and O. Finally, to cut a dull story short, our little roving will-o'-the-wisp returned to us with a bang. That is to say she burst into my room in the middle of the night and proceeded to have hysterics. All the other girls came flocking in to see what the fuss was about and stood around in their night-gowns and dressing-gowns and pyjamas with grease on their faces looking like Christmas night in the whore-house. I gave Bonny some Three Star Martell in a tooth glass which gave her hiccups but calmed her down a bit. Presently, when Jill had made her drink some water backwards and we'd all thumped her on the back, she managed to sob out the garbled story of her star-crossed romance, and it was good and star-crossed believe me. Apparently the Parsee had taken her in an old Ford convertible which broke down three times to visit his family, a happy little group consisting of about thirty souls in all, including goats, who lived in a small town seventy miles away. The house they lived in was not so much a house as a tenement and Bonny was forced to share a room with two of the Parsee's female cousins and a baby that was the teeniest bit spastic. She didn't seem to have exactly hit it off with the Parsee's dear old mother who snarled at her in Hindustani whenever she came within spitting distance. There was obviously no room for fun and games indoors so whatever sex they had had to take place on a bit of waste-land behind the railway station. She didn't enjoy any of this very much on account of being scared of snakes, but being so near the railway station often *did* actually give her the idea of making a getaway. Finally after one of the usual cosy evenings *en famille* with mum cursing away in one corner and the spastic baby having convulsions in the other, she managed to slip out of the house without her loved one noticing and run like a stag to the station. It was a dark night but she knew the way all right having been in that direction so frequently. After waiting four hours in a sort of shed a train arrived and she got onto it and here she was more dead than alive.

By the time she'd finished telling us all this the dawn had come up like thunder and she began to get hysterical again so Avice forced a couple of aspirins down her throat and put her to bed. Three days after this, having given our last triumphant performance to a quarter-full house, we set sail for England, home, and what have you, and that was really the end of Georgie Banks and His Six Bombshells.

Sunday

It's Sunday and all the church bells are ringing and I wish they wouldn't because I had a bad night and feel a bit edgy and the noise is driving me crackers.

It wasn't a bad night from the pain point of view although I felt a little uncomfortable between two and three and Sister Clothilde came in and gave me an injection which was a new departure really because I usually get a pill. Anyway it sent me off to sleep all right but it wasn't really sleep exactly, more like a sort of trance. I wasn't quite off and I wasn't quite on if you know what I mean and every so often I'd wake up completely for a few minutes feeling like I'd had a bad dream and couldn't remember what it was. Then I'd float off again and all sorts of strange things came into my mind. I suppose it was thinking yesterday so much about me and the bombshells that I'd got myself kind of overexcited. I woke up at about eight-thirty with a hangover but I felt better when I'd had a cup of tea. The orderly came in and carried me to the bathroom and then brought me back and put me in the armchair with an eiderdown wrapped round me while the bed was being made and the room done. One of the nicest things about being ill is when you're put back into a freshly made bed and can lie back against cool pillows before they get hot and crumpled and start slipping. The orderly stayed and chatted with me for a bit. He's quite sweet really. He told me he'd got the afternoon and evening off and that a friend of his was arriving from Munich who was a swimming champion and had won a lot of cups. He said this friend was very *"costaud"* and had a wonderfully developed chest but his legs were on the short side. They were going to have dinner in a restaurant by the lake and then go to a movie. I wished him luck and winked at him and wished to God I was going with them.

Later. It's still Sunday but the bells have stopped ringing and it's started to rain. The professor with the blue chin came to see me after I'd had my afternoon snooze. He looked different from usual because he was wearing quite a snappy sports coat and grey-flannel trousers. He told me he'd had lunch in a little restaurant in the country and had only just got back. I watched him looking at me carefully while he was talking to me as though he wanted to find out something. I told him about having had the injection and how it made me feel funny and he smiled and nodded and lit a cigarette. He then asked me whether I had any particular religion and when I said I hadn't he laughed and said that he hadn't either but he supposed it was a good thing for some people who needed something to hang on to. Then he asked me if I had ever talked to Father Lucien who was a Catholic priest who was sort of attached to the clinic. I said he'd come in to see me a couple of times and had been quite nice but that he gave me the creeps. Then he laughed again and started wandering about the room sort of absent-mindedly as though he was thinking of something else, then he came back, stubbed his cigarette out in the ashtray on my bed-table, and sat down again, this time on the side of the bed. I moved my legs to give him a bit more room. There was a fly buzzing about and a long way off one of those bloody church bells started ringing again. I looked at him sitting there so nonchalantly swinging his legs ever so little but frowning as though something were puzzling him. He was a good-looking man all right, somewhere between forty and fifty I should say, his figure was slim and elegant and his face thin with a lot of lines on it and his dark hair had gone grey at the sides. I wondered if he had a nice sincere wife to go home to in the evenings after a busy day cutting things out of people, or whether he lived alone with a faithful retainer and a lot of medical books and kept a tiny vivacious mistress in a flashy little apartment somewhere or other or even whether he was queer as a coot and head over heels in love with a sun-tanned ski instructor and spent madly healthy weekends with him in cosy wooden chalets up in the mountains. He looked at me suddenly as though he had a half guess at what I was thinking and I giggled. He smiled when I giggled and very gently took my hand in his and gave it a squeeze, not in the least a sexy squeeze but a sympathetic one and all at once I realised, with a sudden sinking of the heart, what the whole production was in aid of, why he had come in so casually to see me on a Sunday afternoon, why he had been drifting about the room looking ill at ease and why he had asked me about whether I was religious or not. It was because he knew that I was never going to get well again and was trying to make up his mind whether to let me know the worst or just let me go on from day to day hoping for the best. I knew then, in a sort of panic, that I didn't want him to tell me anything, not in so many words, because once he said them there I'd be stuck with them in my mind and wake up in the night and remember them. What I mean is that although I knew that I knew and had actually known, on and off, for a long time, I didn't want it settled and signed and sealed and done up, gift wrapped, with a bow on top. I still wanted not to be quite sure so that I could get through the days without counting. That was a bad moment all right, me lying there with him still holding my hand and all those thoughts going through my head and trying to think of a way to head him off. I knew that unless I did something quickly he'd blurt it out that I'd be up shit creek without a paddle and with nothing to hang on to and no hope left and so I did the brassiest thing I've ever done in my life and I still blush when I think of it. I suddenly reared myself up on my pillows, pulled him towards me, and gave him a smacking kiss. He jumped back as if he'd been shot. I've never seen anyone so surprised. Then, before he could say anything, I went off into a long spiel—I was a bit hysterical by then and I can't remember exactly what I said—but it was all about me having a "thing" about him ever since I'd first seen him and that that was the way I was and there was nothing to be done about it and that as he was a doctor I hoped he would understand and not be too shocked and that anyway being as attractive as he was he had no right to squeeze people's hands when they were helpless in bed and not expect them to lose control and make a pounce at him and that I'd obeyed an impulse too strong to be resisted—yes I actually said that if you please—and that I hoped he would forgive me but that if he didn't he'd just have to get on with it. I said a lot more than this and it was all pretty garbled because I'd worked myself into a proper state, but that was the gist of it. He sat there quite still while I was carrying on, staring at me and biting his lip. I didn't quite know how to finish the scene so I fell back on the old ham standby and burst into tears and what was so awful was that once I'd started I couldn't stop until he took out his cigarette-case, shoved a cigarette into my mouth, and lit it for me. This calmed me down and I was able to notice that he had stopped looking startled and was looking at me with one of his eyebrows a little higher than the other, quizzically as you might say, and that his lips were twitching as though he was trying not to laugh. Then he got up and said in a perfectly ordinary voice that he'd have to be getting along now as he had a couple more patients to see but that he'd come back and have a look at me later. I didn't say anything because I didn't feel I could really without starting to blub again, so I just lay puffing away like crazy at the cigarette and trying not to look too like Little Orphan Annie. He went to the door, paused for a moment, and then did one of the kindest things I've ever known. He came back to the bed, put both his arms round me, and kissed me very gently, not on the mouth but on the cheek as though he were really fond of me. Then he went out and closed the door quietly after him.

Monday

I woke up very early this morning having slept like a top for nearly nine hours. I rang the bell and when Sister Dominique came clattering in and pulled back the curtains it was a clear, bright morning again, not a bit like yesterday. When she'd popped off to get me my tea I lay quite still watching a couple of jet planes flying back and forth over the mountains and making long trails of white smoke in the pale blue sky. They went terribly quickly and kept on disappearing and coming back into view again. I tried to imagine what the pilots flying them looked like and what they were thinking about. It must be a wonderful feeling whizzing through the air at that tremendous speed and looking down at the whole world. Every now and then the sun caught one of the planes and it glittered like silver. I had some honey with my toast but it was a bit too runny. When the usual routine had been gone through and I was back in bed again I began to think of the professor yesterday afternoon and what I'd done and I felt hot with shame for a minute or two and then started to laugh. Poor love, it must have been a shock and no mistake. And then I got to wondering if after all it had been quite such a surprise to him as all that. Being a doctor he must be pretty hep about the so dainty facts of life, and being as dishy as he is, he can't have arrived at his present age without someone having made the teeniest weensiest pass at him at some time or other. Anyway by doing what I did I at least stopped him from spilling those gloomy little beans, if of course there were any beans to spill. Now, this morning, after a good night, I'm feeling that it was probably all in my imagination. You never know, do you? I mean it might have been something quite silly and unimportant that upset me, like those bloody church bells for instance. They'd been enough to get anybody down. Anyway there's no sense in getting morbid and letting the goblins get you. Maybe I'll surprise them all and be springing about like a mountain goat in a few weeks from now. All the same I shan't be able to help feeling a bit embarrassed when the professor comes popping in again. Oh dear—oh dear!

Here it is only half past eight and I've got the whole morning until they bring me my lunch at twelve-thirty to think about things and scribble my oh so glamorous memories on this pad which by the way is getting nearly used up so I must remember to ask Mavis to bring me another one. She'll probably be coming in this afternoon. It's funny this wanting to get things down on paper. I suppose quite a lot of people do if you only knew, not only professional writers but more or less ordinary people, only as a rule of course they don't usually have the time, whereas I have all the time in the world—or have I? Now then, now then, none of that. At any rate I've at least had what you might call an *interesting life* what with flouncing about all over the globe with those girls and having a close-up of the mysterious Orient and sailing the seven seas and one thing and another. Perhaps when I've finished it I shall be able to sell it to the *Daily Express* for thousands and thousands of pounds and live in luxury to the end of my days. What a hope! All the same it just might be possible if they cut out the bits about my sex life and some of the four-letter words were changed. Up to now I've just been writing down whatever came into my mind without worrying much about the words themselves. After all it's the thought that counts as the actress said to the bishop after he'd been bashing away at her for three hours and a half.

When I got back to London after that first tour with the bombshells I let them all go their own sweet ways and had a long talk to Ted about either working up an act on my own or trying to get into a West End show. Not a lead mind you. I wasn't so silly as to think I'd get more than a bit part, but if I happened to hit lucky and got a *good* bit part and was noticed in it then I'd be on the up and up and nothing could stop me. All this unfortunately came under the heading of wishful thinking. As a matter of fact I *did* get into a show and it *was* a good part with a duet in act one and a short solo dance at the beginning of act two, but the whole production was so diabolical that Fred Astaire couldn't have saved it and we closed after two weeks and a half. Then I decided that what I really needed was acting experience. After all nobody can go on belting out numbers and kicking their legs in the air forever whereas acting, legitimate acting that is, can last you a lifetime providing you're any good at it. Anyhow Ted managed to get me a few odd jobs in reps dotted over England's green and pleasant land and for two whole years, on and off, I slogged away at it. I had a bang at everything. Young juveniles—"Anyone for tennis"—old gentlemen, dope addicts, drunks. I even played a Japanese prisoner-of-war once in a ghastly triple bill at Dundee. My bit came in the first of the three plays and I was on and off so quickly that by the end of the evening none of the audience could remember having seen me at all. Somewhere along the line during those two years it began to dawn on me that I was on the wrong track. Once or twice I did manage to get a good notice in the local paper but I knew that didn't count for much and finally I found myself back in London again with two hundred and ten pounds in the bank, no prospects, and a cold. That was a bad time all right and I can't imagine now, looking back on it, how I ever lived through it. Finally, when I was practically on the bread line and had borrowed forty pounds from Ted, I had to pocket my pride and take a chorus job in a big American musical at the Coliseum which ran for eighteen months and there I was, stuck with it. Not that I didn't manage to have a quite good time one way or another. I had a nice little "combined" in Pimlico—Lupus Street to be exact—and it had a small kitchenette which I shared with a medical student on the next floor. He was quite sweet really but he had a birth mark all down one side of his neck which was a bit off-putting, however one must take the rough with the smooth is what I always say. When the show closed I'd paid back Ted and got a bit put by but not enough for a rainy day by any manner of means, so back I went into the chorus again and did another stretch. This time it lasted two years and I knew that if I didn't get out and do something on my own again I'd lose every bit of ambition I'd ever had and just give up. Once you really get into a rut in show business you've had it. All this was nearly five years ago and I will say one thing for myself, I *did* get out of the rut and although I nearly starved in the process and spent all I'd saved, I was at least free again and my own boss. I owe a great deal to old Ted really. Without him I could never have got these girls together and now of course, just as we were beginning to do really nicely, I have to get ill and bugger up the whole thing. This is where I come to a full stop and I know it and it's no good pretending any more to myself or anybody else. Even if I do get out of this clinic it'll take me months and months to get well enough to work again and by that time all the girls will have got other jobs and I shall have to shop around and find some new ones and redo the act from the beginning, and while we're at it, I should like to know how I'm going to live during those jolly months of languid convalescence! This place and the operation and the treatment must be costing a bloody fortune. Ted and Mavis are the only ones who know exactly what I've got saved and they're coping, but it can't go on for much longer because there just won't be anything left. I tried to say something to Mavis about this the other day but she said that everything was all right and that I wasn't to worry and refused to discuss it any further. I've never had much money sense I'm afraid, Ted's always nagging me about it but it's no use. When I've got it I spend it and when I haven't I don't because I bloody well can't and that's that. All the same I have been careful during the last few years, more careful than I ever was before, and there must still be quite a bit in the bank, even with all this extra expense. I must make Mavis write to Ted and find out just exactly how things are. He's got power of attorney anyhow. Now you see I've gone and got myself low again. It's always the same, whenever I begin to think about money and what I've got saved and what's going to happen in the future, down I go into the depths. I suppose this is another lack in me like not having had just that extra something which would have made me a great big glamorous star. I must say I'm not one to complain much as a rule. I've had my ups and downs and it's all part of life's rich pattern as some silly bitch said when we'd just been booed off the stage by some visiting marines in Port Said. All the same one can't go on being a cheery chappie forever, can one? I mean there are moments when you have to look facts in the face and not go on kidding yourself, and this, as far as I'm concerned, is one of them. I wish to Christ I hadn't started to write at all this morning. I was feeling fine when I woke up, and now, by doing all this thinking back and remembering and wondering, I've got myself into a state of black depression and it's no use pretending I haven't. As a matter of fact it's no use pretending ever, about anything, about getting to the top, or your luck turning, or living, or dying. It always catches up with you in the end. I don't even feel like crying which is funny because I am a great crier as a rule when things get bad. It's a sort of relief and eases the nerves. Now I couldn't squeeze a tear out if you paid me. That really is funny. Sort of frightening. That's the lot for today anyway. The *Daily Express* must wait.

Tuesday

Mavis came yesterday afternoon as promised and I forgot to ask her about getting another writing pad, but it doesn't really matter because there's still quite a lot of this one left. I didn't feel up to talking much so I just lay still and listened while she told me all the gossip. Lily-May had sprained her ankle, fortunately in the last number, not a bad sprain really, not bad enough that is for her to have to stay off. She put on cold compresses last night and it had practically gone down by this morning. Beryl and Sylvia were taken out after the show on Saturday night by a very rich banking gentleman from Basle who Monsieur Philippe had brought backstage. He took them and gave them a couple of drinks some-where or other and then on to an apartment of a friend of his which was luxuriously furnished and overlooked the lake except that they couldn't see much of it on account of it being pitch dark and there being no moon. Anyway the banker and his friend opened a bottle of champagne and sat Beryl and Sylvia down as polite as you please on a sofa with satin cushions on it and while they were sipping the champagne and being thoroughly piss-elegant, which they're inclined to be at the best of times, the banker, who'd gone out of the room for a minute, suddenly came in again stark naked carrying a leather whip in one hand and playing with himself with the other. The girls both jumped up and started screaming and there was a grand old hullabaloo for a few minutes until the friend managed to calm them down and made the banker go back and put on a dressing-gown. While he was out of the room he gave the girls a hundred francs each and apologised for the banker saying that he was a weeny bit eccentric but very nice really and that the whip was not to whack them with but for them to whack him, the banker, with, which just happened to be his way of having fun. Then the twins stopped screaming and got grand as all get-out and said that they were used to being treated like ladies. They didn't happen to mention who by. Then the banker came back in a fur coat not having been able to find a dressing-gown and said he was sorry if he had frightened them and would they please not say a word to Monsieur Philippe. They all had some more champagne and the banker passed out cold and the friend brought them home in a taxi without so much as groping them. Anti-climax department the whole thing. Anyway they got a hundred francs each whichever way you look at it and that's eight pounds a head for doing fuck all. I must say I couldn't help laughing when Mavis told me all this but she wasn't amused at all, oh dear me no. There's a strong governessy streak in our Mavis. She went straight to Monsieur Philippe and carried on as if she were a mother superior in a convent. This made me laugh still more and when she went she looked quite cross.

Friday

I haven't felt up to writing anything for the last few days and I don't feel any too good now but I suppose I'd better make an effort and get on with it. I began having terrible pains in my back and legs last Tuesday night I think it was, anyway it was the same day that Mavis came, and Dr. Pierre was sent for and gave me an injection and I've felt sort of half asleep ever since, so much so that I didn't even know what day it was. I've just asked Sister Dominique and she told me it was Friday. Imagine! That's two whole days gone floating by with my hardly knowing anything about it. I've been feeling better all day today, a bit weak I must admit, but no more pain. The professor came in to see me this afternoon and brought me a bunch of flowers and Mavis brought me a little pot of pâté-de-foie-gras, or maybe it was the other way round, anyway I know that they both came. Not at the same time of course but at different times, perhaps it was the day before yesterday that the professor came. I'm still feeling a bit woozy and can't quite remember. I know he held my hand for quite a long time so he can't have really been upset about me behaving like that. He's a wonderful man the professor is, a gentle and loving character, and I wish, I wish I could really tell him why I did what I did and make him understand that it wasn't just silly camping but because I was frightened. I expect he knows anyhow. He's the sort of man who knows everything that goes on in people's minds and you don't have to keep on saying you're sorry and making excuses to him any more than you'd have to to God if God is anything like what he's supposed to be. The act closes tomorrow night if today really is Friday, and all the girls have promised to come to say good-bye to me on Sunday before they catch the train, at least that's what Mavis said. I had the funniest experience last night. I saw Harry-boy. He was standing at the end of the bed as clear as daylight wearing his blue dungarees and holding up a pair of diabolical old socks which he wanted me to wash out for him. Of course I know I didn't really see him and that I was dreaming, but it did seem real as anything at the time and it still does in a way. Harry never could do a thing for himself, like washing socks I mean, or anything useful in the house. I'm not being quite fair because he did fix the tap in the lavatory basin once when it wouldn't stop running, but then he was always all right with anything to do with machinery, not that the tap in the lavatory basin can really be called machinery but it's the same sort of thing if you know what I mean. All the girls are coming to say good-bye to me on Sunday before they catch the train, at least that's what Mavis said. Good old Mavis. I suppose I'm fonder of her than anybody actually, anybody that's alive I mean. I must try to remember to tell her this the next time she comes. If she doesn't come before Sunday I can tell her then. The weather's changed with a vengeance and it's raining to beat the band which is a shame really because I can't see the mountains any more except every now and then for a moment or two when it lifts. I wonder whatever became of Bonny Macintyre. I haven't had so much as a post-card from her in all these years. She was a tiresome little bitch but she had talent and there's no doubt about it and nobody else ever did the balloon dance quite the way she did it. It wasn't that she danced all that brilliantly, in fact Jill could wipe her eye any day of the week when it came to speed and technique. But she had something that girl.

Sister Clothilde pulled the blinds down a few minutes ago just before Dr. Pierre and Father Lucien came in. Dr. Pierre gave me an injection which hurt a bit when it went in but felt lovely a few seconds later, a sweet warm feeling coming up from my toes and covering me all over like an eiderdown. Father Lucien leant over me and said something or other I don't remember what it was. He's quite nice really but there *is* something about him that gives me the creeps. I mean I wouldn't want him to hold my hand like the professor does. The act closes on Saturday night and the girls are all coming to say good-bye to me on Sunday before they catch the train. I do hope Mavis gets a job or meets someone nice and marries him and settles down. That's what she ought to do really. It isn't that she's no good. She dances well and her voice is passable, but the real thing is lacking. Hark at me! I should talk. I wish Sister Clothilde hadn't pulled the blinds down, not that it really matters because it's dark by now and I shouldn't be able to see them anyhow.

~ *J. R. Ackerley* ~

FROM

My Father
and Myself

A useful vantage point for observing my father and myself together is
the Bois de Boulogne in the spring of 1923. My parents were in
Paris with my sister, who was working as a mannequin for one of the
fashion houses, and I joined them there, coming up from Ragusa, where
I had been with a young artist friend. At this time I had a flat in St.
John's Wood.

I remember sitting with my father one afternoon in the Bois, watching
the procession of people go by. If I had known and thought about him
then as much as I have learnt and thought about him since his death,
what an interesting conversation we might have had. For here was the
city of his romantic youth, hither he had brought Louise after his deser-
tion of de Gallatin, here he had married her and lived with her and her
parents in the Boulevard de Courcelles until she died, hither he had
escorted my mother thirty-one years ago. The place must have been full
of memories for him, happy and sad, and if I could have that day again,
I hope I should make better use of it. But although it was jolly sitting

---

*J. R. ACKERLEY was born and spent most of his life in London, where he was literary
editor of the BBC publication* The Listener. *His books include the Indian memoir* Hindoo
Holiday; *the novel* We Think the World of You *(later made into a film with Alan
Bates and Gary Oldman);* My Dog Tulip, *an account of his fifteen-year "marriage" to
a German Shepherd; and the extraordinary autobiographical work* My Father and Myself,
*excerpted here. Readers interested in this gifted writer's extremely peculiar life should have
a look at Peter Parker's wonderful biography,* Ackerley.

with him in the Bois, we had no interesting talk; instead we were watching a dog's large turd, just pointed out by him, which lay in the middle of the path in front of us. Which of the people passing along would be the first to tread on it? That was our curiosity, and thus, whether it was dogs' turds, or "yarns," or other trivialities, did all our life together senselessly slip away.

To watch the world go by—this "wonderful old world" as he often called it—whether in the Bois, on Richmond Terrace, or elsewhere, was one of my father's pleasurable leisure occupations, and when our little excremental comedy had worked itself out to its messy conclusion, we reverted to observing the faces and dresses of the crowd parading before us. But whereas my father was appraising the women, commenting on those "plump little partridges" he found interesting, I was eyeing the young men. Venus herself could have passed without attracting my gaze or altering the beat of my pulse if my father had pointed her out.

To psychologists, my love-life, into which I must now again go before continuing with my father's, may appear somewhat unsatisfactory; in retrospect it does not look perfectly satisfactory to me, indeed I regard it with some astonishment. It may be said to have begun with a golliwog and ended with an Alsatian bitch; in between there passed several hundred young men, mostly of the lower orders and often clad in uniforms of one sort or another. Even behind the golliwog I have a suspicion that another shadowy figure lurks: a boot-boy. I do not firmly bring him forward because I can't be sure that he existed, though why should I have invented him? In Apsley House, the first of our Richmond residences, I place him, and he is a game, a childish game, possibly and unwittingly suggested by my weekend and sometimes retributive father himself, for in this game my brother, the boot-boy, and I take down each other's trousers by turn and gently beat the bare bottoms that lie, warmly and willingly, across our laps. With this forgotten boot-boy I associate the word "brown," but whether it was his face, or his bottom, or his name that was brown I don't recall.

The golliwog has more substance. He occurred during my convalescence from peritonitis. After the operation ("It has been successful," said Mr. Cuthbert Wallis, the eminent specialist, "but I can't answer for his life") my father, on his early way to town, said he wanted to bring me back a present, what would I like? Expense was no matter, I could have anything in the world I desired. I said, "A golliwog." I was twelve years old and my father could scarcely believe his ears. He got it for me of course; but in later life he referred to it as one of the most extraordinary requests he had ever received. Of the golliwog itself I now remember nothing; possibly the shocked amazement on my father's face smeared it with guilt; afterwards I became more cautious in concealing my weaknesses, in covering up; but the unguarded moment of the golliwog, so to speak, sometimes recurred; repress him as we may, he manages to crop up.

It should not be inferred, however, from golliwogs at twelve and the nickname "Girlie" at my preparatory school that I was in the least effeminate. That I was a pretty boy I have already said, too pretty I fear— beauty, among the gifts of fairy godmothers, is not the one most conducive of happiness (though I remember a man at Cambridge saying to me, "I wish to God I had your looks, I'd have any bloody girl in the world I wanted"); but I was far from girlish, physically or in my nature; there were no marks upon me as I matured from which my father could have suspected the sort of son he had sired; I did not lisp, I could throw overhand, and I could whistle. True, I disliked football and cricket and thought them dangerous recreations, but I was good at hockey (a hard, fast game Rossall played upon the sands of the seashore) and an accurate marksman (I captained the school shooting eight at Bisley for two or three years); I grew a moustache—albeit a wispier one than my father's or the Count de Gallatin's—during the war and took to a pipe: all manly accomplishments. Indeed I was far from needing, I am sorry to say, the fervent warning I received from Teddy Bacon at school. This boy was the son of that wealthy Manchester friend of my father's whose £100 cheque I was later obliged to return, and he unfortunately left Rossall at the end of my first or second term. He was charming, clever, and beautiful, with a pale milky skin and black hair, and he occupied in the regard of our English master, S. P. B. Mais, the pre-eminent place in which I was to succeed him. After he had gone I noticed a photograph of him in the centre of Mais's mantelpiece, and looking at it one day when I was alone in the room, I turned it round and found, to my surprise and jealousy, written upon the back of it in Mais's hand: "The best boy I have ever known or am ever likely to know." Teddy was the school whore; I can't remember whether he was expelled or departed more normally; at any rate, just before he left he took me aside and begged me, whatever I did, not to go the way that he had gone. The reason for this tardy revulsion I don't recall, only the vehemence of it. My father's friendship with his father had brought us together for a time, too short a time; I liked and admired him very much and if ever *he* had sat on my bed after lights out, asking to be let in, I wonder if my life, then and later, would have been happier. Probably not; happiness of that kind, I suspect, was not a thing I was psychologically equipped to find. In any case he was in a different house. He was killed in the first few weeks of the war.

Instead of supplying his place as the school whore, my sexual life was of the dullest. Apart from the furtive fumblings I have already mentioned, I had no physical contact with anyone, not even a kiss, and remained in this virginal state until my Cambridge days more than five years later. Other boys, less attractive than Teddy, became enslaved to me, but speechlessly; I gave them no help, they left, we corresponded, they entered the war and were killed, and when I myself, in my last terms, fell in love with a boy named Snook, I could not bring myself to touch him and it remained a pure and platonic ideal. A clue to the guilty state of my ideas of love as a pure thing, an innocent thing, spoiled and soiled by sex, may be got from a poem I wrote about my feeling for Snook in my last term and published in a magazine called *The Wasp,* of which I was inventor and editor, and most of which I conceitedly wrote myself. It was a counter-blast to the official school publication, and may have been the venture upon which Captain Bacon bestowed his £100. The personal pronouns in this poem are clearer to me than they may be to others.

He loved him for his face,
His pretty head and fair complexion,
His natural lissome grace,
But trusted not his own affection.

He watched him smile, his eyes
All lighted with youth's careless laughter;
His brain rehearsed his lies
And wondered if he'd like him after.

Then love of beauty rose
Untarnished like a woodland flower,
Which never lies but grows
Caressed by sun and kissed by shower. . . .

He would not understand,
This pretty child of many graces,
So with a burning hand
He led him out to quiet places.

This erotic little poem so upset my housemaster that he said his inclination was to beat me, but I replied that he could not do that because
the title I had given the poem was "Millstones." To another master,
William Furness, with whom I was pally, I confided my passion for
Snook. He said he thought it a very good thing that this was my last
term—but for reasons which would have shocked my housemaster almost
as much as the poem had done. Snook, said Furness, was, in his opinion,
a perfectly heartless little boy and quite unworthy of me. A third peda-
gogic view of me may be added. I wish I could recall this master's name.
He was a reserved, sardonic, rather attractive, unsmiling man as I remember him, upon whom the charm of my appearance had failed to have the
disarming effect it had upon everyone else. Bowing low to me instead of
taking my proffered hand when I went to say good-bye, he remarked,
with a faint, chilly smile, "Pride will have a fall, Ackerley, pride will have
a fall." Rebukes such as this are too seldom administered; I never forgot
this shocking remark and think always with respect of the now anonymous man who troubled himself to make it.

The Snook situation continued sporadically into my Army and Cambridge life. Instinctively evading older men who seemed to desire me, I
could not approach the younger ones whom I desired. Eluding "Titchy,"
I admired the younger Thorne at a distance. The working classes also, of
course, now took my eye. Many a handsome farm- or tradesboy was to
be found in the ranks of one's command, and to a number of beautiful
but untouchable NCOs and privates did I allot an early sentimental or
heroic death in my nauseous verse. My personal runners and servants were
usually chosen for their looks; indeed this tendency in war to have the
prettiest soldiers about one was observable in many other officers; whether
they took more advantage than I dared of this close, homogenous, almost
paternal relationship I do not know. Then came capture and imprisonment. In the hospital in Hanover, to which I was taken with my splintered
pelvis, I became enamoured of a Russian medical orderly, a prisoner like
myself, named Lovkin; he was gentle and kind, with a broad Slav face,
but apparently without personal feelings; we had no common language,

but liking to be in his arms I wanted no one else to carry me to and from the operating theatre and to dress my wound, which suppurated for weeks until all the little fragments of bone had been extracted. My memory of the rest of my imprisonment in Germany is emotionally featureless; there were two or three middle-aged officers, among the various lagers I was sent to, with whom I formed friendships and whose feelings I believe I aroused and frustrated, but I remember them only as shadows.

In Switzerland I was attracted to two young men. One was a captain of my own age named Carlyon. He had an artificial eye and a dog, his inseparable companions. To say that he was unapproachable does not mean that I was ever bold enough to approach him. My sentiments for him too were confided only to my notebook in many a sickly verse. Around the other, a consumptive boy who died of his complaint soon after the Armistice, I wrote my play *The Prisoners of War,* which the poor fellow, having identified himself in it, thought awfully unkind, as well he might since I accused him, in the character of Grayle, of a heartless un-responsiveness to love without, in reality, ever having made my own feelings towards him plain—if indeed I knew what my own feelings were. A passage in this play seems to me revealing as showing how little I had developed emotionally since my schooldays. The hero, Captain Conrad (myself of course), is asked by one of the other characters why he is so fond of Lieutenant Grayle. He replies, "I don't know. He's clean. Fills gaps. . . . His life's like an open book." ("Fills gaps" I longed to eradicate when I was older and the play was already in print; I saw that Freud had got away with more than I intended.) "But hardly worth reading!" ex-claims the other. This passage echoes my conversation, four years earlier, with Furness about Snook. I was still on the same tack: purity, innocence, and innocence is untouchable ("Millstones"). Sex remained a desirable but guilty thing.

However, my knowledge of life now began to increase. I met in Switzerland a mocking and amusing fellow with whom I became very thick. He was the second forceful intellectual under whose dominance I fell. His name was Arnold Lunn, and with his energetic, derisive, icon-oclastic mind and rasping demonic laugh he was both the vitality and the terror of the community. Almost the first mischievous question he shot at me was "Are you homo or hetero?" I had never heard either term before; they were explained and there seemed only one answer. He him-self, like Mais, was hetero; so far as I recall I never met a recognisable or self-confessed adult homosexual (except an ancient master at school, called "the Nag," who was mysteriously sacked) until after the war; the Army with its male relationships was simply an extension of my public school. Lunn lent or recommended me books to read, Otto Weininger, Edward Carpenter, Plutarch, and thus and with his malicious, debunking thought opened my mind. When I was at last repatriated and my mother's frequent innuendoes about girls and the eventual arrival of "Miss Right" exasperated me, I lectured her severely on Otto Weininger, while the poor lady lifted the wads of her hair from her shrinking ears, the better to catch, if she must, the appalling things I seemed to be saying. Of Weininger now I recollect little; that I ever got to the end of him I doubt; but I believe that his thesis is that, in respect of the male and female principles, we all have both in some degree, individually and therefore variously blended, as though we were bags of tea; if the human race, then, were sorted out and lined up in one vast single-rank parade, the hermaphrodite would stand in the centre, the 100% male and female at either end, and infinite gradations of the mixture in between. Presumably having got so far, I must have concluded my lecture by placing myself on parade in such a position as to indicate that girls were not for me; at any rate, poor Arnold Lunn became, in my mother's anxious thought, an incarnation of the devil. It did not matter; nothing much, especially of a disturbing nature, remained in her mind for long—worry was bad for the health—and anyway Lunn, like Mais, belonged for me to his time and place; transplanted into my home soil they both soon withered away.

I was now on the sexual map and proud of my place on it. I did not care for the word "homosexual" or any label, but I stood among the men, not among the women. Girls I despised; vain, silly creatures, how could their smooth, soft, bulbous bodies compare in attraction with the muscular beauty of men? Their place was the harem, from which they should never have been released; true love, equal and understanding love, occurred only between men. I saw myself therefore in the tradition of the Classic Greeks, surrounded and supported by all the famous homosexuals of history—one soon sorted them out—and in time I became something of a publicist for the rights of that love that dare not speak its name. Unfortunately in my own private life also it seemed to have some impediment in its speech; love and sex, come together as I believed they should, failed to meet, and I got along at Cambridge no better than anywhere else. In varying degrees and at various times I was attracted to a number of other undergraduates; I had sexual contact with none of them. So far as I know, all but one were normal boys, and the normal, manly boy always drew me most. Certainly effeminacy in men repelled me almost as much as women themselves did. But although I felt that, had I tried to kiss these normal, friendly boys who came so often to my rooms, my advances would not have been rebuffed, I could not take that step. It seemed that I needed a degree of certainty so great that only unambiguous advances from the other side would have suited me; these I never got, and even had I got them I might not, for another reason,★ have been able to cope. To one boy I was so attracted that I bought him an expensive pair of gold and platinum cuff-links at Asprey's which linked our engraved Christian names together. My homosexual undergraduate friend thought him a horrid little boy and I did see that he was perfectly brainless, but he had the kind of dewy prettiness I liked, the innocent look of Snook and "Grayle"—and innocence was difficult to tamper with. Him I managed to kiss, but went no further; the distance between the mouth and the crotch seemed too great. Yet I believe that he himself wished it to be spanned, for our last meeting took place in my Richmond home, to which he had been invited for a dance-party and to stay the night, and having spent a chaste one there he remarked ruefully the following morning, "Every time one meets you, one has to start all over again." Another boy provided a similar but plainer and therefore sadder lesson. He was a Persian and, I thought, the most ravishingly pretty boy I'd ever seen. I knew him only by sight and would trail about Cambridge after him whenever I spied him in the street, wondering how to get into conversation. Once, I followed him to the station and he got into a London train. I got in too, though I had not the least intention or wish to visit London. Not daring to sit beside him I eyed him covertly across the carriage. Whenever he looked at me I looked away. At Liverpool Street he entered a taxi and I returned to Cambridge by the next available train. Some ten years later, when I was well into my sexual stride, I ran into him at Marble Arch and managed to recognise him, though the bloom and the charm had vanished, the wonderful astrakhan hair receded. More surprisingly, he recognised me. I told him of my admiration for him in Cambridge; he said with a laugh that he had been well aware of it, what a pity I had not spoken, he had always hoped I would speak,

---

★ Ejaculatio praecox.

and how about returning with him to his flat now? It was just round the corner. He was no longer attractive to me, but the glamorous memory remained and I went. Our deferred pleasures were, to me, closer to pain; to him a fiasco. He smelt rather nice of some musky perfume with which he and his flat were drenched, but my apparently artless ideas of love had no place in his highly sophisticated repertoire. He disliked being kissed, and the attentions and even acrobatics he required to stimulate his jaded sex were not merely disagreeable to me but actually uncomfortable. Within limits I attempted to oblige him, but he said scathingly at last, "The trouble with you is you're innocent." It was a wounding word, but kinder than the right one.

It was in my Cambridge years that I began to meet and mix with other acknowledged homosexuals. The emotional feelings and desires we shared, which, at any rate in their satisfaction, made us outcasts and criminals in the sight of the impertinent English laws, naturally drove us into each other's company and the society of those who, though not homosexual themselves, or not exclusively homosexual, were our intelligent, enlightened friends. In such company one was able to enjoy perfect freedom of speech. To understand and explain oneself, which I am trying to do, is very difficult, so I don't know whether to attribute to mere bad luck or to the inscrutable perversities of my nature the fact that neither in Cambridge nor afterwards did I ever meet a homosexual with whom I wanted to set up house. The simplest answers to our dilemmas are not always the ones we desire. Many of my friends brought off enduring "marriages" with men of their own class and kind, others with men of their own kind though of a different class, and I myself have had some short episodes with homosexuals who came attractively in my way; but for some reason I never established myself with any of them. Certain, perhaps relevant, notes about my Cambridge character, as I try to discern it, may be put down. I saw myself, in affairs of the heart, in the masculine role, the active agent; the undergraduates who seemed to me attractive were always younger than I. I myself was attractive, but I did not like to be thought so and pursued by others to whom I was not attracted, as sometimes happened. I avoided or repelled undesirable intimacies. I remember that a middle-aged homosexual novelist, whom I had met only twice and whose name I have now forgotten, said to me, "May I call you Joe?" I said, "No." I was not out to give pleasure but to get it. It was particularly embarrassing when my homosexual friends seemed to fall for me if they themselves had no physical appeal. I dodged and frustrated them and hurt their feelings. In later life, when I tried to improve a character which I saw to be ungenerous, I found that, try as I did, I could not produce the smallest physical response to the passions of those who loved me and of whom indeed I was fond, though not in a physical way. Thus did I hurt their feelings again. It is easier to mend one's manners than one's psychology, and it has sometimes seemed to me that, in my case, the feelings of the heart and the desires of the flesh have lain in separate compartments.

One more neurosis, shared with my mother: I was worried about bad breath. I disliked it in others and feared I might have it myself. My mother carried always with her in her bag a supply of cachous called Red Lavender lozenges. I doubt if they still exist. Chemists sold them and they had a distinctive taste and scent, pleasant and pervasive, which I associate with her, her person and her belongings. I too used to buy these lozenges to suck before kissing, and all through my sexual life I have carried something in my pocket, peppermints, chocolate, to sweeten my breath in case it was nasty.

With the homosexual undergraduate friend to whom I have already alluded I was especially thick and had for him indeed some emotional feeling, incipient at least, which he reciprocated. We kissed. He was a few years younger than myself and is my friend still. But he was sexually experienced where I was not and was already having affairs with two men much older than either of us. Perhaps unwisely he described to me their love-making, in which fellatio played the largest part. This seemed to my innocent or puritanical mind so disgusting that for a long time I thought of his friends with utter repulsion as monsters, lower than the beasts, and wondered that their faces, when at length I met them both, should look so ordinary. This boy and I, after discussing and hesitating on the verge of physical love, which was never strong on either side, decided that it would "spoil" our friendship.

Unable, it seemed, to reach sex through love, I started upon a long quest in pursuit of love through sex. Having put that neat sentence down I stare at it. Is it true? At some point in the journey I would certainly have so described it; how serious I was in the beginning, the early twenties, I no longer remember. I was to spend twenty-five years in this search, which began, it may not surprise readers to hear, in Piccadilly, at No. 11 Half Moon Street, a discreet establishment someone had told me about and where I rented a room for a weekend, twice I think, in my Cambridge history. Street prowlers and male prostitutes, not many, were my first prey; of them, strangely enough, I remember nothing at all, but I find in my notebooks the following brief entry: "No. 11 Half Moon Street, the kind of room in which one kills oneself."

However, if I was cheerless then, life brightened for me after I came down. I met socially more and more homosexuals and their boy friends and had an affair with a good-natured normal Richmond tradesboy who delivered groceries to my parents' house but, through some kind of physical apathy, delivered nothing material to me. By the time I reached, with my father, the dog's turd in the Bois de Boulogne I was well into my predatory stride. I had just come up from Ragusa, where I had been idling about with a lisping little artist whose girlishness had ended by sickening me; my homosexual Cambridge friend was now living in Paris and we were exploring the queer bars and Turkish baths where one was able to select one's masseur from photographs displayed by the proprietor; I was busy making assignations with a Corsican waiter in the Café de la Paix under my parents' noses. Later on, when my play was in production in London, actors were added to my social list; I do not like to boast, but Ivor Novello took me twice into his bed. Though I can't remember my state of mind at this period, I expect that much of all this seemed fun. It certainly afforded pleasure and amusement, it was physically exciting, and in England it had the additional thrill of risk. A single instance of this mixture of fun and risk may be described. Early in the decade I travelled up to Liverpool with my father to visit his sisters. In the restaurant car where we were having lunch a good-looking young waiter was instantly recognised by me as a "queer." While my father studied the menu I exchanged smiles and winks with this youth. Towards the end of the meal, when the business of serving it was over, he passed me with a meaning look and backward glance and disappeared down the corridor. Excusing myself to my father for a natural need, I followed him. He was waiting for me by the door of the toilet. We entered together, quickly unbuttoned, and pleasured each other. Then I returned to finish my coffee. I had scribbled down my address for this amusing youth, but never heard from him again.

Yet in spite of such adventures, if anyone had asked me what I was doing I doubt if I should have replied that I was diverting myself. I think I should have said that I was looking for the Ideal Friend. If I had not said that in the beginning I would certainly have said it later. Though two or three hundred young men were to pass through my hands in the course of years, I did not consider myself promiscuous but monogamous, it was all a run of bad luck, and I became ever more serious over this as time went on. Perhaps as a reaction to my school, Army, and Cambridge difficulties, the anxiety, nervousness, guilt that had dogged me all along the line (though I did not think of it then as guilt, if indeed it was), I was developing theories of life to suit myself: sex was delightful and of prime importance; the distance between the mouth and the crotch must be bridged at once, clothes must come off as soon as possible, no courtship, no nonsense, no beating, so to speak, about the bush; the quickest, perhaps the only, way to get to know anyone thoroughly was to lie naked in bed with him—both were at once disarmed of all disguise and pretence, all cards were on the table, and one could tell whether he was the Ideal Friend. What I meant by the Ideal Friend I doubt if I ever formulated, but now, looking back over the years, I think I can put him together in a partly negative way by listing some of his many disqualifications. He should not be effeminate, indeed preferably normal; I did not exclude education but did not want it, I could supply all that myself and in the loved one it had always seemed to get in the way; he should admit me but no one else; he should be physically attractive to me and younger than myself—the younger the better, as closer to innocence; finally he should be on the small side, lusty, circumcised, physically healthy and clean: no phimosis, halitosis, bromidrosis. It may be thought that I had set myself a task so difficult of accomplishment as almost to put success purposely beyond my reach; it may be thought too that the reason why this search was taking me out of my own class into the working class, yet still towards that innocence which in *my* class I had been unable to touch, was that guilt in sex obliged me to work it off on my social inferiors. This occurred to me only as a latter-day question and the answer may be true, I cannot tell; if asked then I would probably have said that working-class boys were more unreserved and understanding, and that friendship with them opened up interesting areas of life, hitherto unknown.

Difficult of discovery though my Ideal Friend might seem, I found him, as I thought, quite soon. He was a sailor, an able-bodied seaman, a simple, normal, inarticulate, working-class boy whom I met by introduction. I already knew some of his family. Small in stature and a lightweight boxer quite famous in the Navy, his silken-skinned, muscular, perfect body was a delight to behold, like the Ephebe of Kritios. His brown-eyed, slightly simian face, with its flattened nose and full thick lips, attracted me at once. If he smelt of anything it was the salt of the sea. He had had no sexual experience with anyone before, but wanted it and instantly welcomed it with me. In fact he satisfied all my undefined specifications, and if men could marry, I would have proposed to him. He might even, in the first delight, have accepted me, for he never manifested the slightest interest in girls (he did not marry until well into his forties), was proud of me and my friendship and excited by all it had to offer—my flat, which became his second home, my car, which I taught him to drive, and the admiration which provided him with such presents as a smart civilian suit.

This boy engrossed my heart and thought for four years, but in a way I had not foreseen he was not Ideal: being a sailor he was too seldom available. Had he been more available, perhaps the affair would not have lasted so long. He was stationed in Portsmouth, free only at weekends, if then. Sometimes he went off for a long cruise on his ship. Whenever he had leave he came to stay with me; but because of his sporadic appearances, his conventional background, his unsophistication, and the "manly respectability" of our relationship (the Greek view of life), all my anxieties found their fullest play. I was not faithful to him (not that he demanded faithfulness), he was too much away, but concealed from him my nature and the kind of life I led (not that he ever exhibited the least curiosity about it). I did not want him to think me "queer" and himself a part of homosexuality, a term I disliked since it included prostitutes, pansies, pouffs, and queans. Though he met some of my homosexual friends, I was always on edge in case they talked in front of him the loose homosexual chatter we talked among ourselves. My sailor was a sacred cow and must be protected against all contamination.

The setting of the nuptial scene whenever he was due to arrive was fraught with anxieties. Idle callers of a "contaminating" kind, of whom I had too many, had to be warned off or turned away from the door; my boiling incontinence had somehow to be concealed; I would have liked instantly to undo his silks and ribbons, but the conventions by which he lived required, I supposed, the delays of conversation, drinks, supper: sex should be postponed to its proper respectable time, bedtime; the Red Lavender lozenges had to be handy, a towel also, though hidden from him, to obviate the embarrassment of turning out naked in search of one to dry us down, and to prevent, if possible, stains on the sheets as a speculation for my char. He liked dancing with me to the gramophone, readily accepting the female role, and often when I had ascertained that he too was in a state of erection we would strip and dance naked, so unbearably exciting that I could not for long endure the pressure of his body against mine. Our pleasures were, I suppose, fairly simple; kisses, caresses, manipulations, intercrural massage; he got his own satisfaction quite soon, though not as soon as I; whether we ever repeated these pleasures during the night (we slept in one bed) I don't recall; I doubt it; since he was an athlete, always boxing or training for it, I expect it was tacitly understood that he should conserve his strength. I am quite sure that if further turnings towards each other occurred, it was never he who turned. There seemed, indeed, always something to worry about—as there had been throughout my sexual life; and when a friend once asked me whether I ever "lost myself" in sex, the answer had to be no.

Careful though I seemed to myself to be with my sailor, my desire for him outran prudence, he began to feel an unwelcome emotional pressure, there were failed appointments when I waited for him in vain, and I started to lose my head. Advice came from a close friend★ of mine:

> I'm sure that if one tries to live only for love one cannot be happy, but perhaps happiness is not your deepest need. . . . The standards which are so obvious to you are very remote to him and his class, and he was bound to relapse from them sooner or later. And by standards I mean not only conventions but methods of feeling. He can quite well be deeply attached to you and yet suddenly find the journey up too much of a fag. It is difficult for us, with our middle-class training, to realise this, but it is so. Also if you want a permanent relationship with him or anyone, you must give up the idea of ownership, and even the idea of being owned. Relationships based on ownership may be the best (I have never known or tried to know them), but I'm certain they never last. Not being you and not knowing him I can't say any more, except to beg you to write nothing to him beyond brief notes of

---

★ The close friend to whom Ackerley refers is E. M. Forster; the text following the first ellipsis is from a letter dated April 9, 1928, in the Harry Ransom Humanities Research Center, University of Texas, Austin. —Editors.

affection until you meet again. Don't rebuke, don't argify, don't apologise. . . .

How much of this excellent advice I took, or was constitutionally able to take, I don't remember; very little, I imagine, for later on I went so far as to rent a flat in Portsmouth for the sailor and myself in order to see more of him than I was seeing in London. There, like any possessive housewife, I catered and cooked for him while he was at work, impatiently awaiting the moment of his return. One evening he said irritably, "What, chicken again!" It is the only speech he ever made that has stuck in my mind. The end was clearly in view, but it came, strangely and sadly enough, not through anything I put into *his* mouth, but through something I took into my own. I did to him the very thing that had so revolted me in Cambridge in the revelations of my homosexual friend's love-life. This was a thing I had never done before, reluctantly since and out of politeness if requested. It is a form of pleasure I myself have seldom enjoyed, passively or actively, preferring the kiss upon the lips, nor have I ever been good at it. Some technical skill seems required and a retraction of the teeth, which, perhaps because mine are too large or unsuitably arranged, seem always to get in the way. Squeamishness with comparative strangers over dirt or even disease disturbs me, and I have noticed that those normal young men who request for themselves this form of amusement never offer it in return. It is also, in my experience, a stimulation usually desired by a somewhat exhausted sex; it may produce quicker results for them than masturbation, but they are not quick, and to be practically choked for ten minutes or so after one's own orgasm has passed is something I have never enjoyed.

I suppose I acted towards my sailor thus because his body was so beautiful and desirable that I simply wanted to eat it. It was a fatal mistake. He cut future appointments, plunging me in despair. When, at length, I saw him again I asked if I had displeased him in any way. Roughly he replied, "You know what you did! You disgusted me!" After that he deserted me entirely for a year and a half, while I pined for him in the darkest dejection of spirit and lost much weight. Then, through the mediation of one of his brothers (a homosexual, oddly enough, and of a far more affectionate character, but unfortunately too effeminate to attract me), he wrote to apologise ("I behaved rottenly to you and you didn't deserve it") and called. He had a new gentleman friend now, I had learned from his brother, who took him for holidays to Nice and Cannes and had doubtless completed his education in matters of sex, thereby arousing his conscience over me; yet I think he would have resumed sex with me too, if only I had been able to control the emotion in my voice and the trembling of the arm I put around his shoulders. He did not want emotion, only fun. He then disappeared out of my life.

The Ideal Friend was never so nearly found again, though, as I interpret my life now, I devoted most of my leisure in the succeeding fifteen years to the search for him, picking up and discarding innumerable candidates. My restlessness at this time was such that two arresting comments made to me by friends concerned for my happiness may be quoted. Forrest Reid, sitting with me one day in Hyde Park, said, "Do you really care about anyone?" To this searching question I do not know the answer, it goes too deep; since people and events vanish so easily from my memory, it may be no. The other friend wrote, "I seize my pen to read you a lecture on your character. . . . I think you are scared or bored by response. Here my lecture ends, for how you are to alter yourself I know not; but sometimes the comment of an outsider helps so I make it. I think love is beautiful and important—anyhow I have found it so in spite of all the pain—and it will sadden me if you fail in this particular way." This reproach was, I suppose, much the same as the first, but I see myself in it more clearly, clearly enough to hazard an answer. I got response, doubtless because of my youth and looks, more readily than my lecturer, who went without either; I was therefore, when it came, less grateful, more "choosy," than he would have been; I was not scared or bored by it when my own physical desires were caught and held, as they were by less than half a dozen chaps in my post-Cambridge life; on the other hand, response from these, the boys who took my fancy, never contented me either, or for long; there seemed always something wrong, disappointing, frustrating. The superficiality of this answer will be plainly seen by the reflective reader; I was not reflective at the time. Another friend of mine once told me that he was able to cut clean out of his life and thought any emotional affair that was causing him unhappiness. *That* I could never do; indeed I may be said to have wallowed in the very miseries he avoided; and I sometimes wonder, though I cannot know, whether that remark in the letter I have just quoted, "perhaps happiness is not your deepest need," may not be profoundly true, whether the hardship of it all was the very thing I wanted, the frustrations, which often seemed to me so starveling and wretched, my subconscious choice.

My restlessness during these fifteen years increased; I was seldom re-laxed and did little writing or reading, for what was happening outside in the streets? what was I missing by staying indoors? I was rarely happy in any one place, for all the other places where I was not appeared, in my imagination, more rewarding than the one I occupied. The Ideal Friend was always somewhere else and might have been found if only I had turned a different way. The buses that passed my own bus seemed always to contain those charming boys who were absent from mine; the ascending escalators in the tubes fiendishly carried them past me as I sank helplessly into hell. Unless I had some actual business or social engagement (often maddening, for then, when punctuality or responsibility was un-avoidable and I was walking with my host or guest, the Ideal Friend would be sure to appear and look deep into my eyes as he passed) I seldom reached my destination, but was forever darting off my buses, occupied always, it seemed, by women or Old Age Pensioners, because on the pavements below, which I was constantly scanning, some attractive boy had been observed. Yet one of my old anxieties, now in public form, persisted: I had to feel an absolute degree of confidence. Industrious pred-ator though I was, I was not a bold or reckless one. One of my father's yarns concerned a man who told a friend that whenever he saw an at-tractive girl he went straight up to her and said, "Do you fuck?" "My word!" said the friend. "Don't you get an awful lot of rebuffs?" "Of course," was the reply; "but I also get an awful lot of fucking." I was not in the least like that. I did not want rebuffs or cuffs, nor did I want the police summoned. I had to feel reasonably safe and developed furtive techniques to aid me. I did not like boys to think I was pursuing them, they might turn nasty; the safest thing was the quick "open" exchange of understanding looks or smiles. For this it was necessary to meet people face to face, a problem if the particular boy was moving in the same direction. In such a case I would hasten after him, pass him without a glance (in the hope of not being noticed), and when I had reached what I considered to be an invisible distance ahead, turn about to retrace my steps for a head-on collision. If then I got a responsive look, a smile, a backward glance, if he then stopped to stare after me or to study the goods in the nearest shop-window (the more incongruous they were the safer I felt) I judged I might act, though still with caution in case he was luring me into some violent trap. The elaborateness of this manoeuvre often lost me the boy, he had gone into a house or disappeared up some side turning behind my back—and therefore remained in my chagrined thought as the Ideal Friend.

This obsession with sex was already taking me, of course, to foreign countries, France, Italy, Denmark, where civilised laws prevailed and one was not in danger of arrest and imprisonment for the colour of one's hair. Many anxieties and strains were therefore lessened abroad; at the same time—a delayed conclusion—what was the good of making friends in other countries? One wanted them in one's own, one wanted them in one's home. In any case I was condemned to my own country for eleven months in the year, for in 1928 I had joined the staff of the BBC and was to remain in it for thirty years. My field of sexual activities was therefore confined chiefly to London, and how, in that enormous, puritanical, and joyless city, could one find the Ideal Friend? Where did one begin to look? One needed a focus, such as the popular promenades, gardens, locales, gay bars, baths, and brothels so generously provided in foreign towns. London offered only some tatty pubs in Soho and elsewhere, the haunts of queans, prostitutes, pimps, pickpockets, pansies, debauched servicemen, and detectives, a few dull clubs frequented by elderly queers, and some dark and smelly urinals, which were not to my taste. To hang about Piccadilly Circus and its tube station, which I often did, was seldom rewarding, and I had not the necessary patience for long-term investigations into such perhaps fruitful foci as public swimming baths, youth hostels, YMCAs, working men's clubs, boy scout organisations, etc. In the thirties I found myself concentrating my attention more and more upon a particular society of young men in the metropolis which I had tapped before and which, it seemed to me, might yield, without further loss of time, what I required. His Majesty's Brigade of Guards had a long history in homosexual prostitution. Perpetually short of cash, beer, and leisure occupations, they were easily to be found of an evening in their red tunics standing about in the various pubs they frequented, over the only half-pint they could afford or some "quids-in" mate had stood them, in Knightsbridge, Victoria, the Edgware Road, and elsewhere, or hanging about Hyde Park and the Marble Arch, with nothing to do and nothing to spend, whistling therefore in vain to the passing "prossies," whom they contemptuously called "bags" (something into which something is put), and alert to the possibility that some kind gentleman might appear and stand them a few pints, in return for which and the subsequent traditional tip—a pound was the recognised tariff for the Foot Guards then, the Horse Guards cost rather more—they were perfectly agreeable to, indeed often eager for, a "bit of fun." In their availability and for other reasons they suited my book; though generally larger than I liked, they were young, they were normal, they were working-class, they were drilled to obedience; though not innocent for long, the new recruit might be found before someone else got at him; if grubby they could be bathed, and if civility and consideration, with which they did not always meet in their liaisons, were extended to them, one might gain their affection.

Evening after evening, for many years, when I was free I prowled Marble Arch, the Monkey Walk, and Hyde Park Corner, or hastened from pub to pub as one unrewarding scene replaced another. Seaport towns also (sailors too were jolly and short of cash) were often combed at weekends. The taint of prostitution in these proceedings nevertheless displeased me and must, I thought, be disagreeable to the boys themselves, accept it though they did. I therefore developed mutually face-saving techniques to avoid it, such as standing drinks and giving cash at once and, without any suggestive conversation, leaving the boy free to return home with me if he wished, out of sexual desire or gratitude, for he was pretty sure to know what I was after. This, I suppose, was akin to my father's technique of bribery in advance for special restaurant service, for of course I too hoped for responsiveness to generosity and was annoyed if I did not get it. A similar but more self-restrained and hazardous form of procedure was to treat the soldier, if he was particularly attractive, to a pleasant evening's entertainment—cinema, supper—give him a present at the end of it when he had to return to barracks, and leave it to him to ask, "When can I see you again?" Thus, by implying that it was more his society then his body that interested me, did I hope to distinguish myself from the other "twanks" (as guardsmen called people like myself) and gain his respect. If he did not turn up to his future appointment I was upset and would loiter about his barracks for days. These methods had another advantage: they disarmed, or could be hoped to disarm, any tendency the guardsman might have to robbery or violence. Such incidents were not frequent but they occurred, sometimes brutal (the homosexual who was found murdered, his penis severed and stuck into his own mouth), sometimes jolly (the Hammersmith quean who, robbed by a guardsman of his fur coat, flew out in a rage and found a policeman, who quickly recovered the conspicuous garment and went to bed with the grateful owner himself). Cautious and nervous as I was, I myself did not get through without a few episodes of extortion and theft, in France of actual violence, so repugnant to my mind that I noticed in course of time that the boys I picked up were almost always mild and characterless, as perhaps they had been from the very beginning; character tended to be difficult, and it was as though some instinct for safety within me recognised and selected boys with no character whatever.

As I have said, I never came so close to finding the Ideal Friend again but, my standards declining, I found a number of decent boys who attracted me, of whom I grew fond as they grew fond of me, who entered my family life as I entered theirs, and who afforded me further rests upon the way. For one reason or another they were all imperfect, a common inperfection being that, though obliging, they were, like the Richmond tradesboy of my early days, physically unresponsive to homosexual love. One of them was married, the others had girls somewhere in the background. This was one of the first things I had to give way on, because it was recurrent. The girl friend was a situation all too liable to be found in the lives of normal boys, and my formula (as I now see it) had to be modified to meet it. Since women could not be excluded they had to be admitted; I never suffered much from jealousy, and the Ideal Friend could have a girl or a wife if he wished, so long as she did not interfere with me. No wife ever failed to interfere with me.

These boys remained my friends for some years, until the second war killed them or they disappeared into marriage. They were what homosexuals call "steadies," that is to say they propped up one's mind, one could call upon their company and comfort if available, if required—and if nothing more hopeful offered. For valuable though they were, the belief remained that one could do better, better, better, and so one continued to hurl oneself into the fray. This *ignis fatuus* caused me to behave inconsiderately to them at times, even to hurt the feelings my genuine affection for them had aroused, and one at least had the spirit to reprove me when I fobbed him off from an appointment with a present of money because some more promising new candidate had since appeared upon the scene. Another of them, to whom in the beginning I had given bad marks, became in the end, I suddenly perceived, the best and most understanding friend I had ever made; a Welsh boy, gentle, kind, cheerful, undemanding, self-effacing, always helpful, always happy to return to me in spite of neglect, and in control (a rare thing) of his jealous wife, I realised his value so deeply at last that he involved my heart. His feet smelt, poor boy, some glandular trouble, and out of politeness he preferred not to take off his boots. He was killed in the war. When I had lost him and remembered the course of our friendship, how it had gradually sprouted and burgeoned out of such, for me, unpropitious soil, I wondered how many other decent boys I had carelessly rejected in pursuit of my *ignis fatuus*. Some, I recalled, had made so little impression upon me at our one and only congress that, seeing them again some months later sunning themselves on the grass of Hyde Park, I could not even remember what had passed between us.

As has already been indicated, I was far from being the only person engaged in these activities; there was indeed considerable competition and as time passed I got to recognise some of my rivals well by sight. Standing at the various bars, with our token half-pints before us, waiting for the soldiers and sailors to appear, we would eye each other surreptitiously, perhaps registering the fact that, with so many eagles about, if any Ganymede did arrive we would have to work fast. A number of my own intellectual friends shared this taste of mine and might pop in; but it was tacitly understood that this was not a social gathering, like a cocktail party, but a serious occasion needing undistracted concentration, like stalking or chess. To speak to each other would have been a breach of etiquette; a nod or a wink might pass, then to the business in hand. Perhaps one would meet them again later, in some other pub, beating, like oneself, all the known coverts for the blue-jacketed or red-breasted game. . . . And as the years rolled by I saw these competitors of mine growing older and older, greyer and greyer, and, catching sight of myself in the mirrors of saloon or public bars, would perceive that the same thing was happening to me, that I was becoming what guardsmen called an "old pouff," an "old twank," and that my chance of finding the Ideal Friend was, like my hair, thinning and receding. Most of my prejudices had now fallen by the way, nothing in the human scene any longer disgusted me (how heart-rending the cry of the pervert to his sexologist: "I want people to shit on my face, but even when I find them they are *never* my type"), dirt and disease worried me no more (though the state of my breath continued to do so forever), I kept a stock of Blue Ointment handy for the elimination of crabs, and weathered a dose of anal clap without much fuss (anal, yes; I *assured* the young Grenadier that I was quite impenetrable, but he begged so hard to be allowed at any rate to try). I wanted nothing now but (the sad little wish) someone to love me. My last long emotional affair, in the torments and frustrations of which I wallowed for years, was with a deserter, who became frontally infected by a prostitute with the disease I have just mentioned. Confessing this to me when I was hoping to go to bed with him, he unbuttoned his flies to exhibit the proof, squeezing out the pus for my enlightenment. Twenty years earlier, I re-flected, such a performance would have dished him for me forever; now I saw it as one of the highest compliments I had ever been paid.

~ *Graham Greene* ~

May We
Borrow Your
Husband?

1

I never heard her called anything else but Poopy, either by her husband or by the two men who became their friends. Perhaps I was a little in love with her (absurd though that may seem at my age) because I found that I resented the name. It was unsuited to someone so young and so open—too open; she belonged to the age of trust just as I belonged to the age of cynicism. "Good old Poopy"—I even heard her called that by the elder of the two interior-decorators (who had known her no longer than I had): a sobriquet which might have been good enough for some vague bedraggled woman of middle age who drank a bit too much but who was useful to drag around as a kind of blind—and those two certainly needed a blind. I once asked the girl her real name, but all she said was, "Everyone calls me Poopy," as though that finished it, and I was afraid of appearing too square if I pursued the question further—too middle-aged perhaps as well, so though I hate the name whenever I write it down, Poopy she has to remain: I have no other.

I had been at Antibes working on a book of mine, a biography of the seventeenth-century poet, the Earl of Rochester, for more than a month before Poopy and her husband arrived. I had come there as soon

---

GRAHAM GREENE was the author of many novels and story collections, among them The Comedians, The Honorary Consul, The Heart of the Matter, *and* The Third Man. *Readers of this anthology might also wish to look at his play* The Return of A. J. Raffles. *Greene died in 1991.*

as the full season was over, to a small ugly hotel by the sea not far from the ramparts, and I was able to watch the season depart with the leaves in the Boulevard Général Leclerc. At first, even before the trees had begun to drop, the foreign cars were on the move homeward. A few weeks earlier, I had counted fourteen nationalities, including Morocco, Turkey, Sweden and Luxembourg, between the sea and the Place de Gaulle, to which I walked every day for the English papers. Now all the foreign number-plates had gone, except for the Belgian and the German and an occasional English one, and, of course, the ubiquitous number-plates of the State of Monaco. The cold weather had come early and Antibes catches only the morning sun—good enough for breakfast on the terrace, but it was safer to lunch indoors or the shadow might overtake the coffee. A cold and solitary Algerian was always there, leaning over the ramparts, looking for something, perhaps safety.

It was the time of year I liked best, when Juan les Pins becomes as squalid as a closed fun-fair with Lunar Park boarded up and cards marked *Fermeture Annuelle* outside the Pam-Pam and Maxim's, and the Concours International Amateur de Striptease at the Vieux Colombiers is over for another season. Then Antibes comes into its own as a small country town with the Auberge de Provence full of local people and old men sit indoors drinking beer or pastis at the *glacier* in the Place de Gaulle. The small garden, which forms a roundabout on the ramparts, looks a little sad with the short stout palms bowing their brown fronds; the sun in the morning shines without any glare, and the few white sails move gently on the unblinding sea.

You can always trust the English to stay on longer than others into the autumn. We have a blind faith in the southern sun and we are taken by surprise when the wind blows icily over the Mediterranean. Then a bickering war develops with the hotel-keeper over the heating on the third floor, and the tiles strike cold underfoot. For a man who has reached the age when all he wants is some good wine and some good cheese and a little work, it is the best season of all. I know how I resented the arrival of the interior-decorators just at the moment when I had hoped to be the only foreigner left, and I prayed that they were birds of passage. They arrived before lunch in a scarlet Sprite—a car much too young for them, and they wore elegant sports clothes more suited to spring at the Cap. The elder man was nearing fifty and the grey hair that waved over his ears was too uniform to be true: the younger had passed thirty and his hair was as black as the other's was grey. I knew their names were Stephen and Tony before they even reached the reception desk, for they had clear, penetrating yet superficial voices, like their gaze, which had quickly lighted on me where I sat with a Ricard on the terrace and registered that I had nothing of interest for them, and passed on. They were not arrogant: it was simply that they were more concerned with each other, and yet perhaps, like a married couple of some years' standing, not very profoundly.

I soon knew a great deal about them. They had rooms side by side in my passage, though I doubt if both rooms were often occupied, for I used to hear voices from one room or the other most evenings when I went to bed. Do I seem too curious about other people's affairs? But in my own defence I have to say that the events of this sad little comedy were forced by all the participants on my attention. The balcony where I worked every morning on my life of Rochester overhung the terrace where the interior-decorators took their coffee, and even when they oc-cupied a table out of sight those clear elocutionary voices mounted up to me. I didn't want to hear them; I wanted to work. Rochester's relations with the actress, Mrs. Barry, were my concern at the moment, but it is almost impossible in a foreign land not to listen to one's own tongue. French I could have accepted as a kind of background noise, but I could not fail to overhear English.

"My dear, guess who's written to me now?"

"Alec?"

"No, Mrs. Clarenty."

"What does the old hag want?"

"She objects to the mural in her bedroom."

"But, Stephen, it's divine. Alec's never done anything better. The dead faun . . ."

"I think she wants something more nubile and less necrophilous."

"The old lecher."

They were certainly hardy, those two. Every morning around eleven they went bathing off the little rocky peninsula opposite the hotel—they had the autumnal Mediterranean, so far as the eye could see, entirely to themselves. As they walked briskly back in their elegant bikinis, or some-times ran a little way for warmth, I had the impression that they took their bathes less for pleasure than for exercise—to preserve the slim legs, the flat stomachs, the narrow hips for more recondite and Etruscan pastimes.

Idle they were not. They drove the Sprite to Cagnes, Vence, St. Paul, to any village where an antique store was to be rifled, and they brought back with them objects of olive wood, spurious old lanterns, painted religious figures which in the shop would have seemed to me ugly or banal, but which I suspect already fitted in their imaginations some scheme of decoration the reverse of commonplace. Not that their minds were altogether on their profession. They relaxed.

I encountered them one evening in a little sailors' bar in the old port of Nice. Curiosity this time had led me in pursuit, for I had seen the scarlet Sprite standing outside the bar. They were entertaining a boy of about eighteen who, from his clothes, I imagine worked as a hand on the boat to Corsica which was at the moment in harbour. They both looked very sharply at me when I entered, as though they were thinking, "Have we misjudged him?" I drank a glass of beer and left, and the younger said "Good evening" as I passed the table. After that we had to greet each other every day in the hotel. It was as though I had been admitted to an intimacy.

Time for a few days was hanging as heavily on my hands as on Lord Rochester's. He was staying at Mrs. Fourcard's baths in Leather Lane, receiving mercury treatment for the pox, and I was awaiting a whole section of my notes which I had inadvertently left in London. I couldn't release him till they came, and my sole distraction for a few days was those two. As they packed themselves into the Sprite of an afternoon or an evening I liked to guess from their clothes the nature of their excursion. Always elegant, they were yet successful, by the mere exchange of one *tricot* for another, in indicating their mood: they were just as well dressed in the sailors' bar, but a shade more simply; when dealing with a Lesbian antique dealer at St. Paul, there was a masculine dash about their handkerchiefs. Once they disappeared altogether for the inside of a week in what I took to be their oldest clothes, and when they returned the older man had a contusion on his right cheek. They told me they had been over to Corsica. Had they enjoyed it? I asked.

"Quite barbaric," the young man Tony said, but not, I thought, in praise.

He saw me looking at Stephen's cheek, and he added quickly, "We had an accident in the mountains."

It was two days after that, just at sunset, that Poopy arrived with her husband. I was back at work on Rochester, sitting in an overcoat on my balcony, when a taxi drove up—I recognized the driver as someone who plied regularly from Nice airport. What I noticed first, because the passengers were still hidden, was the luggage, which was bright blue and of an astonishing newness. Even the initials—rather absurdly PT—shone like newly-minted coins. There were a large suitcase and a small suitcase and a hat-box, all of the same cerulean hue, and after that a respectable old leather case totally unsuited to air travel, the kind one inherits from a father, with half a label still left from Shepheard's Hotel or the Valley of the Kings. Then the passenger emerged and I saw Poopy for the first time. Down below, the interior-decorators were watching too, and drinking Dubonnet.

She was a very tall girl, perhaps five feet nine, very slim, very young, with hair the colour of conkers, and her costume was as new as the luggage. She said, *"Finalmente,"* looking at the undistinguished façade with an air of rapture—or perhaps it was only the shape of her eyes. When I saw the young man I felt certain they were just married; it wouldn't have surprised me if confetti had fallen out from the seams of their clothes. They were like a photograph in the *Tatler;* they had camera smiles for each other and an underlying nervousness. I was sure they had come straight from the reception, and that it had been a smart one, after a proper church wedding.

They made a very handsome couple as they hesitated a moment before going up the steps to the reception. The long beam of the Phare de la Garoupe brushed the water behind them, and the floodlighting went suddenly on outside the hotel as if the manager had been waiting for their arrival to turn it up. The two decorators sat there without drinking, and I noticed that the elder one had covered the contusion on his cheek with a very clean white handkerchief. They were not, of course, looking at the girl but at the boy. He was over six feet tall and as slim as the girl, with a face that might have been cut on a coin, completely handsome and completely dead—but perhaps that was only an effect of his nerves. His clothes, too, I thought, had been bought for the occasion, the sports-jacket with a double slit and the grey trousers cut a little narrowly to show off the long legs. It seemed to me that they were both too young to marry—I doubt if they had accumulated forty-five years between them—and I had a wild impulse to lean over the balcony and warn them away—"Not this hotel. Any hotel but this." Perhaps I could have told them that the heating was insufficient or the hot water erratic or the food terrible, not that the English care much about food, but of course they would have paid me no attention—they were so obviously "booked," and what an ageing lunatic I should have appeared in their eyes. ("One of those eccentric English types one finds abroad"—I could imagine the letter home.) This was the first time I wanted to interfere, and I didn't know them at all. The second time it was already too late, but I think I shall always regret that I did not give way to that madness . . .

It had been the silence and attentiveness of those two down below which had frightened me, and the patch of white handkerchief hiding the shameful contusion. For the first time I heard the hated name: "Shall we see the room, Poopy, or have a drink first?"

They decided to see the room, and the two glasses of Dubonnet clicked again into action.

I think she had more idea of how a honeymoon should be conducted than he had, because they were not seen again that night.

2

I was late for breakfast on the terrace, but I noticed that Stephen and Tony were lingering longer than usual. Perhaps they had decided at last that it was too cold for a bathe; I had the impression, however, that they were lying in wait. They had never been so friendly to me before, and I wondered whether perhaps they regarded me as a kind of cover, with my distressingly normal appearance. My table for some reason that day had been shifted and was out of the sun, so Stephen suggested that I should join theirs: they would be off in a moment, after one more cup . . . The contusion was much less noticeable today, but I think he had been applying powder.

"You staying here long?" I asked them, conscious of how clumsily I constructed a conversation compared with their easy prattle.

"We had meant to leave tomorrow," Stephen said, "but last night we changed our minds."

"Last night?"

"It was such a beautiful day, wasn't it? 'Oh,' I said to Tony, 'surely we can leave poor dreary old London a little longer?' It has an awful staying power—like a railway sandwich."

"Are your clients so patient?"

"My dear, the clients? You never in your life saw such atrocities as we get from Brompton Square. It's always the same. People who pay others to decorate for them have ghastly taste themselves."

"You do the world a service then. Think what we might suffer without you. In Brompton Square."

Tony giggled. "I don't know how we'd stand it if we had not our private jokes. For example, in Mrs. Clarenty's case, we've installed what we call the Loo of Lucullus."

"She was enchanted," Stephen said.

"The most obscene vegetable forms. It reminded me of a harvest festival."

They suddenly became very silent and attentive, watching somebody over my shoulder. I looked back. It was Poopy, all by herself. She stood there, waiting for the boy to show her which table she could take, like a new girl at school who doesn't know the rules. She even seemed to be wearing a school uniform: very tight trousers, slit at the ankle—but she hadn't realized that the summer term was over. She had dressed up like that, I felt certain, so as not to be noticed, in order to hide herself, but there were only two other women on the terrace and they were both wearing sensible tweed skirts. She looked at them nostalgically as the waiter led her past our table to one nearer the sea. Her long legs moved awkwardly in the pants as though they felt exposed.

"The young bride," Tony said.

"Deserted already," Stephen said with satisfaction.

"Her name is Poopy Travis, you know."

"It's an extraordinary name to choose. She couldn't have been *christened* that way, unless they found a very liberal vicar."

"He is called Peter. Of an undefined occupation. Not Army, I think, do you?"

"Oh no, not Army. Something to do with land perhaps—there's an agreeable *herbal* smell about him."

"You seem to know nearly all there is to know," I said.

"We looked at their police *carnet* before dinner."

"I have an idea," Tony said, "that PT hardly represents their activities last night." He looked across the tables at the girl with an expression extraordinarily like hatred.

'We were both taken," Stephen said, "by the air of innocence. One felt he was more used to horses."

"He mistook the yearnings of the rider's crotch for something quite different."

Perhaps they hoped to shock me, but I don't think it was that. I really believe they were in a state of extreme sexual excitement; they had received a *coup de foudre* last night on the terrace and were quite incapable of disguising their feelings. I was an excuse to talk, to speculate about the desired object. The sailor had been a stop-gap: this was the real thing. I was inclined to be amused, for what could this absurd pair hope to gain from a young man newly married to the girl who now sat there patiently waiting, wearing her beauty like an old sweater she had forgotten to change? But that was a bad simile to use: she would have been afraid to wear an old sweater, except secretly, by herself, in the playroom. She had no idea that she was one of those who can afford to disregard the fashion of their clothes. She caught my eye and, because I was so obviously English, I suppose, gave me half a timid smile. Perhaps I too would have received the *coup de foudre* if I had not been thirty years older and twice married.

Tony detected the smile. "A regular body-snatcher," he said. My breakfast and the young man arrived at the same moment before I had time to reply. As he passed the table I could feel the tension.

"*Cuir de Russie,*" Stephen said, quivering a nostril. "A mistake of inexperience."

The youth caught the words as he went past and turned with an astonished look to see who had spoken, and they both smiled insolently back at him as though they really believed they had the power to take him over . . .

For the first time I felt disquiet.

3

Something was not going well; that was sadly obvious. The girl nearly always came down to breakfast ahead of her husband—I have an idea he spent a long time bathing and shaving and applying his *Cuir de Russie*. When he joined her he would give her a courteous brotherly kiss as though they had not spent the night together in the same bed. She began to have those shadows under the eyes which come from lack of sleep— for I couldn't believe that they were the "lineaments of gratified desire." Sometimes from my balcony I saw them returning from a walk—nothing, except perhaps a pair of horses, could have been more handsome. His gentleness towards her might have reassured her mother, but it made a man impatient to see him squiring her across the undangerous road, holding open doors, following a pace behind her like the husband of a princess. I longed to see some outbreak of irritation caused by the sense of satiety, but they never seemed to be in conversation when they returned from their walk, and at table I caught only the kind of phrases people use who are dining together for the sake of politeness. And yet I could swear that she loved him, even by the way she avoided watching him. There was nothing avid or starved about her; she stole her quick glances when she was quite certain that his attention was absorbed elsewhere—they were tender, anxious perhaps, quite undemanding. If one inquired after him when he wasn't there, she glowed with the pleasure of using his name. "Oh, Peter overslept this morning." "Peter cut himself. He's staunching the blood now." "Peter's mislaid his tie. He thinks the floor-waiter has purloined it." Certainly she loved him; I was far less certain of what his feelings were.

And you must imagine how all the time those other two were closing in. It was like a medieval siege: they dug their trenches and threw up their earthworks. The difference was that the besieged didn't notice what they were at—at any rate, the girl didn't, I don't know about him. I longed to warn her, but what could I have said that wouldn't have shocked her or angered her? I believe the two would have changed their floor if that would have helped to bring them closer to the fortress; they probably discussed the move together and decided against it as too overt.

Because they knew that I could do nothing against them, they regarded me almost in the role of an ally. After all, I might be useful one day in distracting the girl's attention—and I suppose they were not quite mistaken in that; they could tell from the way I looked at her how interested I was, and they probably calculated that my interests might in the long run coincide with theirs. It didn't occur to them that, perhaps, I was a man with scruples. If one really wanted a thing scruples were obviously, in their eyes, out of place. There was a tortoiseshell star mirror at St. Paul they were plotting to obtain for half the price demanded (I think there was an old mother who looked after the shop when her daughter was away at a *boîte* for women of a certain taste); naturally, therefore, when I looked at the girl, as they saw me so often do, they considered I would be ready to join in any "reasonable" scheme.

"When I looked at the girl"—realize that I have made no real attempt to describe her. In writing a biography one can, of course, just insert a portrait and the affair is done: I have the prints of Lady Rochester and Mrs. Barry in front of me now. But speaking as a professional novelist (for biography and reminiscence are both new forms to me), one describes a woman not so much that the reader should see her in all the cramping detail of colour and shape (how often Dickens's elaborate portraits seem like directions to the illustrator which might well have been left out of the finished book), but to convey an emotion. Let the reader make his own image of a wife, a mistress, some passer-by "sweet and kind" (the poet required no other descriptive words), if he has a fancy to. If I were to describe the girl (I can't bring myself at this moment to write her hateful name), it would be not to convey the colour of her hair, the shape of her mouth, but to express the pleasure and the pain with which I recall her—I, the writer, the observer, the subsidiary character, what you will. But if I didn't bother to convey them to her, why should I bother to convey them to you, *hypocrite lecteur?*

How quickly those two tunnelled. I don't think it was more than four mornings after the arrival that, when I came down to breakfast, I found they had moved their table next to the girl's and were entertaining her in her husband's absence. They did it very well; it was the first time I had seen her relaxed and happy—and she was happy because she was talking about Peter. Peter was agent for his father, somewhere in Hampshire—there were three thousand acres to manage. Yes, he was fond of riding and so was she. It all tumbled out—the kind of life she dreamed of having when she returned home. Stephen just dropped in a word now and then, of a rather old-fashioned courteous interest, to keep her going. Apparently he had once decorated some hall in their neigh-bourhood and knew the names of some people Peter knew—Winstanley, I think—and that gave her immense confidence.

"He's one of Peter's best friends," she said, and the two flickered their eyes at each other like lizards' tongues.

"Come and join us, William," Stephen said, but only when he had noticed that I was within earshot. "You know Mrs. Travis?"

How could I refuse to sit at their table? And yet in doing so I seemed to become an ally.

"Not *the* William Harris?" the girl asked. It was a phrase which I hated, and yet she transformed even that, with her air of innocence. For she had a capacity to make everything new: Antibes became a discovery and we were the first foreigners to have made it. When she said, "Of course, I'm afraid I haven't actually *read* any of your books," I heard the over-familiar remark for the first time; it even seemed to me a proof of her honesty—I nearly wrote her virginal honesty. "You must know an awful lot about people," she said, and again I read into the banality of the remark an appeal—for help against whom, those two or the husband who at that moment appeared on the terrace? He had the same nervous air as she, even the same shadows under the lids, so that they might have been taken by a stranger, as I wrote before, for brother and sister. He hesitated a moment when he saw all of us there and she called across to him, "Come and meet these nice people, darling." He didn't look any too pleased, but he sat glumly down and asked whether the coffee was still hot.

"I'll order some more, darling. They know the Winstanleys, and this is *the* William Harris."

He looked at me blankly; I think he was wondering if I had anything to do with tweeds.

"I hear you like horses," Stephen said, "and I was wondering whether you and your wife would come to lunch with us at Cagnes on Saturday. That's tomorrow, isn't it? There's a very good racecourse at Cagnes . . ."

"I don't know," he said dubiously, looking to his wife for a clue.

"But, darling, of course we must go. You'd love it."

His face cleared instantly. I really believe he had been troubled by a social scruple: the question whether one accepts invitations on a honeymoon. "It's very good of you," he said, "Mr. . . ."

"Let's start as we mean to go on. I'm Stephen and this is Tony."

"I'm Peter." He added a trifle gloomily, "And this is Poopy."

"Tony, you take Poopy in the Sprite, and Peter and I will go by *autobus*." (I had the impression, and I think Tony had too, that Stephen had gained a point.)

"You'll come too, Mr. Harris?" the girl asked, using my surname as though she wished to emphasize the difference between me and them.

"I'm afraid I can't. I'm working against time."

I watched them that evening from my balcony as they returned from Cagnes and, hearing the way they all laughed together, I thought, "The enemy are within the citadel: it's only a question of time." A lot of time, because they proceeded very carefully, those two. There was no question of a quick grab which I suspect had caused the contusion in Corsica.

4

It became a regular habit with the two of them to entertain the girl during her solitary breakfast before her husband arrived. I never sat at their table again, but scraps of the conversation would come over to me, and it seemed to me that she was never quite so cheerful again. Even the sense of novelty had gone. I heard her say once, "There's so little to do here," and it struck me as an odd observation for a honeymooner to make.

Then one evening I found her in tears outside the Musée Grimaldi. I had been fetching my papers, and, as my habit was, I made a round by the Place Nationale with the pillar erected in 1819 to celebrate—a remarkable paradox—the loyalty of Antibes to the monarchy and her resistance to *les Troupes Etrangères,* who were seeking to re-establish the monarchy. Then, according to rule, I went on by the market and the old port and Lou-Lou's restaurant up the ramp towards the cathedral and the Musée, and there in the grey evening light, before the street-lamps came on, I found her crying under the cliff of the château.

I noticed too late what she was at or I wouldn't have said, "Good evening, Mrs. Travis." She jumped a little as she turned and dropped her handkerchief, and when I picked it up I found it soaked with tears—it was like holding a small drowned animal in my hand. I said, "I'm sorry," meaning that I was sorry to have startled her, but she took it in quite another sense. She said, "Oh, I'm being silly, that's all. It's just a mood. Everybody has moods, don't they?"

"Where's Peter?"

"He's in the museum with Stephen and Tony looking at the Picassos. I don't understand them a bit."

"That's nothing to be ashamed of. Lots of people don't."

"But Peter doesn't understand them either. I know he doesn't. He's just pretending to be interested."

"Oh well . . ."

"And it's not that either. I pretended for a time too, to please Stephen. But he's pretending just to get away from me."

"You are imagining things."

Punctually at five o'clock the *phare* lit up, but it was still too light to see the beam.

I said, "The museum will be closing now."

"Walk back with me to the hotel."

"Wouldn't you like to wait for Peter?"

"I don't smell, do I?" she asked miserably.

"Well, there's a trace of Arpège. I've always liked Arpège."

"How terribly experienced you sound."

"Not really. It's just that my first wife used to buy Arpège."

We began walking back, and the mistral bit our ears and gave her an excuse when the time came for the reddened eyes.

She said, "I think Antibes so sad and grey."

"I thought you enjoyed it here."

"Oh, for a day or two."

"Why not go home?"

"It would look odd, wouldn't it, returning early from a honeymoon?"

"Or go on to Rome—or somewhere. You can get a plane to most places from Nice."

"It wouldn't make any difference," she said. "It's not the place that's wrong, it's me."

"I don't understand."

"He's not happy with me. It's as simple as that."

She stopped opposite one of the little rock houses by the ramparts. Washing hung down over the street below and there was a cold-looking canary in a cage.

"You said yourself . . . a mood . . ."

"It's not his fault," she said. "It's me. I expect it seems very stupid to you, but I never slept with anyone before I married." She gulped miserably at the canary.

"And Peter?"

"He's terribly sensitive," she said, and added quickly, "That's a good quality. I wouldn't have fallen in love with him if he hadn't been."

'If I were you, I'd take him home—as quickly as possible." I couldn't help the words sounding sinister, but she hardly heard them. She was listening to the voices that came nearer down the ramparts—to Stephen's gay laugh. "They're very sweet," she said. "I'm glad he's found friends."

How could I say that they were seducing Peter before her eyes? And in any case wasn't her mistake already irretrievable? Those were two of the questions which haunted the hours, dreary for a solitary man, of the middle afternoon when work is finished and the exhilaration of the wine at lunch, and the time for the first evening drink has not yet come and the winter heating is at its feeblest. Had she no idea of the nature of the young man she had married? Had he taken her on as a blind or as a last desperate throw for normality? I couldn't bring myself to believe that. There was a sort of innocence about the boy which seemed to justify her love, and I preferred to think that he was not yet fully formed, that he had married honestly and it was only now that he found himself on the brink of a different experience. And yet if that were the case the comedy was all the crueller. Would everything have gone normally well if some conjunction of the planets had not crossed their honeymoon with that hungry pair of hunters?

I longed to speak out, and in the end I did speak, but not, so it happened, to her. I was going to my room and the door of one of theirs was open and I heard again Stephen's laugh—a kind of laugh which is sometimes with unintentional irony called infectious; it maddened me. I knocked and went in. Tony was stretched on a double bed and Stephen was "doing" his hair, holding a brush in each hand and meticulously arranging the grey waves on either side. The dressing-table had as many pots on it as a woman's.

"You really mean he told you that?" Tony was saying. "Why, how are you, William? Come in. Our young friend has been confiding in Stephen. Such really fascinating things."

"Which of your young friends?" I asked.

"Why, Peter, of course. Who else? The secrets of married life."

"I thought it might have been your sailor."

"Naughty!" Tony said. "But *touché* too, of course."

"I wish you'd leave Peter alone."

"I don't think he'd like that," Stephen said. "You can see that he hasn't quite the right tastes for this sort of honeymoon."

"Now you happen to like women, William," Tony said. "Why not go after the girl? It's a grand opportunity. She's not getting what I believe is vulgarly called her greens." Of the two he was easily the more brutal. I wanted to hit him, but this is not the century for that kind of romantic gesture, and anyway he was stretched out flat upon the bed. I said feebly enough—I ought to have known better than to have entered into a debate with those two—"She happens to be in love with him."

"I think Tony is right and she would find more satisfaction with you, William dear," Stephen said, giving a last flick to the hair over his right ear—the contusion was quite gone now. "From what Peter has said to me, I think you'd be doing a favour to both of them."

"Tell him what Peter said, Stephen."

"He said that from the very first there was a kind of hungry femininity about her which he found frightening and repulsive. Poor boy—he was really trapped into this business of marriage. His father wanted heirs—he breeds horses too, and then her mother—there's quite a lot of lucre with that lot. I don't think he had any idea of—of the Shape of Things to Come." Stephen shuddered into the glass and then regarded himself with satisfaction.

Even today I have to believe for my own peace of mind that the young man had not really said those monstrous things. I believe, and hope, that the words were put into his mouth by that cunning dramatizer, but there is little comfort in the thought, for Stephen's inventions were always true to character. He even saw through my apparent indifference to the girl and realized that Tony and he had gone too far; it would suit their purpose, if I were driven to the wrong kind of action, or if, by their crudities, I lost my interest in Poopy.

"Of course," Stephen said, "I'm exaggerating. Undoubtedly he felt a bit amorous before it came to the point. His father would describe her, I suppose, as a fine filly."

"What do you plan to do with him?" I asked. "Do you toss up, or does one of you take the head and the other the tail?"

Tony laughed. "Good old William. What a clinical mind you have."

"And suppose," I said, "I went to her and recounted this conversation?"

"My dear, she wouldn't even understand. She's incredibly innocent."

"Isn't he?"

"I doubt it—knowing our friend Colin Winstanley. But it's still a moot point. He hasn't given himself away yet."

"We are planning to put it to the test one day soon," Stephen said.

"A drive in the country," Tony said. "The strain's telling on him, you can see that. He's even afraid to take a siesta for fear of unwanted attentions."

"Haven't you *any* mercy?" It was an absurd old-fashioned word to use to those two sophisticates. I felt more than ever square. "Doesn't it occur to you that you may ruin her life—for the sake of your little game?"

"We can depend on you, William," Tony said, "to give her creature comforts."

Stephen said, "It's no game. You should realize we are saving *him*. Think of the life that he would lead—with all those soft contours lapping him around." He added, "Women always remind me of a damp salad—you know, those faded bits of greenery positively swimming . . ."

"Every man to his taste," Tony said. "But Peter's not cut out for that sort of life. He's very sensitive," he said, using the girl's own words. There wasn't any more I could think of to say.

5

You will notice that I play a very unheroic part in this comedy. I could have gone direct, I suppose, to the girl and given her a little lecture on the facts of life, beginning gently with the régime of an English public school—he had worn a scarf of old-boy colours, until Tony had said to him one day at breakfast that he thought the puce stripe was an error of judgement. Or perhaps I could have protested to the boy himself, but, if Stephen had spoken the truth and he was under a severe nervous strain, my intervention would hardly have helped to ease it. There was no move I could make. I had just to sit there and watch while they made the moves carefully and adroitly towards the climax.

It came three days later at breakfast when, as usual, she was sitting alone with them, while her husband was upstairs with his lotions. They had never been more charming or more entertaining. As I arrived at my table they were giving her a really funny description of a house in Kensington that they had decorated for a dowager duchess who was passionately interested in the Napoleonic wars. There was an ashtray, I remember, made out of a horse's hoof, guaranteed—so the dealer said—by Apsley House to have belonged to a grey ridden by Wellington at the

Battle of Waterloo; there was an umbrella stand made out of a shellcase found on the field of Austerlitz; a fire-escape made of a scaling ladder from Badajoz. She had lost half that sense of strain listening to them. She had forgotten her rolls and coffee; Stephen had her complete attention. I wanted to say to her, "You little owl." I wouldn't have been insulting her—she *had* got rather large eyes.

And then Stephen produced the master-plan. I could tell it was coming by the way his hands stiffened on his coffee-cup, by the way Tony lowered his eyes and appeared to be praying over his *croissant*. "We were wondering, Poopy—may we borrow your husband?" I have never heard words spoken with more elaborate casualness.

She laughed. She hadn't noticed a thing. "Borrow my husband?"

"There's a little village in the mountains behind Monte Carlo— Peille it's called—and I've heard rumours of a devastatingly lovely old bureau there—not for sale, of course, but Tony and I, we have our winning ways."

"I've noticed that," she said, "myself."

Stephen for an instant was disconcerted, but she meant nothing by it, except perhaps a compliment.

"We were thinking of having lunch at Peille and passing the whole day on the road so as to take a look at the scenery. The only trouble is there's no room in the Sprite for more than three, but Peter was saying the other day that you wanted some time to have a hair-do, so we thought . . ."

I had the impression that he was talking far too much to be convincing, but there wasn't any need for him to worry: she saw nothing at all. "I think it's a marvellous idea," she said. "You know, he needs a little holiday from me. He's had hardly a moment to himself since I came up the aisle." She was magnificently sensible, and perhaps even relieved. Poor girl. She needed a little holiday, too.

"It's going to be excruciatingly uncomfortable. He'll have to sit on Tony's knee."

"I don't suppose he'll mind that."

"And, of course, we can't guarantee the quality of food en route."

For the first time I saw Stephen as a stupid man. Was there a shade of hope in that?

In the long run, of the two, notwithstanding his brutality, Tony had the better brain. Before Stephen had time to speak once more, Tony raised his eyes from the *croissant* and said decisively, "That's fine. All's settled, and we'll deliver him back in one piece by dinner-time."

He looked challengingly across at me. "Of course, we hate to leave you alone for lunch, but I am sure William will look after you."

"William?" she asked, and I hated the way she looked at me as if I didn't exist. "Oh, you mean Mr. Harris?"

I invited her to have lunch with me at Lou-Lou's in the old port— I couldn't very well do anything else—and at that moment the laggard Peter came out onto the terrace. She said quickly, "I don't want to interrupt your work . . ."

"I don't believe in starvation," I said. "Work has to be interrupted for meals."

Peter had cut himself again shaving and had a large blob of cottonwool stuck on his chin: it reminded me of Stephen's contusion. I had the impression, while he stood there waiting for someone to say something to him, that he knew all about the conversation; it had been carefully rehearsed by all three, the parts allotted, the unconcerned manner practised well beforehand, even the bit about the food. . . . Now somebody had missed a cue, so I spoke.

"I've asked your wife to lunch at Lou-Lou's," I said. "I hope you don't mind."

I would have been amused by the expression of quick relief on all three faces if I had found it possible to be amused by anything at all in the situation.

6

"And you didn't marry again after she left?"

"By that time I was getting too old to marry."

"Picasso does it."

"Oh, I'm not quite as old as Picasso."

The silly conversation went on against a background of fishing-nets draped over a wallpaper with a design of wine-bottles—interior decoration again. Sometimes I longed for a room which had simply grown that way like the lines on a human face. The fish soup steamed away between us, smelling of garlic. We were the only guests there. Perhaps it was the solitude, perhaps it was the directness of her question, perhaps it was only the effect of the *rosé*, but quite suddenly I had the comforting sense that we were intimate friends. "There's always work," I said, "and wine and a good cheese."

"I couldn't be that philosophical if I lost Peter."

"That's not likely to happen, is it?"

"I think I'd die," she said, "like someone in Christina Rossetti."

"I thought nobody of your generation read her."

If I had been twenty years older, perhaps, I could have explained that nothing is quite as bad as that, that at the end of what is called "the sexual life" the only love which has lasted is the love that has accepted everything, every disappointment, every failure and every betrayal, which has accepted even the sad fact that in the end there is no desire so deep as the simple desire for companionship.

She wouldn't have believed me. She said, "I used to weep like anything at that poem about 'Passing Away.' Do you write sad things?"

"The biography I am writing now is sad enough. Two people tied together by love and yet one of them incapable of fidelity. The man dead of old age, burnt-out, at less than forty, and a fashionable preacher lurking by the bedside to snatch his soul. No privacy even for a dying man: the bishop wrote a book about it."

An Englishman who kept a chandlers' shop in the old port was talking at the bar, and two old women who were part of the family knitted at the end of the room. A dog trotted in and looked at us and went away again with its tail curled.

"How long ago did all that happen?"

"Nearly three hundred years."

"It sounded quite contemporary. Only now it would be the man from the *Mirror* and not a bishop."

"That's why I wanted to write it. I'm not really interested in the past. I don't like costume-pieces."

Winning someone's confidence is rather like the way some men set about seducing a woman; they circle a long way from their true purpose, they try to interest and amuse until finally the moment comes to strike. It came, so I wrongly thought, when I was adding up the bill. She said, "I wonder where Peter is at this moment," and I was quick to reply, "What's going wrong between the two of you?"

She said, "Let's go."

"I've got to wait for my change."

It was always easier to get served at Lou-Lou's than to pay the bill. At that moment everyone always had a habit of disappearing: the old woman (her knitting abandoned on the table), the aunt who helped to serve, Lou-Lou herself, her husband in his blue sweater. If the dog hadn't gone already he would have left at that moment.

I said, "You forget—you told me that he wasn't happy."

"Please, please find someone and let's go."

So I disinterred Lou-Lou's aunt from the kitchen and paid. When we left, everyone seemed to be back again, even the dog.

Outside I asked her whether she wanted to return to the hotel.

"Not just yet—but I'm keeping you from your work."

"I never work after drinking. That's why I like to start early. It brings the first drink nearer."

She said that she had seen nothing of Antibes but the ramparts and the beach and the lighthouse, so I walked her around the small narrow backstreets where the washing hung out of the windows as in Naples and there were glimpses of small rooms overflowing with children and grandchildren; stone scrolls were carved over the ancient doorways of what had once been noblemen's houses; the pavements were blocked by barrels of wine and the streets by children playing at ball. In a low room on a ground floor a man sat painting the horrible ceramics which would later go to Vallauris to be sold to tourists in Picasso's old stamping-ground— spotted pink frogs and mauve fish and pigs with slits for coins.

She said, "Let's go back to the sea." So we returned to a patch of hot sun on the bastion, and again I was tempted to tell her what I feared, but the thought that she might watch me with the blankness of ignorance deterred me. She sat on the wall and her long legs in the tight black trousers dangled down like Christmas stockings. She said, "I'm not sorry that I married Peter," and I was reminded of a song Edith Piaf used to sing, *"Je ne regrette rien."* It is typical of such a phrase that it is always sung or spoken with defiance.

I could only say again, "You ought to take him home," but I wondered what would have happened if I had said, "You are married to a man who only likes men and he's off now picnicking with his boy friends. I'm thirty years older than you, but at least I have always preferred women and I've fallen in love with you and we could still have a few good years together before the time comes when you want to leave me for a younger man." All I said was, "He probably misses the country—and the riding."

"I wish you were right, but it's really worse than that."

Had she, after all, realized the nature of her problem? I waited for her to explain her meaning. It was a little like a novel which hesitates on the verge between comedy and tragedy. If she recognized the situation it would be a tragedy; if she were ignorant it was a comedy, even a farce —a situation between an immature girl too innocent to understand and a man too old to have the courage to explain. I suppose I have a taste for tragedy. I hoped for that.

She said, "We didn't really know each other much before we came here. You know, weekend parties and the odd theatre—and riding, of course."

I wasn't sure where her remarks tended. I said, "These occasions are nearly always a strain. You are picked out of ordinary life and dumped together after an elaborate ceremony—almost like two animals shut in a cage who haven't seen each other before."

"And now he sees me he doesn't like me."

"You are exaggerating."

"No." She added, with anxiety, "I won't shock you, will I, if I tell you things? There's nobody else I can talk to."

"After fifty years I'm guaranteed shockproof."

"We haven't made love—properly, once, since we came here."

"What do you mean—properly?"

"He starts, but he doesn't finish; nothing happens."

I said uncomfortably, "Rochester wrote about that. A poem called 'The Imperfect Enjoyment.' " I don't know why I gave her this shady piece of literary information; perhaps, like a psychoanalyst, I wanted her not to feel alone with her problem. "It can happen to anybody."

"But it's not his fault," she said. "It's mine. I know it is. He just doesn't like my body."

"Surely it's a bit late to discover that."

"He'd never seen me naked till I came here," she said with the candour of a girl to her doctor—that was all I meant to her, I felt sure.

"There are nearly always first-night nerves. And then if a man worries (you must realize how much it hurts his pride) he can get stuck in the situation for days—weeks even." I began to tell her about a mistress I once had—we stayed together a very long time and yet for two weeks at the beginning I could do nothing at all. "I was too anxious to succeed."

"That's different. You didn't hate the sight of her."

"You are making such a lot of so little."

"That's what he tries to do," she said with sudden schoolgirl coarseness and giggled miserably.

"We went away for a week and changed the scene, and everything after that was all right. For ten days it had been a flop, and for ten years afterwards we were happy. Very happy. But worry can get established in a room, in the colour of the curtains—it can hang itself up on coat-hangers; you find it smoking away in the ashtray marked Pernod, and when you look at the bed it pokes its head out from underneath like the toes of a pair of shoes." Again I repeated the only charm I could think of. "Take him home."

"It wouldn't make any difference. He's disappointed, that's all it is." She looked down at her long black legs; I followed the course of her eyes because I was finding now that I really wanted her and she said with sincere conviction, "I'm just not pretty enough when I'm undressed."

"You are talking real nonsense. You don't know what nonsense you are talking."

"Oh no, I'm not. You see—it started all right, but then he touched me"—she put her hands on her breasts—"and it all went wrong. I always knew they weren't much good. At school we used to have dormitory inspection—it was awful. Everybody could grow them big except me. I'm no Jayne Mansfield, I can tell you." She gave again that mirthless giggle. "I remember one of the girls told me to sleep with a pillow on top—they said they'd struggle for release and what they needed was exercise. But of course it didn't work. I doubt if the idea was very scientific." She added, "I remember it was awfully hot at night like that."

"Peter doesn't strike me," I said cautiously, "as a man who would want a Jayne Mansfield."

"But you understand, don't you, that if he finds me ugly, it's all so hopeless."

I wanted to agree with her—perhaps this reason which she had thought up would be less distressing than the truth, and soon enough there would be someone to cure her distrust. I had noticed before that it is often the lovely women who have the least confidence in their looks, but all the same I couldn't pretend to her that I understood it her way. I said, "You must trust me. There's nothing at all wrong with you and that's why I'm talking to you the way I am."

"You are very sweet," she said, and her eyes passed over me rather as the beam from the lighthouse which at night went past the Musée Grimaldi and after a certain time returned and brushed all our windows indifferently on the hotel front. She continued, "He said they'd be back by cocktail-time."

"If you want a rest first"—for a little time we had been close, but now again we were getting further and further away. If I pressed her now she might in the end be happy—does conventional morality demand that a girl remains tied as she was tied? They'd been married in church; she was probably a good Christian, and I knew the ecclesiastical rules: at this moment of her life she could be free of him, the marriage could be annulled, but in a day or two it was only too probable that the same rules would say, "He's managed well enough, you are married for life."

And yet I couldn't press her. Wasn't I after all assuming far too much? Perhaps it was only a question of first-night nerves; perhaps in a little while the three of them would be back, silent, embarrassed, and Tony in his turn would have a contusion on his cheek. I would have been very glad to see it there; egotism fades a little with the passions which engender it, and I would have been content, I think, just to see her happy.

So we returned to the hotel, not saying much, and she went to her room and I to mine. It was in the end a comedy and not a tragedy, a farce even, which is why I have given this scrap of reminiscence a farcical title.

7

I was woken from my middle-aged siesta by the telephone. For a moment, surprised by the darkness, I couldn't find the light-switch. Scrambling for it, I knocked over my bedside lamp—the telephone went on ringing, and I tried to pick up the holder and knocked over a tooth-glass in which I had given myself a whisky. The little illuminated dial of my watch gleamed up at me marking 8:30. The telephone continued to ring. I got the receiver off, but this time it was the ashtray which fell over. I couldn't get the cord to extend up to my ear, so I shouted in the direction of the telephone, "Hullo!"

A tiny sound came up from the floor which I interpreted as "Is that William?"

I shouted, "Hold on," and now that I was properly awake I realized the light-switch was just over my head (in London it was placed over the bedside table). Little petulant noises came up from the floor as I put on the light, like the creaking of crickets.

"Who's that?" I said rather angrily, and then I recognized Tony's voice.

"William, whatever's the matter?"

"Nothing's the matter. Where are you?"

"But there was quite an enormous crash. It hurt my eardrum."

"An ashtray," I said.

"Do you usually hurl ashtrays around?"

"I was asleep."

"At 8:30? William! William!"

I said, "Where are you?"

"A little bar in what Mrs. Clarenty would call Monty."

"You promised to be back by dinner," I said.

"That's why I'm telephoning you. I'm being *responsible*, William. Do you mind telling Poopy that we'll be a little late? Give her dinner. Talk to her as only you know how. We'll be back by ten."

"Has there been an accident?"

I could hear him chuckling up the phone. "Oh, I wouldn't call it an accident."

"Why doesn't Peter call her himself?"

"He says he's not in the mood."

"But what shall I tell her?" The telephone went dead.

I got out of bed and dressed and then I called her room. She answered very quickly; I think she must have been sitting by the telephone. I relayed the message, asked her to meet me in the bar, and rang off before I had to face answering any questions.

But I found it was not so difficult as I feared to cover up; she was immensely relieved that somebody had telephoned. She had sat there in her room from half-past seven onwards thinking of all the dangerous turns and ravines on the Grande Corniche, and when I rang she was half afraid that it might be the police or a hospital. Only after she had drunk two dry Martinis and laughed quite a lot at her fears did she say, "I wonder why Tony rang you and not Peter me?"

I said (I had been working the answer out), "I gather he suddenly had an urgent appointment—in the loo."

It was as though I had said something enormously witty.

"Do you think they are a bit tight?" she asked.

"I wouldn't wonder."

"Darling Peter," she said, "he deserved the day off," and I couldn't help wondering in what direction his merit lay.

"Do you want another Martini?"

"I'd better not," she said, "you've made me tight too."

I had become tired of the thin cold *rosé* so we had a bottle of real wine at dinner and she drank her full share and talked about literature. She had, it seemed, a nostalgia for Dornford Yates, had graduated in the sixth form as far as Hugh Walpole, and now she talked respectfully about Sir Charles Snow, who she obviously thought had been knighted, like Sir Hugh, for his services to literature. I must have been very much in love or I would have found her innocence almost unbearable—or perhaps I was a little tight as well. All the same, it was to interrupt her flow of critical judgements that I asked her what her real name was and she replied, "Everyone calls me Poopy." I remembered the PT stamped on her bags, but the only real names that I could think of at the moment were Patricia and Prunella. "Then I shall simply call you You," I said.

After dinner I had brandy and she had a kümmel. It was past 10:30 and still the three had not returned, but she didn't seem to be worrying any more about them. She sat on the floor of the bar beside me and every now and then the waiter looked in to see if he could turn off the lights. She leant against me with her hand on my knee and she said such things as "It must be wonderful to be a writer," and in the glow of brandy and tenderness I didn't mind them a bit. I even began to tell her again about the Earl of Rochester. What did I care about Dornford Yates, Hugh Walpole or Sir Charles Snow? I was even in the mood to recite to her, hopelessly inapposite to the situation though the lines were:

Then talk not of Inconstancy,
  False hearts, and broken vows;
If I, by miracle, can be
This live-long minute true to thee,
  'Tis all that Heaven allows.

when the noise—what a noise!—of the Sprite approaching brought us both to our feet. It was only too true that all that heaven allowed was the time in the bar at Antibes.

Tony was singing; we heard him all the way up the Boulevard Général Leclerc; Stephen was driving with the greatest caution, most of the time in second gear, and Peter, as we saw when we came out onto the terrace, was sitting on Tony's knee—nestling would be a better description—and joining in the refrain. All I could make out was

> *Round and white*
> *On a winter's night,*
> *The hope of the Queen's Navee.*

If they hadn't seen us on the steps I think they would have driven past the hotel without noticing.

"You *are* tight," the girl said with pleasure. Tony put his arm round her and ran her up to the top of the steps. "Be careful," she said. "William's made me tight too."

"Good old William."

Stephen climbed carefully out of the car and sank down on the nearest chair.

"All well?" I asked, not knowing what I meant.

"The children have been very happy," he said, "and very, very relaxed."

"Got to go to the loo," Peter said (the cue was in the wrong place), and made for the stairs. The girl gave him a helping hand and I heard him say, "Wonderful day. Wonderful scenery. Wonderful . . ." She turned at the top of the stairs and swept us with her smile, gay, reassured, happy. As on the first night, when they had hesitated about the cocktail, they didn't come down again. There was a long silence and then Tony chuckled. "You seem to have had a wonderful day," I said.

"Dear William, we've done a very good action. You've never seen him so *détendu*."

Stephen sat saying nothing; I had the impression that today hadn't gone quite so well for him. Can people ever hunt quite equally in couples or is there always a loser? The too-grey waves of hair were as immaculate as ever, there was no contusion on the cheek, but I had the impression that the fear of the future had cast a long shadow.

"I suppose you mean you got him drunk?"

"Not with alcohol," Tony said. "We aren't vulgar seducers, are we, Stephen?" But Stephen made no reply.

"Then what was your good action?"

"*Le pauvre petit Pierre.* He was in such a state. He had quite convinced himself—or perhaps she had convinced him—that he was *impuissant.*"

"You seem to be making a lot of progress in French."

"It sounds more delicate in French."

"And with your help he found he wasn't?"

"After a little virginal timidity. Or near virginal. School hadn't left him quite unmoved. Poor Poopy. She just hadn't known the right way to go about things. My dear, he has a superb virility. Where are you going, Stephen?"

"I'm going to bed," Stephen said flatly, and went up the steps alone. Tony looked after him, I thought with a kind of tender regret, a very light and superficial sorrow. "His rheumatism came back very badly this afternoon," he said. "Poor Stephen."

I thought it was well then to go to bed before I should become "Poor William" too. Tony's charity tonight was all-embracing.

8

It was the first morning for a long time that I found myself alone on the terrace for breakfast. The women in tweed skirts had been gone for some days, and I had never before known "the young men" to be absent. It was easy enough, while I waited for my coffee, to speculate about the likely reasons. There was, for example, the rheumatism . . . though I couldn't quite picture Tony in the character of a bedside companion. It was even remotely possible that they felt some shame and were unwilling to be confronted by their victim. As for the victim, I wondered sadly what painful revelation the night would certainly have brought. I blamed myself more than ever for not speaking in time. Surely she would have learned the truth more gently from me than from some tipsy uncontrolled outburst of her husband. All the same—such egoists are we in our passions—I was glad to be there in attendance . . . to staunch the tears . . . to take her tenderly in my arms, comfort her . . . oh, I had quite a romantic day-dream on the terrace before she came down the steps and I saw that she had never had less need of a comforter.

She was just as I had seen her the first night: shy, excited, gay, with a long and happy future established in her eyes. "William," she said, "can I sit at your table? Do you mind?"

"Of course not."

"You've been so patient with me all the time I was in the doldrums. I've talked an awful lot of nonsense to you. I know you told me it was nonsense, but I didn't believe you and you were right all the time."

I couldn't have interrupted her even if I had tried. She was a Venus at the prow sailing through sparkling seas. She said, "Everything's all right. Everything. Last night—he loves me, William. He really does. He's not a bit disappointed with me. He was just tired and strained, that's all. He needed a day off alone—*détendu*." She was even picking up Tony's French expressions second-hand. "I'm afraid of nothing now, nothing at all. Isn't it strange how black life seemed only two days ago? I really believe if it hadn't been for you I'd have thrown in my hand. How lucky I was to meet you and the others too. They're such wonderful friends for Peter. We are all going home next week—and we've made a lovely plot together. Tony's going to come down almost immediately we get back and decorate our house. Yesterday, driving in the country, they had a wonderful discussion about it. You won't know our house when you see it—oh, I forgot, you never *have* seen it, have you? You must come down when it's all finished—with Stephen."

"Isn't Stephen going to help?" I just managed to slip in.

"Oh, he's too busy at the moment, Tony says, with Mrs. Clarenty. Do you like riding? Tony does. He adores horses, but he has so little chance in London. It will be wonderful for Peter—to have someone like that because, after all, I can't be riding with Peter all day long, there will be a lot of things to do in the house, especially now, when I'm not accustomed. It's wonderful to think that Peter won't have to be lonely. He says there are going to be Etruscan murals in the bathroom—whatever Etruscan means; the drawing-room *basically* will be eggshell green and the dining-room walls Pompeian red. They really did an awful lot of work yesterday afternoon—I mean in their heads, while we were glooming around. I said to Peter, 'As things are going now we'd better be prepared for a nursery,' but Peter said Tony was content to leave all that side to me. Then there are the stables: they were an old coach-house once, and Tony feels we could restore a lot of the ancient character and there's a lamp he bought in St. Paul which will just fit . . . it's endless the things there are to be done—a good six months' work, so Tony says, but luckily he can leave Mrs. Clarenty to Stephen and concentrate on us. Peter asked him about the garden, but he's not a specialist in gardens. He said, 'Everyone to his own métier,' and he's quite content if I bring in a man who knows all about roses.

"He knows Colin Winstanley too, of course, so there'll be quite a band of us. It's a pity the house won't be all ready for Christmas, but Peter says he's certain to have wonderful ideas for a really original tree. Peter thinks . . ."

She went on and on like that; perhaps I ought to have interrupted her even then; perhaps I should have tried to explain to her why her dream wouldn't last. Instead, I sat there silent, and presently I went to my room and packed—there was still one hotel open in the abandoned fun-fair of Juan between Maxim's and the boarded-up Striptease.

If I had stayed . . . who knows whether he could have kept on pretending for a second night? But I was just as bad for her as he was. If he had the wrong hormones, I had the wrong age. I didn't see any of them again before I left. She and Peter and Tony were out somewhere in the Sprite, and Stephen—so the receptionist told me—was lying late in bed with his rheumatism.

I planned a note for her, explaining rather feebly my departure, but when I came to write it I realized I had still no other name with which to address her than Poopy.

~ *Sherwood Anderson* ~

Hands

U pon the half-decayed veranda of a small frame house that stood near the edge of a ravine near the town of Winesburg, Ohio, a fat little old man walked nervously up and down. Across a long field that had been seeded for clover but that had produced only a dense crop of yellow mustard weeds, he could see the public highway along which went a wagon filled with berry pickers returning from the fields. The berry pickers, youths and maidens, laughed and shouted boisterously. A boy clad in a blue shirt leaped from the wagon and attempted to drag after him one of the maidens, who screamed and protested shrilly. The feet of the boy in the road kicked up a cloud of dust that floated across the face of the departing sun. Over the long field came a thin girlish voice. "Oh, you, Wing Biddlebaum, comb your hair, it's falling into your eyes," commanded the voice to the man, who was bald and whose nervous little hands fiddled about the bare white forehead as though arranging a mass of tangled locks.

Wing Biddlebaum, forever frightened and beset by a ghostly band of doubts, did not think of himself as in any way a part of the life of the town where he had lived for twenty years. Among all the people of

Born in 1876 in Camden, Ohio, SHERWOOD ANDERSON was the author of such works as Poor White, The Triumph of the Egg, *and the autobiography* A Storyteller's Story, *but he will probably be best remembered for the collection* Winesburg, Ohio, *from which "Hands" is excerpted. He died in 1941.*

Winesburg but one had come close to him. With George Willard, son of Tom Willard, the proprietor of the New Willard House, he had formed something like a friendship. George Willard was the reporter on the *Winesburg Eagle* and sometimes in the evenings he walked out along the highway to Wing Biddlebaum's house. Now as the old man walked up and down on the veranda, his hands moving nervously about, he was hoping that George Willard would come and spend the evening with him. After the wagon containing the berry pickers had passed, he went across the field through the tall mustard weeds and climbing a rail fence peered anxiously along the road to the town. For a moment he stood thus, rubbing his hands together and looking up and down the road, and then, fear overcoming him, ran back to walk again upon the porch on his own house.

In the presence of George Willard, Wing Biddlebaum, who for twenty years had been the town mystery, lost something of his timidity, and his shadowy personality, submerged in a sea of doubts, came forth to look at the world. With the young reporter at his side, he ventured in the light of day into Main Street or strode up and down on the rickety front porch of his own house, talking excitedly. The voice that had been low and trembling became shrill and loud. The bent figure straightened. With a kind of wriggle, like a fish returned to the brook by the fisherman, Biddlebaum the silent began to talk, striving to put into words the ideas that had been accumulated by his mind during long years of silence.

Wing Biddlebaum talked much with his hands. The slender expressive fingers, forever active, forever striving to conceal themselves in his pockets or behind his back, came forth and became the piston rods of his machinery of expression.

The story of Wing Biddlebaum is a story of hands. Their restless activity, like unto the beating of the wings of an imprisoned bird, had given him his name. Some obscure poet of the town had thought of it. The hands alarmed their owner. He wanted to keep them hidden away and looked with amazement at the quiet inexpressive hands of other men who worked beside him in the fields, or passed, driving sleepy teams on country roads.

When he talked to George Willard, Wing Biddlebaum closed his fists and beat with them upon a table or on the walls of his house. The action made him more comfortable. If the desire to talk came to him when the two were walking in the fields, he sought out a stump or the top board of a fence and with his hands pounding busily talked with renewed ease.

The story of Wing Biddlebaum's hands is worth a book in itself. Sympathetically set forth it would tap many strange, beautiful qualities in obscure men. It is a job for a poet. In Winesburg the hands had attracted attention merely because of their activity. With them Wing Biddlebaum had picked as high as a hundred and forty quarts of strawberries in a day. They became his distinguishing feature, the source of his fame. Also they made more grotesque an already grotesque and elusive individuality. Winesburg was proud of the hands of Wing Biddlebaum in the same spirit in which it was proud of Banker White's new stone house and Wesley Moyer's bay stallion, Tony Tip, that had won the two-fifteen trot at the fall races in Cleveland.

As for George Willard, he had many times wanted to ask about the hands. At times an almost overwhelming curiosity had taken hold of him. He felt that there must be a reason for their strange activity and their inclination to keep hidden away, and only a growing respect for Wing Biddlebaum kept him from blurting out the questions that were often in his mind.

Once, he had been on the point of asking. The two were walking in the fields on a summer afternoon and had stopped to sit upon a grassy bank. All afternoon Wing Biddlebaum had talked as one inspired. By a fence he had stopped and beating like a giant woodpecker upon the top board had shouted at George Willard, condemning his tendency to be too much influenced by the people about him. "You are destroying yourself," he cried. "You have the inclination to be alone and to dream and you are afraid of dreams. You want to be like others in town here. You hear them talk and you try to imitate them."

On the grassy bank Wing Biddlebaum had tried again to drive his point home. His voice became soft and reminiscent, and with a sigh of contentment he launched into a long rambling talk, speaking as one lost in a dream.

Out of the dream Wing Biddlebaum made a picture for George Willard. In the picture men lived again in a kind of pastoral golden age. Across a green open country came clean-limbed young men, some afoot, some mounted upon horses. In crowds the young men came to gather about the feet of an old man who sat beneath a tree in a tiny garden and who talked to them.

Wing Biddlebaum became wholly inspired. For once he forgot the hands. Slowly they stole forth and lay upon George Willard's shoulders. Something new and bold came into the voice that talked. "You must try to forget all you have learned," said the old man. "You must begin to dream. From this time on you must shut your ears to the roaring of the voices."

Pausing in his speech, Wing Biddlebaum looked long and earnestly at George Willard. His eyes glowed. Again he raised the hands to caress the boy and then a look of horror swept over his face.

With a convulsive movement of his body, Wing Biddlebaum sprang to his feet and thrust his hands deep into his trousers pockets. Tears came to his eyes. "I must be getting along home. I can talk no more with you," he said nervously.

Without looking back, the old man had hurried down the hillside and across a meadow, leaving George Willard perplexed and frightened upon the grassy slope. With a shiver of dread the boy arose and went along the road toward town. "I'll not ask him about his hands," he thought, touched by the memory of the terror he had seen in the man's eyes. "There's something wrong, but I don't want to know what it is. His hands have something to do with his fear of me and of everyone."

And George Willard was right. Let us look briefly into the story of the hands. Perhaps our talking of them will arouse the poet who will tell the hidden wonder story of the influence for which the hands were but fluttering pennants of promise.

In his youth Wing Biddlebaum had been a school teacher in a town in Pennsylvania. He was not then known as Wing Biddlebaum, but went by the less euphonic name of Adolph Myers. As Adolph Myers he was much loved by the boys of his school.

Adolph Myers was meant by nature to be a teacher of youth. He was one of those rare, little-understood men who rule by a power so gentle that it passes as a lovable weakness. In their feeling for the boys under their charge such men are not unlike the finer sort of women in their love of men.

And yet that is but crudely stated. It needs the poet there. With the boys of his school, Adolph Myers had walked in the evening or had sat talking until dusk upon the schoolhouse steps, lost in a kind of dream. Here and there went his hands, caressing the shoulders of the boys, playing about the tousled heads. As he talked his voice became soft and musical. There was a caress in that also. In a way the voice and the hands, the stroking of the shoulders and the touching of the hair, were a part of the schoolmaster's effort to carry a dream into the young minds. By the caress that was in his fingers he expressed himself. He was one of those men in whom the force that creates life is diffused, not centralized. Under the caress of his hands doubt and disbelief went out of the minds of the boys and they began also to dream.

And then the tragedy. A half-witted boy of the school became en-amored of the young master. In his bed at night he imagined unspeakable things and in the morning went forth to tell his dreams as facts. Strange, hideous accusations fell from his loose-hung lips. Through the Pennsyl-vania town went a shiver. Hidden, shadowy doubts that had been in men's minds concerning Adolph Myers were galvanized into beliefs.

The tragedy did not linger. Trembling lads were jerked out of bed and questioned. "He put his arms about me," said one. "His fingers were always playing in my hair," said another.

One afternoon a man of the town, Henry Bradford, who kept a saloon, came to the schoolhouse door. Calling Adolph Myers into the school yard he began to beat him with his fists. As his hard knuckles beat down into the frightened face of the schoolmaster, his wrath became more and more terrible. Screaming with dismay, the children ran here and there like disturbed insects. "I'll teach you to put your hands on my boy, you beast," roared the saloon keeper, who, tired of beating the master, had begun to kick him about the yard.

Adolph Myers was driven from the Pennsylvania town in the night. With lanterns in their hands a dozen men came to the door of the house where he lived alone and commanded that he dress and come forth. It was raining and one of the men had a rope in his hands. They had intended to hang the schoolmaster, but something in his figure, so small, white, and pitiful, touched their hearts and they let him escape. As he ran away into the darkness they repented of their weakness and ran after him, swearing and throwing sticks and great balls of soft mud at the figure that screamed and ran faster and faster into the darkness.

For twenty years Adolph Myers had lived alone in Winesburg. He was but forty but looked sixty-five. The name of Biddlebaum he got from a box of goods seen at a freight station as he hurried through an eastern Ohio town. He had an aunt in Winesburg, a black-toothed old woman who raised chickens, and with her he lived until she died. He had been ill for a year after the experience in Pennsylvania, and after his recovery worked as a day laborer in the fields, going timidly about and striving to conceal his hands. Although he did not understand what had happened he felt that the hands must be to blame. Again and again the fathers of the boys had talked of the hands. "Keep your hands to yourself," the saloon keeper had roared, dancing with fury in the schoolhouse yard.

Upon the veranda of his house by the ravine, Wing Biddlebaum continued to walk up and down until the sun had disappeared and the road beyond the field was lost in the grey shadows. Going into his house he cut slices of bread and spread honey upon them. When the rumble of the evening train that took away the express cars loaded with the day's harvest of berries had passed and restored the silence of the summer night, he went again to walk upon the veranda. In the darkness he could not see the hands and they became quiet. Although he still hungered for the presence of the boy, who was the medium through which he expressed his love of man, the hunger became again a part of his loneliness and his waiting. Lighting a lamp, Wing Biddlebaum washed the few dishes soiled by his simple meal and, setting up a folding cot by the screen door that led to the porch, prepared to undress for the night. A few stray white bread crumbs lay on the cleanly washed floor by the table; putting the lamp upon a low stool he began to pick up the crumbs, carrying them to his mouth one by one with unbelievable rapidity. In the dense blotch of light beneath the table, the kneeling figure looked like a priest engaged in some service of his church. The nervous expressive fingers, flashing in and out of the light, might well have been mistaken for the fingers of the devotee going swiftly through decade after decade of his rosary.

~ *James Kirkup* ~

The Teacher of
American Business
English

I'm a part-time teacher of American Business English at a minor Japanese university in Osaka. Most of the students in my classes, ninety minutes each, are girls aged eighteen to twenty-one, which is something of a disappointment for me. I've nothing against girls, mind you, and I am always scrupulously fair to them in tests and final examinations. In fact, if I may put it this way, I bend over backward to help them. Some of them seem quite grateful. Occasionally I get little gifts from them— toilet soap or little boxes of candy. I always send them a little note of thanks.

But our relationships never go further than that. If I were to start an affair with a student, it would soon be all over the place, and I'd be in big trouble. There are scores of foreigners just waiting to step into my place here. They'd not hesitate to drag my name through the dirt.

When I say the girls are something of a disappointment to me, it's not that I'm ungrateful, and it's not just because most of them are extremely idle students and hopeless at English of any kind, but especially American Business English. No. The fact is, I prefer boys. And there are only a handful of males in each class.

Reared in South Shields, Tyneside, England, JAMES KIRKUP is the author of many books of poetry, novels, and memoirs, among them I, of All People, *in which he reveals that he has "the evil eye." After many years spent living and teaching in Japan, he now makes his home in the Principality of Andorra.*

The girls sit in the front rows, staring at me in a speculative way, as if wondering where I got my necktie (Charvet) or if I have chest hair, and if so, is it the same blond shade as that on my head (tinted). But nearly all the boys sit right at the back of the class, out of the way of my questioning. Well, that's okay by me. If they don't want to work, that's no skin off my nose. But sometimes I jump on one of them and ask him to read or translate, just to throw him. Or to waken him up. Some of them work half the night as "escorts" at what they call here Adonis bars, where they act as "companions" (and sometimes more than that) to frustrated rich businessmen's wives.

I'm not all that attracted to most Japanese boys. They're a bit too girlish and insipid for my tastes—at least most of the college crowd are. Now, the workmen and day laborers—that's another ball game entirely.

I said "nearly all" the male students sit in the back row and try to attract my attention as little as possible. They are the good-looking ones who couldn't put an English sentence together to save their pampered lives. They all look pretty much the same—tall, extremely skinny, sallow, with tightly permed hair and wearing those sloppy, floppy pants and sweaters that pass for the latest fashion here. Some of them have very nice teeth, I'll give you that—whenever they smile at me, which is once in a blue moon. But they look so limp and listless, lanky as rhubarb that has shot up too quickly. They have a spineless appearance, and they're always jigging their knees nervously up and down as they sit at the ancient desks that are now too small for the average Japanese teenager. I hate to see them doing that with their widely spread knees. It gets on my nerves.

But there are always one or two male students who sit near the front of the class. They are always the same type—rather weedy, small, bespectacled, spotty, and dressed in old-fashioned regulation student uniforms. Their faces are pale and intense. They are desperate to learn American Business English. Usually, they are the best students in the class. They practice reading English aloud on their own every day. They listen religiously to the Voice of America radio programs. They have little tape recorders, on which they record every word I say. They do their exercises and write their model American Business English letters faithfully every week. It's nearly always this type of earnest and zealous student who speaks good English. The good-looking ones know they'll never have to bother speaking English, even "broken" English. Their careers are already mapped out for them. Daddy owns a prosperous company. Or a marriage has been arranged for them with the ugly daughter of a rich property developer. Or they've already found an adoring middle-aged mistress who keeps them in luxury; soon they will have enough cash saved to start their own business—probably another Adonis bar—and then they can throw over the old bag with the money and pick up some sexy young schoolgirl chick.

But the plain boys—and God, how plain they can be!—know they have to start at the bottom of the business ladder and work their way painfully up rung by rung, and never to the top. They'll never amount to much more than assistant section chief. And they'll never catch a rich wife. So the plain boys sweat it out for four years at business school, trying to master American Business English, though as they'll never be employed by Americans, and as the companies they'll be working for will always be minor ones with no need for American Business English, I sometimes wonder why they waste their time drafting form letters and staff circulars in this funny kind of stilted, unnatural English. "In reply to yours of the 4th inst. . . ."

They all have to get a graduation diploma. That's the trouble. Without that diploma, no one in Japan can get even a clerk's job in a store or in a bank. I've even met taxi drivers that were college graduates, who had attended special classes in English Conversation for Taxi Drivers:

"Where to?"

"You speak good Japanese."

"How long Japan?"

"You American guy?"

"Where you from?"

And so on and so on, *ad nauseam,* every one of them asking the same standard questions. American Business English is bad enough. Heaven help me if I ever have to try to earn an honest penny teaching an English Conversation for Taxi Drivers class. Though some of these young drivers are really dishy . . .

~ ~ ~

Always at the start of each academic year, as soon as I meet a new class for the first time, I can "place" everyone. By the position they have taken in the rows of desks, I know exactly what their ability in speaking English is.

The better-looking boys, and two or three girls, the dopes, will be at the back or in far-off corners, where they hope I can't see them. They are the hopeless cases. They don't even want to learn to speak or write American Business English. "How to Draft an Inter-Office Memo . . ."

In the middle of the classroom there is a sort of amorphous lump consisting of students of average to below-average ability. They can just about manage to read an English text in a toneless, expressionless voice, but without understanding most of what they're reading. They think reading is just producing (more or less) the sounds they see on the page. What they produce has no relation at all to any kind of comprehensible English: it's a kind of stumbling, giggling gabble that slowly fills me with the deepest depression. "Read the *meaning!*" I keep telling them. But they don't seem to realize that languages other than Japanese can have any "meaning." That's my middle lump.

In the front row, there about six girls with fairly bright, intelligent, and sometimes pretty faces. These are the above-average ones, who don't die of convulsions if I ask them a question in English. Also in the front row, but well separated from the girls, are two or three plain-faced boys, peering at me shortsightedly through thick spectacles. The intensity of that bespectacled gaze, probing yet expressionless, is sometimes unendurable. When it becomes too much for me, I make them write a short essay, and nip out for a smoke and a shot of bourbon in the john. I look in vain for graffiti on the doors of the john, the sort of stuff that covers every inch of space in American colleges, with vivid drawings, addresses, phone numbers, pleas for someone to cut a hole in the partition between the cubicles, offers of dates, fevered erotic fantasies, slogans for Gay Lib. . . . But in Japan, there is none of that: the johns are depressingly spotless, and there are no glory holes.

It's getting more and more difficult to pick up boys and men. It's not just the AIDS scare—most people in Japan believe that the Japanese are immune, though if pressed they will admit there have been some deaths, or that "harmless social diseases" like the clap are slightly on the rise in all ranks of society: school pupils, housewives, masseuses, Adonis bar boys . . . bar hostesses, Self-Defense Force recruits, mountaineers, fishermen, sushi cooks, teachers . . . But not AIDS. It can never happen in Japan.

So the only thing to do at night is to go to a gay bar. But even these are now off limits to foreigners, who might contaminate the purity of the homogeneous Japanese. Foreign gays here are made to feel like pariahs.

Of course, I'm getting on, pushing fifty. But I'm still in fairly good shape. I've got all my hair and teeth, and I never admit to being more than thirty-nine. Fortunately, the Japanese have difficulty in telling a foreigner's age. We all look alike to them. But even those younger and better-looking than I are having a hard time. It's as if Japan had turned overnight into a sexless society. It's really sad to think of all those growing boys just masturbating in secret. They don't even do it with each other now. . . . They are beginning to look like space-age mutants. I've been thinking of starting an anti-AIDS gay bar called Bring Your Own Glass. But things would never go any further than a little thigh squeezing on the barstools. It's a truly grim lookout for all of us.

~ ~ ~

Or is it? The other day, I found a note in my mailbox at the college. At first I thought it must be just another silly thank-you note from one of the girls, because the envelope was lavender, with fairies and violets on the back, and the writing paper was almost entirely covered with cute little purple hearts and pink cupid's-bow lipstick impressions.

But when I opened it in the staff room, I found that it was from one of my male students, Tomohiro Matsubara. He was one of the "good" students—hardworking but without a scrap of imagination, initiative, or humor. He was also one of the ugliest students I have ever had: low, wrinkled forehead, short but unruly black hair sprinkled with white, a big, slack, puffy mouth, a sickly complexion, and mean little close-set eyes behind abnormally large, thick, heavy-rimmed eyeglasses. On his upper lip and chin there were always a few sparse black bristles: he never seemed to shave, yet those scattered bristles never seemed to grow any longer. As far as I could tell, his body was as unformed as his face, though his hands were hairless, surprisingly broad, with long fingers. I had also noticed that he was left-handed, which did not prevent him from writing the most legible English in the class. I always used to hold up his immaculate essays as an example to the rest of the students, who were incredibly sloppy writers. Tomohiro had a neat italic hand, which he must have learned from an older person: in his grandfather's day, there was a great fad for italic script, and many of the older professors today still delight me by their mastery of it when they write letters to me in English.

But my name on this kitschy envelope had been typed, and the letter inside it was typed too, on an old-fashioned machine with a frayed ribbon, and there were some mistypings, which I shall not perpetuate here:

Dear Prof. Richards,

How are you? We, the boy students in your American Business English class, are very fine thank you very much.

It was the conventional opening of the usual student letter. I felt a wave of irritation at being addressed as "Prof." which I consider to be a most humiliating abbreviation, though I must admit it is used by the Japanese in imitation of the style of American teachers who should know better. When I receive a letter beginning "Dear Prof." I know I'm going to hate the writer. Why can't they address me as *Sensei,* which is an old term of respect for a teacher, and greatly to be preferred to the almost universal "Prof." or "Dr." But my irritation soon subsided. After all, this was the first letter I had received from a group of male students. What on earth could they be wanting? The letter continued:

Sorry to say, sir, we the boy students of your American Business English class can't understand you. Every time you are kind to the foolish girls in our class. You smile at them and say nice things and give them good grades. But you are not kind to us boys. You never give smile when you speak to us. You do not say nice things so often to us.

We boys have asked me, Tomohiro Matsubara, to write to you because I am best at English and you sometimes praise my handwriting. Some of the girls are better at English than me, so at first I asked them to make one of the girls write this letter. But they did not want to ask a favor of those foolish girls. So they asked me. Please be kind to the boys in your class, Prof. Richards. We hope you give us better grades and do not fail us in the final exam. We like you teaching very much.

Please excuse my poor English. I asked my foreign friend who is a *judoka* at the judo school where I go to correct my mistakes. But not all maybe,

Your boy student,

Tomohiro Matsubara (in the front row)

To say that I was surprised by the letter would be to put it mildly. It gave me a completely new insight into my male students. And particularly into Tomohiro Matsubara. Who ever would have thought he practiced judo? Whoever would have expected him to have a foreign friend? Well, yes—a missionary perhaps, or one of those dedicated speakers of Japanese, the young Mormon boys who go around in pairs seeking Japanese converts. But not a *judoka,* a judo expert . . . But what was I to do about this odd situation? To be kind to the boys in my class—especially to the silent, better-looking ones—was one of my permanent fantasies. But how kind could I get?

~ ~ ~

When I entered the classroom that morning, I could feel a certain tension in the air. All eyes were trained upon me, but that was nothing unusual. It was a certain intensity in the silence after we had said good morning that struck me. . . . They were expecting me to say something about the letter.

To defuse the tension, I asked one of the boys in the back row: "Kinoshita, will you please open the window?"

As I expected, the words did not sink in at once. Kinoshita gaped at me, giving the usual bewildered little yelp: "Eh?"

I repeated my request, even more slowly and clearly: "Mr. Kinoshita, will you please open the window."

Lowering his head in confusion, he giggled and looked sideways at his neighbors, asking them in hissing tones what I wanted. But before they had time to make him understand, Tomohiro Matsubara, the writer of the joint letter, jumped up and, amid titters from the girls who had understood the question, went to open the window. He returned to his seat in the front row. Today he was sitting right in front of me, gazing up at me with those sharp little slanting eyes in an even more penetrating way than usual.

"Thank you, Mr. Matsubara." I gave him a slight bow, to which he did not respond: he seemed to be transfixed by the sight of me only about one foot in front of his desk.

After that inauspicious start, I decided not to mention the letter. But after the class, I wrote a note to Tomohiro Matsubara, inviting him and the male students to come and discuss the matter at my apartment, only a short distance from the campus. They all knew where it was, and on several occasions the girls had invited themselves to tea, bringing sickly cakes and idiotic letters from their foreign pen friends. But the male students had never been to my apartment. I had announced in class that

I would be glad to see them there on my "at home day" on Wednesday afternoons from three to five. But for some reason they had never accepted the invitation. Perhaps they did not want to be seen entering my apartment with "foolish girls."

Wednesday was the day after my class. So I cleaned my apartment on Tuesday evening and bought some cakes, fruit, and cookies for the men. I knew they would scorn to bring cakes as the girls did. Then I did a special flower arrangement for them and placed it in the *tokonoma* of my living room, which is in traditional Japanese style, with a matted tatami floor and sliding paper doors and windows.

By the time I had finished, it was after nine o'clock, and I was making an evening snack and sipping a flask of warm saké when I heard my front doorbell ring—melodious saccharin chimes for which I am not to blame: each apartment in the house was fitted with exactly the same chimes.

Who could it be? The young ladies selling insurance and the young salesmen with encyclopedias did not usually call so late in the evening. Before opening the front door, I peeped through the little spyhole, and to my astonishment saw that it was my student Tomohiro Matsubara. He was dressed not in his usual drab uniform but in baggy sports pants and a sweater bearing the Janglish slogan "All we boys do honorable sports and art."

I took a deep breath and opened the door.

"Good evening, Professor," said Matsubara, with his particularly intense scrutiny of my person, yet giving a bow at the same time. I had had a hot bath and changed into a light cotton kimono and sash. Matsubara-san also seemed to have just showered. He was carrying one of those oblong sports bags.

"Good evening," I replied. "Come on in."

He appeared not to have heard my invitation. "May I come in?" he said.

I realized that he must have looked up this phrase and rehearsed it many times, so that in spite of my invitation he did not want to waste it. I made the ushering gesture with my left hand that Japanese usually make when asking someone to enter or sit down. He came into the entry and shuffled off his scuffed white sneakers.

"I came from *dojo*," he told me, looking up intently into my face in the narrow confines of the entry. "Tonight I have judo practice."

So that explained the sports bag, which must contain his *sashiko* judo gear, and his spiky hair, still damp from the showers. I seemed to smell the sweat rising through the zipper on that long, oblong sports bag marked with the legend "Harvard Business School." Such bags, Japanese imitations, are sold by the millions in sports shops all over Japan.

We went along the little corridor to my living room and sat down opposite each other on the flat, square cushions on either side of the low table. I knew the Japanese too well to ask immediately for an explanation of his unannounced visit. It would emerge gradually.

I jumped up. "I was just making some supper," I said. "Would you like some Cup Noodle?"

He bowed, and rose, and seemed unable to say anything. He followed me into the kitchen, where the saké bottle and the little cup stood on the table. I took another cup out of the cupboard and poured him a cup of warm saké. He stood with it in his big hand, as if wondering what to do with it. His glasses appeared to be misting over with the steam from my cooking—or was it from the fumes of the saké?

I made him a bowl of noodles and another for myself, and we sat down at the kitchen table. Before beginning to eat, we toasted each other with cups of saké: *"Kampai!"*

"Kampai!"

His voice was a little hoarse. As soon as he had sipped one cup of the rice wine, his high cheekbones with their taut sallow skin were suffused by a very delicate and most becoming pink. We slurped our noodles. Then we had some of the cakes intended for tomorrow's tea party and some of the fruit. He gave a little sigh of repletion. I knew that the moment of explanation was arriving, so I filled another bottle with hot saké and we moved back to the living room, where we sat side by side at the low table, exchanging saké cups, as is the custom.

"I show your kind letter to boy students," he suddenly said.

"Are they coming tomorrow?"

"No."

There was a silence. I filled his empty cup again. By now, his eyelids, too, had taken on a rosy glow, and his eyes seemed larger and brighter behind those awful spectacles. "But we all like you very much, sir, Professor Richards."

I thought that was perhaps another phrase he had learned by heart, especially for this occasion.

"They are not good boys, sir, Professor," he blurted out, fixing me with that strangely persistent gaze, as if waiting for me to do something or say something. "They not want come. They too shy, not speak any good English. Me too—shy. I ashamed my poor English ability, so sorry, sir."

"I understand," I said. "It's all right. And I'm glad you came to tell me."

"Yes," he replied inscrutably, fixing liquid brown eyes upon me.

There was another silence, rather longer. We sat drinking. I got up to go to the kitchen and fetch another bottle. Like a pet dog, he also got up and followed me, walking a little unsteadily. Perhaps sitting on the floor had given him cramps in his feet, as it always does me? But as I was heating the saké he suddenly became expansive.

"It is first time I drink saké," he said, with a smile that revealed a perfect set of white teeth, only slightly protruding. It was the first time I had seen him smile.

"And first time I visit foreigner's house."

"And first time I see you smile."

(Even native speakers sometimes drop into the peculiar grammar of Japanese English. After hearing it in classes all day long, it's no wonder.)

"And first time you smile at me, sir, Professor Richards."

Without warning, he started to cry and flung his arms around me. I was taken by surprise, but after a moment I put my arms around his shaking shoulders and hugged him.

We found ourselves in my Western-style bedroom, undressing. He removed his glasses and at once, in his frail nakedness, looked touchingly vulnerable. We got into bed, and I took him in my arms and kissed him. He kissed me back, with astonishing passion, and hugged me close, with a fervor totally unsuspected from someone as mysteriously reserved as Tomohiro Matsubara. And as I explored his body, and he explored mine, I discovered silken, hairless skin, powerful muscles on delicate bones, an intoxicating male adolescent scent, musky and faintly sour. We made love again and again. It was after midnight when he started to get dressed again, and I slipped into my *yukata* to see him to the front door.

There, in the dimness of the little entry, we embraced and kissed again, as he shuffled his feet into his scuffed loafers.

He put on his spectacles and regained his former appearance: but I did not mind—I now knew all the wonders that were concealed beneath his unappetizing exterior. Looking up at me gravely, again with his former curious fixity and piercing intentness, greatly magnified because of my closeness to him, he said:

"You not tell other boys, sir?"

"Tell them what?"

He paused, hunting for suitable words.

"That I love you tonight?"

"Of course not, Matsubara-san."

"It is secret only?"

"Yes."

"They not know I homo."

I was silent. I refrained from saying that no one would ever suspect it.

"Even girl students not know."

"Why would they know such a thing?"

"Girl students very interested homo. Japanese girls very foolish. Like homo men, homo movies, *Cruising, Midnight Express, Another Country.*"

This was news to me, though now that he had mentioned it, I remembered noticing a large number of teenage girls at those particular movies. In fact, I was one of the few men present. The films were being constantly revived, I had noticed. But not for males, most of whom were ashamed to be seen at such movies, in case they should be suspected of sharing the feelings of the actors in them.

"Don't worry," I told Matsubara-san.

"All students like you, sir."

"I'm glad to hear that."

"Especially foolish girl students."

"Oh, really? I wonder why? Because I'm kind to them, I suppose. Kinder than I am to the boys."

"No, sir. It because they know you are homo."

"The girls know I am homo?"

"Yes, Professor Richards. Boys also, of course."

There was a silence. Then Matsubara-san opened the door and stepped out on the landing.

He bowed.

I bowed in return.

"Sayonara, sir."

Before I had time to whisper "Sayonara" in return, he was gone, and I could hear him running downstairs two steps at a time.

I closed the door and stood a long time in the dark entry, almost afraid to return to my empty bed.

So I sat down at the kitchen table to prepare the outlines for tomorrow's classes—my three classes in American Business English.

~ *John Cheever* ~

FROM

Falconer

Farragut was still limping, but his hair had begun to grow back, when he was asked to cut a ditto sheet for an announcement that read: THE FIDUCIARY UNIVERSITY OF BANKING WILL OFFER A COURSE IN THE ESSENCE OF BANKING FOR ANY QUALIFIED INMATE. SEE YOUR CELL-BLOCK OFFICER FOR FURTHER INFORMATION. That night Farragut asked Tiny about the news. Tiny told him that the class was going to be limited to thirty-six. Classes would be on Tuesdays and Thursdays. Anyone could apply, but the class would be chosen on the strength of an intelligence quotient test furnished by the university. That's all Tiny knew. Toledo mimeographed the announcements, and they were stuck into the cells along with the evening mail. Toledo should have mimeographed two thousand, but he seemed to have run off another two thousand, because the fliers were all over the place. Farragut couldn't figure out where they came from, but when a wind sprang up in the yard you could see the Fiduciary University announcements circling on the air, not by the tens but by the hundreds. A few days after the announcements were circulated, Farragut had to ditto an announcement for the bulletin

---

A fantasist of suburbia, JOHN CHEEVER lived most of his life with his wife and family in Ossining, New York. His stories are about men torn between the need for familial security and the lure of attractive demons—alcohol and adultery chief among them. Cheever dealt explicitly with the demon of homosexuality, however, only in his journals and in the novel Falconer, *the prison setting of which made love between men permissible.*

board. ANY MAN FOUND USING FIDUCIARY UNIVERSITY ANNOUNCE-
MENT FOR TOILET PAPER WILL BE GIVEN THREE DAYS CELL LOCK. THEY
CLOG THE PLUMBING. Paper was always in short supply, and this snow
of fliers was a bounty. They were used for handkerchiefs, airplanes, and
scrap paper. The jailhouse lawyers used them for drafting petitions to the
Pope, the President, the governor, the Congress, and the Legal Aid Society. They were used for poems, prayers, and illustrated solicitations. The
greenhouse crew picked them up with nailed sticks, but for some time
the flow of fliers seemed mysterious and inexhaustible.

This was in the autumn, and mixed with the Fiduciary University
announcements were the autumn leaves. The three swamp maples within
the wall had turned red and dropped their leaves early in the fall, but
there were many trees beyond the wall, and among the Fiduciary announcements Farragut saw the leaves of beech trees, oaks, tulips, ash,
walnut, and many varieties of maple. The leaves had the power to remind
Farragut, an hour or so after methadone, of the enormous and absurd
pleasure he had, as a free man, taken in his environment. He liked to
walk on the earth, swim in the oceans, climb the mountains, and, in the
autumn, watch the leaves fall. The simple phenomenon of light—brightness angling across the air—struck him as a transcendent piece of good
news. He thought it fortunate that as the leaves fell, they turned and spun,
presenting an illusion of facets to the light. He could remember a trustees
meeting in the city over a matter of several million dollars. The meeting
was on the lower floor of a new office building. Some ginkgo trees had
been planted in the street. The meeting was in October, when the gink-
gos turn a strikingly pure and uniform yellow, and during the meeting
he had, while watching these leaves fall across the air, found his vitality
and his intelligence suddenly stimulated and had been able to make a
substantial contribution to the meeting founded foursquare on the brightness of leaves.

Above the leaves and the fliers and the walls were the birds. Farragut
was a little wary about the birds, since the legend of cruelly confined
men loving the birds of the air had never moved him. He tried to bring
a practical and informed tone to his interest in birds, but he had very little
information. He became interested in a flock of red-winged blackbirds.
They lived in swamps, he knew, so there must have been a swamp near
Falconer. They fed at dusk in some stagnant water other than the swamp
where they lived. Night after night, all through the summer and deep

into the fall, Farragut stood at his window and watched the black birds cross the blue sky above the walls. There would be one or two in the beginning, and while they must have been leaders, there was nothing adventurous about their flight. They all had the choppy flight of caged birds. After the leaders came a flock of two or three hundred, all of them flying clumsily but given by their numbers a sense of power—the magnetic stamina of the planet—drawn through the air like embers on a strong draft. After the first flock there were more laggards, more adventurers, and then another flock of hundreds or thousands and then a third. They made their trip back to their home in the swamp after dark, and Farragut could not see this. He stood at the window waiting to hear the sound of their passage, but it never happened. So in the autumn he watched the birds, the leaves, and the Fiduciary University announcements moving as the air moved, like dust, like pollen, like ashes, like any sign of the invincible potency of nature.

Only five men in cellblock F applied for the course in banking. Nobody much took it seriously. They guessed that the Fiduciary University was either newborn or on the skids and had resorted to Falconer for publicity. The bounteous education of unfortunate convicts was always good for some space in the paper. When the time came, Farragut and the others went down to the parole board room to take the intelligence quotient test. Farragut knew that he tested badly. He had never tested over 119 and had once gone as low as 101. In the army this had kept him from any position of command and had saved his life. He took the test with twenty-four other men, counting blocks and racking his memory for the hypotenuse of the isosceles triangle. The scores were supposed to be secret, but for a package of cigarettes Tiny told him he had flunked out with 112. Jody scored at 140 and claimed he had never done so badly.

Jody was Farragut's best friend. They had met in the shower, where Farragut had noticed a slight young man with black hair smiling at him. He wore around his neck a simple and elegant gold cross. They were not allowed to speak in the shower, but the stranger, soaping his left shoulder, spread out his palm so that Farragut could read there, written in indelible ink: "Meet me later." When they had dressed they met at the door. "You the professor?" the stranger asked. "I'm 734-508-32," said Farragut. He was that green. "Well, I'm Jody," said the stranger brightly, "and I know you're Farragut but so long as you ain't homosexual I don't care what

your name is. Come on with me. I'll show you my hideout." Farragut
followed him across the grounds to an abandoned water tower. They
climbed up a rusty ladder to a wooden catwalk where there was a mattress,
a butt can, and some old magazines. "Everybody's got to have a hideout,"
said Jody. "This is mine. The view is what they call the Millionaire's
View. Next to the death house, this is the best place for seeing it." Farragut saw, over the roofs of the old cellblocks and the walls, a two-mile
stretch of river, with cliffs and mountains on the western shore. He had
seen or glimpsed the view before, at the foot of the prison street, but this
was the most commanding sight he had been given of the world beyond
the wall, and he was deeply moved.

"Sit down, sit down," his friend said, "sit down and I'll tell you about
my past. I ain't like most of the dudes, who won't tell you nothing.
Everybody knows that Freddy, the Mad Dog Killer, iced six men, but
you ask him, he'll tell you he's in for stealing flowers from some park.
He ain't kidding. He means it. He really believes it. But when I have a
buddy I tell him everything if he wants to hear it. I talk a lot, but I listen
a lot too. I'm a very good listener. But my past is really my past. I don't
have no future at all. I don't see the parole board for twelve years. What
I do around here don't matter much, but I like to stay out of the hole.
I know there ain't no medical evidence for brain damage, but after you
hit yourself about fourteen times you get silly. Once I banged myself
seven times. There wasn't nothing more to come out, but I went on
banging myself. I couldn't stop. I was going crazy. That ain't healthy.
Anyhow, I was indicted on fifty-three counts. I had a forty-five-thousand-
dollar house in Levittown, a great wife, and two great sons: Michael and
Dale. But I was in this bind. People with your kind of life-style don't
ever understand. I didn't graduate from high school, but I was up for an
office in the mortgage department of Hamilton Trust. But nothing was
moving. Of course, my not having an education was a drawback, and
they were laying people off, left and right. I just couldn't make enough
money to support four people, and when I put the house up for sale I
discover that every fucking house on the block is on the market. I thought
about money all the time. I dreamed about money. I was picking dimes,
nickels, and pennies off the sidewalk. I was bananas about money. So I
had a friend named Howie, and he had this solution. He told me about
this old guy—Masterman—who ran a stationery store in the shopping
center. He had two seven-thousand-dollar pari-mutuel tickets. He kept

them in a drawer beside his bed. Howie knew this because he used to let the old man blow him for a fin. Howie had this wife, kids, a wood-burning fireplace, but no money. So we decided to get the tickets. In those days you didn't have to endorse them. It was fourteen thousand in cash and no way to trace it. So we watched the old man for a couple of nights. It was easy. He closed up the store at eight, drove home, got drunk, ate something, and watched TV. So one night when he closed the store and got into his car we got into it with him. He was very obedient, because I was holding this loaded gun against his head. This gun was Howie's. He drove home, and we lock-stepped him up to the front door, poking the gun into any soft part of him that was convenient. We marched him into the kitchen and handcuffed him to this big god-damned refrigerator. It was very big, a very recent model. We asked him where the tickets was, and he said they was in the lockbox. If we pistol-whipped him like he said we did, it wasn't me. It could have been Howie, but I didn't see it. He kept telling us the two tickets was in the bank. So then we turned the house upside down looking for tickets, but I guess he was right. So we turned on the TV for neighbors and left him chained to this ten-ton refrigerator and took off in his car. The first car we saw was a police car. This was just an accident, but we got scared. We drove his car into one of those car washes where you have to get out of the car when it hits the shower. We put the car in the slot and took off. We got a bus into Manhattan and said good-bye at the terminal.

"But you know what that old sonofabitch Masterman did? He ain't big and he ain't strong, but he starts inching this big, fucking refrigerator across the kitchen floor. Believe me, it was enormous. It was really a nice house, with lovely furniture and carpets, and he must have had one hell of a time with all those carpets bunching up under the refrigerator, but he got out of the kitchen and down the hall and into the living room, where the telephone was. I can imagine what the police saw when they got there: this old man chained to a refrigerator in the middle of his living room with hand-painted pictures all over the walls. That was Thursday. They picked me up the following Tuesday. They already had Howie. I didn't know it, but he already had a record. I don't blame the state. I don't blame nobody. We did everything wrong. Burglary, pistol-whipping, kidnapping. Kidnapping's a big no-no. Of course, I'm the next thing to dead, but my wife and sons are still alive. So she sold the house at a big loss and goes on welfare. She comes to see me once in a while, but you know what the boys do? First they got permission to write me letters, and then Michael, the big one, wrote me a letter saying that they would be on the river in a rowboat at three on Sunday and they would wave to me. I was out at the fence at three on Sunday, and they showed up. They were way out in the river—you can't come too close to the prison—but I could see them and feel my love for them and they waved their arms and I waved my arms. That was in the autumn, and they stopped coming when the place where you rent boats shut down, but they started again in the spring. They were much bigger, I could see that, and then it occurs to me that for the length of time I'm here they'll get married and have children and I know they won't stuff their wives or their kids into no rowboat and go down the river to wave to old Daddy. So I ain't got no future, Farragut, and you ain't got no future either. So let's go down and wash up for chow."

Farragut was working then part-time with the greenhouse crew, cutting lawns and hedges, and part-time as a typist, cutting ditto sheets for the prison announcements. He had the key to an office near the squad room and the use of a typewriter. He continued to meet Jody at the water tower and later, when the afternoons got cold, in his office. They had known one another a month when they became lovers. "I'm so glad you ain't homosexual," Jody kept saying when he caressed Farragut's hair. Then, saying as much one afternoon, he had unfastened Farragut's trousers and, with every assistance from Farragut, got them down around his knees. From what Farragut had read in the newspapers about prison life, he had expected this to happen, but what he had not expected was that this grotesque bonding of their relationship would provoke in him so profound a love. Nor had he expected the administration to be so lenient. For a small ration of cigarettes, Tiny let Farragut return to the shop between chow and lockup. Jody met him there, and they made love on the floor. "They like it," Jody explained. "At first they didn't like it. Then some psychologist decided that if we got our rocks moved regularly we wouldn't riot. They'll let us do anything if they think it will keep us from rioting. Move over, Chicken, move over. Oh, I love you very much."

They met two or three times a week. Jody was the beloved, and now and then he stood Farragut up, so that Farragut had developed a preternatural sensitivity to the squeak of his lover's basketball sneakers. On some nights his life seemed to hang on the sound. When the classes in banking began, the two men met always on Tuesdays and Thursdays, and Jody reported on his experience with the university. Farragut had boosted a mattress from the shop, and Jody had hustled a hot plate from somewhere, and they lay on the mattress and drank hot coffee and were fairly comfortable and happy.

But Jody spoke skeptically to Farragut about the university. "It's the same old shit," said Jody. "Success School. Charm School. Elite School. How to Make a Million School. I been to them all, and they're all the same. You see, Chicken, banking arithmetic and all that shit is done by computers today, and what you have to concentrate on is to inspire the confidence of the potential investor. That's the big mystery of modern banking. For instance, you come on with the smile. Every class I took begins with lessons in this smile. You stand outside the door thinking about all the great things that happened to you that day, that year, for your whole life. It has to be real. You can't fake this selling smile. I mean you remember a great girl who made you happy or winning a long shot if you ever had one or a new suit or a race you won or a great day when you really had everything going for you. Well, then you open the door and go in and smack him with this smile. Only they don't know nothing, Chicken. I mean about smiling. They don't know nothing at all about smiling.

"It's all right to smile, I mean you have to smile to sell anything, but if you don't smile in the right way you get terrible lines on your face like you have. I love you, Chicken, but you don't know how to smile. If you knew how to smile you wouldn't have those wrinkles all around your eyes and those big, disgusting cuts like scars on your face. Look at me, for example. You think I'm twenty-four, don't you? Well, I'm actually thirty-two, but most people when they're asked to guess my age put me down for eighteen or nineteen at the most. That's because I know how to smile, how to use my face. This actor taught me. He was in on a morals charge, but he was very beautiful. He taught me that when you use your face you spare your face. When you throw your face recklessly into every situation you come up against, you come out looking like *you* do, you come out looking like shit. I love you, Chicken, I really do, otherwise I wouldn't tell you that you got a ruined face. Now watch me smile. See? I look real happy—don't I, don't I, don't I?—but if you'll notice, I keep my eyes wide open so I won't get disgusting wrinkles all around the edges like you have and when I open my mouth I open it very, very wide so that it won't destroy the beauty of my cheeks, their beauty and smoothness. This teacher from the university tells us to smile, smile, smile, smile, but you go around smiling all the time like he teaches us to, you get to look like a very old person, a very old and haggard person who nobody wants anything to do with, especially in the line of banking investments."

When Jody talked scornfully about the Fiduciary University, Farragut's attitude seemed parental, seemed to express some abiding respect for anything that was taught by an organization, however false the teaching and however benighted the organization. Listening to Jody describe the Fiduciary University as shit made Farragut wonder if disrespect was not at the bottom of Jody's criminal career and his life in prison. He felt that Jody should bring more patience, more intelligence, to his attacks on the university. It may have been no more than the fact that the word "fiduciary" seemed to him to deserve respect and inspire honesty; and in its train were thrift, industry, frugality, and honest strife.

In fact, Jody's attacks on the university were continuous, predictable, and, in the end, monotonous. Everything about the school was wrong. The teacher was ruining his face with too broad and committed a smile. The spot quizzes were too easy. "I don't do no work," Jody said, "and I always get the highest marks in the class. I got this memory. It's easy for me to remember things. I learned the whole catechism in one night. Now, today we had Nostalgia. You think it's got something to do with your nose. It don't. It's what you remember with pleasure. So what you do is your homework on what the potential investor remembers with pleasure and you play on his pleasant memories like a fucking violin. You not only stir up what they call Nostalgia with talk, you wear clothes and look and talk and use body language like something they're going to remember with pleasure. So the potential investor likes history, and can't you see me coming into the bank in a fucking suit of armor?"

"You're not taking it seriously, Jody," Farragut said. "There must be something worthwhile in it. I think you ought to pay more attention to what is useful in the course."

"Well, there may be something in it," Jody said. "But you see, I had it all before in Charm School, Success School, Elite School. It's all the same shit. I had it ten times before. Now, they tell me a man's name is for him the sweetest sound in the language. I know this when I was three, four years old. I know the whole thing. You want to hear it? Listen."

Jody ticked off his points on the bars of Farragut's cell. "One. Let the other fellow feel that all the good ideas are his. Two. Throw down a challenge. Three. Open up with praise and honest appreciation. Four. If you're wrong admit it quickly. Five. Get the other person saying yes. Six. Talk about your mistakes. Seven. Let the other man save his face. Eight. Use encouragement. Nine. Make the thing you want to do seem easy. Ten. Make the other person seem happy about doing what you want. Shit, man, any hustler knows that. That's my life, that's the story of my life. I've been doing all this ever since I was a little kid, and look where it got me. Look where my knowledge of the essence of charm and success and banking dumped me. Shit, Chicken, I feel like quitting."

"Don't, Jody," said Farragut. "Stay with it. You'll graduate and it'll look good on your record."

"Nobody's going to look at my record for another forty years," said Jody.

He came one night. It was snowing. "Put in for sick call tomorrow," Jody said. "Monday. There'll be a crowd. I'll wait for you outside the infirmary." He was gone. "Don't he love you no more?" asked Tiny. "Well, if he don't love you no more it's a weight off my shoulders. You're really a nice guy, Farragut. I like you, but I got no use for him. He's blown half the population, and he's hardly begun. Last week, the week before last—I can't remember—he did this fan dance on the third tier. Toledo told me about it. He had this piece of newspaper pleated, you know, like a fan, and he kept switching it from his cock to his asshole and doing this dance. Toledo said it was very disgusting. Very disgusting." Farragut tried to imagine this and couldn't. What he felt was that Tiny was jealous. Tiny had never experienced the love of a man. Tiny was insecure. He made out his sick-call slip, put it between the bars, and went to bed.

The waiting room at the infirmary was full, and he and Jody stood outside where no one could hear them. "Now, listen," Jody said. "Now, before you get upset, listen to me. Don't say nothing until I stop talking. I quit the university yesterday. Now, don't say nothing. I know you're not going to like it because you got this father image thing about me being a big success in the world, but wait until I tell you my plan. Don't say anything. I said don't say anything. Graduation is planned. Nobody but us in the school knows what's going to happen, but you will in a few days. Listen to this. The cardinal, the cardinal of the diocese, is going to come here in a helicopter and present the diplomas to the graduating class. I'm not shitting you, and don't ask me why. I guess the cardinal's some kind of a relation to somebody in the university, but it'll be great publicity and that's what's going to happen. Now, one of the dudes in the class is the chaplain's assistant. His name is DiMatteo. He's a very close friend to me. So he's in charge of all those dresses they wear on the altar, you know. So what he's got is a red one, in my size, a perfect fit. He's going to give it to me. So when the cardinal comes there'll be a lot of confusion. So I'll hang back, hide in the boiler room, get into my red dress, and when the cardinal celebrates mass I'll get my ass on the altar. Listen. I know what I'm doing. I know. I served on the altar beginning when I was eleven. That was when I was confirmed. I know you think they'll catch me, but they won't. At mass you don't look at the other acolytes. That's the thing about prayer. You don't look. When you see a stranger on the altar you don't go around asking who's the stranger on the altar. This is holy business, and when you're doing holy business you don't see nothing. When you drink the blood of Our Savior you don't look to see if the chalice is tarnished or if there's bugs in the wine. You get to be transfixed, you're like transfixed. Prayer. That's why it is. Prayer is what's going to get me out of this place. The power of prayer. So when the mass is over I'll get in the helicopter in my red dress and if they ask me where I'm from I'll say I'm from Saint Anselm's, Saint Augustine's, Saint Michael's, Saint Anywhere's. When we land I'll get out of my robes in the vestry and walk out on the street. What a miracle! I'll panhandle subway fare up to 174th Street, where I got friends. I'm telling you this, Chicken, because I love and trust you. I'm putting my life in your hands. Greater love hath no man. But don't expect to see very much of me from now on. This dude with the red dress likes me. The chaplain brings him in food from the outside, and so I'm taking the electric plate. I may never see you again, Chicken, but if I can I'll come back and say good-bye." Jody then put his hands on his stomach, stooped, and, groaning softly with pain, went into the waiting room. Farragut followed, but they didn't speak again. Farragut complained of headaches and the doctor gave him an aspirin. The doctor wore dirty clothes and had a large hole in his right sock.

Jody didn't return, and Farragut missed him painfully. He listened through all the million sounds of the prison for the squeak of basketball sneakers. It was all he wanted to hear. Soon after their parting at the infirmary he was given the ditto sheet to type announcing that His Eminence Cardinal Thaddeus Morgan would arrive at Falconer by helicopter on the twenty-seventh of May to present diplomas to the graduating class of the Fiduciary University. He would be assisted by the governor and the commissioner of correction. Mass would be celebrated. Attendance at the ceremony would be mandatory and cellblock officers would have further information.

Toledo mimeographed the ditto, but he didn't overdo it this time and there was no blizzard of paper. In the beginning the announcement had almost no impact at all. Only eight men were going to be graduated. The thought of Christ's Advocate descending from heaven onto the gallows field seemed to excite no one. Farragut, of course, went on listening for the squeak of basketball sneakers. If Jody came to say good-bye it would probably be the night before the cardinal's arrival. That gave Farragut a month of waiting to see his lover and then for only a moment. He had to settle for this. Jody, he guessed, was thrashing around with the chaplain's dude, but he did not experience any real jealousy. He could not honestly guess at whether or not Jody's plan to escape would succeed, since both the cardinal's and Jody's plans were preposterous, although the cardinal's plans were reported in the newspaper.

Farragut lay on his cot. He wanted Jody. The longing began in his speechless genitals, for which his brain cells acted as interpreter. The longing then moved up from his genitals to his viscera and from there to his heart, his soul, his mind, until his entire carcass was filled with longing. He waited for the squeak of basketball sneakers and then the voice, youthful, calculatedly so perhaps, but not too light, asking: Move over, Chicken. He waited for the squeak of basketball sneakers as he had waited for the sound of Jane's heels on the cobbles in Boston, waited for the sound of the elevator that would bring Virginia up to the eleventh floor, waited for Dodie to open the rusty gate on Thrace Street, waited for Roberta to get off the C bus in some Roman piazza, waited for Lucy to install her diaphragm and appear naked in the bathroom door, waited for telephone bells, doorbells, church bells that told the time, waited for the end of the thunderstorm that was frightening Helen, waited for the bus, the boat, the train, the plane, the hydrofoil, the helicopter, the ski lift, the five o'clock whistle, and the fire alarm to deliver his beloved into his arms. It seemed that he had spent an inordinate amount of his life and his energies waiting, but that waiting was not, even when no one came, an absolute frustration; it took some of its nature from the grain of the vortex.

But why did he long so for Jody when he had often thought that it was his role in life to possess the most beautiful women? Women possessed the greatest and the most rewarding mysteriousness. They were approached in darkness and sometimes, but not always, possessed in darkness. They were an essence, fortified and besieged, worth conquering and, once conquered, flowing with spoils. At his horniest he wanted to reproduce, to populate hamlets, towns, villages, and cities. It seemed to be his desire to fructify that drove him to imagine fifty women quickening with his children. Women were Ali Baba's cave, they were the light of the morning, they were waterfalls, thunderstorms, they were the immensities of the planet, and a vision of this had led him to decide on something better when he rolled naked off his last naked scoutmaster. There was a trace of reproach in his memory of their splendor, but reproach was not what he meant. Considering the sovereignty of his unruly cock, it was only a woman who could crown that redness with purpose.

There was, he thought, some sameness of degree in sexual possession and sexual jealousy; and accommodations and falsehoods were needed to equate this with the inconstancy of the flesh. He had often overlooked anything expedient in his loves. He had desired and pursued women who charmed him with their lies and enchanted him with their absolute irresponsibility. He had bought their clothes and their tickets, paid their hairdressers and their landlords and, in one case, a facial surgeon. When he bought some diamond earrings he had deliberately judged the sexual mileage he could expect from these jewels. When women had faults he often found them charming. When, while dieting rigorously and continuously talking about their diet, they are found eating a candy bar in a parking lot, one is enchanted. He did not find Jody's faults enchanting. He did not find them.

His radiant and aching need for Jody spread out from his crotch through every part of him, visible and invisible, and he wondered if he could bring off his love for Jody in the street. Would he walk down the street with his arm around Jody's waist, would he kiss Jody at the airport, would he hold Jody's hand in the elevator, and if he refrained from any of this, wouldn't he be conforming to the cruel edicts of a blasphemous society? He tried to imagine Jody and himself in the world. He remembered those pensions or European boardinghouses where he and Marcia and their son sometimes spent the summer. Young men, women, and their children—if they were not young they were at least agile—set the tone. One avoided the company of the old and the infirm. Their haunts were well known and word got around. But here and there, in this familial landscape, one saw at the end of the bar or the corner of the dining room two men or two women. They were the queers, a fact that was usually established by some conspicuous dynamism of opposites. One of the women would be docile; the other commanding. One of the men would be old; the other a boy. One was terribly polite to them, but they were never asked to crew in the sailboat races or take a picnic up the mountain. They were not even asked to the marriage of the village black-smith. They were different. How they gratified their venereal hungers would remain, for the rest of the company, acrobatic and bizarre. They would not, as the rest of the company did, inaugurate the siesta with a good, sweaty fuck. Socially the prejudice against them was very light; at a more profound level it was absolute. That they enjoyed one another's company, as they sometimes did, seemed astonishing and subversive. At one pension Farragut remembered, the queers seemed to be the only happy couple in the dining room. That had been a bad season for holy matrimony. The wives wept. The husbands sulked. The queers won the sailboat race, climbed the highest mountain, and were asked to lunch by the reigning prince. That was an exception. Farragut—extending things out to the street—tried to imagine Jody and himself at some such pension. It was five. They were at the end of the bar. Jody was wearing a white duck suit that Farragut had bought him; but that was as far as he could go. There was no way he could wrench, twist, screw, or otherwise force his imagination to continue the scene.

If love was a chain of resemblances, there was, since Jody was a man, the danger that Farragut might be in love with himself. He had seen self-love only once that he could remember in a man, someone he had worked with for a year or so. The man played a role of no consequence in his affairs, and he had, perhaps to his disadvantage, only casually ob-served this fault, if it was a fault. "Have you ever noticed," the man had asked, "that one of my eyes is smaller than the other?" Later the man had asked with some intensity: "Do you think I'd look better with a beard, a mustache perhaps?" Walking down a sidewalk to a restaurant, the man had asked: "Do you like your shadow? When the sun is behind me and I see my shadow I'm always disappointed. My shoulders aren't broad enough and my hips are too wide." Swimming together, the man asked: "Frankly now, what do you think of my biceps? I mean do you think they're overdeveloped? I do forty push-ups every morning to keep them firm, but I wouldn't want to look like a weight lifter." These questions were not continuous, they were not even daily, but they came often enough to appear eccentric and had led Farragut to wonder, and then to the conviction that the man was in love with himself. He spoke about himself as some other man, in a chancy marriage, might ask for approval of his wife. Do you think she's beautiful? Do you think she talks too much? Don't you like her legs? Do you think she ought to cut her hair? Farragut did not think that he was in love with himself, but once, when he got off the mattress to piss, Jody had said, "Shit, man, you're beautiful. I mean you're practically senile and there isn't much light in here, but you look very beautiful to me." Bullshit, said Farragut, but in some part of the considerable wilderness that was himself, a flower seemed to bloom and he could not find the blossom and crush it with his heel. It was a whore's line, he knew, but he seemed helplessly susceptible. It seemed that he had always known he was beautiful and had been waiting all his life to hear this said. But if in loving Jody he loved himself, there was that chance that he might, hell for leather, have become infatuated with his lost youth. Jody posed as a youth, he had the sweet breath and the sweet-smelling skin of youth, and in possessing these Farragut possessed an hour of greenness. He missed his youth, missed it as he would miss a friend, a lover, a rented house on one of the great beaches where he had been a young man. To embrace one's self, one's youth, might be easier than to love a fair woman whose nature was rooted in a past that he could never comprehend. In loving Mildred, for example, he had had to learn to accommodate her taste for anchovies at breakfast, scalding bathwater, tardy orgasms, and lemon-yellow wallpaper, toilet paper, bed linen, lamp shades, dinner plates, table linen, upholstery, and cars. She had even bought him a lemon-yellow jockstrap. To love oneself would be an idle, an impossible, but a delicious pursuit. How simple to love oneself!

And then there was to think upon the courting of death and death's dark simples, that in covering Jody's body he willingly embraced decay and corruption. To kiss a man on the throat, to gaze into a man's eyes with passion, was as unnatural as the rites and procedures in a funeral

parlor; while kissing, as he had, the tight skin of Jody's belly, he might
have been kissing the turf that would cover him.

With Jody gone—with the removal of this erotic and sentimental
schedule—Farragut found his sense of time and space somewhat imper-
iled. He owned a watch and a calendar, and his surroundings had never
been so easily catalogued, but he had never faced with such deep apprehension the fact that he did not know where he was. He was at the head
of a slalom trail, he was waiting for a train, he was waking after a bad
drug trip in a hotel in New Mexico. "Hey, Tiny," he would shout,
"where am I?" Tiny understood. "Falconer Prison," he would say. "You
killed your brother." "Thanks, Tiny." So, on the strength of Tiny's voice,
the bare facts would return. In order to lessen this troubling sense of
otherness, he remembered that he had experienced this in the street as
well. The sense of being simultaneously in two or three places at the same
instant was something he had known beyond the walls. He remembered
standing in an air-conditioned office on a sunny day while he seemed, at
the same time, to be standing in a shabby farmhouse at the beginning of
a blizzard. He could, standing in a highly disinfected office, catch the
smell of a woodbox and catalogue his legitimate concerns about tire
chains, snowplows, and supplies of groceries, fuel, and liquor—everything
that concerns a man in a remote house at the beginning of a tempest.
This was a memory, of course, seizing someplace in the present, but why
should he, in an antiseptic room in midsummer, have unwillingly received
such a memory? He tried to track it down on the evidence of smell. A
wooden match burning in an ashtray might have provoked the memory,
and he had been skeptical about his sensual responsiveness ever since he
had, while watching the approach of a thunderstorm, been disconcerted
by a wet and implacable erection. But if he could explain this duality by
the smoke of a burning match, he could not explain that the vividness of
his farmhouse memory deeply challenged the reality of the office where
he stood. To weaken and dispel the unwanted memory, he forced his
mind beyond the office, which was indeed artificial, to the incontestable
fact that it was the nineteenth of July, the temperature outside was ninety-
two, the time was three-eighteen, and he had eaten for lunch scallops or
cod cheeks with sweet tartar sauce, sour fried potatoes, salad, half a roll
with butter, ice cream, and coffee. Armed with these indisputable details,
he seemed to scourge the farmhouse memory as one opens doors and
windows to get the smoke out of a room. He was successful at establishing

the reality of the office, and while he was not truly uneasy about the experience, it had very definitely raised a question for which he had no information at all.

With the exception of organized religion and triumphant fucking, Farragut considered transcendent experience to be perilous rubbish. One saved one's ardor for people and objects that could be used. The flora and fauna of the rain forest were incomprehensible, but one could comprehend the path that led to one's destination. However, at Falconer the walls and the bars had sometimes seemed to threaten to vanish, leaving him with a nothingness that would be worse. He was, for example, waked early one morning by the noise of the toilet and found himself among the receding fragments of some dream. He was not sure of the depth of the dream—of its profundity—but he had never (nor had his psychiatrists) been able to clearly define the moraines of consciousness that compose the shores of waking. In the dream he saw the face of a beautiful woman he enjoyed but had never much loved. He also saw or felt the presence of one of the great beaches on a sea island. A nursery rhyme or jingle was being sung. He pursued these receding fragments as if his life, his self-esteem, depended upon his bringing them together into a coherent and useful memory. They fled, they fled purposefully like the carrier in a football game, and one by one he saw the woman and the presence of the sea disappear and heard the music of the jingle fade away. He checked his watch. It was three-ten. The commotion in the toilet subsided. He fell asleep.

Days, weeks, months, or whatever later, he waked from the same dream of the woman, the beach, and the song, pursued them with the same intensity that he had in the beginning, and one by one lost them while the music faded. Imperfectly remembered dreams—if they were pursued—were a commonplace, but the dispersal of this dream was unusually deep and vivid. He asked himself, from his psychiatric experience, if the dream was in color. It had been, but not brilliantly. The sea had been dark and the woman wore no lipstick, but the memory was not limited to black and white. He missed the dream. He was genuinely irritated at the fact that he had lost it. It was, of course, worthless, but it seemed like a talisman. He checked his watch and saw that it was three-ten. The toilet was still. He went back to sleep.

This happened again and again and perhaps again. The time was not always precisely three-ten, but it was always between three and four in the morning. He was always left irritable at the fact that his memory could, quite independently of anything he knew about himself, manipulate its resources in controlled and repeated designs. His memory enjoyed free will, and his irritability was increased by his realization that his memory was as unruly as his genitals. Then one morning, jogging from the mess to shop along the dark tunnel, he heard the music and saw the woman and the sea. He stopped so abruptly that several men banged into him, scattering the dream galley-west. That was that for the morning. But the dream was to reappear again and again in different places around the prison. Then one evening in his cell, as he was reading Descartes, he heard the music and waited for the woman and the sea. The cellblock was quiet. The circumstances for concentration were perfect. He reasoned that if he could pin down a line or two of the jingle, he would be able to reassemble the rest of the reverie. The words and the music were receding, but he was able to keep abreast of their retreat. He grabbed a pencil and a scrap of paper and was about to write down the lines he had captured when he realized that he did not know who or where he was, that the uses of the toilet he faced were completely mysterious, and that he could not understand a word of the book he held in his hands. He did not know himself. He did not know his own language. He abruptly stopped his pursuit of the woman and the music and was relieved to have them disappear. They took with them the absolute experience of alienation, leaving him with a light nausea. He was more shaken than wounded. He picked up the book and found that he could read. The toilet was for waste. The prison was called Falconer. He was convicted of murder. One by one he gathered up the details of the moment. They were not particularly sweet, but they were useful and durable. He did not know what would have happened had he copied down the words of the song. Neither death nor madness seemed involved, but he did not feel committed to discover what would happen if he pieced the reverie together. The reverie returned to him again and again, but he shrugged it off vigorously since it had nothing to do with the path he took or his destination.

"Knock, knock," said the Cuckold. It was late, but Tiny hadn't called lockup. Chicken Number Two and the Mad Dog Killer were playing rummy. Television was shit. The Cuckold came into Farragut's cell and sat in the chair. Farragut disliked him. His round pink face and his thin hair had not been changed at all by prison. The brilliant pinkness of the

Cuckold, his protuberant vulnerability—produced, it seemed, by alcohol and sexual embarrassment—had not lost its striking hue. "You miss Jody?" he asked. Farragut said nothing. "You score with Jody?" Farragut said nothing. "Hell, man, I know you do," said the Cuckold, "but I don't hold it against you. He was beautiful, he was just beautiful. Do you mind if I talk?"

"I've got a cab downstairs, waiting to take me to the airport," said Farragut. Then he said, sincerely, "No, no, no, I don't mind if you talk, I don't mind at all."

"I scored with a man," said the Cuckold. "That was after I had left my wife. That time I found her screwing this kid on the floor of the front hall. My thing with this man began in a Chinese restaurant. In those days I was the kind of lonely man you see eating in Chinese restaurants. You know? Anywhere in this country and in some parts of Europe where I've been. The Chung Fu Dynasty. The One Hung Low. Paper lanterns with teakwood frames all over the place. Sometimes they keep the Christmas lights up all year round. Paper flowers, many paper flowers. Large family groups. Also oddballs. Fat women. Square pegs. Jews. Sometimes lovers and always this lonely man. Me. We never eat the Chinese food, we lonely men. We always have the London broil or the Boston baked beans in Chinese restaurants. We're international. Anyhow, I'm a lonely man eating the London broil in a Chinese restaurant on the strip outside Kansas City. Any place that used to have a local option has a place outside the town limits where you used to have to go for liquor, cunt, a motel bed for a couple of hours.

"The place, this Chinese restaurant, is about half full. At a table is this young man. That's about it. He's good-looking, but that's because he's young. He'll look like the rest of the world in ten years. But he keeps looking at me and smiling. I honestly don't know what he's after. So then when I get my pineapple chunks, each one with a toothpick, and my fortune cookie, he comes over to my table and asks me what my fortune is. So I tell him I can't read my fortune without my glasses and I don't have my glasses and so he takes this scrap of paper and he reads or pretends to read that my fortune is I am going to have a beautiful adventure within the next hour. So I ask him what his fortune is and he says it's the same thing. He goes on smiling. He speaks real nicely but you could tell he was poor. You could tell that speaking nicely was something he learned. So when I go out he goes out with me. He asks where I'm staying at and I say I'm staying at this motel which is attached to the restaurant. Then he asks if I have anything to drink in my room and I say yes, would he like a drink, and he says he'd love a drink, and he puts his arm around my shoulder, very buddy-buddy, and we go to my room. So then he says can he make the drinks and I say sure and I tell him where the whiskey and the ice is and he makes some nice drinks and sits beside me and begins to kiss me on the face. Now, the idea of men kissing one another doesn't go down with me at all, although it gave me no pain. I mean a man kissing a woman is a plus and minus situation, but a man kissing a man except maybe in France is a very worthless two of a kind. I mean if someone took a picture of this fellow kissing me it would be for me a very strange and unnatural picture, but why should my cock have begun to put on weight if it was all so strange and unnatural? So then I thought what could be more strange and unnatural than a man eating baked beans alone in a Chinese restaurant in the Middle West—this was something I didn't invent—and when he felt for my cock, nicely and gently, and went on kissing me, my cock put on its maximum weight and began pouring out juice and when I felt for him he was halfway there.

"So then he made some more drinks and asked me why I didn't take off my clothes and I said what about him and he dropped his pants displaying a very beautiful cock and I took off my clothes and we sat bare-ass on the sofa drinking our drinks. He made a lot of drinks. Now and then he would take my cock in his mouth and this was the first time in my life that I ever had a mouth around my cock. I thought this would look like hell in a newsreel or on the front page of the newspaper, but evidently my cock hadn't ever seen a newspaper because it was going crazy. So then he suggested that we get into bed and we did and the next thing I knew the telephone was ringing and it was morning.

"It was all dark. I was alone. I had a terrible headache. I picked up the telephone and a voice said, 'The time is now seven-thirty.' Then I felt around in bed to see if there was any evidence of a come but there wasn't. Then I went to the closet and looked at my wallet and all the money—about fifty dollars—was gone. Nothing else, none of my credit cards. So the hustler had teased me, given me a Mickey Finn, and taken off with my money. I lost fifty dollars but I guessed I'd learned something. So while I was shaving the phone rang. It was the hustler. You'd think I'd be angry with him, wouldn't you, but I was all sweetness and friendliness. First he said he was sorry that he made my drinks so strong I had passed out. Then he said I shouldn't have given him all that money, that he wasn't worth it. Then he said he was sorry, that he wanted to give me a marvelous time for free, and when could we meet. So I knew he had teased me and stoned me and robbed me, but I wanted him badly and I said I would be in at about half past five and why didn't he come around then.

"I had four calls to make that day and I made them and I made three sales, which was good for that territory. I was feeling all right when I got back to the motel and I had some drinks and he came in at half past five and I mixed his drinks this time. He laughed when I did this but I didn't say anything about the Mickey. Then he took off his clothes and folded them neatly on a chair and he took off my clothes with some assistance from me and kissed me all over. Then he got a look at himself in the big mirror on the bathroom door and this was the first time I ever saw a man who was narcissistic, what they call. One look at himself naked in the mirror and he couldn't get away. He couldn't get enough of it. He couldn't tear himself away. So then I figured out my options. I had cashed a check and I had about sixty dollars in my wallet. I had to hide this. While he was loving himself I was worried about money. Then when I saw how deep he was, how really absorbed he was in the way he looked, I picked my clothes up off the floor and hung them in the closet. He didn't notice me, he didn't see anything but himself. So there he was, fondling his balls in the mirror, and there I was in the closet. I took the cash out of my wallet and stuffed it into the toe of my shoe. So then he finally separated from himself in the looking glass and joined me on the sofa and loved me up and when I came I nearly blew my eyeballs out. So then we got dressed and went out to the Chinese restaurant.

"When I got dressed I had some trouble getting into my shoe with the sixty dollars in the toe. I had credit cards to pay for dinner. When we walked to the restaurant he said why are you limping and I said I wasn't limping, but I guessed he knew where the money was. They took Carte Blanche at the restaurant and so I wasn't a lonely man in a Chinese restaurant anymore, I was an old queer with a young queer in a Chinese restaurant. I've been looking down my nose at couples like this all my life, but I've felt worse. We had this very big, very good dinner and so then I paid the check with my Carte Blanche and he said didn't I have any cash and I said no, I'd given it all to him, hadn't I, and he laughed and we went back to my room although I was very careful not to limp and wondered what I would do with the sixty dollars because I wasn't going to pay him that much. So then I hid my shoe in a dark corner and we got into bed and he loved me up again and then we talked and I asked him who he was and he told me.

"He said his name was Giuseppe or Joe but he changed it to Michael. His father was Italian. His mother was white. His father had a dairy farm in Maine. He went to school but he worked for his father in his time off and he was about nine when the chief at the dairy farm started to blow him. He liked it and it got to be a daily thing until the dairy chief asked him if he would take it up the ass. He was eleven or twelve then. It took four or five tries before he got it all the way in but when it worked it felt wonderful and they did this all the time. But it was a very hard life going to school and working on the farm and never seeing anybody but the dairy chief so then he began to hustle, first in the nearest town and then the nearest city and then all the way across the country and around the world. He said that that's what he was, a hustler, and that I shouldn't feel sorry for him or wonder what would become of him.

"All the time he was talking I listened very carefully to him, expecting him to sound like a fairy, but he never did, not that I could hear. I have this very strong prejudice against fairies. I've always thought they were silly and feebleminded, but he talked like anybody else. I was really very interested in what he had to say because he seemed to me very gentle and affectionate and even very pure. Lying in bed with me that night he seemed to me about the purest person I have ever known because he didn't have any conscience at all, I guess I mean he didn't have any prefabricated conscience. He just moved through it all like a swimmer through pure water. So then he said he was sleepy and tired and I said I was sleepy and tired and he said he was sorry he robbed me of the money but he hoped he'd made it up to me and I said he had and then he said that he knew I had some cash in my shoe but that he wasn't going to steal it and that I shouldn't worry and so we fell asleep. It was a nice sleep and when we woke in the morning I made some coffee and we joked and shaved and dressed and there was all the money in my shoe and I said I was late and he said he was late too and I said late for what and he said he had a client waiting in room 273 and then he asked did I mind and I said no, I guessed I didn't mind, and then he said could we meet at around half past five and I said sure.

"So he went his way and I went mine and I made five sales that day and I thought that he wasn't only pure, he was lucky, and I felt very happy coming back to the motel and I took a shower and had a couple of drinks. There was no sign of him at half past five and no sign of him at half past six or seven and I guessed he'd found a customer who didn't keep his money in his shoe and I missed him, but then sometime after seven the phone rang and I slid a base to get it, thinking it was Michael, but it was the police. They asked if I knew him and I said sure I knew him, because I did. So then they asked could I come down to the county courthouse and I asked what for and they said they'd tell me when I got there so I said I would be there. I asked the man in the lobby how to get to the county courthouse and he told me and then I drove there. I thought perhaps he'd been picked up on some charge like vagrancy and needed bail and I was willing, I was willing and eager to bail him out. So when I spoke to the lieutenant who called me he was nice enough but also sad and he said how well did I know Michael and I said I'd met him at the Chinese restaurant and had some drinks with him. He said they weren't charging me with anything but did I know him well enough to identify him and I said of course, thinking that he might be in some lineup although I had already begun to sense that it would be something more serious and grave, as it was. I followed him down some stairs and I could tell by the stink where we were going and there were all these big drawers like a walk-in filing cabinet and he pulled one out and there was Michael, very dead, of course. The lieutenant said they got him with a knife in the back, twenty-two times, and the cop, the lieutenant, said he was very big in drugs, very active, and I guess somebody really hated him. They must have gone on knifing him long after he was dead. So then the lieutenant and I shook hands and I think he gave me a searching look to see if I was an addict or a queer and then he gave me a broad smile of relief which meant that he didn't think I was either although I could have made this all up. I went back to the motel and had about seventeen more drinks and cried myself to sleep."

~   ~   ~

It was not that night but sometime later that the Cuckold told Farragut about the Valley. The Valley was a long room off the tunnel to the left of the mess hall. Along one wall was a cast-iron trough of a urinal. The light in the room was very dim. The wall above the urinal was white tiling with a very limited power of reflection. You could make out the height and the complexion of the men on your left and your right, and that was about all. The Valley was where you went after chow to fuck yourself. Almost no one but killjoys strayed into the dungeon for a simple piss. There were ground rules. You could touch the other man's hips and shoulders, but nothing else. The trough accommodated twenty men, and twenty men stood there, soft, hard, or halfway in either direction, fucking themselves. If you finished and wanted to come again you went to the end of the line. There were the usual jokes. How many times, Charlie? Five coming up, but my feet are getting sore.

Considering the fact that the cock is the most critical link in our chain of survival, the variety of shapes, colors, sizes, characteristics, dispositions, and responses found in this rudimentary tool are much greater than those shown by any other organ of the body. They were black, white, red, yellow, lavender, brown, warty, wrinkled, comely, and silken, and they seemed, like any crowd of men on a street at closing time, to represent youth, age, victory, disaster, laughter, and tears. There were the frenzied and compulsive pumpers, the long-timers who caressed themselves for half an hour, there were the groaners and the ones who sighed, and most of the men, when their trigger was pulled and the fusillade began, would shake, buck, catch their breath, and make weeping sounds, sounds of grief, of joy, and sometimes death rattles. There was some rightness in having the images of the lovers around them opaque. They were universal, they were phantoms, and any skin sores, or signs of cruelty, ugliness, stupidity, or beauty, could not be seen. Farragut went here regularly after Jody was gone.

When Farragut arced or pumped his rocks into the trough he endured no true sadness—mostly some slight disenchantment at having spilled his energy onto iron. Walking away from the trough, he felt that he had missed the train, the plane, the boat. He had missed it. He experienced some marked physical relief or improvement: the shots cleared his brain. Shame and remorse had nothing to do with what he felt, walking away from the trough. What he felt, what he saw, was the utter poverty of erotic reasonableness. That was how he missed the target, and the target was the mysteriousness of the bonded spirit and the flesh. He knew it well. Fitness and beauty had a rim. Fitness and beauty had a dimension, had a floor, even as the oceans have a floor, and he had committed a trespass. It was not unforgivable—a venal trespass—but he was reproached by the majesty of the realm. It was majestic; even in prison he knew the world to be majestic. He had taken a pebble out of his shoe in the middle of mass. He remembered the panic he had experienced as a boy when he found his trousers, his hands, and his shirttails soaked with crystallizing gism. He had learned from the *Boy Scout Handbook* that his prick would grow as long and thin as a shoelace, and that the juice that had poured out of his crack was the cream of his brain power. This miserable wetness proved that he would fail his College Board exams and have to attend a broken-down agricultural college somewhere in the Middle West. . . .

~ ~ ~

Then Marcia returned in her limitless beauty, smelling of everything provocative. She did not kiss him, nor did he try to cover her hand with his. "Hello, Zeke," she said. "I have a letter here from Pete."

"How is he?"

"He seems very well. He's either away at school or camp, and I don't see anything of him. His advisers tell me that he is friendly and intelligent."

"Can he come to see me?"

"They think not, not at this time of his life. Every psychiatrist and counselor I've talked with, and I've been very conscientious about this, feels that since he's an only child, the experience of visiting his father in prison would be crippling. I know you have no use for psychologists, and I'm inclined to agree with you, but all we can do is to take the advice of the most highly recommended and experienced men, and that is their opinion."

"Can I see his letter?"

"You can if I can find it. I haven't been able to find anything today. I don't believe in poltergeists, but there are days when I can find things and there are days when I cannot. Today is one of the worst. I couldn't find the top to the coffeepot this morning. I couldn't find the oranges. Then I couldn't find the car keys, and when I found them and drove to get the cleaning woman I couldn't remember where she lived. I couldn't find the dress I wanted, I couldn't find my earrings. I couldn't find my stockings, and I couldn't find my glasses to look for my stockings." He might have killed her then had she not found an envelope on which his name was written clumsily in lead pencil. She put this on the counter. "I didn't ask him to write the letter," she said, "and I have no idea of what it contains. I suppose I should have shown it to the counselors, but I knew you would rather I didn't."

"Thank you," said Farragut. He put the letter into his shirt, next to his skin.

"Aren't you going to open it?"

"I'll save it."

"Well, you're lucky. So far as I know, it's the first letter he's ever written in his life. So tell me how you are, Zeke. I can't say that you look well, but you look all right. You look very much like yourself. Do you still dream about your blonde? You do, of course; that I can easily see. Don't you understand that she never existed, Zeke, and that she never will? Oh, I can tell by the way you hold your head that you still dream about that blonde who never menstruated or shaved her legs or challenged anything you said or did. I suppose you have boyfriends in here?"

"I've had one," said Farragut, "but I didn't take it up the ass. When I die, you can put on my headstone: 'Here lies Ezekiel Farragut, who never took it up the ass.' "

She seemed suddenly touched by this, suddenly she seemed to find in herself some admiration for him; her smile and her presence seemed accommodating and soft. "Your hair has turned white, dear," she said. "Did you know that? You haven't been here a year, and yet your hair has turned snow white. It's very becoming. Well, I'll have to go. I've left your groceries in the package room." He carried the letter until the lights and the television were extinguished and read, in the glare from the yard, "I love you."

As the day of the cardinal's arrival approached, even the lifers said they had never seen such excitement. Farragut was kept busy cutting dittos for order sheets, instructions, and commands. Some of the orders seemed insane. For example: "It is mandatory that all units of inmates marching to and from the parade grounds will sing 'God Bless America.' " Common sense killed this one. No one obeyed the order, and no one tried to enforce it. Every day for ten days the entire population was marshaled out onto the gallows field, the ballpark, and what had now become the parade grounds. They were made to practice standing at attention, even in the pouring rain. They remained excited, and there was a large element of seriousness in the excitement. When Chicken Number Two did a little hornpipe and sang: "Tomorrow's the day they give cardinals away with a half pound of cheese," no one laughed, no one at all. Chicken Number Two was an asshole. On the day before his arrival, every man took a shower. The hot water ran out at around eleven in the morning, and cellblock F didn't get into the showers until after chow. Farragut was back in his cell, shining his shoes, when Jody returned.

He heard the hooting and whistling and looked up to see Jody walking toward his cell. Jody had put on weight. He looked well. He walked toward Farragut with his nice, bouncy jock walk. Farragut much preferred this to the sinuous hustle Jody put on when he was hot and his pelvis seemed to grin like a pumpkin. The sinuous hustle had reminded Farragut of vines, and vines, he knew, had to be cultivated or they could harass and destroy stone towers, castles, and cathedrals. Vines could pull down a basilica. Jody came into his cell and kissed him on the mouth. Only Chicken Number Two whistled. "Good-bye, sweetheart," he said. "Good-bye," said Farragut. His feelings were chaotic and he might have cried, but he might have cried at the death of a cat, a broken shoelace, a wild pitch. He could kiss Jody passionately, but not tenderly. Jody turned and walked away. Farragut had done nothing with Jody so exciting as to say good-bye. Among the beaches and graves and other matters he had unearthed in seeking the meaning of his friendship, he had completely overlooked the conspiratorial thrill of seeing his beloved escape.

Tiny called the lockup for eight and made the usual jokes about beauty sleep and meat beating. He said, of course, that he wanted his men to look beautiful for the cardinal. He pulled the light switch at nine. The only light was the television. Farragut went to bed and to sleep. The roar of the toilet woke him, and then he heard thunder. At first the noise pleased and excited him. The random explosions of thunder seemed to explain that heaven was not an infinity but a solid construction of domes, rotundas, and arches. Then he remembered that the flier had said that in case of rain the ceremony would be canceled. The thought of a thunderstorm inaugurating a rainy day deeply disturbed him. Naked, he went to the window. This naked man was worried. If it rained, there would be no escape, no cardinal, no nothing. Have pity upon him, then; try to understand his fears. He was lonely. His love, his world, his everything, was gone. He wanted to see a cardinal in a helicopter. Thunderstorms, he thought hopefully, could bring in anything. They could bring in a cold front, a hot front, a day when the clearness of the light would seem to carry one from hour to hour. Then the rain began. It poured into the prison and that part of the world. But it lasted only ten minutes. Then the rain, the storm, swept mercifully off to the north, and just as swiftly and just as briefly that rank and vigorous odor that is detonated by the rain flew up to and above where Farragut stood at his barred window. He had, with his long, long nose, responded to this cutting fragrance wherever he had been—shouting, throwing out his arms, pouring a drink. Now there was a trace, a memory, of this primitive excitement, but it had been cruelly eclipsed by the bars. He got back into bed and fell asleep, listening to the rain dripping from the gun towers.

~ ~ ~

Farragut got what he had bargained for: a day of incomparable beauty. Had he been a free man, he would have claimed to be able to walk on the light. It was a holiday; it was the day of the big rugby game; it was the circus; it was the Fourth of July; it was the regatta; and it dawned as it should, clear and cool and beautiful. They had two pieces of bacon for breakfast, through the bounty of the diocese. Farragut went down the tunnel to the methadone line, and even this rat tail of humanity seemed to be jumping with high spirits. At eight they stood by their cell doors, shaved, wearing their white shirts and some of them with ointment in their hair; you could tell by the clash of perfumes that floated up and down the cellblock. Tiny inspected them and then there was, as there is for any holiday or ceremony, time to kill.

There was a cartoon show on television. They could hear whistles blowing on other cellblocks and guards with military backgrounds trying to shout their men into sharp formations. It was only a little after eight then, and the cardinal wasn't expected until noon, but men were already being marched out onto the gallows field. The walls checked the force of the late spring sun, but it would hit the field by noon. Chicken and the Cuckold shot dice. Farragut killed the time easily at the top of his methadone high. Time was new bread, time was a sympathetic element, time was water you swam in, time moved through the cellblock with the grace of light. Farragut tried to read. He sat on the edge of his bunk. He was a man of forty-eight, sitting on the edge of his bunk in a prison to which he had been unjustly confined for the murder of his brother. He was a man in a white shirt sitting on the edge of a bunk. Tiny blew his whistle, and they stood at attention in front of their cells again. They did this four times. At half past ten they were lined up two by two and marched down the tunnel, where they formed up in a pie-shaped area marked "F" with lime.

The light had begun to come into the field. Oh, it was a great day. Farragut thought about Jody and wondered if he didn't bring it off would he get cell lock or the hole or maybe seven more years for attempted escape. So far as he knew, he and the chaplain's dude were the only ones in on the plot. Then Tiny called them to attention. "Now, I got to have your cooperation," Tiny said. "It ain't easy for any of us to have two thousand shitheads out here together. The tower guards today is been replaced with crack shots, and as you know, they got the right to shoot any inmate they got suspicions about. We got crack shots today, so they won't be no spray firing. The leader of the Black Panthers has agreed not to give the salute. When the cardinal comes you stand at parade rest. Any of you ain't been in the service, ask some friend what parade rest is. It's like this. Twenty-five men has been picked to take the Holy Eucharist. The cardinal's got lots of appointments, and he's going to be here only twenty minutes. First we hear from the warden and then the commissioner, who's coming down from Albany. After this he gives out the diplomas, celebrates mass, blesses the rest of you assholes, and takes off. I guess you can sit down if you want. You can sit down, but when you get the order for attention I want you all straight and neat and clean, with your heads up. I want to be proud of you. If you have to piss, piss, but don't piss where anybody's going to be sitting." Cheers for Tiny, and then most of them pissed. There was, Farragut thought, some universality to a full bladder. For this length of time they perfectly understood one another. Then they sat down.

Somebody was testing the public address system: "Testing, one, two, three. Testing, one, two, three." The voice was loud and scratchy. Time passed. God's advocate was punctual. At a quarter to twelve they got the command for attention. They shaped up nicely. The sound of the chopper could be heard then, bounding off the hills, loud at low altitudes, faintly, faintly in the deep river valley; soft and loud, hills and valleys, the noise evoked the contour of the terrain beyond the walls. The chopper, when it came into view, had no more grace than an airborne washing machine, but this didn't matter at all. It lofted gently onto the target, and out the door came three acolytes, a monsignor in black, and the cardinal himself, a man either graced by God with great dignity and beauty or singled out by the diocese for these distinctions. He raised his hand. His ring flashed with spiritual and political power. "I seen better rings on hustlers," Chicken Number Two whispered. "No fence would give you thirty. The last time I hit a jewelry store I fenced the lot for—" Looks shut him up. Everybody turned and put him down.

The crimson of the cardinal's robes seemed living and pure, and his carriage was admirable and would have quelled a riot. He stepped out of the helicopter, lifting his robes not at all like a woman leaving a taxi but like a cardinal leaving his airborne transport. He made a sign of the cross as high and wide as his reach, and the great spell of worship fell over that place. *In nomine Patris et Filii et Spiritus Sancti.* Farragut would have liked to pray for the happiness of his son, his wife, the safety of his lover, the soul of his dead brother, would have liked to pray for some enlargement of his wisdom, but the only word he could root out of these massive intentions was his *Amen. Amen,* said a thousand others, and the word, from so many throats, came up from the gallows field as a solemn whisper.

Then the public address system began to work so well that the confusion that followed could be heard by everyone. "Now you go first," said the commissioner to the warden. "No, you go," said the warden to the commissioner. "It says here that you go." "I said you go," said the commissioner angrily to the warden, and the warden stepped forward, knelt, kissed the cardinal's ring, and, standing, said: "The graciousness of Your Eminence in endangering life and limb in order to come and visit us in the Falconer Rehabilitation Center is greatly appreciated by me and the deputy wardens, the guards, and all the inmates. It reminds me of how when I was a little boy and sleepy my father carried me from the car into the house at the end of a long trip. I was a load to carry, but I knew how kind he was being to me, and that's the way I feel today."

There was applause—exactly the noise of water striking stone—but unlike the indecipherable noise of water, its intent was clearly grateful and polite. Farragut remembered applause most vividly when he had heard it outside the theater, hall, or church where it sounded. He had heard it most clearly as a bystander waiting in a parking lot on a summer night, waiting for the show to break. It had always astonished and deeply moved him to realize that so diverse and warlike a people could have agreed on this signal of enthusiasm and assent. The warden passed the public address system to the commissioner. The commissioner had gray hair, wore a gray suit and a gray tie, and reminded Farragut of the grayness and angularity of office filing cabinets in the far, far away. "Your Eminence," he said, reading his speech from a paper and evidently for the first time. "Ladies and gentlemen." He frowned, raised his face and his heavy eyebrows at this error of his speechwriter. "Gentlemen!" he exclaimed. "I want to express my gratitude and the gratitude of the governor to the cardinal, who for the first time in the history of this diocese and perhaps in the whole history of mankind has visited a rehabilitation center in a helicopter. The governor sends his sincere regrets at not being able to express his gratitude in person, but he is, as you must all know, touring the flood-disaster areas in the northwestern part of the state. We hear these days"—he picked up a head of steam—"a great deal about prison reform. Best-sellers are written about prison reform. Professional so-called penologists travel from coast to coast, speaking on prison reform. But where does prison reform begin? In bookstores? In lecture halls? *No.* Prison reform, like all sincere endeavors at reform, begins at home, and where is home? Home is prison! We have come here today to commemorate a bold step made possible by the Fiduciary University of Banking, the archdiocese, the Department of Correction, and above all the prisoners themselves. All four of us together have accomplished what we might compare—compare only, of course—to a miracle. These eight humble men have passed with honors a most difficult test that many well-known captains of industry have failed. Now, I know that you all have, unwillingly, sacrificed your right to vote upon coming here—a sacrifice that the governor intends to change—and should you, at some later date, find his name on a ballot, I'm sure you will remember today." He shot his cuff to check the time. "As I present these coveted diplomas, please refrain from applause until the presentation is completed. Frank Masullo, Herman Meany, Mike Thomas, Henry Phillips . . ." When the last of the diplomas had been presented, he lowered his voice in a truly moving shift from secular to spiritual matters and said, "His Eminence will now celebrate mass." At exactly that moment Jody came out of the boiler room behind the bench, genuflected deeply at the cardinal's back, and took his place at the right of the altar, the consummate figure of a tardy acolyte who has just taken a piss.

Adiutorium nostrum in Nomine Domini. The raptness of prayer enthralled Farragut as the raptness of love. *Misereatur tui omnipotens Deus et dismissis pecatis tuis. Misereatur vestri omnipotens Deus et dismissis pecatis vestris perducat vos ad vitam aeternam. Indulgentiam, absolutionem, et remissionem pecatorum nostrorum tribuat nobis omnipotens et misericors Dominus. Deus tu conversus vivificabis nos. Ostende nobis, Domine misericordiam tuam.* On it drummed to the *Benedicat* and the last *Amen.* Then he performed another large cross and returned to the helicopter, followed by his retinue, including Jody.

The props kicked up a cloud of dust, and the engine ascended. Someone put a recording of cathedral bells on the public address system, and up they went to this glorious clamor. Oh, glory, glory, glory! The exaltation of the bells conquered the scratching of the needle and a slight warp in the record. The sound of the chopper and the bells filled heaven and earth. They all cheered and cheered and cheered, and some of them cried. The sound of the bells stopped, but the chopper went on playing its geodetic survey of the surrounding terrain—the shining, lost, and beloved world.

~   ~   ~

The cardinal's helicopter landed at La Guardia, where two large cars were waiting. Jody had seen cars like this in the movies and nowhere else. His Eminence and the monsignor took one. The acolytes filled the second. Jody's excitement was violent. He was shaking. He tried to narrow his thinking down to two points. He would get drunk. He would get laid. He held to these two points with some success, but his palms were sweaty, his ribs were running with sweat, and sweat ran down his brows into his eyes. He held his hands together to conceal their shaking. He was afraid that when the car reached its destination he would be unable to walk as a free man. He had forgotten how. He imagined that the paving would fly up and strike him between the eyes. He then convinced himself that he was playing a part in a miracle, that there was some congruence between his escape and the will of God. Play it by ear. "Where are we going?" he asked one of the others. "To the cathedral, I guess," he said. "That's where we left our clothes. Where did you come from?" "Saint Anselm's," said Jody. "I mean how did you get to the prison?" "I went out early," Jody said. "I went out on the train."

The city out of the car windows looked much wilder and stranger than beautiful. He imagined the length of time it would take—he saw time as a length of road, something measured by surveyors' instruments —before he could move unselfconsciously. When the car stopped he opened the door. The cardinal was going up the steps of the cathedral, and two of the people on the sidewalk knelt. Jody stepped out of the car.

There was no strength at all in his legs. Freedom hit him like a gale wind. He fell to his knees and broke the fall with his hands. "Shit, man, you drunk?" the next acolyte asked. "Fortified wine," said Jody. "That wine was fortified." Then his strength returned, all of it, and he got to his feet and followed the others into the cathedral and to a vestry much like any other. He took off his robe and while the other men put on ties and jackets he tried to invest his white shirt, his issue fatigues, and his basketball sneakers with respectability. He did this by bracing his shoulders. He saw himself in a long glass, and he saw that he looked emphatically like an escaped convict. There was nothing about him—his haircut, his pallor, his dancy step—that a half-blind drunk wouldn't have put down as a prison freak. "His Eminence would like to speak to you," the monsignor said. "Please follow me."

A door was opened, and he went into a room a little like the priest's front parlor at home. The cardinal stood there, now in a dark suit, and held out his right hand. Jody knelt and kissed the ring. "Where are you from?" "Saint Anselm's, Your Eminence," said Jody. "There is no Saint Anselm's in the diocese," said the cardinal, "but I know where you're from. I don't know why I asked. Time must play an important part in your plans. I expect you have about fifteen minutes. It is exciting, isn't it? Let's get out of here." They left the parlor and the cathedral. On the sidewalk a woman knelt and the cardinal gave her his ring to kiss. She was, Jody saw, an actress he had seen on television. Another woman knelt and kissed his ring before they reached the end of the block. They crossed the street and a third woman knelt and kissed his ring. For her he wearily made a sign of the cross; and then they went into a store. The acknowledgment of their arrival was a matter of seconds. Someone of authority approached them and asked if the cardinal wanted a private room. "I'm not sure," he said. "I'll leave it up to you. This young man and I have an important appointment in fifteen minutes. He is not wearing the right clothes." "We can manage," the authority said. Jody was measured with a tape. "You're built like a tailor's dummy," said the man. This went to Jody's head, but he definitely felt that vanity was out of place in the miracle. Twenty minutes later he walked up Madison Avenue. His walk was springy—the walk of a man going to first on balls, which can, under some circumstances, seem to be a miracle.

~ *William Maxwell* ~

FROM

The Folded
Leaf

T he fraternity house which was referred to with such a carefully casual
air in LeClerc's was a one-room basement apartment that Bud Griesenauer got for five dollars a month through an uncle in the real estate
business.

They took possession on Groundhog Day and spent Saturday and
Sunday calcimining the walls a sickly green. The woodwork, the floor,
and the brick fireplace were scrubbed with soap and water, but there was
nothing much that they could do about the pipes on the ceiling, and they
decided not to bother with curtains even though small boys peered in
the windows occasionally and had to be chased away.

The apartment was furnished with a worn grass rug, a couch, a bookcase, and three uncomfortable chairs from the Edwards' attic. Carson
brought an old Victrola, which had to be wound before and then again
during every record, and sometimes it made terrible grinding noises. Mark
Wheeler contributed a large framed picture of a handsome young collegian with his hair parted in the middle, enjoying his own fireside, his
pennants, and the smoke that curled upward from the bowl of his long-

*WILLIAM MAXWELL may be the most underappreciated great American fiction writer
of the century. A longtime editor at* The New Yorker, *he is the author of many extraordinary novels, among them* So Long, See You Tomorrow; The Chateau, *an incan-
descent account of a young couple's experience of France just after the Second World War;
and of course* The Folded Leaf, *an excerpt from which is included here.*

210

stemmed clay pipe. The title of the picture was "Pipe-Dreams," and they gave it the place of honor over the mantel. The only other picture they were willing to hang in the apartment was of an ugly English bulldog looking out through a fence. This had been given to Mr. and Mrs. Snyder twenty-two years before, as a wedding present. The glass was underneath the slats in the fence, and they were real wood, varnished and joined at the top and bottom to the picture frame.

To get to the fraternity from school the boys had to take a southbound Clark Street car and get off and wait on a windy street corner, by a cemetery, until a westbound Montrose Street car came along. It was usually dark when they reached the apartment, and a grown person would have found the place dreary and uninviting, but they had a special love for it, from the very beginning. This was partly because it had to be kept secret. They could talk about it safely in LeClerc's but not at school, in their division rooms, where the teacher might overhear them and report it to the principal. And partly because they knew instinctively that sooner or later the apartment would be taken away from them. They were too young to be allowed to have a place of their own, and so they lived in it as intensely and with as much pleasure as small children live in the houses which they make for themselves on rainy days, out of chairs and rugs, a fire screen, a footstool, a broomstick, and the library table.

Sometimes the boys came in a body, after school; sometimes by two and threes. Carson and Lynch were almost always there, and when Ray Snyder came it was usually with Bud Griesenauer or Harry Hall. Catanzano and deFresne came together, as a rule, and Bob Edwards and Mark Wheeler. Lymie Peters attached himself to any group or any pair of friends he could find, and once Spud Latham turned up with a blond boy from Lake View High School, who kept tossing his hair out of his eyes. He didn't think much of the apartment and made Spud go off with him somewhere on his bicycle. Later, without being exactly unpleasant to Spud, they managed to convey to him that he had made a mistake in bringing an outsider to the fraternity house, and after that, when Spud came, which was not very often, he came alone. Ford also came alone. As a result of his refusing to jump off a stepladder blindfolded, he was now known as "Steve Brodie" and sometimes "Diver" and he had stopped going to LeClerc's.

The fraternity house was a place to try things. Catanzano and deFresne smoked their first cigars there and were sick afterwards, out in the areaway. Ray Snyder fought his way through "I Dreamt I Dwelt in Marble Halls" on the ukulele, and Harry Hall appeared one day with a copy of Balzac's *Droll Stories,* which he had swiped from the bookcase at his grandfather's. It was referred to as the dirty book, and somebody was always off in a corner or stretched out on the couch, reading it.

One afternoon when Carson and Lynch walked in they found Dede Sandstrom and a fat-cheeked girl named Edith Netedu side by side on the couch, with an ashtray and a box of Pall Malls between them. The girl sat up and began to fuss with her hair, and Dede said, "Haven't you two guys got any home to go to?"

Carson and Lynch had a feeling that maybe they weren't wanted, but they took off their caps and coats and stayed. Dede wound the Victrola and put a record on, and after the girl had danced with him a couple of times she asked Carson and then Lynch to dance with her. Both of them were conscious of her perfume and of her arm resting lightly on their shoulders, and they felt that the place was different. Something that had been lacking before (the very thing, could it have been, that made them want the apartment in the first place?) had been found. They went off to the drugstore and came back with four malted milks, in cardboard containers, and it was like a party, like a housewarming.

The other girls who ate lunch at LeClerc's knew about the apartment and were curious about it, but they wouldn't go there. Edith Netedu was the only one. She was there quite often. She came with Dede Sandstrom, but she belonged to all of them. They dressed up in her hat and coat and teased her about her big hips and snatched her high-heeled pumps off and hid or played catch with them and fought among each other for the privilege of dancing with her. She was a very good dancer, and the boys liked particularly to waltz with her. She never seemed to get dizzy, no matter how much they whirled. They took turns, trying to make her fall down, and when one of the boys began to stagger, another would step in and take his place. Finally, when they were all sprawling on the couch or the floor, Dede Sandstrom would take over and dance with her quietly, cheek to cheek.

When she was there, the place was at its best. They sang and did card tricks. Ray Snyder's ukulele was passed around, and sometimes they just talked, in a relaxed way, about school and what colleges were the best and how much money they were going to make when they finished studying and got out into the world. Edith Netedu said she was going to marry a millionaire and have three children, all boys; and she was going to name them Tom, Dick, and Harry. When she and Dede Sandstrom put on their coonskin coats and tied their woolen mufflers under their chins and went out, they left sadness behind them. . . .

~ ~ ~

In April there was trouble over the fraternity house. It began on a rainy Monday afternoon. Six of them were there. Catanzano had a sprained ankle and was enthroned on the couch. The others were trying out his crutches. Lynch was about to play a medley of songs from "No, No, Nanette" on the Victrola when the janitor, who was a Belgian, walked in. He had a couple with him—a very tall man whose wrists hung down out of the sleeves of his black overcoat and a woman in a purple suit with a cheap fur neckpiece, blondined hair, blue eyes, and very red skin. She looked around critically and then said, "Fourteen dollars?"

The janitor nodded.

"Well," the woman said, "I don't know." She crossed the room and would have tripped over Catanzano's bandaged foot if he hadn't drawn it hastily out of the way. The other boys stood still, like figures in some elaborate musical parlor game.

The man couldn't have been more than five years older than Mark Wheeler, but life had already proved too much for him. There was no color in his long thin face. The skin was drawn tight over his cheekbones. His hair was receding from his temples, and something about him—the look in his eyes, mostly—suggested a conscious determination to shed his flesh at the earliest possible moment and take refuge in his dry skeleton.

The woman was almost old enough to be his mother, but there was nothing maternal or gentle about her. She went into the bathroom and came out again, inspected the only closet, discovered that there were no wall plugs, and sniffed the air, which smelled strongly of wet wool. Still undecided, she wandered back to the door.

"I've never lived in a basement apartment before," she said, turning to the man, "and I'm kind of afraid of the dampness. On account of my asthma."

"Is not damp," the janitor said.

"Maybe not now with the heat on, but in summer I bet it's good and damp. . . . What about it, Fred?"

The young man was looking at the picture of the English bulldog. "It's up to you," he said. "I'll be away all day."

"Well, I guess I'll have to think about it," the woman said, shifting her fur. The expression on her face was like a pout, but she wasn't pouting, actually; she was thinking. "I don't want to move in and unpack everything and then find out that I can't breathe," she said. And then, turning to the janitor, "We'll let you know."

She looked once more at the boys without seeing them and walked out. The janitor followed, and after him the young man, who had a sudden coughing fit in the areaway and left the door wide open behind him.

Lymie Peters was the first to recover. He was standing in a draft and he sneezed. Dede Sandstrom walked over to the door and slammed it. As if a spell had been lifted, the Victrola needle came to rest on the opening bars of "I Want to Be Happy," and they all started talking at once. Their excitement, the pitch of their immature voices, the gestures which they made with their hands, and their uneasy profanity were all because of one thing which none of them dared say: Their house, their fraternity (which stood in the minds of all of them like a beautiful woman that they were too young to have) was as good as gone. If these people didn't take it, the next ones would.

The record came to an end, and the turntable of the Victrola went round and round slower and slower until at last it stopped. Mark Wheeler and Dede Sandstrom went out and called Bud Griesenauer, who wasn't home. His mother didn't know where they could reach him. On their way back to the apartment they met the janitor in the areaway. Mark Wheeler walked up to him and said, "What's the big idea?"

The janitor shrugged his shoulders. "I show the apartment, that's all."

"But it's our apartment," Dede Sandstrom said. "We pay rent on it."

"Maybe somebody else pay more rent on it," the janitor said, and disappeared into the boiler room.

The second indignation meeting lasted until almost dinnertime. On the way home Lymie Peters stopped in a drugstore and called Bud Griesenauer. This time he was at home. They'd all been calling him, he said. Wheeler and Hall and Carson and Lynch and everybody. And he'd called his uncle. It was probably a misunderstanding of some kind, his uncle said, and maybe the people wouldn't rent the apartment after all. But if they did decide to take it, there was nothing anybody could do. The boys didn't have a lease, and the owner of the building naturally had a right to try to get as much money out of it as possible.

They held a special meeting the next afternoon, and it was decided that somebody should come down to the fraternity house every afternoon after school, in case the janitor showed the place to any more people; and that they should take turns staying there at night. The rest of the time they would lock the door with a padlock. They wrote days of the week on slips of paper and put them in Mark Wheeler's hat and passed the hat around. Lymie drew the following Friday, and Spud Latham offered to stay with him.

When they arrived Friday night, Lymie had three army blankets under one arm and a coffeepot under the other. Spud carried a knapsack containing all the equipment and food necessary for a large camp breakfast.

The apartment was very warm when they got there, but they built a fire in the fireplace anyway. Lymie sat on the floor in front of the fire and took off his shoes, which were wet, and loosened his tie and unbuttoned his shirt collar. Spud took all his clothes off except his shorts. Then he emptied the knapsack out on the hearth, arranging the skillet, the coffeepot, the iron grill, the plates, knives, forks, salt, and pepper so that they would all be ready and convenient the next morning. The food he put in the bathroom, on the windowsill, and the blankets he spread one by one, on the couch. Every movement of his body was graceful, easy, and controlled. Lymie, who was continually being surprised by what his own hands and feet were up to, enjoyed watching him. With the firelight shining on his skin and no other light in the room, Spud looked very much like the savage that he was playing at being.

When he had finished with the couch, he stretched out on top of the blankets, and there was so much harmony in the room that he said, "This is the life. No school tomorrow. Nobody to tell you when to go to bed. Plenty to eat and a good fire. Why didn't we think of this before?"

"I don't know," Lymie said. "Why didn't we?"

"There's always something," Spud said. The full implications of this remark, in spite of its vagueness, were deeply felt by both of them. Spud picked up the volume of Balzac's stories and read for a while, lying on his back with his knees raised. Lymie continued to sit in front of the fire, facing him. The expression in his eyes was partly pride (he had never had a friend before) and partly envy, though he didn't recognize it as that. He was comparing his own wrists, which were so thin that he could put his thumb and forefinger around one of them and still see daylight, to Spud's, which were strong and square. The wish closest to Lymie's heart, if he could have had it for the asking, would have been to have a well-built body, a body as strong and as beautifully proportioned as Spud's. Then all his troubles would have been over.

When Spud turned and lay on his stomach, Lymie got up and sat down beside him on the edge of the couch and began to read over Spud's shoulder: . . . *woman will heal thy wound, stop the waste hole in thy bag of tricks. Woman is thy wealth; have but one woman, dress, undress, and fondle that woman, make use of the woman . . . woman is everything . . . woman has an inkstand of her own; dip thy pen into that bottomless inkpot . . .* Without looking up, Spud rolled over on his back, so that Lymie could stretch out and read in comfort. But Lymie didn't move. His face was troubled. He started to say something, and then, after a second's hesitation, he went on reading: . . . *Woman makes love . . . make love to her with the pen only, tickle her fantasies and sketch merrily for her a thousand pictures of love in a thousand pretty ways. Woman is generous and all for one or one for all . . . must pay the painter and furnish the hairs of the brush . . .* At the bottom of the page Spud looked up to see if Lymie was still reading. Lymie had been finished for some time. He was staring at Spud's chest.

"Let's do something else," he said.

"Why?" Spud asked. "This is interesting." He rolled over on his stomach again and was about to go on reading when Lymie surprised him by grabbing the book out of his hands. It sailed across the room, into the blazing fire. Spud sat up and saw with a certain amount of regret that the flames were already licking at the open pages.

"What did you do that for?" he asked.

Instead of explaining, Lymie prodded at the book with the poker, so that the leaves burned faster. Pieces of charred paper detached themselves and were drawn, still glowing, up the chimney.

"You're going to have a hell of a time explaining to Hall about his book," Spud said.

"I'm not going to explain about it," Lymie said. His jaw was set, and Spud, realizing that Lymie was very close to tears, sank back on the couch as if nothing had happened.

After a week in which no one, so far as the boys knew, was shown through the apartment, they gave up staying there at night, and with the warm weather they stopped going to the fraternity house altogether. It took too long, and besides, they were suffering from spring fever. When they emerged from the school building at three o'clock with their ties loosened and their collars undone, they had no energy and no will. They stood around in the schoolyard watching baseball practice and leaning against each other for support. Any suggestion that anybody made always turned out to be too much trouble.

There is no telling how long it would have taken them to find out about the fraternity if Carson hadn't wanted suddenly to play his record of "I'll See You in My Dreams." The record was at the fraternity, and he asked Lynch to ride down there with him. Lynch's last report card was unsatisfactory and he wasn't allowed out after supper on week nights, so Carson went alone. When he came around the corner of the apartment building and saw the furniture clogging the areaway, he stopped short, unable to believe his eyes.

The couch was soggy and stained from being rained on. The chairs were coming unglued. There were wrinkles in the picture of the collegian, where the water had got in behind the glass, and the grass rug gave off a musty odor. The English bulldog was missing, but Lynch was too upset to notice this. It was his Victrola, the condition of his Victrola, that upset him most. The felt pad on the turntable had spots of mildew, the oak veneer of the case peeled off in strips, and both the needle and the arm were rusted. When he tried to wind it, the Victrola made such a horrible grinding sound that he gave up and went in search of the janitor. There was no one in the boiler room or in any of the various storerooms in the basement. He came back and tried the door of the apartment. The padlock that they had used was gone, and in its place was a new Yale lock. No one came to the door.

The Victrola records were warped and probably ruined, but he took them anyway and walked around to the front of the building, intending to peer in at the basement windows. They had net curtains across them, and he could see nothing. He went off down the street with the records under his arm and his spirits held up by anger and the melancholy pleasure of spreading the news.

~ ~ ~

With school almost over for the year and summer vacation looming ahead, the loss of a meeting place made very little difference to any of them. Spud Latham and Lymie Peters met in the corridor by Spud's locker after school and went off together. Lymie had a malted milk and Spud had a milk shake and then they came out of the stale air of LeClerc's and separated. Or else Lymie went home with Spud. He never asked Spud to come home with him, and Spud never suggested it. So far as he was concerned, Lymie belonged at his house and had no other home.

No matter how often Lymie went there, Mrs. Latham always seemed glad to see him. She treated him casually and yet managed to watch over him. When she caught him helping himself out of the icebox as if he lived there, all she said was "Lymie, there's some fudge cake in the cake-box. Wouldn't you rather have a piece of that?"

At mealtime there was a place for him at the dining room table, next to Spud. From the other side of the table Helen teased him because he didn't like parsnips or because he needed a haircut, and Mr. Latham used him as an excuse to tell long stories about the heating business.

After supper Lymie and Spud studied together in Spud's room until their minds wandered from the page and they started yawning. Then they got up and went across the street to the park and lay on the grass and stared into the evening sky and thought out loud about what the future had in store for them. Spud's heart was fixed on a cabin in the North Woods where they (it was understood that Lymie was to be with him) could fish in the summertime and in winter set trap lines and then sit around and be warm and comfortable indoors, with the wind howling and the snow banked up higher than the windows of the cabin. Lymie chewed on a blade of grass and didn't commit himself. It all seemed possible. Something that would require arranging perhaps (pleasant though such a life might be, there was obviously not going to be much money in it) but perfectly possible.

At nine-thirty or a quarter of ten he pulled Spud up off the grass and they went back across the street. Lymie gathered up his books and papers. As he passed by the living room door he said "Good night, everybody," and Helen and Mr. and Mrs. Latham looked up and nodded affection-ately, as if he had told them that he was going down to the drugstore on the corner and would be right back.

One day Mrs. Latham discovered that there was a button missing from his shirt after he and Spud had been doing push-ups on the living room rug. They looked under all the furniture without being able to find it, and then she made Lymie come into her bedroom with her while she hunted through her sewing box for another white button to sew on in place of the one he had lost. Something in the tone of her voice caught Spud's attention. He stood still in the center of the living room and listened, with a troubled expression on his face. His mother was talking to Lymie in a scolding way that was not really scolding at all and that he had never heard her use with anybody but him. He felt a sharp stab of jealousy. It was one thing to have a friend, but another to . . . He raised the sleeve of his coat and looked at it thoughtfully. A piece of brown thread dangled from the cuff where a button should have been.

"Speaking of buttons," he said quietly.

"Oh, all right," Mrs. Latham answered him from the bedroom. "I've been meaning to fix it, but I just didn't get around to it, with all there is to do in this house. Leave it on your bed when you go to school tomorrow. . . . Stand still, Lymie. I don't want to stick you. . . . And next time remember to save the button, do you hear? It isn't always easy to—"

She didn't bother to finish the sentence, but Spud's face cleared. He was reassured. His mother still loved him the most. She had heard him two rooms away, even though he hadn't raised his voice; and she knew exactly what button he was talking about.

Another afternoon when they got home from school, Spud was restless and wanted to go walking in the rain. They walked a long way west until they came to the Northwestern Railway tracks, where further progress was blocked by an interminable freight train. They stood and counted boxcars and coal cars and oil tankers, and the train shuddered violently once or twice and came to a dead stop. By that time they were tired of waiting for it to pass, and so they turned back. The soles of their shoes were soaked through, and the bottoms of their trousers were wet and kept flapping about their ankles. When they got home they hung their yellow slickers on the back porch to dry and retired to Spud's room with a quart of milk and a box of Fig Newtons. Noticing the hollows under Lymie's eyes, Spud decided that he ought to take a nap. There was plenty of time before dinner, and he began to undo Lymie's tie. Lymie refused, for no reason; or perhaps because Spud hadn't given him a chance to consider whether he was tired or not. Spud got the tie off, but when he tried to unbutton Lymie's shirt, Lymie began to fight him off. He had never really fought anybody before, and he fought with strength that he had no idea he possessed.

At first Spud was amused, and then suddenly it became a life-and-death matter. He wasn't quite sure how to come at Lymie, because Lymie didn't know the rules. He fought with his hands and his feet and his knees. He gouged at and he grabbed anything that he could lay hands on. Each time that Spud managed to get his arms around Lymie he twisted and fought his way free. The noise they made, banging against the furniture, climbing up on the bed and down again, drew Mrs. Latham, who stood in the doorway for a while, trying to make them stop. Neither of them paid any attention to her. The expression on Lymie's tormented face was almost but not quite hate. Spud was calm and possessed and merely bent on making Lymie lie still under the covers and take a nap before dinner. He pried one of Lymie's shoes off and then the other. His trousers took much longer and were harder to manage, but in the end they came off, too, and one of Lymie's striped socks. With each loss, like a country defending itself against an invader, Lymie fought harder. He fought against being made to do something against his will, and he fought also against the unreasonable strength in Spud's arms. He butted. He kicked. All of a sudden, with no warning, the last defense gave way. Lymie quit struggling and lay still. As in a dream, he let Spud cover him with a blanket. Something had burst inside of him, something more important than any organ, and there was a flowing which was like blood. Though he kept on breathing and his heart after a while pounded less violently, there it was all the same, an underground river which went on and on and was bound to keep on like that for years probably, never stopping, never once running dry.

He watched Spud pull the shades down and leave the room without having any idea of what he had done.

~ *Donald Windham* ~

Servants
with
Torches

S ergio was thinking.
　　I am tired of pigeons, he was thinking. I am tired of their red feet
and orange eyes. I am tired of their feathers blowing about the court
every afternoon. I am bored.

He was standing guard at the entrance of the court to the caserma.
The caserma was a pink building on a side street. The court, which was
paved with stones, had a white marble well head in the centre, but nothing else. At the far end, after lunch, Pancrazio had amused himself by
tying a wad of paper to the cat's back leg with a string and watching the
cat run and roll on its back, playing with the paper ball. And Luigi and
Rosario had amused themselves by hanging a piece of paper on Pancrazio's back while he was absorbed with the kitten and then igniting the
paper. Everyone, except Sergio, had been amused with the results. He
had seen them do the same thing too many times. He was bored.

I may as well be a portiere, he thought. I did not become a carabiniere
to stand in a doorway all afternoon, or to sit at a table tearing pieces of
paper in half and then tearing the halves in quarters as I did all morning.

A native of Atlanta, DONALD WINDHAM is the author of Lost Friendships, *a memoir of his relationships with Truman Capote and Tennessee Williams, as well as five novels—among them the highly esteemed* Two People—*all of which have now sadly lapsed out of print. He is also the author of an autobiography,* Emblems of Conduct, *and a short story collection,* The Warm Country, *for which E. M. Forster wrote the introduction.*

I would like to do something important, or I would like at least to walk up and down the streets where I can see and be seen.

The court in which he was standing guard was deserted, but only a few feet away, Pancrazio, who was standing guard with him, was sitting in the small dark entrance to the office. Very few people came to the caserma except the carabinieri who worked there. Sometimes, however, tourists who had been robbed came, and Sergio wished that one would come now. He would ask her as many questions, talk to her as long and find out as much as possible before he let her go inside to see an officer who could help her. Pancrazio would not interfere; Pancrazio would only stand and listen. Besides, if the tourist spoke English he would speak English to her and Pancrazio would not understand. But I, Sergio thought, I was a prisoner in an American army camp in North Africa, and I can understand and speak English, which is more than most of the officers can do.

Walking to the small mirror which was stuck on the wall by the door, half concealed by the moulding, he looked at his reflection. In the light of the setting sun which poured through the portal, his skin glowed as though he were made of pink Venetian glass, and his small black moustache was very black and elegant over his mouth. He took off his cap, with its silver insignia of globe and flames, and holding it in one hand, he ran his other hand gently over the surface of his black hair and watched its reflection in the mirror. Then he frowned and thought: The one thing I like about working in the office is that I do not have to wear my cap there. And what I would not like about it if I were stationed outside is that I would have to wear my cap all the time.

He put his cap back on, walked to the portal again, and looked out. Maybe someone interesting was coming toward the caserma now. But only a group of boys passed, their arms about each other's waists, and a pigeon at his feet scurried a little distance away and then looked back expectantly. The street was almost dark, and Sergio felt the beginning of the restlessness which always rose in him as, from pastel day, the city sank to dark and brilliant night.

"Sergio."

Pancrazio, who had gone into the building and returned, was calling him.

"What do you want?"

"The commissario has just spoken to me. You and I are to stand duty tonight in Campo Sant' Angelo, where there is to be the outdoor opera. Let's go, we must get ready."

～　～　～

When it was dark, the half-moon over San Giorgio silvered the whole sky as though it were a great blue mirror suspended behind the city, and the lights above the piazza were like the many coloured threads of an agate curving across the mirror's surface.

This is the kind of world men should live in, Sergio thought as he stood in the entrance to the crowded square. From the women about him came the luxurious odour of perfume, making him visualise little glass bottles filled with liquids the tints of the lights in the sky, and on the men and women ornaments of gold flashed like the gold ornaments of gondolas. Nowhere did he see any of the poor or even any of the ordinary people of the city; here were only the rich, and among the rich there was nothing to do but to stand and wait.

Pancrazio had bought an ice cream and offered one to Sergio, but he had refused. Even though there was nothing for them to do, until the opera began he felt that it was their duty to stand at attention; so while Pancrazio retired into a corner and ate his ice cream with the firemen who were on duty there as they would have been in a theatre, although there did not seem to be much in the square which could burn, Sergio stood as near to the entrance as he could. The women brushed past him as they entered, some of them wearing jackets of fur, although their arms were bare and white, most of them talking and laughing, their voices as clear and light as the moonlight, and all of them so oblivious of him that he could not help thinking of the pleasure it would be to catch their elbows in his hand, turn them toward him, and smother their laughter, or at least demand, first roughly and then tenderly, why they were laughing. But the idea of disrespect to people of a better class appalled him as much as the other idea pleased him, and he watched silently until the lights dimmed for the opera to begin.

Then Pancrazio came up to him and took his arm, saying:

"Quick, let's go and find a seat before they are all taken."

The opera was *Otello,* the story of a dark man loved by a fair woman. Sergio was extremely fond of it, and he hurried with Pancrazio and climbed toward the back benches near the electricians' booth, where the remaining free space was rapidly filling with sellers of drinks and candies.

But he kept his eyes open for anyone slipping in, and even before they sat down he was watching a boy who had entered and was wandering back and forth through the seats below them. All the lower seats were taken, and as the boy mounted nearer, Sergio saw that he was well dressed, probably a foreigner, and in any case no one for him to question. He turned his attention to the stage, where, there before him, was the isle of Cyprus with the sail of a Venetian ship in the background.

He was aware, however, when the boy sat beside him, for the undivided wooden bench was crowded and the empty space beside Sergio would not comfortably have accommodated even a small child. But he did not object. He wanted to keep his attention on the stage, and he supposed that the boy had paid for a ticket and had more right to the space than he had.

There was no back to the seat, and after a while the boy, leaning back, spread himself out so that one of his hands was beneath Sergio's leg. Sergio had not objected to the boy's crowding him, but he was nevertheless determined not to give up his own space, and he did not move. Apparently the boy also was determined, for though he removed his hand several times he replaced it always in the same position, and it at last occurred to Sergio, in a sensation received together with the swell of the music, that the boy was touching him deliberately, for the pleasure of it. The idea rose in his mind without in the least distracting him from the music. In fact, he was so intent on the opera that it seemed to lessen his feeling of separation from the drama and to bring the music closer to him; and while he sat listening as though he were in the centre of the stage itself, his emotions rising and falling with Verdi's notes, he acted to discover if his idea was true. Not only did he refuse to make room but he pressed back, asserting his presence immovably. Then he turned his head and looked defiantly into the boy's face.

The boy was fair and blue-eyed, his face colder and calmer than an Italian's. But the boy showed no awareness of Sergio and, without removing his eyes from the stage, concealed whatever surprise Sergio had given him by taking a package of cigarettes from his pocket. For a moment Sergio thought that the boy was going to offer him a cigarette. But he did not. After taking one for himself, the boy returned the package to his pocket; and Sergio, seeing that the cigarettes were English, turned away with contempt. The English tourists since the war were notoriously stingy, and he had no use for them. He even thought of telling the boy that smoking was forbidden; but people were smoking all about them, so he turned his attention back to the stage, where Desdemona and the Moor were beginning their duet. Then the boy replaced his hand on the seat, and Sergio, swept away from himself by the music, was brought back again with his realisation of the hand's pressure.

This boy probably has a sister like Desdemona, he thought, only she would be feelingless, the way foreigners are, and would not deign to notice the people her brother comes and sits next to and touches. Or maybe he is travelling with his mother, who would still be young, and she is looking for another husband because his father has died. And if I should marry her and be his father, then I would put the fear of me into him. I would make him tell me what he means and if he often does this sort of thing when he goes out in the evening, and I would threaten to beat him if I found him among people of whom I did not approve. I would tie him in a chair for three days and give him only bread and water to eat. But even as it is, he remembered, I am a carabiniere and I can tell him that he cannot act in this manner in my country, that he must be careful how he acts with me.

For despite the ecstasy of the music, Sergio's awareness of the boy had increased, and it seemed to him that the very palm of the boy's hand was beneath his leg, motionlessly, almost tenderly waiting. The boy was touching him, yet like all foreigners who do not speak and assert themselves, the boy would not acknowledge Sergio and put himself under obligation to him.

Suddenly, Sergio hissed in a whisper:

"What do you want?"

The boy made no sign that he knew Sergio had spoken; but as low as Sergio's voice had been, Pancrazio on the other side of him had heard and asked:

"What, Sergio? What?"

Sergio shushed him and pointed to the stage. But he could not give all of his attention to the music now, as the boy seemed to be doing. If I had touched his sister or mother like that, he thought, when I was a soldier or before when I was a boy like him, they would not have allowed me simply to look as though nothing had happened. Not if I had put my hand on her white thigh. And she would be embarrassed to know that he has put his hand on mine, for I would show her just how he did it. He touched me here, I would say, and touch myself, looking at her. She

would have to commit herself then, as he has not. She would have to
say: But you are handsome, and because of this you must excuse him.
He is a bad boy and I shall send him to bed. But you must understand
that this has happened because you are handsome, and you must excuse
him. You must stay and have a glass of wine with me.

As the music ended and the applause drowned out his thoughts, he
knew that that was not the way it would happen. But she would think
of it, as he had thought of it, and that would please him.

"What did you say?" Pancrazio was asking.

But Sergio did not look at Pancrazio.

"Here," he said, taking the boy's arm. "You will have to come
with me."

The boy looked at him indignantly and tried to pull away. Then he
said something which Sergio did not understand. But Sergio held on to
his arm and repeated his own statement in English.

"Why?" the boy demanded.

"Because I have said so," Sergio responded. "And I am a carabiniere."

And turning to Pancrazio, he added in Italian:

"Take his other arm."

"Why?" Pancrazio asked.

"Do as I tell you," Sergio told him. "This is important."

His tone was authoritative, and Pancrazio obeyed. Awkwardly, the
three of them started down the steps, the boy in the middle, not resisting
but not easily able to step from tier to tier of the seats with Sergio holding
him in front and Pancrazio behind. When they reached the level of the
piazza, Sergio said in English:

"Show me your documents."

"What?"

"Your documents. Documents."

"I don't have any documents," the boy said. "I'm not an Italian."

"Then show me your passport."

"I don't have my passport with me. Why should I?"

The boy tried to pull his arm away again, but Sergio held on to him.

"Where is your passport?" he asked.

"At the hotel."

"What hotel?"

"I don't remember the name."

Sergio became indignant.

"Do you tell me that you do not know where you live?"

"Certainly I know where I live," the boy said. "I can find my way there, but I do not remember the name."

"With whom do you live in the hotel?" Sergio asked. "Your father and mother?"

"I don't have to tell you all these things," the boy replied. "What have I done that's wrong? You have no right to treat me this way."

"Perhaps you are staying with your sister," Sergio suggested.

"I don't have to tell you with whom I am staying," the boy insisted. "What have I done that's wrong?"

Nearly everyone in the crowd was pouring obliviously toward the exit, but a few people around them were watching, and Sergio thought: This will be a good thing for me to report. If the commissario is here he will be pleased. He does not like foreigners who get in trouble like this, even with boys of the streets, and if they come to the caserma he laughs at them behind their backs. But I must do everything correctly.

"You watch him while I go and see if the commissario is on duty here," he said to Pancrazio. "I will be back soon."

"Very well," Pancrazio answered.

But Sergio had gone only a few steps when he heard Pancrazio shout, and turning around he saw that the boy had broken away and was running through the crowd toward the exit. He began to run also, knocking people from his path, and before the boy managed to reach the exit Sergio overtook him and grabbed hold of the arm of his jacket. The jacket tore, and the boy, the momentum of his run broken by the carabiniere's sudden grasp, swung around toward him with his feet completely off the ground and crashed against his body. The two of them stood close together and gasping. Pancrazio ran up and jerked the boy out of Sergio's grasp.

"Idiot!" Sergio cried, and slapped Pancrazio's hand from the boy's arm. "If it had been up to you the boy would have escaped. I will take care of him from now on."

Dragging the boy with him, he started toward the exit. But the boy fought back with anger.

"Look what you have done to my coat," he shouted. "You've torn my coat. What right have you to tear my coat? I haven't done anything wrong."

Sergio stopped, also angry at the unfavourable attention which was beginning to centre on them, and demanded:

"No? If you had not done anything wrong, then why did you run?"

"Who wouldn't run," the boy demanded, "with a lot of carabinieri dragging him around and threatening to arrest him?"

"Very well," Sergio said. "But you must show your passport to a carabiniere when he asks to see it."

The boy said nothing more; and Sergio, motioning for Pancrazio to follow, led the way alongside the strip of rough white cloth which was stretched at the back of the seats to screen off the view of the opera from passersby, and out into the narrow space between the cloth and the iron railing of the bridge which ran up and down several steps into a narrow street of closed shops. For a moment the three of them were only three more dark shapes in the crowd jamming its way through the narrow passage. Then they passed the aromatic stream of light from the open door of a pastry shop, on the sill of which a white cat was sitting, and came out into a long bright square filled with cafés and hung with paper lanterns. Sergio looked at the boy again, and even in the reflection of the coloured lanterns, curved in bright agate lines across the blue glass sky which roofed the crowded cafés, he could see that the boy was frightened and pale. He appeared even younger than Sergio had thought him, and despite his rather haughty coldness he had an air of nurtured innocence. Even with his jacket torn, he looked rich. He was wearing a beautiful shirt and tie.

They were almost to the middle of the square when someone called and the boy stopped. Sergio was alert, ready to grab the boy if he tried to escape again. But the boy merely stood where he was.

"Where are you going?" a man seated at an outdoor table of a café called to him.

"To the hotel with these carabinieri," the boy replied. "They say they are going to arrest me."

"Oh, Christ, how stupid," the man said. "I'll come with you."

And turning to the other person at the table, he added:

"You pay, please; I'm going with him."

Hurriedly, the man rose from the table and joined them. He walked on the outside of Sergio and spoke across him to the boy. They spoke so rapidly that Sergio could not understand what they were saying, and he did not like the man's coming with them. The man was not old enough to be the boy's father, and it was the boy's family that he wanted to encounter.

At the middle of the square they turned into another dark passage, which led up and down over several bridges. The man, who spoke fair Italian, demanded of Sergio:

"What has my friend done that is wrong?"

"He behaved to me in a most insulting manner," Sergio replied. "He touched my leg with his hand."

"Yes, but that is only an accident," the man said. "What is wrong with that?"

"You do not understand," Sergio replied indignantly. "He felt my leg, like this."

And he improvised the most indecent gesture he could conceive.

"He says that you groped him," the man said across Sergio to the boy.

"Then he's a liar," the boy replied.

"Do you understand?" Sergio demanded.

"Yes, I understand," the man said flatly. "Well?"

"You may do things like that where you come from," Sergio said with contempt, "but we do not behave that way toward carabinieri in Italy."

"In the first place," the man replied, "my friend says that he did not do what you said that he did. And in the second, even if he did, it isn't against the law to touch someone, as far as I know."

"Your friend says that he did not touch me?" Sergio asked incredulously.

"Yes."

"And I say that he did touch me. And my word is worth more than his."

"Nevertheless," the man replied, "I believe him."

"But I am a carabiniere. I am the law."

"That is not my fault," the man said.

"In your country do you not believe the word of the law?"

"I believe the word of whoever speaks the truth," the man said smugly.

"Ha," Sergio cried, "and that is what I believe, also."

They had arrived at the entrance of one of the most elegant hotels, and the boy stopped, bringing the others to a halt around him.

"Is this where you live?" Sergio demanded.

"Yes," the boy answered.

"Very well, let us go inside."

The lobby was enormous. The floors were of polished marble, the walls were hung with silks and decorated with great glass figures of gondoliers and masqueraders surrounded by exotic flowers. Sergio allowed the two foreigners to enter before him, then he followed, leaving Pancrazio to come behind. The lobby was empty except for a few employees in the distance and the portiere, who hurried from the desk to meet them as they entered. Sergio was impressed by the size and beauty of the hotel, in which he had never been before; but without allowing the foreigners to speak, he ordered the portiere to bring the key to the boy's room. When the portiere brought the key, Sergio saw with annoyance that the man accepted it. He had expected the boy to go up and return with his mother.

"It is the boy's passport that I want," he said.

"Yes," the man replied. "I will bring it."

"Go with him," Sergio instructed Pancrazio, "and have him bring his passport also."

When they were gone Sergio removed his cap, and holding it in one hand, he smoothed his hair with the other. Then he put his cap under his arm and crossed to the portiere's desk.

"Show me the register," he said. "Is this boy with his family?"

"No," the portiere replied. "The two gentlemen are alone."

Sergio turned the ledger around so that he could read it and looked across the column from the two names which the portiere pointed out. Under nationality he read: American.

"But they are not American," he said. "They are English."

"No, they are American," the portiere said. "They have American passports."

With a feeling more of unhappiness than of annoyance, Sergio turned and walked to the boy, who was standing in the middle of the lobby and watching him.

"You are American?" he asked.

"Certainly," the boy replied. "Isn't that why you are trying to make trouble for me? Because you are a communist and do not like Americans?"

"I am not a communist," Sergio replied, "and I like Americans very much. Our government is very friendly to Americans. Besides, I was a prisoner with the Americans in North Africa and they were very good to me."

"Then maybe you don't like Americans because you were a prisoner of war," the boy said. "But you don't like us. I like the Italians, but you don't like us."

"Ah, yes," Sergio said sentimentally. "You like the Italians too much."

"Not any more," the boy replied.

The elevator door opened. The man came across the lobby toward them, followed by Pancrazio, to whom Sergio held out his hand for the passports.

"He has them," Pancrazio said, indicating the man. "He would not give them to me."

Sergio turned to the man, who gave him the passports. They were American. Sergio looked at the photographs and at the man and boy in turn. He did not know what to look for next, for although he could speak English he could not read it. Then he remembered the permesso di soggiorno, the police permit which all foreigners must have.

"Your permesso di soggiorno," he said.

Without hesitating the man handed him the two folded papers which he was already holding in his hand.

With these Sergio knew what to look for, and he read them carefully while the others, aggregated now by a group of hotel employees at a short distance, stood and waited. He read on, hardly interested in what he was reading, wishing that there was some pleasant way in which the whole affair could be ended. Then, with an intense focussing of his attention, he realised that one of the permits was expired.

"Whose is this?" he asked, holding it out.

"Mine," the man replied.

"It is expired," Sergio said. "It has been expired almost a month."

"Yes, I know," the man answered. "I have requested a renewal, but it has not arrived yet."

Sergio looked at the paper for several minutes, while everyone waited. It was not merely possible, it was proper now for him to take the man to the caserma, but he felt disinclined to do so.

"I am afraid I shall have to take you to the caserma," he said.

"Why?" the man demanded. "I have applied for a renewal."

"It does not say here that a renewal has been applied for," Sergio said, examining the piece of paper again.

"That is not my fault," the man objected. "I applied for it, and that is all that I can do. If I am to be taken anywhere, I wish to telephone the American consul first."

"Excuse me, but that cannot be permitted," Sergio said quickly. "Besides, the consul's office would be closed now."

"Very well, if he takes me away you telephone the American consul at his home and tell him what has happened, do you understand?" the man said to the boy.

Then, turning to the portiere, he added:

"And if he takes us both with him, I want you to telephone the American consul for us and to continue telephoning until you receive an answer."

"Yes, sir," the portiere replied.

"Two minutes, please," Sergio said.

Going into the corner of the lobby, away from the others, he called Pancrazio to him.

"This is a very complicated situation," he began.

"Yes," Pancrazio said.

"Yes, a very complicated situation," Sergio repeated. "One of the Americans has a permesso di soggiorno which is expired, but he has requested a renewal. It would be regular to take him to the commissario and report this, but I have already frightened both of the foreigners so much that I do not want to frighten them any more. After all, our government is friendly to the Americans and the E.R.P., and if we take them to the office we will have to report the other American's incivility to me and that will be most unpleasant for them. On the other hand, if we do not take them we must not mention the expired permesso di soggiorno. If we are asked, we must say that we examined the foreigners' documents and that they are in order. Do you understand?"

"Yes, I understand," Pancrazio said.

"Very well. Then, if I do what I think is best and most civil to the foreigners, you will not say anything at the caserma which will get us into trouble with the commissario?"

"No, I will not say anything which will get us into trouble," Pancrazio agreed.

"Very well."

With an air of decision, Sergio returned to the group in the middle of the lobby.

"How long will you remain in Venice?" he asked the man.

"We intend to leave tomorrow," the man replied.

"And where will you go?"

"To Rome, where I am staying."

"Ah, in that case," Sergio said happily, "the matter of your permesso di soggiorno should be taken up there. If you will be sure to report to the Questura in Rome when you return and inquire if your renewal has been made, that will be all that is necessary."

"Thank you," the man said.

"And the other matter," Sergio conceded, "I will be willing to forget."

"Thank you," the man said.

"What about my coat that he tore?" the boy asked crossly. "Is he just going to forget that too?"

"Really," the man said. "Let him go. Don't you know when you are well off?"

~ ~ ~

Out in the dark street again, Sergio heard the chimes of a nearby church ringing the hour. The half-moon was higher and smaller in the sky. Sergio turned back in the direction from which they had come and led the way toward the square in which the opera was being performed. Pancrazio walked at his side, waiting for him to say something, but he did not say anything. He was thinking.

It was very clever of me to be kind to them, he was thinking; it is better for everyone that way. But already he regretted that everything had not happened differently from the beginning. I am tired of nights at half-moon, he thought. I am bored with events which never come to a climax. I am bored with these dark narrow streets, up and down bridges. I am bored with these stupid pigeons. I hope that we get back to the opera in time to see Otello strangle Desdemona.

~ *Desmond Hogan* ~

Jimmy

H er office overlooked the college grounds; early in the spring they
were bedecked with crocuses and snowdrops. Looking down upon
them was to excel oneself. She was a fat lady, known as "Windy" by the
students, her body heaved into sedate clothes and her eyes somehow
always searching despite the student gibes that she was profoundly stupid
and profoundly academic.

She lectured in ancient Irish history, yearly bringing students to view
Celtic crosses and round towers marooned in spring floods. The college
authorities often joined her on these trips; one administrator insisted on
speaking in Irish all the time. This was a college situated near Connemara,
the Gaelic-speaking part of Ireland. Irish was a big part of the curriculum;
bespectacled pioneer pin-bearing administrators insisted on speaking Irish
as though it was the tongue of foolish crows. There was an element of
mindlessness about it. One spoke Irish because a state that had been both
severe and regimental on its citizens had encouraged it.

Emily delayed by the window this morning. It was spring, and fool-
ishly she remembered the words of the blind poet Raftery. "Now that
it's spring the days will be getting longer. And after the feast of Brigid I'll
set foot to the roads." There was that atmosphere of instinct abroad in
Galway today. Galway as long as she recalled was a city of travelling

A native of Ireland, DESMOND HOGAN is the author of the short story collections
Diamonds at the Bottom of the Sea *and* Children of Lir.

people: red-petticoated tinkers, clay-pipe-smoking sailors, wandering beggars.

In Eyre Square sat an austere statue of Padhraic O Connaire, an Irish scribe who'd once walked to Moscow to visit Chekhov and found him gone for the weekend.

In five minutes she would lecture on Brigid's crosses, the straw symbols of renewal in Ireland.

There was now evidence that Brigid was a lecher, a Celtic whore who was ascribed to sainthood by those who had slept with her, but that altered nothing. She was one of the cardinal Irish holy figures, the Isis of the spring-enchanted island.

Emily put words together in her mind.

In five minutes they'd confront her, pleased faces pushing forward. These young people had been to New York or Boston for their summer holidays. They knew everything that was to be known. They sneered a lot, they smiled little. They were possessed of good looks, spent most of the day lounging in the cellar bar, watching strangers: even students had the wayward Galway habit of eyeing a stranger closely, for it was a city tucked away in a corner of Ireland, peaceable, prosperous, seaward-looking.

After class that day she returned to the college canteen, where she considered the subject of white sleeveless jerseys. Jimmy used to have one of those. They'd gone to college in the thirties, Earlsfort Terrace in Dublin, and Jimmy used to wear one of those jerseys. They'd sit in the dark corridor, a boy and a girl from Galway, pleased that the trees were again in bloom, quick to these things by virtue of coming from Galway, where nature dazzled.

Their home was outside Galway city, six miles from it, a big house, an elm tree on either side of it and in spring two pools of snowdrops like hankies in front of it.

Jimmy had gone to Dublin to study English literature. She had followed him in a year to study history. They were respectable children of a much-lauded solicitor, and they approached their lives gently. She got a job in the university in Galway. He got a job teaching in Galway city.

Mrs. Carmichael, lecturer in English, approached.

Mrs. Carmichael wore her grandmother's Edwardian clothes, because, though sixty, she considered it in keeping with what folk were wearing in Carnaby Street in London.

"Emily, I had trouble today," she confessed. "A youngster bit a girl in class."

Emily smiled, half from chagrin, half from genuine amusement.

Mrs. Carmichael was a bit on the Anglo-Irish side, taut, upper-class, looking on these Catholic students as one might upon a rare and rather charming breed of radishes.

"Well, tell them to behave themselves," Emily said. "That's what I always say."

She knew from long experience that they did not obey, that they laughed at her, and that her obesity was hallmarked by a number of nicknames. She could not help it, she ate a lot, she enjoyed cakes in Lydons' and more particularly when she went to Dublin she enjoyed Bewley's and country-shop cakes.

In fact the country shop afforded her not just a good pot of tea and nice ruffled cream cakes but a view of the green, a sense again of student days, here in Dublin, civilized, parochial. She recalled the woman with the oval face who became famous for writing stories and the drunkard who wrote strange books that now young people read.

"I'll see you tomorrow," Mrs. Carmichael said, leaving.

Emily watched her. She'd sail in her Anglia to her house in the country, fleeing this uncivilized mess.

Emily put her handkerchief into her handbag and strolled home.

What was it about this spring? Since early in the year strange notions had been entering her head. She'd been half-thinking of leaving for Paris for a few days or spending a weekend in West Cork.

There was both desire and remembrance in the spring.

In her parents' home her sister, Sheila, now lived. She was married. Her husband was a vet.

Her younger brother, George, was working with the European Economic Community in Brussels.

Jimmy alone was unheard of, unlisted in conversation.

He'd gone many years ago, disappearing on a mail train when the war was waging in the outside world. He'd never come back; some said he was an alcoholic on the streets of London. If that was so he'd be an eloquent drunkard. He had so much, Jimmy had, so much of his race, astuteness, learning, eyes that danced like Galway Bay on mornings when the islands were clear and when gulls sparkled like flecks of foam.

She considered her books, her apartment, sat down, drank tea. It was already afternoon, and the Dublin train hooted, shunting off to arrive in Dublin in the late afternoon.

Tom, her brother-in-law, always said Jimmy was a moral retrograde, to be banished from mind. Sheila always said Jimmy was better off gone. He was too confused in himself. George, the youngest of the family, recalled only that he'd read him Oscar Wilde's *The Happy Prince* once and that tears had broken down his cheeks.

The almond blossom had not yet come and the war trembled in England and in a month Jimmy was gone and his parents were glad. Jimmy had been both a nuisance and a scandal. Jimmy had let the family down.

Emily postured over books on Celtic mythology, taking notes.

It had been an old custom in Ireland to drive at least one of your family out, to England, to the mental hospital, to sea, or to a bad marriage. Jimmy had not fallen easily into his category. He'd been a learned person, a very literate young man. He'd taught in a big school, befriended a young man, the thirties prototype with blond hair, went to Dublin one weekend with him, stayed in Buswell's Hotel with him, was since branded by names they'd put on Oscar Wilde. Jimmy had insisted on his innocence, but the boy had lied before going to Dublin, telling his parents that he was going to play a hurling match.

Jimmy had to resign his job; he took to drink, he was banished from home, slipping in in the afternoons to read to George. Eventually he'd gone. The train had registered nothing of his departure as it whinnied in the afternoon. He just slipped away.

The boy, Johnny Fogarthy, whom Jimmy had abducted to Dublin, himself left Ireland.

He went to the States, ended up in the antique trade, and in 1949, not yet twenty-seven, was killed in Pacifica. Local minds construed all elements of this affair to be tragic.

Jimmy was safely gone.

The dances at the crossroads near their home ceased, and that was the final memory of Jimmy, dancing with a middle-aged woman and she wearing earrings and an accordion bleating "The Valley of Slieve-namban."

Emily heard a knock on the door early next morning. Unrushed, she went to the door. She was wearing a pink gown. Her hair was in a net. She had been expecting no caller, but then again the postman knocked when he had a parcel.

For years afterwards she would tell people of the thoughts that had been haunting her mind in the days previously.

She opened the door.

A man aged but not bowed by age, derelict but not disarrayed, stood outside.

There was a speed in her eyes which detected the form of a man older than Jimmy her brother but yet holding his features and hiding nothing of the graciousness of which he was possessed.

She held him. He held her. There was anguish in her eyes. Her fat hands touched an old man.

"Jimmy," she said simply.

Jimmy the tramp had won £100 at the horses and chosen from a variety of possibilities a home visit. Jimmy the tramp lived on Charing Cross Road.

Jimmy the tramp was a wino, yes, but like many of his counterparts near St.-Martin-in-the-Field in London was an eloquent one. Simply Jimmy was home.

News brushed swiftly to the country. His brother-in-law reared. His sister, Sheila, silenced. Emily, in her simple way, was overjoyed.

News was relayed to Brussels. George, the younger brother, was expected home in two weeks.

That morning Emily led Jimmy to a table, laid it as her own mother would have done ceremoniously with breakfast things, and near a pitcher, blue and white, they prayed.

Emily's prayer was one of thanksgiving.

Jimmy's too was one of thanksgiving.

Emily poured milk over porridge and dolled the porridge with honey from Russia, invoking for Jimmy the time Padhraic O Connaire walked to Moscow.

In the afternoon he dressed in clothes Emily bought for him, and they walked the streets of Galway. Jimmy by the Claddagh, filled as it was with swans, wept the tears of a frail human being.

"Emily," he said. "This should be years ago."

For record he said there'd been no interest other than platonic in the young boy, that he'd been wronged and this wrong had driven him to drink. "I hope you don't think I'm apologizing," he said. "I'm stating facts."

Sheila met him, and Tom, his brother-in-law, who looked at him as though at an animal in the zoo.

Emily had prepared a meal the first evening of his return. They ate veal, drank rosé d'Anjou, toasted by a triad of candles. "One for love, one for luck, one for happiness," indicated Emily.

Tom said the EEC made things good for farmers, bad for businessmen. Sheila said she was going to Dublin for a hairdo.

Emily said she'd like to bring Jimmy to the old house next day.

Sure enough the snowdrops were there when they arrived, and the frail trees.

Jimmy said, as though in speed, he'd lived as a tramp for years, drinking wine, beating his breast in pity.

"It was all an illusion," he said. "This house still stands."

He entered it, a child, and Tom, his brother-in-law, looked scared.

Jimmy went to the library, and sure enough the works of Oscar Wilde were there.

"Many a time *The Happy Prince* kept me alive," he said.

Emily dressed newly; her dignity cut a hole in her pupils. They silenced and listened to talk about Romanesque doorways.

She lit her days with thoughts of the past: rooms not desecrated, appointments under the elms.

Her figure cut through Galway. Spring came in a rush. There was no dalliance. The air shattered with freshness.

As she lectured, Jimmy walked. He walked by the Claddagh, by Shop Street, by Quay Street. He looked, he pondered, his gaze drifted to Clare.

Once, Johnny Fogarthy had told him he was leaving for California on the completion of his studies. He left all right.

He was killed.

"For love," Jimmy told Emily. He sacrificed himself for the speed of a car on the Pacific coast.

They dined together and listened to Bach. Tom and Sheila kept away.

Emily informed Jimmy about her problems. Jimmy was wakeful to them. In new clothes, washed, he was the aged poet, distinguished, alert to the unusual, the charming, the indirect.

"I lived in a world of craftsmen," he told Emily. "Most alcoholics living on the streets are poets driven from poetry, lovers driven from their beloved, craftsmen exiled from their craft."

They assuaged those words with drink.

Emily held Jimmy's hand. "I hope you are glad to be here," she said. "I am, I am," he said.

The weekend in Dublin with Johnny Fogarthy he'd partaken of spring lamb with him on a white-lain table in Buswell's, he told Emily.

"We drank wine then too, rosé. Age made no difference between us. We were elucidated by friendship, its acts, its meaning. Pity love was mistaken for sin."

Jimmy had gone during the war, and he told Emily about the bombs, the emergencies, the crowded air-raid shelters.

"London was on fire. But I'd have chosen anything, anything to the gap in people's understanding in Ireland."

They drank to that.

Emily at college was noted now for a new beauty.

Jimmy in his days walked the streets.

Mrs. Kenny in Kenny's bookshop recognized him and welcomed him. Around were writers' photographs on the wall. "It's good to see you," she said.

He had represented order once, white sleeveless jumpers, fairish hair evenly parted, slender volumes of English poetry.

"Remember," Mrs. Kenny said, "the day O'Duffy sailed to Spain with the blueshirts, and you, a boy, said they should be beaten with their own rosary beads."

They laughed.

Jimmy had come home not as an aged tramp but as a poet. It could not have been more simple if he'd come from Cambridge, a retired don. Those who respected the order in him did not seek undue information. Those puzzled by him demanded all the reasons.

Those like Tom, his brother-in-law, who hated him, resented his presence. "I sat here once with Johnny," Jimmy told Emily one day on the Connemara coast. "He said he needed something from life, something Ireland could not give him. So he went to the States."

"Wise man."

"But he was killed."

"We were the generation expecting early and lucid deaths," he told Emily.

Yes. But Jimmy's death had been his parents' mortification with him, his friends' disavowal of him, Emily's silence in her eyes. He'd gone, dispirited, rejected. He'd gone, someone who'd deserted his own agony.

"You're back," Emily said to him cheerily. "That's the most important thing."

His brother, George, came back from Brussels, a burly man in his forties.

He was cheerful and gangly at encountering Jimmy. He recognized integrity, recalled Jimmy reading him *The Happy Prince,* embraced the old man.

Over gin in Emily's he said, "The EEC is like everything else, boring. You'll be bored in Tokyo, bored in Brussels, bored in Dublin." Emily saw that Jimmy was not bored.

In the days, he walked through town, wondering at change, unable to account for it, the new buildings, the supermarkets. His hands were held behind his back. Emily often watched him, knowing that like De Valera he represented something of Ireland. But an element other than pain, fear, loneliness. He was the artist. He was the one foregone and left out in a rush to be acceptable.

They attended mass in the pro-cathedral. Jimmy knelt, prayed; Emily wondered, were his prayers sincere? She looked at Christ, situated quite near the mosaic of President Kennedy, asked him to leave Jimmy, for him not to return. She enjoyed his company as though that of an erstwhile lover.

Sheila threw a party one night.

The reasoning that led to this event was circumspect. George was home. He did not come home often. And when he did he stayed only a few days.

It was spring. The house had been spring-cleaned. A new carpet now graced the floor. Blossom threatened; lace divided the carpet with its shadows.

All good reasons to entertain the local populace.

But deep in Sheila, that aggravated woman's mind, must have been the knowledge that Jimmy, being home, despite his exclusion from all ceremony, despite his rather nebulous circumstances, his homecoming had by some decree to be both established and celebrated.

So neighbours were asked, those who'd borne rumour of him once, those who rejected him and yet were only too willing to accept his legend, young teacher in love with blond boy, affair discovered, young teacher flees to the gutters of London, blond boy ends up in a head-on collision in Pacifica, a town at the toe of San Francisco, California.

The first thing Jimmy noticed was a woman singing "I Have Seen the Lark in the Morning" next to a sombre ancient piano.

Emily had driven him from Galway, she beside him in a once-a-lifetime cape saw his eyes and the shadow that crossed them. He was back in a place which had rejected him. He had returned bearing no triumph but his own humility.

Emily chatted to Mrs. Connaire and Mrs. Delaney. To them, though a spinster, she was a highly erudite member of the community and as such acknowledged by her peers.

Emily looked about. Jimmy was gone. She thrust herself through the crowds and discovered Jimmy after making her way up a stairway hung with paintings of cattle marts and islands, in a room by himself, the room in which he had once slept.

"Jimmy." He turned.

"Yes."

"Come down."

Like a lamb he conceded.

They walked again into the room where a girl aged seventeen sang "The Leaving of Liverpool."

It was a party in the old style, with pots of tea and whiskey and slender elegant cups.

George said, "It's great to see the country changing, isn't it? It's great to see people happy."

Emily thought of the miles of suburban horror outside Galway and thought otherwise.

Tom slapped Jimmy's back. Tom, it must be stated, did not desire this party, not at least until Jimmy was gone. His wife's intentions he suspected, but he let it go ahead.

"It's great having you," he said to Jimmy, bitter and sneering from drink. "Isn't it you that was the queer fellow throwing up a good job for a young lad."

Emily saw the pain, sharp, smitten, like an arrow.

She would have reached for him as she would have for a child smitten by a bomb in the North of Ireland, but the crowd churned and he was lost from sight.

Tom sang "If I Had a Hammer." Sheila, plagued by the social success of her party, wearing earrings like toadstools, sang 'I Left My Heart in San Francisco."

A priest who'd eyed Jimmy but had not approached him sang "Lullaby of Broadway."

George, Jimmy's young brother working in the EEC, got steadily drunker. Tom was slapping the precocious backsides of young women. Sheila was dancing attendance with cucumber sandwiches.

Jimmy was talking to a blond boy who if you stretched memory greatly resembled Johnny Fogarthy.

The fire blazed.

Their parents might have turned in their grave, hating Jimmy their child because he was the best of their brood and sank the lowest.

Emily sipped sherry and talked to neighbours about cows and sheep and daughters with degrees in medicine and foreign countries visited.

She saw her brother and mentally adjusted his portrait: he was again a young man, very handsome, if you like, in love in an idle way with one of his pupils.

In love in a way one person gives to another a secret, a share in their happiness.

She would have stopped all that was going to happen to him but knew that she couldn't.

Tom, her brother-in-law, was getting drunker and viler.

He said out loud, "What is it that attracts men to young fellows?" surprising Jimmy in a simple conversation with a blond boy.

The party ceased, music ceased. All looked towards Jimmy, looked away. The boy was Mrs. McDonagh's son, going from one pottery to another in Ireland to learn his trade, never satisfied, always moving, recently taken up with the Divine Light, some religious crowd in Galway.

People stared. The image was authentic. There was not much sin in it but a lot of beauty. They did not share Tom's prejudice but left the man and the boy. It was getting late. The country was changing, and if there had been wounds, why couldn't they be forgotten?

Tom was slobbering. His wife attended him. He was slobbering about

Jimmy, always afraid of that element of his wife's family, always afraid strange children would be born to him but none came anyway. His wife brought him to the toilet, where presumably he got sick.

George, drunk on gin, talked about the backsides of secretaries in Brussels, and Jimmy, alone among the crowd, still eloquent with drink, spoke to the blond teenager about circuses long ago.

"Why did you leave Ireland?" the boy asked him.

"Searching," he said, "searching for something. Why did you leave your last job?"

"Because I wasn't satisfied," the boy said. "You've got to go on, haven't you? There's always that sense that there's more than this."

The night was rounded by a middle-aged woman who'd once met Count John McCormack singing "Believe Me if All Those Endearing Young Charms."

On the way back into Galway, Emily felt revered and touched by time, recalled Jimmy, his laughter once, that laughter more subdued now.

She was glad he was back; glad of his company and, despite everything, clear in her mind that the past was a fantasy. People had needed culprits then, people had needed fallen angels.

She said good night to Jimmy, touched him on the cheek with a kiss.

"See you in the morning," she said.

She didn't.

She left him asleep, made tea for herself, contemplated the spring sky outside.

She went to college, lectured on Celtic crosses, lunched with Mrs. Carmichael, drove home in the evening, passing the sea, the Dublin train sounding distantly in her head. The party last night had left a strange colour inside her, like light in wine or a reflection on a saxophone.

What was it that haunted her about it? she asked herself.

Then she knew.

She remembered Jimmy on a rain-drenched night during the war coming to the house and his parents turning him away.

Why was it Sheila had thrown that party? Because she had to requite the spirit of the house.

Why was it Jimmy had come back to the house? Because he needed to reassert himself to the old spirits there.

Why was it she was glad? Because her brother was home and at last she had company to glide into old age.

She opened the door. Light fell, guiltily.

Inside was a note.

"Took the Dublin train. Thanks for everything. Love, Jimmy."

The note closed in her hand like a building falling beneath a bomb, and the scream inside her would have dragged her into immobility had not she noticed the sky outside, golden, futuristic, the colour of the sky over their home when Easter was near and she, a girl in white, not fat, beautiful even, walked with her brother, a boy in a sleeveless white jersey, by a garden drilled in daffodils, expecting nothing less than the best life could offer.

~ *William Trevor* ~

Torridge

Perhaps nobody ever did wonder what Torridge would be like as a man—or what Wiltshire or Mace-Hamilton or Arrowsmith would be like, come to that. Torridge at thirteen had a face with a pudding look, matching the sound of his name. He had small eyes and short hair like a mouse's. Within the collar of his grey regulation shirt the knot of his House tie was formed with care, a maroon triangle of just the right shape and bulk. His black shoes were always shiny.

Torridge was unique in some way: perhaps only because he was beyond the pale and appeared, irritatingly, to be unaware of it. He wasn't good at games and had difficulty in understanding what was being explained in the classroom. He would sit there frowning, half smiling, his head a little to one side. Occasionally he would ask some question that caused an outburst of groaning. His smile would increase then. He would glance around the classroom, not flustered or embarrassed in the least, seeming to be pleased that he had caused such a response. He was naïve to the point where it was hard to believe he wasn't pretending, but his naïveté was real and was in time universally recognized as such. A master called Buller Yeats reserved his cruellest shafts of scorn for it, sighing

WILLIAM TREVOR's books include the novels Mrs. Eckdorf in O'Neill's Hotel, Fools of Fortune, *and* Two Lives, *part of which was nominated for the Booker Prize, as well as the recent* Collected Stories. *A native of Ireland, he is reputed to put his stories away in a drawer for a year before sending them out for publication.*

whenever his eyes chanced to fall on Torridge, pretending to believe his name was Porridge.

Of the same age as Torridge, but similar in no other way, were Wiltshire, Mace-Hamilton, and Arrowsmith. All three of them were blond-haired and thin, with a common sharpness about their features. They wore, untidily, the same clothes as Torridge, their House ties knotted any old how, the laces in their scuffed shoes often tied in several places. They excelled at different games and were quick to sense what was what. Attractive boys, adults had more than once called them.

The friendship among the three of them developed because, in a way, Torridge was what he was. From the first time they were aware of him —on the first night of their first term—he appeared to be special. In the darkness after lights-out someone was trying not to sob and Torridge's voice was piping away, not homesick in the least. His father had a button business was what he was saying; he'd probably be going into the button business himself. In the morning he was identified, a boy in red and blue striped pyjamas, still chattering in the wash-room. "What's your father do, Torridge?" Arrowsmith asked at breakfast, and that was the beginning. "Dad's in the button business," Torridge beamingly replied. "Torridge's, you know." But no one did know.

He didn't, as other new boys, make a particular friend. For a while he attached himself to a small gang of homesick boys who had only their malady in common, but after a time this gang broke up and Torridge found himself on his own, though it seemed quite happily so. He was often to be found in the room of the kindly housemaster of Junior House, an ageing white-haired figure called Old Frosty, who listened sympathetically to complaints of injustice at the hands of other masters, always ready to agree that the world was a hard place. "You should hear Buller Yeats on Torridge, sir," Wiltshire used to say in Torridge's presence. "You'd think Torridge had no feelings, sir." Old Frosty would reply that Buller Yeats was a frightful man. "Take no notice, Torridge," he'd add in his kindly voice, and Torridge would smile, making it clear that he didn't mind in the least what Buller Yeats said. "Torridge knows true happiness," a new young master, known as Mad Wallace, said in an unguarded moment one day, a remark which caused immediate uproar in a Geography class. It was afterwards much repeated, like "Dad's in the button business" and "Torridge's, you know." The true happiness of Torridge became a joke, the particular property of Wiltshire and Mace-

Hamilton and Arrowsmith. Furthering the joke, they claimed that know-ing Torridge was a rare experience, that the private realm of his innocence and his happiness was even exotic. Wiltshire insisted that one day the school would be proud of him. The joke was worked to death.

At the school it was the habit of certain senior boys to "take an interest in" juniors. This varied from glances and smiles across the dining-hall to written invitations to meet in some secluded spot at a stated time. Friend-ships, taking a variety of forms, were then initiated. It was flattering, and very often a temporary antidote for homesickness, when a new boy re-ceived the agreeable but bewildering attentions of an important fifth-former. A meeting behind Chapel led to the negotiating of a barbed-wire fence on a slope of gorse bushes, the older boy solicitous and knowl-edgeable. There were well-trodden paths and nooks among the gorse where smoking could take place with comparative safety. Farther afield, in the hills, there were crude shelters composed of stones and corrugated iron. Here, too, the emphasis was on smoking and romance.

New boys very soon became aware of the nature of older boys' in-terest in them. The flattery changed its shape, an adjustment was made —or the new boys retreated in panic from this area of school life. Andrews and Butler, Webb and Mace-Hamilton, Dillon and Pratt, Tothill and Goldfish Stewart, Good and Wiltshire, Sainsbury Major and Ar-rowsmith, Brewitt and King: the liaisons were renowned, the combina-tions of names sometimes seeming like a music-hall turn, a soft-shoe shuffle of entangled hearts. There was faithlessness too: the Honourable Anthony Swain made the rounds of the senior boys, a fickle and tartish *bijou,* desired and yet despised.

Torridge's puddingy appearance did not suggest that he had *bijou* qual-ities, and glances did not readily come his way in the dining-hall. This was often the fate, or good fortune, of new boys and was not regarded as a sign of qualities lacking. Yet quite regularly an ill-endowed child would mysteriously become the object of fifth- and sixth-form desire. This remained a puzzle to the juniors until they themselves became fifth-or sixth-formers and desire was seen to have to do with something deeper than superficial good looks.

It was the apparent evidence of this truth that caused Torridge, first of all, to be aware of the world of *bijou* and protector. He received a note from a boy in the upper fifth who had previously eschewed the sexual life offered by the school. He was a big, black-haired youth with glasses and a protruding forehead, called Fisher.

"Hey, what's this mean?" Torridge enquired, finding the note under his pillow, tucked into his pyjamas. "Here's a bloke wants to go for a walk."

He read the invitation out: *"If you would like to come for a walk meet me by the electricity plant behind Chapel. Half past four Tuesday afternoon. R.A.J. Fisher."*

"Jesus Christ!" said Armstrong.

"You've got an admirer, Porridge," Mace-Hamilton said.

"Admirer?"

"He wants you to be his *bijou,*" Wiltshire explained.

"What's it mean, *bijou?*"

"Tart, it means, Porridge."

"Tart?"

"Friend. He wants to be your protector."

"What's it mean, protector?"

"He loves you, Porridge."

"I don't even know the bloke."

"He's the one with the big forehead. He's a half-wit actually."

"Half-wit?"

"His mother let him drop on his head. Like yours did, Porridge."

"My mum never."

Everyone was crowding around Torridge's bed. The note was passed from hand to hand. "What's your dad do, Porridge?" Wiltshire suddenly asked, and Torridge automatically replied that he was in the button business.

"You've got to write a note back to Fisher, you know," Mace-Hamilton pointed out.

"Dear Fisher," Wiltshire prompted, "I love you."

"But I don't even—"

"It doesn't matter, not knowing him. You've got to write a letter and put it in his pyjamas."

Torridge didn't say anything. He placed the note in the top pocket of his jacket and slowly began to undress. The other boys drifted back to their own beds, still amused by the development. In the wash-room the next morning Torridge said:

"I think he's quite nice, that Fisher."

"Had a dream about him, did you, Porridge?" Mace-Hamilton enquired. "Got up to tricks, did he?"

"No harm in going for a walk."

"No harm at all, Porridge."

In fact a mistake had been made. Fisher, in his haste or his excitement, had placed the note under the wrong pillow. It was Arrowsmith, still allied with Sainsbury Major, whom he wished to attract.

That this error had occurred was borne in on Torridge when he turned up at the electricity plant on the following Tuesday. He had not considered it necessary to reply to Fisher's note, but he had, across the dining-hall, essayed a smile or two in the older boy's direction: it had surprised him to meet with no response. It surprised him rather more to meet with no response by the electricity plant. Fisher just looked at him and then turned his back, pretending to whistle.

"Hullo, Fisher," Torridge said.

"Hop it, look. I'm waiting for someone."

"I'm Torridge, Fisher."

"I don't care who you are."

"You wrote me that letter." Torridge was still smiling. "About a walk, Fisher."

"Walk? What walk?"

"You put the letter under my pillow, Fisher."

"Jesus!" said Fisher.

The encounter was observed by Arrowsmith, Mace-Hamilton, and Wiltshire, who had earlier taken up crouched positions behind one of the chapel buttresses. Torridge heard the familiar hoots of laughter, and because it was his way, he joined in. Fisher, white-faced, strode away.

"Poor old Porridge," Arrowsmith commiserated, gasping and pretending to be contorted with mirth. Mace-Hamilton and Wiltshire were leaning against the buttress, issuing shrill noises.

"Gosh," Torridge said, "*I* don't care."

He went away, still laughing a bit, and there the matter of Fisher's attempt at communication might have ended. In fact it didn't, because Fisher wrote a second time, and this time he made certain that the right boy received his missive. But Arrowsmith, still firmly the property of Sainsbury Major, wished to have nothing to do with R.A.J. Fisher.

When he was told the details of Fisher's error, Torridge said he'd guessed it had been something like that. But Wiltshire, Mace-Hamilton, and Arrowsmith claimed that a new sadness had overcome Torridge. Something beautiful had been going to happen to him, Wiltshire said: just as the petals of friendship were opening, the flower had been crudely snatched away. Arrowsmith said Torridge reminded him of one of Picasso's sorrowful harlequins. One way or the other, it was agreed that the experience would be beneficial to Torridge's sensitivity. It was seen as his reason for turning to religion, which recently he had done, joining a band of similarly inclined boys who were inspired by the word of the chaplain, a figure known as God Harvey. God Harvey was ascetic, seeming dangerously thin, his face all edge and as pale as paper, his cassock odorous with incense. He conducted readings in his room, offering coffee and biscuits afterwards, though not himself partaking of these refreshments. "God Harvey's linnets" his acolytes were called, for often a hymn was sung to round things off. Welcomed into this fold, Torridge regained his happiness.

R.A.J. Fisher, on the other hand, sank into greater gloom. Arrowsmith remained elusive, mockingly faithful to Sainsbury Major, haughty when Fisher glanced pleadingly, ignoring all his letters. Fisher developed a look of introspective misery. The notes that Arrowsmith delightedly showed around were full of longing, increasingly tinged with desperation. The following term, unexpectedly, Fisher did not return to the school.

There was a famous Assembly at the beginning of that term, with much speculation beforehand as to the trouble in the air. Rumour had it that once and for all an attempt was to be made to stamp out the smiles and the glances in the dining-hall, the whole business of *bijous* and protectors, even the faithless behaviour of the Honourable Anthony Swain. The school waited, and then the gowned staff arrived in the Assembly Hall and waited also, in grim anticipation on a raised dais. Public beatings for past offenders were scheduled, it was whispered: the sergeant-major —the school's boxing instructor, who had himself told tales of public beatings in the past—would inflict the punishment at the headmaster's bidding. But that did not happen. Small and bald and red-skinned, the headmaster marched to the dais unaccompanied by the sergeant-major. Twitching with anger that many afterwards declared had been simulated, he spoke at great length of the school's traditions. He stated that for fourteen years he had been proud to be its headmaster. He spoke of decency and then of his own dismay. The school had been dishonoured;

he would wish certain practices to cease. "I stand before you ashamed," he added, and paused for a moment. "Let all this cease," he commanded. He marched away, tugging at his gown in a familiar manner.

No one understood why the Assembly had taken place at that particular time, on the first day of a summer term. Only the masters looked knowing, as though labouring beneath some secret, but pressed and pleaded with, they refused to reveal anything. Even Old Frosty, usually a most reliable source on such occasions, remained awesomely tight-lipped.

But the pronounced dismay and shame of the headmaster changed nothing. That term progressed, and the world of *bijous* and their protectors continued as before, the glances, the meetings, cigarettes, and romance in the hillside huts. R.A.J. Fisher was soon forgotten, having never made much of a mark. But the story of his error in placing a note under Torridge's pillow passed into legend, as did the encounter by the electricity plant and Torridge's deprivation of a relationship. The story was repeated as further terms passed by; new boys heard it and viewed Torridge with greater interest, imagining what R.A.J. Fisher had been like. The liaisons of Wiltshire with Good, Mace-Hamilton with Webb, and Arrowsmith with Sainsbury Major continued until the three senior boys left the school. Wiltshire, Mace-Hamilton, and Arrowsmith found fresh protectors then, and later these new liaisons came to an end in a similar manner. Later still, Wiltshire, Mace-Hamilton, and Arrowsmith ceased to be *bijous* and became protectors themselves.

Torridge pursued the religious side of things. He continued to be a frequent partaker of God Harvey's biscuits and spiritual uplift, and a useful presence among the chapel pews, where he voluntarily dusted, cleaned brass, and kept the hymn-books in a state of repair with Sellotape. Wiltshire, Mace-Hamilton, and Arrowsmith continued to circulate stories about him which were not true: that he was the product of virgin birth, that he possessed the gift of tongues but did not care to employ it, that he had three kidneys. In the end there emanated from them the claim that a liaison existed between Torridge and God Harvey. "Love and the holy spirit," Wiltshire pronounced, suggesting an ambience of chapel fustiness and God Harvey's grey boniness. The swish of his cassock took on a new significance, as did his thin, dry fingers. In a holy way the fingers pressed themselves onto Torridge, and then their holiness became a passion that could not be imagined. It was all a joke, because Torridge was

Torridge, but the laughter it caused wasn't malicious, because no one hated him. He was a figure of fun; no one sought his downfall, because there was no downfall to seek.

~ ~ ~

The friendship between Wiltshire, Mace-Hamilton, and Arrowsmith continued after they left the school, after all three had married and had families. Once a year they received the Old Boys' magazine, which told of the achievements of themselves and the more successful of their schoolfellows. There were Old Boys' cocktail parties and Old Boys' Day at the school every June and the Old Boys' cricket match. Some of these occasions, from time to time, they attended. Every so often they received the latest rebuilding programme, with the suggestion that they might like to contribute to the rebuilding fund. Occasionally they did.

As middle age closed in, the three friends met less often. Arrowsmith was an executive with Shell and stationed for longish periods in different countries abroad. Once every two years he brought his family back to England, which provided an opportunity for the three friends to meet. The wives met on these occasions also, and over the years the children. Often the men's distant schooldays were referred to, Buller Yeats and Old Frosty and the sergeant-major, the little red-skinned headmaster, and above all Torridge. Within the three families, in fact, Torridge had become a myth. The joke that had begun when they were all new boys together continued, as if driven by its own impetus. In the minds of the wives and children the innocence of Torridge, his true happiness in the face of mockery, and his fondness for the religious side of life all lived on. With some exactitude a physical image of the boy he'd been took root: his neatly knotted maroon House tie, his polished shoes, the hair that resembled a mouse's fur, the pudding face with two small eyes in it. "My dad's in the button business," Arrowsmith had only to say to cause instant laughter. "Torridge's, you know." The way Torridge ate, the way he ran, the way he smiled back at Buller Yeats, the rumour that he'd been dropped on his head as a baby, that he had three kidneys, all this was considerably appreciated, because Wiltshire and Mace-Hamilton and Arrowsmith related it well.

What was not related was R.A.J. Fisher's error in placing a note beneath Torridge's pillow, or the story that had laughingly been spread about concerning Torridge's relationship with God Harvey. This would

have meant revelations that weren't seemly in family circles, the explanation of the world of *bijou* and protector, the romance and cigarettes in
the hillside huts, the entangling of hearts. The subject had been touched
upon among the three husbands and their wives in the normal course of
private conversation, although not everything had been quite recalled.
Listening, the wives had formed the impression that the relationships between older and younger boys at their husbands' school were similar to
the platonic admiration a junior girl had so often harboured for a senior
girl at their own schools. And so the subject had been left.

One evening in June, 1976, Wiltshire and Mace-Hamilton met in a
bar called the Vine, in Piccadilly Place. They hadn't seen one another
since the summer of 1974, the last time Arrowsmith and his family had
been in England. Tonight they were to meet the Arrowsmiths again, for
a family dinner in the Woodlands Hotel, Richmond. On the last occasion
the three families had celebrated their reunion at the Wiltshires' house in
Cobham and the time before with the Mace-Hamiltons in Ealing. Arrowsmith insisted that it was a question of turn and turn about, and every
third time he arranged for the family dinner to be held at his expense at
the Woodlands. It was convenient because, although the Arrowsmiths
spent the greater part of each biennial leave with Mrs. Arrowsmith's parents in Somerset, they always stayed for a week at the Woodlands in
order to see a bit of London life.

In the Vine in Piccadilly Place, Wiltshire and Mace-Hamilton hurried
over their second drinks. As always, they were pleased to see one another,
and both were excited at the prospect of seeing Arrowsmith and his family
again. They still looked faintly alike. Both had balded and run to fat.
They wore inconspicuous blue suits with a discreet chalk stripe, Wiltshire's a little smarter than Mace-Hamilton's.

"We'll be late," Wiltshire said, having just related how he'd made a
small killing since the last time they'd met. Wiltshire operated in the
import-export world; Mace-Hamilton was a chartered accountant.

They finished their drinks. "Cheerio," the barman called out to them
as they slipped away. His voice was deferentially low, matching the softly
lit surroundings. "Cheerio, Gerry," Wiltshire said.

They drove in Wiltshire's car to Hammersmith, over the bridge and
on to Barnes and Richmond. It was a Friday evening; the traffic was
heavy.

"He had a bit of trouble, you know," Mace-Hamilton said.

"Arrows?"

"She took a shine to some guy in Mombasa."

Wiltshire nodded, poking the car between a cyclist and a taxi. He wasn't surprised. One night six years ago Arrowsmith's wife and he had committed adultery together at her suggestion. A messy business it had been, and afterwards he'd felt terrible.

~ ~ ~

In the Woodlands Hotel, Arrowsmith, in a grey flannel suit, was not entirely sober. He, too, had run a bit to fat although, unlike Wiltshire and Mace-Hamilton, he hadn't lost any of his hair. Instead, it had dramatically changed colour: what Old Frosty had once called "Arrows' blond thatch" was grey now. Beneath it his face was pinker than it had been, and he had taken to wearing spectacles, heavy and black-rimmed, making him look even more different from the boy he'd been.

In the bar of the Woodlands he drank whisky on his own, smiling occasionally to himself because tonight he had a surprise for everybody. After five weeks of being cooped up with his in-laws in Somerset, he was feeling good. "Have one yourself, dear," he invited the barmaid, a girl with an excess of lipstick on a podgy mouth. He pushed his own glass towards her while she was saying she didn't mind if she did.

His wife and his three adolescent children, two boys and a girl, entered the bar with Mrs. Mace-Hamilton. "Hi, hi, hi," Arrowsmith called out to them in a jocular manner, causing his wife and Mrs. Mace-Hamilton to note that he was drunk again. They sat down while he quickly finished the whisky that had just been poured for him. "Put another in that for a start," he ordered the barmaid, and crossed the floor of the bar to find out what everyone else wanted.

Mrs. Wiltshire and her twins, girls of twelve, arrived while drinks were being decided about. Arrowsmith kissed her, as he had kissed Mrs. Mace-Hamilton. The barmaid, deciding that the accurate conveying of such a large order was going to be beyond him, came and stood by the two tables that the party now occupied. The order was given; an animated conversation began.

The three women were different in appearance and in manner. Mrs. Arrowsmith was thin as a knife, fashionably dressed in a shade of ash grey that reflected her ash-grey hair. She smoked perpetually, unable to abandon the habit. Mrs. Wiltshire was small. Shyness caused her to coil herself up in the presence of other people, so that she often resembled a ball. Tonight she was in pink, a faded shade. Mrs. Mace-Hamilton was carelessly plump, a large woman attired in a carelessly chosen dress that had begonias on it. She rather frightened Mrs. Wiltshire. Mrs. Arrowsmith found her trying.

"Oh, heavenly little drink!" Mrs. Arrowsmith said, briefly drooping her blue-tinged eyelids as she sipped her gin and tonic.

"It *is* good to see you," Mrs. Mace-Hamilton gushed, beaming at everyone and vaguely raising her glass. "And how they've all grown!" Mrs. Mace-Hamilton had not had children herself.

"Their boobs have grown, by God," the older Arrowsmith boy murmured to his brother, a reference to the Wiltshire twins. Neither of the two Arrowsmith boys went to their father's school: one was at a preparatory school in Oxford, the other at Charterhouse. Being of an age to do so, they both drank sherry and intended to drink as much of it as they possibly could. They found these family occasions tedious. Their sister, about to go to university, had determined neither to speak nor to smile for the entire evening. The Wiltshire twins were quite looking forward to the food.

Arrowsmith sat beside Mrs. Wiltshire. He didn't say anything, but after a moment he stretched a hand over her two knees and squeezed them in what he intended to be a brotherly way. He said without conviction that it was great to see her. He didn't look at her while he spoke. He didn't much care for hanging about with the women and children.

In turn Mrs. Wiltshire didn't much care for his hand on her knees and was relieved when he drew it away. "Hi, hi, hi," he suddenly called out, causing her to jump. Wiltshire and Mace-Hamilton had appeared.

The physical similarity that had been so pronounced when the three men were boys and had been only faintly noticeable between Wiltshire and Mace-Hamilton in the Vine was clearly there again, as if the addition of Arrowsmith had supplied missing reflections. The men had thickened in the same way; the pinkness of Arrowsmith's countenance was a pinkness that tinged the other faces too. Only Arrowsmith's grey thatch of hair seemed out of place, all wrong beside the baldness of the other two: in their presence it might have been a wig, an impression it did not otherwise give. His grey flannel suit, beside their pinstripes, looked like something put on by mistake. "Hi, hi, hi," he shouted, thumping their shoulders.

Further rounds of drinks were bought and consumed. The Arrow-smith boys declared to each other that they were drunk and made further *sotto voce* observations about the forming bodies of the Wiltshire twins. Mrs. Wiltshire felt the occasion becoming easier as Cinzano Bianco coursed through her bloodstream. Mrs. Arrowsmith was aware of a certain familiar edginess within her body, a desire to be elsewhere, alone with a man she did not know. Mrs. Mace-Hamilton spoke loudly of her garden.

In time the party moved from the bar to the dining-room. "Bring us another round at the table," Arrowsmith commanded the lipsticked bar-maid. "Quick as you can, dear."

In the large dim dining-room, waiters settled them around a table with little vases of carnations on it, a long table beneath the chandelier in the centre of the room. Celery soup arrived at the table, and smoked salmon and pâté, and the extra round of drinks Arrowsmith had ordered, and bottles of Nuits St. Georges, and bottles of Vouvray and Anjou Rosé, and sirloin of beef, chicken à la king, and veal escalope. The Arrowsmith boys laughed shrilly, openly staring at the tops of the Wiltshire twins' bodies. Potatoes, peas, spinach, and carrots were served. Mrs. Arrowsmith waved the vegetables away and smoked between courses. It was after this dinner six years ago that she had made her suggestion to Wiltshire, both of them being the worse for wear and it seeming not to matter because of that. "Oh, *isn't* this jolly?" the voice of Mrs. Mace-Hamilton boomed above the general hubbub.

Over Chantilly trifle and Orange Surprise the name of Torridge was heard. The name was always mentioned just about now, though some-times sooner. "Poor old bean," Wiltshire said, and everybody laughed because it was the one subject they all shared. No one really wanted to hear about the Mace-Hamiltons' garden; the comments of the Arrow-smith boys were only for each other; Mrs. Arrowsmith's needs could naturally not be voiced; the shyness of Mrs. Wiltshire was private too. But Torridge was different. Torridge in a way was like an old friend now, existing in everyone's mind, a family subject. The Wiltshire twins were quite amused to hear of some freshly remembered evidence of Torridge's naïveté; for the Arrowsmith girl it was better at least than being ques-tioned by Mrs. Mace-Hamilton; for her brothers it was an excuse to bellow with simulated mirth. Mrs. Mace-Hamilton considered that the boy sounded frightful, Mrs. Arrowsmith couldn't have cared less. Only Mrs. Wiltshire had doubts: she thought the three men were hard on the memory of the boy, but of course had not ever said so. Tonight, after Wiltshire had recalled the time when Torridge had been convinced by Arrowsmith that Buller Yeats had dropped dead in his bath, the younger Arrowsmith boy told of a boy at his own school who'd been convinced that his sister's dog had died.

"Listen," Arrowsmith suddenly shouted out. "He's going to join us. Old Torridge."

There was laughter, no one believing that Torridge was going to arrive, Mrs. Arrowsmith saying to herself that her husband was pitiful when he became as drunk as this.

"I thought it would be a gesture," Arrowsmith said. "Honestly. He's looking in for coffee."

"You bloody devil, Arrows," Wiltshire said, smacking the table with the palm of his hand.

"He's in the button business," Arrowsmith shouted. "Torridge's, you know."

As far as Wiltshire and Mace-Hamilton could remember, Torridge had never featured in an Old Boys' magazine. No news of his career had been printed, and certainly no obituary. It was typical, somehow, of Arrowsmith to have winkled him out. It was part and parcel of him to want to add another dimension to the joke, to recharge its batteries. For the sight of Torridge in middle age would surely make funnier the reported anecdotes.

"After all, what's wrong," demanded Arrowsmith noisily, "with old school pals all meeting up? The more the merrier."

He was a bully, Mrs. Wiltshire thought: all three of them were bullies.

~ ~ ~

Torridge arrived at half past nine. The hair that had been like a mouse's fur was still like that. It hadn't greyed any more; the scalp hadn't balded. He hadn't run to fat; in middle age he'd thinned down a bit. There was even a lankiness about him now, which was reflected in his movements. At school he had moved slowly, as though with caution. Jauntily attired in a pale linen suit, he crossed the dining-room of the Woodlands Hotel with a step as nimble as a tap dancer's.

No one recognized him. To the three men who'd been at school with him the man who approached their dinner table was a different person, quite unlike the figure that existed in the minds of the wives and children.

"My dear Arrows," he said, smiling at Arrowsmith. The smile was different too, a brittle snap of a smile that came and went in a matter-of-fact way. The eyes that had been small didn't seem so in his thinner face. They flashed with a gleam of some kind, matching the snap of his smile.

"Good God, it's never old Porridge!" Arrowsmith's voice was slurred. His face had acquired the beginnings of an alcoholic crimson, sweat glistened on his forehead.

"Yes, it's old Porridge," Torridge said quietly. He held his hand out towards Arrowsmith and then shook hands with Wiltshire and Mace-Hamilton. He was introduced to their wives, with whom he shook hands also. He was introduced to the children, which involved further handshaking. His hand was cool and rather bony: they felt it should have been damp.

"You're nicely in time for coffee, Mr. Torridge," Mrs. Mace-Hamilton said.

"Brandy more like," Arrowsmith suggested. "Brandy, old chap?"

"Well, that's awfully kind of you, Arrows. Chartreuse I'd prefer, really."

A waiter drew up a chair. Room was made for Torridge between Mrs. Mace-Hamilton and the Arrowsmith boys. It was a frightful mistake, Wiltshire was thinking. It was mad of Arrowsmith.

Mace-Hamilton examined Torridge across the dinner table. The old Torridge would have said he'd rather not have anything alcoholic, that a cup of tea and a biscuit were more his line in the evenings. It was impossible to imagine this man saying his dad had a button business. There was a suavity about him that made Mace-Hamilton uneasy. Because of what had been related to his wife and the other wives and their children, he felt he'd been caught out in a lie, yet in fact that wasn't the case.

The children stole glances at Torridge, trying to see him as the boy who'd been described to them, and failing to. Mrs. Arrowsmith said to herself that all this stuff they'd been told over the years had clearly been rubbish. Mrs. Mace-Hamilton was bewildered. Mrs. Wiltshire was pleased.

"No one ever guessed," Torridge said, "what became of R.A.J. Fisher." He raised the subject suddenly, without introduction.

"Oh God, Fisher," Mace-Hamilton said.

"Who's Fisher?" the younger of the Arrowsmith boys enquired.

Torridge turned to flash his quick smile at the boy. "He left," he said. "In unfortunate circumstances."

"You've changed a lot, you know," Arrowsmith said. "Don't you think he's changed?" he asked Wiltshire and Mace-Hamilton.

"Out of recognition," Wiltshire said.

Torridge laughed easily. "I've become adventurous. I'm a late developer, I suppose."

"What kind of unfortunate circumstances?" the younger Arrowsmith boy asked. "Was Fisher expelled?"

"Oh no, not at all," Mace-Hamilton said hurriedly.

"Actually," Torridge said, "Fisher's trouble all began with the writing of a note. Don't you remember? He put it in my pyjamas. But it wasn't for me at all."

He smiled again. He turned to Mrs. Wiltshire in a way that seemed polite, drawing her into the conversation. "I was an innocent at school. But innocence eventually slips away. I found my way about eventually."

"Yes, of course," she murmured. She didn't like him, even though she was glad he wasn't as he might have been. There was malevolence in him, a ruthlessness that seemed like a work of art. He seemed like a work of art himself, as though in losing the innocence he spoke of he had re-created himself.

"I often wonder about Fisher," he remarked.

The Wiltshire twins giggled. "What's so great about this bloody Fisher?" the older Arrowsmith boy murmured, nudging his brother with an elbow.

"What're you doing these days?" Wiltshire asked, interrupting Mace-Hamilton, who had also begun to say something.

"I make buttons," Torridge replied. "You may recall my father made buttons."

"Ah, here're the drinks," Arrowsmith rowdily observed.

"I don't much keep up with the school," Torridge said as the waiter placed a glass of Chartreuse in front of him. "I don't so much as think about it, except for wondering about poor old Fisher. Our headmaster was a cretin," he informed Mrs. Wiltshire.

Again the Wiltshire twins giggled. The Arrowsmith girl yawned, and her brothers giggled also, amused that the name of Fisher had come up again.

"You will have coffee, Mr. Torridge?" Mrs. Mace-Hamilton offered, for the waiter had brought a fresh pot to the table. She held it poised above a cup. Torridge smiled at her and nodded. She said:

"Pearl buttons d'you make?"

"No, not pearl."

"Remember those awful packet peas we used to have?" Arrowsmith enquired. Wiltshire said:

"Use plastics at all? In your buttons, Porridge?"

"No, we don't use plastics. Leathers, various leathers. And horn. We specialize."

"How very interesting!" Mrs. Mace-Hamilton exclaimed.

"No, no. It's rather ordinary really." He paused, and then added, "Someone once told me that Fisher went into a timber business. But of course that was far from true."

"A chap was expelled a year ago," the younger Arrowsmith boy said, contributing this in order to cover up a fresh outburst of sniggering. "For stealing a transistor."

Torridge nodded, appearing to be interested. He asked the Arrowsmith boys where they were at school. The older one said Charterhouse and his brother gave the name of his preparatory school. Torridge nodded again and asked their sister, and she said she was waiting to go to university. He had quite a chat with the Wiltshire twins about their school. They considered it pleasant the way he bothered, seeming genuinely to want to know. The giggling died away.

"I imagined Fisher wanted me for his *bijou*," he said when all that was over, still addressing the children. "Our place was riddled with fancy larks like that. Remember?" he added, turning to Mace-Hamilton.

"Bijou?" one of the twins asked before Mace-Hamilton could reply.

"A male tart," Torridge explained.

The Arrowsmith boys gaped at him, the older one with his mouth actually open. The Wiltshire twins began to giggle again. The Arrowsmith girl frowned, unable to hide her interest.

"The Honourable Anthony Swain," Torridge said, "was no better than a whore."

Mrs. Arrowsmith, who for some minutes had been engaged with her own thoughts, was suddenly aware that the man who was in the button business was talking about sex. She gazed diagonally across the table at him, astonished that he should be talking in this way.

"Look here, Torridge," Wiltshire said, frowning at him and shaking his head. With an almost imperceptible motion he gestured towards the wives and children.

"Andrews and Butler. Dillon and Pratt. Tothill and Goldfish Stewart. Your dad," Torridge said to the Arrowsmith girl, "was always very keen. Sainsbury Major in particular."

"Now look here," Arrowsmith shouted, beginning to get to his feet and then changing his mind.

"My gosh, how they broke chaps' hearts, those three!"

"Please don't talk like this." It was Mrs. Wiltshire who protested, to everyone's surprise, most of all her own. "The children are quite young, Mr. Torridge."

Her voice had become a whisper. She could feel herself reddening with embarrassment, and a little twirl of sickness occurred in her stomach. Deferentially, as though appreciating the effort she had made, Torridge apologized.

"I think you'd better go," Arrowsmith said.

"You were right about God Harvey, Arrows. Gay as a grig he was, beneath that cassock. So was Old Frosty, as a matter of fact."

"Really!" Mrs. Mace-Hamilton cried, her bewilderment turning into outrage. She glared at her husband, demanding with her eyes that instantly something should be done. But her husband and his two friends were briefly stunned by what Torridge had claimed for God Harvey. Their schooldays leapt back at them, possessing them for a vivid moment: the dormitory, the dining-hall, the glances and the invitations, the meetings behind Chapel. It was somehow in keeping with the school's hypocrisy that God Harvey had had inclinations himself, that a rumour begun as an outrageous joke should have contained the truth.

"As a matter of fact," Torridge went on, "I wouldn't be what I am if it hadn't been for God Harvey. I'm what they call queer," he explained to the children. "I perform sexual acts with men."

"For God's sake, Torridge," Arrowsmith shouted, on his feet, his face the colour of ripe strawberry, his watery eyes quivering with rage.

"It was nice of you to invite me tonight, Arrows. Our *alma mater* can't be too proud of chaps like me."

People spoke at once, Mrs. Mace-Hamilton and Mrs. Wiltshire, all three men. Mrs. Arrowsmith sat still. What she was thinking was that she had become quietly drunk while her husband had more boisterously reached the same condition. She was thinking, as well, that by the sound of things he'd possessed as a boy a sexual urge that was a lot livelier than the one he'd once exposed her to and now hardly ever did. With boys who had grown to be men he had had a whale of a time. Old Frosty had been a kind of Mr. Chips, she'd been told. She'd never ever heard of Sainsbury Major or God Harvey.

"It's quite disgusting," Mrs. Mace-Hamilton's voice cried out above the other voices. She said the police should be called. It was scandalous to have to listen to unpleasant conversation like this. She began to say the children should leave the dining-room, but changed her mind because it appeared that Torridge himself was about to go. "You're a most horrible man," she cried.

Confusion gathered, like a fog around the table. Mrs. Wiltshire, who knew that her husband had committed adultery with Mrs. Arrowsmith, felt another bout of nerves in her stomach. "Because she was starved, that's why," her husband had almost violently confessed when she'd discovered. "I was putting her out of her misery." She had wept then, and he had comforted her as best he could. She had not told him that he had never succeeded in arousing in her the desire to make love: she had always assumed that to be a failing in herself, but now for some reason she was not so sure. Nothing had been directly said that might have caused this doubt, but an instinct informed Mrs. Wiltshire that the doubt should be there. The man across from her smiled his brittle, malevolent smile at her, as if in sympathy.

With his head bent over the table and his hands half hiding his face, the younger Arrowsmith boy examined his father by glancing through his fingers. There were men whom his parents warned him against, men who would sit beside you in buses or try to give you a lift in a car. This man who had come tonight, who had been such a joke up till now, was apparently one of these, not a joke at all. And the confusion was greater: at one time, it seemed, his father had been like that too.

The Arrowsmith girl considered her father also. Once she had walked into a room in Lagos to find her mother in the arms of an African clerk. Ever since, she had felt sorry for her father. There'd been an unpleasant scene at the time; she'd screamed at her mother and later in a fury had told her father what she'd seen. He'd nodded, wearily seeming not to be surprised, while her mother had miserably wept. She'd put her arms around her father, comforting him; she'd felt no mercy for her mother, no sympathy or understanding. The scene formed vividly in her mind as she sat at the dinner table: it appeared to be relevant in the confusion and yet not clearly so. Her parents' marriage was messy, messier than it had looked. Across the table her mother grimly smoked, focusing her eyes with difficulty. She smiled at her daughter, a soft, inebriated smile.

The older Arrowsmith boy was also aware of the confusion. Being at a school where the practice which had been spoken of was common enough, he could easily believe the facts that had been thrown about. Against his will, he was forced to imagine what he had never imagined before: his father and his friends as schoolboys, engaged in passion with other boys. He might have been cynical about this image, but he could not be. Instead, it made him want to gasp. It knocked away the smile that had been on his face all evening.

The Wiltshire twins unhappily stared at the white tablecloth, here and there stained with wine or gravy. They, too, found they'd lost the urge to smile and instead shakily blinked back tears.

"Yes, perhaps I'd better go," Torridge said.

With impatience Mrs. Mace-Hamilton looked at her husband, as if expecting him to hurry Torridge off or at least to say something. But Mace-Hamilton remained silent. Mrs. Mace-Hamilton licked her lips, preparing to speak herself. She changed her mind.

"Fisher didn't go into a timber business," Torridge said, "because poor old Fisher was dead as a doornail. Which is why our cretin of a headmaster, Mrs. Mace-Hamilton, had that Assembly."

"Assembly?" she said. Her voice was weak, although she'd meant it to sound matter-of-fact and angry.

"There was an Assembly that no one understood. Poor old Fisher had strung himself up in a barn on his father's farm. I discovered that," Torridge said, turning to Arrowsmith, "years later: from God Harvey actually. The poor chap left a note, but the parents didn't care to pass it on. I mean it was for you, Arrows."

Arrowsmith was still standing, hanging over the table. "Note?" he said. "For me?"

"Another note. Why d'you think he did himself in, Arrows?"

Torridge smiled, at Arrowsmith and then around the table.

"None of that's true," Wiltshire said.

"As a matter of fact it is."

He went, and nobody spoke at the dinner table. A body of a school-boy hung from a beam in a barn, a note on the straw below his dangling feet. It hung in the confusion that had been caused, increasing the confusion. Two waiters hovered by a sideboard, one passing the time by arranging sauce bottles, the other folding napkins into cone shapes. Slowly Arrowsmith sat down again. The silence continued as the conversation of Torridge continued to haunt the dinner table. He haunted it himself, with his brittle smile and his tap dancer's elegance, still faithful to the past in which he had so signally failed, triumphant in his middle age.

Then Mrs. Arrowsmith quite suddenly wept and the Wiltshire twins wept and Mrs. Wiltshire comforted them. The Arrowsmith girl got up and walked away, and Mrs. Mace-Hamilton turned to the three men and said they should be ashamed of themselves, allowing all this to happen.

Some of
These
Days

What my landlord's friends said about me was in a way the gospel truth, that is he was good to me and I was mean and ungrateful to him. All the two years I was in jail, nonetheless, I thought only of him, and I was filled with regret for the things I had done against him. I wanted him back. I didn't exactly wish to go back to live with him now, mind you, I had been too mean to him for that, but I wanted him for a friend again. After I got out of jail I would need friendship, for I didn't need to hold up even one hand to count my friends on, the only one I could even name was him. I didn't want anything to do with him phys-ically again, I had kind of grown out of that somehow even more while in jail, and wished to try to make it with women again, but I did require my landlord's love and affection, for love was, as everybody was always saying, his special gift and talent.

He was at the time I lived with him a rather well-known singer, and he also composed songs, but even when I got into my bad trouble, he was beginning to go downhill, and not to be so in fashion. We often quarreled over his not succeeding way back then. Once I hit him when he told me how much he loved me, and knocked out one of his front teeth. But that was only after he had also criticized me for not keeping

JAMES PURDY is the author of such novels and story collections as Malcolm, 63: Dream Palace, In the Hollow of His Hand, *and* The Candles of Your Eyes. *He lives in Brooklyn, New York.*

the apartment tidy and clean and doing the dishes, and I threatened him with an old gun I kept. Of course I felt awful bad about his losing this front tooth when he needed good teeth for singing. I asked his forgiveness. We made up and I let him kiss me and hold me tight just for this one time.

I remember his white face and sad eyes at my trial for breaking and entering and possession of a dangerous weapon, and at the last his tears when the judge sentenced me. My landlord could cry and not be ashamed of crying, and so you didn't mind him shedding tears somehow. At first, then, he wrote me, for as the only person who could list himself as nearest of kin or closest tie, he was allowed by the authorities to communicate with me, and I also received little gifts from him from time to time. And then all upon a sudden the presents stopped, and shortly after that, the letters too, and then there was no word of any kind, just nothing. I realized then that I had this strong feeling for him which I had never had for anybody before, for my people had been dead from the time almost I was a toddler, and so they are shadowy and dim, whilst he is bright and clear. That is, you see, I had to admit to myself in jail (and I choked on my admission), but I had hit bottom, and could say a lot of things now to myself, I guess I was in love with him. I had really only loved women, I had always told myself, and I did not love this man so much physically, in fact he sort of made me sick to my stomach to think of him that way, though he was a good-looker with his neat black straight hair, and his robin's-egg-blue eyes, and cheery smile. . . . And so there in my cell I had to confess what did I have for him if it was not love, and yet I had treated him meaner than anybody I had ever knowed in my life, and once come close to killing him. Thinking about him all the time now, for who else was there to think about, I found I got to talking to myself more and more, like an old geezer of advanced years, and in place of calling on anybody else or any higher power, since he was the only one I had never met in my twenty years of life who said he cared. I would find myself saying, like in church, *My landlord*, though that term for him was just a joke for the both of us, for all he had was this one-room flat with two beds, and my bed was the little one, no more than a cot, and I never made enough to pay him no rent for it, he just said he would trust me. So there in my cell, especially at night, I would say *My landlord*, and finally, for my chest begin to trouble me about this time and I was short of breath often, I would just manage to get out *My lord*. That's what I would call him for short. When I got out, the first thing I made up my mind to do was find him, and I was going to put all my efforts behind the search.

And when there was no mail now at all, I would think over all the kind and good things he done for me, and the thought would come to me which was blacker than any punishment they had given me here in the big house that I had not paid him back for his good deeds. When I got out I would make it up to him. He had took me in off the street, as people say, and had tried to make a man of me, or at least a somebody out of me, and I had paid him back all in bad coin, first by threatening to kill him, and then by going bad and getting sent to jail. . . . But when I got out, I said, I will find him if I have to walk from one ocean shore to the other.

And so it did come about that way, for once out, that is all I did or found it in my heart to do, find the one who had tried to set me straight, find the one who had done for me, and shared and all.

One night after I got out of jail, I had got dead drunk and stopped a guy on Twelfth Street, and spoke, *Have you seen my lord?* This man motioned me to follow him into a dark little theater, which later I was to know all too well as one of the porno theaters, he paid for me, and brought me to a dim corner in the back, and then the same old thing started up again, he beginning to undo my clothes, and lower his head, and I jumped up and pushed him and ran out of the movie, but then stopped and looked back and waited there as it begin to give me an idea.

Now a terrible thing had happened to me in jail. I was beat on the head by another prisoner, and I lost some of the use of my right eye, so that I am always straining by pushing my neck around as if to try to see better, and when the convict hit me that day and I was unconscious for several weeks and they despaired of my life, later on, when I come to myself at last, I could remember everything that had ever happened in my whole twenty years of life except my landlord's name, and I couldn't think of it if I was to be alive. That is why I have been in the kind of difficulty I have been in. It is the hardest thing in the world to hunt for somebody if you don't know his name.

I finally though got the idea to go back to the big building where he and I had lived together, but the building seemed to be under new management, with new super, new tenants, new everybody. Nobody anyhow remembered any singer, they said, nor any composer, and then after a time, it must have been though six months from the day I returned to

New York, I realized that I had gone maybe to a building that just looked like the old building my landlord and I have lived in, and so I tore like a blue streak straight away to this "correct" building to find out if any such person as him was living there, but as I walked around through the halls looking, I become somewhat confused all over again if this was the place either, for I had wanted so bad to find the old building where he and I had lived. I had maybe been overconfident of this one also being the correct place, and so as I walked the halls looking and peering about I become puzzled and unsure all over again, and after a few more turns, I give up and left.

That was an awesome fall, and then winter coming on and all, and no word from him, no trace, and then I remembered a thing from the day that man had beckoned me to come follow him into that theater, and I remembered something, I remembered that on account of my land-lord being a gay or queer man, one of his few pleasures when he got an extra dollar was going to the porno movies in Third Avenue. My re-membering this was like a light from heaven, if you can think of heaven throwing light on such a thing, for suddenly I knowed for sure that if I went to the porno movie I would find him.

The only drawback for me was these movies was somewhat expensive by now, for since I been in jail prices have surely marched upwards, and I have very little to keep me even in necessities. This was the beginning of me seriously begging, and sometimes I would be holding out my hand on the street for three fourths of a day before I got me enough to pay my way into the porno theater. I would put down my three bucks, and enter the turnstile, and then inside wait until my eyes got used to the dark, which because of my prison illness took nearly all of ten minutes, and then I would go up each aisle looking for my landlord. There was not a face I didn't examine carefully. . . . My interest in the spectators earned me several bawlings-out from the manager of the theater, who took me for somebody out to proposition the customers, but I paid him no mind. . . . But his fussing with me gave me an idea too, for I am attractive to men, both young and old, me being not yet twenty-one, and so I began what was to become regular practice, letting the audience take any liberty they was in a mind to with me in the hopes that through this contact they would divulge the whereabouts of my landlord.

But here again my problem would surface, for I could not recall the very name of the person who was most dear to me, yes that was the real sore spot. But as the men in the movie theater took their liberties with me, which after a time I got sort of almost to enjoy, even though I could barely see their faces, only see enough to know they was not my landlord, I would then, I say, describe him in full to them, and I will give them this much credit, they kind of listened to me as they went about getting their kicks from me, they would bend an ear to my asking for this information, but in the end they never heard of him nor any other singer, and never knowed a man who wrote down notes for a living.

But strange as it might seem to anybody who will ever see these sheets of paper, this came to be my only connection with the world, my only life—sitting in the porno theater. Since my only purpose was to find him and from him find my own way back, this was the only thoroughfare there was open for me to reach him. And yet I did not like it, though at the same time, even disliking it as much as I did, it give me some little feeling of a resemblance to warmth and kindness as the unknown men touched me with their invisible faces and extracted from me all I had to offer, such as it was. And then when they had finished me, I would ask them if they knew my landlord (or as I whispered to myself, my lord). But none ever did.

Winter had come in earnest, was raw in the air. The last of the leaves in the park had long blown out to sea, and yet it was not to be thought of giving up the search and going to a warmer place. I would go on here until I had found him or I would know the reason why, yes, I must find him, and not give up. (I tried to keep the phrase *My lord* only for myself, for once or twice when it had slipped out to a stranger, it give him a start, and so I watched what I said from there on out.)

And then I was getting down to the last of the little money I had come out of jail with, and oh the porno theater was so dear, the admission was hiked another dollar just out of the blue, and the leads I got in that old dark hole was so few and far between. Toward the end one man sort of perked up when I mentioned my landlord, the singer, and said he thought he might have known such a fellow, but with no name to go on, he too soon give up and said he guessed he didn't know after all.

And so I was stumped. Was I to go on patronizing the porno theater, I would have to give up food, for my panhandling did not bring in enough for both grub and movies, and yet there was something about bein' in that house, getting the warmth and attention from the stray men, that meant more to me than food and drink. So I began to go without eating in earnest so as to keep up my regular attendance at the films. That was maybe, looking back on it now, a bad mistake, but what is one bad mistake in a lifetime of them.

As I did not eat now but only give my favors to the men in the porno, I grew pretty unsteady on my feet. After a while I could barely drag to the theater. Yet it was the only place I wanted to be, especially in view of its being now full winter. But my worst fear was now realized, for I could no longer afford even the cheap lodging place I had been staying at, and all I had in the world was what was on my back, and the little in my pockets, so I had come at last to this, and yet I did not think about my plight so much as about him, for as I got weaker and weaker he seemed to stand over me as large as the figures of the film actors that raced across the screen, and at which I almost never looked, come to think of it. No, I never watched what went on on the screen itself. I watched the audience, for it was the living that would be able to give me the word.

"Oh come to me, come back and set me right!" I would whisper, hoping someone out of the audience might rise and tell me they knew where he was.

Then at last, but of course slow gradual like, I no longer left the theater. I was too weak to go out, anyhow had no lodging now to call mine, knew if I got as far as a step beyond the entrance door of the theater, I would never get back inside to its warmth, and me still dressed in my summer clothes.

Then after a long drowsy time—days, weeks, who knows?—my worse than worst fears was realized, for one—shall I say day? for where I was now there was no day or night, and the theater never closed its doors—one time, then, I say, they *come* for me, they had been studying my condition, they told me later, and they come to take me away. I begged them with all the strength I had left not to do so, that I could still walk, that I would be gone and bother nobody again.

When did you last sit down to a bite to eat? A man spoke this direct into my ear, a man by whose kind of voice I knew did not belong to the porno world, but come from some outside authority.

I have lost all track of time, I replied, closing my eyes.

All right, buddy, the man kept saying, and *Now, bud,* and then as I fought and kicked, they held me and put the straitjacket on me, though didn't they see I was too weak and dispirited to hurt one cruddy man jack of them.

Then as they was taking me finally away, for the first time in months I raised my voice, as if to the whole city, and called, and shouted, and explained: "*Tell him if he comes, how long I have waited and searched, that I have been hunting for him, and I cannot remember his name. I was hit in prison by another convict and the injury was small, but it destroyed my one needed memory, which is his name. That is all that is wrong with me. If you would cure me of this one little defect, I will never bother any of you again, never bother society again. I will go back to work and make a man of myself, but I have first to thank this former landlord for all he done for me.*"

"He is hovering between life and death."

I repeated aloud the word "hovering" after the man who had pronounced this sentence somewhere in the vicinity of where I was lying, in a bed that smelled strong of carbolic acid.

And as I said the word "hovering," I knew his name. I raised up. Yes, my landlord's name had come back to me. . . . It had come back after all the wreck and ruin of these weeks and years.

But then one sorrow would follow upon another, as I believe my mother used to say, though that is so long ago I can't believe I had a mother, for when they saw that I was conscious and in my right mind, they come to me and begun asking questions, especially what was my name. I stared at them then with the greatest puzzlement and sadness, for though I had fished up his name from so far down, I could no more remember my own name now when they asked me for it than I could have got out of my straitjacket and run a race, and I was holding on to the just-found landlord's name with the greatest difficulty, for it, too, was beginning to slip from my tongue and go disappear where it had been lost before.

As I hesitated, they begun to persecute me with their kindness, telling me how they would help me in my plight, but first of all they must have my name, and since they needed a name so bad, and was so insistent, I could see their kindness beginning to go, and the cruelty I had known in jail coming fresh to mind, I said, "I am Sidney Fuller," giving them you see my landlord's name.

"And your age, Sidney?"

"Twenty, come next June."

"And how did you earn your living?"

"I have been without work now for some months."

"What kind of work do you do?"

"Hard labor."

"When were you last employed?"

"In prison."

There was a silence, and the papers was moved about, then: "Do you have a church or faith?"

I waited quite a while, repeating his name, and remembering I could not remember my own, and then I said, "I am of the same faith as my landlord."

There was an even longer silence then, like the questioner had been cut down by his own inquiry, anyhow they did not interrogate me any more after that, they went away and left me by myself.

After a long time, certainly days, maybe weeks, they announced the doctor was coming.

He set down on a sort of ice cream chair beside me, and took off his glasses and wiped them. I barely saw his face.

"Sidney," he began, after it sounded like he had started to say something else first and then changed his mind. "Sidney, I have some very serious news to impart to you, and I want you to try to be brave. It is hard for me to say what I am going to say. I will tell you what we have discovered. I want you, though, first, to swallow this tablet, and we will wait together for a few minutes, and then I will tell you."

I had swallowed the tablet it seemed a long time ago, and then all of a sudden I looked down at myself, and I saw I was not in the straitjacket, my arms was free.

"Was I bad, Doctor?" I said, and he seemed to be glad I had broke the ice, I guess.

"I believe, Sidney, that you know in part what I am going to say to you," he started up again. He was a dark man, I saw now, with thick eyebrows, and strange, I thought, that for a doctor he seemed to have no wrinkles, his face was smooth as a sheet.

"We have done all we could to save you, you must believe us," he was going on as I struggled to hear his words through the growing drowsiness given me by the tablet. "You have a sickness, Sidney, for which unfortunately there is today no cure. . . ."

He said more, but I do not remember what, and was glad when he left, no, amend that, I was sad I guess when he left. Still, it didn't matter one way or another if anybody stayed or lit out.

But after a while, when I was a little less drowsy, a new man come in, with some white papers under his arm.

"You told us earlier when you were first admitted," he was saying, "that your immediate family is all dead. . . . Is there nobody to whom you wish to leave any word at all? . . . If there is such a person, we would appreciate your writing the name and address on each of these four sheets of paper, and add any instructions which you care to detail."

At that moment, I remembered my own name, as easily as if it had been written on the paper before me, and the sounds of it placed in my mouth and on my tongue, and since I could not give my landlord's name again, as the someone to whom I could bequeath my all, I give the inquirer with the paper my own real name:

James De Salles

"And his address?" the inquirer said.

I shook my head.

"Very well, then, Sidney," he said, rising from the same chair the doctor had sat in. He looked at me some time, then kind of sighed, and folded the sheaf of papers.

"Wait," I said to him then, "just a minute. . . . Could you get me writing paper, and fountain pen and ink to boot. . . ."

"Paper, yes. . . . We have only ballpoint pens, though. . . ."

So then he brought the paper and the ballpoint, and I have written this down, asking another patient here from time to time how to say this, or spell that, but not showing him what I am about, and it is queer indeed, isn't it, that I can only bequeath these papers to myself, for God only knows who would read them later, and it has come to me very clear in my sleep that my landlord is dead also, so there is no point in my telling my attendants that I have lied to them, that I am really James De Salles, and that my lord is or was Sidney Fuller.

But after I done wrote it all down, I was quiet in my mind and heart, and so with some effort I wrote my own name on the only thing I have to leave, and which they took from me a few moments ago with great puzzlement, for neither the person was known to them, and the address of course could not be given, and they only received it from me, I suppose, to make me feel I was being tended to.

~ *Barbara Pym* ~

FROM

A Glass of
Blessings

"Perhaps you will see Piers's lodgings," said Sybil, when I told her of the invitation, so much more respectable than my secret expedition would have been.

"Lodgings" sounded old-fashioned and sordid, and for a moment I felt as if it were wrong to be looking forward to the afternoon so much.

"He's asked me to have tea with him, but I suppose we may go to some public place," I said.

"It's a pity the Derry Roof Gardens aren't open on Saturday afternoons," said Sybil drily, "but I expect you'd enjoy a tea he had prepared himself better than anything else. Women like to see men doing domestic things, especially if they are not done very well—if the tea is too weak or too strong, or the toast burnt."

"I don't suppose Piers is very domesticated," I said happily, imagining the sort of tea we might have. Perhaps not toast, as it was a hot day, but roughly cut bread and butter and sickly bought cakes. "It won't be like having tea with Mr. Bason."

BARBARA PYM wrote many charming and infectiously readable novels, among them Excellent Women, Quartet in Autumn, *and* No Fond Return of Love. *Renowned for her stylistic panache, gentility, humor, and modesty, she is less widely recognized as one of the first English writers to include homosexual characters in her work without sensationalizing or condemning them. Readers interested in pursuing this substratum of the Pym universe should have a look at* A Glass of Blessings, *excerpted here, and* The Sweet Dove Died, *without doubt her darkest and most savage novel. She died in 1980.*

"I should think not indeed." Sybil laughed. "Well, you look very nice and I hope you will enjoy yourself. Give Piers my kindest regards and tell him that I have composed six sentences showing—I hope correctly—the use of the personal infinitive."

If it had seemed odd, and it had a little, for Sybil to send me off to Piers with her blessing, I was now reminded that to her he was after all our Portuguese teacher and the brother of my best friend. She could not know the delicious walking-on-air feeling that pervaded me as I hurried across the park, hardly able to bear being even the prudent few minutes late.

May has always seemed to me, as indeed it has to poets, the most romantic of all the months. There are so many days when the air really is like wine—a delicate white wine, perhaps Vouvray drunk on the banks of the Loire. This afternoon had about it something of the quality of that day when Piers and I had walked through the Temple and seen the cat crouching among the tulips and the new leaves covering up the old sad fruits on the fig tree.

I was wearing a dress of deep coral-coloured poplin, very simple, with a pair of coral and silver earrings, and a bracelet to match. I always like myself in deep clear colours, and I felt at my best now and wondered if people were looking at me as I passed them. They seemed to be mostly lovers absorbed in each other, and I did not mind this, but when a drab-looking woman in a tweed skirt and crumpled pink blouse looked up from her sandwich and *New Statesman,* I felt suddenly embarrassed and was reminded of poor Miss Limpsett in Piers's office. What could her life have held? What future was there for her and the woman in the crumpled pink blouse?

I was glad when I reached our meeting place and saw Piers standing with his back to me, apparently absorbed in a border of lupins. I wanted to rush up to him with some silly extravagant gesture, like covering his eyes with my hands; and my hands were outstretched, waiting to be taken in his, when I called his name and he turned round to face me.

"I hope I'm not late," I said, discarding as one does the other, more exciting openings I had prepared.

"Not very," he said, evading my outstretched hands without seeming to do so in any obvious way. "You look very charming. That colour suits you."

I had hoped he would say this, but I was pleased when the words actually came. We stood for a few moments looking at the lupins.

"How I should love to get right in among them and smell their warm peppery smell!" I said exuberantly. "I do so adore it!"

"My dear, it isn't quite you, this enthusiasm," said Piers. "You must be cool and dignified, and behave perfectly in character—not plunging in among lupins."

"Oh." I was a little cast down. "Is that how I am—cool and dignified? I don't mind being thought elegant, of course—but cool and dignified. It doesn't sound very lovable."

"Lovable? Is that how you want to be?" He sounded surprised.

"I should have thought everyone did on this sort of an afternoon," I said, rather at a loss. It was evident that his mood did not quite match mine, and that I should have to—as women nearly always must—damp down my own exuberant happiness until we were more nearly in sympathy.

"Wilmet, what's the matter with you? You're talking like one of the cheaper women's magazines." Piers's tone was rather petulant.

Love is the cheapest of all emotions, I thought; or such a universal one that it makes one talk like a cheap magazine. What, indeed, was the matter with me?

"I shouldn't have thought *you'd* know much about those," I said.

"We don't read them at the press, certainly, but one sees them somehow. Have we been long enough at these lupins? Shall we walk on?"

"Yes," I said, for I could think of nothing else to say.

"Poor girl," he said teasingly, after we had been walking in silence for some time. "Don't mind my ill humour. You said yourself that I was a moody person."

"All people are strange," I said crossly. Then I began telling him about Mr. Bason and the Fabergé egg. The story seemed to amuse him, and by the time we had walked across the park to the end of the Bayswater Road he was in a much better temper and I was feeling almost happy again.

"Imagine that scene in the choir vestry!" he exclaimed. "Taking the egg out of the pocket of his cassock and tossing it into the air. How I should love to have seen that! Now, Wilmet, what would you like to do next? Go to the pictures, have a nice sit-down in a deck chair, or what?"

"I should like to see where you live," I said firmly.

"All right. Tea at home, then. But don't expect too much. We must get a bus to Shepherd's Bush, first of all."

"Goodness—is it a very long way, then?"

"*You* would think it a long way—certainly too far to go by taxi."

"I always like a long bus ride," I said. "Do you remember Father Lester, who was at Rowena's cocktail party? He'd been at a church in Shepherd's Bush. He and his wife spoke so nostalgically of it."

"It's rather that kind of place, though it's a *nostalgie de la boue,* really."

"I suppose theirs wouldn't be that," I said. "I do hope they have settled down better now."

"It will be hard going for them there," said Piers. "I think that in some ways religion in the country *is* harder going than in town. Has it ever occurred to you that it's really the country words that rhyme with God in our language?"

"Yes, I suppose they do—clod, sod, and trod—what heavy words they are!"

"How hymn writers have struggled with them, poor things—it's a wonder all hymns aren't harvest hymns or for the burial of the dead. Those are really the only kind that the rhymes would fit."

"This must be Shepherd's Bush Green," I said. "Do we get out here?"

"No, we must go on a little way and then walk."

"Will your colleague be at home this afternoon?" I asked, as we stood on an island amid a swirl of trolley buses.

"My colleague?"

"The person you share the flat with."

"Oh, of course. Yes, it's quite likely he'll be doing the weekend shopping at this very minute."

We walked along a street full of cheap garish-looking dress shops, their windows crammed with blouses and skirts in crude colours, and butchers' and greengrocers' smelling sickly in the heat. When we came to a grocer's, Piers went into the doorway and looked inside.

"Yes, there he is," he said.

We went into the shop. I had imagined that I would immediately recognize the colleague when I saw him, but although there were several people at the counter, none of them seemed quite right. There were two men and three women, two elderly and the other young and flashily dressed, with dyed golden hair and long earrings. Surely, I wondered in horror, it couldn't be *her?* But no, Piers had said "he," so it must be one of the nondescript-looking men.

"Oh, there you are—I thought we'd probably find you here." Piers had gone over into a corner, where a small dark young man wearing black jeans and a blue tartan shirt, whom I had not noticed before, was peering into some biscuit tins.

"Wilmet, this is Keith—I don't think you've met before," said Piers in a rather jolly tone which did not seem quite natural to him.

Keith gave a stiff little bow and looked at me warily. He was about twenty-five years old, with a neat-featured rather appealing face and sombre brown eyes. His hair was cropped very short in the fashionable style of the moment. I noticed that it glistened like the wet fur of an animal.

"No, we haven't actually met, but I've heard a lot about you, Mrs. Forsyth," he said politely.

"I think we've spoken on the telephone, haven't we?" I said, recognizing the flat, rather common little voice as the one which had answered me the evening I had tried to ring up Piers. I could not reciprocate by saying that I had heard a lot about him, when I had heard nothing whatsoever. Indeed, I was so taken aback and confused by the encounter that I did not know what to say or even what to think. I stood rather awkwardly, my hand mechanically stroking a large black and white cat which was asleep on a sack of lentils. So *this* was the colleague.

Keith turned to Piers with some question about bacon.

"What do you think, Wilmet?" asked Piers. "Which is the best kind of bacon?"

"I don't know," I said, unable to give my attention to bacon. "It depends what you like."

"These two gentlemen will never make up their minds," said the motherly-looking woman behind the counter. "I have to help them choose every time. Now, what's the matter with that, dear?" she said to Keith. "Is it too fat for your liking?"

"We like it more striped, as it were," said Piers.

"*Striped!* Isn't that sweet—did you ever!" She turned to me. "You mean *streaky,* dear—that's what we call it. Let me cut you some off here—this is nice." She thrust a side of bacon towards us and then placed it in the machine.

It began to go backwards and forwards with a swishing noise, while the three of us stood in silence, watching it. There was an air of unreality about the whole scene—Keith, with his absurd clothes and bristly hair like a hedgehog or porcupine, was almost a comic figure. And yet I felt sad too, as if something had come to an end. The sadness, however, was underneath, and my most conscious feeling as I waited for somebody to break the silence was one of indignation.

"Have we finished yet?" Piers asked rather impatiently.

"I think we need custard powder," said Keith.

"*Custard powder?*" exclaimed Piers in horror. "Good God, whatever do we want custard powder for?"

"To make custard," said Keith flatly.

"You mean *you* want to make custard with it. Well, all right then, as long as you don't expect *me* to eat it."

"He'll eat anything, really," said Keith to me in a confidential tone, gathering his purchases together into a canvas bag not unlike Mr. Bason's. "I always think custard is nice with stewed fruit, don't you, Mrs. Forsyth?"

His respectful manner and constant use of my name were a little disconcerting, I found.

"Yes," I said inadequately, "I do."

We walked along the pavement, Keith and I together, with Piers a little in front. Nobody seemed to be saying anything, and perhaps conversation is not always necessary; but I felt that there was a kind of awkwardness about our silence, so I said to Keith, "You're not really at all as I'd imagined you."

"Had you imagined me, Mrs. Forsyth?" There was a note of eagerness in the flat little voice. "How did Piers describe me?"

Perhaps if I had said "he didn't" he would have been hurt, and it was lucky that Piers broke in rather impatiently before I had time to think of a tactful answer.

"We cross the road here," he said, "and take this turning opposite."

We were soon in a street of peeling stuccoed houses, which were not even noble in their shabbiness. I saw that some of them had been painted, while others, which had presumably been bombed, had had their façades rebuilt in a way which did not harmonize with the rest. There were rather a lot of children running about, and old women in bedroom slippers sunning themselves on ramshackle balconies crowded with plants in pots. Various kinds of music were blaring from the open windows.

"It's rather continental here, isn't it," I said. "It reminds me of Naples, you know."

"Thank you," said Piers. "That's really the best one can say about this district, and it's nice of you to say it."

"Where do you live, Mrs. Forsyth?" asked Keith.

I told him.

He paused a moment in what seemed a respectful silence, then said seriously, "I should think rents are very high there."

"Wilmet doesn't have to bother about dreary things like that," said Piers.

"No—I mean, the house belongs to my husband's mother, so I've never had to."

"I wish we could get a nice place, somewhere in a cleaner district," said Keith. "I have to wash the paint every week here. I just use plain soda and water—detergents make it go yellow. Do you find that, Mrs. Forsyth?"

"Well, I don't know," I said, ashamed of my ignorance.

"Keith, you must realize that Wilmet wouldn't know about dreary things like that," said Piers. "I don't suppose she's ever washed paint in her life."

"No, I haven't," I said crossly, "except perhaps when I was first in the Wrens. But am I any the worse for that? I could do it if I had to."

"But do remember about not using detergents," said Keith.

"Well, here we are," said Piers, with a note of relief in his tone.

We had stopped outside one of the newly painted houses. It had a flight of steps up to the front door and three bells, two of which had cards by them. One had HALIBURTON written in block capitals, the other a Polish name of daunting complexity on a printed visiting card.

"I suppose yours is the top bell, as it has no card on it," I said.

"Yes, we've got the top flat," said Keith chattily. "Two rooms with kitchenette, and we share the bathroom with Mr. Sienkiewicz."

"No relation to the author of *Quo Vadis?*, as far as we know, but the name is comforting in a way," said Piers.

We entered the hall and began to walk upstairs. I remembered how I had imagined the narrow hall with prams and bicycles and the smell of stale cooking or even other things, but there was a kind of deadness about this house on this fine Saturday afternoon. People were either out or behind closed doors, and I had the feeling that I ought to walk on tiptoe up the stairs, carpeted in maroon with a white squiggle pattern. And yet the silence was somehow unlike that of the clergy house, though I could not have said exactly why.

At last we reached the top floor.

"Where are we to have tea?" Piers asked. "My room is the obvious one, but I think I may have forgotten to make my bed, and I don't think Wilmet could stand the sight of that."

"I shouldn't mind," I said, for I had been preparing myself for the unmade bed—perhaps littered with galley proofs—for the bottle of gin, the unwashed glasses and cups, and the unemptied ashtrays.

"I tidied and cleaned your room while you were out," said Keith primly. "And I've laid tea in there."

"Good heavens!" Piers flung open a door. "It's hardly recognizable. Flowers, too." He glanced over to the bookcase, where some blue irises were arranged in a cut-glass vase. "Did you do all this?"

Keith smiled but said nothing.

I had wanted so much to see where Piers lived, and was disappointed that Keith should have tidied away the more obvious personal touches. The room was, of course, full of books; but I have rather ceased to regard books as being very personal things—everybody one knows has them and they are really rather obvious. It was no doubt significant that Mary Beamish should have the novels of Miss Goudge while Piers had those of Miss Compton-Burnett, but I should have been able to guess that for myself without actually seeing. I suppose I really *had* hoped for the py-jamas on the unmade bed and the shaving things on the mantelpiece, though perhaps, as Piers had said, I could not really have stood the sight of them.

Keith came back from the kitchen with the teapot and kettle, but he had evidently made most of his preparations in advance. There was a check tablecloth on a low table, and plates of sandwiches and biscuits and a pink and white gateau arranged on plastic doilies. Each plate had a paper table napkin laid across it. It was not at all like Mr. Bason's tea, but I had the feeling that it had been even more anxiously prepared and that I must therefore eat more than I wanted—which was really nothing—and praise it judiciously or even extravagantly. It was quite obvious that I was going to find it impossible to dislike Keith.

After we had finished tea I was taken on a tour of the flat.

"Of course the flat is furnished," Keith explained, "so we can't really have exactly what we want, but I got this contemporary print for my divan cover—do you like it, Mrs. Forsyth?"

I said that I did, though it was not particularly distinguished. His room was painfully neat and unlived in, as if everything had been arranged for effect. There were only two books on the table by the divan, a French grammar and a paperbacked novel with a lurid cover. A trailing plant of a kind which had lately become fashionable stood on another table, its pot in a white-painted metal cover. A print of Van Gogh's irises in a light oak frame hung on one wall.

"You're much tidier than Piers," I said. "And I think your room has a nice view, hasn't it?" I went over to the window hopefully.

"Yes, it is rather nice, isn't it, Mrs. Forsyth?" said Keith in a pleased tone. "You can even see trees in the distance."

"It's amazing how one can in London, isn't it?" I said.

"Yes," said Piers. "Even in the worst parts of London there is always a distant glimpse of some trees or Battersea power station or the top of Westminster Cathedral."

"I expect Mrs. Forsyth sees *many* trees where she lives," said Keith wistfully.

"Why don't you call her Wilmet?" Piers suggested. "I'm sure she wouldn't mind?"

"No, of course I shouldn't," I said, rather embarrassed.

"I expect your home is very nice, Wilmet," said Keith.

"You must come and have tea one day," I found myself saying, as I suspected I was meant to.

"Thank you, Wilmet," said Keith with quiet satisfaction. "I should like that."

He stood on the doorstep and waved as Piers and I went out of the house. I was surprised that he should be so friendly towards me, but then it occurred to me that he had no reason to be otherwise. It was a situation I had not met before, and I did not know what to say to Piers as we walked along the hot noisy street.

We were silent for a while, then I said rather stiffly, "So that is the person with whom you live."

"Yes. He's obviously taken a great fancy to you." Piers smiled. "Do you like him?"

"He seems a nice boy," I said, "but rather unexpected."

"In what way unexpected?"

"You said you lived with a colleague from the press. I suppose I'd imagined a different sort of person."

"*You* always said that I lived with a colleague. But aren't we all colleagues, in a sense, in this grim business of getting through life as best we can?"

I said nothing, so he went on. "My dear girl, what's the matter? Do you think I've been deceiving you, or something absurd like that?"

"No, of course I don't," I said indignantly. But of course, in a way, he had deceived me. "It would have been more friendly if you'd told me, though," I added.

"Well, now you and Keith have met, I'm sure you'll like each other. You really will have to ask him to tea, you know. He's dying to see your home, as he calls it."

I noticed that there was no malice in this last remark.

"Of course I shall," I said. "Where did you meet him, if I may be so inquisitive?"

"Why—at my French class."

"I see—that accounts for the French grammar by the bed, then."

"Yes—imagine it, Wilmet. The pathos of anyone not knowing French—I mean, not at all!"

"It does seem strange," I admitted. "So he was one of your pupils! Of course I had no idea . . ."

"No, why should you have?"

"But, Piers, why did you choose him of all people? I shouldn't have thought you had anything in common."

"This having things in common," said Piers impatiently, "how overrated it is! Long dreary intellectual conversations, capping each other's obscure quotations—it's so exhausting. It's much more agreeable to come home to some different remarks from the ones one's been hearing all day."

"I'm sure you get *those*," I said spitefully. "What does Keith do for a living, anyway?"

"Various things. At the moment he's working in a coffee bar in the evenings, and he sometimes gets modelling jobs."

"Good heavens!" I suppose I must have been unable to keep the note of horror out of my voice, for Piers said sharply, "Well, hasn't it ever occurred to you that somebody must pose for those photographs of handsome young men you see in knitting patterns and women's magazines?"

"Yes, but not people one actually *knows*."

"Not people *you* know, you mean, but there *are* others in the world—in fact quite a few million people outside the narrow select little circle that makes up Wilmet's world."

I had a dreadful feeling that I might be going to cry, but even that seemed impossible in the hot garish street with the Saturday evening shopping crowds and trolley buses swirling around us.

Piers looked at me curiously. "I'm sorry," he said more gently. "Perhaps I've gone too far. After all, I didn't really mean to imply that you're to blame for what you are. Some people are less capable of loving their fellow human beings than others," he went on in an almost academic way. "It isn't necessarily their fault."

"You're being horrid," I protested.

"But I often am—you should know that by now." He was smiling most charmingly as he spoke, which increased the confusion of my feelings still further. Perhaps I had never really known him, or—what was worse—myself. That anyone could doubt my capacity to love! But strangely enough my immediate thought was that I could not bear to go home by bus. I must get a taxi.

"This will take you most of the way," said Piers, as a bus approached the stop.

"I think I'd rather find a taxi."

"Dear Wilmet, so deliciously in character! Don't ever try to make yourself any different."

He waved to a passing taxi. They were no doubt easier to get here than in the better districts, I reflected.

"I've just remembered that Mary Beamish is coming back from the convent today," I said, trying to pull myself together. "She's coming to stay with us for a while, and I must be home before she arrives."

"Whatever will you say to her?" Piers asked. "Do you often have this kind of experience?"

"No," I said. "It will make two new experiences in one day."

"I hope they will both have been equally interesting and rewarding," said Piers. "Well, all experience is said to be that, isn't it?"

I got into the taxi and we waved good-bye. I could now imagine Piers going back to the house, climbing the stairs, perhaps sitting down heavily in an armchair, letting out an exaggerated sigh, while Keith's flat little voice began discussing me, criticizing my clothes and manner. I felt battered and somehow rather foolish, very different from the carefree girl who had set out across the park to meet Piers. But I was not a girl. I was a married woman, and if I felt wretched, it was no more than I deserved for having let my thoughts stray to another man. And the ironical thing was that it was Keith, that rather absurd little figure, who had brought about the change I thought I had noticed in Piers and which I had attributed to my own charms and loving care!

I lay back in the taxi and lit a cigarette. Into my temporarily blank mind there came a sudden picture of Father Bode, toothy and eager, talking about hiring a coach for the parish retreat. It was obscurely comforting to let my mind dwell on such things, and I suppose I must have been unconsciously preparing myself to meet Mary, covering up the humiliation and disappointment to be looked at later when I had more time.

I had hoped to be back before she arrived, but as soon as I opened the front door I knew that she had forestalled me. A suitcase and a brown canvas bag stood in the hall. I wondered irrelevantly that she should have so much luggage.

"Is that Wilmet?" I heard her eager voice say, and soon we were embracing and apologizing—she for being early, I for being late. I was glad to have something to do, to show her her room and sit with her while she unpacked the drab clothes she had worn in the convent— including the dyed black dress with the dye showing up the worn patches, which I should so much have disliked wearing myself.

"I really shall have to do some shopping," she said. "I've no summer things. Will you help me, Wilmet, please?"

I saw us shopping together, having lunch or tea in a restaurant, perhaps going to the pictures. It gave me the same comfortable feeling as thinking of Father Bode hiring a coach for the parish retreat. I knew that time would pass and that I should feel better.

After dinner we sat—Sybil, Mary, and I—in the drawing-room by the open window, looking out at the trees in the square. I heard again Keith's wistful voice saying, "I expect Mrs. Forsyth sees *many* trees where she lives." Rodney had decided to be out; he was rather nervous of meeting Mary, perhaps fearing that his conversational powers would not be up to the situation. It might be, after all, that I with my sheltered life was in some ways more fitted to deal with certain things, for which Rodney's, with public school and university, the war in Italy, and the

Civil Service, was inadequate. For there could, I felt, be situations for which even these varied experiences might have failed to equip him.

As it happened, Mary went to bed quite early, and Sybil and I were left alone, feeling that we could hardly discuss her the moment she had left the room. In any case she had seemed to be so very much her old self that there was little we could have said, especially when another more important and interesting subject was on our minds.

"So you saw Piers's lodgings," said Sybil, in the tone she used to invite discussion of a topic when no information had yet been offered.

"Yes, he has quite a nice flat, not properly self-contained but on the top floor, which does make it *seem* more self-contained," I found myself saying quickly.

"And the mysterious colleague—was he there?"

"Oh yes—we all had tea together."

"What is he like?"

"Younger than I'd expected—rather nice, really."

"I suppose he works at the press?"

"I'm not sure what he does," I said. For if I had ever thought that Sybil and I might enjoy a good laugh over Keith not knowing French, and posing for photographs of knitting patterns, I now realized that he had aroused in me some kind of—protective or maternal?—instinct which would save him from being turned into an object of ridicule.

Sybil yawned and rolled up her knitting.

"Well, it doesn't seem to have been a very exciting afternoon," she said. "I suppose I was hoping for some little bit of scandal—very wicked of me, I know, and wickedness is particularly distressing in *old* people don't you think? Do you want that knitting book, dear?"

"I thought I'd look through it and see if there's anything I could make for Rodney. I seem to want to knit when I see other people doing it."

I took the book up to my room and put it on the table by my bed. As I sat brushing my hair I caught sight of the little box which Harry had given me at Christmas.

If you will not when you may
When you will you shall have nay . . .

I pondered over the words in the light of the new character Piers had given me. How had Harry meant them to be taken? As a rather naughty little joke, or had there been a grain of truth in the words? I put the box into a drawer, not wanting to have to look at it every time I went to my dressing table.

In bed I turned the pages of the knitting book, looking for Keith. I soon found him, on the opposite page to a rugged-looking pipe-smoking man who was wearing a cable-stitch sweater which took thirty ounces of double knitting wool. Keith was leaning against a tree, one hand absently playing with a low-hanging branch. He wore a kind of lumber jacket with a shawl collar, knitted crossways in an intricate and rather pleasing stitch. "For Leisure Hours," the pattern said. "To fit a 36–38-inch chest. Commence at right cuff by casting on 64 sts. on No. 11 needles. . . ." It seemed as if he might have stood there patiently while some busy woman knitted the jacket onto him. The expression in the dark eyes was sombre and unfathomable, the lips unsmiling. If one ignored the slightly ridiculous setting, it was easy to see how he could become an object of devotion. This thought led me to consider the religious and secular meanings of the word "devotion," and how "devout" did not mean the same as "devoted." I was not sure why this was, but it seemed suitable that my life should have this confusion in it.

I went on looking at the patterns, comparing the expressions, and finding that though most were smiling and jolly, the sort of men one could imagine pottering about in the garden at the weekend or playing a round of golf, some were a little shamefaced, as if they hoped nobody they knew would come upon them posing for knitting patterns. None seemed to me to have Keith's air of romantic detachment. Was he thinking of French verbs, dreaming of the day when he could read Baudelaire with ease? I wondered. Or was his mind a blank, in the way that the minds of beautiful people are sometimes said to be? I began to want to know more of his origins and history. I thought he might be a colonial, perhaps a New Zealander; I remembered clever moody passionate girls, like Katherine Mansfield, striving to break away from the narrowness of their environment, almost nineteenth-century Russian in their yearnings, hating the traditional English Christmas in the middle of summer and the sentimental attitude towards the Mother Country. They would come to London and live wretchedly, perhaps starving in an attic, exulting in their freedom, and yet keeping underneath everything their innate primness and respectability. Was Keith like this, or did he just come from Fulham or Brixton or some dreary English provincial town? I supposed that if I kept my promise to ask him to tea I should be able to find out all about him.

I closed the knitting book and took a sleeping pill. I was just conscious of Rodney coming in very much later, but I did not open my eyes or speak to him.

~ *Edmund White* ~

Reprise

A novel I'd written, which had flopped in America, was about to come out in France, and I was racing around, vainly trying to assure its success in translation. French critics seldom give nasty reviews to books, but they often ignore a novel altogether, especially one by a foreign writer, even one who like me lives in Paris.

In the midst of these professional duties I suddenly received a phone call. A stifled baritone voice with a Midwestern accent asked if I was "Eddie." No one had called me that since my childhood. "It's Jim Grady. Your mother gave me your number."

I hadn't seen him in almost forty years, not since I was fourteen and he twenty, but I could still taste the Luckies and Budweiser beer on his lips, feel his powerful arms closing around me, remember the deliberate way he'd folded his trousers on the crease rather than throwing them on the floor in romantic haste as I'd done.

I met Jim through our parents. My mother was dating his father, an arrangement she'd been falling back on intermittently for years, although she mildly despised him. She went out with him when there was no one

EDMUND WHITE has written several novels, among them Nocturnes for the King of Naples, A Boy's Own Story, *and* The Beautiful Room Is Empty, *as well as a biography of Jean Genet. He was editor of* The Faber Book of Gay Short Fiction, *an estimable anthology that deserves a place next to this one on every bookshelf. He lives in Paris.*

better around. She was in her fifties, fat, highly sexed, hardworking, by turns bitter and wildly optimistic (now I'm all those things, so I feel no hesitation in describing her in those terms, especially since she was to change for the better in old age). My father and she had divorced seven years earlier, and she'd gone to work partly out of necessity but partly to make something out of herself. Her Texas relations expected great things from her, and their ambitions had shaped hers.

Before the divorce she'd studied psychology, and now she worked in the Chicago suburban public schools, traveling from one to another, systematically testing all the slow learners, problem cases, and "exceptional" children ("exceptional" meant either unusually intelligent or retarded). She put great stock in making an attractive, even a stunning appearance at those smelly cinder-block schools and rose early in the morning to apply her make-up, struggle into her girdle, and don dresses or suits that followed the fashions better than the contours of her stubby body.

In the gray, frozen dawns of Chicago winters she would drive her new Buick to remote schools where the assistant principal would install her in an empty classroom and bring her one child after another. Shy, dirty, suspicious kids would eye her warily, wag their legs together in a lackluster parody of sex, fall into dumb trances, or microscopically assay the hard black riches they'd mined from their nostrils, but nothing could dim my mother's glittering determination to be cheerful.

She never merely went through the motions or let a more appropriate depression muffle her performance. She always had the highly colored, fatuously alert look of someone who is listening to compliments. Perhaps she looked that way because she was continuously reciting her own praises to herself as a sort of protective mantra. Most people, I suspect, are given a part in which the dialogue keeps running out, a supporting role for which the lazy playwright has scribbled in, "Improvise background chatter" or "Crowd noises off." But my mother's lines had been fully scored for her (no matter that she'd written them herself), and she couldn't rehearse them often enough. Every night she came home, kicked off her very high heels, and wriggled out of her orthopedically strong girdle, shrinking and filling out and sighing, "Whooee!"—something her Ranger, Texas, mother would exclaim after feeding the chickens or rustling up some grub in the summer heat.

Then our mother would pour herself a stiff bourbon and water, first of the many highballs she'd need to fuel her through the evening. "I saw fifteen patients today—twelve Stanford-Binets, one Wexford, one House-Tree-Person. I even gave a Rorschach to a beautiful little epileptic with high potential." On my mother's lips, "beautiful" meant not a pretty face but a case of grimly classic textbook orthodoxy. "The children loved me. Several of them were afraid of me—I guess they'd never seen such a pretty, stylish lady all smiling and perfumed and bangled. But I put them right at ease. I know how to handle those backward children; they're just putty in my hands."

She thought for a moment, regarding her hands, then lit up. "The assistant principal was so grateful to me for my fine work. I guess she'd never had such an efficient, skilled state psychologist visit her poor little school before. She accompanied me to my automobile, and boy, you should have seen her eyes light up when she realized I was driving a fine Buick." Mother slung her stocking feet over the arm of the upholstered chair. "She grabbed my hand and looked me right in the eye and said, 'Who *are* you?' " This was the part of the litany I always hated, because it was so obviously a lie. " 'Why, whatever do you mean?' I asked her. 'You're no ordinary psychologist,' she said. 'I can see by your fine automobile and your beautiful clothes and your fine mind and lovely manners that you are a real lady.' " It was the phrase "fine automobile" that tipped me off, since only Southerners like my mother said that. Chicagoans said "nice car." Anyway, I'd never heard any Midwesterner praise another in such a gratifying way; only in my mother's scenarios were such heady scenes a regular feature.

As the night wore on and my sister and I would sit down to do our homework on the cleared dining room table, as the winter pipes would knock hypnotically and the lingering smell of fried meat would get into our hair and heavy clothes, our mother would pour herself a fourth highball and put on her glasses to grade the tests she'd administered that day or to write up her reports in her round hand, but she'd interrupt her work and ours to say, "Funny, that woman simply couldn't get over how a fine lady like me could be battling the Skokie slush to come out to see those pitiful children." The note of pity was introduced only after the fourth drink, and it was, I imagine, something she felt less for her patients than for herself as the telephone stubbornly refused to ring.

At that time in my mother's life she had few friends. Going out with other unmarried women struck her as a disgrace and defeat; she was convinced couples looked down on her as a divorcée, and those single men who might want to date a chubby, penniless middle-aged woman with two brats hanging around her neck were, as she'd say, scarce as hen's teeth.

That's where Mr. Grady came in. He was forty-five, going on sixty, overweight and utterly passive. He, too, liked his drinks, although in his case they were Manhattans; he fished the maraschino cherries out with his fingers. He didn't have false teeth, but there was something weak and sunken around his mouth as he mumbled his chemically bright cherries. His hairless hands were liver-spotted, and the nails were flaky, bluish, and unusually flat, which my mother, drawing on her fragmentary medical knowledge, called "spatulate," although I forget which malady this symptom was supposed to indicate. His wife had left him for another man, much richer, but she considerately sent Mr. Grady cash presents from time to time. He needed them. He lived reasonably well, and he didn't earn much. He worked on the city desk of a major Chicago daily, but he'd been there for nearly twenty years, and in that era, before the Newspaper Guild grew strong, American journalists were badly paid unless they were flashy, opinionated columnists. Mr. Grady wrote nothing and had few opinions. He occasionally assigned stories to reporters, but most of the time he filled out columns that ran short with curious scraps of information. These items were called, for some reason, "boilerplate" and were composed weeks, even months in advance. For all I know, they were bought ready-made from some Central Bureau of Timeless Information. Although Mr. Grady seldom said anything interesting and was much given to dithering over the practical details of his daily life, his work furnished him with the odd bit of startling knowledge.

"Did you realize that Gandhi ate meat just once in his life and nearly died of it?" he'd announce. "Did you know there is more electric wire in the Radio City Music Hall organ than in the entire city of Plattsburgh?"

He was capable of going inert, like a worm that poses as a stick to escape a bird's detection (I have my own stock of boilerplate). When my mother would hector him for not demanding a raise or for not acting like a man, his face would sink into his jowls, his chin into his chest, his chest into his belly, and the whole would settle lifelessly onto his elephantine legs. His eyes behind their thick glasses would refuse all contact. In that state he could remain nearly indefinitely, until at last my mother's irritation would blow over and she would make a move to head off for

Miller's Steak House, a family restaurant with a menu of sizzling T-bones, butter and rolls, French-fried onions, hot fudge sundaes, that would contribute to Mr. Grady's early death by cardiac arrest.

In September 1954 the Kabuki Theater came from Tokyo to Chicago for the first time, and my mother and Mr. Grady bought tickets for themselves and me and Mr. Grady's son, Jim, whom we had never met (my sister didn't want to go; she thought it sounded "weird," and the prospect of meeting an eligible young man upset her).

The minute I saw Jim Grady I became sick with desire—sick because I knew from my mother's psychology textbooks, which I'd secretly consulted, just how pathological my longings were. I had looked up "homosexuality" and read through the frightening, damning diagnosis and prognosis so many times with an erection that finally, through Pavlovian conditioning, fear instantly triggered excitement, guilt automatically entailed salivating love or lust or both.

Jim was tall and tan and blond, with hair clipped soldier-short and a powerful upper lip that wouldn't stay shaved and always showed a reddish-gold stubble. His small, complicated eyes rapidly changed expression, veering from manly impenetrability to teenage shiftiness. He trudged rather than walked, as though he were shod with horseshoes instead of trim oxford lace-ups. He wore a bow tie, which I usually associated with chipper incompetence but that in Jim's case seemed more like a tourniquet hastily tied around his large, mobile Adam's apple in a makeshift attempt to choke off its pulsing maleness. If his Adam's apple was craggy, his nose was small and thin and well made, his bleached-out eyebrows so blond they shaded off into his tanned forehead, his ears small and neat and red and peeling on top and on the downy lobes.

He seemed eerily unaware of himself—the reason, no doubt, he left his mouth open whenever he wasn't saying "Yes, ma'am" or "No, ma'am" to my mother's routine questions, although once he smiled at her with the seductive leer of a lunatic, as though he were imitating someone else. He had allergies or a cold that had descended into his larynx and made his monosyllables sound becomingly stifled—or maybe he always talked that way. He could have been a West Point cadet, so virile and impersonal did his tall body appear, except for that open mouth, those squirming eyes, his fits of borrowed charm.

Someone had dressed him up in a hairy alpaca suit jacket and a cheap white shirt that was so small on him that his red hands hung down out of the cuffs like hams glazed with honey, for the backs of his hands were brushed with gold hair. The shirt, which would have been dingy on anyone less tan, was so thin that his dark chest could be seen breathing through it like a doubt concealed by a wavering smile. He wasn't wearing a T-shirt, which was unusual in those days, even provocative.

Mr. Grady was seated at one end, my mother next to him, then Jim, then me. My mother took off her coat and hat and combed her hair in a feathery, peripheral way designed to leave the deep structure of her permanent intact. "You certainly got a good tan this summer," she said.

"Thank you, ma'am."

His father, heavily seated, said tonelessly, without lifting his face from his chin or his chin from his chest, "He was working outside all summer on construction, earning money for his first year in med school."

"Oh, really!" my mother exclaimed, suddenly fascinated by Jim since she had a deep reverence for doctors. I, too, felt a new respect for him as I imagined the white surgical mask covering his full upper lip. "I want you on your hands and knees," I could hear him telling me. "Now bend forward, cross your arms on the table, turn your face to one side, and lay your cheek on the back of your forearm. Arch your back, spread your knees still wider." He was pulling on rubber gloves, and from my strange, sideways angle I could see him dipping his sheathed finger into the cold lubricant. . . .

"Have you chosen a specialty already?" my mother asked as the auditorium lights dimmed.

"Gynecology," Jim said—and I clamped my knees together with a start.

Then the samisens squealed, kotos thunked dully, and drums kept breaking rank to race forward faster and faster until they fell into silence. A pink spotlight picked out a heavily armored and mascaraed warrior frozen in mid-flight on the runway, but only the scattered Japanese members of the audience knew to applaud him. The program placed a Roman numeral IV beside the actor's name, which lent him a regal importance. Soon Number IV was stomping the stage and declaiming something in an angry gargle, but we hadn't paid for the earphones that would have given us the crucial simultaneous translation, since my mother said she always preferred the Gestalt to the mere details. "On the Rorschach I always score a very high W," she had coyly told the uncomprehending and uninterested Mr. Grady earlier over supper. I knew from her frequent elucidations that a high W meant she saw each inkblot as a whole rather than as separate parts and this grasp of the Gestalt revealed her global intelligence, which she regarded as an attribute of capital importance.

A mincing, tittering maiden with a homely powdered white face and an impractical hobble skirt (only later did I read that the performer was a man and the fifth member of his improbably dynasty) suddenly metamorphosed into a sinister white fox. With suicidal daring I pressed my leg against Jim's. First I put my shoe against his, sole planted squarely against sole. Then, having staked out this beachhead, I slowly cantilevered my calf muscles against his, at first just lightly grazing him. I even withdrew for a moment, proof of how completely careless and unintended my movements were, before I sat forward, resting my elbows on my knees in total absorption, leaning attentively into the exotic squealing and cavorting on stage—an intensification of attention that of course forced me to press my slender calf against his massive one, my knobby knee against his square, majestic one.

As two lovers rejoiced or despaired (one couldn't be sure which) and tacky paper blossoms showered them, Jim's leg held fast against mine. He didn't move it away. I stole a glance at his profile, but it told me nothing. I pulsed slightly against his leg but still didn't move away. I rubbed my palms together and felt the calluses that months of harp practice had built up on my fingertips.

If I kept up my assaults would he suddenly and indignantly withdraw, even later make a remark to his father, who would feel obliged to tip off my mother about her son the fairy? I'd already been denounced at the country club where I'd worked as a caddy last summer. While waiting on the benches in the stifling hot caddy house for golfers to arrive, I'd pressed my leg in just this way against that of an older caddy named Mikey, someone who until then had liked shooting the shit with me. Now he stood up and said, "What the hell are you anyway, some sort of fuckin' Liberace?" He'd tried to pull away several times, but I'd ignored his hints.

This time I'd wait for reciprocal signals. I wouldn't let my desire fool me into seeing mutual longing where only mine existed. I was dreading the intermission because I didn't know if I could disguise my tented crotch or the blush bloom that was slowly drifting up my neck and across my face.

I flexed my calf muscle against Jim's, and he flexed back. We were football players locked into a tight huddle or two wrestlers, each struggling to gain the advantage over the other (an advantage I was only too eager to concede). We were about to pass over the line from accident into intention. Soon he'd be as incriminated as I. Or did he think this dumb show was just a joke, indicative of other intentions, anything but sexual?

I flexed my calf muscles twice, and he signaled back twice; we were establishing a Morse code that was undeniable. On stage, warriors were engaged in choreographed combat, frequently freezing in mid-lunge, and I wondered where we would live, how I would escape my mother, when I could kiss those full lips for the first time.

A smile, antic with a pleasure so new I scarcely dared to trust it, played across my lips. Alone with my thoughts but surrounded by his body, I could imagine a whole long life with him.

When the intermission came at last, our parents beat a hasty retreat to the bar next door, but neither Jim nor I budged. We had no need of highballs or a Manhattan; we already had them and were already in New York or someplace equally magical. The auditorium emptied out. Jim looked at me matter-of-factly as his Adam's apple rose and fell and he said, "How are we ever going to get a moment alone?"

"Do you have a television set?" I asked (they were still fairly rare).

"Of course not. Dad never has a damn cent; he throws his money away with both hands."

"Why don't you come over to our place on Saturday to watch the Perry Como show, then drink a few too many beers and say you're too tight to drive home and ask to stay over. The only extra bed is in my room."

"Okay," he said in that stifled voice. He seemed startled by my efficient deviousness as much as I was by his compliance. When our much livelier parents returned and the lights went back down, I wedged a hand between our legs and covertly stroked his flexed calf, but he didn't reciprocate and I gave up. We sat there, knee to knee, in a stalemate of lust. I'd been erect so long my penis began to ache and I could see a pre-come stain seeping through my khakis. I turned bitter at the prospect of waiting three whole days till Saturday. I wanted to pull him into the men's room right now.

Once at home, my mother asked me what I thought of Jim and I said he seemed nice but dumb. When I was alone in bed and able at last to strum my way to release (I thought of myself as the Man with the

Blue Guitar), I hit a high note (my chin), higher than I'd ever shot before, and I licked myself clean and floated down into the featherbed luxury of knowing that big tanned body would soon be wrapped around me.

Our apartment was across the street from the beach, and I loved to jump the Lake Michigan waves. Now I'm astonished I enjoyed doing anything that athletic, but then I didn't think of it as sport so much as opera, for just as in listening to 78 records I breasted one soaring outburst after another sung by Lauritz Melchior or Flagstad, in the same way I was thrilled by the repeated crises staged by the lake in September—a menacing crescendo that melted anticlimatically away into a creamy glissando, a minor interval that swelled into a major chord, all of it as abstract, excited, and endless as Wagner's *Ring,* which I'd never bothered to dope out motif by leitmotif since I, too, preferred an ecstatic Gestalt to tediously detailed knowledge. We were careless in my family, careless and addicted to excitement.

Jim Grady called my mother and invited himself over on Saturday evening to watch the Perry Como show on television. He told her he was an absolute fanatic about Como, that he considered Como's least glance or tremolo incomparably cool, and that he specially admired his long-sleeved golfer's sweaters with the low-slung yoke necks, three buttons at the waist, coarse spongy weave, and bright colors. My mother told me about these odd enthusiasms; she was puzzled by them because she thought fashion concerned women alone and that its tyranny even over women extended only to clothes, certainly not to ways of moving, smiling, or singing. "I wouldn't want to imitate anyone else," she said with her little mirthless laugh of self-congratulation and a disbelieving shake of her head. "I like being me just fine, thank you very much."

"He's not the first young person to swoon over a pop star," I informed her out of my infinite world-weariness.

"Men don't swoon over men, dear," Mother reminded me, peering at me over the tops of her glasses. Now that I unscramble the signals she was emitting, I see how contradictory they were. She said she admired the sensitivity of a great dancer such as Nijinsky, and she'd even given me his biography to read to make sure I knew the exact perverse composition of that sensitivity. ("What a tragic life. Of course, he ended up psychotic, with paranoid delusions, a martyr complex, and degenerative ataxia.") She'd assure me just as often, with snapping eyes and carnivorous smile, that she liked men to be men and a boy to be all boy (as who did not), although the hearty heartlessness of making such a declaring to her willowy, cake-baking, harp-playing son thoroughly eluded her. Nor would she have tolerated a real boy's beer brawls, bloody noses, or stormy fugues. She wanted an obedient little gentleman to sit placidly in a dark suit when he wasn't helping his mother until, at the appropriate moment and with no advance fuss, he would marry a plain Christian girl whose unique vocation would be the perpetual adoration of her *belle-mère*.

At last Jim Grady arrived after our dispirited Saturday night supper, just in time for a slice of my devil's food cake and the Perry Como show. My sister skulked off to her room to polish her hockey stick and read through fan magazine articles on Mercedes McCambridge and Barbara Stanwyck. Jim belted back the six-pack he'd brought along and drew our attention with repulsive connoisseurship to every cool Como mannerism. I now realize that maybe Como was the first singer who'd figured out that the TV lens represented twenty million horny women dateless on Saturday night, and he looked searchingly into its glass eye and warbled with the calm certainty of his seductive charm.

As a homosexual I understood the desire to possess an admired man, but I was almost disgusted by Jim's ambition to imitate him. My mother saw men as nearly faceless extras who surrounded the diva, a woman; I regarded men as the stars; but both she and I were opposed to all forms of masculine self-fabrication, she because she considered it unbecomingly narcissistic, I because it seemed a sacrilegious parody of the innate superiority of a few godlike men. Perhaps I was just jealous that Jim was paying more attention to Como than to me.

Emboldened by beer, Jim called my mother by her first name, which I'm sure she found flattering since it suggested he saw her as a woman rather than as a parent. She drank one of her many highballs with him, sitting beside him on the couch, and for an instant I coldly appraised my own mother as a potential rival, but she lost interest in him when he dared to shush her during a bit of the singer's studied patter. In those days before the veneration of pop culture, unimaginative highbrows such as my mother and I swooned over opera, foreign films of any sort, and "problem plays" such as *The Immoralist* and *Tea and Sympathy,* but we were guiltily drawn to television in spite of ourselves with a mindless, vegetable-like tropism best named by the vogue word of the period, "apathy." We thought it beneath us to study mere entertainment.

Jim was so masculine in the way he held his Luckies cupped between his thumb and middle finger and kept another, unlit cigarette behind his ear, he was so inexpressive, so devoid of all gesture, that when he stood up to go, shook his head like a wet dog, and said, "Damn! I've had one too many for the road," he was utterly convincing. My mother said, "Do you want me to drive you home?" Jim laughed insultingly and said, "I think you're feeling no pain yourself. I'd better stay over, Delilah, if you have an extra bed."

My mother was much more reluctant to put Jim up than I'd anticipated. "I don't know, I could put my girdle back on. . . ." Had she picked up the faint sex signal winking back and forth between her son and Jim? Or was she afraid he might sneak into her bedroom after lights-out? Perhaps she worried how it might look to Mr. Grady—drunk son spends night in lakeside apartment, and such a son, the human species at its peak of physical fitness, mouth open, eyes shifting, Adam's apple working.

At last we were alone, and operatically I shed my clothes in a puddle at my feet, but Jim, undressing methodically, whispered, "You should hang your clothes up, or your mother might think we were up to some sort of monkey business." Hot tears sprang to my eyes, but they dried as I looked at the long torso being revealed, with its small, turned waist and the wispy hairs around the tiny brown nipples like champagne grapes left to wither on a vine gone pale. His legs were pale because he'd worn jeans on the construction site, but he must have worn them low. For an instant he sat down to pull off his heavy white socks, and his shoulder muscles played under the overhead light with all the demonic action of a Swiss music box, the big kind with its works under glass.

He lay back with a heavy-lidded cool expression I suspected was patterned on Como's, but I didn't care; I was even pleased he wanted to impress me as I scaled his body, felt his great warm arms close over me, as I tasted the Luckies and Bud on his lips, as I saw the sharp focus in his eyes fade into a blur. "Hey," he whispered, and he smiled at me as his hands cupped my twenty-six-inch waist and my hot penis planted its flag on the stony land of his perfect body. "Hey," he said, hitching me higher and deeper into his presence.

Soon after that I came down with mononucleosis, the popular "kissing disease" of the time, although I'd kissed almost no one but Jim. I was tired and depressed. I dragged myself with difficulty from couch to bed, but at the same time I was so lonely and frustrated that I looked down from the window at every man or boy walking past and willed him to look up, see me, join me, but the will was weak.

Jim called one afternoon and we figured out he could come by the next evening, when my mother was going somewhere with my sister. I warned him he could catch mono if he kissed me, but I was proud that after all he did kiss me, long and deep. Until now the people I'd had sex with were boys at camp who pretended to hypnotize each other or married men who cruised the Howard Street Elevated toilets and drove me down to the beach in a station wagon filled with their children's toys. Jim was the first man who took off his clothes, held me in his arms, looked me in the eye, and said, "Hey." He who seemed so stiff and ill at ease otherwise became fluent in bed.

I was bursting with my secret, all the more so because mononucleosis had reduced my world to the size of our apartment and the books I was almost too weak to hold (that afternoon it had been Oscar Wilde's *Lady Windermere's Fan*). In the evening my mother was washing dishes and I was drying, but I kept sitting down to rest. She said, "Mr. Grady and I are thinking of getting married." The words just popped out of my mouth: "Then it will have to be a double wedding." My brilliant repartee provoked not a laugh but an inquisition, which had many consequences for me over the years, both good and bad. The whole story of my homosexual adventures came out, my father was informed, I was sent off to boarding school and a psychiatrist—my entire life changed.

My mother called up Jim Grady and boozily denounced him as a pervert and a child molester, although I'd assured her I'd been the one to seduce him. I never saw him again until almost forty years later in Paris. My mother, who'd become tiny, wise, and sober with age, had had several decades to get used to the idea of my homosexuality (and my sister's, as it turned out). She had run into Jim Grady twice in the last three years; she'd warned me he'd become maniacally stingy, to the point that he'd wriggle out of a drinks date if he thought he'd have to pay.

And yet when he rang me up from London, where he was attending a medical conference, he didn't object when I proposed to book him into the pricey hotel next door to me on the Île St. Louis.

He called from his hotel room and I rushed over. He was nearly sixty years old, with thin gray hair, clear glasses frames he'd mended with black electrician's tape, ancient Corfam shoes, an open mouth, a stifled voice. We shook hands, but a moment later he'd pulled me into his arms. He said he knew, from a magazine interview I'd given, that this time I was infected with a virus far more dangerous than mononucleosis, but he kissed me long and deep, and a moment later we were undressed.

Over the next four days with him I had time to learn all about his life. He hadn't become a gynecologist after all but a sports doctor for a Catholic boys' school, and he spent his days bandaging the bruised and broken bodies of teenage athletes. His best friend was a fat priest nick-named "The Whale," and they frequently got drunk with one of Jim's soldier friends, who'd married a real honey, a little Chinese gal. Jim owned his own house. He'd always lived alone and seemed never to have had a lover. His father had died from an early heart attack, but Jim felt nothing but scorn for him and his spendthrift ways. Jim himself had a tricky heart, and he was trying to give a shape to his life. He was about to retire.

It was true he'd become a miser. He bought his acrylic shirts and socks in packs of ten. His glasses came from public welfare. At home he went to bed at sunset to save on electricity. We spent hours looking for prints that would cost less than five dollars, as presents for The Whale, the army buddy, and the Chinese gal. He wouldn't even let me invite him to a good restaurant. We were condemned to eating at the Maubert Self, a cafeteria, or nibbling on cheese and apples we'd bought at the basement supermarket next to the Métro St. Paul. He explained his econ-omies to me in detail. Proudly he told me he was a millionaire several times over and that he was leaving his fortune to the Catholic Church, although he was an atheist.

I took him with me to my literary parties and introduced him as my cousin. He sat stolidly by like an old faithful dog as people said brilliant, cutting things in French, a language he did not know. He sent every hostess who'd received us a thank-you letter, which in English was once so common it's still known as a "bread-and-butter note," although in French it was always so sufficiently rare as to be called a *lettre de château.* The same women who'd ignored him when he sat at their tables were retrospectively impressed by his New World courtliness.

During his trip to Paris I slept with him just that first time in his hotel room, but then, as we kissed, he removed his smudged, taped welfare glasses and revealed his darting young blue eyes. He undressed my sagging body and embraced my thirty-six-inch waist and bared his own body, considerably slimmer but just as much a ruin with its warts and wattles and long white hair. And yet, when he hitched me into his embrace and said, "Hey," I felt fourteen again. "You were a moron to tell your mom everything about us," he said. "You made us lose a lot of time." And if we had spent a life together, I wondered, would we each be a bit less deformed now?

As his hands stroked my arms and belly and buttocks, everything the years had worn down or undone, I could hear an accelerating drum and see, floating just above the rented bed, our young, feverish bodies rejoicing or lamenting, one couldn't be sure which. The time he'd come over when I had mono ("glandular fever," as the English call it), my hot body had ached and shivered beside his. Now each time I touched him I could hear music, as though a jolt had started the clockwork after so many years. We watched the toothed cylinder turn under glass and strum the long silver notes.

~ *Edna O'Brien* ~

Dramas

W hen the new shopkeeper arrived in the village he aroused great
curiosity along with some scorn. He was deemed refined because
his fingernails looked as if they had been varnished a tinted ivory. He had
a horse, or as my father was quick to point out, a glorified pony, which
he had brought from the Midlands, where he had previously worked.
The pony was called Daisy, a name unheard of in our circles for an animal.
The shopkeeper wore a long black coat, a black hat, talked in a low
voice, made his own jams and marmalades, and could even darn and sew.
All that we came to know of, in due course, but at first we only knew
him as Barry. In time the shop would have his name, printed in beautiful
silver sloping script, above the door. He had bought the long-disused
bakery, had all the ovens thrown out, and turned it into a palace which
had not only gadgets but gadgets that worked: a lethal slicer for the ham,
a new kind of weighing scale that did not require iron weights hefted
onto one side but that simply registered the weight of a bag of meal and
told it by a needle that spun round, wobbling dementedly before coming
to a standstill. Even farmers praised its miraculous skills. He also had a

*Widely considered one of Ireland's most important writers—an heir to the legacy of James
Joyce—EDNA O'BRIEN is the author of such novels as* The Country Girls, A Pagan
Place, Zee & Co., *and* Time and Tide, *as well as many story collections. "Dramas" is
from her most recent collection,* Lantern Slides, *the title story of which deserves particular
attention: it is a kind of contemporary answer to Joyce's "The Dead."*

meat safe with a grey gauze door, a safe in which creams and cheeses could be kept fresh for an age, free of the scourge of flies or gnats.

Straightaway he started to do great business as the people reneged on the shops where they had dealt for years and where many of them owed money. They flocked to look at him, to hear his well-mannered voice, and to admire dainties and things that he had in stock. He had ten different-flavored jellies and more than one brand of coffee. The women especially liked him. He leant over the counter, discussed things with them, their headaches, their knitting, patterns for suits or dresses that they might make, and along with that he kept an open tin of biscuits so that they could have them if they felt peckish. The particular favorite was a tiny round biscuit, like a Holy Communion wafer with a thin skin of rice paper as a lining. These were such favorites that Barry would have to put his hand down beneath the ruffs of ink paper and ferret up a few from the bottom. The rice paper did not taste like paper at all but like a disk of some magical metamorphosed sugar. Besides that coveted biscuit, there were others, a sandwich of ginger with a soft white filling that was as sturdy as putty, and another in which there was a blend of raspberry and custard, a combination that engendered such ecstasy that one was torn between the pleasure of devouring it or tasting each grain slowly so as to isolate the raspberry from the custard flavour. There were also arrowroot and digestives, but these were the last to be eaten. He called the biscuits "bikkies" and cigarettes "ciggies."

He was not such a favorite with the men, both because he raved to the women and because he voiced the notion of bringing drama to the town. He said that he would find a drama that would embody the talents of the people and that he would direct and produce it himself. Constantly he was casting people, and although none of us knew precisely what he meant, we would agree when he said, "Rosalind, a born Rosalind," or, "Cordelia, if ever I met one." He did not, however, intend to do Shakespeare, as he feared that, being untrained, the people would not be able to get their tongues around the rhyming verse and would not feel at home in bulky costumes. He would choose something more suitable, something that people could identify with. Every time he went to the city to buy stock, he also bought one or two plays, and if there was a slack moment in the shop he would read a speech or even a whole scene, he himself acting the parts, the men's and the women's. He was very convincing when he acted the women or the girls. One play was about a young girl who saw a dead seagull, and in seeing it, her tragedy was predestined: she was crossed in love, had an illegitimate child, and drove a young man to suicide. Another time he read scenes about two very unhappy people in Scandinavia who scalded each other, daily, with accusation and counter-accusation, and to buoy himself up, the man did a frenzied dance. Barry did the dance too, jumping on and off the weighing scales or even onto the counter when he got carried away. He used to ask me to stay on after the shop closed, simply because I was as besotted as he was by these exotic and tormented characters. It was biscuits, sweets, lemonade, anything. Yet something in me trembled, foresaw trouble.

The locals were suspicious, they did not want plays about dead birds and illegitimate children, or unhappy couples tearing at each other, because they had these scenarios aplenty. Barry decided, wisely, to do a play that would be more heartening, a simple play about wholesome people and wholesome themes, such as getting the harvest in safely. I was always privy to each new decision, partly because of my mania for the plays and partly because I had to tell him how his pony was doing. The pony grazed with us, and consequently we were given quite a lot of credit. I shall never forget my mother announcing this good news to me flushed with pride, almost suave as she said, "If ever you have the hungry grass on the way from school, just go into Barry and say you feel like a titbit." By her telling me this so casually, I saw how dearly she would have loved to have been rich, to entertain, to give lunch parties and supper parties, to show off the linen tablecloths and the good cutlery which she had Vaselined over the years to keep the steel from rusting. In these imaginary galas she brandished the two silver salvers, the biscuit barrel, and the dinner plates with their bouquets of violets in the center and scalloped edging that looked like crochet work. We had been richer, but over the years the money got squandered.

Barry to her did not talk wisely about dramas but about the ornaments in our house, commenting on her good taste. It was the happiest half year in my life, being able to linger in Barry's shop and while he was busy read some of these plays and act them silently inside my head. With the customers all gone, I would sit on the counter, swing my legs, gorge biscuits, and discuss both the stories and the characters. Barry in his white shop coat and with a sharpened pencil in his hand would make notes of the things we said. He would discuss the scenery, the lights, the intonation of each line, and when an actor should hesitate or then again when an actor should let rip. Barry said it was a question of contrast, of nuance versus verve. I stayed until dark, until the moon came up or the first star. He walked home, but he did not try to kiss one or put his hand on the tickly part of the back of the knee, the way other men did, even the teacher's first cousin, who pretended he wasn't doing it when he was. Barry was as pure as a young priest and like a priest had pale skin with down on it. His only blemish was his thinning hair, and the top of his head was like an egg, with big wisps, which I did not like to look at.

Business for him was not quite as flush as in those first excitable weeks, but as he would say to my mother, things were "ticking over," and also he was lucky in that his Aunt Milly in the Midlands was going to leave him her farm and her house. Meanwhile, if there were debts she would come to the rescue, so that he would never be disgraced by having his name printed in a gazette where all the debtors' names were printed so that the whole country knew of it.

As it neared autumn Barry had decided on a play and had started auditions. "All for Hecuba and Hecuba for me," he said to the mystified customers. It was a play about travelling players, so that, as he said, the actors and actresses could have lots of verve and camp it up. No one knew quite what he meant by "camp it up." He mulled over playing the lead himself, but there were objections from people in the town. So each evening men and women went to the parlour that adjoined the shop, read for him, and often emerged disgruntled and threatening to start up a rival company because he did not give them the best part. Then an extraordinary thing happened. Barry had written on the spur of the moment to a famous actor in Dublin for a spot of advice. In the letter he had also said that if the actor was ever passing through the vicinity he might like "to break bread." Barry was very proud of the wording of this letter. The actor replied on a postcard. It was a postcard on which four big white cats adhered together, in a mesh. Spurred by this signal, Barry made a parcel of country stuffs and sent them to the actor by registered post. He sent butter, fowl, homemade cake, and eggs wrapped in thick twists of newspaper and packed in a little papier-mâché box.

Not long after, I met him in the street, in a dither. The most extraordinary thing had happened. The actor and his friend were coming to visit, had announced it without being invited, said they had decided to help Barry in his artistic endeavour and would teach him all the rudiments of theatre that were needed for his forthcoming production. "A business lunch à *trois*" was how Barry described it, his voice three octaves higher, his face unable to disguise his fervid excitement. My mother offered to loan linen and cutlery, the Liddy girl was summoned to scrub, and Oona, the sacristan, was cajoled to part with some of the flowers meant for the altar, while I was enlisted to go around the hedges and pick anything, leaves, branches, anything.

"His friend is called Ivan," Barry said, and added that, though Ivan was not an actor, he was a partner and saw to the practical aspect of things. How he knew this I have no idea, because I doubt that the actor would have mentioned such a prosaic thing. Preparations were begun. My mother made shortbread and cakes, orange and Madeira; she also gave two cockerels, plucked and ready for the oven, with a big bowl of stuffing which the Liddy girl could put in the birds at the last minute. She even put in a darning needle and green thread so that the rear ends of the chickens could be sewn up once the stuffing was added. The bath was scoured, the bathroom floor so waxed that the Liddy girl slipped on it and threatened to sue, but was pacified with the gift of a small packet of cigarettes. A fire was lit in the parlour for days ahead, so as to air it and give it a sense of being lived in. It was not certain if the actor and Ivan would spend the night, not clear from the rather terse bulletin that was sent, but, as Barry pointed out, he had three bedrooms, so that if they did decide to stay, there would be no snag. Naturally he would surrender his own bedroom to the actor and give Ivan the next-best one and he could be in the box room.

Nobody else was invited, but that was to be expected, since after all it was a working occasion and Barry was going to pick their brains about the interpretation of the play, about the sets and the degree to which the characters should exaggerate their plights. The guests were seen emerging from a big old-fashioned car with coupe bonnet, the actor holding an umbrella and sporting a red carnation in his buttonhole. Ivan wore a raincoat and was a little portly, but they ran so quickly to the hall door that only a glimpse of them was caught. Barry had been standing inside the door since after Mass, so that the moment he heard the thud of the knocker, the door was swung open and he welcomed them into the cold but highly polished corridor. We know that they partook of lunch because the Liddy girl told how she roasted the birds to a T, added the potatoes for roasting at the correct time, and placed the lot on a warmed platter with carving knife and carving fork to one side. She had knocked on the parlour door to ask if Barry wanted the lunch brought in, but he had simply told her to leave it in the hatch and that he would get it himself, as they were in the thick of an intense discussion. She grieved at not being able to serve the lunch, because it meant both that she could not have a good look at the visitors and that she would not get a handsome tip.

It was about four o'clock in the afternoon when the disturbance happened. I had gone there because of being possessed by a mad hope that they would do a reading of the play and that I would be needed to play some role, even if it was a menial one. I stood in the doorway of the drapery shop across the street, visible if Barry should lift the net curtain and look out. Indeed, I believed he would and I waited quite happily. The village was quiet and sunk in its after-dinner somnolence, with only myself and a few dogs prowling about. It had begun to spatter with rain. I heard a window being raised and was stunned to see the visitors on the small upstairs balcony, dressed in outlandish women's clothing. I should have seen disaster then, except that I thought they were women, that other visitors, their wives perhaps, had come unbeknownst to us. When I saw Barry in a maroon dress, larking, I ducked down, guessing the awful truth. He was calling, "Friends, Romans, countrymen." Already three or four people had come to their doorways, and soon there was a small crowd looking up at the appalling spectacle of three drunk men pretending to be women. They were all wearing pancake make-up and were heavily rouged. The actor also wore a string of pearls and kept hitting the other two in jest. Ivan was wearing a pleated skirt and a low-cut white blouse, with falsies underneath. The actor had on some kind of toga and was shouting wild endearments and throwing kisses.

The inflamed owner of the drapery shop asked me how long these antics had been going on.

"I don't know," I said, my face scarlet, every bit of me wishing to vanish. Yet I followed the crowd as they moved, inexorably, towards the balcony, all of them speechless, as if the spectacle had robbed them of their reason. It was in itself like a crusade, this fanatic throng moving towards assault.

Barry wore a tam-o'-shanter and looked uncannily like a girl. It gave me the shivers to see this metamorphosis. He even tossed his neck like a girl, and you would no longer believe he was bald. The actor warmed to the situation and starting calling people "Ducky" and "Cinders," while also reciting snatches from Shakespeare. He singled people out. So carried away was he by the allure of his performance that the brunette wig he was wearing began to slip, but determined to be a sport about this, he took it off, doffed it to the crowd, and replaced it again. One of the women, a Mrs. Gleeson, fainted, but more attention was being paid to the three performers than to her, so she had to stagger to her feet again. Seeing that the actor was stealing the scene, Ivan did something terrible: he opened the low-cut blouse, took out the falsies, tossed them down to the crowd, and said to one of the young men, "Where there's that, there's plenty more." The young man in question did not know what to do, did not know whether to pick them up and throw them back or challenge the strangers to a fight. The actor and Ivan then began arguing and vied with each other as to who was the most fetching. Barry had receded and was in the doorway of the upper room, still drunk, but obviously not so drunk as to be indifferent to the calamity that had occurred.

The actor, it seemed, had also taken a liking to the young man whom Ivan had thrown the falsies to, and now holding a folded scroll, he leant over the wrought iron, looked down directly at the man, brandished the scroll, and said, "It's bigger than that, darling." At once the locals got the gist of the situation and called on him to come down so that they could beat him to a pulp. Enthused now by their heckling, he stood on the wobbly parapet and began to scold them, telling them there were some naughty skeletons in their lives and that they couldn't fool him by all pretending to be happily married men. Then he said something awful: he said that the great Oscar Wilde had termed the marriage bed "the couch of lawful lust." A young guard arrived and called up to the actor to please recognize that he was causing a disturbance of the peace as well as scandalizing innocent people.

"Come and get me, darling," the actor said, and wriggled his forefinger like a saucy heroine in a play. Also, on account of being drunk he was swaying on this very rickety parapet.

"Come down now," the guard said, trying to humour him a bit, because he did not want the villagers to have a death on their hands. The actor smiled at this note of conciliation and called the guard "Lola" and asked if he ever used his big baton anywhere else, and so provoked the young guard and so horrified the townspeople that already men were taking off their jackets to prepare for a fight.

"Beat me, I love it," he called down while they lavished dire threats on him. Ivan, it seemed, was now enjoying the scene and did not seem to mind that the actor was getting most of the attention and most of the abuse. Two ladders were fetched, and the young guard climbed up to arrest the three men. The actor teased him as he approached. The doctor followed, vowing that he would give them an injection to silence their filthy tongues. Barry had already gone in, and Ivan was trying to mollify them, saying it was all clean fun, when the actor put his arms around the young guard and lathered him with frenzied kisses. Other men hurried up the ladder and pushed the culprits into the bedroom so that people would be spared any further display of lunacy. The French doors were closed, and shouting and arguments began. Then the voices ceased as the offenders were pulled from the bedroom to the room downstairs, so that they could be carted into the police van which was now waiting. People feared that maybe these theatrical villains were armed, while the women wondered aloud if Barry had had these costumes and falsies and things, or if the actors had brought them. It was true that they had come with two suitcases. The Liddy girl had been sent out in the rain to carry them in. The sergeant who now arrived on the scene called to the upper floor, but upon getting no answer went around to the back of the house, where he was followed by a straggle of people. The rest of us waited in front, some of the opinion that the actor was sure to come back onto the balcony, to take a bow. The smaller children went from the front to the back of the house and returned to say there had been a terrible crash of bottles and crockery. The dining room table was overturned in the fracas. About ten minutes later they came out by the back door, each of the culprits held by two men. The actor was wearing his green suit, but his makeup had not been fully wiped off, so that he looked vivid and startled, like someone about to embark on a great role. Ivan was in his raincoat and threatening aloud to sue unless he was allowed to speak to his solicitor. He called the guards and the people "rabble." The woman who had fainted went up to Barry and vehemently cursed him, while one of the town girls had the audacity to ask the actor for his autograph. He shouted the name of the theatre in Dublin to which she could send for it. Some said that he would never again perform in that or any theatre, as his name was mud.

When I saw Barry waiting to be bundled into the van like a criminal, I wanted to run over to him, or else to shout at the locals, disown them in some way. But I was too afraid. He caught my eye for an instant. I don't know why it was me he looked at, except perhaps he was hoping he had a friend, he was hoping our forays into drama had made a bond between us. He looked so abject that I had to look away and instead concentrated my gaze on the shop window, where the weighing scales, the ham slicer, and all the precious commodities were like props on an empty stage. From the corner of my eye I saw him get into the big black van and saw it drive away with all the solemnity of a hearse.

~ *Larry Kramer* ~

"Mrs. Tefillin"

I

On the day in January 1982 when her husband, Peter, finally died —he was eighty-eight and she was eighty-one, and they'd been married fifty-two years and lived in a tiny room in the Hotel Eden in Miami Beach for over twenty of them—Rivka Trout realized she had no place to turn for help but to Gertrude Jewsbury in Palm Beach.

Rivka hadn't seen Gertrude since 1930. That was the year Herman Levy divorced Gertrude, then tried one last time to convince Rivka to marry him. But Rivka married Peter Trout, Herman went to live in New York, never to be seen by Rivka again, and Gertrude departed for what were to become decades of world travel: postcards came to Rivka from farther and farther away until they came no more. Yes, Rivka had turned Herman down time after time and married his best friend, Peter, in the ugly industrial city of Bridgeport, Connecticut, where Herman's father had made a great fortune manufacturing light bulbs.

Many times over the years, Peter told Rivka, "I won't have enough money to leave you when I die. Find Herman. Tell him I'm dead." Rivka wanted to respond like the schoolteacher she'd been—she had specialized

LARRY KRAMER is the author of a novel, Faggots, *several screenplays, and the plays* The Normal Heart, Just Say No, *and* The Destiny of Me. *He was cofounder of both the Gay Men's Health Crisis and ACT-UP and has been the preeminent voice in AIDS activism since the early eighties. His story* " 'Mrs. Tefillin' " *will probably surprise the expectations of both his admirers and his enemies.*

313

in teaching English to foreigners, and she'd prided herself on imparting to them an ability to take each problem and deal with it logically, step by step: "Number One, you don't even know Herman is still alive. Number Two, you don't know if he has any money left. Number Three, if he does, why should he take care of me? Number Four, why would he do either of us such a favor?" She could go on, probably up to several dozen, and often did, until Peter cried out, "Stop it, you're driving me nuts."

"You're not going to die," Rivka would answer. "What an awful thing to say."

He would always yell back: "Can't you listen to me for once!"

He'd told her many times he was waiting to die. Each day he waited for it and each night he went to sleep expecting it and each morning he was surprised when he woke up still in this world. Sometimes she thought Peter had been waiting to die for as long as she'd known him.

She couldn't go to Herman. He was still sending her the letters. He never gave up! Rivka had never told Peter about the letters. But she could go to Gertrude. Gertrude had all that money Herman had settled on her, money that would have been Rivka's if Rivka had been Herman's bride. Gertrude had to help. Rivka had only two thousand dollars in the bank. Peter's benefits from social security and his pension from the City of Bridgeport for being an assistant high school superintendent would now be halved and they'd hardly been enough as it was. She couldn't afford to stay at the Hotel Eden anymore. She couldn't afford to go anywhere she could think of that was remotely pleasant. She couldn't remember any friends still alive in any position to help her. Yes, she would go to Gertrude, who would get word to Herman, whom Gertrude was no doubt in touch with via lawyers, and of course Herman would take care of Rivka. This way was just a little more roundabout than Peter's way. How could her oldest friend in the world not help her?

The photograph in the Miami newspaper of the Palm Beach charity ball was five or six years old. There she was, identified as Mrs. Gertrude Jewsbury of The Breakers. Rivka would have recognized her anywhere, even if she hadn't changed back to her distinctive maiden name. There she was, looking very Gertrude, very grand, very haughty, very beautiful. How could her oldest friend in the world not be alive?

Rivka Wishenwart Trout had always lived by one rule. She tried not to allow herself to dwell on anything unhappy. Her life was and had been a fine one. She had many wonderful memories. She'd even been around the world herself, with Peter, and seen London and Paris and Rome, where Peter's ankles swelled up and a doctor who could hardly speak English told them to fly home right away, in case anything happened, which it didn't. Oh, that had been a lovely trip while it lasted!

Rivka found Peter's body when she returned home from the Cuban store on Collins Avenue where she bought cheap fruit. Peter's last words to her had been, "We're running out. Go buy some more."

He'd been drying off from a shower and he was lying sprawled out naked on the floor. In all their marriage, she had never really looked at his body. So this is what you look like. She poked the fat in his stomach with a finger. He rolled over onto his back and the sudden, unexpected movement startled her. He didn't seem to have any genitals. They were hidden under layers of flesh. She was amazed that she wanted to see them. She was amazed that her fingers were poking under and lifting up the rolls of fat and fumbling around trying to find something she had never seen and pulling them into view as best she could. This is what you put into me, four, five, perhaps six times in all our life together?

Miami Beach ambulances arrived very quickly. They were not called ambulances; they were called Life Support Vehicles. The old people everywhere always became immobilized as they watched, their hands over their mouths, the attendants rushing in and rushing up and carrying down and carrying out. It was a scene that happened every day at this southern end of the beach. Looking out her window, Rivka could see old people in rocking chairs on porches stretching to eternity, old people setting up aluminum folding chairs in groups by the water to deepen their suntans, old people craning their heads out of their windows so they could get a better view. They all had their hands over their mouths.

She could also see the ocean and the sunshine and that it was a lovely day outside.

Should there be a funeral? Who would come? The few friends they'd made down here were dead. Why have a funeral just for herself? Even Peter had said, "Just burn me up." She told the attendants that's what she wanted and they gave her extra papers to sign. She wondered if they were shocked by her decision. They didn't seem to mind. They were both very young.

What would the Rabbi say?

After they took his body away, she thought, Now I must cry. But the overwhelming heaviness that had filled this tiny room for so long was gone and she felt lighter and almost giddy. She wanted to buy a new dress made of something like clouds. Yes, she'd find Gertrude. Her life was still a fine one.

The Hotel Eden was completed in 1930, and the Trouts came here that year on their honeymoon; they were the first guests to stay in this very room, which they retired to in 1960, not having seen it or Florida in-between. Peter wouldn't listen when, in Bridgeport, she tried to read him the newspaper reports of riots and bad times. "The Hotel Eden will be cheaper," was his answer. He was going to retire there, and that was that. Decisive he often was, impetuous rarely: she never understood why this place had so delighted him. For most of their years here guests couldn't even go out at night for fear of street gangs and muggings, and even during the daytime it was necessary to walk to the grocery in a group or take your chances. But now things were changing. Preservationists. The neighborhood and the Hotel Eden and its three-story pink stucco art deco refinements were suddenly of great interest to preservationists. Architects and designers and real estate people were always sticking their noses into corridors and closets and admiring essentials the inhabitants had prayed would be updated. The only time their son, Tim, who was a decorator (he had dropped out of architecture school halfway), ever came to visit them, he said all these buildings with all their gewgaws were going to be worth a great deal someday; he advised them to put any spare money they had into local real estate. Peter yelled at him, calling him a fool, the way he always did all the days of Tim's youth in Bridgeport. "*Spare* money! Who do you think I am? Rockefeller? Herman Levy?" The Trouts' 16 × 19 third-floor room was a tough enough fit for two. Tim stayed only one night, and he never called, and Rivka wasn't even certain the voice on the New York answering machine on which she'd left word of Peter's death was her son's.

As soon as they arrived at the Hotel Eden, on February 12, 1960, which was not only Lincoln's birthday but Peter's, Peter had a slight stroke. He became numb in his left leg. The doctor said he was okay and must not let this get him down. Peter rarely left his room again. For over twenty years he watched the television, sitting in the middle of the sea-green plush sofa, which also had art deco curvatures, and developed, as he got fatter, a sag where he sat.

Another thing Rivka never told Peter about was Norman's tefillin. She still had the set of tefillin in her bottom drawer. She didn't know how to get rid of it. You just can't throw away tefillin. It was against some holy religious law. And women weren't meant to have tefillin, which made it frighten her even more.

Tefillin are small black boxes of hide and long black leather thongs that secure these boxes to certain parts of the man's body. The boxes are filled with prayers from God. The tefillin, bound around head and arm, are a symbol of bondage. For it is written in Exodus: "Remember this day, in which you came out of Egypt, out of the house of bondage. By strength of hand He brought you out from the house of bondage." This passage from Exodus, and others from it and from Deuteronomy, are inside the tefillin's boxes.

She had watched her father put on his two phylacteries and give himself over to God. He went into swoons and cried out in a strange guttural voice Rivka never heard anywhere else, except once when Herman, during one of his last attempts at persuading her to marry him, had come unannounced to her house when she was the only one home and she let him in and—no sooner had the front door been closed—he let down his trousers and underpants and showed himself to her. "See! See! Take mine! Peter is smaller." Then he masturbated himself. She was less shocked than absorbed: like a New England tourist in some exotic non-English-speaking land. When he climaxed, he cried out, "I love you! I love *you!*" in that same ecstatic tone she'd heard from her father in this very room. When her father finished celebrating the miraculous release from bondage God performed for his Jewish people, which is so commemorated by and in and with tefillin, he would open his eyes and see Rivka staring at him from behind the upright piano no one ever played and instead of punishing her for her witnessing of his act he took her into a huge embrace and she could feel his body, which seemed furiously hot, and hear his heart pounding, and also the swollen bump between his legs. Then his hand would take her hand, leading it to the tefillin, guiding her fingers to untie his thongs so the two black boxes sticking to him were released, helping her to catch them as they slithered down his perspiring skin, lest these boxes touch the ground and be stained and rendered impure and unholy. She wanted to ask questions, but he would shush her, answering only: "Who are we to question the mysteries of

God?" Rivka stared at the wet spot Herman had left on the floor; he buckled his pants and stalked out, saying, "That is our son." She cleaned up Herman's mess. The next day he married Gertrude.

Rivka worked part-time as a volunteer in the office at Temple Emanu-El. She had to get out of the Hotel Eden and that small room and the television never shutting up. At the temple, she answered the Rabbi's telephone and she licked stamps for the Rabbi's mail and she spoke out through the hole in the glass partition to direct various repairmen who needed to get to ailing parts of the building. The temple had many reception rooms and suites for meetings and a huge auditorium that was called a sanctuary, and a library upstairs that was always kept locked. A notice posted on the library door said that its key was available in the office. Rivka was the key's keeper; it was in her top desk drawer, though no one ever asked her for it.

Rabbi Chesterfield had been seventy-five when Rivka took this job; he was the Rabbi Emeritus and he was in good health, though his wife wasn't. He was tall and slender, one of the few old men in the entire town who had no fat and still had all his hair, which was a lustrous silver; his voice was deep and mellifluous, and he had what sounded like an English accent. It was said he had studied at Oxford.

No, she would not have a funeral and she wouldn't have to ask Rabbi Chesterfield his opinion about burning Peter up because he'd died too, almost a year ago, at eighty-five. They could have had ten good years together.

A week or so after he originally interviewed her, when they were both leaving the temple at noon, Rabbi Chesterfield invited her to join him for lunch.

"Oh, I promised my husband," she said with a demureness she was unaware she possessed.

She bought a peach and sat by the ocean eating it. She thought about Rabbi Chesterfield, and about his wife. Mrs. Rabbi Chesterfield wore a mink coat and handsome jewelry and spoke perfect Hebrew and often translated articles from Israeli publications for the temple's newsletter; she had a bad cancer spreading inside her; both her breasts were already gone. The Rabbi must have been waiting for his mate to die, too.

Rabbi Chesterfield continued to smile at Rivka regularly, and to ask her to join him for luncheon, and, finally, to say quietly to her at the end of the day when he was on his way to his condominium on Indian Creek Drive, "We're not getting any younger, Rivka Trout."

On a sunny, beautiful day, just before his unexpected death, Rabbi Chesterfield suddenly yanked open the door of his study and marched into the outer office, right up to where Rivka sat by the glass partition.

"Please give me the key to the library," he said to her in a voice so insistent she wondered if he thought for some reason she wouldn't.

She took the key from her desk drawer and handed it to him.

"Please come with me," he further commanded, walking quickly out of the office.

She hurried to keep him in sight, past the Sisterhood Room, the Meeting Lounge, the Banqueting Manager's Office, the rooms belonging to the kindergarten, past all the walls of framed photographs, through the years, of this class and that class, all the net gowns and bouffant hairdos and talliths and yarmulkes and smiling, bright, hopeful, young Jewish faces, gathered around the comforting centerpiece of Rabbi Chesterfield himself, in his flowing black robe, as he gently aged through all the Sabbath School Beginner's Classes on the ground floor, through the Bar Mitzvah classes going up the stairway, through the Confirmation classes hanging along the second floor corridor, all the way to the locked library door itself.

He stood there fumbling with the key in the lock. Rivka, slightly out of breath, caught up with him and stood behind him as he yanked at the doorknob. He pushed the door open and she followed him into one of the few rooms in this entire religious complex she'd never entered.

He closed the library door and the windowless room was black for an instant before the fluorescent lights flickered on.

Rivka was wearing a light lime-colored dress with a pattern of dark-green twigs and branches and fernlike leaves. It had been an expensive dress she'd bought for Tim's graduation from some school of fashion and interior decorating in New York City, a graduation Peter refused to attend because he said it was a school for sissies.

Under the bright fluorescent lights, Rivka followed Rabbi Chesterfield's gaze to the large gleaming mahogany table that was the centerpiece of the room, the walls of which were lined floor to ceiling with shelves of religious books. There, on the table, lay a high pile of intertwining black leather straps, nestled with their small black leather boxes.

"These are the wounded ones," he said, "waiting for their straps to be mended before they can be worn again and put back to use in the congregation. The Talmud tells us we mustn't lay tefillin when the straps are broken. I have summoned these back from all the old men who are too tired to get them repaired and instead use them anyway, in their decrepit state. Old tefillin mustn't be abused. They must be repaired."

As he spoke, the Rabbi nervously moved piles of straps and boxes around, sliding them over the shiny, polished wood, first with one hand, then with the other, then with both, rearranging them as if he were playing three-card monte. He was sweating lightly, though the room was cool. He was dressed as he was always dressed, in a beautifully cut black suit tailored for him in London, with a blazing-white pima cotton shirt that always remained impeccably unwrinkled and a dark-gray heavy silk cravat from France. He patted his brow dry with a handkerchief. He cleared his throat.

"Tefillin are our antenna to God. Like a radio, or a TV, we must . . . tune in . . . to receive God's signal. When I wear these knots and these straps and these boxes and I say my prayers, I am under His protection. I am guided. The Lord is my shepherd. Did you . . . have a religious upbringing?"

"My father was very religious. But there was no time for Mama and the children. I feel . . . inside of me, I feel . . ."

"Yes?" He was looking at her and he was not looking at her.

"I feel that I am religious."

"No matter how far astray we may have traveled," he said, suddenly focusing and looking at her so intently her heart began quite unexpectedly to ache with pain, "it is not too late."

She nodded, even though she wasn't certain what he was asking or what she was agreeing to.

"The Torah has told us so."

She found this disappointing.

His hands had pulled out from the pile one set of tefillin, and he clutched it to him, its two boxes sagging down, dangling its straps.

"I laid my first tefillin on the day of my bar mitzvah. We don't have so many men who do it anymore."

Now he closed his eyes, and his tone was so intimate that Rivka closed her eyes as well.

"We tighten the knot. We make the coils. We press it into my bicep, directing it toward my heart. We make the windings around my middle finger . . ." He had taken off his jacket and rolled up his shirtsleeve and he was doing it. His arm was smooth and pale white, like an arm from some marble statue. She was peeking intently through her closed eyes. His submission was like her father's. Even his voice had changed its timbre to one of imprecation. "I am ready. I am ready. I submit. I come. 'I will wed You to me forever. I will wed You to me forever. I will wed You to me forever with right and justice, with love and mercy. I will wed You to me with faith and we shall know God.' "

So this is how a man knew God. Why could women not have tefillin? She'd asked her father that in her childhood, and he had hit her.

The Rabbi's last words came out in gasps. She opened her eyes. He was still sweating. His eyes were glistening with tears of fervor and the fear of transgression. He looked into her eyes, which were also filled with tears. When she said nothing, he appeared to be defeated.

"Please forgive me," he said so softly that she had to lean forward to hear him. "My wife has been dying for many years. I know your husband is also an invalid. I have lusted after you for ten years. I promised myself I must . . . ask you . . . before it is too late. I am sorry."

He unbound himself from the tefillin. His hands released it.

He started toward the door. He turned out the lights. He opened the door and stood by it, his hand on the inside knob, waiting to usher her out before him. But she hadn't moved. She was standing in the dark, and he couldn't see her at all, not even a dark shadowy presence, because he'd looked into the lighted hallway and his eyes were blinded.

"This has been a lovely experience," she said softly. "I'm very flattered by your interest. I keep waiting for something inside me to tell me what to do. Perhaps . . . if you could close the door . . . I would allow a short embrace . . . and a kiss."

After Rabbi Norman Chesterfield embraced and kissed her tenderly in the darkness and then took her out to luncheon at the Eden Roc, where, under the table, he held her hand, Rivka, back behind her plate of glass in the temple office, took the key and came back upstairs to the library alone. She felt breathless; she was gasping for air; she felt not hungry, but so empty, so empty inside. She stood in front of the table and its pile of tefillin. There it was, the one he had worn. Terrified she might be discovered, she plucked it up, this lonely, broken connection to God that he'd held to his heart. Norman said it wasn't too late to try.

Suddenly she felt exhausted. It seemed as if she'd been trying all her life. But no, it must never be too late. For whatever it might be. She stuffed the tefillin into her pocketbook.

The next day, after another luncheon at the Eden Roc, Norman took her for a long drive in his Cadillac, and the next day, after a third luncheon, by which time they were each beginning to tell themselves, No, it is not too late, Norman and Rivka slept in each other's arms in the afternoon. They'd tried to make love, but they had eaten a lovely meal, with champagne, and they were, after all, old-timers, if not in their desires.

The Rabbi died that night and Peter died a year later and how could she have believed a tefillin would bring her luck?

Too, she had been accused by Mrs. Annunciata Springstein of having killed the Rabbi. Mrs. Annunciata Springstein, a rich widow who herself had lusted rabbinically, had seen Rivka and the Rabbi entering and leaving the small motel. Mrs. Annunciata Springstein was not silent. It wasn't long before all the old Jews in the rocking chairs on the porches and in the aluminum folding chairs on the beach were not talking to Rivka, were looking the other way when she came near. Matters got even worse the night she was discovered trying to throw the tefillin into the ocean in the moonlight. The tefillin would not sink or float away. An old man actually ran from his room in the Hotel Ponce de Leon all the way down to the water and waded in his bedroom slippers to save the tefillin and forced the slithering wet straps back into her hands, barking at her rudely, most harshly. After this, she was known, behind her back, as "Mrs. Tefillin."

After the removal of Peter's body, Rivka went for a long walk along the ocean. She took off her sandals and walked in the sand for hours and miles. She didn't care who saw her or whispered behind her back. The sun was down, and there was a chill creeping in. She walked past all the third- and second- and first-class examples of gewgaws and froufrous and folderols that excited preservationists. She walked all the way up to the Eden Roc. Here she could hear orchestra music softly playing a nice romantic tune. Old songs were always being played in Miami Beach. The Mills Brothers could always be heard, somewhere, singing "Be my life's companion and you'll never grow old."

When she finally returned home, she fell asleep in exhaustion. Just before her eyes closed, she realized for the first time that Peter's heavy body was not weighing down the bed, forcing her to sleep on a tilt.

II

When she woke, it was another day. It was time to find Gertrude. She went to her bottom drawer and pulled out Herman's hidden letters and Norman's tefillin. Kissing them both for good luck, she placed them, with the toiletries and clean underwear she needed, in her ancient traveling bag. She dressed herself in a comfortable outfit that was wrinkle-free and that she hoped was fashionable enough for a day in Palm Beach. She left the Hotel Eden. She stopped at the savings bank and withdrew one thousand dollars. On Collins Avenue, she went to the car rental with the biggest billboard.

"Insurance?" the Cuban young man asked her.

She'd waited for him to serve her because his English was so poor. Her Connecticut driver's license had long since expired. Oh, wasn't she becoming the schemer!

She shook her head no.

"You take the big chances!" He smiled at her. "Here initial." He pointed to a maze of boxes. She initialed with a flourish. "Credit card." It was not a question but an assumption. She would have to surprise him. "I pay cash."

This caused some consternation. He'd never dealt with a cash transaction, and it took a while to locate a staff member who could explain in Spanish what must be done. It was necessary to leave a deposit of two hundred dollars. She handed him the bills, and he looked at them as if they lay in the hands of his grandmother, whose life of sacrifice such bills, held in such old and wrinkled palms, represented, making it difficult for him to take them from her without feelings of sadness and guilt. She patted his hand, having felt this way with her own mother and exploited it with her own son.

He nodded and smiled back and didn't even notice that her license had run out, as he copied its many numbers, exerting the necessary pressure on his pen to ensure their soaking into triplicate.

"Please outside. Space Five. Is Malibu or Capri. Very big. You like."

In the lot she found her enormous chariot, all silver and light blue and chrome and freshly glistening with the dewdrops of its recent hosing-down. She threw open its front door with the carefree strength of a much younger woman and she sat herself down regally behind the wheel and pulled her door closed and inserted her key. Somewhere, an engine started. Her driving skills were still intact.

She decided she'd drive along the ocean. She'd not had a vacation since she arrived in Florida, which was meant to have been a vacation for life. "For twenty years you waited to die! Twenty years I was healthy!" she heard her voice yell out. Then she said to the gray imitation-leather traveling bag sitting beside her: "You are very, very ugly. I want a new one."

The car, the Malibu or Capri, jumped and bucked with each emphatic statement. Drivers were already giving her wide berth.

In Bal Harbour, she stopped at the expensive shops. The four hundred dollars she discovered herself calmly paying for the new genuine-leather shoulder bag at Gucci's left her with four hundred dollars. She transferred her possessions from old world to new and on her way out told the saleslady, who was only too happy to do so quickly, to throw away the old. Her new bag had intertwining G's, which could only be an omen that Gertrude was alive and beckoning.

As she drove north, she realized that she was enjoying herself. Cars certainly drove themselves nowadays: she hardly had to do a thing. She was grateful she'd noted new car advertising over the years and understood, in concept at least, the idea of automatic transmission. She turned all the buttons she could find—air-conditioning and FM stereo radio and windshield wipers and directional indicators—on and off. Perhaps she could live in this car, this Malibu or Capri. She waved happily at the outside world and someone in a passing car waved back.

She was whizzing by so many expensive places to live! At first the pro-liferating repetition of elaborate high-rise condominiums and evocatively-themed motels impressed her. Of course she'd known the world was not completely filled with retired fixed-income people like herself and Peter, or with the criminally inclined and the blighted towns and cities as fea-tured each evening on the local and national news. Still, she felt she'd not been properly prepared for Eldorado, Versailles, Tiffany, Park Ave-nue, Monte Carlo, Hollywood, The Riviera, as replicated in oceanfront towers in an unbroken line. She imagined Gertrude, certainly, to be living so grandly—but not so many others as well. Something had certainly been happening in the outside world since she'd last thought about it.

When she became hungry, she saw signs that proclaimed she was in Fort Lauderdale. Fort Lauderdale had always sounded such a long way away! She pulled into a diagonal space facing the beach and sallied forth. Oh, courage was now her middle name! When she asked the pimple-faced youth in the submarine-sandwich store what was good, she was told that everything was good and its cost was calculated by the inch. She held up her hands, measuring goodness. "Eight, nine . . . how much would this many inches of tuna fish salad be?"

She sat on the low stone wall in front of her car, five inches in her lap and five in her hands and entering her body, her skirt up a tiny bit so her knees might catch some sun. She was watching some extremely beautiful young golden gods and goddesses frolicking on the beach. Rivka had never seen so many beautiful children before. Tim had black hair all over his body. He looked like an ape. Sometimes she wondered how he could have been created inside her and come out of her. These children were hairless, relaxed, and confident. Tim never acted like anything but a malcontent. She had been glad when he grew up and went out into the world. Now she was looking at a handsome boy and a beautiful girl, lying in each other's arms on a large white towel on the white sand, their lips touching and their arms and legs all tangled together as they slept peacefully under this sun. She could not believe that such bliss was available, and in public.

Her eyes followed a group of effeminate young men in the scantiest of bathing suits as they skipped across the highway and into a hotel on the other side. She knew what they were. Her son didn't skip and he wasn't effeminate, but before he left home he'd told her he was one of those. Why did he have to tell her? She jumped up. She threw away her unfinished sandwich and her half-drunk Tab and she locked herself back in her car, fighting against being overwhelmed by the sweater of heat she'd jumped into. She jabbed at a button marked Colder and pumped her accelerator like a pro, pulling her car out and into the stream like some crotchety old animal unexpectedly let free. There was no point, was there, in dwelling on memories of disappointing sons who left home and rabbis who'd wanted to love her. Were her eyes wet with tears or sweat?

I want to love you.

Those had been Norman's words.

"I want to love you."

He'd said them to her at the beginning of the one and only week they were to have together after the embrace in the library and before his death. (He tripped and fell down two steps descending into his sunken living room on Indian Creek Drive; he hit his head and had a stroke; he became paralyzed; and he died—all on the same day.)

He was holding her hand under the table at their first luncheon.

"I want to love you but you are not letting me."

She said nothing.

"If I rented a room somewhere, would you come with me?'

"No!" she said too loudly.

"Why not?"

"What could possibly be gained by two such old bodies getting into bed together?"

"You're shy."

"Of course I'm shy," she said, accepting his excuse.

When she didn't accept his first invitation, the Rabbi said to her: "We are just like the Jewish people. Our timing is always a little bit off. At another time, perhaps God will let His daughter out of His house of bondage."

Now she was suddenly frightened. She tried not to think of death and bodies and love that was taken away. And of no money to live on for much longer, to pay for the Hotel Eden. She tried not to cry out, "Where is my son to take care of me now?" Pompano, Hillsboro, Deerfield, Boca Raton—she forced herself to look at even more slabs of luxury sating the view. She tried not to feel poor. And old and tired and sweaty and unloved.

Quickly, she gave herself a talking-to. Always, when she found herself succumbing to negative moods, she'd give herself a talking-to.

"I'm going to visit Gertrude Jewsbury!"

But utter terror was her companion. What folly! What could Gertrude Jewsbury do for her?

The honking horns from behind her penetrated her fear. Her speed had decreased and she bravely put her foot on the gas. Going forward calmed her. How could she go back and live in a tiny room where her husband of over fifty years, whom she'd never loved in the first place, had died, a big flabby tank of flesh, a beached whale?

I never loved him?

Now guilt replaced her terror.

"I was unfair to you, Peter. I ruined your life. You might have had a better life if you had married somebody else." (No name occurred to her.) "No, I loved you, I loved you."

A policeman stopped her in Lake Worth. She was driving too slowly and holding up traffic for miles behind her and the law required greater speed. Finally, something made her laugh. "It is a funny law that requires greater speed."

She knew she was in Palm Beach because everything looked perfect. Nothing she'd ever seen had prepared her for this. She was in the capital of the rich world. She closed her eyes tight for just a second of intense, prayerful meditation. Gertrude Jewsbury *must* be alive. She reached in her bag and grabbed for the tefillin and kissed it over and over.

There it was. Right in front of her. Without her even having to look for it. The Breakers. She let out a loud belch, tasting of tuna fish salad a stomach her age should not have eaten. She parked and locked her rental car in the large lot in front of the hotel. She placed her Gucci bag on the fender and used her hands to smooth down her dress and tidy her hair. It was just after six. She was chilly. She poked around in her bag before realizing she hadn't brought her soft cashmere sweater decorated with bursts of tiny beads. Why hadn't she brought it? It was the one item of clothing she owned that Gertrude would have applauded. Soon I'll be with Gertrude, she thought. We'll hug and embrace and cry over old memories, and she'll help me. No, I mustn't wish in advance. That brings bad luck. She tried to walk into The Breakers jauntily, with a bouncy assertiveness reminiscent of her younger self.

III

She was stunned by the scale of the hotel's insides. The huge vaults of space made everyone look tiny. All the guests were very dressed up. Everyone seemed to be taking indoor strolls before dinner, walking back and forth, up and down, in their finery. Some people were bent over, or used aluminum walkers for support, or walked holding on to attendants. Everyone was quite old. Everyone looked more helpless than in Miami Beach.

She went to the front desk. It seemed ages before the clerk paid attention to her. "What may I do for you, madam?" he asked in an accent unmistakably German.

"I'm hoping you'll have a room for one night only." Her voice sounded too meek.

"A room," he repeated, as if he'd heard a most peculiar word.

"I'm meeting a friend here. Mrs. Gertrude Jewsbury."

"Ah, of course. Mrs. Jewsbury. She has not told us."

Rivka felt enormously relieved. Gertrude was still alive. Her smile was so large the clerk lowered his eyes.

"I'm afraid my arrival here is quite unexpected. I'm afraid I just came. I want to surprise my old friend. I hope that's all right."

"May I have your credit card, please?" Now he was staring at her.

"I'll be paying cash." Was cash suspicious here, too? Jewish people had always had trouble with Germans. She tried to return his stare, to convince him of her honesty.

He punched keys on a computer and studied an apparition of numbers. Finally, he spoke. "In the end, I have nothing for this night."

She felt tiny.

She'd not expected to be turned away. She'd imagined she'd be settled in a room under the same roof before dialing Gertrude. Was there likely to be a cancellation? He thought it most unlikely. From where could she telephone Mrs. Jewsbury? The house phone was just over there. She thanked him, and started out, but then returned to ask him softly, "Do you know where I can spend the night nearby?" Suddenly he became kinder. He pulled out a small map and traced the route to a Holiday Inn just across the lake in West Palm Beach. He repeated the directions when she seemed uncertain. She thanked him. She felt like crying from this encounter. Should she have tipped him a dollar? I wanted to stay *here!* She picked up the phone, beaten.

Gertrude Jewsbury's voice was exactly as it had been in memory. Rivka Trout felt better the moment she heard it. Gertrude was here!

"Hello!" Gertrude barked louder the second time. "Who is there!"

"Gertrude . . . would you believe this is Rivka Trout speaking?"

"Oh, my God!" came the immediate response, without so much as a pause. "Where are you?"

"Below you, in the very lobby of your hotel." She was sounding like a schoolgirl and she was even standing on tiptoe and she hoped Gertrude felt so excited too. "I tried to get a room here—it's all so sudden that I didn't have time to call or write, I just hoped you'd be here—and there is no room here, I must stay in a Holiday Inn in West Palm Beach, and Gertrude . . . Peter is dead."

"You come up to me immediately! Hurry! Hurry, because we must dine in twenty minutes. Room 1012."

Rivka walked to the elevator on a cloud.

Her thoughts became confused again in the elevator. Does she remember me fondly? Maybe she's in a wheelchair and needs someone to push her around. I don't want to live with another invalid. There was a small bench and she sat down. The black woman who operated the elevator inquired if she was all right.

"Do you know, I'm very frightened."

"Do you want to see the house physician?"

"No, no, I'm not sick."

She looked at the woman and suddenly wanted to say: You look like Meredith who came once a month to me in Bridgeport. She used to steal from me . . . pillowcases she thought I wasn't using . . . potatoes. I knew she was stealing and she knew I knew and . . . She was so poor. How much did a few potatoes amount to? And pillowcases? To sleep on.

"Here's the tenth floor, honey. You take care of yourself."

Rivka followed the arrows toward 1012. The hallway reminded her of Peter's descriptions of the hotels he'd visited with Herman Levy on their grand tour of the British Isles in 1925. It had been Rivka's listening to Peter tell of this trip that made her seriously consider him as a potential husband, even though he had no money. His descriptive powers were then so magical! He wove captivating stories about that trip and Rivka longed to travel. Oh, why didn't I fire her for stealing? Rivka Trout marched down the long, endless, empty corridor, her fingers, like a little girl's, trailing along the embossed wallpaper and reaching toward the height of the chandeliers and to the reflection in the gilt-framed mirrors. Rivka Wishenwart, for one second in time, was now a young woman walking down the hall of some fancy foreign rich hotel Peter hadn't taken her to at all.

"Here I am!"

And there she was, Gertrude Jewsbury, staring at Rivka, waiting for Rivka, standing there regally outside her room. You look so dignified, Rivka thought. You're not in a wheelchair at all.

Rivka, who knew she'd been studied from head to toe as well, and found wanting, gallantly kept on her smile. "And here I am."

They did not throw themselves into each other's arms. They did not hug or kiss or embrace. Overcome with nervousness, neither knew what to do with the other. So for this moment they did nothing. Gertrude stood back and allowed Rivka to enter her suite before her. They were both inside and Gertrude closed the door. They were in a tiny vestibule, giving onto rooms beyond, and they were almost on top of each other, hardly breathing, each shyly and slyly looking the other over, these two friends from long ago, and noting what changes time and fortune had wrought.

Gertrude pushed ahead and led the way into a living room. The drapes and slipcovers and scattered pillows were of a gray and crimson French provincial pattern and made of chintz, a material Rivka associated with goods beyond her reach.

"How absolutely beautiful," she gasped out loud. "At the Hotel Eden we faced the ocean. But of course there's no comparison."

"As one of the investors in this hotel, my suite does not face the ocean because such rooms fetch higher prices and when I am here, which is not for so very long, I sacrifice my creature comforts to my greed. Now, I have several kinds of cheeses and some biscuits. I don't drink, but there is bottled water. Do you wish to freshen up? Can I lend you a fresh dress? I have some that are too big for me. No, of course, you look lovely. Let me look at you. Let me look at you."

Gertrude looked at Rivka's wrinkled and unstylish dress and at what looked to be an imitation Gucci bag that didn't go with anything and at hair that needed cutting and shaping and styling and . . .

"We *could* eat here in my room," Gertrude said.

"Life has been good to you. But then I knew it would be."

The first time Rivka saw Gertrude Jewsbury was the day Gertrude married Herman Levy. It was in 1926, at the Barnum Circus Café Grande in Bridgeport (P. T. Barnum had made his home in this small city, been its mayor, and died here, and many things were named after him), and Rivka was relieved that this beautiful woman had come from across the sea to marry the pest so that she wouldn't have to. Her parents had put great pressure on her. "Herman's so rich," her mother said longingly. "Think of us," her father said bluntly. Herman had met Gertrude, who was British, in London on that trip with Peter; he left him each day to go and be with her; he married her at the Barnum because she wasn't Jewish, which ruled out a religious ceremony. It was a very large wedding anyway, because Gertrude was one thing Herman and his parents wanted to show off big.

Herman and Gertrude moved into an enormous house near Seaside Park and Rivka became her best friend. Every day the two women walked on the beach, past the big brown shingled mansions facing Long Island Sound, holding hands like schoolgirls, planning imaginary trips around the world. Gertrude had much to learn about America and Rivka, ever the teacher, was happy to impart everything she knew. One day shortly after the wedding, Herman asked Rivka to walk outside, not along the beach but around the bleak neighborhood in the North End where she still lived with her parents; since he apologized for behaving so shockingly the last time they'd been alone, and since he seemed sad and subdued, Rivka had felt sorry for him and agreed to the walk. He told her the story of Gertrude's past, which was not nearly so fancy as he'd led everyone in Bridgeport to believe.

"She was just a poor girl, like you. She worked in a dress shop in Mayfair. Her parents are dead. She had no one and nothing. I transformed her. I gave *her* a new life."

Rivka waited for more, but Herman just looked at her, like a petulant child who wants something his mommy won't give him. She realized the implications of his words. When would he leave her alone? She ran from him, before their walk had even started.

Within four years Gertrude gave birth to four sons. Each of them died not long after birth. Gertrude became very depressed, and then she became a recluse. Herman moved to New York. Finally, Gertrude left Bridgeport and disappeared, without even saying good-bye to Rivka. On Rivka and Peter's wedding day, a bolt of delicate lace arrived from Barcelona, with a note—"Until we meet again, my dear friend"—but there was no return address, as there was none on the occasional postcard that arrived from abroad. Also, on the day of the wedding, Herman sent a telegram saying that Rivka was the only woman he'd ever wanted and since she wouldn't have him she would be punished—both she and Peter would be punished—for her refusal to marry *him*.

And from that year to this one Herman kept his promise, which is how Rivka knew Herman was still alive. From that year to this one, the letters came. As every sort of success continued to remain outside Peter's realization, as years and years went by and they had no more money than they'd begun with, once each year came the unsigned letter, each with only a monetary figure writ large. Once a year Rivka stared at those huge, black, accusatory numbers. "$575,809." *You didn't marry me.* "$1,000,212." *You should have.* "$2,000,201." *See what you're missing.* "$4,890,092." *Aren't you sorry you were so stupid as to marry such a dummy?* The most recent letter had arrived last week, as had all the others, on their wedding anniversary. "$53,987,503." Rivka believed these figures to be the amount of money Herman was worth—money that would have been hers to share if only she'd married Herman Levy and not Peter Trout. Once a year she got that letter, in the envelope from the Bank of Bridgeport, which was also her bank and Peter's, and she would stare at it and not want to open it, not want to stare at that figure, which was now so big. Then she'd sneak off to a bench by the ocean and rip it open and gasp as if someone had kicked her in the stomach. No tears, though. If Herman thought he'd caused her tears, he was wrong.

"Yes, Peter has died," Rivka said to Gertrude. "We had a wonderful life together."

The women were seated in two stiff chairs, picking at some hard cheddar cheese and water biscuits. Rivka, who now was famished, ate hungrily, oblivious to the crumbs falling down her front. Everything in the room looked as if it was from some distant place: tables with intricate carvings; rugs that were shining and delicately thin. Gertrude wore a red Chanel suit and an ivory silk blouse and navy kid pumps.

"You are an *investor!*"

"In this and many other beautiful places. I still must pay my expenses. Though of course I do receive special attentions."

Rivka suddenly cried out: "Gertrude, I simply cannot get over how beautiful you look!"

And Gertrude jumped up and hastened to doors that she pulled open to reveal an entire wall of closet filled with glorious swaths of every color; she returned to Rivka with an armful of soft violet. "Please! I insist. Put this on. It will look lovely on you. Please!" Her voice was pinched, and she tried to soften her appeal. "To please me. I . . . I have so much."

And Gertrude took Rivka's elbow and led her into an adjoining bedroom, a huge room where there were twin beds, and helped her off with her old garment and slipped the new one over her head. Then they looked at Rivka in a mirror. The dress, its shades of purple cascading in panels from a high bodice, made her look tall and thin and elegant. Rivka turned in front of the mirror, for a second obscuring her view of Gertrude, and for a second, it was her room. She lived here.

"Now take a comb to your hair." Gertrude led her to a bathroom. "And wash your face and use any of my cosmetics and scent. But quickly. We must get down to dinner. They don't wait, even for me. If you're a First Sitting person, as I am, they don't take you at the Second Sitting if they're full up. Two thousand dollars a week, and it's just like the army."

"Our entire retirement income was only fifteen thousand dollars a year," Rivka said involuntarily. She must stop saying things like this. She was not a supplicator. She was not!

In the elevator going down, the operator smiled at Rivka. "You must be feeling better! Good!"

"Yes, thank you. What is your name?"

"Oh, I have a funny name, ma'am." She offered nothing further.

"Well, I understand and so do I. And it's very nice to be served by such courteous and attentive and considerate people."

"Thank you, ma'am."

"You're very welcome."

Gertrude looked ahead while this conversation, which she obviously considered odd, played itself out. The doors opened, and she led the way, just a few steps in front of Rivka, down the long corridors to the dining room, nodding to an occasional acquaintance.

The enormous dining room was filled as far as the eye could see. Gertrude, followed by Rivka, threaded her way among the aisles and seated herself in the very center of the room at a table for two. Rivka sat down across from her. It was as if everything all around was radiating from them. "They're all relics and crones," Gertrude said as Rivka gazed about. "They are nothing but old relics and crones with nothing to do but band together for gin rummy and chomp-chomp their way through plates of lean meat and boiled chicken and salt-free everything, meal after meal, until one day one more of them's not here." She was not looking around her at all.

Soup had appeared before them. "It's a lovely old hotel," Rivka said, to make up for Gertrude's being so critical. She leaned forward, trying to be intimate and confidential. "We have so much to catch up on."

Gertrude ate none of her soup and only picked at her salad. "I don't look bad for seventy-five, do I? I thought I might stay in England. I went home for a while. But I found I got cold very easily. I couldn't tolerate the cold anymore."

"That's exactly what Peter said! He couldn't tolerate the cold anymore. That's why we moved here." She'd thought she and Gertrude had been the same age.

" 'Toleration' is everyone in Florida's favorite word for moving here. And it is the most intolerant place in the entire universe. There is only one thing anyone in this state is interested in, and that is money. And, of course, staying alive. You do know, don't you, that you are the person I've known longest in the world? Does someone from the first part arrive at the end? Some attempt at order and structure after all? Save room for dessert. The desserts are the only good things they do."

Rivka was busy ordering from the waiter, roast beef and several vegetables and more rolls and butter. "I don't like desserts very much," Rivka said, vaguely aware that something had just been said that troubled her but unable to retrace the steps of the conversation.

"It's all I'd eat if it would keep me alive. I can eat a pint of ice cream and a box of chocolates *and* an entire cake or pie and not gain one single ounce. I don't sleep well, though."

"How have you kept your figure?"

"Rivka, do you think fate has sent you to me just at this particular moment as an omen?" She pulled the collar of her Chanel jacket tight around her neck, as if she were suddenly cold.

"Why, Gertrude? Do you need me now?"

"Need? I don't *need* anything. I still have all my faculties. My health has been extremely good."

"And Herman has taken good care of you." Rivka was looking at the far end of the room, where there was an entire window banked with fresh flowers. She was surprised, though, not to hear any music. Were the romantic old songs played only in Miami Beach?

"Herman? Herman does not take care of me."

Rivka was uncertain she had heard correctly. "He doesn't?"

Rivka had taken a roll and was slowly buttering it. It was her second or third roll, she couldn't remember which. She was eating as if she'd been deprived of food for life. The butter was in little gold-colored foil packets, and Rivka spread the hard bits as best she could on a surface so brittle flakes of crust scattered everywhere. She was feeling more uncomfortable than she'd bargained for. Was she on the wrong track? "Why

. . . why did you change your name back? If you don't mind my asking."

"When you travel, the best places don't take Jews. But I could call myself Mrs. Jewsbury, which isn't Jewish at all. It shocks the pants off everybody. Which amuses me."

"Where does it come from?"

"It's a very common Yorkshire name. Jewsbury. Dewsbury. It can be spelled half a dozen ways."

"I read somewhere there's a Jewtown, Georgia. Isn't that awful?"

"Why? Why is it? It's not dissimilar to Jewsbury, Yorkshire."

"It's not the same at all! It's much more . . . hateful."

Roast beef and broiled fish had arrived. Gertrude didn't touch a bit of food. She didn't return one of Rivka's smiles. I've lost, Rivka thought. What do I do now? "The Yorkshire people are filled with a great deal of common sense," Gertrude was continuing. "Not religion. Just common sense. Religion does so get in the way of common sense."

"Gertrude, I should tell you that Herman writes me letters every year."

Gertrude winced. "Herman writes to you?"

"Yes. I've saved all his letters. They're here in my bag." There had been a confusing scuffle upstairs when Rivka put the bag on her shoulder and Gertrude tried to take it off. "It doesn't look right; let's just leave it here for now," Gertrude had said. "Really, Gertrude." Rivka had fought back. "I feel undressed without it. I bought it at Gucci's on the way up here this morning, thinking you'd approve." She looked to see if it still hung from the back of her chair, and of course it did.

Gertrude removed her hand from her neck. Apparently she no longer felt a chill, was no longer considering the possible mystical implications of Rivka's appearance from out of the blue. She'd snapped to attentiveness. "What do these letters say?"

"They say he's worth over fifty million dollars!"

The busgirl was taking away the plates, and the waiter was ready for orders for dessert. "I'm sorry the salmon was frozen after all, Mrs. Jewsbury," he said, noting Gertrude's untouched food.

"What makes you think he writes and tells you that?" Gertrude asked, waving the waiter away.

"Wait!" Rivka called after the waiter. "I want some dessert."

"Wheel over the trolley," Gertrude ordered.

"Because he wanted me to marry him and I wouldn't. I thought you knew all this. He told me he told you. When I turned him down he went on that trip to London and that's where he met you working in a shop and he brought you to Bridgeport and just before the ceremony he asked me again and I said no again and he married you. And after he married you he . . . came back again. And before I married Peter he tried one last time. And when I got married he said he would never let me forget him. And once a year he writes me a letter telling me how much money he's worth. It's very cruel to do that, don't you think?" She'd wanted the words to come out in a calmer, more orderly fashion, and instead they'd rushed out, as in some child's game, ready or not, here I come.

"Why didn't you marry him?"

"I . . . I don't know. His breath always smelled. Why did you? For his money? He made you very rich."

"Yes, his breath always smelled."

"Do you feel guilty?"

"He discarded me! I must tell you something, Rivka. His entire settlement upon me amounted to four hundred thousand dollars. One hundred thousand dollars for each dead son, he said. I am worth far, far more than that, and not because of Herman."

Questions were coming to Rivka faster than any answers. "That's all? . . . You are? . . . Did you know Peter would always be poor?"

"Of course."

"How did you know?"

"One senses these things."

"You could have told me. We were best friends."

"Well, I only . . . surmised."

"I surmised, too."

The waiter was standing there, at attention, beside a trolley laden with a confectioner's enthusiasms. Rivka pointed to one, then another, then a third. "Mrs. Jewsbury says I can have as many as I want."

Then she said everything out loud that she'd said to herself in the Hotel Eden in Miami Beach.

"If I had married Herman you wouldn't be here and you should be very grateful to me and now I don't have anything and Peter said Herman would always take care of me after he died, Peter died, and I don't know how to get in touch with Herman, and I thought you could tell him Peter's dead and could he please take care of me now." There were tears in her eyes. "I'm ready now."

"Herman is dead."

The waiter was serving the many pieces of pie and cake, and some eclairs, too. He placed forks down for both women.

"Herman is dead?"

"He died over twenty years ago. He took his own life."

"Why did I order so much? I don't even like cake. You say they are good?"

"Yes, about the only thing they do well here."

"Twenty years?" His letters were the only valid things in her life. "My letters aren't from Herman?"

"I don't see how they could be."

"Look! Look!" Hysteria was building inside her as she practically turned out the contents of her bag on the table and the letters in their bundle fell out and she ripped off the restraining bands of string and ribbon and fanned them out awkwardly on the cloth, among the sea of sweets. "Take one. Look at any one!"

Gertrude looked at several of them expressionlessly. What was she thinking? Why doesn't she say anything! Rivka was trying hard not to scream out, "What do you know!"

It was a long time before Gertrude answered.

"Herman was not in love with you. Nor was he in love with me. He was in love with Peter. I found them in bed with each other several times, both in London and in Bridgeport. He'd made no secret of it. That is why he purchased me in Mayfair. Because my circumstances, which were not dissimilar to yours at present, necessitated that I be for sale. These things—all of these things—happen."

Rivka wanted to cover her ears forever. "He badgered me to marry him! Over and over and over! He wouldn't leave me alone!" Falteringly, trying to speak words she was not accustomed to speaking, much less to even think, she told Gertrude about the awful experience, the sight of Herman waving his erect penis in her face.

Gertrude's eyes closed momentarily, and her hands became small fists. Was she angry at Rivka? At Herman? At herself? "It sounds a most desperate act," she finally said.

Then she continued: "Herman was a tortured man. He scared me to death too, many times. Had any one of ours sons lived, I still should have left him." Then she stopped, and she took both of Rivka's hands. "Peter rejected Herman. Peter told him he would marry you. Herman then

338 ~ The Penguin Book of Gay Short Stories

convinced himself that capturing you was the only way he could have Peter. Do you understand any of this? At first he used me to make Peter jealous. That did not work. So he brought me back and paraded me before his entire town. That did not work either. Peter would not go away with him or live with him.''

"So Peter did not love him!" She was about to say, He loved me!

"Love? You lived with him. Do you think Peter Trout was capable of love? He married you to be taken care of.''

"But Herman could have taken care of him on the grandest scale . . . What am I saying?" She understood none of this. A man taking care of a man? A man caring for another man as would a wife? Tending and cooking and mending and shopping and buying the fruit from the cheapest market?

"Jewish boys did not run off with other Jewish boys and have sex with them in 1930! My dear Rivka, he married you to escape these feelings, and to hope for the best.''

"You knew all this when you married him and you knew all this when I married him and you knew all this when you and I walked along the ocean, silly young girls, holding hands, dreaming of seeing the entire world?''

Gertrude looked away. She took her fork and started picking at one of Rivka's eclairs. "I could also say to you that if you had not been so blind as to be unable to sense the man did not love you, I would not have been purchased and involved. We would not be here.''

Rivka said softly, "I don't want to know any more.''

"But there is more.''

"I have heard too much already.''

"It was not over between them, even after both of their marriages. They continued to meet here and there. Herman would call Peter at his office and they would meet somewhere, and yes, Peter would call Herman. I would hold my hand over the receiver and listen. 'I need to see you right away,' I would hear Peter say. It was like he was in some sort of pain and Herman was the doctor with the medicine to make him feel better. I don't know where they met. I think Herman had another apartment somewhere, just for them.''

"Why didn't you tell me any of this! We were like sisters!''

"How could I tell you any of this? It is hard for me to tell you even now, so many years later! 'My husband is sleeping with your husband.'

How could I tell you this when we and the world seemed both so young? I was a poor girl who'd been given some perverse, outlandish opportunity to come to a new country and earn money for her future. So what if there were strings attached. There are always strings attached!"

"Peter wrote me those letters."

Gertrude was silent to this supposition.

"Did he hate me that much for marrying him that he would punish me all these years? Did Peter know when Herman died? He must have known. So Peter pushed me into finding you—to discover all of this. What a very vengeful man I married! Why didn't Herman leave some of his money to Peter?"

Gertrude suddenly got up and started from the table, threading her way back through the crowded aisles. Rivka jumped up and stuffed the letters into her bag and clutched it to her and, once again, rushed to catch up with her.

They walked down the long ornate vaulted corridor toward the ocean entrance, past old men and women sitting in big overstuffed chairs and staring into space; past the room full of gin rummy and bridge and pinochle players, all of them old too; past the male couples and female couples, strolling indoors after dinner, arm in arm, to while away the hours before bedtime. Gertrude had said earlier she found The Breakers most depressing after dinner: there was nothing to do but walk or sit; it was a certain prelude to the end of life itself. They walked out the ocean entrance and along the path between the grand old hotel and its protective seawall. They could hear the ocean.

Gertrude sat down on the wall. "I want to make you understand something, and I don't know how to do it. I hope my words will lead you toward some safe harbor.

"Herman located me before he killed himself. He told me he wished to leave his estate to Peter's son and that if I could find him, he would reward me as well. I found your son in New York, rather down on his luck. As was I. My money had run out. I had traveled too far and too wide and too long. Herman left Timothy several millions. We all had misguided notions of how wealthy he ever really was. Timothy and I traveled at first. He was a shy man, with little knowledge of the world beyond its pain. He felt exceedingly unloved, and somehow I was able to help him rise above self-pity. We made each other laugh. For myself —well, I discovered I had a great deal of pent-up motherhood within me, just waiting for release. In Paris, he convinced me we should take our money and buy an old hotel on the Left Bank that required extensive renovation. It became popular, and profitable, quite swiftly. So we went on from there. We bought a much larger one in Rome. We performed the same renovation and achieved the same rewards. I was, to my surprise, quite good at business. In twenty years we rescued ten old buildings, each one larger and grander than the one before. We became, and I hesitate to say this, millionaires ourselves. I wanted to locate you, to share some of our good fortune. But . . . he forbade me. He is dead now, from a disease no one could identify or cure. Herman took his own life when Peter had his stroke. Did you realize that? Herman came to Miami to see Peter, and Peter would not see him. Timothy and I pieced all this together. Herman left diaries, and Peter wrote Herman love letters full of tantalizing ardor he could not deliver in real life. I have been wanting you to know all this for so many years, Rivka! I should have told you. But how could I tell you! How could I tell you all of *this?*"

"My baby is dead?"

Gertrude nodded.

"He felt we never loved him?"

Gertrude said nothing at first. Then, "I hope you realize that, now, we both are . . . free."

"He was right. He was most unlovable. Both of them were."

"So here we are, my dear Rivka, two old ladies, unloved all our lives, scorned by men who couldn't even love each other, sitting together by a mighty ocean. Can you see that the rest of your life is not very long at all?"

"The tide is so high," Rivka said, raising herself on tiptoe and peering over the wall and down at the waves. "They want me to look back and say it was all so awful. I won't. I won't at all."

There was a balcony jutting out over the seawall, and onto this Rivka ran. Gertrude ran after her to prevent her jump, for that was what she thought the distraught woman contemplated. But it was not herself that Rivka threw out into the distance. First it was her letters, clutched angrily in her fists as she ripped them into little pieces, then watched while, like some wedding's confetti, they fluttered and drifted away. Then came a strange and tangled object that Gertrude did not recognize—the tefillin, the straps and the prayers and the boxes and their blackness, all hurled out into the twilight and falling fast, like something dying and losing blood. God could not punish Rivka any harsher for disposing of His attributes than He had punished her for being drawn to hold them.

Then, like a siren heard only dimly through the fog and from a distance, or like a high-pitched croon from some animal Rivka herself had certainly never seen or heard or known, some animal or bird or mate suddenly let free from captivity and understanding it not a whit, she wailed her availability out into the wind. The nighttime answered her at first with only silence, not even a rustle of a breeze off the ocean, not even a distant hint of a tune from an orchestra gathered in some far-off ballroom, playing for the rich.

Gertrude embraced her. And held her tight. And kissed her forehead as she smoothed her hair.

Stories like this are never over. There is always a future to be haunted by a ghost or two. Did Rivka stay with Gertrude? (Yes.) Did two old ladies finally and at last have some kind of happy ending, now that the Jew among them had been led out of the house of bondage?

~ *Paul Bailey* ~

Spunk

W here had I read that this was the hour of the damned, when the tormented are startled out of quiet slumber? I remember asking myself that literary question as I lay awake in a state much like terror early one morning in my fifteenth year. I had just masturbated, in my brown-skinned idol's imagined embrace. Thoughts of pleasure were succeeded by feelings of shame and guilt. I sat up in bed, in the absolute darkness of the long hour that only ends with dawn, and realized I was among the lost.

Three years before, in pre-spunk times, I had known desire of the kind other boys knew. I could speak of it, if I wanted to, with the voice of experience. On that memorable Saturday evening, my parents told me I would have to sleep with the two girls who lived on the ground floor. My mother and father were having a party, and some of the guests would be staying the night. There was no room for me upstairs.

"You can lie between us," said the older girl, who was well into adolescence. I was under orders, and obeyed. She and her sister pulled back the bedclothes and made a space for me. In clean pyjamas, with my face freshly scrubbed, my teeth brushed and hair neatly combed, I had passed my mother's test for immaculacy: "You've washed behind your ears, for once. Miracles will never cease."

A renowned novelist, PAUL BAILEY is the author most recently of the memoir An Immaculate Mistake, *from which "Spunk" is excerpted. He lives in London.*

I wonder, now, who were the more innocent—the four trusting parents or their three apparently guileless children. Into the bed I went, with no anticipation of the bliss that was to ensue. I had been instructed to go off to sleep as quickly as possible, and when the girls' mother wished us sweet dreams and turned out the light, I closed my eyes and kept them closed.

They opened, in surprise, when the older girl guided my right hand to her large, round breasts, which seemed to grow larger and rounder at the touch. I was soon aware that one hand was insufficient to cope with the abundance of flesh I was being offered. She pushed me aside, asked me to wait a minute, and then made her nightdress ride up until it was like a vast collar round her throat. I had complete access to the swollen beauties, and pressed and squeezed them while she whispered that I should try to be more gentle and not be so rough. She then commanded me to kiss her nipples, which I did. From kissing I progressed to sucking and licking. In the meantime, the younger sister, determined to join in the fun, had lowered my pyjama trousers from the rear and now held my throbbing penis in a firm grip. It was still in her possession when I had the first "moment"—for such was the name I gave it—of my life. I trembled with delicious excitement as it happened. At the age of twelve, I was too young to leave incriminating stains on the sheet.

~ ~ ~

"Semen" and "sperm" were unknown words to us. It was "spunk" we talked of, in and out of class. The more extroverted boys held competitions in the lavatories to see who could produce most and who could send it flying farthest. We were spunk-obsessed, in our different ways, in the spring of 1950. The sticky stuff had us in its thrall.

"You're getting through rather a lot of handkerchiefs," observed my suspicious mother. "Yet you don't seem to have the sniffles."

There were not many advantages in being immaculate, but this was one of them. Every morning throughout my schooldays, my mother folded a clean handkerchief into the breast pocket of my blazer, above the arms and motto of the school's founder: "Rather Deathe than False of Faythe." I rarely had colds, thanks to my love of oranges, and seldom sneezed, but now I could use what she called the sniffles as the reason for the stiffened squares of cotton collecting under my pillow.

"You never took a hanky to bed with you before."

Often, during the night, guessing that she was awake in the next room, I pretended to sneeze at the moment of ejaculation. Cunning and deceit can be born of guilt, I discovered.

There was a boy in our year, I recall, who knew neither shame nor deception. He masturbated whenever he needed to, and his need was limitless. His desk shook with him as orgasm was frantically achieved, and only subsided when he was calm again. As soon as the word went round that he was "at it," we tried not to snigger and the master tried not to notice. One teacher, and one alone, was openly amused by the spectacle. This dapper man, who wore floppy bow-ties, taught chemistry. "Today I shall communicate to the class the ideas of a certain Avogadro, who is not to be confused with a certain Ava Gardner. Those of you who wish to learn about the Italian physicist's work on gases will have pens and paper to the ready—with the exception, that is, of the single-minded student in your midst who would appear to be interested in more stimulating pursuits." He looked at the boy, whose eyes had already glazed over. Shortly afterwards, when the boy let out a resounding gasp, he diverted from the subject of Avogadro for an instant and enquired if E—— was "better now"? E—— replied that he was, thank you, sir. "That's good," said the teacher, and went on with the lesson.

~ ~ ~

It was always at the hour of the damned—the time when most people die—that I felt ashamed and miserable. I tried, with infrequent success, to curb the need to masturbate. Boys who indulged in self-abuse could expect fearsome manifestations of that indulgence in later life—blindness, hairy growths on the palms of the hands, and complete loss of memory were but three of the promised signs.

How did I know this? We did not talk of sex at home, and if anyone attempted to, my mother brought discussion to an abrupt halt with "Go and wash your mouth out with carbolic soap" or "I didn't bring you up to think filth." My knowledge was a common one: it was in the air, it was all about us. At school, in religious instruction, we learned that God slew Onan, the son of Judah, for spilling the seed his father had ordered him to put into Tamar, the wife of his wicked brother, Er, whom God had also dispatched. I did not view this episode, then, as yet another example of God's customary perverseness—I simply understood, as I was meant to, that Onan had committed a terrible sin, for which he was duly punished.

Seed-spilling was bad for you, morally and physically, but doing what the men of Sodom wanted to do to the two angels who put up for the night at Lot's house was infinitely worse. We had to know that "to know" in the Bible was not "to know" as we knew it. When the young and old males of that soon-to-be-destroyed city (by God, of course) demanded of Lot that he bring his visitors "unto us, that we may know them," they had something more than a friendly handshake in mind. The scribe responsible for Chapter 19 of Genesis is annoyingly vague on the subject of the methods employed by Sodom's welcome committee, and our teacher emulated his vagueness. We had to read between the lines.

My feelings of shame were founded on nonsense, on unexamined superstition. Yet they persisted long after I had sent God packing. I continued to believe that I was unnatural, though a healthy strain of arrogance in me occasionally translated this as "different." That I wasn't really ashamed of being a coward and a hypocrite is what shames me, in retrospect, for I never rose to the defence of my fellow pansies when they were insulted or mocked. I stayed silent when I should have spoken, and was even a party to the mockery.

Two events, both comic in essence, signalled the beginning of the end of shame. In the first, a congenial young woman with whom I was endeavouring to make love on a friend's divan suddenly began to giggle. I persevered. "What's the matter?" I asked, when her giggling became uncontrollable. "You are," she answered, pushing me off. "You're the matter. You're soft where you shouldn't be. You want a man, don't you?"

"Yes," I astonished myself by admitting.

"So do I," she said, without malice. "Let's go and get drunk."

Her honesty and kindliness were beneficial to me, and we remained friends for years. In the second deciding event, it was I who laughed— inwardly. I had gone to bed with an actor who had converted to Roman Catholicism in his twenties. His tiny flat, at the top of a huge Victorian house, was decorated with icons. We had eaten a sparse dinner, which he had made sure we had washed down with a surfeit of red wine. Incense was burning in the bedroom when we undressed, in the dark. He did not care for kissing, he told me. What *did* he care for? "Playing," he revealed. The play, when it took place, was not inventive. My hand having fulfilled its required duty, he moaned and turned away from me. I pretended to doze off. Some time later, when he felt certain that I was asleep, he left the bed, stealthily. Then I heard him muttering, and made out the words "forgive me," which he repeated. I opened my eyes and saw him on his knees before a crucifix. He was begging forgiveness— from Jesus, from the Virgin Mary—for wasting his seed.

In the morning, when he invited me to play again, I said, truthfully, that I was not in the mood. He demanded a reason. "I'm just not in the mood," I replied.

"Try to be," he pleaded.

"I can't. I honestly can't."

He glowered at me as I put my clothes on. I said good-bye, and thanked him for the meal and the wine and the play. I could not thank him, then, for the gift of his abjectness, which helped to release me from mine.

~ ~ ~

"That girl's got more spunk than any boy I've ever met"—the sentence, encountered in a children's adventure story, caused me to stop and think. A girl with spunk? The only spunk I was conscious of was the stuff I couldn't resist spilling, despite the example of slaughtered Onan. I consulted the *Oxford Dictionary* in the school library and was initially bewildered. Was the fictional girl a spark, a touchwood, or tinder, a fungoid growth on a tree, a match or Lucifer? The fifth definition made sense: "Spirit, mettle; courage, pluck." To have spunk is to have courage, I learned. This spunk is rarer, much rarer, than the other kinds, and it does not stain.

~ *Allen Barnett* ~

The
Times as It
Knows Us

Time will say nothing but I told you so,
Time only knows the price we have to pay.
—W. H. AUDEN

"With regard to human affairs," Spinoza said, "not to laugh, not to cry, not to become indignant, but to understand." It's what my lover, Samuel, used to repeat to me when I was raging at the inexplicable behavior of friends or at something I had read in the newspaper. I often intend to look the quote up myself, but that would entail leafing through Samuel's books, deciphering the margin notes, following underlined passages back to where his thoughts were formed, a past closed off to me.

"Not to laugh, not to cry, not to become indignant, but to understand," he would say. But I can't understand, I'd cry, like a child at the end of a diving board afraid to jump into the deep end of the pool.

"Then let go of it," he would say. "I can't," I'd say about whatever had my heart and mind in an insensible knot. And he would come up behind me and put his arms around me. "Close your eyes," he'd say. "Close them tight. Real tight. Tighter."

ALLEN BARNETT's collection The Body and Its Dangers *was the finalist for the 1991 PEN/Hemingway Prize. Eloquent and feverish, his stories defined masterfully the experience of AIDS in the 1980s. Barnett was quoted as saying that AIDS gave him something to write about and took away the strength with which to write about it. He died not long after the publication of this, his first and only book.*

Samuel would tell me to reach out my arms and clench my fists. "Squeeze as hard as you can," he would say, and I would, knowing that he believed in the physical containment of emotions in a body's gesture. "Now, let go," he would say, and I did. If I felt better, though, it was because his mustache was against the back of my neck, and I knew full well that when I turned my head, his mouth would be there to meet mine.

The day that Samuel went into the emergency room, he took a pile of college catalogues with him, not suspecting this hospital was the only thing he would ever be admitted to again. I got to him just as a nurse was hanging a garnet-colored sack above his bed. Soon a chorus of red angels would be singing in his veins. He told me he wanted to go back to school to get a degree in Biomedical Ethics, the battlefront he believed least guarded by those most affected by Acquired Immune Deficiency Syndrome. "Do you think you'll need an advanced degree?" I asked. His eyes opened, and his head jerked, as if the fresh blood had given him new insight, anagnorisis from a needle.

"That's not what I meant to say," I said. He said, "Not to worry." He died before they knew what to treat him for, what an autopsy alone would tell them, before he could even be diagnosed.

Vergil said, "Perhaps someday even this stress will be a joy to recall." I'm still waiting.

I

Noah called Perry a "fat, manipulative sow who doesn't hear anything he doesn't want to hear."

The endearments "fat" and "sow" meant that the argument we were having over brunch was still on friendly terms, but "manipulative" cued us all to get our weapons out and to take aim. Perry was an easy target, and we had been stockpiling ammunition since Tuesday, when an article on how AIDS had affected life in the Pines featured the seven members of our summer house. Perry had been the reporter's source. It was Saturday.

"What I resent," Joe said, newspaper in hand, "is when she writes, 'They arrive at the house on Friday night to escape the city. When everyone is gathered, the bad news is shared: A friend died that morning. They are silent while a weekend guest, a man with AIDS, weeps for a few moments. But grief does not stop the party. Dinner that night is fettucine in a pesto and cream-cheese sauce, grilled salmon, and a salad created at one of New York's finest restaurants.' "

Perry said, "That's exactly what happened that night."

"You made it sound as if we were hanging streamers and getting into party dresses," said Enzo, who had cooked that meal. "It was dinner, not the Dance of the Red Masque." He put a plate of buttered English muffins in front of us, and four jars of jam from the gourmet shop he owned in Chelsea.

Joe said, "I don't like the way she implies that death has become so mundane for us, we don't feel it anymore: Paul died today. Oh, that's too bad; what's for dinner? Why couldn't you tell her that we're learning to accommodate grief. By the way, Enzo, what's the black stuff on the pasta?"

"Domestic truffles. They're from Texas," he answered from the kitchen counter, where he was mixing blueberries, nectarines, apricots, and melon into a salad.

Stark entered the fight wearing nothing but the Saks Fifth Avenue boxer shorts in which he had slept. "Just because our lives overlap on the weekend, Perry, doesn't give you rights to the intimate details of our health." His large thumb flicked a glob of butter and marmalade off the front of his shorts and into his mouth. Our eyes met. He smiled, and I looked away.

"What intimate details?"

Stark took the paper from Joe and read aloud, " 'The house is well accustomed to the epidemic. Last year, one member died, another's lover died over the winter. This year, one has AIDS, one has ARC, and three others have tested positive for antibodies to the AIDS virus."

"She doesn't identify anybody," Perry protested.

"The article is about us, even if our names are not used," Enzo said. He placed a cake ring on the coffee table. Noah, who had just had liposuction surgery done on his abdomen, looked at it nostalgically.

Perry, on the other hand, was eating defensively, the way some people drive a car. "I was told this was going to be a human-interest piece," he said. "They wanted to know how AIDS is impacting on our lives—"

"Please don't use *impact* as a verb."

"—and I thought we were the best house on the Island to illustrate how the crisis had turned into a lifestyle. But none of you wanted your name in the paper."

I said, "How we represent ourselves is never the way the *Times* does."

"They officially started using the word *gay* in that article," Perry said, pointing to the paper like a tour guide to the sight of a famous battle.

"It didn't cost them anything," I said. Indeed, the *Times* had just started using the word *gay* instead of the more clinical *homosexual*, a semantic leap that coincided with the adoption of Ms. instead of Miss, and of publishing photographs of both the bride and the groom in Sunday's wedding announcements. And in the obituaries, they had finally agreed to mention a gay man's lover as one of his survivors.

"You're mad at me because she didn't write what you wouldn't tell her," Perry said to me.

Noah said, "We are mad at you because we didn't want to be in the piece and we are. And you made us look like a bunch of shallow faggots."

"Me?" Perry screamed. "I didn't write it."

Noah slapped the coffee table. "Yes, you, the media queen. You set up the interview because you wanted your name in the paper. If it weren't for AIDS, you'd still be doing recreation therapy at Bellevue."

"And you'd still be stealing Percodan and Demerol from the nurses' station."

"Yeah," Noah shouted. "You may have left the theater, but you turned AIDS into a one-man show. The more people die, the brighter your spotlight gets."

"I have done nothing I am ashamed of," Perry said. "And you are going to be hard-pressed to find a way to apologize for that remark." The house shook on its old pilings as Perry stamped out. Noah glared into space. The rest of us sat there wondering whether the weekend was ruined.

"I don't think that the article is so awful," Horst said. He was Perry's lover. "She doesn't really say anything bad about anybody."

Horst was also the one in the article with AIDS. Every day at 4:00 A.M., he woke to blend a mixture of orange juice and AL721—a lecithin-based drug developed in Israel from egg yolks and used for AIDS treatment—because it has to be taken when there is no fat in the stomach. For a while, he would muffle the blender in a blanket, but he stopped, figuring that if he woke us, we would just go back to sleep. He laughed doubtfully when I told him that the blender had been invented by a man named

Fred who had died recently. It was also the way he laughed when Perry phoned to say their cat had died.

Stark asked Noah, "Don't you think you were a little hard on Perry?"

Noah said, "The next thing you know, he'll be getting an agent."

I said, "We're all doing what we can, Noah. There's even a role for personalities like his."

He would look at none of us, however, so we let it go. We spoke of Noah among ourselves as not having sufficiently mourned Miguel, as if grief were a process of public concern or social responsibility, as if loss was something one just *did*, like jury duty, or going to high school. His late friend had been a leader at the beginning of the epidemic; he devised a training program for volunteers who would work with the dying; he devised systems to help others intervene for the sick in times of bureaucratic crisis. He was the first to recognize that AIDS would be a problem in prisons. A liberal priest in one of the city prisons once asked him, "Do you believe your sexuality is genetic or environmentally determined?" Miguel said, "I think of it as a calling, Father." Dead, however, Miguel could not lead; dead men don't leave footsteps in which to follow. Noah floundered.

And we all made excuses for Noah's sarcasm and inappropriate humor. He once said to someone who had put on forty pounds after starting AZT, "If you get any heavier, I won't be your pallbearer." He had known scores of others who had died before and after Miguel, helped arrange their funerals and wakes. But each death was beginning to brick him into a silo of grief, like the stones in the walls of old churches that mark the dead within.

"Let's go for a walk," his lover, Joe, said.

Noah didn't budge, but their dog, Jules, came out from under a couch, a little black Scottie that they had had for seventeen years. Jules began to cough, as if choking on the splintered bones of chicken carcass.

"Go for it, Bijou," Noah said. (Even the dog in our house had a drag name.) One of his bronchial tubes was collapsed, and several times a day he gagged on his own breath. He looked up at us through button eyes grown so rheumy with cataracts that he bumped into things and fell off the deck, which was actually kind of cute. Taking one of the condoms that were tossed into the shopping bag like S & H green stamps at the island grocery store, Joe rolled it down the length of Jules's tail.

"Have you ever thought of having Jules put to sleep?" Stark asked.

"Yes, but Joe won't let me," Noah said. But we knew it was Noah keeping Jules alive, or half-alive, stalling one more death.

Stark said, "I noticed that his back is sagging so much that his stomach and cock drag along the boardwalk."

"Yeah," Joe said, "but so do Noah's."

~ ~ ~

I took The Living Section containing the offending article and threw it on the stack of papers I had been accumulating all summer. My role as a volunteer was speaking to community groups about AIDS, and I collected articles to keep up with all facets of the epidemic. But I had actually been saving them since they first appeared in the *Times* on a Saturday morning in July several years ago. RARE CANCER SEEN IN 41 HOMOSEXUALS, the headline of the single-column piece announced, way in the back of the paper. I read it and lowered the paper to my lap. "Uh-oh," I said.

I remember how my lover, Samuel, had asked from our bedroom, "What is it?" He was wearing a peach-colored towel around his waist, from which he would change into a raspberry-colored polo shirt and jeans. There was a swollen bruise in the crook of his arm, where he had donated plasma the day before for research on the hepatitis vaccine. As he read the article, I put the lid on the ginger jar, straightened the cushions of the sofa we had bought together, and scraped some dried substance from its plush with my thumbnail. I looked at him leaning against the door arch. He was always comfortable with his body, whether he stood or sat. Over the years, we had slipped without thinking into a monogamous relationship, and space alone competed with me for his attention. No matter where he was, space seemed to yearn for Samuel, as if he gave it definition. He once stood me in the middle of an empty stage and told me to imagine myself being projected into the entire theater. From way in the back of the house, he said, "You have a blind spot you're not filling above your right shoulder." I concentrated on that space, and he shouted, "Yes, yes, do you feel it? That's stage presence." But I could not sustain it the way he did.

Samuel looked up from the article. "It says here that there is evidence to point away from contagion. None of these men knew one another."

"But they all had other infections," I said. Hepatitis, herpes, amebiasis—all of which I had had. Samuel used to compare me to the

Messenger in Greek tragedies, bearing news of some plague before it hit the rest of the populace.

"It also says cytomegalovirus," he said. "What's that?"

"*Cyto* means cell; *megalo* is large," I said. "That doesn't tell you much."

"Well, if you haven't had it," he said, "there's probably nothing to worry about."

～　～　～

Perry's guest for the week came in with the day's paper, a generous gesture, I thought, since our house's argument had embarrassed him into leaving through the back door. His name was Nils, but we called him Mr. Norway, for that was where he was from, and where he was a crowned and titled body builder. By profession, he was an anthropologist, but he preferred being observed over observing, even if the mirror was his only audience. I didn't like him much. When he sat down and began to read the paper I assumed he had bought for us, I tried to admire him, since it was unlikely that I would read the Oslo *Herald* were I in Norway. I couldn't help thinking, however, that the steroids Nils took to achieve his award-winning mass had made him look like a Neanderthal man. On the other hand, I thought, perhaps that was appropriate for an anthropologist.

I picked up the last section of the paper and turned to the obituaries. "Gosh, there are a lot of dead people today," I said.

"You are reading the death notices every day," Nils said. "I thought so."

"We all do," said Stark, "then we do the crossword puzzle."

We deduced the AIDS casualties by finding the death notices of men, their age and marital status, and then their occupation. Fortunately, this information usually began the notice, or we would have been at it for hours. If the deceased was female, old, married, or worked where no one we knew would, we skipped to the next departed. A "beloved son" gave us pause, for we were all that; a funeral home was a clue, because at the time, few of them would take an AIDS casualty—those that did usually resembled our parents' refinished basements.

Stark looked over my shoulder and began at the end of the columns. "Here's a birthday message in the In Memoriams for someone who died thirty-six years ago. 'Till memory fades and life departs, you live forever in my heart.' "

"Who do people think read these things?" Enzo asked.

"I sometimes wonder if the dead have the *Times* delivered," I said.

We also looked for the neighborhood of the church where a service would be held, for we knew the gay clergy. We looked at who had bought the notice, and what was said in it. When an AIDS-related condition was not given as the cause of death, we looked for coded half-truths: cancer, pneumonia, meningitis, after a long struggle, after a short illness. The dead giveaway, so to speak, was to whom contributions could be made in lieu of flowers. Or the lyrics of Stephen Sondheim.

It was good we had this system for finding the AIDS deaths, otherwise we might have had to deal with the fact that other people were dying too, and tragically, and young, and leaving people behind wondering what it was all about. Of course, the difference here was that AIDS was an infectious disease and many of the dead were people with whom we had had sex. We also read the death notices for anything that might connect us to someone from the past.

"Listen to this." I read, " 'Reyes, Peter. Artist and invaluable friend. Left our sides after a courageous battle. His triumphs on the stage are only footnotes to the starring role he played in our hearts. We will deeply miss you, darling, but will carry the extra richness you gave us until we build that wall again together. Contributions in his name can be made to The Three Dollar Bill Theater. Signed, The people who loved you.' "

Stark said, "You learn who your friends are, don't you?"

Horst looked thoughtfully into the near distance; his eyes watered. He said, "That is touching."

"You know what I want my death notice to read?" Enzo asked. " 'Dead GWM, loved 1950s rock and roll, Arts & Crafts ceramics, back issues of *Gourmet* magazine. Seeking similar who lived in past for quiet nights leading to long-term relationship.' "

"There's another one," Stark said, his head resting on my shoulder, his face next to mine. "Mazzochi, Robert."

"Oh, God," I said into the open wings of the newspaper.

The newsprint began to spread in runnels of ink. I handed the paper over to Stark, who read out loud, " 'Mazzochi, Robert, forty-four on July —, 1987. Son of Victor and Natalia Mazzochi of Stonington, Connecticut. Brother of Linda Mazzochi of Washington, D.C. Served as lieutenant in the United States Army. Came back from two terms of duty in Vietnam, unscarred and unblaming. With the Department of Health and Human Services NYC since 1977. A warm, radiant, much-loved man.' "

"What a nice thing to say," Horst said. "Did you know him well?" "He was that exactly," I said.

There was another one for him, which Stark read. " 'Robert, you etched an indelible impression and left. Yes, your spirit will continue to enrich us forever, but your flesh was very particular flesh. Not a day will go by. Milton.' "

The others sat looking at me as I stood there and wept. There was Stark, an investment banker from Scotland; Horst, a mountain peasant from a farm village in Switzerland; and Enzo, who grew up in Little Italy and studied cooking in Bologna (he dressed like a street punk and spoke like a Borghese); and there was Mr. Norway on his biennial tour of gay America. They were waiting for a cue from me, some hint as to what I needed from them. I felt as if I had been spun out of time, like a kite that remains aloft over the ocean even after its string breaks. I felt awkward, out of time and out of place, like not being able to find the beat to music, which Samuel used to say that even the deaf could feel surging through the dance floor. Robert's funeral service was being held at that very moment.

The last time I had seen him was a Thursday afternoon in early October, a day of two funerals. Two friends had died within hours of one another that week. I went to the funeral of the one who had been an only child and whose father had died before him. I went, I guess, for his mother's sake. Watching her weep was the saddest thing I had ever seen.

Afterward, I made a bargain with myself. If Robert Mazzochi was still alive, I would go to work. If he was dead, I would take the day off. When he did not answer his home phone, I called the hospital with which his doctor was associated, and the switchboard gave me his room number. I visited him on my way to work, a compromise of sorts.

"How did you know I was here?" he asked.

"Deduction."

Eggplant-colored lesions plastered his legs. Intravenous tubes left in too long had bloated his arms. Only strands were left to his mane of salt and pepper hair. He was in the hospital because thrush had coated his esophagus. The thrush irritated his diaphragm and made him hiccup so violently he could not catch his breath. Robert believed that he would have suffocated had his lover, Milton, not been there to perform the Heimlich maneuver. He was waiting for the nurse to bring him Demerol, which relaxed him and made it easier to breathe.

I finally said, "I can't watch you go through this."

He looked at me for a long moment. "If I've learned anything through all this, it's about hope," he said. "Hope needs firmer ground to stand on than I've got. I'm just dangling here."

" 'Nothing is hopeless. We must hope for everything,' " I said. "That's Euripides. It's a commandment to hope. It would be a sin not to."

"Then why are you leaving me?" he asked, and I couldn't answer him. He said, "Don't worry. I am surrounded by hopeful people. Milton's hope is the most painful. But I could be honest with you."

"The truth hurts too," I said.

"Yes, but you could take it."

"For a while."

We used to meet after work for an early supper before he went to his KS support group. One night he said to me, "I never knew that I was handsome until I lost my looks." He was still handsome as far as I was concerned, but when he pulled his wallet out to pay the check, his driver's license fell to the table. He snatched it back again, but I had seen the old picture on it, seen what must have told him that he had been a beautiful man.

The nurse came in and attached a bag of Demerol to the intravenous line feeding his arm. "We might have been lovers," Robert said to me, "if it hadn't been for Milton."

"And Samuel," I said.

The Demerol went right to his head. He closed his eyes and splayed his fingers and smiled. "My feet may never touch ground again," he said, and floated there briefly. "This is as good as it will ever get."

~ ~ ~

The rest of the day passed slowly, like a book that doesn't give one much reason to turn the page, leaving the effort all in your hands. Perry was sulking somewhere. Stark and Nils had gone to Cherry Grove. A book of Rilke's poetry, which he was not reading, lay open on Horst's lap.

"Genius without instinct," he said during the second movement of

Mozart's *Jeunehomme* piano concerto. "He knew exactly what he was doing."

"Are you all right?" I asked Enzo, who was lying in the sun, in and out of a doze.

"It's just a cold," he said. "Maybe I'll lie down for a while."

"You didn't eat breakfast today. I was watching you," I said.

"I couldn't."

"You should have something. Would you like some pasta al'burro?" Enzo smiled. "My mother used to make that for me when I was sick."

"I could mix it with Horst's AL721. It might taste like spaghetti alla carbonara."

Horst said, "You should have some of that elixir my brother sent me from Austria. It has lots of minerals and vitamins."

"Elixir?" Enzo asked.

"That potion that's in the refrigerator."

Enzo and I worried what Horst meant by potion, for Horst went to faith healers, he had friends who were witches, he ate Chinese herbs by the fistful and kept crystals on his bedside. These he washed in the ocean and soaked in the sun to reinvigorate them when he figured they'd been overworked. He said things like "Oh, I am glad you wore yellow today. Yellow is a healing color." Around his neck, he wore an amulet allegedly transformed from a wax-paper yogurt lid into metal by a hermit who lived in Peru, and which had been acquired by a woman who had sought him out to discuss Horst's illness. "You don't have to say anything," the hermit told her at the mouth of his cave, "I know why you're here." Fabulous line, I said to myself, that should come in handy.

Enzo and I found a silver-colored canister in the refrigerator. Its instructions were written in German, which neither of us could read. I wet a finger and stuck it in the powder. "It tastes safe," I said.

"Athletes drink it after a workout," Horst said.

"I'll have some after my nap," Enzo said.

"If you have a fever, you sweat out a lot of minerals."

"I'll mix it with cranberry juice," Enzo assured him.

"You lose a lot of minerals when you sweat," Horst said. He had been repeating himself a lot lately, as if by changing the order of the words in a sentence, he could make himself better understood.

"If you want me to cook tonight, I will," I said.

Enzo said, "The shopping's done already," and handed me a large manila envelope from the city's health department, in which he kept his recipes. They were all cut from the *Times*, including the evening's menu: tuna steaks marinated in oil and herbs (herbs that Horst had growing in pots on the deck) and opma.

"What is opma?"

"It's an Indian breakfast dish made with Cream of Wheat."

"We're having a breakfast dish for dinner?" I asked.

"If this gets out, we'll be ruined socially," he said, and went to bed, leaving Horst and me alone.

Horst and I had been alone together most of the summer, except for a visit by his sister and brother, both of whom were too shy to speak whatever English they knew. Gunther cooked Horst's favorite meals. Katja dragged our mattresses, pillows, and blankets out on the deck to air. When she turned to me and said in perfect, unaccented English, "I have my doubts about Horst," I wondered how long it had taken her to put that sentence together. Gunther and I walked the beach early in the morning, before Horst was up. He wanted to know all he could about Horst's prognosis, but I was afraid to tell him what I knew, because I did not know what Horst wanted him to think. But fear translates, and hesitant truth translates instantly. I did not enjoy seeing them return to Switzerland, for when they thanked me for looking after their brother, I knew I had done nothing to give them hope.

"Remember my friend you met in co-op care?" I asked Horst. "He has lymphoma. The fast-growing kind."

"He should see my healer. Lymphoma is her specialty," he said. "Oh, I just remembered. Your office called yesterday. They said it was very important. Something about not getting rights for photographs. They need to put something else in your movie."

"What time did they call?"

"In the morning."

"Did you write it down?"

"No, but I remember the message. I'm sorry I forgot to tell you. I figured if it was important that they would have called back."

"They are respecting my belated mourning period," I said.

"What does this mean?"

"I'll have to go into town on Monday."

"That's too bad. How long will you stay?"

"Three or four days."

I began to look over the recipes that Enzo had handed me, angry at Horst for not telling me sooner but far more angry that I would have to leave the Island and go back to editing films I had thought were finished. Samuel had died when we were behind schedule and several hundred thousand dollars over budget on a documentary series titled *Auden in America*. Working seven-day weeks and twelve-hour days, it took a case of shingles to remind me of how much I was suffering the loss of what he had most fulfilled in me.

Perry came in while I was banging drawers and pans about the kitchen. "What's with her?" he asked Horst.

"Oh, she's got a craw up her ass," Horst said.

"I beg your pardon," I said.

"He is mad at me for not taking a message, but I say to hell with him." He raised a long, thin arm, flicked his wrist, and said, "Hoopla."

"I am not mad at you," I said, although I was. I believed that he had been using his illness to establish a system of priorities that were his alone. No one else's terrors or phone messages carried weight in his scheme of things. If he said something wasn't important, like the way he woke us up with the blender, knowing we would eventually go back to sleep, we had to take his word for it because he was dying.

And that was something we could not deny; the skeleton was rising in his face. Every two steps Death danced him backward, Horst took one forward. Death was the better dancer, and who could tell when our once-around-the-floor was next, when the terrible angel might extend a raven wing and say, "Shall we?"

And then I was angry at myself for thinking that, for elevating this thing with a metaphor. What was I doing personifying Death as a man with a nice face, a way with the girls? This wasn't a sock hop, I thought, but a Depression-era marathon with a man in a black suit who probably resembled Perry calling, "Yowsa, yowsa, yowsa, your lover's dead, your friends are dying."

As I cleared aside the kitchen counter, I came across another note in Horst's spindly handwriting. I read it out loud: " 'Sugar, your mother called. We had a nice chat. Love, Heidi.' "

"Oh, I forgot again," Horst said.

"It's all right," I said, and paused. "I'm more concerned with what you talked about."

"We talked female talk for ten minutes."

"Does that mean you talked about condoms or bathroom tiles?"

"We talked about you too."

"What did you say?" I asked.

"I said that you were fabulous."

"Oh, good. Did you talk about . . . yourself?"

"Yes, I told her about the herb garden," he said. "I'm going to bed now for a little nap. I want to preserve my energy for tonight's supper that you are cooking." Then he went into his room and closed the door.

I looked at Perry, who registered nothing—neither about the exchange nor about the fact that his lover, who had been a bundle of energy for three days, was taking a nap.

"Aren't you out to your mother?" he asked.

"She probably knows. We just never talk about it."

"I'm surprised you don't share this part of your life with her."

"What part?" I asked.

"You shouldn't close yourself off to her, especially now."

"It wouldn't be any different if AIDS hadn't happened," I said.

"You'd have less to talk about."

"I almost called her when Samuel died."

Perry said, "I think we should get stoned and drunk together."

Horst came back out of his room. "I forgot to show you these pictures of us my sister took when I was home for harvest last time."

He showed me pictures of him and Perry carrying baskets and sitting on a tractor together. In my favorite, they were both wearing overalls, holding pitchforks, and smoking cigars.

"You two were never more handsome," I said. I looked at Perry, who pulled the joint out of his pocket. He had recently taken up smoking marijuana again after three years of health-conscious abstinence.

"Look how big my arms were then," Horst said. Then suddenly he pounded the counter with both his fists. Everything rattled. "I hate this thing!" he said. And then he laughed at his own understatement.

"What time is dinner?" he asked.

"At nine, *liebchen*."

Horst nodded and went to bed, closing the door behind him.

Perry looked at me. I poured the vodka that was kept in the freezer, while he lit the joint. I knew what was coming. It was the first time we had been alone together since Sam's death. Perry had known Sam from their days together working with a theater company for the deaf. Samuel loved sign language, which he attempted to teach me but which I would not learn, for it seemed a part of his life before we met, and I was jealous of the years I did not know him, jealous of the people as well, even the actors in their deafness, rumored to be sensuous lovers. When Samuel danced, he translated the lyrics of songs with his arms and fingers, the movement coming from his strong, masculine back and shoulders the way a tenor sings from his diaphragm. Sometimes I would leave the dance floor just to watch him.

"It was easier for you," Perry said, referring to Sam's sudden death. "It was all over for you fast."

"You make it sound as if I went to Canada to avoid the draft."

"You didn't have to force yourself to live in hope. It's hard to sustain all this denial."

"Maybe you shouldn't make such an effort," I said.

He looked at me. "Do you want to hear some bad news?" Perry asked, knowing what the effect would be but unable to resist it. The Messenger in Greek tragedies, after all, gets the best speeches. "Bruce was diagnosed this week. PCP."

I heard a bullet intended for me pass through a younger man's lungs. I backed away from the kitchen counter for a few minutes, wiping my hands on a dish towel in a gesture that reminded me of my mother.

"Are you all right?" Perry asked.

"Actually, I'm not sure how much longer I can take this."

"You're just a volunteer," he said. "I work with this on a daily basis."

"I see," I said. "How does that make you feel when you pay your rent?"

There are people who are good at denying their feelings; there are those who are good at denying the feelings of others. Perry was good at both. "Touché," he said.

"Have you ever thought about leaving the AIDS industry for a while?" I asked him.

"I couldn't," Perry said, as if asked to perform a sexual act he had never even imagined. "AIDS is my mission."

I finished my drink and poured myself another. "Someone quoted Dylan Thomas in the paper the other day: 'After the first death there is no other.'"

"What does it mean?"

"I don't know, except that I believed it once."

"We need more occasions to mourn our losses," he said.

"What do you want, Grieve-a-thons?"

The *Times* had already done the article "New Rituals Ease Grief as AIDS Toll Increases": white balloons set off from courtyards; midnight cruises around Manhattan; catered affairs and delivered pizzas. It was the "bereavement group" marching down Fifth Avenue on Gay Pride Day bearing placards with the names of the dead that made me say, No, no, this has gone too far.

"I'm very distrustful of this sentimentality, this tendency toward willful pathos," I said. "A kid I met on the train was going to a bereavement counselor."

"You've become a cynic since this all began."

"That's not cynicism, that's despair."

"I haven't been of much help to you," Perry said. "I never even called to see how you were doing when you had shingles."

"I didn't need help," I said, although I had mentioned this very fact in my journal: "March 30. I am blistered from navel to spine. My guts rise and fall in waves. Noah paused a long time when I told him what I had and then asked about my health in general. Dr. Dubreuil said that shingles are not predictive of AIDS, but I know that the herpes zoster virus can activate HIV in vitro. So should that frighten me? We pin our hopes on antivirals that work in vitro. What should we fear? What should we draw hope from? What is reasonable? I worry: How much fear is choice of fear in my case? Horst has them now, as well. When I called Perry to ask him what shingles looked like, he said, 'Don't worry, if you had them, you would know it.' He hasn't called back, though the word is out."

"I have a confession to make," Perry said. "I read your journal, I mean, the Reluctant Journal."

That is what I called my diary about daily life during the epidemic: who had been diagnosed, their progress, sometimes their death. I wrote what I knew about someone who had died: what he liked in bed, his smile, his skin, the slope of his spine.

I asked Perry: "Did you read the whole thing or just the parts where your name was mentioned?"

"I read the whole thing. Out loud. To the rest of the house when you weren't here," he said. "You just went white under your tan, Blanche."

I laid Saran Wrap over the tuna steaks that I had been preparing. The oil made the cellophane adhere to the fish in the shape of continents; the herbs were like mountain ridges on a map.

"I was just joking," Perry said.

"Right."

"You had that coming to you."

"I suppose I did."

"I don't know what to say to you about Samuel that you haven't already said to yourself," he said. "I think of him every time you enter the room. I don't know how that makes me feel about you."

"Sometimes I miss him so much I think that I am him."

I took things to the sink in order to turn my back on Perry for a moment, squaring my shoulders as I washed the double blade of the food processor's knife. What connected the two of us, I asked myself, but Samuel, who was dead? What did we have in common but illness, sexuality, death? Perry had told himself that asking me to share the house this summer was a way of getting back in touch with me after Samuel died. The truth was that he could no longer bear the sole burden of taking care of Horst. He wanted Horst to stay on the Island all summer and me to stay with him. "It would be good for you to take some time off between films, and Horst loves you," he had said, knowing all along that I knew what he was asking me to do.

Perry was silent while I washed dishes. Finally, he said, "I saw Raymond Dubreuil in co-op care last Friday night. He was still doing his rounds at midnight."

"There aren't enough doctors like him," I said, still unable to turn around.

"He works eighteen-hour days sometimes. What would happen to us if something should happen to him?"

"I asked him what he thought about that *Times* article that said an infected person had a greater chance of developing AIDS the longer he was infected. Ray said the reporter made years of perfect health sound worse than dying within eighteen months of infection."

Perry had brought up a larger issue and placed it between us like a branch of laurel. I turned around. His hand was on the counter, middle two fingers folded under and tucked to the palm, his thumb, index, and little finger extended in the deaf's sign for "I love you." But he did not raise his hand. I thought of Auden's lines from *The Rake's Progress*, "How strange! Although the heart dare everything / The hand draws back and finds no spring of courage." For a passing moment, I loathed Perry, and I think the feeling was probably mutual. He had what I was certain was a damaged capacity to love.

Joe came in, followed by Stark and Nils. Joe kissed me and put his arm around my shoulder. "Nils told me a friend of yours died. I'm sorry. Are you okay?"

Perry slapped the counter.

"Don't get me started," I said. "Where's Noah?"

"We've been visiting a friend with a pool," Joe said. "Here's something for your diary. This guy just flew all the way to California and back to find a psychic who would assure him that he won't die of AIDS."

"Why didn't he just get the antibody test?" I asked.

"Because if it came out positive, he'd commit suicide. Anyway, Noah's coming to take you to tea. Where's Enzo?"

Stark came out of the room he shared with Enzo. "His body's there, but I can't attest to anything else. Does this mean you're cooking dinner?"

Nils came out of my room, which had the guest bed in it. He had changed into a pastel-colored muscle shirt bought in the Grove. I stiffened as he put an arm around me. "Come to tea and I will buy you a drink," Nils said.

"We'll be there soon," Perry said in a tone that implied wounds from the morning were being healed. Nils left to save us a place before the crowd got there. While the others were getting ready, Perry began to scour the kitchen counter. Someone was always cleaning the sink or dish rack for fear of bacteria or salmonella, mainly because of Horst, but you never know. Perry asked, "You don't like Nils, do you?"

"No. He has ingrown virginity."

"Meaning he wouldn't put out for you?"

"And another thing . . . all I've heard this week is that the Pines is going to tea later, that we're eating earlier, that there's more drag, fewer drugs, more lesbians, and less sexual tension. For an anthropologist, he sounds like *The New York Times*."

Noah's long, slow steps could be heard coming around the house. When he saw Perry in the kitchen, he stopped in the center of the deck. Noah looked at Perry, raised his eyebrows, then turned and entered the house through the sliding door of his and Joe's room. Perry turned to the mirror and ran a comb through his mustache. From a tall vase filled

with strings of pearls bought on Forty-second Street for a dollar, he selected one to wrap around his wrist. The pearls were left over from the
previous summer, when the statistics predicting the toll on our lives were
just beginning to come true; there were dozens of strands, in white, off-
white, the colors of after-dinner mints. This will be over soon, my friend
Anna says, they will find a cure, they have to. I know what she is saying.
When it began, we all thought it would be over in a couple of years;
perhaps the *Times* did as well and did not report on it much, as if the
new disease would blow over like a politician's sex scandal. AIDS to them
was what hunger is to the fed, something we think we can imagine
because we've been on a diet.

From behind the closed door of their bedroom, I heard Joe whisper
loudly to Noah, "You're not going to change anything by being angry
at him." Perry stared at the door for a moment as if he should prepare
to bolt. Instead, he asked, "Are you still mad at me about the article?"

"I never was."

"But you were angry."

I looked over at the stack of papers accumulating near the couch, only
then beginning to wonder what I achieved by saving them, what comfort
was to be gained. "I always expect insight and consequence from their
articles, and I'm disappointed when they write on our issues and don't
report more than what we already know," I said. "And sometimes I
assume that there is a language to describe what we're going through,
and that they would use it if there was."

"You should have told me about your friend," Perry said.

"This is one I can't talk about," I said. "As for your suggestion . . .
I don't know how I would begin to tell my mother about my life as I
know it now."

"You could say, 'I've got some good news and some bad news.' "

"What's the good news?"

"You don't have AIDS."

~   ~   ~

Noah was still taking a shower when the others left for tea. He came out
of the bathroom with an oversized towel wrapped around his waist and
lotion rubbed into his face and hands. I could see the tiny scar on his
back where the liposuction surgery had vacuumed a few pounds of fat.
Tall and mostly bald, older than he would confess to, he was certainly as

old as he looked. For a moment, he regarded me as if I were a dusty sock found under the bed. Then his face ripened.

"Dish alert," he said. "Guess who's having an affair with a twenty-two-year-old and I'm not supposed to tell anyone?"

"Perry," I said almost instantly. "The bastard."

"They were together in Washington for the international AIDS conference, supposedly in secret, but word has gotten back that they were making out in public like a couple of Puerto Rican teenagers on the subway."

"Does Horst know?"

"Of course. Perry thinks that talking about dishonest behavior makes it honest. As far as I'm concerned, it's another distraction from Horst's illness. Perry distanced himself from everyone when it became obvious that they were dying. Last year it was Miguel, this year it's Horst. When I confronted him, he said, 'Don't deny me my denial.' "

"Oh, that's brilliant. As long as he claims to be in denial, he doesn't even have to appear to suffer," I said. "One of these days, all this grief he's avoiding is going to knock him on his ass."

"But then he'll wear it around town like an old cloth coat so that everyone will feel sorry for him. He won't be happy until people in restaurants whisper 'Brava' as he squeezes past them to his table."

"What's the boyfriend like?"

"What kind of person has an affair with a man whose lover is dying of AIDS?" Noah asked.

I said, "The kind that probably splits after the funeral."

"He's what my Aunt Gloria would call a mayonnaise Jew, someone trying to pass for a WASP."

"I don't know if I should be offended by that or not," I said.

"But get this: He's had three lovers since he graduated from Harvard. The first one's lover died of AIDS. The second one had AIDS. Now there's Perry. So this kid gets the antibody test. It came back negative, and now he's got survivor's guilt." Noah gave me one of his bland, expressionless looks. "Perry acts as if this were the most misunderstood love affair since Abélard and Héloïse. He told me it was one of those things in life you just have no control over."

"For someone so emotionally adolescent, he's gotten a lot of mileage out of this epidemic," I said.

"Where else would he be center stage with a degree in drama therapy?" Noah asked. "He even quoted your journal at the last AIDS conference."

"What?"

"In Washington. He quoted you in a paper he presented. I knew he hadn't told you yet," Noah said. "He was certain you'd be honored. He would have been."

"Do you know what he used?"

"Something about an air of pain, the cindered chill of loss. It was very moving. You wondered if there wasn't a hidden cost to constant bereavement. You know Perry, he probably presented your diary as the work of a recent widower whose confidentiality had to be protected. That way he didn't have to give you credit."

I once went to an AIDS conference. Perry treated them like summer camp—Oh, Mary, love your hat, let's have lunch. I had seen him deliver papers that were barely literate and unprepared, and what was prepared was plagiarized. Claiming he was overwhelmed with work, he feigned modesty and said he could only speak from his heart. When social scientists provided remote statistics on our lives, Perry emoted and confessed. "My personal experience is all I can offer as the essence of this presentation." And it worked. It gave everyone the opportunity to cry and feel historic.

Noah asked, "Are you coming to tea? There's someone I want you to meet."

"Another widower?" I asked. "More damaged goods?"

"I'll put it to you this way," Noah said. "You have a lot in common."

With regard to human affairs, Noah was efficient. "Let me count the ways," I said. "A recent death, the ache of memory, reduced T-cell functions, positive sero status . . ."

"Yes, well, there's that."

"And maybe foreshortened futures, both of us wary of commitment should one or the other get sick, the dread of taking care of someone else weighed against the fear of being sick and alone."

"I doubt that Samuel would like your attitude."

"Samuel will get over it," I said. "And I'm not interested in a relationship right now. I'm only interested in sex."

"Safer sex, of course."

"I want to wake up alone, if that's what you mean."

Noah raised his eyebrows and lowered them again, as if to say that he would never understand me. I said, "Let me tell you a story. I hired a Swedish masseur recently because I wanted to be touched by someone, and no one in particular, if you get my innuendo. At one point, he worked a cramped muscle so hard that I cried out. And he said, 'That's it, go ahead, let it out'—as if I was holding something back, you know, intellectualizing a massage. I asked him if he felt anything, and he said, 'I feel'—long pause—'sorrow.' I told him that I had been a little blue lately but it wasn't as bad as all that."

Noah nodded. He said, "The real reason I didn't want to be interviewed for the piece in the *Times* was because Perry invited the reporter for dinner and told her we'd all get into drag if she brought a photographer."

Before I went down to the beach, I looked in on Enzo. Stark was right. The only time I'd ever seen anyone like this before was when Horst was first diagnosed. Perry had scheduled people just to sit with him, when none of us thought he would even survive. Enzo's skin was moist, his lips dry, his breath light. He was warm, but not enough for alarm.

These summer evenings I sat on the beach in a sling-back chair, listening to my cassette player and writing things about Samuel. I recalled our life together backward. The day he went into the hospital, he had cooked himself something to eat and left the dishes in the sink. Then he was dead, and washing his dishes was my last link to him as a living being. This evening, the pages of my journal felt like the rooms of my apartment when I came home and found it burglarized. Like my apartment, I knew I had to either forsake it or reclaim it as my own. Though in this case something had been taken, nothing was missing. I was angry with Perry, but it was not the worst thing he could have done. The worst is not when we can say it is the worst.

I started to write about Robert. The words of his obituary, "warm, radiant, much-loved man," somewhat assuaged my remorse at having abandoned him to the attention of the more hopeful. The beach was nearly empty at this time of the day—as it was in the morning—except for those like me who were drawn by the light of the early evening, the color of the water, the sand, the houses seen without the protection of sunglasses. Others passed, and I nodded from my beach chair. We smiled. Everyone agreed that the Island was friendlier this year, as if nothing were at stake when we recognized one another's existence. Verdi's Requiem was on my Walkman, a boat was halfway between the shore and the horizon. One full sail pulled the boat across the halcyon surface of the water. Near me a man stood with his feet just in the waves. He turned and held his binoculars as if he were offering me a drink. "They're strong," he said. I found the sailboat in the glasses. I found a handsome and popular Episcopal priest who I knew from experience to be a fine lover in bed. He was in collar and was praying. There was another handsome man. He was indistinct, but I recognized his expression. He reached into a box and released his fist over the boat's rail. Another man and a woman repeated the gesture. *Libera me.* The surviving lover shook the entire contents of the cloth-wrapped box overboard. The winds that spin the earth took the ashes and grains of bones and spilled them on the loden-green sea. He was entirely gone now but for the flecks that stuck to their clothes and under their nails, but for the memory of him, and for the pleasure of having known him. The boaters embraced with that pleasure so intense they wept at it. *Dies magna et amara valde.* I returned the binoculars to the man. It was a beautiful day and it was wonderful to be alive.

II

Two old couches, one ersatz wicker, the other what my mother used to call colonial, sat at a right angle to one another in the middle of our living room. Enzo and Horst were lying on them with their heads close together, like conspiring convalescents. Horst's cheeks were scarlet.

"You aren't feeling well, are you?" I asked.

Horst said, "No, but I didn't want to tell Perry and spoil his weekend."

"How is Enzo doing?"

"He thinks he has a cold, but I don't think so."

From where I stood, I could lay my hand on both their foreheads. I felt like a television evangelist. Enzo's forehead was the warmer of the two.

"I hear there's a flu going around," Horst said.

"Where did you hear that? You haven't been in town in a week."

"I had a flu shot," he said. "I think I'm not worried."

Without opening his eyes, Enzo said, "You had better get started if you are going to cook supper before everyone gets back. I put all the ingredients out for you."

I heated oil as the recipe instructed. "When the oil is very hot add mustard seeds," it read. "Keep the lid of the pan handy should the seeds sputter and fly all over." In the first grade, I recalled giving a girl named Karen Tsakos a mustard-seed bracelet in a Christmas exchange, selecting it myself from the dollar rack at a store called Gaylord's. "Aren't mustard seeds supposed to be a symbol of something?" I asked as they began to explode between me and the cabinet where the lids were kept.

"Hope, I think," Enzo said.

"Perhaps I should put more in."

"No, faith," Horst said, lying down in his bedroom.

"Faith is a fine invention, as far as I can see, but microscopes are prudent, in case of emergency," I said, approximating a poem by Emily Dickinson. Horst laughed, but Enzo showed no sign whatsoever that he knew what I was talking about. I wasn't so sure myself what Dickinson meant by an emergency: Could a microscope confirm one's belief in a crisis of faith, or, in a crisis of nature, such as an epidemic illness, was man best left to his own devices?

"How's dinner coming?" Stark asked, returning five minutes before it was to have been on the table.

"It's not ready," I said.

"Why not?"

"I didn't start it in time," I said.

"Why not?"

"Because I was at a funeral."

He picked up one of Miguel's old porno magazines and disappeared into the bathroom with it. He emerged ten minutes later and asked, "Is there anything I could be doing?"

"You can light the coals, and grill the tuna steaks. I've got to watch the opma," I said. "Enzo, what are gram beans?"

"The little ones."

Perry returned next and kissed me. "I forgot to tell you that Luis is in the hospital again," he said loudly. "His pancreas collapsed but he seems to be getting better."

"Enzo, I think I burned the gram beans."

"Luis's lover, Dennis, just took the antibody test," Perry said. "He was sero-negative."

"Oh, that's good."

"Yeah. Luis said, 'Thank God for hemorrhoids.' "

"Enzo, which of these is the cumin?"

"Don't cumin my mouth," Perry said, going into his room to check on Horst. I watched him brush the hair off Horst's forehead and take the thermometer out of Horst's mouth to kiss him. Perry's face darkened when he read the thermometer, as if he didn't know what to think. I added the Cream of Wheat to the gram beans.

Nils came up to me and wrapped a huge arm around my shoulder. "They told me down at tea that if dinner was scheduled for nine, that meant ten in Fire Island time."

"Dinner would have been ready at nine o'clock if I hadn't been given this god-awful recipe to make," I said, sounding more angry than I intended, and Nils hastened away. Noah came to the stove. "You are bitter, aren't you?"

"He's like Margaret Mead on steroids," I said.

"He's writing a book," Noah said.

"Yeah, sure, *Coming of Age in Cherry Grove.*"

"What's this here?" Noah asked.

"Opma."

"Where did you get the recipe?"

"From *The New York Times.*"

"I hate that paper."

Stark came running into the kitchen with the tuna steaks and put them in the electric broiler. The recipe said to grill them four minutes on each side.

"The grill will never get hot enough," he said. "Is that opma?"

"In the flesh."

"It looks like Cream of Wheat with peas in it."

Noah found the radio station we always listened to during dinner on Saturday nights. "Clark, what's the name of this song?" he asked, a game we played as part of the ritual. Enzo usually played along as he did the cooking.

" 'The Nearness of You,' " I answered.

"Who's singing?"

"Julie London."

"Who wrote it?"

"Johnny Mercer." Enzo didn't say anything, though the correct answer was Hoagy Carmichael. Perry sang as he helped Joe set the table, making up his own lyrics as he went along, the way a child does, with more rhyme than reason. We were all aware that he and Noah were behaving as if the other were not in the room, but their orbits were getting closer. As the song closed, Perry and I turned to one another and imitated the deep voice of the singer: "It's just the queerness of you." Then I made everyone laugh by stirring the thickening opma with both hands on the spoon. Jules, the dog, began hacking in the center of the room.

"Did you have a productive cough, dear?" Joe asked. Horst laughed from his bedroom.

"Enzo, come tell me if the opma is done," I said. He kind of floated up off the couch as if he was pleasantly drunk. I knew then that he was seriously ill. He took the wooden spoon from me and poked the opma twice. "It's done," he said.

We went to the table. I sat in the center, with Enzo on my right, Nils across from me, Joe on my left. Perry and Noah faced each other from the opposite ends, like parents. This was how we sat, each and every week. The guest was always in the same chair, whether he knew it or not. For the first several minutes of dinner, the table was a tangle of large arms passing the salad and popping open beer cans.

"Eat something, darling," I said to Enzo, who was only staring at the fish on his plate. "You haven't eaten anything all day."

Perry said, "This is the best opma I ever had."

Horst looked up as if he had something to announce, his fork poised in the air. We all turned to him. His fork fell to his plate with a clatter, and he said, "I think I have to lie down."

Perry said, "This opma will taste good reheated."

"So Fred told me this story at tea about the last of the police raids on the Meat Rack in the early seventies," Noah said.

"You're going to love this, Clark," Perry said.

"The cops came in one night with huge flashlights and handcuffs. There were helicopters and strobe lights; they had billy clubs and German shepherds. And they started dragging away dozens of men. The queens were crying and screaming and pleading with the cops because they would get their names in the paper and lose their jobs, you know, this was when it was still illegal for two men to dance with one another. The guys that got away hid under the bushes until everything was clear. Finally, after everything was perfectly quiet, some queen whispered, 'Mary, Mary!' And someone whispered back, 'Shhh, no names!' "

"Nils, would you like this?" Enzo asked. I looked up at Nils, whose forearms circled his plate. Everyone looked at me looking at him. I picked up Enzo's tuna steak with my fork and dropped it on Nils's plate. Enzo got up and stumbled to the couch.

Stark and Joe cleared the table. Perry went outside and smoked a cigar. With his back turned toward the house, he was calling attention to himself. I sat on the arm of the couch, looking down at Enzo and looking out at Perry, wondering who needed me most. But Noah was also looking at Perry. I could see him in his room, a finger on his lip, looking through the doors that opened out onto the deck. He stepped back from my sight and called, "Perry, this doesn't fit me. Would you like to try it on?"

The next thing I knew, Perry was wearing a black velvet Empress gown, like the one Madame X wears in the Sargent painting. In one hand, he held its long train, in the other, a cigar. Between the cleavage of the dress was Perry's chest hair, the deepest part of which was gray.

"Where'd you get that dress?" Stark asked.

"Noah inherited Miguel's hope chest. It was in the will."

Enzo was smiling, but I knew he was faking it. I whispered, "Do you need help to your bed?"

He clutched my hand and I helped him into his room. His forehead was scalding. "I'll be right back," I told him. I ran into the kitchen and pulled a dish towel from the refrigerator handle and soaked it under cold water. By this time, Noah was wearing the silver-lined cape that went with Perry's gown, a Frederick's of Hollywood merry widow, and silver lamé high heels. On his bald head was a tiny silver cap. I smiled as I passed through them, but they didn't see me.

Horst was sitting on Enzo's bed when I got back to him. This was the room in which Miguel had died the year before, and which Horst did not want this summer, though it was bigger and cooler than his own room and its glass doors opened onto the deck. "I could hear his breathing over all the commotion," Horst said. "Have you taken any aspirin?"

"I've been taking aspirin, Tylenol, and Advil every two hours," Enzo said, his voice strengthened by fear's adrenaline.

Horst asked, "Did you take your temperature?"

"I don't have a thermometer."

Horst got his own. "I cleaned it with peroxide," he said. "I hope that is good enough." Before I could ask him how to use it, he was on his way back to bed.

I pulled the thermometer from its case, pressed a little button, and placed it in Enzo's mouth. Black numbers pulsed against a tiny gray screen. I watched its numbers climb like a scoreboard from hell. Outside, Nils's arms were flailing because the high heels he was wearing were stuck between the boards of the deck. The thermometer beeped. Perry and Noah, in full drag, walked off with Nils between them.

"You have a temperature of a hundred and three point two," I said. This was the first time in my life I had ever been able to read a thermometer. "Do you want me to get the Island doctor?"

"Let's see if it goes down. Can you get me some cranberry juice?"

I went into the kitchen. Stark and Joe were reading. "How's he doing?" Joe asked.

"I think we should get him to a doctor."

"The number's on the ferry schedule," Joe said, and went back to his book.

A machine at the doctor's office said in the event of an emergency, to leave a number at the sound of the beep. I could not imagine the doctor picking up messages that late at night. But what I really feared was the underlying cause of Enzo's fever. I put the phone in its cradle.

"Don't we know any doctors?" I asked.

Stark and Joe shook their heads. Joe said that Noah or Perry might. I suddenly realized how isolated the Island was at night. At this point, there was no way of getting Enzo off the Island short of a police helicopter.

He was asleep when I took him his juice. He was not the handsomest of men, but at this moment he was downright homely. He cooked all our meals for us, meals to which even Horst's fickle appetite responded. He overstocked the refrigerator with more kinds of foodstuff than we could identify. We wondered why he did it, even as we stored away a few extra pounds, telling ourselves we were delaying the sudden weight loss associated with the first signs of AIDS. Perry had put on so much weight, his posture changed. He tilted forward as he walked. If he should develop the AIDS-associated wasting-away syndrome, Noah told him, months might go by before anyone would notice. I took the towel off Enzo's head and soaked it in cold water again.

"You'll be sure to clean Horst's thermometer before you give it back to him," he said, holding my hand, which held the towel to his face.

"Yes, of course."

"I mean it."

"Let me take your temperature again. This thermometer is really groovy." His temperature had risen to just shy of 104. With all I knew about AIDS, I suddenly realized I did not even know what this meant. "When was the last time you took some aspirin?"

"An hour ago. I'll give it another one."

The house shook as Perry, Noah, and Nils returned, all aglow with the success of their outing. Perspiration hung off Perry's chest hair like little Italian lights strung about the Tavern on the Green. Nils got into a clean tank top and went dancing.

Noah snapped open a Japanese fan and waved it at his face. "Dish alert," he said. He could be charming. For a moment, I forgot Enzo, the thermometer in my hand.

Joe said, "Clark thinks Enzo needs a doctor."

Noah asked, "What's his temperature?"

I stood in the doorway. "It's one hundred and four," I said, exaggerating a little.

"That's not too bad."

"It isn't?"

"Is he delirious?" Noah asked.

"What if he's too sick to be delirious?"

Perry said, "Miguel's temperature used to get much higher than that. He'd be ranting and raving in there sometimes."

"Yes, but Miguel is dead," I said.

When we opened the house this summer, I threw away his sheets, the polyester bathrobes, the towels from Beth Israel, St. Vincent's, Sloan-Kettering, and Mount Sinai, that filled our closets and dresser drawers from all of Miguel's hospital visits. Noah had watched me, neither protesting nor liking what I was doing. But I could not conceive of any nostalgia that would want to save such souvenirs. The hospital linen was part and parcel of the plastic pearls, the battery-operated hula doll, the Frederick's of Hollywood merry widow, five years' worth of porno magazine subscriptions—the measure of the extremes they went to for a laugh last year, the last summer of Miguel's life. Why did we need them when we were still getting post-dated birthday presents from Miguel: sweaters on our birthday, Smithfield hams at Christmas, magazine subscriptions in his name care of our address—anything he could put on his Visa card once he realized that he would expire before it did.

"If Enzo's temperature gets too high, we can give him an alcohol bath, or a shower, to bring it down," Noah said.

"So can I go to bed now?" Stark asked.

"Sure," I said. "Just don't sleep too soundly."

I went into my own room, which smelled of Nils's clothes, his sweat and the long trip, of coconut suntan lotion and the salty beach. I missed Samuel at moments like this, missed his balance of feelings, of moderated emotions as if he proportioned them out, the pacifying control he had over me. I fell asleep, woke and listened for Enzo's breath, and fell asleep again. I halfway woke again and sensed my longing even before Nils's presence woke me completely. In the next bed, a sheet pulled up to his nipples, Nils's chest filled the width of the bed.

Drunk one night on the beach, he had said to me, "Perry doesn't think there's hope for anyone who is diagnosed in the next few years."

"We've pinned our hopes on so many," I said, aware that Nils was delving for useful information, "that I don't know what role hope plays anymore. They're predicting as many deaths in 1991 alone as there were Americans killed in Vietnam. Some of those are bound to be people one knows."

"Hope is the capacity to live with the uncertain," he said.

I had read that line myself somewhere. "Bullshit," I said. Nils stepped back and looked at me as if I had desecrated the theology of some deified psychotherapist.

"You don't need hope to persevere," I said.

"What do you need, then?" Nils asked.

"Perseverance," I answered, and laughed at myself. And then I told him a story I had heard at a funeral service. It was the story of a Hasidic rabbi and a heckler. The rabbi had told his congregation that we must try to put everything into the service of God, even that which was negative and we didn't like. The heckler called out, "Rabbi, how do we put a disbelief in God into His service?" The rabbi's answer made me think that God and hope are interchangeable. He told the heckler, "If a man comes to you in a crisis, do not tell him to have faith, that God will take care of everything. Act instead as if God does not exist. Do what you can do to help the man."

Nils put his arm around me and pulled me up close to him as we walked. There was a strong wind that night, and the waves were high. The moon was low across the water and illuminated the waves as they reached for it. I felt massive muscles working in Nils's thighs and loins, a deep and deeper mechanism than I had ever felt in a human body and which seemed to have as its source of energy that which lifted the waves and kept the moon suspended. He was that strong, and I would feel that secure. A bulwark against the insentient night, his body: if I did not need hope to persevere, I needed that. He stopped and held me, kissed my head politely, and pushed me out at arms' length. He made me feel like the canary sent down the mine to warn him of dangerous wells of feeling, wells that he could draw upon but needn't descend himself.

~ ~ ~

When I woke again, the oily surface of his back was glowing. The sky held more prophecy than promise of light. I got up to check on Enzo. He was not in bed. Stark was sitting up waiting for him to come out of the bathroom. He patted the bed next to him. I sat down and he put his arm around me.

"Has he been sleeping?" I asked.

"Like the dead."

"Do you think we should have gotten a helicopter off the Island?"

"No, but I wish we had."

Enzo could be heard breathing through the thin door. Stark said, "It's been like that all night."

The toilet flushed; we heard Enzo moan, then the thud of his body falling against the bathroom door.

Stark carefully pushed it opened and looked in. "All hell broke loose," he said.

Enzo was lying in a puddle of excrement. In his delirium, he had forgotten to pull his pajamas down before sitting on the toilet. When he tried to step out of them, his bowels let go a spray of watery stool. His legs were covered, as were the rugs and the wall against which he fainted.

"You're burning up, darling," Stark whispered to him.

"I'm afraid he'll dehydrate," I said.

I pulled off Enzo's soiled pajamas, turned the shower on, and took off the old gym shorts I slept in. "Hand him over," I said from within the lukewarm spray.

Enzo wrapped his arms around my back and laid his hot head on my shoulder. Our visions of eternal hell must come from endless febrile nights like this, I thought. I gradually made the water cooler and sort of two-stepped with him so that it would run down his back, and sides, and front. The shower spray seemed to clothe our nakedness. If I closed my eyes, we were lovers on a train platform. We could have been almost anywhere, dancing in the sad but safe aftermath of some other tragedy, say the Kennedy assassinations, the airlift from Saigon, the bombing of a Belfast funeral. Stark used the pump bottle of soap—bought to protect Horst from whatever bacteria, fungus, or yeast might accumulate on a shared bar—to lather Enzo's legs. I slowly turned the water cooler.

"Can we get your head under water a little bit?" I asked, though Enzo was barely conscious. "Let's see if we can get your fever down."

"I think we're raising it," Stark murmured. He was washing Enzo's buttocks, and his hand would reach through Enzo's legs and wash his genitals almost religiously. He reached through Enzo's legs and lathered my genitals as well. He pulled on my testicles and loosened them in their sac. He pulled and squeezed them just to the pleasure point of pain. He winked at me, but he didn't smile. I noticed there were interesting shampoos on the shelf that I had never tried.

"I can't stand much longer, you guys," Enzo whispered in my ear. "I'm sorry."

I maneuvered him around to rinse the soap off. Stark waited with huge towels. While I dried us both, Stark changed Enzo's bedclothes, tucking the fresh sheets in English style. Then he helped me carry him back to bed.

"Let's take his temperature before he falls asleep," I said. Stark stared in my face as we waited. The thermometer took so long, I was afraid it was broken. It finally went off with a tremulous beep. "Dear God," I said.

"What is it?"

Despite the shower, his fever was over 105. "Do we have any rubbing alcohol?" I asked.

Stark couldn't find any after checking both bathrooms. I said, "Get the vodka, then."

He returned with the ice-covered bottle from the freezer; the liquor within it was gelatinous. "Do you think this wise?" he asked.

"Not the imported. Get the stuff we give the guests. Wait," I said. "Leave that one here and bring me a glass."

Stark brought the domestic vodka and a sponge. "Do you know what you're doing?" he asked.

"Alcohol brings a temperature down by rapidly evaporating off the body," I said. "Vodka happens to evaporate faster than rubbing alcohol. Other than that, no, I don't have the faintest idea."

Stark watched me for a while, then took Enzo's temperature himself. It had fallen to 104.8. "I think we should get some aspirin in him," he said, which we woke Enzo to do. He drank a little juice. Fifteen minutes later, I took his temperature again. Enzo's temperature had gone down to 104.6. While waiting for this reading, Stark had fallen back asleep. I wondered whether he didn't want me in bed with him. That would have been pleasant, temporary; he was a solid man, like a park bench.

But instead I went out to the living room. My stack of newspapers was near the couch. I could look in on Enzo if I clipped the articles I intended to save. Just the night before, Noah had shaken his head at all the papers and said, "It looks like poor white trash lives here."

"My roots must be showing," I said.

I clipped my articles and put them in an accordion file that I kept closed with an old army-issue belt. Sometimes margin notes reminded me why I was saving something, such as the obituary of an interior designer, in which, for the first time, the lover was mentioned as a survivor. Or the piece in which being sero-positive for HIV antibodies became tantamount to HIV infection, indicating that our language for talking about AIDS was changing. "With the passage of time, scientists are beginning to believe that all those infected will develop symptoms and die," the article said. It really doesn't sit well to read about one's mortality in such general terms.

In the magazine section, a popular science writer wrote that there was no moral message in AIDS. Over the illustration, I scrawled, "When late is worse than never." Scientists had been remiss, he said, for "viewing it as a contained and peculiar affliction of homosexual men." In the margin I wrote, "How much did they pay you to say this?"

Then there were those living-out-loud columns written by a woman who had given up on actual journalism to raise her children. Some of them were actually quite perceptive, but I had never forgiven her for the one in which the writer confessed that she had been berated by a gay man in a restaurant for saying, "They were so promiscuous—no wonder they're dying."

Horst emerged from his bedroom to blend his AL721, which was kept in the freezer in ice-cube trays. He did not see me, and I did not say anything for fear of frightening him because he concentrated so severely on his task. If you did not know him, you would not think he was ill, but very, very old. He had always been a vulnerable and tender man, but now he was fragile. He hoped that the elixir in his blender could keep the brush of death's wings from crushing him entirely.

When Samuel called to tell me two years ago that Horst had been diagnosed, I began to weep mean, fat tears. My assistant editor sent me out for a walk. I wandered aimlessly around SoHo for a while, once trying to get into the old St. Patrick's, its small walled-in cemetery covered with the last of autumn's spongy brown leaves. I fingered cowhide and pony pelts hanging in a window; I bought a cheap stopwatch from a street vendor, some blank tapes, and spare batteries for my tape cassette. Eventually, hunger made me find a place to rest, a diner with high ceilings and windows looking onto a busy street. After I ordered, I thought of Horst again, and something odd happened: the room—no, not the room but my vision went, as when you've looked at the sun too long. All I could see was a glowing whiteness, like a dentist's lamp, or the inside of a nautilus shell. For a brilliant moment, I saw nothing, and knew nothing, but this whiteness that had anesthetized and cauterized the faculties by which one savors the solid world. Like a film dissolving from one scene to another, the room came back, but the leftover whiteness limned the pattern of one man's baldness, glittered off the earring of his companion, turned the white shirt my waitress wore to porcelain, fresh and rigid, as it was from the Chinese laundry. She stood over me with a neon-bright plate in one hand and the beer's foam glowing in the other, waiting for me to lift my elbows and give her room to put down my lunch.

"Oh, shit," Horst said, knocking the orange-juice carton over and spilling some into the silverware drawer.

"I'll clean it up," I said softly.

"I knew you were there," he said. "I heard you in here. How is Enzolina?"

"His temperature was very high. We got it down a little bit."

"You must sleep too." He leaned over me and kissed my cheek. "It's okay about Perry and his boyfriend," he said, obviously having heard Noah speaking that afternoon. "Perry is still affectionate and he takes care of me. And I don't feel so sexual anymore. But Noah shouldn't have told you, because it would only make you angry."

Whether it was the lateness of the hour or the sensitive logic of pain, I thought I heard resignation in Horst's voice, as if he were putting one foot in the grave just to test the idea of it.

"Have you met the boyfriend?"

"Oh, yes. He's very bland. I don't know what Perry sees in him," Horst said. "Perry thinks the three of us should go into therapy together, but I'm not doing it. I don't have to assuage their guilt."

"Where will Perry be when you get really sick?"

"Probably at a symposium in Central Africa." He laughed and waved his hand like an old woman at an off-color joke. Horst used to be hardy, real peasant stock. He was the kind of man who could wear a ponytail and make it look masculine. Here was a man gang-banged for four days by a bunch of Turks on the Orient Express who lived to turn the memory into a kind of mantra. He said, "Perry needs so many buffers from reality."

"Most of us do."

"Not you."

"You're wrong," I said. Then I showed him the article on the death of an iconoclastic theater director that had started on the front page of the *Times*. "Look, there's a typo. It says he died of AIDS-related nymphoma."

He laughed and laid his head in my lap. "I am homesick for Switzerland," he said. "I'd like to go home, but I don't know if I could handle the trip. And I don't want to be a burden on my family."

"You wouldn't be."

"I've been thinking lately I don't want to be cremated. I want to be buried in the mountains. But it's so expensive."

"Horst, don't worry about expenses," I said.

"How is Samuel?" he asked.

"He's dead, honey. He died this winter."

"Oh, I'm sorry," he said, and covered his face with his hands. Memory lapses are sometimes part of the deterioration. I wondered whether

Perry had noticed or ignored them. "I forget these things," he added. "It's late, you're tired." He started up. I said, "Horst, I think you should go home if you want to. Just make sure you come back."

My fingertips were pungent with the smell of newsprint, like cilantro, or the semen smell of ailanthus seeds in July. "Did you see that piece in today's paper?" we asked one another over the phone when a point we held dear was taken up on the editorial page. "Yes, haven't they come far and in such a short time," we responded. I filed it all away, with little science and what was beginning to feel like resignation: *C* for condoms, *S* for Heterosexuals, *P* for Prevention and Safer Sex, *R* for Race and Minorities, *O* for Obits.

"I can't tell you how bored I am with this," a man said to me on the beach one evening when he learned that another friend had gone down for the count. He said, "Sometimes I wish there was something else to talk about," which is what my mother used to say as she put her make-up on for a night out with my father. "I just wish we could go out and talk about anything but you kids and the house," she'd say with the vague longing I recall with numbing resonance. "I just wish there was something else to talk about."

They would eat at a place called D'Amico's Steak House, where the menus were as large as parking spaces. She would have frogs' legs, which she told me tasted like chicken but were still a leap toward the exotic, no matter how familiar the landing. Her desire had no specific object; she was not an educated woman; she did not even encourage fantasy in her children; but it still arouses whatever Oedipal thing there is left un-resolved in me, and I often wish to be able to satisfy it—to give her nights and days of conversation so rooted in the present that no reference to when we were not happy could ever be made, and no dread of what to come could be imagined. But we both know that there's no forgetting that we were once unhappy. Our conversation is about my sisters' lives and their children. She ends our infrequent telephone conversations with "Please take care of yourself," emphasizing, without naming, her fear of losing me to an illness we haven't talked about, or to the ebbs of time and its hostilities that have carried me further and further away from perfect honesty with her.

But language also takes you far afield. Metaphors adumbrate; facts mitigate. For example, "Nothing is hopeless; we must hope for every-thing." I had believed this until I realized the lie of its intrinsic metaphor, that being without hope is not being, plunged into the abyss that noth-ingness fills. We have not come far since the world had one language and few words. Babel fell before we had a decent word for death, and then we were numb, shocked at the thought of it, and this lisping dumb word—*death, death, death*—was the best we could come up with.

And simply speak, disinterested and dryly, the words that fill your daily life: "Lewis has KS of the lungs," or "Raymond has endocarditis but the surgeons won't operate," or "Howard's podiatrist will not remove a bunion until he takes the test," or "Cytomegalovirus has inflamed his stomach and we can't get him to eat," or "The DHPG might restore the sight in his eye," or "The clinical trial for ampligen has filled up," or "They've added dementia to the list of AIDS-related illnesses," or "The AZT was making him anemic," or "His psoriasis flaked so badly, the maid wouldn't clean his room," or "They found tuberculosis in his glands," or "It's a form of meningitis carried in pigeon shit; his mother told him he should never have gone to Venice," or "The drug's available on a compassionate basis," or "The drug killed him," or "His lung col-lapsed and stopped his heart," or "This is the beginning of his decline," or "He was *so* young." What have you said and who wants to hear it?

"Oh, your life is not so awful," a woman at my office told me. She once lived in India and knew whereof she spoke. At Samuel's funeral, a priest told me, "I don't envy you boys. This is your enterprise now, your vocation." He kissed me, as if sex between us was an option he held, then rode to the altar on a billow of white to a solitary place setting meant to serve us all.

Enzo's temperature remained the same through the night. I poured myself a drink—though I did not need it—to push myself over the edge of feeling. I took it down to the beach. There were still a few bright stars in the sky. Everything was shaded in rose, including the waves and the footprints in the sand, deceiving me and the men coming home from dancing into anticipating a beautiful day.

Since the deaths began, the certified social workers have quoted Shakespeare at us: "Give sorrow words." But the words we used now reek of old air in churches, taste of the dust that has gathered in the crevices of the Nativity and the Passion. Our condolences are arid as leaves. We are actors who have overrehearsed our lines. When I left the Island one beautiful weekend, Noah asked, "Were you so close to this man you have to go to his funeral?" I told myself all the way to Philadelphia that I did not have to justify my mourning. One is responsible for feeling something and being done with it.

Give sorrow occasion and let it go, or your heart will imprison you in constant February, a chain-link fence around frozen soil, where your dead will stack in towers past the point of grieving. *Let your tears fall for the dead, and as one who is suffering begin the lament . . . do not neglect his burial.* Think of him, the one you loved, on his knees, on his elbows, his face turned up to look back in yours, his mouth dark in his dark beard. He was smiling because of you. You tied a silky rope around his wrists, then down around the base of his cock and balls, his anus raised for you. When you put your mouth against it, you ceased to exist. All else fell away. You had brought him, and he you, to that point where you are most your mind and most your body. His prostate pulsed against your fingers like a heart in a cave, *mind, body, body, mind,* over and over. Looking down at him, he who is dead and gone, then lying across the broken bridge of his spine, the beachhead of his back, you would gladly change places with him. *Let your weeping be bitter and your wailing fervent; then be comforted for your sorrow.* Find in grief the abandon you used to find in love; grieve the way you used to fuck.

~ ~ ~

Perry was out on the deck when I got back. He was naked and had covered himself with one hand when he heard steps on our boardwalk. With the other hand, he was hosing down the bathroom rugs on which Enzo had been sick. I could tell by the way he smiled at me that my eyes must have been red and swollen.

"There's been an accident," he said.

"I was a witness. Do you need help?"

"I've got it," he said, and waddled back inside for a bucket and disinfectant to do the bathroom floors.

Enzo opened the curtains on his room. I asked him how he was feeling.

"My fever's down a little. And my back hurts."

Stark asked him, "Do you think you can stay out here a couple of days and rest? Or do you want to go into the hospital?"

"You can fly in and be there in half an hour," I said.

"One of us will go in with you," Stark said.

"I'm not sure. I think so," Enzo said, incapable of making a decision.
"What if I call your doctor and see what he says?" I asked.

The doctor's service answered, and I left as urgent a message as I
could. I began breaking eggs into a bowl, adding cinnamon and almond
concentrate. The doctor's assistant called me back before the yolks and
egg whites were beaten together. "What are the symptoms?" he asked.

"Fever, diarrhea."

"Back pain?"

"Yes."

"Is his breathing irregular?" the assistant asked.

"His breathing is irregular, his temperature is irregular, his pulse is
irregular, and his bowel movement is irregular. My bet is he's dehydrated.
What else do you need to know?"

"Has he been diagnosed with AIDS yet?"

"No," I said, "but he had his spleen removed two years ago. And
Dr. Williams knows his medical history."

"I'll call you back," he said.

"How is he?" asked Noah. It was early for him to be out of bed. I
began to suspect that no one had slept well.

"He's weak and now his back hurts. I think he'd like to go to the
hospital."

"It's Sunday. They aren't going to do anything for him. All they'll
do is admit him. He might as well stay here, and I'll drive him in
tomorrow."

Horst came out of Enzo's room. "That's not true. They can test
oxygen levels in his blood for PCP and start treatment right away. And
the sooner they catch these things, the easier they are to treat."

Horst had said what none of us would say—PCP—for if it was *Pneu-
mocystis carinii* pneumonia, then Enzo did have AIDS. One more person
in the house would have it, one more to make it impossible to escape
for a weekend, one more to remind us of how short our lives were
becoming.

The phone rang. Dr. Williams's assistant told me to get Enzo in right
away. "Get yourself ready," I said. "Your doctor will be coming in just
to see you. I'll call the airline to get you a seat on the seaplane."

"Okay," Enzo said, relieved to have the decision made for him. He
put his feet on the floor and got his bearings. Stark helped him fill a bag.

Then I looked outside and saw what appeared to be a sheet unfurling over the trees. Fog was coming through the brambles the way smoke unwraps from a cigarette and lingers in the heat of a lamp.

"Oh, my God, will you look at that," Joe said. "Another lousy beach day. This has been the worst summer."

Perry called the Island airline. All flights were canceled for the rest of the morning. Visibility of three miles was needed for flight to the Island, and we couldn't even see beyond our deck. Even voices from the neighboring houses sounded muffled and far away, for the first time all summer.

"We're going to have to find someone who will drive him in," Perry said. "Unless he thinks he can handle the train."

"He's too sick for the train," I said.

"Who do we know with a car?" Perry asked. Joe took Jules out for a walk. Noah went behind the counter, where the batter for French toast was waiting. He began slicing challah and dipping it into batter, though no one was ready to eat.

Perry said, "I wonder if Frank is driving back today."

"Call him," I said.

But Perry didn't get the response he expected. We heard him say, "Frank, he's very sick. His doctor said to get him in right away." He turned to us. "Frank says he'll drive Enzo in if the fog doesn't clear up."

"Well, I can understand why he would feel put upon," Noah said. "I wouldn't want to give up my weekend either."

At that point, I said, "I'm going in with Enzo."

Noah said, "He can go into the emergency room by himself. He doesn't need anyone with him." I said nothing, but I did not turn away from him either. Perry looked at me and then to Noah. His lower lip dropped from under his mustache. Noah said, "Well, doesn't he have someone who could meet him there?"

"Enzo," I called, "is there anyone who could meet you in the city?"

"I guess I could call my friend Jim," he said.

"See," Noah said.

"Jim's straight," I said, not that I thought it really made any difference, but it sounded as if it did. We did, supposedly, know the ropes of this disease. "Enzo, who would you rather have with you, me or Jim?"

"You."

Noah raised his eyebrows and shrugged one shoulder. "I don't know why you feel you have to go into the emergency room."

"Because I am beginning to see what it will be like to be sick with this thing and not have anyone bring me milk or medication because it isn't convenient or amusing any longer."

Noah said, "I have been working at the Gay Men's Health Crisis for the past six years. I was one of the first volunteers."

"Oh, good, the institutional response. That reassures me," I said. Starting into my room to pack a bag, I bumped into Nils, who was coming out of the shower and didn't have any clothes on, not even a towel. Although Nils walked the beach in a bikini brief that left nothing to—nor satisfied—the imagination, he quickly covered himself and pressed his body against the wall to let me pass.

"I'm sorry if I kept you up last night," he said to me.

"It wasn't you. I was worried about Enzo," I said.

By eleven-thirty the fog was packed in as tight as cotton in a new jar of aspirin. Our friend with the car decided that since it was not a beach day, he could be doing things in the city. We were to meet him at the dock for the twelve o'clock ferry. He could not, however, take me as well, for he had promised two guests a ride and only had room for four in his jaunty little car.

Enzo and Perry seemed embarrassed by this. "I don't mind taking the train," I said. "I'll be able to read the Sunday *Times*."

Nils put his arm around me and walked me to the door. "I'll be gone when you come back. I'd like to leave you my address." I wanted to say a house gift would be more appropriate, something for the kitchen or a flowering plant. "It's unlikely that I'll ever get that far north," I said, "but thanks all the same. Maybe I'll drop you a line." The last thing I saw as I was leaving was his large head down over his plate, his arms on the table, a fork in a fist. He was a huge and odd-looking man. Stark said he had a face like the back of a bus, but it was actually worse than that. Nils was also the author of two books, was working on a third, about the Nazi occupation of Oslo. I saw the others join him around the table. He was probably ten times smarter than anyone there. Sharp words and arguments often defined the boundaries of personalities in this house, but Nils did not touch any of our borders. He simply did not fit in. And though tourists are insufferable after a point, I knew I should ask his forgiveness for my sin of inhospitality, but I couldn't make the overture to deserve it.

On the ferry, Enzo said, "I'm glad you're coming."

"I wanted out of that house," I said.

"I know."

We listened to our tape players so as not to speak about what was on our minds. People wore white sweaters and yellow mackintoshes. They held dogs in their laps, or the Sports section, or a beach towel in a straw purse; a man had his arm around his lover's shoulder, his fingertips alighted on the other's collarbone. No one spoke. It didn't seem to matter that the weekend was spoiled. We were safe in this thoughtless fog. The bay we crossed was shallow; it could hide neither monsters from the deep nor German submarines. It seemed all we needed to worry about was worrying too much; what we had to fear was often small and could be ignored. But as we entered the harbor on the other side, a dockworker in a small motorboat passed our ferry and shouted, "AIDS!" And in case we hadn't heard him, shouted again, "AIDS, AIDS!"

A man slid back the window and shouted back, "Crib death!" Then he slunk in his seat, ashamed of himself.

I read the paper on the train. I listened to Elgar, Bach, Barber, and Fauré. An adagio rose to its most poignant bar; the soprano sang the Pie Jesù with a note of anger, impatient that we should have to wait so long for everlasting peace, or that the price was so high, or that we should have to ask at all. I filled the empty time between one place and another with a moderate and circumspect sorrow delineated by the beginning, middle, and end of these adagios. Catharsis is not a release of emotion; it is a feast. Feel this. Take that. And you say, Yes, sir, thank you, sir. Something hardens above the eyes and your throat knots and you feel your self back into being. Friends die and I think, Good, that's over, let go of these intolerable emotions, life goes on. The train ride passed; I finished mourning another one. The train ride was not as bad as people say it is.

And Enzo had arrived at the hospital only ten minutes before me. The nurses at the emergency desk said I couldn't see him.

"I'm his care partner from the Gay Men's Health Crisis," I said, telling them more than they were prepared to hear. "Can I just let him know I'm here?" The lie worked as I was told it would.

Dr. Williams was there as well, standing over Enzo's gurney, which was in the middle of the corridor. "Was there any diarrhea?" he asked. Enzo said no, I said yes. "Fever?" "Over a hundred and five." "Did you have a productive cough?" he asked, and Enzo smiled. He pounded on the small of Enzo's back. "Does that hurt?" It did. The doctor was certain that Enzo's infection was one to which people who have had their spleens removed are vulnerable. We were moved to a little curtained room in the emergency ward.

"I'm not convinced it isn't PCP," Enzo said to me.

"Neither am I," said the attending physician, who had been outside the curtain with Enzo's chart. "Dr. Williams's diagnosis seems too logical. I want to take some tests just to make sure."

He asked for Enzo's health history: chronic hepatitis; idiopathic thrombocytopenia purpura; the splenectomy; herpes. Enzo sounded as if he were singing a tenor aria from *L'Elisir d'Amore*. The attending physician leaned over him, listened for the high notes, and touched him more like a lover than a doctor.

"You don't have to stay," Enzo said to me.

"I want to see if he comes back," I said.

"He reminds you of Samuel."

"A little bit."

"Do you think he's gay?"

"I don't think he'd be interested in me even if he was. Maybe you, though," I said.

Enzo smiled at that and fell asleep. The afternoon passed with nurses coming in to take more blood. He was wheeled out twice for X rays. A thermos of juice had broken in his overnight bag. I rinsed his sodden clothes and wrapped them in newspaper to take back to the house to wash. But his book about eating in Paris was ruined. He had been studying all summer for his trip to France the coming fall. Restaurants were highlighted in yellow, like passages in an undergraduate's philosophy book; particular dishes were starred.

He woke and saw me with it. "My shrink told me that we couldn't live our lives as if we were going to die of AIDS. I've been putting off this vacation for years," he said. "If there's anything you want to do, Clark, do it now."

"Do you want me to call anyone?" I asked.

"Have you called the house yet?"

"I thought I'd wait until we had something to tell them."

"Okay," he said, and went back to sleep. I read what I hadn't thrown away of the *Times*. In the magazine was an article titled "She Took the Test." I began to read it but skipped past the yeasty self-examination to get to the results. Her test had come back negative. I wondered whether she would have written the piece had it come back positive.

Enzo woke and asked again, "Have you called the house yet?"

"No, I was waiting until we knew something certain."

"If I had PCP, you would tell them right away," he said.

"Yes, Enzo, but we don't know that yet," I said, but he had already fallen back asleep. He hadn't had anything to eat all day and hadn't been given anything to reduce the fever. Because he was dehydrated, they had him on intravenous, but he seemed to be sweating as quickly as the fluid could go into his body. I felt the accusation anyway, and it was just. I had not called the house precisely because they were waiting for me to call and because I was angry at them.

It was eight o'clock that evening before the handsome doctor returned again. "There is too much oxygen in your blood for it to be PCP," he told us. "But we found traces of a bacterial pneumonia, the kind of infection Dr. Williams was referring to. Losing your spleen will open you up to these kinds of things, and there's no prevention. We'll put you on intravenous penicillin for a week, and you'll be fine."

Enzo grinned. He would not have to cancel his trip to Paris. His life and all the things he had promised himself were still available to him. An orderly wheeled him to his room, and I followed behind with his bag. It was not AIDS, but it would be someday, a year from now, maybe two, unless science or the mind found prophylaxis. He knew this as well as I did. Not this year, he said, but surely within five. No one knows how this virus will affect us over the years, what its impact will be on us when we are older, ten years after infection, fifteen—fifteen years from now? When I was eleven years old, I never thought I would live to be twenty-six, which I thought to be the charmed and perfect age. I think fifteen years from now, and I come to fifty. How utterly impossible that seems to me, how unattainable. I have not believed that I would live to the age of forty for two years now.

"You'll call the house now," he said as I was leaving.

"Yes."

"I appreciate your being here."

I turned in the doorway. Several responses came to mind—that I hadn't really done so much, that anybody would have done what I had done. Enzo saw me thinking, however, and smiled to see me paused in thought. "I wanted to say that reality compels us to do the right thing if

we live in the real world," I said. "But that's not necessarily true, is it?"
"It can put up a compelling argument," Enzo said. "Don't be mad at Noah. I didn't expect him to drive me in."

With Enzo in his room, the penicillin going into his veins, feeling better simply at the idea of being treated, I submitted to my own exhaustion and hunger. I went home and collected a week's worth of mail from a neighbor. There was nothing to eat in the refrigerator, but on the door was a review from the *Times* of a restaurant that had just opened in the neighborhood and that I had yet to try. The light was flashing on my answering machine, but I could not turn it on, knowing the messages would be from my housemates. I called the man who drove Enzo in to tell him how much suffering he had saved Enzo from, exaggerating for the answering machine, which I was glad had answered for him. I turned my own off so that I couldn't receive any more messages and left my apartment with the mail I wanted to read.

Walking down a dark street of parking garages to the restaurant that had been reviewed, I saw a gold coin-shaped wrapper—the kind that chocolate dollars and condoms come in—embedded in the hot asphalt. Pop caps glittered in the street like an uncorked galaxy stuck in the tar.

~ ~ ~

Horst's prediction came true. While Horst was dying two years later, Perry was at an AIDS conference with his new little boyfriend. When confronted, he'd say, "Horst wanted me to go." Perry would include Horst's death notice with fund-raising appeals for the gay youth organization he volunteered for. Everyone who knows him learns to expect the worst from him. And Enzo would be right also. A year or so later, he was diagnosed with KS, then with lymphoma.

The *Times* would eventually report more on the subject and still get things wrong. Not journalism as the first draft of history, but a rough draft, awkward and splintered and rude and premeditated. They will do a cover story on the decimation of talent in the fashion industry and never once mention that the designers, stylists, illustrators, showroom assistants, make-up artists, or hairdressers were gay. How does one write about a battle and not give name to the dead, even if they are your enemy?

The dead were marching into our lives like an occupying army. Noah's defenses were weakening, but the illness did not threaten him personally. He was sero-negative and would stay that way. Even so, he

had found himself in a standstill of pain, a silo of grief, which I myself
had not entered, though I knew its door well. Perry thought of Samuel
every time he saw me and, in turn, probably thought of Horst. I suspected
he saw his new boyfriend as a vaccine against loneliness and not as an
indication that he had given up hope. We had found ourselves in an
unacceptable world. And an unacceptable world can compel unacceptable
behavior.

~ ~ ~

But that night, I turned around without my supper and went back home
to listen to my messages. The first was from Horst, who would have been
put up to call because he was the closest to me and the closest to death.
"Clark, are you there? It's Horst," he said, as if I wouldn't have recognized his accent. "We want to know how Enzolina is. Please call. We
love you."

For a long stretch of tape, there was only the sound of breathing, the
click of the phone, over and over again. Perry's voice came next.

"I was very touched by your going into the hospital today and how
you took care of Enzo last night. I want to tell you that now," he said,
in a low voice. "I hope you understand that there was nothing to be
done last night, and you were doing it. Sometimes I don't think Horst
understands that the nights he is almost comatose that I am suffering beside
him, fully conscious. I saw your face when Noah did not offer to drive
Enzo in. I thought perhaps it was because they can't take the dog on the
train, or because he had taken tomorrow off to spend with Joe. But I
can't make any excuses for him. You are so morally strict sometimes, like
an unforgiving mirror. Oh, let's see . . . Horst is feeling much better.
Call us, please."

Then Stark called to find out whether either Enzo or I needed anything, and told me when he would be home if I wanted to call. And
then Joe. "Where are you, Clark? Oh, God, you should have seen Noah
go berserk today when he took the garbage out and found maggots in
the trash cans. He screamed, 'I can't live like this the rest of the summer.'
He's been cleaning windows and rolling up rugs. She's been a real mess
all day. Oh, God, now he's sweeping under the bed. I can't decide if I
should calm him down or stay out of his way. The house should look
nice when you get back."

Finally, Noah called. "Clark, where are you, Superman? I have to tell you something. You know the novel you lent me to read? I accidentally threw it in the washing machine with my bedclothes. Please call."

My lover Samuel used to tell a story about himself. It was when he was first working with the Theater of the Deaf. The company had been improvising a new piece from an outline that Samuel had devised, when he said something that provoked a headstrong and violent young actor, deaf since birth. "I understand you," Samuel said in sign, attempting to silence him, if that's the word. The young actor's eyes became as wild as a horse caught in a burning barn; his arms flew this way and that, as if furious at his own imprecision. Samuel needed an interpreter. "You do not understand this," the actor was saying, pointing to his ears. "You will never understand."

You let go of people, the living and the dead, and return to your self, to your own resources, like a widower, a tourist alone in a foreign country. Your own senses become important, and other people's sensibilities a kind of Novocaine, blocking out your own perceptions, your ability to discriminate, your taste. There is something beyond understanding, and I do not know what it is, but as I carried the phone with me to the couch, a feeling of generosity came over me, of creature comforts having been satisfied well and in abundance, like more than enough to eat and an extra hour of sleep in the morning. Though I hadn't had either, I was in a position to anticipate them both. The time being seeps in through the senses: the plush of a green sofa; the music we listen to when we attempt to forgive ourselves our excesses; the crazing pattern on the ginger jar that reminds us of why we bought it in the first place, not to mention the shape it holds, the blessing of smells it releases. The stretch of time and the vortex that it spins around, thinning and thickening like taffy, holds these pleasures, these grace notes, these connections to others, to what it is humanly possible to do.

~ *David Plante* ~

The
Princess
from Africa

T his is the happy story of how Daniel first made love.
At what point should the story begin? Should it begin with Daniel, a student at a Jesuit college in Boston, going to Europe for the first time, on his way to spend his junior year at a European university, and meeting on the ship a black woman named Angela? Should the story start with him seeing her, in a tight white satin strapless cocktail dress, spangled in silver, sing in the tourist-class lounge after dinner to pay, as she later told him, her fare—hers and the fares of her two young children?

She was in the spotlight before the microphone, singing. He was sitting with a Belgian family, a husband and wife and their daughter, with whom he'd danced, and her parents, assuming him to be a nice young man, had invited him to sit at their table for a glass of wine. They all listened to the black woman sing. Daniel didn't want to be a nice young man, and politely (he was always polite) he excused himself when the black woman (in 1959, when this happened, he would have thought of her as a Negro) finished her blues song and sat by herself at a table and, he saw, delicately brought a cigarette to her lips, and he went toward her with a matchbook taken from the ashtray on the Belgians' table, striking a match as he went to light her cigarette. The match went out, and the

---

Among DAVID PLANTE's many novels are The Native, The Catholic, The Woods, *and* The Foreigner. *A formidable stylist and a master of literary understatement, he lives in London and in Lucca, Italy.*

next, and the next, but, finally, one flared and she lit her cigarette from it, then leaned back and smiled. Her bare black shoulders gleamed, as if lightly smeared with Vaseline, as did the slopes of her black breasts, which appeared not to be supported by but to be loose in the pointed cups of her stiff bodice. Her entire dress appeared a fraction separated from her thin, soft, tender, black body, which moved within the stiff dress. Her black hair was dense, almost solid, and, at the back, was as if pulled out in jagged points from the density. She wore dangling silver earrings. The spangles on her bodice shaking as her earrings did, she looked about the lounge as she smoked, not at Daniel but, maybe, for someone she was expecting, her irises as black as her pupils, and little flecks of black in the whites. When the band struck up, Daniel asked her to dance. She laughed and said sure. He was a good dancer. He guided her by the Belgian family, who didn't look at him. He was nineteen, and she must have been, oh, about thirty.

She left him early to go to her cabin and her two kids, a boy and a girl from, she said, a white Australian guy, an alcoholic, she'd left behind in Harlem, where she was from.

Daniel walked about the illuminated decks. He had never before in his life been close to a black person.

He shared a compartment on the Le Havre–to–Paris boat train with Angela and her two children, the four of them laughing about a French orange soda pop called Pssshit. Angela said there were other drinks in Europe with funny names like Bols. Ashley and Charlotte, the kids, invented funny names for drinks. The train, swaying from side to side, raced past small grey towns.

Angela asked Daniel, "So what are your plans?"

He thought he'd told her. She had a way of forgetting what he'd told her, as if she never really paid attention. "I'll travel during the summer before I start at the university in the fall."

She said, "Why don't you come to Spain? I'm going to Spain with the kids."

Ashley said, "I thought we were going to stay in Paris."

"No," his mother said. "I've decided we're going to Spain."

"On the boat, you said we were going to stay in Paris," Charlotte said.

The two kids were pale brown.

"We're going to Barcelona," Angela said.

The kids accepted that. They accepted going anywhere she said, and also accepted her changing her mind when they got there and going on to somewhere else.

On the way to Paris, night fell and they saw from the train a farmhouse burning in a field, the high, raging flames rising out of the roof timbers, and people in the field staring at the conflagration, their shadows cast back from them. In the compartment, Ashley and Charlotte pressed against the window to look out, Angela and Daniel behind them.

"Write to me care of American Express, Barcelona," Angela said later, "and tell me when you'll be coming."

In Paris, Daniel stayed with other students in the apartment of an elderly woman. The floors were parquet, and there were porcelain figures everywhere, which the students were warned not to touch. One of the students was German, named Werner, who stayed to himself and didn't have Sunday morning croissants and coffee with Madame and the other students. Madame said about him:

"Il est un peu efféminé, mais il a une très belle musculature."

Werner went out early and came back late. All Daniel knew of him was the creaking sounds of parquet from his room.

Daniel believed he was not good-looking. In his room, he looked at himself in the mirror over the fireplace, and for a moment he thought he had really fine features, but then, looking more closely, he thought his features were gaunt. A Jesuit back at college in Boston would have said he needed a haircut, but away from his college, he liked the way his sideburns came down to points. He had no idea if he was *efféminé* or not, but he was sure he, with a thin, flat, hairless body, did not have anything like a *belle musculature*.

It meant taking a little risk, but he wrote to Angela, care of American Express in Barcelona, to say he was coming, and he was surprised to have a letter back from her to tell him to come to a little town called Sitges, outside Barcelona, where she and the kids had found an apartment, cheap.

On the train, he was in a crowded second-class compartment. Sweating, he tried to sleep sitting up among the others in the compartment, illuminated only by a dim blue bulb overhead, but couldn't. No one could. From time to time one of the men lit a cigarette, and in the light he saw the faces of the other travellers. The women wore black kerchiefs and had callused, square hands they held crossed in their laps. A chicken in a burlap sack on the luggage rack moved. Daniel couldn't imagine

Angela existed. Next to the window, he stood and pulled it open to breathe in the cold night air. All he could see was the looming outline of a high, dark mountain.

In the Barcelona station, he changed to a local train with wooden seats. The sea appeared in the bright Mediterranean light, and he felt he had come very far. And it was odd that in coming so far he was going to Angela Hughs. At every station, he stood to look out the window at the names of the towns. He was from a region of pines and oaks and birch, and he saw, for the first time, palm trees.

As the train slowed down at a station, he spotted Angela, in a man's white shirt, not tucked in and with the collar turned up at the nape, and tight black pedal pushers and espadrilles, waiting with Ashley and Charlotte. He waved, and they, laughing, waved back, and he became excited and, on the cement platform, dropped his bag and put his arms around Angela and kissed her cheek. She, too, was excited and moved as if jiving. The kids, too, were excited, and each in turn carried Daniel's bag along the narrow streets through the white town. He was going to stay with black people. The sunlight on the white walls was brilliant.

As if it were an expression of her excitement, Angela said, "This place is a dump."

Angela, Daniel learned, always put down, offhand, the place where she was: Sitges was a dump, and they should move to Barcelona; Barcelona was a dump, and they should move to Berlin; Berlin was a dump . . .

Daniel said, "But look at the flowers in pots everywhere."

"Yeah," Angela said.

The apartment had tile floors and stark white walls, and all the furniture in the living-dining room, including the dining table, was covered with clothes, mostly evening wear, cocktail dresses and gowns and even a ball gown, and the floor was littered with shoes with stiletto heels. There were also large, glossy black-and-white photographs, some curling at the edges and torn, of Angela wearing the clothes thrown around, and one of the photographs showed Angela, with a bouffant wig, turning so the gown swirled out about her. She pushed clothes off the dining table, and Ashley and Charlotte went out and came back with plates, knives and forks, and a cold Spanish omelette. Charlotte wore wooden clogs that rang against the tile floor.

Ashley asked Daniel, "Will you climb the mountain with us?"

From the open double windows at the side of the room was a view of a purple mountain.

"Yes," Daniel said.

"Can I come?" Charlotte asked.

"We'll all go," Angela said.

She always said they would do things they never did do, but the kids didn't seem to mind not doing anything but sitting in the apartment, Charlotte brushing her long frizzy hair and Ashley drawing the mountain.

Angela said to Daniel, "I'll show you where you'll sleep."

He followed her down a long corridor with his bag, and he saw, through open doorways to left and right, bedrooms with clothes thrown everywhere. Angela opened a door onto a room that had in it only two beds and a chair between them. Angela and Daniel stood together in the room, both looking about as if at what wasn't there.

She had to say something. She asked, "What bed will you sleep in?"

He felt a strange looseness in his body. "Any one will do."

"What about this one?" she said, pointing with a long, thin black finger with a long, clear, manicured nail.

"That's fine."

She looked about the room again, then at him, and asked, "What would you like to do now?"

"Oh," he said.

"The kids are going to the beach."

He was very tired and wanted to sleep.

As if she felt a little sorry for him, she said, "You must be tired."

Hunching a shoulder, he said, "Not really." He would do anything she said.

Angela put a hand on his hunched shoulder and, more sorry for him, said, "Why don't you go out to the beach with the kids."

"You won't come?"

"No, I've got a lot to do here," she said.

He would have done anything she'd said, and, suddenly, he felt free to do anything he wanted.

The beach was three streets away, beyond a road along the seafront and below a stone seawall. Fishing boats were pulled up on it, and people in bikinis lay on the sand among the boats. Daniel's large swimsuit had a tartan pattern. High above the seawall was a brown church tower, and as he, Ashley and Charlotte on either side of him, ran into the sea, the church bell rang.

"People just got married," Ashley said.

Lying between boats on the beach were, Daniel saw when he and the kids were lying in the sunlight, two men, hairy and fat, one with a skimpy green bikini and one with a skimpy blue bikini, which were shoved into mounds by their penises; the fingers of their hands, extended towards one another, intertwined. The sight amused Daniel a lot.

He had thought he would have been, with Angela, intimidated in some way, he wasn't sure in what way.

When he and the kids got back to the apartment, Angela wasn't there. Daniel said he'd have a nap and, in his room, wondered if he should shut his door or not, and he shut it. He woke in the purple light of after-sunset. The kids were in the living room, sitting quietly among all the clothes.

"Where's your mum?" he asked.

"Gone to Barcelona," Ashley said.

Charlotte explained, "She's gone for the afternoon show at the club."

"Then she should be back soon," Daniel said.

Charlotte laughed, a high, delicate laugh from a delicate girl. "Afternoon means night here. She gets back about five or six in the morning."

"If she doesn't stay on in Barcelona," Ashley said.

Daniel spent the day with the kids, all of them sitting around the living room, in the midst of the clothes, where for supper they ate fried eggs.

In the morning when he woke, Daniel heard Charlotte and Ashley speaking in Spanish to someone who spoke Spanish rapidly and with a shrill, and in the living room, he found a very small girl in a striped dress that was too big for her. Her face was blunt, and her hair was in a Dutch cut with a topknot, and her feet were bare.

Charlotte said, "She's the idiot girl who comes to see us."

Ashley said something to her in Spanish, and she wrinkled up her nose and laughed so her teeth and gums showed.

Charlotte said, "She takes me to mass on Sunday mornings."

"You go to mass?" Daniel asked.

Raising and lowering her chin slowly, Charlotte said, "She brought me the first time. I never went before. Now we go every Sunday."

Daniel hadn't been to mass since he'd arrived in Europe, and he couldn't imagine what going for the first time must mean to someone.

Charlotte said, "Mum bought me a black veil to wear over my head when I go to mass."

For lunch, Daniel took the kids to a café, where they ate ham sandwiches. As if they were used to sitting around a lot, they sat at the café table a long while, then, when Charlotte said she thought they had digested their sandwiches, they went to the beach.

Studying one of his bare arms, Daniel said, "I'm getting tan."

With a thumb, Ashley drew the waistband of his bathing suit, which was snug, away from his smooth tummy and a little down, and he said, "Look how tan I've become," and Daniel leaned forward to look while the boy held his bathing suit open.

Charlotte said, "And look at me," and she raised her one-piece bathing suit at her thigh to reveal the paler skin under.

Beyond her, Daniel saw, coming between two beached boats, Angela, deep black, with a lighter, brown woman, and a white man, all together. Angela was jumping around a little, as if jiving, as they came forward. They were laughing.

Angela called out to Daniel, as though he were part of her family, "We've got guests who'll be staying."

Aware of his naked chest and shoulders, Daniel shook hands with the brown woman, Hilary, who was elegant, each movement she made, even the movement of raising her hand towards him, seeming to start with a slight swaying or rolling motion backwards and then forwards. She held out just the tips of her fingers and pursed her lips and slowly opened them to say "Hello" with what Daniel thought an English accent. She had a sharp, narrow jaw and a long, thin nose and a high forehead, and her black hair was pulled tightly back against her oval head.

She stood away, and the man stepped forward, and as he held out his hand to Daniel, Angela asked him, "What's your name again?"

He said something in a strange accent Daniel didn't understand.

Angela didn't either. She said, "Anyway, this is Daniel."

Daniel held his hand out to the man, who had close-cropped hair and black eyes with delicate lashes, and whose lips, faintly curving at the corners into a smile, were full and yet delicately defined. He was wearing a shirt open onto his chest, and his neck, his clavicle, the curves of an exposed pectoral muscle and nipple, appeared solid yet delicate. Raising his arm, he moved slowly, almost lazily, smiling all the while that slight smile, as if he were very amused to find himself where he was, but he was keeping his amusement, which he thought no one else could appreciate, to himself. He pursed his lips a little, perhaps to keep even his smile to himself. The black irises of his eyes were sharp and bright.

Holding his dry, warm hand, Daniel asked, "What did you say your name is?"

"I'll spell it," the man said, and he spelled, slowly and with that strange accent, which was partly English and partly something very far from being English, "O, umlaut, c, cedilla, i, dot—Öçi," and he smiled despite himself.

Very seriously, Daniel asked, "Öçi?"

"That's right," Öçi answered.

He seemed to Daniel to be a man much older than he was, but Öçi was in fact only two years older than Daniel. He was twenty-one.

"What kind of name is that?" Charlotte asked him.

"A funny name," he answered.

With that slight, slow, undulating, backward and forward movement, Hilary unbuttoned her long white beach robe and dropped it from her slender shoulders and, in her bathing suit, walked barefoot into the sea without pausing, always keeping her head high and tilted back on her slender neck.

As Öçi undressed, stripping his body to a brief European bathing suit, Daniel watched him. With a slow leap, because he was capable even of jumping in a slow and lazy way, Öçi ran to the sea and dived in and swam past Hilary, whose head, still tilted back, she held high out of the waves as she floated about. Öçi swam slowly round her.

Squinting in the sea glare, Angela asked Charlotte to give her her straw hat, and she put it on and rolled down the sleeves of her green blouse.

Charlotte asked her mother, "Who's Hilary?"

"Some Nigerian," Angela said.

"Where'd you meet her?"

"In Barcelona."

"And who's the guy?" Ashley asked.

"I don't know," Angela said. "He was with Hilary, and I asked them to come and stay."

"What's his name?" Charlotte asked.

"I didn't understand," Angela said. "Something like Archie."

"Öçi," Daniel said.

"Oh," Angela said. "Anyway, it was Hilary I wanted to invite."

"I never met a Nigerian before," Ashley said.

"She's a princess," Angela said.

"A princess!" Charlotte exclaimed. "I never met a princess before."

"Maybe she'll invite us to Africa," Angela said.

Charlotte shook her arms as with fright. "Brrr, I don't know if I'd go to Africa," she said.

"I'd go," Ashley said. "I wouldn't be scared."

Angela told the kids they had to come home with her. The priest would be there soon to give them lessons, and she bet they hadn't studied. They were going to grow up knowing nothing. Maybe she'd made a mistake taking them to Europe and should have left them with her mother in Harlem. Their father wouldn't look after them. They dressed silently and followed her across the sand.

Alone, Daniel sat and watched Öçi emerge from the sea. As Öçi came towards him, he thought Öçi looked right at him, and he sat up more. Dripping, Öçi sat right before him, his legs crossed. Hilary's head was still floating in the sea.

Öçi's wet body shone as with a fine oil, an unguent, lightly smeared all over his skin, and this shine made his body appear very solid and, again, delicate. Öçi's shoulders shone, and his chest, and his thighs and shins. Daniel was aware, too, of Öçi having internal organs, of his heart and lungs and liver. The presence of Öçi made Daniel aware of his own presence, and he felt the solidity of his own body. When Öçi spoke, Daniel was as attentive to the liquid-pink inside of his mouth, of his tongue and teeth, as to what Öçi said. Daniel felt the warm saliva in his own mouth, and when he swallowed he felt the swallow go all the way down into his stomach. Though he had of course never met him before, Öçi leaned towards him as if he had always known him.

"You're American," Öçi said.

"I am," Daniel said, aware of his own smile as Öçi smiled.

"What kind of American are you?"

"What do you mean?"

"Well, all Americans are Irish or Italian or Jewish—"

"I'm French," Daniel said.

Öçi shifted sand from one hand to another.

"Have you been to America?" Daniel asked.

"No," Öçi said.

Daniel asked, "Where are you from?"

With a slight sigh, Öçi let the sand run through his fingers and said, "From what was one time, when my family would have been powerful and rich and I totally spoiled, called Byzantium."

"Where do you live?"

"My parents live in London."

"Is that where you live, then? London?"

"Now, I'm living in Spain."

"Why?"

Öçi said, "I don't know myself, really." He brushed his hands against one another. "And so I'll leave Spain."

"And go where?"

Öçi turned towards the sea and said, "I would like to go to America." When he turned back to Daniel, he smiled his smile with the fine corners of his lips.

Daniel, smiling also, lowered his head.

Then Hilary, seeming, as she walked towards them, still to be floating upright in water with her head above it, came and sat with them.

She said to Daniel, "Tell me about Angela."

"I don't know much about her," he said.

"You don't?"

"I got here just yesterday."

Hilary laughed.

But the fact that Daniel had arrived only the day before interested Öçi. He asked, "Didn't you know her?"

"Oh, sure," Daniel said. "I met her on the boat from New York to France. We became friends."

"I see," Öçi said.

Daniel had no idea what Öçi, who kept his smile curling the corners of his lips, saw. In fact, he felt more at ease talking with Hilary than Öçi. He said to her, "Angela told me you're from Nigeria."

Hilary laughed in a reserved way, smoothing back with her pink palms strands of hair that had come undone. "What else did Angela say?"

"That she'd like to go to Africa."

"I hope she doesn't think she's African."

Daniel wondered if he should have said anything about Angela and Africa. He asked Hilary, "What are you doing in Spain?"

Again, Hilary laughed. "You might well ask. I'm supposed to be at a Catholic school for girls run by nuns. It's like being in a convent, and I hate it, and somehow I escaped." Hilary said to Öçi, "You'd love the convent."

As if he had just eaten something delicious, Öçi said, "My harem."

Hilary laughed a rich laugh from deep in her throat.

She said she couldn't wait to get back to Nigeria. She had her house, though she always had trouble with servants. She could only get maids from the bush, and no matter how much she beat them, they would never learn to wash the pots on the table but would wash them on the floor.

It was Öçi who said they should go, he'd had enough, and he wanted a drink at a café.

After Hilary brushed the sand from her feet and her hands, she said, holding her palms upward, "I'm ashamed of having white palms and soles. I should dye them red."

Öçi said, "Then you'd leave red handprints everywhere."

Again, Hilary laughed from deep in her throat.

Light-spirited, Daniel said to Hilary, "Blue handprints would be nice too."

The sun was setting when they got back to the apartment house. As none of them had a key, they rang the one bell without a name, and the door clicked open with no one asking who was there. The door to the apartment was open. In the late, deep violet light of the living-dining room, Charlotte and Ashley, at a corner of the dining table, were writing out lessons. Charlotte said her mother was sleeping, but just then Angela, yawning, came into the room. She was wearing a blue silk *robe de chambre* that clung to her sharp hips and was open deep between her breasts. Her hair stood out in points.

She dropped into an armchair, the back of it draped with a black dress hanging upside down so the straps trailed on the floor, and she asked, blinking, "So what do you all want to do?"

"Aren't you going to the club today?" Charlotte asked.

Angela made a gesture with a hand, which she left hanging loosely from her bent wrist. "That club is a dump. I keep telling them to get rid of the whores, but do they listen to me? And it's not only the whores who make it a dump. No, I'm not going. I'll tell them my ulcer was acting up. I'll stay home, and we'll have some fun." Rubbing one eye, she looked with the other at Öçi, Hilary, Daniel, standing in a row before her, and she asked, "What kind of fun do you want to have?"

Doors opened and closed again and again around the apartment as they all went into and out of rooms to wash and change, even the kids, and then they all went to the outside market to shop. Bare bulbs hung lit over the fish, the pigs' hocks, eggs, tomatoes. Angela held a basket over her arm. The vendors stared at the group as it moved from stall to stall, talking loudly and laughing. Angela was the one to stop at stalls to buy sausages, then cooked beans, then oranges, which she paid for with small, frayed peseta notes. The gang invaded the small bakery shop to buy bread, and the baker's wife joked in Spanish with Angela. As the gang moved around one another, crisscrossing back and forth, Öçi sometimes, as if to keep himself from bumping into him, put his hand on Daniel's shoulder or passed his hand across his back, and Daniel felt that this physical contact was the result of the nonphysical contact among them all in their excitement, which was caused by Angela.

The kids asked for *caramelas*, and Angela bought them a big paper cone of them.

Öçi said he'd buy the wine, and Daniel said he'd share, and they all went into the wine bodega, where a wrinkled, toothless man in a black vest unbuttoned over a white shirt filled, from a tun with a wooden spigot, a demijohn encased in a basket with two handles, and Öçi and Daniel each held a handle and were the rear of the gang going through the narrow, intimate streets back to the apartment.

Hilary, though with them, seemed to hold herself, or her head, just a little above them.

The kids were fighting about who would hold the cone of candies, and Angela shouted at them, "Shut up, you two, I want to have a good time," and they shut up. Ashley let Charlotte hold the cone.

The night air smelled of sea, of suntan lotion, of jasmine, and voices resounded everywhere. The sloshing wine in the demijohn at times pulled Öçi and Daniel towards one another, and they tried, pulling away from one another, then giving way a little, and again pulling back, to synchronize their movements. The demijohn was stoppered with rolled-up newspaper.

Only Hilary, her arms resting along the overstuffed armrests of the armchair, sat, while the others, with the continuing spirit of a dance, got the table cleared and set the grilled sausages and beans and bread and a bowl of oranges on it, and then Hilary came to the table. The wine, Angela said, had to be drunk, first gulp, holding the edge of the table to keep yourself steady. She did this and said, "To hell with my ulcer," and she held out her glass to Öçi for more of the wine. She said to him, "Give Daniel more too."

Then all the lights went out. They went out all over the town. Angela called out, "Candles, candles," and the kids, who were used to this happening, left the table and in other parts of the room lit candles, which they brought to the table. The shadows of the circle of people were cast large and flickering against the white walls.

Hilary, svelte, slender, told them all she would teach them a Nigerian dance. She beat the rhythm by clapping her hands, and, occasionally tripping on the high-heel shoes littering the floor, Angela and Öçi and Daniel and the kids, too, danced separately, in imitation of Hilary, who kept her neck and head and body from the waist up bent forward but as if inflexible, her arms, bent at the elbows, raised as she clapped softly and thrust her pelvis out again and again.

Öçi said to her, "You must have invented this dance," and Hilary gave one of her rich laughs from deep in her throat.

Angela took up the clapping and danced with deeper thrusts than Hilary, who said to her, "You're moving your upper body too much," and Angela answered, "That's the way I am."

On impulse, Daniel grabbed Angela to dance with her, and she laughed. Whatever they were doing, it was not a Nigerian dance, and Hilary turned away from them. Perhaps it was an American dance. Angela and Daniel, both drunk, laughed a lot. The streetlamp outside, lights in other apartments, the lights in the apartment, suddenly came on, and Daniel separated from Angela.

She shouted, "Shut off the lights," and the kids ran to switches to turn the lights off, and they and Angela and Daniel continued to dance in the candlelight, thrusting out their hips again and again, sweating. But Öçi and Hilary had stopped dancing. Hilary sat in the armchair, and Öçi went out onto the balcony beyond the windows that opened towards the sea. Daniel danced exaggeratedly with Angela, both stumbling, the kids bumping into them. Daniel's impulse, which only Angela seemed to understand, was to go someplace from where he would never be able to come back.

He stopped moving, and Angela did. In a loud voice, he said, "Let's go for a swim."

Angela exclaimed that that was a great idea. They'd all go for a swim. That was a really great idea.

Hilary said she'd come along to the beach, but she didn't think she'd swim.

Öçi came in from the balcony, and he said, with a quiet smile, that, yes, he'd like that.

The kids said they wanted to go too, but their mother said no, they had to go to bed, and they went without protesting to their rooms.

Arm in arm, Öçi walked with Hilary ahead of Daniel and Angela, who were not arm in arm, towards the sea. Daniel was all at once frightened of touching Angela. The empty streets were lit with dim bulbs under fluted tin shades attached to the stucco walls of houses.

Angela said to Daniel, "I don't like him."

"Who?"

"Archie. Do you like him?" Angela asked.

Laughing, Daniel took Angela's arm in his, and, together, they skipped, then ran, across the road along the seafront, which was empty and where only one café was lit up. They ran past Öçi and Hilary.

On the dark beach, Daniel and Angela separated to undress. She went a long way away and, undressing, disappeared in the night.

As Daniel undressed he felt himself go into erection, and shivering a little, he stood naked on the sand, his erection sticking out at a lopsided angle. He hoped everyone saw him, white in the night.

He heard laughter, Hilary's, on the beach, but he couldn't see her or Öçi, and then he saw a naked white body run past him towards the sea, and he heard a splash and Öçi exclaim, "Oh, the delight," and then the splashing sound of swimming.

Daniel ran and, all his roused body exposed to the dark, threw himself into the sea, sank, rose, and as he rose he heard Angela, somewhere in the sea, yell, "Daniel." He couldn't see her. He couldn't see anyone. Then he saw, in the swelling and falling waves, a pale body swim underwater towards him, and close by him, and pass by him, and disappear.

Again, Daniel dived down, took deep, slow strokes, and rose only when he felt his lungs about to burst, and he faced total darkness. He heard Angela call, "Daniel, Daniel," and he turned towards the few lights along the sea road.

Shivering, he ran to his clothes and dressed, his underpants and shirt sticking to him, and joined Angela, also dressed, and Hilary. He shivered more, as with fear, when he saw Öçi, dressed, come across the beach carrying his loafers. No one laughed, and they went back through the streets, empty but for them, in silence. Daniel almost thought a sadness had descended on them. He was still shivering, not, he knew, from the cold. Only Öçi smiled, and Daniel was grateful for the smile. In the apartment, candles were burning, and Angela snuffed them out with her fingers and didn't light the ceiling light.

She said to Öçi, "You'll sleep in Daniel's room, and Hilary will sleep in my room."

Daniel shivered more.

The door to the bedroom was shut. Daniel and Öçi reached for the handle together. Öçi put his hand on it first, then he went still. Daniel, his extended fingers almost touching Öçi's hand, also went still, and the moment fixed them. It was a moment that would fix them, for Daniel, forever, even, years and years later, beyond the death of Öçi in New York, where he, an American citizen, finally made his home.

Öçi opened the door.

Daniel woke to the sunlight blazing through the open window onto the empty bed on the other side of the room with its sheets neatly folded on the mattress. He fell back asleep. He woke again, and it seemed odd to him that the sheets were still folded on the bed. The apartment was very quiet.

Naked, he got up and went to the window and leaned out, and in the sunlight his body smelled as it warmed of a pungent odor, and he turned his head and pressed his nose into his shoulder to smell the odor more deeply, and then he licked himself lightly. He didn't smell of himself. He didn't taste of himself. His body was tender to his touch when he soaped it in the shower.

Dressed, he felt he was not himself but someone else. He went into the sunlit living room, where Angela, sitting in a square of light through a window, was combing her hair with an electrically heated metal comb attached to a socket by a wire, so steam was rising from her head. She was wearing her blue silk *robe de chambre*. Her face severe, she looked at

Daniel as he came into the room as if to reprimand him for having slept late, or for something.

But she said, "I've prepared breakfast for us on the balcony."

On the balcony a table with a white cloth was set. The cutlery and china gleamed.

"Just the two of us," Angela said. "Hilary and Archie have gone."

"Where are the kids?" Daniel asked.

"They went to mass."

"Is today Sunday?"

Angela laughed. "You're like me. You never know what day it is."

She reached out and unplugged her comb and stood and told Daniel to give her five minutes to get dressed.

He went out onto the balcony and leaned against the balustrade, towards the sea he saw down the narrow street, and he knew that if he leaned further forward, leaned so far over that he wouldn't be able to draw back, he wouldn't fall but would fly out over the sea. He turned back only when he heard Angela pull a chair away from the table.

She was placing a coffeepot on a straw mat. There was orange juice in tall glasses, milk in a pitcher, strawberry jam in a little glass bowl, butter, and a basket of bread slices folded into a napkin.

They didn't talk as they ate, but kept looking down the street at the sea, where the waves rose to points that flashed, over and over, in small, brilliantly luminous globes.

Angela poured more coffee into Daniel's cup and asked, "Did Archie make love with you last night?"

"He did, yes," he said.

"I thought he would."

Angela pressed her lips together and drew them in so they disappeared, and the space between her nose and her upper lip swelled out far, the two ridges of the narrow concavity forming a half-circle. He thought the black flecks in the whites of her eyes jumped about. Her round nose twitched, and she rubbed it with a knuckle. She glanced away, looked back at him, glanced the other way, and looked back, considering him. Again her nose twitched and she rubbed it, then kept her finger crooked over the bridge. She had painted her long fingernails red. She asked, "Was it your first time?"

"Yes," Daniel said.

Dropping her hand from her face and letting it hang loose in the air, she said, "Why didn't you do it with me first time?"

"It just happened this way," Daniel said.

Angela sighed and said, "Yeah." She put her hand flat on the table. "What would your mother think?"

"I don't know what she would think."

"All right, all right," Angela said, as if what Daniel had said, or the way he'd said it, was a protest against her question. Her hand rose and, the thin, long, red-nailed fingers extended far out, she took up a pack of cigarettes from the table and a box of matches, lit the cigarette, inhaled, then picked a shred of tobacco off her tongue, exhaled, and all these little movements seemed to be the outward signs of her inner deliberation. When she exhaled, the smoke was blown back against her face and she winced. Still wincing, she said, "All right, then. I'll become your European mother."

Daniel laughed and reached his hand across the table to touch Angela on her shoulder.

Angela didn't laugh. She inhaled again, exhaled, and, wincing against the smoke about her face, said, "He's coming back. He asked me this morning if he could come back in a week's time, and I said, yeah, he could."

"With Hilary?"

"Hilary went back to the convent, and I suppose she won't be allowed to get away again for a long time. I don't care if I don't see her again. She didn't invite me to Africa."

With the little idiot girl, Ashley and Charlotte came in from mass. Charlotte was wearing her black mantilla over her head.

For once, Angela stuck to her promise of doing something. That afternoon they all climbed the mountain, even the little idiot girl, for whom Angela had bought sandals. The little girl laughed a lot and made everyone else laugh.

Having said nothing to him, Angela went, the next day, to Barcelona, as the kids informed him when he got up. Daniel asked them if they'd like to go to the beach with him, and they said they wanted to stay in and play. He'd never make them do what they didn't want to do. He went to the beach alone.

Lying on the hot sand, he fell asleep, and when, with a little jolt of his body, he opened his eyes, the sky appeared to have become a brilliant black.

In the apartment, he found Ashley and Charlotte walking along the corridor, he—wearing one of his mother's strapless cocktail dresses, one of his mother's wigs, his lips coated with red lipstick—wavering on stiletto-heel shoes. The bodice of the dress slipped down his smooth chest below his nipples, and he raised it. Behind him, Charlotte, her hair shoved under a knitted cap, was wearing Daniel's clothes, a shirt and trousers rolled up at the bottoms, and his shoes.

"What are you two doing?" Daniel asked.

Charlotte said, "We're playing queers."

From his bed, Daniel heard Angela come in, singing, as dawn was rising. He thought he heard a man's voice in the midst of Angela's singing, and he listened, but he imagined he had made a mistake, as he didn't hear it again. But he did hear Angela laugh.

Again, he slept late, and he hoped, when he woke, that Angela would have gone. But he found her in the kitchen, looking for something to eat.

"Where are the kids?" he asked.

"They've gone out somewhere."

"They seem to have a lot of fun together."

"If they don't, it's their own fault." She chewed on a piece of stale bread. "Why don't you come to Barcelona with me today?" she said. "Come with me to the club."

They took an afternoon train, and a yellow taxi from the station to the Plaza Real, where the Jazz Club was. The neon sign over the doorway was off. They walked around the square, looked in the windows of the taxidermist at the stuffed animals, then, in an arcade, had beers and shrimp on a saucer. When they went back to the club, the red neon sign was lit in the soft darkness.

Daniel got to know some of the whores. They spoke a little English and were friendly. With the saxophonist of the band he played craps on the bar while Angela was changing. Daniel won, but the saxophonist didn't pay. The saxophonist said, "It's only beginner's luck." The club filled up, and Daniel sat at a corner table, near the little stage, and listened to Angela sing her blues songs. During the break, Angela came and sat at the table with Daniel and drank crème de menthe, which she said was the only alcoholic drink her stomach ulcer tolerated. When the whores approached the table, Angela shouted at them in Spanish to go away. "Dumb whores," she said, but added, "Not that some of them aren't nice." The saxophonist wanted to play more craps with Daniel, but Angela wouldn't let him.

At four o'clock in the morning, Angela announced that she would sing her last song for the night. She was standing before the microphone, the band behind her. The club went silent. She said, "This song is for Daniel," and she sang a sad blues song.

The ceiling lights that revealed scratches in the tables and the threadbare carpet were lit in the club, but there were still a few people at tables. Three American sailors, slouched back in chairs and their knees wide apart, were drinking. The saxophonist and the drummer were sitting at the table with Daniel, and Angela, who seemed to have just come into their own now that the club was closing, was standing and jiving before them.

One of the sailors, watching Angela jive, sat up and leaned forward and, his eyes narrowed, said, "You come far, and all you find's a nigger," and Angela, her long, thin fingers out, turned to him and jumped, so he, startled, drew back. Close enough to claw him, she said, "You'll go even further if you don't say you're sorry, fast." The sailor, with a drunken wobble throughout his body, said, "I'm sorry." Angela said, "You're just drunk." "That's right," the sailor said, "I'm drunk." Angela put a hand on his shoulder and said, "I like being drunk myself."

Drunk also, Daniel wondered what it meant to be aware, day after day, all your life, that you were black, and he suddenly thought: such awareness makes you free.

He, who knew about being aware of yourself, now felt free, free and happy in his freedom, and this, he had never imagined before, was all because of such awareness.

Angela came back to the table and said to Daniel, "Look, I'm going to stay in Barcelona until I've had some fun. How do you feel about going back to Sitges on your own?" He said he felt all right about it.

At the taxi, she asked him to keep his eye on the kids. "Tell them," she said, "that I've stayed in Barcelona for fun, and they'll understand." She kissed him and said, "And you have fun."

When Daniel got back he found, not Ashley and Charlotte, but the little idiot girl. He asked her where the kids were, and she, shrugging, indicated the wide world with his hands. He didn't see much of them during the week.

On Saturday morning, Daniel went in the early afternoon to wait in the train station, though he didn't know when Öçi was supposed to arrive. He saw, past the ticket controller, the trains arrive and leave on the platform. Whenever a train stopped, he went to the entrance to the platform. The doors opened, people descended with bundles, then the doors were slammed shut, and whistles blew, and the brown, dusty train with dirty windows started off slowly. Many, many trains stopped, then left.

The sky clouded and rain fell. Daniel stood at the entrance to the station, facing the square. The rain was falling heavily, so the drops exploded on the square as if in silver flashes, and through the flashes a young man on a bicycle pedalled fast in one direction, and going in another direction, an old man, holding a burlap sack over his head with one hand, was goading the donkey he was riding to go faster. The big raindrops exploded brilliantly on the dripping fronds of the palm trees.

Daniel stared, and as he did he had a sense of removal from what he saw, but the greater his sense of removal, the more acute his awareness of what he saw became. He stared, as if from a far, far distance, at a lottery ticket on the ground near him, at a burnt match stick, at the petals of a crushed geranium blossom. He thought he wouldn't be able to touch the stone of the wall he was next to if he reached his hand out to it, because it appeared to him so far away, and yet he was aware of the faint chisel marks in it.

The rain stopped, and he thought, Öçi isn't coming, and he walked back to the apartment.

Charlotte was brushing her hair. She asked, "Where were you?"

"I was out."

"Archie came," she said.

"Did he?"

"He waited for the rain to stop, and then he went out to buy some food for supper. Ashley went with him. We didn't know where you were. Archie wondered if you were gone."

"Gone where?"

"People go," Charlotte said.

Daniel heard the door to the apartment open and Öçi's voice speaking to Ashley in Spanish. Ashley came into the room first and he turned round to Öçi and said, "Here he is," and Öçi came in.

Rain fell again as they ate, the four of them, and with the rain cool darkness fell.

Charlotte said, "I like it when it rains."

"So do I," Ashley said.

"I like shutting the windows and hearing the rain on the glass."

Ashley shut the windows for her.

With the windows shut and the rain falling, the electric lights reflected in the glass, the apartment was calm. They remained at the table after they ate and drew pictures of one another, using sheets from Ashley's drawing pad and his colored pencils. They held up the results to show one another, and laughed, or, in Öçi's case, smiled. Daniel would never quite understand Öçi's smile, never. They all helped wash and dry the dishes and put them away, and then, in the domestic calm, Ashley and Charlotte went to the bathroom and then their rooms and shut their doors.

In the living room with Daniel, Öçi opened the windows. The rain-fresh sea air circulated around them, and Daniel thought the world would have taken delight in their own delight, in their freedom, if only it had been aware, for even one moment, of them, two young men revolving together, round and round, in one another's arms.

~ *Allan Gurganus* ~

Adult
Art

For George Hackney Eatman
and Hiram Johnson Cuthrell, Jr.

I've got an extra tenderness. It's not legal.

~ ~ ~

I see a twelve-year-old boy steal a white Mercedes off the street. I'm sitting at my official desk—Superintendent of Schools. It's noon on a weekday and I watch this kid wiggle a coat hanger through one front window. Then he slips into the sedan, straight-wires its ignition, squalls off. Afterward, I can't help wondering why I didn't phone the police. Or shout for our truant officer just down the hall.

Next, a fifty-nine Dodge, black, mint condition, tries to parallel park in the Mercedes' spot (I'm not getting too much paperwork done today). The driver is one of the worst drivers I've ever seen under the age of eighty. Three pedestrians take turns waving him in, guiding him back out. I step to my window and hear one person yell, "No, left, sharp *left*. Clown." Disgusted, a last helper leaves.

A native of Rocky Mount, North Carolina, ALLAN GURGANUS is the author of the massive and amazing novel Oldest Living Confederate Widow Tells All. His astute, unpredictable short stories have been collected in the volume White People, and he is currently at work on a new novel, The Erotic History of a Southern Baptist Church. He lives mostly in Chapel Hill, North Carolina; occasionally in New York City.

When the driver stands and stretches, he hasn't really parked his car, just stopped it. I've noticed him around town. About twenty-five, he's handsome, but in the most awkward possible way. His clothes match the old Dodge. His belt's pulled up too high. White socks are a mistake. I watch him comb his hair, getting presentable for downtown. He whips out a handkerchief and stoops to buff his shoes. Many coins and pens spill from a shirt pocket.

While he gathers these, a second boy (maybe a brother of the Mercedes thief?) rushes to the Dodge's front, starts gouging something serious across its hood. I knock on my second-story window—nobody hears. The owner rises from shoe-polishing, sees what's happening, shouts. The vandal bolts. But instead of chasing him, the driver touches bad scratches, he stands—patting them. I notice that the guy is talking to himself. He wets one index fingertip, tries rubbing away scrawled letters. Sunlight catches spit. From my second-floor view, I can read the word. It's an obscenity.

I turn away, lean back against a half-hot radiator. I admire the portrait of my wife, my twin sons in Little League uniforms. On a far wall, the art reproductions I change every month or so. (I was an art history major, believe it or not.) I want to rush downstairs, comfort the owner of the car, say, maybe, "Darn kids nowadays." I don't dare.

They could arrest me for everything I like about myself.

At five sharp, gathering up valise and papers, I look like a regular citizen. Time to leave the office. Who should pass? The owner of the hurt Dodge. His being in the Municipal Building shocked me, as if I'd watched him on TV earlier. In my doorway, I hesitated. He didn't notice me. He tripped over a new two-inch ledge in the middle of the hall. Recovering, he looked around, hoping nobody had seen. Then, content he was alone, clutching a loaded shirt pocket, the guy bent, touched the spot where the ledge had been. There was no ledge. Under long fingers, just smoothness, linoleum. He rose. I stood close enough to see, in his pocket, a plastic caddy you keep pens in. It was white, a gift from WOOTEN'S SMALL ENGINES, NEW AND LIKE-NEW. Four old fountain pens were lined there, name-brand articles. Puzzled at why he'd stumbled, the boy now scratched the back of his head, made a face. "Gee, *that's* funny!" An antiquated cartoon drawing would have shown a decent cheerful hick doing and saying exactly that. I was charmed.

～ ～ ～

I've got this added tenderness. I never talk about it. It only sneaks up on me every two or three years. It sounds strange but feels so natural. I know it'll get me into big trouble. I feel it for a certain kind of other man, see. For any guy who's even clumsier than me, than *I*.

You have a different kind of tenderness for everybody you know. There's one sort for grandparents, say. But if you waltz into a singles bar and use that type of affection, you'll be considered pretty strange. When my sons hit pop flies, I get a strong wash of feeling—and yet, if I turned the same sweetness on my Board of Education, I'd soon find myself both fired and committed.

～ ～ ～

Then he saw me.

He smiled in a shy cramped way. Caught, he pointed to the spot that'd given him recent trouble, he said of himself, "Tripped." You know what I said? When I noticed—right then, this late—how kind-looking he was, I said, "Happens all the time. Me too." I pointed to my chest, another dated funny-paper gesture. "No reason." I shrugged. "You just *do*, you know. Most people, I guess."

Well, he liked that. He smiled. It gave me time to check out his starched shirt (white, buttoned to the collar, no tie). I studied his old-timey overly wide belt, its thunderbird-design brass buckle. He wore black pants, plain as a waiter's, brown wingtips with a serious shine. He took in my business suit, my early signs of graying temples. Then he decided, guileless, that he needed some quick maintenance. As I watched, he flashed out a green comb and restyled his hair, three backward swipes, one per side, one on top. Done. The dark waves seemed either damp or oiled, suspended from a part that looked incredibly white, as if my secretary had just painted it there with her typing correction fluid.

This boy had shipshape features—a Navy recruiting poster, forty years past due. Some grandmother's favorite. Comb replaced, grinning, he lingered, pleased I'd acted nice about his ungainly little hop. "What say to a drink?" I asked. He smiled, nodded, followed me out. —How simple, at times, life can be.

～ ～ ～

I'm remembering: During football practice in junior high gym class, I heard a kid's arm break. He was this big blond guy, nice but out of it. He whimpered toward the bleachers and perched there, grinning, sweating. Our coach, twenty-one years old, heard the fracture too. He looked around: somebody should walk the hurt boy to our principal's office. Coach spied me, frowning, concerned. Coach decided that the game could do without me. I'd treat Angier right. (Angier was the kid—holding his arm, shivering.)

"Help him." Coach touched my shoulder. "Let him lean against you."

Angier nearly fainted halfway back to school. "Whoo . . ." He had to slump down onto someone's lawn, still grinning apologies. "It's okay," I said. "Take your time." I finally got him there. The principal's secretary complained—Coach should've brought Angier in himself. "These *young* teachers." She shook her head, phoning the rescue squad. It all seemed routine for her. I led Angier to a dark waiting room stacked with textbooks and charts about the human body. He sat. I stood before him holding his good hand. "You'll be fine. You'll see." His hair was slicked back, as after a swim. He was always slow in class—his father sold fancy blenders in supermarkets. Angier dressed neatly. Today he looked so white his every eyelash stood out separate. We could hear the siren. Glad, he squeezed my hand. Then Angier swooned back against the bench; panting, he said something hoarse. "What?" I leaned closer. "Thank you." He grinned, moaning. Next he craned up, kissed me square, wet, on the mouth. Then Angier fainted, fell sideways.

Five days later, he was back at school sporting a cast that everybody popular got to sign. He nodded my way. He never asked me to scribble my name on his plaster. He seemed to have forgotten what happened. I remember.

~ ~ ~

As we left the office building, the Dodge owner explained he'd been delivering insurance papers that needed signing—flood coverage on his mother's country property. "You can never be too safe. That's Mother's motto." I asked if they lived in town; I was only trying to get him talking, relaxed. If I knew his family, I might have to change my plans.

"Mom died," he said, looking down. "A year come March. She left me everything. Sure burned my sisters up, I can tell you. But they're both in Florida. Where were *they* when she was so sick? She appreciated it. She said she'd remember me. And Mom did, too." Then he got quiet, maybe regretting how much he'd told.

We walked two blocks. Some people spoke to me; they gave my companion a mild look as if thinking, What does Dave want with *him*?

~ ~ ~

He chose the bar. It was called The Arms, but whatever word had been arched between the "The" and the "Arms"—six Old English golden letters—had been stolen; you could see where glue had held them to the bricks. He introduced himself by his first name: Barker. Palms flat on the bar, he ordered beers without asking. Then he turned to me, embarrassed. "Mind reader," I assured him, smiling, and—for a second—cupped my hand over the bristled back of his, but quick. He didn't seem to notice or much mind.

My chair faced the street. His aimed my way, toward the bar's murky back. Bathrooms were marked KINGS and QUEENS. Some boy played a noisy video game that sounded like a jungle bird in electronic trouble.

Barker's head and shoulders were framed by a window. June baked each surface on the main street. Everything out there (passersby included) looked planned, shiny and kind of ceramic. I couldn't see Barker's face that clearly. Sun turned his ears a healthy wax red. Sun enjoyed his cheekbones, found highlights waiting in the wavy old-fashioned hair I decided he must oil. Barker himself wasn't so beautiful—a knotty wiry kid—only his pale face was. It seemed an inheritance he hadn't noticed yet.

Barker sitting still was a Barker almost suave. He wasn't spilling anything (our beer hadn't been brought yet). The kid's face looked, backlit, negotiable as gems. Everything he said to me was heartfelt. Talking about his mom put him in a memory-lane kind of mood. "Yeah," he said. "When *I* was a kid . . ." and he told me about a ditch that he and his sisters would wade in, building dams and making camps. Playing doctor. Then the city landfill chose the site. No more ditch. Watching it bulldozed, the kids had cried, holding on to one another.

Our barman brought us a huge pitcher. I just sipped; Barker knocked four mugs back fast. Foam made half a white mustache over his sweet slack mouth; I didn't mention it. He said he was twenty-nine but still felt about twelve, except for winters. He said after his mother's death he'd joined the Air Force but got booted out.

"What for?"

"Lack of dignity." He downed a fifth mug.

"You mean . . . 'lack of discipline'?"

He nodded. "What'd I say?" I told him.

" 'Dignity,' 'discipline.' " He shrugged to show they meant the same thing. The sadder he seemed, the better I liked it, the nicer Barker looked.

Women passing on the street (he couldn't see them) wore sundresses. How pretty their pastel straps, the freckled shoulders; some walked beside their teenaged sons; they looked good too. I saw folks I knew. Nobody'd think to check for me in here.

Only human, under the table, my knee touched Barker's, lingered a second, shifted. He didn't flinch. He hadn't asked about my job or home life. I got the subject around to things erotic. With a guy as forthright as Barker, you didn't need posthypnotic suggestion to manage it. He'd told me where he lived. I asked wasn't that out by Adult Art Film and Book. "You go in there much?"

He gave me a mock-innocent look, touched a fingertip to his sternum, mouthed Who, me? Then he scanned around to make sure nobody'd hear. "I guess it's me that keeps old Adult Art open. Don't tell, but I can't help it, I just love that stuff. You too?"

I nodded.

"What kind?"

I appeared bashful, one knuckle rerouting sweat beads on my beer mug. "I like all types, I guess. You know, boy/girl, girl/girl, boy/boy, girl/dog, dog/dog." Barker laughed, shaking his fine head side to side. "Dog/dog," he repeated. "That's a good one. *Dog*/dog!"

He was not the most brilliantly intelligent person I'd ever met. I loved him for it.

~   ~   ~

We went in my car. I didn't care to chance his driving. Halfway to Adult Art, sirens and red lights swarmed behind my station wagon. This is it, I thought. Then the white Mercedes (already mud-splattered, a fender dented, doing a hundred and ten in a thirty-five zone) screeched past. Both city patrol cars gave chase, having an excellent time.

We parked around behind; there were twelve or fourteen vehicles jammed back of Adult Art's single Dumpster; seven phone-repair trucks had lined up like a fleet. Adult's front asphalt lot, plainly visible from US 301 Business, provided room for forty cars but sat empty. This is a small town, Falls. Everybody sees everything, almost. So when you *do* get away with something, you know it; it just means more. Some people will tell you sin is old hat. Not for me. If, once it starts, it's not going to be naughty, then it's not worth wasting a whole afternoon to set up. Sin is bad. Sex is good. Sex is too good not to have a whole lot of bad in it. I say, Let's keep it a little smutty, you know?

Barker called the clerk by name. Barker charged two films—slightly discounted because they'd been used in the booths—those and about thirty bucks in magazines. No money changed hands; he had an account. The section marked LITERATURE milled with phone linemen wearing their elaborate suspension belts. One man, his pelvis ajangle with wrenches and hooks, held up a picture book, called to friends, "Catch *her*, guys. She has got to be your foxiest fox so far." Under his heavy silver gear, I couldn't but notice on this hearty husband and father, jammed up against work pants, the same old famous worldwide pet and problem poking.

~ ~ ~

I drove Barker to his place; he invited me in for a viewing. I'd hoped he would. "World premiere." He smiled, eyes alive as they hadn't been before. "First show on Lake Drive anyways."

The neighborhood, like Barker's looks, had been the rage forty years ago. I figured he must rent rooms in this big mullioned place, but he owned it. The foyer clock showed I might not make it home in time for supper. Lately I'd overused the excuse of working late; even as superintendent of schools there're limits on how much extra time you can devote to your job.

I didn't want to miff a terrific wife.

I figured I'd have a good hour and a half; a lot can happen in an hour and a half. We were now safe inside a private place.

The house had been furnished expensively but some years back. Mission stuff. The Oriental rugs were coated with dust or fur; thick hair hid half their patterns. By accident, I kicked a chewed rubber mouse. The cat toy jingled under a couch, scaring me.

In Barker's kitchen, a crockpot bubbled. Juice hissed out under a Pyrex lid that didn't quite fit. The room smelled of decent beef stew. His counter was layered with fast-food takeout cartons. From among this litter, in a clay pot, one beautiful amaryllis lily—orange, its mouth wider than the throat of a trombone, startled me. It reminded you of something from science fiction, straining like one serious muscle toward daylight.

In the dark adjacent room, Barker kept humming, knocking things over. I heard the clank of movie reels. "Didn't expect company, Dave," he called. "Just clear off a chair and make yourself at home. Momma was a cleaner-upper. Me . . . less. I don't *see* the junk till I get somebody to . . . till somebody drops over, you know?"

I grunted agreement, strolled into his pantry. Here were cans so old you could sell them for the labels. Here was a 1950s tin of vichyssoise I wouldn't have eaten at gunpoint. I slipped along the hall, wandered upstairs. An archive of *National Geographics* rose in yellow columns to the ceiling. "Dave?" he was hollering. "Just settle in or whatever. It'll only take a sec. See, they cut the leaders off both our movies. I'll just do a little splice. I'm fast, though."

"Great."

~ ~ ~

On the far wall of one large room (windows smothered by outside ivy) a calendar from 1959, compliments of a now-defunct savings and loan. Nearby, two Kotex cartons filled with excelsior and stuffed, I saw on closer inspection, with valuable brown-and-white Wedgwood place settings for forty maybe. He really should sell them—I was already mothering Barker. I'd tell him which local dealer would give top dollar.

In one corner, a hooked rug showed a Scottie terrier chasing one red ball downhill. I stepped on it, three hundred moths sputtered up, I backed off, arms flailing before me. Leaning in the doorway, waiting to be called downstairs for movietime, still wearing my business clothes, I suddenly felt a bit uneasy, worried by a famous thought: What are you *doing* here, Dave?

Well, Barker brought me home with him, is what. And, as far back as my memory made it, I'd only wanted just such guys to ask me over. Only they held my interest, my full sympathy.

The kid with the terrible slouch but (for me) an excellent smile, the kid who kept pencils in a plastic see-through satchel that clamped into his loose-leaf notebook. The boy whose mom—even when the guy'd turned fourteen—*made* him use his second-grade Roy Rogers/Dale Evans lunchbox showing them astride their horses, Trigger and Buttermilk. He was the kid other kids didn't bother mocking because—through twelve years of schooling side by side—they'd never noticed him.

Of course, I could tell there were other boys, like me, studying the other boys. But they all looked toward the pink and blond Stephens and Andrews: big-jawed athletic officeholders, guys with shoulders like baby couches, kids whose legs looked turned on lathes, solid newels—calves that summer sports stained mahogany brown, hair coiling over them, bleached by overly chlorinated pools and an admiring sun: yellow-white-gold. But while others' eyes stayed locked on them, I was off admiring finer qualities of some clubfooted Wendell, a kindly bespectacled Theodore. I longed to stoop and tie their dragging shoestrings, ones unfastened so long that the plastic tips had worn to frayed cotton tufts. Math geniuses who forgot to zip up: I wanted to give them dating hints. I'd help them find the right barber. I dreamed of assisting their undressing—me, bathing them with stern brotherly care, me, putting them to bed (poor guys hadn't yet guessed that my interest went past buddyhood). While they slept (I didn't want to cost them any shut-eye), I'd just reach under their covers (always blue) and find that though the world considered these fellows minor minor, they oftentimes proved more major than the muscled boys who frolicked, unashamed, well-known, pink-and-white in gym showers.

What was I *doing* here? Well, my major was art history. I was busy being a collector, is what. And not just someone who can spot (in a museum with a guide to lead him) any old famous masterpiece. No, I was a detective off in the odd corner of a side-street thrift shop. I was uncovering (on sale for the price of the frame!) a little etching by Wyndham Lewis—futuristic dwarves—or a golden cow by Cuyp, one of Vuillard's shuttered parlors painted on a shirt cardboard.

Maybe this very collector's zeal had drawn me to Carol, had led me to fatherhood, to the underrated joys of community. See, I wanted everything—even to be legit. Nothing was so obvious or subtle that I wouldn't try it once. I prided myself on knowing what I liked and going shamelessly after it. Everybody notices grace. But appreciating perfect clumsiness, that requires the real skill.

"Won't be long now!" I heard Barker call.

"All *right*," I hollered, exactly as my sons would.

~ ~ ~

I eased into a messy office upstairs and, among framed documents and pictures, recognized Barker's grandfather. He looked just like Barker but fattened up and given lessons. During the fifties, the granddad served as mayor of our nearby capital city. Back then, such collar-ad looks were still admired, voted into office.

A framed news photo showed the mayor, hair oiled, presenting horse-topped trophies to young girls in jodhpurs. They blinked up at him, four fans, giggling. Over the wide loud tie, his grin showed an actor's worked-at innocence. He'd been a decent mayor—fair to all, paving streets in the black district, making parks of vacant lots. Good till he got nabbed with his hand in the till. Like Barker's, this was a face almost too pure to trust. When you observed the eyes of young Barker downstairs—it was like looking at a *National Geographic* close-up of some exotic Asian deer—you could admire the image forever, it wouldn't notice or resist your admiration. It had the static beauty of an angel. Designed. That unaffected and willing to serve. His character was like an angel's own—the perfect gofer.

I heard Barker humming Broadway ballads, knocking around ice trays. I opened every door on this hall. Why not? The worse the housekeeping got, the better I liked it. The tenderer I felt about the guy downstairs. One room had seven floor lamps in it, two standing, five resting on their sides, one plugged in. Shades were snare-drum shaped, the delicate linings frayed and split like fabric from old negligees.

I closed all doors. I heard him mixing drinks. I felt that buzz and ringing you learn to recognize as the sweet warning sign of a sure thing. Still, I have been wrong.

I checked my watch. "Ready," he called, "when you are." I passed the bathroom. I bet Barker hadn't done a load of laundry since last March or April. A thigh-high pile made a moat around the tub. I lifted some boxer shorts. (Boxers show low self-esteem, bodywise; my kind of guy always wears them and assumes that every other man on earth wears boxers too.) These particular shorts were pin-striped and had little red New York Yankee logos rashed everywhere. They surely needed some serious bleaching.

~ ~ ~

There he stood, grinning. He'd been busy stirring instant iced tea, two tall glasses with maps of Ohio stenciled on them. I didn't ask, Why Ohio? Barker seemed pleased, quicker-moving, the host. He'd rolled up his sleeves, the skin as fine as sanded ashwood. The icebox freezer was a white glacier dangling roots like a molar's. From one tiny hole in it, Barker fished a gin bottle; he held the opened pint to one tea glass and smiled. "Suit you?"

"Gin and iced tea? Sure." Seducers/seducees must remain flexible.

"Say when, pal." I said so. Barker appeared full of antsy mischief.

For him, I saw, this was still his mother's house. With her dead, he could do as he liked; having an illicit guest here pleased him. Barker cultivated the place's warehouse look. He let cat hair coat his mom's prized rugs; it felt daring to leave the stag-movie projector and screen set up in the den full-time, just to shock his Florida sisters.

I couldn't help myself. "Hey, buddy, where *is* this cat?" I nodded toward the hallway's gray fluff balls.

"Hunh? Oh. There's six. Two mother ones and four kid ones. All super-shy but each one's really different. Good company."

He carried our tea glasses on a deco chrome tray; the film-viewing room was just ten feet from the kitchen. Dark in here. Ivy vines eclipsed the sunset; leaf green made our couch feel underwater. I slumped deep into its dated scalloped cushions.

Sipping, we leaned back. It seemed that we were waiting for a signal: Start. I didn't want to watch a movie. But, also, I did. I longed to hear this nice fellow tell me something, a story, anything, but I worried: talking could spoil whatever else might happen. I only half knew what I hoped for. I felt scared Barker might not understand my particular kind of tenderness. Still, I was readier and readier to find out, to risk making a total fool of myself. Everything worthwhile requires that, right?

I needed to say something next.

"So," is what I said. "Tell me. So tell me something . . . about yourself. Something I should know, Barker." And I added that, oh, I really appreciated his hospitality. It was nothing; he shrugged, then pressed back. He made a throaty sound like a story starting. "Well. Something plain, Dave? Or something . . . kind of spicy?"

"Both," I said. Education does pay off. I know to at least ask for everything.

~ ~ ~

"Okay." His voice dipped half an octave. The idea of telling had relaxed Barker. I could see it. Listening to him relax relaxed me.

~ ~ ~

"See, they sent my granddad to jail. *For* something. I won't say what. He did do it; still, we couldn't picture prison—for him. My mom and sisters were so ashamed that at first they wouldn't drive out to see him. I wanted to. Nobody'd take me. I called up prison to ask about visiting hours. I made myself sound real deep, like a man, so they'd tell me. I was eleven. So when the prison guy gave me the times, he goes, 'Well, thank you for calling, ma'am.' I had to laugh.

"They'd put him in that state pen out on the highway, the work farm. It's halfway to Tarboro, and I rode my bike clear out there. It was busy, a Saturday. I had to keep to the edge of the interstate. Teenagers in two convertibles threw beer cans at me. Finally, when I got to the prison, men said I couldn't come in, being a minor and all. Maybe they smelled the beer those hoods'd chucked at my back.

"I wondered what my granddad would do in the same spot (he'd been pretty well known around here), and so I started mentioning my rights, *loud*. The men said 'Okay, okay' and told me to pipe down. They let me in. He sat behind heavy-gauge chicken wire. He looked good, about the same. All the uniforms were gray, but his was pressed and perfect on him—like he'd got to pick the color of everybody else's outfit. You couldn't even hold hands with him. Was like going to the zoo except it was your granddaddy. Right off, he thanks me for coming and he tells me where the key is hid. Key to a shack he owned at the back side of the fairgrounds. You know, out by the pine trees where kids go park at night and do you-know-what?

"He owned this cottage, but seeing as how he couldn't use it—for six to ten—he wanted me to hang out there. Granddad said I should use it whenever I needed to hide or slack off or anything. He said I could keep pets or have a club, whatever I liked.

"He said there was one couch in it, plus a butane stove, but no electric lights. The key stayed under three bricks in the weeds. He said, 'A boy needs a place to go.' I said, 'Thanks.' Then he asked about Mom and the others. I lied: how they were busy baking stuff to bring him, how they'd be out soon, a carful of pies. He made a face and asked which of my sisters had driven me here.

"I said, 'Biked it.' Well, he stared at me. 'Not nine miles and on a Saturday. No. I've earned this, but you shouldn't have to.' He started crying then. It was hard, with the wire between us. Then, you might not believe this, Dave, but a black guard comes over and says, 'No crying.' I didn't know they could do that—boss you like that—but in jail I guess they can do anything they please. Thing is, Granddad stopped. He told me, 'I'll make this up to you, Barker. Some of them say you're not exactly college material, Bark, but we know better. You're the best damn one. But listen, hey, you walk that bike home, you hear me? Concentrate on what I'm saying. It'll be dark by the time you get back to town, but it's worth it. Walk, hear me?" I said I would. I left and went outside. My bike was missing. I figured that some convict's kid had taken it. A poor kid deserved it more than me. Mom would buy me another one. I walked."

~ ~ ~

Barker sat still for a minute and a half. "What else?" I asked.

"You sure?" He turned my way. I nodded. He took a breath.

~ ~ ~

"Well, I hung out in my new cabin a lot. It was just two blocks from the busiest service station in town, but it seemed way off by itself. Nobody used the fairgrounds except during October and the county fair. You could smell pine straw. At night, cars parked for three and four hours. Up one pine tree, a bra was tied—real old and gray now—a joke to everybody but maybe the girl that'd lost it. Out there, pine straw was all litterbugged with used rubbers. I thought they were some kind of white snail or clam or something. I knew they were yucky; I just didn't know *how* they were yucky.

"I'd go into my house and I'd feel grown. I bought me some birds at the old mall with my own money. Two finches. I'd always wanted some Oriental type of birds. I got our dead parakeet's cage, a white one, and I put them in there. They couldn't sing; they just looked good. One was red and the other one was yellow, or one was yellow and one was red, I forget. I bought these seed balls and one pink plastic bird type of toy they could peck at. After school, I'd go sit on my man-sized sofa, with my birdcage nearby, finches all nervous, hopping, constant, me reading my comics—I'd never felt so good, Dave. I knew why my granddad liked it there—no phones, nobody asking him for favors. He'd take long naps on the couch. He'd make himself a cup of tea. He probably paced around the three empty rooms—not empty really: full of cobwebs and these coils of wire.

"I called my finches Huey and Dewey. I loved my Donald Duck comics. I kept all my funny books in alphabetical order in the closet across from my brown sofa. Well, I had everything I needed—a couch, comics, cups of hot tea. I hated tea, but I made about five cups a day because Granddad had bought so many bags in advance and I did like holding a hot mug while I read. So one day I'm sitting there curled up with a new comic—comics are never as good the second time, you know everything that's next—so I'm sitting there happy and I hear my back door slam wide open. Grownups.

"Pronto, I duck into my comics closet, yank the door shut except for just one crack. First I hoped it'd be Granddad and his bust-out gang from the state pen. I didn't believe it, just hoped, you know.

"In walks this young service-station guy from our busy Sunoco place, corner of Sycamore and Bolton. I heard him say, 'Oh yeah, I use this place sometimes. Owner's away awhile.' The mechanic wore a khaki uniform that zipped up its front. 'Look, birds.' A woman's voice. He stared around. 'I guess somebody else is onto Robby's hideaway. Don't sweat it.' He heaved right down onto my couch, onto my new comic, his legs apart. He stared—mean-looking—at somebody else in the room with us. Robby had a reputation. He was about twenty-two, twice my age then—he seemed pretty old. Girls from my class used to hang around the Coke machine at Sunoco just so they could watch him, arm-deep up under motors. He'd scratch himself a lot. He had a *real* reputation. Robby was a redhead, almost a blond. His cloth outfit had so much oil soaked in, it looked to be leather. All day he'd been in sunshine or up underneath leaky cars, and his big round arms were brown and greasy, like . . . cooked food. Well, he kicked off his left loafer. It hit my door and about gave me a heart attack. It did. Then—he was flashing somebody a double-dare kind of look. Robby yanked down his suit's big zipper maybe four inches, showing more tanned chest. The zipper made a chewing sound.

"I sat on the floor in the dark. My head tipped back against a hundred comics. I was gulping, all eyes, arms wrapped around my knees like going off the high dive in a cannonball.

"When the woman sat beside him, I couldn't believe this. You could of knocked me over with one of Huey or Dewey's feathers. See, she was my best friend's momma. I decided, No, must be her identical twin sister (a bad one), visiting from out of town. This lady led Methodist Youth Choir. Don't laugh, but she'd been my Cub Scout den mother. She was about ten years older than Robby, plump and prettyish but real, real scared-looking.

"He says, 'So, you kind of interested, hunh? You sure been giving old Rob some right serious looks for about a year now, ain't it? I was wondering how many lube jobs one Buick could take, lady.'

"She studies her handbag, says, 'Don't call me Lady. My name's Anne. Anne with an *e*.' She added this like to make fun of herself for being here. I wanted to help her. She kept extra still, knees together, holding on to her purse for dear life, not daring to look around. I heard my birds fluttering, worried. I thought: If Robby opens this door, I am dead.

" 'Anne with a *e*, huh? An-nie? Like Little Orphan. Well, Sandy's here, Annie. Sandy's been wanting to get you off by yourself. You ready for your big red dog Sandy?'

" 'I didn't think you'd talk like that,' she said.

"I wanted to bust out of my comics closet and save her. One time on a Cub Scout field trip to New York City, the other boys laughed because I thought the Empire State Building was called something else. I said I couldn't wait to see the Entire State Building. Well, they sure ragged me. I tried to make them see how it *was* big and all. I tried to make them see the logic. She said she understood how I'd got that. She said it was right 'original.' We took the elevator. I tried to make up for it by eating nine hot dogs on a dare. Then I looked off the edge. That didn't help. I got super-sick, Dave. The other mothers said I'd brought it on myself. But she was so nice, she said that being sick was nobody's fault. Mrs. . . . the lady, she wet her blue hankie at a water fountain and held it to my head and told me not to look. She got me a postcard, so when I got down to the ground I could study what I'd almost seen. Now, with her in trouble in my own shack, I felt like I should rescue her. She was saying, 'I don't know what I expected you to talk like, Robby. But not like this, not cheap, please.'

"Then he grinned, he howled like a dog. She laughed anyway. Huey and Dewey went wild in their cage. Robby held both his hands limp in front of him and panted like a regular hound. Then he asked her to help him with his zipper. She wouldn't. Well then, Robby got mad, said, 'It's my lunch hour. You ain't a customer *here*, lady. It's your husband's silver-gray Electra parked out back. You brought me here. You've got yourself into this. You been giving me the look for about a year. I been a gentleman so far. Nobody's forcing you. It ain't a accident you're here with me. But hey, you can leave. Get out. Go on.'

"She sighed but stayed put, sitting there like in a waiting room. Not looking, kneecaps locked together, handbag propped on her knees. Her fingers clutched that bag like her whole life was in it. 'Give me that.' He snatched the purse and, swatting her hands away, opened it. He prodded around, pulled out a tube of lipstick, said, 'Annie, sit still.' She did. She seemed as upset as she was interested. I told myself, She *could* leave. I stayed in the dark. So much was happening in a half-inch stripe of sunshine. The lady didn't move. Robby put red on her mouth—past her mouth, too much of it. She said, 'Please, Robby.' ' "Sandy," ' he told her, 'You Annie, me Sandy Dog. Annie Girl, Sandy Boy. Sandy show Annie.' He made low growling sounds. 'Please,' she tried, but her mouth was stretched from how he kept painting it. 'I'm not sure,' the lady said. 'I wanted to know you better, yes. But now I don't feel . . . sure.' 'You will, Annie Mae. Open your Little Orphan shirt.' She didn't understand him. ' "Blouse" then, fancy pants, open your "Blouse," lady.' She did it but so slow. 'Well,' she said. 'I don't know about you, Robby. I really don't.' But she took her shirt off anyhow.

"My den mother was shivering in a bra, arms crossed over her. First his black hands pushed each arm down, studying her. Then Robby pulled at his zipper so his whole chest showed. He put the lipstick in her hand and showed her how to draw circles on the tops of his—you know, on his nipples. Then he took the tube and made X's over the dots she'd drawn. They both looked down at his chest. I didn't understand. It seemed like a kind of target practice. Next he snapped her bra up over her collarbones and he lipsticked hers. Next he threw the tube across the room against my door—but, since his shoe hit, this didn't surprise me so much. Robby howled like a real dog. My poor finches were just chirping and flying against their cage, excited by animal noises. She was shaking her head. 'You'd think a person such as myself . . . I'm having serious second thoughts here, Robert, really . . . I'm just not too convinced . . . that . . . that we . . .'

"Then Robby got up and stood in front of her, back to me. His hairdo was long on top, the way boys wore theirs then. He lashed it side to side, kept his hands, knuckles down, on his hips. Mrs. . . . . the lady must have been helping him with the zipper. I heard it slide. I only guessed what they were starting to do. I'd been told about all this. But, too, I'd been told, say, about the Eiffel Tower (we called it the Eye-ful). I no more expected to have this happening on my brown couch than I thought the Eye-ful would come in and then the Entire State Building would come in and they'd hop onto one another and start . . . rubbing girders, or something.

"I wondered how Bobby had forced the lady to. I felt I should holler, 'Methodist Youth Choir!' I'd remind her who she really was around town. But I knew it'd be way worse for her—getting caught. I had never given this adult stuff much thought before. I sure did now. Since, I haven't thought about too much else for long. Robby made worse doggy yips. He was a genius at acting like a dog. I watched him get down on all fours in front of the lady—he snouted clear up under her skirt, his whole noggin under cloth. Robby made rooting and barking noises— pig, then dog, then dog and pig mixed. It was funny but too scary to laugh at.

"He asked her to call him Big Sandy. She did. 'Big Sandy,' she said. Robby explained he had something to tell his Orphan gal but only in dog talk. 'What?' she asked. He said it, part-talking, part-gargling, his mouth all up under her white legs. She hooked one thigh over his shoulder. One of her shoes fell off. The other—when her toes curled up, then let loose—would snap, snap, snap.

"I watched her eyes roll back, then focus. She seemed to squint clear into my hiding place. She acted drowsy then completely scared awake— like at a horror movie in the worst part—then she'd doze off, then go dead, perk up overly alive, then half dead, then eyes all out like being electrocuted. It was something. She was leader of the whole Methodist Youth Choir. Her voice got bossy and husky, a leader's voice. She went, 'This is wrong, Robby. You're so low, Bobert. You are a sick dog, we'll get in deep trouble, Momma's Sandy. Hungry Sandy, thirsty Sandy. Oh —not that, not there. Oh Jesus Sandy God. You won't tell. How *can* we. I've never. What are we *doing* in this shack? Whose shack? We're just too . . . It's not me here. I'm not *like* this.'

"He tore off her panties and threw them at the birdcage. (Later I found silky britches on top of the cage, Huey and Dewey going ga-ga, thinking it was a pink cloud from heaven.) I watched grownups do every-thing fast, then easy, back to front, speeding up. They slowed down and seemed to be feeling sorry, but I figured this was just to make it all last longer. I never heard such human noises. Not out of people free from jail or the state nuthouse. I mean, I'd heard boys make car sounds, 'Uh-dunn. Uh-dunn.' But this was like Noah's ark or every zoo and out of two white people's mouths. Both mouths were lipsticked ear to ear. They didn't look nasty but pink as babies. It was wrestling. They never got all the way undressed—I saw things hooking them. Was like watching grownups playing, making stuff up the way kids'll say, 'You be this and I'll be that.' They seemed friskier and younger, nicer. I didn't know how to join in. If I'd opened my door and smiled, they would have perished and *then* broke my neck. I didn't join in, but I sure was dying to.

"By the end, her pale Sunday suit had black grease handprints on the bottom and up around her neck and shoulders. Wet places stained both people where babies get stained. They'd turned halfway back into babies. They fell against each other, huffing like they'd forgot how grownups sit up straight. I mashed one hand over my mouth to keep from crying or panting, laughing out loud. The more they acted like slobbery babies, the older I felt, watching.

"First she sobbed. He laughed, and then she laughed at how she'd cried. She said, 'What's come over me, Sandy?'

" 'Sandy has.' He stroked her neck. 'And Annie's all over Sandy dog.' He showed her. He blew across her forehead, cooling her off.

"She made him promise not to tell. He said he wouldn't snitch if she'd meet him and his best buddy someplace else. 'Oh, no. No way.' She pulled on her blouse and buttoned it. 'That wasn't part of our agreement, Robert.'

" ' "Agreement"? I like that. My lawyers didn't exactly talk to your lawyers about no agreement. Show me your contract, Annie with a *e*.' Then he dives off the couch and is up under her skirt again. You could see that he liked it even better than the service station. She laughed, she pressed cloth down over his whole working head. Her legs went straight. She could hear him snuffling down up under there. Then Robby hollered, he yodeled right up into Mrs. . . . up into the lady.

"They sort of made up.

"After adults finally limped from sight and even after car doors slammed, I waited—sure they'd come back. I finally sneaked over and picked the pants off my birds' roof. What a mess my couch was! I sat right down on such wet spots as they'd each left. The room smelled like nothing I'd ever smelled before. Too, it smelled like everything I'd ever smelled before but all in one room. Birds still went crazy from the zoo sounds and such tussling. In my own quiet way, Dave, I was going pretty crazy too.

"After that I saw Robby at the station, him winking at everything that moved, making wet sly clicking sounds with his mouth. Whenever I bent over to put air into my new bike's tires, I'd look anywhere except Robby. But he noticed how nervous I acted, and he got to teasing me. He'd sneak up behind and put the toe of his loafer against the seat of my jeans. Lord, I jumped. He liked that. He was some tease, that Robby, flashing his hair around like Lash LaRue. He'd crouch over my Schwinn. The air nozzle in my hand would sound like it was eating the tire. Robby'd say, real low and slimy, 'How you like your air, regular or hi-test, slick?' He'd make certain remarks—'Cat got your tongue, Too-Pretty-By-Half?' He didn't know what I'd seen, but he could smell me remembering. I dreaded him. Of course, Dave, Sunoco was not the only station in town. I worried Robby might force me into my house and down onto the couch. I thought: But he couldn't do anything to *me*. I'm only eleven. Plus, I'm a boy. But next I made pictures in my head, and I knew better. There were ways, I bet. . . .

"I stayed clear of the cabin. I didn't know why. I'd been stuck not nine feet from everything they did. I was scared of getting trapped again. I wanted to just live in that closet, drink tea, eat M&M's, praying they'd come back. Was about six days later I remembered: my birds were alone in the shack. They needed water and feeding every other day. I'd let them down. I worried about finches, out there by their lonesomes. But pretty soon it'd been over a week, ten days, twelve. The longer you stay away from certain things, the harder it is, breaking through to do them right. I told myself, 'Huey and Dewey are total goners now.' I kept clear of finding them—stiff, feet up, on the bottom of the cage. I had dreams.

"I saw my den mother uptown running a church bake sale to help hungry Koreans. She was ordering everybody around like she usually did, charming enough to get away with it. I thought I'd feel super-ashamed to ever see her again. Instead I rushed right up. I chatted too much, too loud. I wanted to show that I forgave her. Of course, she didn't know I'd seen her do all such stuff with greasy Robby. She just kept looking at me, part-gloating, part-fretting. She handed me a raisin cupcake, free. We gave each other a long look. We partly smiled.

"After two and a half weeks, I knew my finches were way past dead.

I didn't understand why I'd done it. I'd been too lazy or spooked to bike out and do my duty. *I* belonged in prison—finch murderer. Finally I pedaled my bike in that direction. One day, you have to. The shack looked smaller, the paint peeled worse. I found the key under three bricks, unlocked, held my breath. I didn't hear one sound from the front room, no hop, no cheep. Their cage hung from a hook on the wall, and to see into it, I had to stand up on my couch. Millet seed ground between my bare feet and the cushions. Birds had pecked clear through the back of their plastic food dish. It'd been shoved from the inside out, it'd skidded to a far corner of the room. My finches had slipped out their dish's slot. Birds were gone—flown up a chimney or through one pane of busted window glass. Maybe they'd waited a week. When I didn't show up and treat them right, birds broke out. They were now in pinewoods nearby. I wondered if they'd known all along that they could leave, if they'd only stayed because I fed them and was okay company.

"I pictured Huey and Dewey in high pines, blinking. I worried what dull local sparrows would do to such bright birds, hotshots from the mall pet store. Still, I decided that being free sure beat my finches' chances of hanging around here, starving.

"Talk about relief. I started coughing from it, I don't know why. Then I sat down on the couch and cried. I felt something slippery underneath me. I wore my khaki shorts, nothing else—it was late August. I stood and studied what'd been written on couch cushions in lipstick, all caked. Words were hard to read on nappy brown cloth. You could barely make out 'I will do what Robby wants. What Sandy needs worst. So help me Dog.'

"I thought of her. I wanted to fight for her, but I knew that, strong as the lady was, she did pretty much what she liked. She wouldn't be needing me. I sat again. I pulled my shorts down. Then I felt cool stripes get printed over my brown legs and white butt. Lipstick, parts of red words stuck onto my skin—'wi' from 'will,' the whole word 'help.' I stretched out full length. My birds didn't hop from perch to perch or nibble at their birdie toy. Just me now. My place felt still as any church. Something had changed. I touched myself, and—for the first time, with my bottom all sweetened by lipstick—I got real results.

"Was right after this I traded in my model cars, swapped every single comic for one magazine. It showed two sailors and twin sisters in a hotel, doing stuff. During the five last pictures, a dark bellboy joined in. Was then that my collection really started. The End, I guess. The rest is just being an adult."

~ ~ ~

Barker sat quiet. I finally asked what'd happened to his grandfather. How about Robby and the den mother?

"In jail. My granddad died. Of a broken heart, Mom said. Robby moved. He never was one to stay anyplace too long. One day he didn't show up at Sunoco and that was it. Mrs. . . . the lady, she's still right here in Falls, still a real leader. Not two days back, I ran into her at the mall, collecting canned goods to end world hunger. We had a nice chat. Her son's a lawyer in Marietta, Georgia, now. She looks about the same, really—I love the way she looks, always have. Now, when we talk, I can tell she's partly being nice to me because I never left town or went to college and she secretly thinks I'm not too swift. But since I kept *her* secret, I feel like we're even. I just smile back. I figure, whatever makes people kind to you is fine. She can see there's something extra going on, but she can't name it. It just makes her grin and want to give me little things. It's one of ten trillion ways you can love somebody. We do, love each other. I'm sure. Nobody ever knew about Robby. She got away with it. More power to her. Still leads the Youth Choir. Last year they won the Southeast Chorus prize, young people's division. They give concerts all over. Her husband loves her. She said winning the prize was the most fulfilling moment of her life. I wondered. I guess everybody does some one wild thing now and then. They should. It's what you'll have to coast on when you're old. You know?" I nodded. He sat there, still.

"Probably not much of a story." Barker shrugged. "But back then it was sure something, to see all that right off the bat, your first time out. I remember being so shocked to know that men want to. *And* women. I'd figured that only one person at a time would need it, and they'd have to knock down the other person and force them to, every time. But when I saw that, no, everybody wants to do it and how there are no rules in it, I couldn't look straight at a grownup for days. I'd see that my mom's slacks had zippers in them, I'd near about die. I walked around town, hands stuffed deep in my pockets. My head was hanging, and I acted like I was in mourning for something. But hey, I was really just waking up. What got me onto all *that*? You about ready for a movie, Dave? Boy, I haven't talked so much in months. It's what you get for asking, I guess." He laughed.

I thanked Barker for his story. I told him it made sense to me.

"Well, thanks for saying so anyhow."

~ ~ ~

He started fidgeting with the projector. I watched. I knew him better now. I felt so much for him. I wanted to save him. I couldn't breathe correctly.

"Here goes." He toasted his newest film, then snapped on the large and somehow sinister antique machine.

The movie showed a girl at home reading an illustrated manual, hand in dress, getting herself animated. She made a phone call; you saw the actor answering, and even in a silent film, even given this flimsy premise, you had to find his acting absolutely awful. Barker informed me it was a Swedish movie; they usually started with the girl phoning. "Sometimes it's one guy she calls, sometimes about six. But always the telephones. I don't know why. It's like they just got phones over there and are still proud of them or something." I laughed. What a nice funny thing to say. By now, even the gin and iced tea (with lemon and sugar) tasted like a great idea.

He sat upright beside me. The projector made its placid motorboat racket. Our couch seemed a kind of quilted raft. Movie light was mostly pink; ivy filtered sun to a thin green. Across Barker's neutral white shirt, these tints carried on a silent contest. One room away, the crockpot leaked a bit, hissing. Hallway smelled of stew meat, the need for maid service, back issues, laundry in arrears, one young man's agreeable curried musk. From a corner of my vision, I felt somewhat observed. Cats' eyes. To heck with caution. Let them look!

Barker kept elbows propped on knees, tensed, staring up at the screen, jaw gone slack. In profile against windows' leaf-spotted light, he appeared honest, boyish, wide open. He unbuttoned his top collar button.

~ ~ ~

I heard cars pass, my fellow Rotarians, algebra teachers from my school system. Nobody would understand us being here, beginning to maybe do a thing like this. Even if I went public, dedicated an entire Board of

Education meeting to the topic, after three hours of intelligent confession, with charts and flannel boards and slide projections, I knew that when lights snapped back on I'd look around from face to face, I'd see they still sat wondering your most basic question:

Why, Dave, why?

I no longer noticed what was happening on-screen. Barker's face, lit by rosy movie light, kept changing. It moved me so. One minute, drowsy courtesy; next, a sharp manly smile. I set my glass down on a Florida-shaped coaster. Now, slow, I reached toward the back of his neck—extra-nervous, sure, but that's part of it, you know? My arm wobbled, fear of being really belted, blackmailed, worse. I chose to touch his dark hair, cool as metal.

"Come *on*." He huffed forward, clear of my hand. He kept gazing at the film, not me. Barker grumbled, "The guy she phoned, he hasn't even got to her *house* yet, man."

I saw he had a system. I figured I could wait to understand it.

~ ~ ~

I felt he was my decent kid brother. Our folks had died; I would help him even more now. We'd rent industrial-strength vacuum cleaners. We'd purge this mansion of dinge, yank down tattered maroon draperies, let daylight in. I pictured us, stripped to the waist, painting every upstairs room off-white, our shoulders flecked with droplets, the hair on our chests flecked with droplets.

I'd drive Barker and his Wedgwood to a place where I'm known, Old Mall Antiques. I bet we'd get fifteen to nineteen hundred bucks. Barker would act amazed. In front of the dealer, he'd say, "For *that* junk?" and, laughing, I'd have to shush him. With my encouragement, he'd spend some of the bonus on clothes. We'd donate three generations of *National Geographic*s to a nearby orphanage, if there are any orphanages anymore and nearby. I'd scour Barker's kitchen, defrost the fridge. Slowly, he would find new shape and meaning in his days. He'd commence reading again—nonporn, recent worthy hardbacks. We'd discuss these.

He'd turn up at Little League games, sitting off to one side. Sensing my gratitude at having him high in the bleachers, he'd understand we couldn't speak. But whenever one of my sons did something at bat or out in center field (a pop-up, a body block of a line drive), I would feel

Barker nodding approval as he perched there alone; I'd turn just long enough to see a young bachelor mumbling to himself, shaking his head yes, glad for my boys.

After office hours, once a week, I'd drive over, knock, then walk right in, calling, "Barker? Me."

No answer. Maybe he's napping in a big simple upstairs room, one startling with fresh paint. Six cats stand guard around his bed, two old Persians and their offspring, less Persian, thinner, spottier. Four of them pad over and rub against my pant cuffs; by now they know me.

I settle on the edge of a single bed, I look down at him. Barker's dark hair has fallen against the pillow like an open wing. Bare-chested, the texture of his poreless skin looks finer than the sheets. Under a blue blanket, he sleeps, exhausted from all the cleaning, from renewing his library card, from the fatigue of clothes shopping. I look hard at him; I hear rush-hour traffic crest, then pass its peak. Light in here gets ruddier.

A vein in his neck beats like a clock, only liquid.

—I'm balanced at the pillow end of someone's bed. I'm watching somebody decent sleep. If the law considers this so wicked—then why does it feel like my only innocent activity? Barker wakes. The sun is setting. His face does five things at once: sees somebody here, gets scared, recognizes me, grins a good blurry grin, says just, "You."

~ ~ ~

(They don't want a person to be tender. They could lock me up for everything I love about myself, for everything I love.)

~ ~ ~

Here on the couch, Barker shifted. "Look *now*, Dave. Uh oh, she hears him knocking. See her hop right up? Okay, walking to the door. It's him, all right. He's dressed for winter. That's because they're in Sweden, right, Dave?"

I agreed, with feeling. Then I noted Barker taking the pen caddy from his pocket, placing it on the table before him. Next, with an ancient kind of patience, Barker's torso twisted inches toward me; he lifted my hand, pulled my whole arm up and around and held it by the wrist, hovering in air before his front side as if waiting for some cue. Then Barker, clutching the tender back part of my hand, sighed, "Um-kay.

Now they're really starting to." And he lowered my whole willing palm
—down, down onto it.

I touched something fully familiar to me, yet wholly new.

～　～　～

He bucked with that first famous jolt of human contact after too long,
too long alone without. His spine slackened, but the head shivered to
one side, righted itself, eager to keep the film in sight. I heard six cats go
racing down long hallways, then come thumping back, relaxed enough
to play with me, a stranger, in their house. Praise.

Barker's voice, all gulpy: "I think . . . this movie's going to be a real
good one, Dave. Right up there on my Ten Favorites list. And, you
know? . . ." He *almost* ceased looking at the screen, he *nearly* turned his
eyes my way instead. And the compliment stirred me. "You know?
You're a regular fellow, Dave. I feel like I can trust you. You seem like
. . . one real nice guy."

Through my breathing, I could hear him, breathing, losing breath,
breathing, losing breath.

"Thank you, Barker. Coming from you, that means a lot."

～　～　～

Every true pleasure is a secret.

~ *Ann Beattie* ~

The
Cinderella
Waltz

M ilo and Bradley are creatures of habit. For as long as I've known
him, Milo has worn his moth-eaten blue scarf with the knot hanging so low on his chest that the scarf is useless. Bradley is addicted to
coffee and carries a Thermos with him. Milo complains about the cold,
and Bradley is always a little edgy. They come out from the city every
Saturday—this is not habit but loyalty—to pick up Louise. Louise is even
more unpredictable than most nine-year-olds; sometimes she waits for
them on the front step, sometimes she hasn't even gotten out of bed
when they arrive. One time she hid in a closet and wouldn't leave
with them.

Today Louise has put together a shopping bag full of things she wants
to take with her. She is taking my whisk and my blue pottery bowl, to
make Sunday breakfast for Milo and Bradley; Beckett's *Happy Days*,
which she has carried around for weeks, and which she looks through,
smiling—but I'm not sure she's reading it; and a coleus growing out of
a conch shell. Also, she has stuffed into one side of the bag the fancy
Victorian-style nightgown her grandmother gave her for Christmas, and
into the other she has tucked her octascope. Milo keeps a couple of

---

ANN BEATTIE's novels and short story collections include Secrets and Surprises, Chilly
Scenes of Winter, The Burning House, Falling in Place, Picturing Will, Where
You'll Find Me, *and* What Was Mine. *A brilliantly observant interpreter of contemporary
American manners and mores, Beattie lives in Charlottesville, Virginia.*

dresses, a nightgown, a toothbrush, and extra sneakers and boots at his apartment for her. He got tired of rounding up her stuff to pack for her to take home, so he has brought some things for her that can be left. It annoys him that she still packs bags, because then he has to go around making sure that she has found everything before she goes home. She seems to know how to manipulate him, and after the weekend is over she calls tearfully to say that she has left this or that, which means that he must get his car out of the garage and drive all the way out to the house to bring it to her. One time, he refused to take the hour-long drive, because she had only left a copy of Tolkien's *The Two Towers*. The following weekend was the time she hid in the closet.

"I'll water your plant if you leave it here," I say now.

"I can take it," she says.

"I didn't say you couldn't take it. I just thought it might be easier to leave it, because if the shell tips over, the plant might get ruined."

"Okay," she says. "Don't water it today, though. Water it Sunday afternoon."

I reach for the shopping bag.

"I'll put it back on my windowsill," she says. She lifts the plant out and carries it as if it's made of Steuben glass. Bradley bought it for her last month, driving back to the city, when they stopped at a lawn sale. She and Bradley are both very choosy, and he likes that. He drinks French-roast coffee; she will debate with herself almost endlessly over whether to buy a coleus that is primarily pink or lavender or striped.

"Has Milo made any plans for this weekend?" I ask.

"He's having a couple of people over tonight, and I'm going to help them make crepes for dinner. If they buy more bottles of that wine with the yellow flowers on the label, Bradley is going to soak the labels off for me."

"That's nice of him," I say. "He never minds taking a lot of time with things."

"He doesn't like to cook, though. Milo and I are going to cook. Bradley sets the table and fixes flowers in a bowl. He thinks it's frustrating to cook."

"Well," I say, "with cooking you have to have a good sense of timing. You have to coordinate everything. Bradley likes to work carefully and not be rushed."

I wonder how much she knows. Last week, she told me about a

conversation she'd had with her friend Sarah. Sarah was trying to persuade Louise to stay around on the weekends, but Louise said she always went to her father's. Then Sarah tried to get her to take her along, and Louise said that she couldn't. "You could take her if you wanted to," I said later. "Check with Milo and see if that isn't right. I don't think he'd mind having a friend of yours occasionally."

She shrugged. "Bradley doesn't like a lot of people around," she said.

"Bradley likes you, and if she's your friend I don't think he'd mind."

She looked at me with an expression I didn't recognize; perhaps she thought I was a little dumb, or perhaps she was just curious to see if I would go on. I didn't know how to go on. Like an adult, she gave a little shrug and changed the subject.

~ ~ ~

At ten o'clock Milo pulls into the driveway and honks his horn, which makes a noise like a bleating sheep. He knows the noise the horn makes is funny, and he means to amuse us. There was a time just after the divorce when he and Bradley would come here and get out of the car and stand around silently, waiting for her. She knew that she had to watch for them, because Milo wouldn't come to the door. We were both bitter then, but I got over it. I still don't think Milo would have come into the house again, though, if Bradley hadn't thought it was a good idea. The third time Milo came to pick her up after he'd left home, I went out to invite them in, but Milo said nothing. He was standing there with his arms at his sides like a wooden soldier, and his eyes were as dead to me as if they'd been painted on. It was Bradley whom I reasoned with. "Louise is over at Sarah's right now, and it'll make her feel more comfortable if we're all together when she comes in," I said to him, and Bradley turned to Milo and said, "Hey, that's right. Why don't we go in for a quick cup of coffee?" I looked into the back seat of the car and saw his red Thermos there; Louise had told me about it. Bradley meant that they should come in and sit down. He was giving me even more than I'd asked for.

It would be an understatement to say that I disliked Bradley at first. I was actually afraid of him, afraid even after I saw him, though he was slender, and more nervous than I, and spoke quietly. The second time I saw him, I persuaded myself that he was just a stereotype, but someone who certainly seemed harmless enough. By the third time, I had enough courage to suggest that they come into the house. It was embarrassing for all of us, sitting around the table—the same table where Milo and I had eaten our meals for the years we were married. Before he left, Milo had shouted at me that the house was a farce, that my playing the happy suburban housewife was a farce, that it was unconscionable of me to let things drag on, that I would probably kiss him and say, "How was your day, sweetheart?" and that he should bring home flowers and the evening paper. "Maybe I would!" I screamed back. "Maybe it would be nice to do that, even if we were pretending, instead of you coming home drunk and not caring what had happened to me or to Louise all day." He was holding on to the edge of the kitchen table, the way you'd hold on to the horse's reins in a runaway carriage. "I care about Louise," he said finally. That was the most horrible moment. Until then, until he said it that way, I had thought that he was going through something horrible— certainly something was terribly wrong—but that, in his way, he loved me after all. *"You don't love me?"* I had whispered at once. It took us both aback. It was an innocent and pathetic question, and it made him come and put his arms around me in the last hug he ever gave me. "I'm sorry for you," he said, "and I'm sorry for marrying you and causing this, but you know who I love. I told you who I love." "But you were kidding," I said. "You didn't mean it. You were kidding."

When Bradley sat at the table that first day, I tried to be polite and not look at him much. I had gotten it through my head that Milo was crazy, and I guess I was expecting Bradley to be a horrible parody—Craig Russell doing Marilyn Monroe. Bradley did not spoon sugar into Milo's coffee. He did not even sit near him. In fact, he pulled his chair a little away from us, and in spite of his uneasiness he found more things to start conversations about than Milo and I did. He told me about the ad agency where he worked; he is a designer there. He asked if he could go out on the porch to see the brook—Milo had told him about the stream in the back of our place that was as thin as a pencil but still gave us our own watercress. He went out on the porch and stayed there for at least five minutes, giving us a chance to talk. We didn't say one word until he came back. Louise came home from Sarah's house just as Bradley sat down at the table again, and she gave him a hug as well as us. I could see that she really liked him. I was amazed that I liked him too. Bradley had won and I had lost, but he was as gentle and low-key as if none of it mattered. Later in the week, I called him and asked him to tell me if any free-lance jobs opened in his advertising agency. (I do a little free-lance artwork, whenever I can arrange it.) The week after that, he called and told me about another agency, where they were looking for outside artists. Our calls to each other are always brief and for a purpose, but lately they're not just calls about business. Before Bradley left to scout some picture locations in Mexico, he called to say that Milo had told him that when the two of us were there years ago I had seen one of those big circular bronze Aztec calendars and I had always regretted not bringing it back. He wanted to know if I would like him to buy a calendar if he saw one like the one Milo had told him about.

Today, Milo is getting out of his car, his blue scarf flapping against his chest. Louise, looking out the window, asks the same thing I am wondering: "Where's Bradley?"

Milo comes in and shakes my hand, gives Louise a one-armed hug.

"Bradley thinks he's coming down with a cold," Milo says. "The dinner is still on, Louise. We'll do the dinner. We have to stop at Gristede's when we get back to town, unless your mother happens to have a tin of anchovies and two sticks of unsalted butter."

"Let's go to Gristede's," Louise says. "I like to go there."

"Let me look in the kitchen," I say. The butter is salted, but Milo says that will do, and he takes three sticks instead of two. I have a brainstorm and cut the cellophane on a left-over Christmas present from my aunt—a wicker plate that holds nuts and foil-wrapped triangles of cheese—and sure enough: one tin of anchovies.

"We can go to the museum instead," Milo says to Louise. "Wonderful."

But then, going out the door, carrying her bag, he changes his mind. "We can go to America Hurrah, and if we see something beautiful we can buy it," he says.

They go off in high spirits. Louise comes up to his waist, almost, and I notice again that they have the same walk. Both of them stride forward with great purpose. Last week, Bradley told me that Milo had bought a weather vane in the shape of a horse, made around 1800, at America Hurrah, and stood it in the bedroom, and then was enraged when Bradley draped his socks over it to dry. Bradley is still learning what a perfectionist Milo is and how little sense of humor he has. When we were first married, I used one of our pottery casserole dishes to put my jewelry in, and he nagged me until I took it out and put the dish back in the kitchen cabinet. I remember his saying that the dish looked silly on my dresser because it was obvious what it was and people would think we left our dishes lying around. It was one of the things that Milo wouldn't tolerate, because it was improper.

~ ~ ~

When Milo brings Louise back on Saturday night they are not in a good mood. The dinner was all right, Milo says, and Griffin and Amy and Mark were amazed at what a good hostess Louise had been, but Bradley hadn't been able to eat.

"Is he still coming down with a cold?" I ask. I was still a little shy about asking questions about Bradley.

Milo shrugs. "Louise made him take megadoses of vitamin C all weekend."

Louise says, "Bradley said that taking too much vitamin C was bad for your kidneys, though."

"It's a rotten climate," Milo says, sitting on the living room sofa, scarf and coat still on. "The combination of cold and air pollution . . ."

Louise and I look at each other, and then back at Milo. For weeks now, he has been talking about moving to San Francisco, if he can find work there. (Milo is an architect.) This talk bores me, and it makes Louise nervous. I've asked him not to talk to her about it unless he's actually going to move, but he doesn't seem to be able to stop himself.

"Okay," Milo says, looking at us both. "I'm not going to say anything about San Francisco."

"*California* is polluted," I say. I am unable to stop myself, either.

Milo heaves himself up from the sofa, ready for the drive back to New York. It is the same way he used to get off the sofa that last year he lived here. He would get up, dress for work, and not even go into the kitchen for breakfast—just sit, sometimes in his coat as he was sitting just now, and at the last minute he would push himself up and go out to the driveway, usually without a good-bye, and get in the car and drive off either very fast or very slowly. I liked it better when he made the tires spin in the gravel when he took off.

He stops at the doorway now, and turns to face me. "Did I take all your butter?" he says.

"No," I say. "There's another stick." I point into the kitchen.

"I could have guessed that's where it would be," he says, and smiles at me.

~ ~ ~

When Milo comes the next weekend, Bradley is still not with him. The night before, as I was putting Louise to bed, she said that she had a feeling he wouldn't be coming.

"I had that feeling a couple of days ago," I said. "Usually Bradley calls once during the week."

"He must still be sick," Louise said. She looked at me anxiously. "Do you think he is?"

"A cold isn't going to kill him," I said. "If he has a cold, he'll be okay."

Her expression changed; she thought I was talking down to her. She lay back in bed. The last year Milo was with us, I used to tuck her in and tell her that everything was all right. What that meant was that there had not been a fight. Milo had sat listening to music on the phonograph, with a book or the newspaper in front of his face. He didn't pay very much attention to Louise, and he ignored me entirely. Instead of saying a prayer with her, the way I usually did, I would say to her that everything was all right. Then I would go downstairs and hope that Milo would say the same thing to me. What he finally did say one night was "You might as well find out from me as some other way."

"Hey, are you an old bag lady again this weekend?" Milo says now, stooping to kiss Louise's forehead.

"Because you take some things with you doesn't mean you're a bag lady," she says primly.

"Well," Milo says, "you start doing something innocently, and before you know it it can take you over."

He looks angry and acts as though it's difficult for him to make conversation, even when the conversation is full of sarcasm and double entendres.

"What do you say we get going?" he says to Louise.

In the shopping bag she is taking is her doll, which she has not played with for more than a year. I found it by accident when I went to tuck in a loaf of banana bread that I had baked. When I saw Baby Betsy, deep in the bag, I decided against putting the bread in.

"Okay," Louise says to Milo. "Where's Bradley?"

"Sick," he says.

"Is he too sick to have me visit?"

"Good heavens, no. He'll be happier to see you than to see me."

"I'm rooting some of my coleus to give him," she says. "Maybe I'll give it to him like it is, in water, and he can plant it when it roots."

When she leaves the room, I go over to Milo. "Be nice to her," I say quietly.

"I'm nice to her," he says. "Why does everybody have to act like I'm going to grow fangs every time I turn around?"

"You were quite cutting when you came in."

"I was being self-deprecating." He sighs. "I don't really know why I come here and act this way," he says.

"What's the matter, Milo?"

But now he lets me know he's bored with the conversation. He walks over to the table and picks up a *Newsweek* and flips through it. Louise comes back with the coleus in a water glass.

"You know what you could do," I say. "Wet a napkin and put it around that cutting and then wrap it in foil, and put it in water when you get there. That way, you wouldn't have to hold a glass of water all the way to New York."

She shrugs. "This is okay," she says.

"Why don't you take your mother's suggestion," Milo says. "The water will slosh out of the glass."

"Not if you don't drive fast."

"It doesn't have anything to do with my driving fast. If we go over a bump in the road, you're going to get all wet."

"Then I can put on one of my dresses at your apartment."

"Am I being unreasonable?" Milo says to me.

"I started it," I say. "Let her take it in the glass."

"Would you, as a favor, do what your mother says?" he says to Louise. Louise looks at the coleus and at me.

"Hold the glass over the seat instead of over your lap, and you won't get wet," I say.

"Your first idea was the best," Milo says.

Louise gives him an exasperated look and puts the glass down on the floor, pulls on her poncho, picks up the glass again and says a sullen good-bye to me, and goes out the front door.

"Why is this my fault?" Milo says. "Have I done anything terrible? I—"

"Do something to cheer yourself up," I say, patting him on the back.

He looks as exasperated with me as Louise was with him. He nods his head yes, and goes out the door.

~ ~ ~

"Was everything all right this weekend?" I ask Louise.

"Milo was in a bad mood, and Bradley wasn't even there on Saturday," Louise says. "He came back today and took us to the Village for breakfast."

"What did you have?"

"I had sausage wrapped in little pancakes and fruit salad and a rum bun."

"Where was Bradley on Saturday?"

She shrugs. "I didn't ask him."

She almost always surprises me by being more grown-up than I give her credit for. Does she suspect, as I do, that Bradley has found another lover?

"Milo was in a bad mood when you two left here yesterday," I say.

"I told him if he didn't want me to come next weekend, just to tell me." She looks perturbed, and I suddenly realize that she can sound exactly like Milo sometimes.

"You shouldn't have said that to him, Louise," I say. "You know he wants you. He's just worried about Bradley."

"So?" she says. "I'm probably going to flunk math."

"No, you're not, honey. You got a C-plus on the last assignment."

"It still doesn't make my grade average out to a C."

"You'll get a C. It's all right to get a C."

She doesn't believe me.

"Don't be a perfectionist, like Milo," I tell her. "Even if you got a D, you wouldn't fail."

Louise is brushing her hair—thin, shoulder-length, auburn hair. She is already so pretty and so smart in everything except math that I wonder what will become of her. When I was her age, I was plain and serious and I wanted to be a tree surgeon. I went with my father to the park and held a stethoscope—a real one—to the trunks of trees, listening to their silence. Children seem older now.

"What do you think's the matter with Bradley?" Louise says. She sounds worried.

"Maybe the two of them are unhappy with each other right now."

She misses my point. "Bradley's sad, and Milo's sad that he's unhappy."

I drop Louise off at Sarah's house for supper. Sarah's mother, Martine Cooper, looks like Shelley Winters, and I have never seen her without a glass of Galliano on ice in her hand. She has a strong candy smell. Her husband has left her, and she professes not to care. She has emptied her living room of furniture and put up ballet bars on the walls and dances in a purple leotard to records by Cher and Mac Davis. I prefer to have Sarah come to our house, but her mother is adamant that everything must be, as she puts it, "fifty-fifty." When Sarah visited us a week ago and loved the chocolate pie I had made, I sent two pieces home with her. Tonight, when I left Sarah's house, her mother gave me a bowl of Jell-O fruit salad.

The phone is ringing when I come in the door. It is Bradley.

"Bradley," I say at once, "whatever's wrong, at least you don't have a neighbor who just gave you a bowl of maraschino cherries in green Jell-O with a Reddi Whip flower squirted on top."

"Jesus," he says. "You don't need me to depress you, do you?"

"What's wrong?" I say.

He sighs into the phone. "Guess what?" he says.

"What?"

"I've lost my job."

It wasn't at all what I was expecting to hear. I was ready to hear that he was leaving Milo, and I had even thought that that would serve Milo right. Part of me still wanted him punished for what he did. I was so out of my mind when Milo left me that I used to go over and drink Galliano with Martine Cooper. I even thought seriously about forming a ballet group with her. I would go to her house in the afternoon, and she would hold a tambourine in the air and I would hold my leg rigid and try to kick it.

"That's awful," I say to Bradley. "What happened?"

"They said it was nothing personal—they were laying off three people. Two other people are going to get the ax at the agency within the next six months. I was the first to go, and it was nothing personal. From twenty thousand bucks a year to nothing, and nothing personal, either."

"But your work is so good. Won't you be able to find something again?"

"Could I ask you a favor?" he says. "I'm calling from a phone booth. I'm not in the city. Could I come talk to you?"

"Sure," I say.

It seems perfectly logical that he should come alone to talk—perfectly logical until I actually see him coming up the walk. I can't entirely believe it. A year after my husband has left me, I am sitting with his lover—a man, a person I like quite well—and trying to cheer him up because he is out of work. ("Honey," my father would say, "listen to Daddy's heart with the stethoscope, or you can turn it toward you and listen to your own heart. You won't hear anything listening to a tree." Was my persistence willfulness, or belief in magic? Is it possible that I hugged Bradley at the door because I'm secretly glad he's down-and-out, the way I used to be? Or do I really want to make things better for him?)

He comes into the kitchen and thanks me for the coffee I am making, drapes his coat over the chair he always sits in.

"What am I going to do?" he asks.

"You shouldn't get so upset, Bradley," I say. "You know you're good. You won't have trouble finding another job."

"That's only half of it," he says. "Milo thinks I did this deliberately. He told me I was quitting on him. He's very angry at me. He fights with me, and then he gets mad that I don't enjoy eating dinner. My stomach's upset, and I can't eat anything."

"Maybe some juice would be better than coffee."

"If I didn't drink coffee, I'd collapse," he says.

I pour coffee into a mug for him, coffee into a mug for me.

"This is probably very awkward for you," he says. "That I come here and say all this about Milo."

"What does he mean about your quitting on him?"

"He said . . . he actually accused me of doing badly deliberately, so they'd fire me. I was so afraid to tell him the truth when I was fired that I pretended to be sick. Then I really *was* sick. He's never been angry at me this way. Is this always the way he acts? Does he get a notion in his head for no reason and then pick at a person because of it?"

I try to remember. "We didn't argue much," I say. "When he didn't want to live here, he made me look ridiculous for complaining when I knew something was wrong. He expects perfection, but what that means is that you do things his way."

"I *was*. I never wanted to sit around the apartment, the way he says I did. I even brought work home with me. He made me feel so bad all week that I went to a friend's apartment for the day on Saturday. Then he said I had walked out on the problem. He's a little paranoid. I was listening to the radio, and Carole King was singing 'It's Too Late,' and he came into the study and looked very upset, as though I had planned for the song to come on. I couldn't believe it."

"Whew," I say, shaking my head. "I don't envy you. You have to stand up to him. I didn't do that. I pretended the problem would go away."

"And now the problem sits across from you drinking coffee, and you're being nice to him."

"I know it. I was just thinking we look like two characters in some soap opera my friend Martine Cooper would watch."

He pushes his coffee cup away from him with a grimace.

"But anyway, I like you now," I say. "And you're exceptionally nice to Louise."

"I took her father," he says.

"Bradley—I hope you don't take offense, but it makes me nervous to talk about that."

"I don't take offense. But how can you be having coffee with me?"

"You invited yourself over so you could ask that?"

"Please," he says, holding up both hands. Then he runs his hands through his hair. "Don't make me feel illogical. He does that to me, you know. He doesn't understand it when everything doesn't fall right into line. If I like fixing up the place, keeping some flowers around, therefore I can't like being a working person too, therefore I deliberately sabotage myself in my job." Bradley sips his coffee.

"I wish I could do something for him," he says in a different voice.

This is not what I expected, either. We have sounded like two wise adults, and then suddenly he has changed and sounds very tender. I realize the situation is still the same. It is two of them on one side and me on the other, even though Bradley is in my kitchen.

"Come and pick up Louise with me, Bradley," I say. "When you see Martine Cooper, you'll cheer up about your situation."

He looks up from his coffee. "You're forgetting what I'd look like to Martine Cooper," he says.

~   ~   ~

Milo is going to California. He has been offered a job with a new San Francisco architectural firm. I am not the first to know. His sister, Deanna, knows before I do and mentions it when we're talking on the phone. "It's middle-age crisis," Deanna says sniffily. "Not that I need to tell you." Deanna would drop dead if she knew the way things are. She is scandalized every time a new display is put up in Bloomingdale's window. ("Those mannequins had eyes like an Egyptian princess, and *rags*. I swear to you, they had mops and brooms and ragged gauze dresses on, with whores' shoes—stiletto heels that prostitutes wear.")

I hang up from Deanna's call and tell Louise I'm going to drive to the gas station for cigarettes. I go there to call New York on their pay phone.

"Well, I only just knew," Milo says. "I found out for sure yesterday, and last night Deanna called and so I told her. It's not like I'm leaving tonight."

He sounds elated, in spite of being upset that I called. He's happy in the way he used to be on Christmas morning. I remember him once running into the living room in his underwear and tearing open the gifts we'd been sent by relatives. He was looking for the eight-slice toaster he was sure we'd get. We'd been given two-slice, four-slice, and six-slice toasters, but then we got no more. "Come out, my eight-slice beauty!" Milo crooned, and out came an electric clock, a blender, and an expensive electric pan.

"When are you leaving?" I ask him.

"I'm going out to look for a place to live next week."

"Are you going to tell Louise yourself this weekend?"

"Of course," he says.

"And what are you going to do about seeing Louise?"

"Why do you act as if I don't like Louise?" he says. "I will occasionally come back East, and I will arrange for her to fly to San Francisco on her vacations."

"It's going to break her heart."

"No it isn't. Why do you want to make me feel bad?"

"She's had so many things to adjust to. You don't have to go to San Francisco right now, Milo."

"It happens, if you care, that my own job here is in jeopardy. This is a real chance for me, with a young firm. They really want me. But anyway, all we need in this happy group is to have you bringing in a couple of hundred dollars a month with your graphic work and me destitute and Bradley so devastated by being fired that of course he can't even look for work."

"I'll bet he is looking for a job," I say.

"Yes. He read the want ads today and then fixed a crab quiche."

"Maybe that's the way you like things, Milo, and people respond to you. You forbade me to work when we had a baby. Do you say anything encouraging to him about finding a job, or do you just take it out on him that he was fired?"

There is a pause, and then he almost seems to lose his mind with impatience.

"I can hardly *believe*, when I am trying to find a logical solution to all our problems, that I am being subjected, by telephone, to an unflattering psychological analysis by my ex-wife." He says this all in a rush.

"All right, Milo. But don't you think that if you're leaving so soon you ought to call her, instead of waiting until Saturday?"

Milo sighs very deeply. "I have more sense than to have important conversations on the telephone," he says.

∼ ∼ ∼

Milo calls on Friday and asks Louise whether it wouldn't be nice if both of us came in and spent the night Saturday and if we all went to brunch together Sunday. Louise is excited. I never go into town with her.

Louise and I pack a suitcase and put it in the car Saturday morning. A cutting of ivy for Bradley has taken root, and she has put it in a little green plastic pot for him. It's heartbreaking, and I hope that Milo notices and has a tough time dealing with it. I am relieved I'm going to be there when he tells her, and sad that I have to hear it at all.

In the city, I give the car to the garage attendant, who does not remember me. Milo and I lived in the apartment when we were first married, and moved when Louise was two years old. When we moved, Milo kept the apartment and sublet it—a sign that things were not going well, if I had been one to heed such a warning. What he said was that if we were ever rich enough we could have the house in Connecticut *and* the apartment in New York. When Milo moved out of the house, he went right back to the apartment. This will be the first time I have visited there in years.

Louise strides in in front of me, throwing her coat over the brass coatrack in the entranceway—almost too casual about being there. She's the hostess at Milo's, the way I am at our house.

He has painted the walls white. There are floor-length white curtains in the living room, where my silly flowered curtains used to hang. The walls are bare, the floor has been sanded, a stereo as huge as a computer stands against one wall of the living room, and there are four speakers.

"Look around," Milo says. "Show your mother around, Louise."

I am trying to remember if I have ever told Louise that I used to live in this apartment. I must have told her, at some point, but I can't remember it.

"Hello," Bradley says, coming out of the bedroom.

"Hi, Bradley," I say. "Have you got a drink?"

Bradley looks sad. "He's got champagne," he says, and looks nervously at Milo.

"No one *has* to drink champagne," Milo says. "There's the usual assortment of liquor."

"Yes," Bradley says. "What would you like?"

"Some bourbon, please."

"Bourbon." Bradley turns to go into the kitchen. He looks different; his hair is different—more wavy—and he is dressed as though it were summer, in straight-legged white pants and black leather thongs.

"I want Perrier water with strawberry juice," Louise says, tagging along after Bradley. I have never heard her ask for such a thing before. At home, she drinks too many Cokes. I am always trying to get her to drink fruit juice.

Bradley comes back with two drinks and hands me one. "Did you want anything?" he says to Milo.

"I'm going to open the champagne in a moment," Milo says. "How have you been this week, sweetheart?"

"Okay," Louise says. She is holding a pale-pink, bubbly drink. She sips it like a cocktail.

Bradley looks very bad. He has circles under his eyes, and he is ill at ease. A red light begins to blink on the phone-answering device next to where Bradley sits on the sofa, and Milo gets out of his chair to pick up the phone.

"Do you really want to talk on the phone right now?" Bradley asks Milo quietly.

Milo looks at him. "No, not particularly," he says, sitting down again. After a moment, the red light goes out.

"I'm going to mist your bowl garden," Louise says to Bradley, and slides off the sofa and goes to the bedroom. "Hey, a little toadstool is growing in here!" she calls back. "Did you put it there, Bradley?"

"It grew from the soil mixture, I guess," Bradley calls back. "I don't know how it got there."

"Have you heard anything about a job?" I ask Bradley.

"I haven't been looking, really," he says. "You know."

Milo frowns at him. "Your choice, Bradley," he says. "I didn't ask you to follow me to California. You can stay here."

"No," Bradley says. "You've hardly made me feel welcome."

"Should we have some champagne—all four of us—and you can get back to your bourbons later?" Milo says cheerfully.

We don't answer him, but he gets up anyway and goes to the kitchen. "Where have you hidden the tulip-shaped glasses, Bradley?" he calls out after a while.

"They should be in the cabinet on the far left," Bradley says.

"You're going with him?" I say to Bradley. "To San Francisco?"

He shrugs and won't look at me. "I'm not quite sure I'm wanted," he says quietly.

The cork pops in the kitchen. I look at Bradley, but he won't look up. His new hairdo makes him look older. I remember that when Milo left me I went to the hairdresser the same week and had bangs cut. The next week, I went to a therapist, who told me it was no good trying to hide from myself. The week after that, I did dance exercise with Martine Cooper, and the week after that the therapist told me not to dance if I wasn't interested in dancing.

"I'm not going to act like this is a funeral," Milo says, coming in with the glasses. "Louise, come in here and have champagne! We have something to have a toast about."

Louise comes into the living room suspiciously. She is so used to being refused even a sip of wine from my glass or her father's that she no longer even asks. "How come I'm in on this?" she asks.

"We're going to drink a toast to me," Milo says.

Three of the four glasses are clustered on the table in front of the sofa. Milo's glass is raised. Louise looks at me, to see what I'm going to say. Milo raises his glass even higher. Bradley reaches for a glass. Louise picks up a glass. I lean forward and take the last one.

"This is a toast to me," Milo says, "because I am going to be going to San Francisco."

It was not a very good or informative toast. Bradley and I sip from our glasses. Louise puts her glass down hard and bursts into tears, knocking the glass over. The champagne spills onto the cover of a big art book about the Unicorn Tapestries. She runs into the bedroom and slams the door.

Milo looks furious. "Everybody lets me know just what my insufficiencies are, don't they?" he says. "Nobody minds expressing himself. We have it all right out in the open."

"He's criticizing me," Bradley murmurs, his head still bowed. "It's because I was offered a job here in the city and I didn't automatically refuse it."

I turn to Milo. "Go say something to Louise, Milo," I say. "Do you think that's what somebody who isn't brokenhearted sounds like?"

He glares at me and stomps into the bedroom, and I can hear him talking to Louise reassuringly. "It doesn't mean you'll *never* see me," he says. "You can fly there, I'll come here. It's not going to be that different."

"You lied!" Louise screams. "You said we were going to brunch."

"We are. We are. I can't very well take us to brunch before Sunday, can I?"

"You didn't say you were going to San Francisco. What *is* San Francisco, anyway?"

"I just said so. I bought us a bottle of champagne. You can come out as soon as I get settled. You're going to like it there."

Louise is sobbing. She has told him the truth, and she knows it's futile to go on.

~ ~ ~

By the next morning, Louise acts the way I acted—as if everything were just the same. She looks calm, but her face is small and pale. She looks very young. We walk into the restaurant and sit at the table Milo has reserved. Bradley pulls out a chair for me, and Milo pulls out a chair for Louise, locking his finger with hers for a second, raising her arm above her head, as if she were about to take a twirl.

She looks very nice, really. She has a ribbon in her hair. It is cold, and she should have worn a hat, but she wanted to wear the ribbon. Milo has good taste: the dress she is wearing, which he bought for her, is a hazy purple plaid, and it sets off her hair.

"Come with me. Don't be sad," Milo suddenly says to Louise, pulling her by the hand. "Come with me for a minute. Come across the street to the park for just a second, and we'll have some space to dance, and your mother and Bradley can have a nice quiet drink."

She gets up from the table and, looking long-suffering, backs into her coat, which he is holding for her, and the two of them go out. The waitress comes to the table, and Bradley orders three Bloody Marys and a Coke, and eggs Benedict for everyone. He asks the waitress to wait awhile before she brings the food. I have hardly slept at all, and having a drink is not going to clear my head. I have to think of things to say to Louise later, on the ride home.

"He takes so many *chances*," I say. "He pushes things so far with people. I don't want her to turn against him."

"No," he says.

"Why are you going, Bradley? You've seen the way he acts. You know that when you get out there he'll pull something on you. Take the job and stay here."

Bradley is fiddling with the edge of his napkin. I study him. I don't know who his friends are, how old he is, where he grew up, whether he believes in God, or what he usually drinks. I'm shocked that I know so little, and I reach out and touch him. He looks up.

"Don't go," I say quietly.

The waitress puts the glasses down quickly and leaves, embarrassed because she thinks she's interrupted a tender moment. Bradley pats my hand on his arm. Then he says the thing that has always been between us, the thing too painful for me to envision or think about.

"I love him," Bradley whispers.

We sit quietly until Milo and Louise come into the restaurant, swinging hands. She is pretending to be a young child, almost a baby, and I wonder for an instant if Milo and Bradley and I haven't been playing house too—pretending to be adults.

"Daddy's going to give me a first-class ticket," Louise says. "When I go to California we're going to ride in a glass elevator to the top of the Fairman Hotel."

"The Fairmont," Milo says, smiling at her.

Before Louise was born, Milo used to put his ear to my stomach and say that if the baby turned out to be a girl he would put her into glass slippers instead of bootees. Now he is the prince once again. I see them in a glass elevator, not long from now, going up and up, with the people below getting smaller and smaller, until they disappear.

~ *Stephen Greco* ~

Good
with
Words

L ast night I dreamed I went back to the Mineshaft. I knew I had come
home even before entering the unmarked door and climbing the
flight of stairs to pay my five dollars. Outside, on the sidewalk—where
I'd sometimes linger and survey the street action that was often hot
enough to induce me to skip the bar entirely—I savored the exhaust that
was being sucked out of the bar's downstairs suite by powerful industrial
fans. Beer, piss, poppers, leather, sweat—the smells blended into a perfume more reassuringly familiar than the Bal à Versailles I remember from
my mother's dressing table.

The first beer at the upstairs bar was just a formality. I gulped it down
and immediately asked the tattooed bartender for another, the second one
to sip—a prop, really, to keep my hands occupied until something better
came along. Inside, a typical evening was under way: someone in the
sling, ingeniously concealing someone else's arm up to the elbow; on-
lookers rapt, then moving on casually, to survey some of the other at-
tractions that were taking form in the shadows; assorted human
undergrowth here and there, some of it inert and some gently undulating
like deep-sea flora. On the platform toward the back, a tall blond man

---

STEPHEN GRECO is an editor with Interview. *Originally published as a safe-sex
porn story in the magazine* Advocate Men, *"Good with Words" has gone on to have a
mythic life of its own; it is as incendiary, unflinching, and erotic a response to the AIDS
epidemic as has yet been written.*

was getting blown. I stood nearby for a while and watched—evaluating his musculature with a touch, scrutinizing his gestures for a flaw in that impeccable attitude, observing the degree to which his arched posture expressed a belief in this kind of recreation—then I turned and went downstairs.

I always spit in the back stairway, as a sort of a ritual of purification, I suppose. Below, things were steamier, and I adjusted my fly accordingly. The piss room was packed, unnavigable, with dense clumps of flesh around each tub and growing outward from the corners. So noting who was doing what, I passed along the edge of it all, slowly, as if in a dream—which it was, of course—though even when it wasn't, back when the Mineshaft was open, it all seemed to be. A wet dream; some kind of prenatal fantasy, dark and sheltered; bathed in the music the management knew was perfect for down there, slowish, hazy waves of taped sound that always struck me as exactly what music would sound like if heard from inside the womb; a dream engulfed, as the evening built to its climax, by the fluids—no, the tides—of life itself.

I walked past the posing niche and entered the club's farthest recess, the downstairs bar. There, on his knees, was Paul. Known more widely than seemed possible as the Human Urinal, Paul had installed himself in one of his favorite spots for the early part of an evening, a relatively open and well-lighted place that invited inspection but did not permit extended scenes. Paul moved around, you see. As an evening progressed he would migrate to increasingly more auspicious locations until, around dawn, you would probably find him in what was by then a hub of the Mineshaft's hardest-core action, the upstairs men's room, where he planted himself efficiently, mouth gaping, eyes glazed, between the two nonhuman fixtures.

How I admired that man and his dedication! What fun we would have in the old days, both here and with the straight boys at the Hellfire Club! Paul is immobile as I pass, but I see by his slowly shifting eyes that he knows I've arrived. And he's glad: even in the dark I sense that his pupils have dilated a fraction when he notices I'm carrying a can of beer. I raise it slightly in his direction in a kind of toast. He understands. I stop for a moment opposite him, the constant flow of men between us. Then, because I feel I should follow through with a sympathetic gesture, I bring the can to my lips while pissing, almost incidentally, in my jeans.

I don't look down, of course, but I know that a dark patch has appeared at the top of my right thigh. And I know that Paul sees it too—but since manners are everything in affairs of the heart, we smile no acknowledgment. Burping unceremoniously, I move off toward the bar. . . .

I was intending to return to Paul after getting another beer, but then I woke up. A garbage truck was roaring outside my bedroom window, and the dream was over.

~   ~   ~

Later that day I called my friend Albert, with whom I'd visited the Mineshaft on occasion. When I mentioned my dream he was unimpressed.

"Of course you're dreaming about the place, puss. It's because you can't go there anymore. What other options *do* we have nowadays for handling our genius, we who have dared to build a world that allowed us to encounter it repeatedly?"

It was like Albert to use the word *genius* that way, with overtones of "essential spirit," even "demon." Albert's good with words, which he says is lucky. He's one of those people who seem able to enjoy exchanging them during sex almost as much as he did those fluids that are now forbidden. Albert sighed and added that we should be thankful to have glimpsed the "golden age."

We discussed some of the old faces. It turns out that he'd been talking to the real Paul, whom I hadn't run into for quite some time. I was surprised to learn that my fastidious friend actually once traded phone numbers with the Human Urinal and recently has been indulging in a bit of phone J.O. with him. It was "nothing kinky," Albert insisted. "We just chat for hours like schoolgirls, about choking body-builder cops with the severed penises of their teenage sons. What could be safer than that?"

I was happy to hear that Paul is still kicking. In fact, I was relieved, since it won't do to make assumptions anymore about people we used to see around. Yeah, Paul always maintained that he was exclusively oral, never anal, but the fact is that none of us is sure whether that or any particular limit is enough to guarantee someone's safety under present conditions. Wasn't one of Paul's favorite numbers, after all, to beg feverishly for "clap dick" and to revel in the disgust this elicited from many men who took him literally? I don't know—maybe the request was meant literally; since gonorrhea was so readily curable, it never seemed to matter much. It was strange, I know, but I realized when talking to Albert how fond of Paul's creative perversity I'd become, how much I missed his "genius" in a way that would be difficult to explain to someone who'd never experienced firsthand the catalytic charm of old-fashioned sex clubs.

I knew Paul slightly. Though not a chatty sort, he would sometimes expose a portion of his outside persona to me, especially if a biographical detail or two could help add luster to a scene we were building. He was thirty-five, the only child of Polish immigrant parents who were now retired. He lived alone in a tenement on the Lower East Side and was involved with a man he called his lover, a man who also had a live-in girlfriend. All three—Paul, lover, girlfriend—were somehow involved in big real estate deals and would often go jetting off for weekends in Europe or North Africa, though it was clear that Paul himself was not in the lucrative end of the business, since he spoke of having to take occasional jobs waiting on tables. Thin and darkly handsome, Paul was nonetheless at pains to downplay his appearance. I remember his pride when he arrived at the bar one night with a new haircut, a brutishly uneven head-shave that he said with a grin made him look "even more" like a survivor of Auschwitz.

I was a little apprehensive about seeing this man again. Sure, I had gradually come to understand his unspoken language and to sense how far his attraction to dangerous things really went. But the world has changed. Who knew what mischief he might be up to these days, what I might have to frown upon sternly, what I might even find myself somehow drawn into doing? Yet things have been *so* dry lately, I whined to Albert. Could it do any harm to just *talk*? Albert laughed as he gave me Paul's number.

~   ~   ~

Paul was napping when I rang. A ballet gala the night before had kept him out until breakfast, and he confessed he was still in his tuxedo pants. After we brought each other up-to-date (and admitted indirectly that our health was fine), he said he'd be happy to get together again, "to see what develops." Nothing was said about conditions—more, I think, because neither of us wanted to queer an incipient liaison with ill-timed reality talk. We set a time for later that day. Paul suggested a secluded men's room on a downtown university campus. That's a good sign, I thought—if he's fooling around with those finicky college boys, he can't be too heedless.

When I arrived at the men's room I found a scene already in progress that would have seemed innocuous enough four or five years ago, but now, in the era of AIDS, took on a faintly unsettling quality. Paul and someone else had positioned themselves not in a stall but right out in the open, and they were talking about death.

The other guy, a bearded man in his forties whom I'd not seen before, was dressed in a beat-up leather jacket, no shirt, and a pair of those drab, baggy chinos that janitors wear. Out of his fly was hanging a cock that must be described as substantial as much for its apparent weight and density as for its obvious size. Semisoft and just at the point of unwrinkling, the thing had a thick, meandering vein down the top that looked more like an exhaust pipe than a detail of human anatomy. He was lighting a cigarette when I entered and seemed unconcerned that his twosome had just become a threesome. And he was wearing a wedding ring. Paul was kneeling in front of the guy, his head hung low, dressed only in a yellow-stained T-shirt and a pair of pulled-down sweatpants. After a moment I saw that his legs had been bound behind him with a length of rope, which struck me as risky, since someone else always could just walk in unannounced. His hands were tied too, though in front of him, so he was able to reach and clumsily manipulate his cock. The room reeked of pine cleanser.

I'd entered during a short lull—or maybe they'd been waiting for me. Instantly I found myself shedding the everyday state of mind that allows us to do things like hold jobs and get through city traffic and assuming a more intuitive, timeless disposition that's much better suited to the consumption of pleasure. Respectfully I approached. Understanding that this wasn't the time for a kiss and introduction, I grunted for them to continue.

"I want it, okay?" Paul said. It was that low, trancelike monotone I remember.

"Yeah? You like this fucker?" The other guy handled himself appreciatively.

"Uh-huh. I need it. Put it in my mouth?"

A pause. The other guy farted.

"Why do you need it?" he asked.

Paul did something obscene with his tongue.

Seeing that this was indeed going to work, I took out my own cock and began to pull on it. Already it felt pleasantly *intrusive,* like a complication worth solving. I couldn't have said exactly why, but there was something palpably right about our little scene, something perhaps reflected in subtle linguistic details like the register of Paul's voice and the rhythm of the other guy's responses, as well as in grosser ones like choice of vocabulary and subject matter. I know from experience that arranging these things is far from easy, and even after this preliminary exchange I understood perfectly why Paul had wanted me to meet this guy. The scene heated up rapidly.

"I live for that dick," said Paul, his gaze fixed on it.

"Then tell me about it, man. Let me hear it."

Paul's drone became more animated.

"Please, let me have your dick. Slip it into my head."

Then he looked up at the guy's face.

"I'll take your load, okay? Let me suck it out of you. I don't care if I get sick."

I guess that was what they both wanted to hear. The other guy narrowed his eyes.

"I don't give a fuck about you, cocksucker—I just wanna get off. You gonna eat my come?"

Paul nodded: "Anything."

Both were pumping faster.

"Okay, let me feel that pussy mouth on my meat. I'll feed you my fucking load and get out of this shithole."

"If I get sick . . . ," Paul began.

"So you get sick," was the reply. "I guess you die, man."

And at that moment—or one like it, since I was too deeply engaged by all this bad-boy stuff to remember more than the drift of the dialogue—the three of us shot. I think we'd all been close for a while, and we shot powerfully—me, off to the side, near the radiator; Paul, onto the floor in front of him, grazing my foot; the other guy, past Paul's shoulder and onto the wall and paper towel dispenser. It took only a couple of minutes for us to button up, undo Paul, and perform a thorough wordless cleanup. Then our guest silently signaled his farewell, pulling Paul toward him and grazing him on the cheek with an affectionate peck.

After he left I raised an eyebrow.

"I know," Paul said. "Sweet man."

"Who is he?" I asked.

"Just a man," was the answer.

As I stood drying my hands, I couldn't help thinking how dismal a conclusion a stranger would have drawn simply by reading a transcript of our encounter. And even if he'd been there himself, would a *Times* reporter or health department official have understood how loving it all was? Or how safe? Paul and his friend must have agreed fairly explicitly, though in their own language, to stay within certain limits. They wanted to raise a little hell, anyway.

I winked at myself in the mirror. Well, boys, I thought, we did it.

~ ~ ~

Hearing that word "die" during sex did leave me feeling a little clammy, though. I've lost so many friends. So has Albert, I know, yet afterward he made light of my reservations.

"Isn't the best way to honor their memory to care for ourselves and the friends we've got left?" he asked. "It sounds to me like the three of you were eminently careful. If you'd only invited me."

But using death in that way. It felt so . . . odd.

"Look," Albert explained, "is it really so different from the old days, when we used to talk about things like getting worked over by a gang of Nazi motorcycle Satanists? Death by gang rape is hardly more attractive than death from AIDS. Sex is theater, darling, even now. And words are only words, even if they do bring the big, bad world into the bedroom, where we can play at controlling it."

When I equivocated, he grew stern.

"Stephen, if you can't tell the difference between talking about something and the thing itself, then you belong in a cave, drawing bison on the wall."

I thought of that remark sometime later, when I attended a play at which I was seated two rows away from someone who was so stirred up by an onstage murder that he began talking violently back to the actors. . . .

~ *Dennis McFarland* ~

Nothing
to Ask
For

I nside Mack's apartment, a concentrator—a medical machine that looks like an elaborate stereo speaker on casters—sits behind an orange swivel chair, making its rhythmic, percussive noise like ocean waves, taking in normal filthy air, humidifying it, and filtering out everything but the oxygen, which it sends through clear plastic tubing to Mack's nostrils. He sits on the couch, as usual, channel grazing, the remote-control button under his thumb, and he appears to be scrutinizing the short segments of what he sees on the TV screen with Zen-like patience. He has planted one foot on the beveled edge of the long oak coffee table, and he dangles one leg—thinner at the thigh than my wrist—over the other. In the sharp valley of his lap, Eberhardt, his old long-haired dachshund, lies sleeping. The table is covered with two dozen medicine bottles, though Mack has now taken himself off all drugs except cough syrup and something for heartburn. Also, stacks of books and pamphlets—though he has lost the ability to read—on how to heal yourself, on Buddhism, on Hinduism, on dying. In one pamphlet there's a long list that includes most human ailments, the personality traits and character flaws that cause these ail-

---

DENNIS McFARLAND *is the author of the highly praised novel* The Music Room. *His story "Nothing to Ask For," which originally appeared in* The New Yorker, *is something rare: a tale of friendship between a gay and a straight man told sensitively and forthrightly from the straight man's point of view. He lives in Massachusetts with his wife and family.*

ments, and the affirmations that need to be said in order to overcome them. According to this well-intentioned misguidedness, most disease is caused by self-hatred, or rejection of reality, and almost anything can be cured by learning to love yourself—which is accomplished by saying, aloud and often, "I love myself." Next to these books are pamphlets and Xeroxed articles describing more unorthodox remedies—herbal brews, ultrasound, lemon juice, urine, even penicillin. And, in a ceramic dish next to these, a small waxy envelope that contains "ash"—a very fine, gray-white, spiritually enhancing powder materialized out of thin air by Swami Lahiri Baba.

As I change the plastic liner inside Mack's trash can, into which he throws his millions of Kleenex, I block his view of the TV screen—which he endures serenely, his head perfectly still, eyes unaverted. "Do you remember old Dorothy Hughes?" he asks me. "What do you suppose ever happened to her?"

"I don't know," I say. "I saw her years ago on the nude beach at San Gregorio. With some black guy who was down by the surf doing cartwheels. She pretended she didn't know me."

"I don't blame her," says Mack, making bug eyes. "I wouldn't like to be seen with any grown-up who does cartwheels, would you?"

"No," I say.

Then he asks, "Was everybody we knew back then crazy?"

What Mack means by "back then" is our college days, in Santa Cruz, when we judged almost everything in terms of how freshly it rejected the status quo: the famous professor who began his twentieth-century-philosophy class by tossing pink rubber dildos in through the classroom window; Antonioni and Luis Buñuel screened each weekend in the dormitory basement; the artichokes in the student garden, left on their stalks and allowed to open and become what they truly were—enormous, purple-hearted flowers. There were no paving-stone quadrangles or venerable colonnades—our campus was the redwood forest, the buildings nestled among the trees, invisible one from the other—and when we emerged from the woods at the end of the school day, what we saw was nothing more or less than the sun setting over the Pacific. We lived with thirteen other students in a rented Victorian mansion on West Cliff Drive, and at night the yellow beacon from the nearby lighthouse invaded our attic windows; we drifted to sleep listening to the barking of seals. On weekends we had serious softball games in the vacant field next to the house—us against a team of tattooed, long-haired townies—and afterward, keyed up, tired and sweating, Mack and I walked the north shore to a place where we could watch the waves pound into the rocks and send up sun-ignited columns of water twenty-five and thirty feet tall. Though most of what we initiated "back then" now seems to have been faddish and wrongheaded, our friendship was exceptionally sane and has endured for twenty years. It endured the melodramatic confusion of Dorothy Hughes, our beautiful shortstop—I loved her, but she loved Mack. It endured the subsequent revelation that Mack was gay—any tension on that count managed by him with remarks about what a homely bastard I was. It endured his fury and frustration over my low-bottom alcoholism and my sometimes raging (and *en*raging) process of getting clean and sober. And it has endured the onlooking fish eyes of his long string of lovers and my two wives. Neither of us had a biological brother—that could account for something—but at recent moments when I have felt most frightened, now that Mack is so ill, I've thought that we persisted simply because we couldn't let go of the sense of *thoroughness* our friendship gave us; we constantly reported to each other on our separate lives, as if we knew that by doing so we were getting more from life than we would ever have been entitled to individually.

In answer to his question—was everybody crazy back then—I say, "Yes, I think so."

He laughs, then coughs. When he coughs these days—which is often—he goes on coughing until a viscous, bloody fluid comes up, which he catches in a Kleenex and tosses into the trash can. Earlier, his doctors could drain his lungs with a needle through his back—last time they collected an entire liter from one lung—but now that Mack has developed the cancer, there are tumors that break up the fluid into many small isolated pockets, too many to drain. Radiation or chemotherapy would kill him; he's too weak even for a flu shot. Later today, he will go to the hospital for another bronchoscopy; they want to see if there's anything they can do to help him, though they have already told him there isn't. His medical care comes in the form of visiting nurses, physical therapists, and a curious duo at the hospital: one doctor who is young, affectionate, and incompetent but who comforts and consoles, hugs and holds hands; another—old, rude, brash, and expert—who says things like "You might as well face it. You're going to die. Get your papers in order." In fact, they've given Mack two weeks to two months, and it has now been ten weeks.

"Oh, my God," cries Lester, Mack's lover, opening the screen door, entering the room, and looking around. "I don't recognize this hovel. And what's that wonderful smell?"

This morning, while Lester was out, I vacuumed and generally straightened up. Their apartment is on the ground floor of a building like all the buildings in this southern California neighborhood—a two-story motel-like structure of white stucco and steel railings. Outside the door are an X-rated hibiscus (blood red, with its jutting yellow powder-tipped stamen), a plastic macaw on a swing, two enormous yuccas; inside, carpet, and plainness. The wonderful smell is the turkey I'm roasting; Mack can't eat anything before the bronchoscopy, but I figure it will be here for them when they return from the hospital, and they can eat off it for the rest of the week.

Lester, a South Carolina boy in his late twenties, is sick too—twice he has nearly died of pneumonia—but he's in a healthy period now. He's tall, thin, and bearded, a devotee of the writings of Shirley MacLaine—an unlikely guru, if you ask me, but my wife, Marilyn, tells me I'm too judgmental. Probably she is right.

The dog, Eberhardt, has woken up and waddles sleepily over to where Lester stands. Lester extends his arm toward Mack, two envelopes in his hand, and after a moment's pause Mack reaches for them. It's partly this typical hesitation of Mack's—a slowing of the mind, actually—that makes him appear serene, contemplative, these days. Occasionally, he really does get confused, which terrifies him. But I can't help thinking that something in there has sharpened as well—maybe a kind of simplification. Now he stares at the top envelope for a full minute, as Lester and I watch him. This is something we do: we watch him. "Oh-h-h," he says, at last. "A letter from my mother."

"And one from Lucy too," says Lester. "Isn't that nice?"

"I guess," says Mack. Then: "Well, yes. It is."

"You want me to open them?" I ask.

"Would you?" he says, handing them to me. "Read 'em to me too."

They are only cards, with short notes inside, both from Des Moines. Mack's mother says it just makes her *sick* that he's sick, wants to know if there's anything he needs. Lucy, the sister, is gushy, misremembers a few things from the past, says she's writing instead of calling because she knows she will cry if she tries to talk. Lucy, who refused to let Mack enter her house at Christmastime one year—actually left him on the stoop in subzero cold—until he removed the gold earring from his ear. Mack's mother, who waited until after the funeral last year to let Mack know that his father had died; Mack's obvious illness at the funeral would have been an embarrassment.

But they've come around, Mack has told me in the face of my anger. I said better late than never.

And Mack, all forgiveness, all humility, said that's exactly right: much better.

"Mrs. Mears is having a craft sale today," Lester says. Mrs. Mears, an elderly neighbor, lives out back in a cottage with her husband. "You guys want to go?"

Eberhardt, hearing "go," begins leaping at Lester's shins, but when we look at Mack, his eyelids are at half mast—he's half asleep.

We watch him for a moment, and I say, "Maybe in a little while, Lester."

~ ~ ~

Lester sits on the edge of his bed reading the newspaper, which lies flat on the spread in front of him. He has his own TV in his room, and a VCR. On the dresser, movies whose cases show men in studded black leather jockstraps, with gloves to match—dungeon masters of startling handsomeness. On the floor, a stack of gay magazines. Somewhere on the cover of each of these magazines the word "macho" appears; and inside some of them, in the personal ads, men, meaning to attract others, refer to themselves as pigs. "Don't putz," Lester says to me as I straighten some things on top of the dresser. "Enough already."

I wonder where he picked up "putz"—surely not in South Carolina. I say, "You need to get somebody in. To help. You need to arrange it now. What if you were suddenly to get sick again?"

"I know," he says. "He's gotten to be quite a handful, hasn't he? Is he still asleep?"

"Yes," I answer. "Yes and yes."

The phone rings, and Lester reaches for it. As soon as he begins to speak I can tell, from his tone, that it's my four-year-old on the line.

After a moment, Lester says, "Kit," smiling, and hands me the phone, then returns to his newspaper.

I sit on the other side of the bed, and after I say hello, Kit says, "We need some milk."

"Okay," I say. "Milk. What are you up to this morning?"

"Being angry mostly," she says.

"Oh?" I say. "Why?"

"Mommy and I are not getting along very well."

"That's too bad," I say. "I hope you won't stay angry for long."

"We won't," she says. "We're going to make up in a minute."

"Good," I say.

"When are you coming home?"

"In a little while."

"After my nap?"

"Yes," I say. "Right after your nap."

"Is Mack very sick?"

She already knows the answer, of course. "Yes," I say.

"Is he going to die?"

This one too. "Most likely," I say. "He's that sick."

"Bye," she says suddenly—her sense of closure always takes me by surprise—and I say, "Don't stay angry for long, okay?"

"You already said that," she says, rightly, and I wait for a moment, half expecting Marilyn to come on the line; ordinarily she would, and hearing her voice right now would do me good. After another moment, though, there's the click.

Marilyn is back in school, earning a Ph.D. in religious studies. I teach sixth grade, and because I'm faculty adviser for the little magazine the sixth graders put out each year, I stay late many afternoons. Marilyn wanted me home this Saturday morning. "You're at work all week," she said, "and then you're over there on Saturday. Is that fair?"

I told her I didn't know—which was the honest truth. Then, in a possibly dramatic way, I told her that fairness was not my favorite subject these days, given that my best friend was dying.

We were in our kitchen, and through the window I could see Kit playing with a neighbor's cat in the backyard. Marilyn turned on the hot water in the kitchen sink and stood still while the steam rose into her face. "It's become a question of where you belong," she said at last. "I think you're too involved."

For this I had no answer, except to say, "I agree"—which wasn't really an answer, since I had no intention of staying home, or becoming less involved, or changing anything.

Now Lester and I can hear Mack's scraping cough in the next room. We are silent until he stops. "By the way," Lester says at last, taking the telephone receiver out of my hand, "have you noticed that he *listens* now?"

"I know," I say. "He told me he'd finally entered his listening period."

"Yeah," says Lester, "as if it's the natural progression. You blab your whole life away, ignoring other people, and then right before you die you start to listen."

The slight bitterness in Lester's tone makes me feel shaky inside. It's true that Mack was always a better talker than a listener, but I suddenly feel that I'm walking a thin wire and that anything like collusion would throw me off balance. All I know for sure is that I don't want to hear any more. Maybe Lester reads this in my face, because what he says next sounds like an explanation: he tells me that his poor old backwoods mother was nearly deaf when he was growing up, that she relied almost entirely on reading lips. "All she had to do when she wanted to turn me off," he says, "was to just turn her back on me. Simple," he says, making a little circle with his finger. "No more Lester."

"That's terrible," I say.

"I was a terrible coward," he says. "Can you imagine Kit letting you get away with something like that? She'd bite your kneecaps."

"Still," I say, "that's terrible."

Lester shrugs his shoulders, and after another moment I say, "I'm going to the Kmart. Mack needs a padded toilet seat. You want anything?"

"Yeah," he says. "But they don't sell it at Kmart."

"What is it?" I ask.

"It's a *joke*, Dan, for chrissake," he says. "Honestly, I think you've completely lost your sense of humor."

When I think about this, it seems true.

"Are you coming back?" he asks.

"Right back," I answer. "If you think of it, baste the turkey."

"How could I not think of it?" he says, sniffing the air.

In the living room, Mack is lying with his eyes open now, staring blankly at the TV. At the moment, a shop-at-home show is on, but he changes channels, and an announcer says, "When we return, we'll talk about tree pruning," and Mack changes the channel again. He looks at me, nods thoughtfully, and says, "Tree pruning. Interesting. It's just like the way they put a limit on your credit card, so you don't spend too much."

"I don't understand," I say.

"Oh, you know," he says. "Pruning the trees. Didn't the man just say something about pruning trees?" He sits up and adjusts the plastic tube in one nostril.

"Yes," I say.

"Well, it's like the credit cards. The limit they put on the credit cards is . . ." He stops talking and looks straight into my eyes, frightened. "It doesn't make any sense, does it?" he says. "Jesus Christ. I'm not making sense."

~ ~ ~

Way out east on University, there is a video arcade every half mile or so. Adult peep shows. Also a McDonald's, and the rest. Taverns—the kind that are open at eight in the morning—with clever names: Tobacco Rhoda's, the Cruz Inn. Bodegas that smell of cat piss and are really fronts for numbers games. Huge discount stores. Lester, who is an expert in these matters, has told me that all these places feed on addicts. "What do you think—those peep shows stay in business on the strength of the occasional customer? No way. It's a steady clientele of people in there every day, for hours at a time, dropping in quarters. That whole strip of road is *made* for addicts. And all the strips like it. That's what America's all about, you know. You got your alcoholics in the bars. Your food addicts sucking it up at Jack-in-the-Box—you ever go in one of those places and count the fat people? You got your sex addicts in the peep shows. Your shopping addicts at the Kmart. Your gamblers running numbers in the bodegas and your junkies in the alleyways. We're all nothing but a bunch of addicts. The whole fucking addicted country."

In the arcades, says Lester, the videos show myriad combinations and arrangements of men and women, men and men, women and women. Some show older men being serviced by eager, selfless young women who seem to live for one thing only, who can't get enough. Some of these women have put their hair into pigtails and shaved themselves—

they're supposed to look like children. Inside the peep show booths there's semen on the floor. And in the old days, there were glory holes cut into the wooden walls between some of the booths, so if it pleased you, you could communicate with your neighbor. Not anymore. Mack and Lester tell me that some things have changed. The holes have been boarded up. In the public men's rooms you no longer read, scribbled in the stalls, "All faggots should die." You read, "All faggots should die of AIDS." Mack rails against the moratorium on fetal-tissue research, the most promising avenue for a cure. "If it was legionnaires dying, we wouldn't have any moratorium," he says. And he often talks about Africa, where governments impede efforts to teach villagers about condoms: a social worker, attempting to explain their use, isn't allowed to remove the condoms from their foil packets; in another country, with a slightly more liberal government, a field nurse stretches a condom over his hand, to show how it works, and later villagers are found wearing the condoms like mittens, thinking this will protect them from disease. Lester laughs at these stories but shakes his head. In our own country, something called "family values" has emerged with clarity. "*Whose* family?" Mack wants to know, holding out his hands palms upward. "I mean, we *all* come from families, don't we? The dizziest queen comes from a family. The ax murderer. Even Dan *Quayle* comes from a family of some kind."

But Mack and Lester are dying, Mack first. As I steer my pickup into the parking lot at the Kmart, I almost clip the front fender of a big, deep-throated Chevy that's leaving. I have startled the driver, a young Chicano boy with four kids in the back seat, and he flips me the bird—aggressively, his arm out the window—but I feel protected today by my sense of purpose: I have come to buy a padded toilet seat for my friend.

~ ~ ~

When he was younger, Mack wanted to be a cultural anthropologist, but he was slow to break in after we were out of graduate school—never landed anything more than a low-paying position assisting someone else, nothing more than a student's job, really. Eventually, he began driving a tour bus in San Diego, which not only provided a steady income but suited him so well that in time he was managing the line and began to refer to the position not as his job but as his calling. He said that San Diego was like a pretty blond boy without too many brains. He knew just how to play up its cultural assets while allowing its beauty to speak for itself. He said he liked being "at the controls." But he had to quit work over a year ago, and now his hands have become so shaky that he can no longer even manage a pen and paper.

When I get back to the apartment from my trip to the Kmart, Mack asks me to take down a letter for him to an old high school buddy back in Des Moines, a country-and-western singer who has sent him a couple of her latest recordings. *"Whenever I met a new doctor or nurse,"* he dictates, *"I always asked them whether they believed in miracles."*

Mack sits up a bit straighter and rearranges the pillows behind his back on the couch. "What did I just say?" he asks me.

" 'I always asked them whether they believed in miracles.' "

"Yes," he says, and continues. *"And if they said no, I told them I wanted to see someone else. I didn't want them treating me. Back then, I was hoping for a miracle, which seemed reasonable.* Do you think this is too detailed?" he asks me.

"No," I say. "I think it's fine."

"I don't want to depress her."

"Go on," I say.

"But now I have lung cancer," he continues. *"So now I need not one but two miracles. That doesn't seem as possible somehow.* Wait. Did you write 'possible' yet?"

"No," I say. " 'That doesn't seem as . . .' "

"Reasonable," he says. "Didn't I say 'reasonable' before?"

"Yes," I say. " 'That doesn't seem as reasonable somehow.' "

"Yes," he says. "How does that sound?"

"It sounds fine, Mack. It's not for publication, you know."

"It's not?" he says, feigning astonishment. "I thought it was: 'Letters of an AIDS Victim.' " He says this in a spooky voice and makes his bug eyes. Since his head is a perfect skull, the whole effect really is a little spooky.

"What else?" I say.

"Thank you for your nice letter," he continues, *"and for the tapes."* He begins coughing—a horrible, rasping seizure. Mack has told me that he has lost all fear; he said he realized this a few weeks ago, on the skyride at the zoo. But when the coughing sets in, when it seems that it may never stop, I think I see terror in his eyes: he begins tapping his breastbone with the fingers of one hand, as if he's trying to wake up his lungs, prod them to do their appointed work. Finally he does stop, and he sits for a

moment in silence, in thought. Then he dictates: *"It makes me very happy that you are so successful."*

~ ~ ~

At Mrs. Mears's craft sale, in the alley behind her cottage, she has set up several card tables: Scores of plastic dolls with hand-knitted dresses, shoes, and hats. Handmade doll furniture. Christmas ornaments. A whole box of knitted bonnets and scarves for dolls. Also, some baked goods. Now, while Lester holds Eberhardt, Mrs. Mears, wearing a large straw hat and sunglasses, outfits the dachshund in a bonnet and scarf. "There now," she says. "Have you ever seen anything so *precious*? I'm going to get my camera."

Mack sits in a folding chair by one of the tables; next to him sits Mr. Mears, also in a folding chair. The two men look very much alike, though Mr. Mears is not nearly as emaciated as Mack. And of course, Mr. Mears is eighty-seven. Mack, on the calendar, is not quite forty. I notice that Mack's shoelaces are untied, and I kneel to tie them. "The thing about reincarnation," he's saying to Mr. Mears, "is that you can't remember anything and you don't recognize anybody."

"Consciously," says Lester, butting in. "*Sub*consciously you do."

"Subconsciously," says Mack. "What's the point? I'm not the least bit interested."

Mr. Mears removes his houndstooth-check cap and scratches his bald, freckled head. "I'm not, either," he says with great resignation.

As Mrs. Mears returns with the camera, she says, "Put him over there, in Mack's lap."

"It doesn't matter whether you're interested or not," says Lester, dropping Eberhardt into Mack's lap.

"Give me good old-fashioned Heaven and Hell," says Mr. Mears.

"I should think you would've had enough of that already," says Lester.

Mr. Mears gives Lester a suspicious look, then gazes down at his own knees. "Then give me nothing," he says finally.

I stand up and step aside just in time for Mrs. Mears to snap the picture. "Did you ever *see* anything?" she says, all sunshades and yellow teeth, but as she heads back toward the cottage door, her face is immediately serious. She takes me by the arm and pulls me along, reaching for something from one of the tables—a doll's bed, white with a red strawberry painted on the headboard. "For your little girl," she says aloud. Then she whispers, "You better get him out of the sun, don't you think? He doesn't look so good."

But when I turn again, I see that Lester is already helping Mack out of his chair. "Here—let me," says Mrs. Mears, reaching an arm toward them, and she escorts Mack up the narrow, shaded sidewalk, back toward the apartment building. Lester moves alongside me and says, "Dan, do you think you could give Mack his bath this afternoon? I'd like to take Eberhardt for a walk."

"Of course," I say, quickly.

But a while later—after I have drawn the bath, after I've taken a large beach towel out of the linen closet, refolded it into a thick square, and put it into the water to serve as a cushion for Mack to sit on in the tub; when I'm holding the towel under, against some resistance, waiting for the bubbles to stop surfacing, and there's something horrible about it, like drowning a small animal—I think Lester has tricked me into this task of bathing Mack, and the saliva in my mouth suddenly seems to taste of Scotch, which I have not actually tasted in nine years.

There is no time to consider any of this, however, for in a moment Mack enters the bathroom, trailing his tubes behind him, and says, "Are you ready for my Auschwitz look?"

"I've seen it before," I say.

And it's true. I have, a few times, helping him with his shirt and pants after Lester has bathed him and gotten him into his underwear. But that doesn't feel like preparation. The sight of him naked is like a powerful, scary drug: you forget between trips, remember only when you start to come on to it again. I help him off with his clothes now and guide him into the tub and gently onto the underwater towel. "That's nice," he says, and I begin soaping the hollows of his shoulders, the hard washboard of his back. This is not human skin as we know it but something already dead—so dry, dense, and pleasantly brown as to appear manufactured. I soap the cage of his chest, his stomach—the hard, depressed abdomen of a greyhound—the steep vaults of his armpits, his legs, his feet. Oddly, his hands and feet appear almost normal, even a bit swollen. At last I give him the slippery bar of soap. "Your turn," I say.

"My poor cock," he says as he begins to wash himself.

When he's done, I rinse him all over with the hand spray attached to the faucet. I lather the feathery white wisps of his hair—we have to remove the plastic oxygen tubes for this—then rinse again. "You know," he says, "I know it's irrational, but I feel kind of turned off to sex."

The apparent understatement of this almost takes my breath away. "There are more important things," I say.

"Oh, I know," he says. "I just hope Lester's not too unhappy." Then, after a moment, he says, "You know, Dan, it's only logical that they've all given up on me. And I've accepted it mostly. But I still have days when I think I should at least be given a chance."

"You can ask them for anything you want, Mack," I say.

"I know," he says. "That's the problem—there's nothing to ask for."

"Mack," I say. "I think I understand what you meant this morning about the tree pruning and the credit cards."

"You do?"

"Well, I think your mind just shifted into metaphor. Because I can see that pruning trees is like imposing a limit—just like the limit on the credit cards."

Mack is silent, pondering this. "Maybe," he says at last, hesitantly— a moment of disappointment for us both.

I get him out and hooked up to the oxygen again, dry him off, and begin dressing him. Somehow I get the oxygen tubes trapped between his legs and the elastic waistband of his sweatpants—no big deal, but I suddenly feel panicky—and I have to take them off his face again to set them to rights. After he's safely back on the living room couch and I've returned to the bathroom, I hear him: low, painful-sounding groans. "Are you all right?" I call from the hallway.

"Oh, yes," he says. "I'm just moaning. It's one of the few pleasures I have left."

The bathtub is coated with a crust of dead skin, which I wash away with the sprayer. Then I find a screwdriver and go to work on the toilet seat. After I get the old one off, I need to scrub around the area where the plastic screws were. I've sprinkled Ajax all around the rim of the bowl and found the scrub brush, when Lester appears at the bathroom door, back with Eberhardt from their walk. "Oh, Dan, really," he says. "You go too far. Down on your knees now, scrubbing our toilet."

"Lester, leave me alone," I say.

"Well, it's true," he says. "You really do."

"Maybe I'm working out my survivor's guilt," I say, "if you don't mind."

"You mean because your best buddy's dying and you're not?"

"Yes," I say. "It's very common."

He parks one hip on the edge of the sink. And after a moment he says this: "Danny boy, if you feel guilty about surviving . . . that's not irreversible, you know. I could fix that."

We are both stunned. He looks at me. In another moment, there are tears in his eyes. He quickly closes the bathroom door, moves to the tub and turns on the water, sits on the side, and bursts into sobs. "I'm sorry," he says. "I'm so sorry."

"Forget it," I say.

He begins to compose himself almost at once. "This is what Jane Alexander did when she played Eleanor Roosevelt," he says. "Do you remember? When she needed to cry she'd go in the bathroom and turn on the water, so nobody could hear her. Remember?"

~ ~ ~

In the pickup, on the way to the hospital, Lester—in the middle, between Mack and me—says, "Maybe after they're down there you could doze off, but on the *way* down, they want you awake." He's explaining the bronchoscopy to me—the insertion of the tube down the windpipe— with which he is personally familiar: "They reach certain points on the way down where they have to ask you to swallow."

"*He's* not having the test, is he?" Mack says, looking confused.

"No, of course not," says Lester.

"Didn't you just say to him that he had to swallow?"

"I meant *anyone*, Mack," says Lester.

"Oh," says Mack. "Oh, yeah."

"The general 'you,' " Lester says to me. "He keeps forgetting little things like that."

Mack shakes his head, then points at his temple with one finger. "My mind," he says.

Mack is on tank oxygen now, which comes with a small caddy. I push the caddy, behind him, and Lester assists him along the short walk from the curb to the hospital's front door and the elevators. Nine years ago, it was Mack who drove *me* to a different wing of this same hospital—against my drunken, slobbery will—to dry out. And as I watch him struggle up the low inclined ramp toward the glass-and-steel doors, I recall the single irrefutable thing he said to me in the car on the way.

"You stink," he said. "You've puked and probably pissed your pants and you *stink*," he said—my loyal, articulate, and best friend, saving my life, and causing me to cry like a baby.

Inside the clinic upstairs, the nurse, a sour young blond woman in a sky-blue uniform who looks terribly overworked, says to Mack, "You know better than to be late."

We are five minutes late to the second. Mack looks at her incredulously. He stands with one hand on the handle of the oxygen-tank caddy. He straightens up, perfectly erect—the indignant, shockingly skeletal posture of a man fasting to the death for some holy principle. He gives the nurse the bug eyes and says, "And you know better than to keep me waiting every time I come over here for some goddamn procedure. But get over yourself: shit happens."

He turns and winks at me.

Though I've offered to return for them afterward, Lester has insisted on taking a taxi, so I will leave them here and drive back home, where again I'll try—successfully, this time—to explain to my wife how all this feels to me, and where, a few minutes later, I'll stand outside the door to my daughter's room, comforted by the music of her small high voice as she consoles her dolls.

Now the nurse gets Mack into a wheelchair and leaves us in the middle of the reception area; then, from the proper position at her desk, she calls Mack's name, and says he may proceed to the laboratory.

"Dan," Mack says, stretching his spotted, broomstick arms toward me. "Old pal. Do you remember the Christmas we drove out to Des Moines on the motorcycle?"

We did go to Des Moines together, one very snowy Christmas—but of course we didn't go on any motorcycle, not in December.

"We had fun," I say, and put my arms around him, awkwardly, since he is sitting.

"Help me up," he whispers—confidentially—and I begin to lift him.

~ *Michael Cunningham* ~

Ignorant
Armies

Tim and I would have been incest. We've been together longer than we've been alone; when he bites his tongue I feel it in my mouth. I used to ask: Did we grow up gay because we were friends, or did we veer together in an Illinois schoolyard out of creaturely recognition? At the age of ten did we already carry homing devices, little silver beads of difference? It doesn't matter. We found one another. Our blood just spoke.

Plenty of others have fallen. Tim is the beauty of us, the one with the vast, reluctant smile. He has the shoulders, the heavy blond forearms; he has some serious business between his legs for anyone who gets that far. People always knew, even when he was ten. By the time our voices started changing, he'd turned dangerous.

He wasn't stupid. He just came from silence. He was a farm boy— he'd grown up with a father who knew the Bible through rumors and a mother who couldn't read flour off the sack. The hogs and chickens did more speaking. Tim listened. He watched. Anyone who called him stupid had never looked inside his head, where the mute wonders lived. There were grottoes inside him. There were underground caverns and schools of luminous fish.

Nancy was the first one. I fell in love with her too, or thought I had.

A native of southern California, MICHAEL CUNNINGHAM is the author of the extraordinary novel A Home at the End of the World. *He lives in New York City.*

This was high school—you lived by telling stories. Tim and Nancy used to kiss, they showed their flesh to one another, but that was as far as it went. She called it respect; she joked about marriage. Nancy was a figure skater, with all that implies about strength and a flashing, razor-edged ambition. She had dark-blond hair, thighs like the branches of an ash tree. Tim and I would pick her up after practice. We got there early to watch her turn and jump, the blades making their immaculate sounds on the cloudy ice. Tim said, "Beautiful."

"She's a vision," I said. "She's an ice goddess. Don't you wonder what it's like to be inside her skin?"

"Mm-hm," he said.

At fifteen, it was still possible to confuse desire with the ordinary love of beauty. It was possible to dream of knives on the ice and tell yourself it was all you wanted.

When she was finished, Nancy would cut over to us, stop in a little shiver of crystals. She'd kiss Tim on the lips, and sometimes she had a quick dry kiss for me too. "Hi, boys," she'd say breathlessly. Because she was going places, because she acted generous, I could imagine she loved us both. You live by telling stories.

As we left the rink, I said to Nancy, "You look complete out there on the ice. You look like a whole world, all by yourself."

She laughed. She considered me comical, but she didn't mind hearing what I had to say. She slipped her slender hand under Tim's big elbow.

"I just want to qualify for the Springfield finals," she said. She had a jock's habit of modesty. "I don't need to be a poem or anything. I want to skate in Chicago."

"So do you think being a vision of perfection could keep you from skating in Chicago?" I asked. "Would the judges hold it against you? Speak into the microphone, please."

"Oh, be quiet, you," she said, but I knew she was glad enough to be reminded of her beauty. Tim smiled, either at Nancy herself or at the living ghost of her, spinning on the ice, touching her own dim reflection at the two electrified points of the blades. We walked together across the parking lot of the mall. Scraps of bright paper from McDonald's scudded past us in the wind.

~ ~ ~

This is Nancy, Tim, and me on a summer night in Illinois, out by the reservoir. There are starfields and the racket of bugs; there's a moon sliding over black water. Nancy sits on a rock, slightly apart, with her chin on her knees. Tim and I pass a wine bottle.

I say, " 'And we are here as on a darkling plain, swept with confused alarms of struggle and flight, where ignorant armies clash by night.' " Back then, I had a few lines of poetry memorized, and I used to mumble them as if I were consoling myself for a loss so huge it could only be expressed by someone already dead. I offered scraps of poetry in place of height or handsomeness.

"You're such a weirdo," Nancy says.

"I know." I'm happy to be called anything by her.

Tim swigs at the bottle. A cold circle of moonlight slips along the dark-green shaft. He says, "It's a pretty night." He offers the bottle to Nancy, who doesn't want it. She wants something, but she won't say what.

"You want to go swimming?" I ask.

"In that water?" she says. "No, thanks."

"It'd be like swimming right out into the stars," I say. "It'd be blacker and more silent than anywhere you've ever been."

"Sure," Tim says. "I'll go."

"Go ahead," Nancy tells him. "I'll watch."

"Okay," Tim says.

"Okay," she answers.

Tim and I stand up tipsily on the rocks, get out of our clothes. I work myself around so that Tim's size, his arms and haunches, are closer to Nancy. I say, " 'The sea is calm tonight, the moon lies fair upon the straits,' " and am just drunk enough to imagine that in the dark, for a moment, she'll put together the sight of Tim's body and the sound of my voice.

She says, "I can't stay out too late, you know. I've got early practice tomorrow."

Tim and I step into the black water, the cool ooze and suck of the bottom. Sinking in this water is like disappearing—that much less of you, then that much, then that. We're just heads and flashing white arms, swimming out. We make soft splashes, no other sound. The sky is crazy with stars, and for a moment it seems we'll have everything, all our delirious dreams. We swim a distance, float. I say to him, "This is heaven. It could be heaven. I mean, if we turn out to spend eternity floating around in dark water watching the stars, that would be okay with me."

"Yeah," he says. "Me too."

We stay there until the ecstasy starts to pale, until it's edged away by thoughts of snapping turtles and pet alligators from Florida that were dumped here years ago and have somehow survived the winters. We swim back with a certain speed, pull ourselves out onto the rocks. Nancy says, "Have a nice swim?"

"Uh-huh." We stand there, naked and glistening. I reach for my shirt. Nancy sits on her rock, a thin girl in jeans and a Mexican peasant blouse. Tim, wet in the starlight, is big and quiet and glossy as a horse. He lifts his arm, pushes a lock of wet hair off his forehead, and looks around as if he's surprised and delighted to find himself here, on earth, where specks of light flick over water and dark smells of grass and manure blow up from the fields. For a moment—for the first time in memory—beauty reverses itself, and it is Nancy and I who are the witnesses. She shrinks, a practical and reluctant little figure sitting on a gray slab of rock. Tim expands. I watch it happen. I watch beauty become what Tim is, innocent and powerful, heavy with muscle, looking out at the world and finding there aren't words for what he wants to say. I check Nancy's face to see if she's seen it too, but Nancy is a practical person. She wants satisfaction. She wants to skate in Chicago.

Tim says, "That was great. Wow, Nance, you don't know what you missed."

"You'd better take me home," she says. "I've got to be on the ice at seven."

~ ~ ~

Tim and I didn't fight, though the ordinary clock of friendship suggested it was time. We were getting our final size, sprouting our hair and finding our voices. We loved the same girl. But we just never fought; it wasn't something that could happen between us. When Nancy left him, I was there to share the bottle of gin. I was beside him when he drove his father's truck off the road, and I was there, howling with him, as he tumbled out of the cab and screamed his curses up at the white sky. That was the day we left his father's truck, nose down in the ditch, its radio still playing, and walked out across the fields as if we both lived somewhere out there, in the huge shimmering heat that buzzed and crackled beyond the orderly streets of town.

"Goddamn her," he said. His voice was thick with the gin. Grasshoppers whirred around us. Cornstalks flashed their leaves, put out a hot green smell.

"She's just stupid," I told him. "Forget her. She doesn't know what she wants."

I was lying. She knew exactly what she wanted. She wanted more than kisses, more than ordinary admiration. She wanted a boyfriend as devoted to her body as she was to the ice.

"Stupid," Tim said. "Right, stupid. Shit, man."

He stopped to take a long draw from the bottle. The gin was clear and bright in the sun. After he'd swallowed he sat down hard. He disappeared among the corn. I went and found him.

"Forget her," I said. The corn leaves crisscrossed over his pale hair. He wore cut-offs and a Rolling Stones T-shirt among the dusty shadows.

"She's got my favorite shirt," he said. He spoke into the bottle. "She's got all my Springsteen records."

"You can get a new shirt."

I sat down beside him. His face was square, clouded, lost in his study of the bottle.

"You can get more records," I said.

"I can. Yeah, sure I can."

"We can go shopping tomorrow."

"Yeah. Okay."

He looked up from the bottle and we kissed, just once, down in the shadows of the corn. We'd been waiting to do it since we were ten. For a moment we left our lives, and kissing became something we could do, drunk, dazzled by the heat. His mouth tasted of gin and of something else, his blood and being, a taste particular to him. We kissed without touching at any other point. Then he was up and running. "Shit, Charlie," he said. I got up, unsteadily. I saw him run off into the fields, frantic, weaving and swaying, as if a flock of invisible crows were chasing him, trying to peck off his clothes and his flesh, everything he owned.

~ ~ ~

We fell away for a while, but I always knew him. I was a radio that picked up his station. He went west, tried acting, not because he had

talent but because he hoped it might help explain his precise and languorous beauty, his exact way of carrying himself. It might help explain
his trouble with the flesh—he was otherworldly, an artist.

Men changed everything. Suddenly there was no bottom to what Tim
could inspire. Suddenly he was valuable, and he didn't need to perform.
It was enough to lie naked beside a pool. It was enough to sit in the
passenger seat, to drink whatever was poured. He made a brief career out
of being who he was, a farm boy with cheerful compliancy and shoulders
broad and graceful as the wings of a plow. He went to Paris. He made
two movies, in which he appeared as a fireman and a mechanic. In both
of them, he obeys the commands of dark-haired, insistent men. In both
he has a shy, beatific smile and visible trouble staying hard.

I'd guessed all that, more or less. When Tim moved back to Illinois,
almost ten years later, I could tell him the story of his life nearly as fluently
as he could tell it to himself.

We kissed hello, a quick dry peck on the lips. We stood together in
adult bodies in my Chicago apartment. By then, Tim's beauty had darkened. It hadn't faded, but his face had taken on a new gravity. His skin
was stitched directly to the bone now. He had pale feathery hair and a
tan. As he sat on my sofa, drinking Scotch, he told me he'd come back
to the Midwest because it was real.

"Isn't every place real?" I asked.

"Man," he said, "I guess you haven't gone on a casting call and gotten
in an elevator with six other guys who all look exactly like you."

"No," I said. "I go to committee meetings instead."

He smiled. It hadn't changed, his smile. He had a talent for making
you believe you were the answer. You were what he'd been waiting for,
and whatever you wanted was what he wanted too.

"You like being a teacher?" he asked.

"No one likes being a teacher. But hey. There are moments, not
many, but there *are* moments when I feel like I'm doing something
useful."

"That's good," he said. "I always knew you'd end up doing something like this. You know. Something good in the world."

"Well, at least I'm not doing any harm," I said.

"Come on, Charlie," he said. "You always been too modest. I'm
proud of you, man. I am."

Though he was like my brother, it was impossible not to think of how many men, ten times richer and more powerful than I'd ever be, had paid real money for this: Tim sitting on their sofas, drinking their Scotch. I thought, for a moment or two, that we might become lovers. That our stories were carrying us there. But it would have been incest. When Tim fell asleep on my sofa that night, he looked the way he had at ten. He muttered fretfully over a dream and curled up with his hands tucked between his thighs.

~ ~ ~

He found an apartment on the North Side, got a job tending bar. We saw one another often, and I admit that, for a while, I let people believe we were together. It's something to walk into a restaurant with a man like Tim. He didn't understand about that. He'd always lived inside his beauty, the tick and moment of it. He didn't know how little happens to most of us, how time can lie in a room.

He cut a path across Chicago. If his beauty hadn't quite been enough to make him famous in Hollywood, it was more than sufficient along the curve of Lake Michigan. I heard all the stories. I heard about the farm boy, Tim's own ghost, who stole the sheets they'd made love on and the teacup Tim had drunk from. I heard about the chef so devoured by jealousy he slapped his hands down flat on the grill and grinned at Tim as the flesh began to sizzle and smoke, saying it hurt less than the ordinary moments.

I had affairs myself. I didn't live in solitude. But no one filled me with panic or crazy light. There was sex shot through with kindness, coffee in the morning. There were new movies, the movements of nations, everything to talk about. I dated an Edward, a Stanley, a Dan. Sometimes, not often, I spent money I couldn't spare on big blond hustlers who, for an hour, would do everything I told them to. Yes, they tended to look like Tim. No, I didn't bring cornstalks to the hotel rooms. I didn't dress them in cut-offs and T-shirts, or ask them to gargle with gin.

I'm not stupid. I know about desire's shallow bottom; I know the dances envy can make us do. A tin cup and a little hat, a serrated smile. What did I want? Not Tim, exactly, though I loved him. I seemed to want something I couldn't quite name. I wanted other skin. I worried that I would always just be more of this: a small man, light in the chin, already losing hair on top. No one ever stole a cup because I'd drunk from it.

Tim had been in Chicago almost two years before he met Mark. Every man like Tim may have a Mark waiting for him, someone older, prosperous, handsome as a good leather suitcase. A man with a country house and crystal glasses, a man who's been so many places he's had all the little fears scoured off. Tim was thirty that year. He was ready. He'd grown tired of smiling at drunks from behind the bar. A pair of brackets had started etching themselves on either side of his mouth. He and Mark found one another at a party, and all Tim had to do was not say no.

This is Mark, Tim, and me on the dock at Mark's house in Michigan. July sun flicks over the water, sailboats belly and sigh. Mark lays his hand on Tim's blond kneecap and says, "You know, sometimes I think there might be order in the universe. There might be something out there that wants us to be happy."

At twenty, Mark had had a lethal beauty, and now, at fifty, he lives inside what's left of it. Big jaw, straight solid jut of nose; an aura of proud, bulky sorrow. He is precise and certain as a carpenter. He loves Tim the way a carpenter loves wood.

I say, "Order in the universe is probably easiest to imagine when you're sitting by a lake and the maid is making lunch." I can't quite pick up the habit of being kind to Mark, though I accept his invitations. I'm an in-law, with attendant privileges.

"Oh, okay," he says. "Let me put it another way. I'd like to formally thank whatever agency might be responsible for this moment. And Carla's not a maid, she's a friend with a catering business. This is a gift she's giving us today."

Maybe Mark's most insulting gesture is his unwillingness to be insulted by me. He runs his big square hand along Tim's calf, cups the arch of Tim's foot in his palm. There is something about that, the sight of a masculine hand tenderly holding a graceful, powerful foot. For a moment, I can imagine what their sex is like.

Tim says, "You want to go for a swim?"

"Sure," Mark answers.

"Come on, Charlie," Tim says, and I say all right. Tim dives in, Mark follows. They send drops sparking up into the air. I'm about to follow, but I change my mind. Something closes in front of me—the moment doesn't have enough room. I sit on the warm boards of the dock and watch them as they swim out. They speak to one another, laugh, speak again. I can't hear what they're saying.

~ ~ ~

I admit that I was jealous, at first. I admit I could be bitter about simple fairness. Didn't I work hard, listen compassionately, treat my students with respect and my friends with honor? I was a good man—where were my surprises, my gaudy nights? Where was the love that pierced? But time passed, and I got used to Tim's new happiness. I did well in my job. I joined more committees, started in on a reputation. I finished my first book, a study of the inverse relationship between beauty and power in medieval society. I graded my weight in papers.

On their second anniversary, Tim and Mark bought rings. They were simple gold bands, marriage rings, with that pure businesslike shine. Mark didn't want a ceremony—he said he'd feel like a fool—but he did want the rings. He and Tim lived together in his apartment on the fifteenth floor. As far as I know, they were faithful. I saw less and less of them, I was so busy with my work, but when I did see them they looked complete. They had that telepathy; they laughed over invisible jokes. For the first time, Tim didn't tell me stories. It was Mark who made the conspicuous efforts in my direction. It was Mark who invited me to dinners and weekends, Mark who asked me to come along and help them pick out the rings.

"Hey, Charlie," he said once after dinner, when Tim was out of the room. "Do you know how much Tim cares about you?"

We sat together in the gray and black silence of his apartment, with candles shivering. City lights blazed behind the gauzy curtains.

I shrugged. I said, "We've been friends a long time, Mark."

"You're almost more than friends. You're Tim's family, don't you think? Much more so than his blood relations."

I nodded. Tim's mother was dead, his father had remarried and moved to Canada, where he could keep a disapproving eye on the earth's icy curve. His sister lived in a trailer park, screaming her religion at the passing cars.

"You're like his brother and his father at the same time," Mark said. "It's an interesting combination." Mark had solemnity, a steady kindness, alert gray eyes. At moments, I may have been in love with him myself.

"I suppose so," I said.

"No question about it," Mark said.

There was something in his eyes, a cloud of meaning. I had some unkind things ready to say about a friendship so old it outranked money and sex, the temporary comforts of the flesh. I was deciding how to phrase them when Tim came back, and Mark looked away from me. We talked about whether we'd go to the movies or just stay in for the night.

There was only a moment, half a moment, that I felt simple vindication when Mark received the news. I never told anyone. I left it behind and took up my truer, more complicated feelings. When Tim found out about himself I held him so hard he choked. We wept together, we three. I'm still not certain whether, mixed with my sorrow, I felt a certain thread of relief. I hate to think that I did.

~ ~ ~

Mark's family couldn't keep us from the funeral, but they refused to let him wear his ring. They buried him in a blue suit, with foundation caught in the corners of his nose. A week after the funeral, Tim and I rented a car and drove back to the cemetery in Wisconsin, a vast field of crosses and tablets and angels bent under the weight of their stone wings. We found Mark's grave, still without its headstone, and sat down on it. We ran our hands over the grass. We could have been touching the place where Mark's chest was, or his head, or his crotch. Tim dug out a plug of grass and put the ring in the dirt. He said, "I hope I'm not putting this over his feet."

We sat for a while. Birds carried on in the trees. Dragonflies blued the air. "When I go," Tim said, "make sure I've got my ring on my finger, okay? Make sure I'm buried with it."

I nodded. I didn't speak.

"Promise?" he said.

"Sure."

He sat with the sun on his milky skin, looking at the place where he'd planted the ring. I saw a vine creeping out of Mark's grave, pale as new asparagus, quiet as an eel. I watched Tim's face and saw—it couldn't have been for the first time—how much he'd lost. His face was empty, and worse than empty. He might have had all the blood sucked out of him. Trees shimmered over the field of stones. Our rented Honda Civic gleamed nearby. When we couldn't sit there anymore we got back in the rented car and had breakfast at a diner. We ate in silence, like old people who've been married so long they've outlived everything they had to say to one another.

~ ~ ~

When we got back to my apartment Tim lay down on my bed and I lay beside him, as we'd done a hundred times before. But this time, after twenty years of chaste friendship, I leaned over and kissed his lips. This time he responded, maybe out of love, maybe out of loneliness. Now I was all he had. We kissed, and I ran my hands along his rib cage. We worked our clothes off. I touched the new smallness of him, the hard little knots of muscle. I put my lips on his lesions. I lathered his cock with spit, took a breath, and put it inside me.

"Hey," he said. "What are you doing?"

"Nothing."

"Oh, no. Stop."

I didn't stop. I said, "I'll take it out before you come." I wanted to have this awful beauty in me, this pale sure knowledge. I pictured him gone. I pictured a wave crashing over the land and soaking everything, the stores and the carpets and the bread. I could see windows breaking, green water rushing in. I moved up and down on his cock. I saw the hairline network of his blood, the crazy pattern of it. I saw the whole of his being, the bloom of his end. I wanted to enter it.

"No," he said, after a minute.

"Come on," I said. "I've been waiting twenty years for this."

"No, oh no," he said, and he shrank inside me. I kept after him. When he fell out I turned around and put it, limp, in my mouth. I could taste both our smells. He took handfuls of my hair and pulled, hard.

"Charlie, stop," he said. "Stop."

"No."

He pushed away from me, got out of bed. It wasn't easy for him. He stood breathing, terrified, on the rug. He looked at me as if I'd betrayed him, told his most precious secret, and I realized we'd finally reached a moment all the others had passed through before me. This moment had been waiting for all of us, when we went too far. When we showed him how much we wanted to walk through the world in his skin, to inhabit the hush and shimmer. To take possession.

"Okay," I said. "Sorry. Come back, I won't do anything."

"Charlie. Aw, Charlie. Please."

"I know. I got a little nuts. Come here, I just want to hold you for a little while."

"Please don't, man. I can't stand it."

"It's all right. Come on."

He got back into bed, uncertainly. He had nowhere else to go. His flesh was sparse now, his hair dull and brittle-looking. I held him, thinking he'd fall asleep. He didn't sleep. He kept turning the ring around on his finger. After a while he got up and found a Kool I'd had in my dresser drawer for over a year and we lay smoking it together, watching the ceiling as if we had, in fact, made love. I ran my palm over his chest, breathed the changing smell of him, though I knew he didn't like my touching him that way. Smoke curled up from his fingers, and he passed the cigarette to me. He coughed, the same sound Mark had made. A squeaky cough, bone dry, wire brushes scrubbing a balloon. "You shouldn't smoke," I said.

"This is my last one."

We lay there, not speaking. It seemed we should have had so much to say. It seemed we should have examined the history of our devotions, explained ourselves, told the final truths. But once the silence established itself, it was impossible to break. I stroked his hair. We lay smoking that stale Kool, while cars bleated in the street below.

~ ~ ~

Today, he has a different beauty. He's a figure drawn with a hot wire in white cement. He has a greyhound's economy of flesh; beside him, the nurses look bloated as manatees. They squeak on the linoleum, they bump one another with their soft heavy flanks. It's not hard to imagine them lolling in brown water, moaning, slapping their flukes. Tim is pale and exact as a fire, prickly with what he knows. You can't touch him. His fingers are thin enough to pick a lock.

He says, "Girls, give it a rest, you're just going to set the alarms off, and then where'll we be?"

Over a month ago, he stopped making sense. He doesn't need to anymore; he's got a gaunt dignity that's better than logic. Now, finally, he's found his voice. He has a large crazy presence, a self-assurance that borders on the regal. When you see him these days, big-eyed and ivory-colored, surrounded by machinery, you think of kings who ordered castles and monuments that broke their country's banks, that crushed slaves and starved peasants for generations and then lived forever as evidence of human accomplishment. Only the insane and the almost-dead can see the ferocious splendor that lies beyond regular pain and loss.

"Everything's fine here," the older nurse says. "Don't worry, you're just going to feel a little pressure."

"Don't *you* worry," Tim says suavely to the young nurse who can't find the vein. "We can just phone this one in, really, there's no point in alarming the public." I can't think where this style came from, this pilot's voice he's developed. Think of Van Heflin at the wheel of a 747, that gruff sense of command.

"Here," the young nurse says, and the older one nods. The older nurse wears a badge that says her name is Florida.

"Got it," the young nurse says, and the needle slides into the vein like it had always belonged there, like there was some magic attraction between steel and flesh. Tim doesn't wince. He has a new set of priorities—the needles don't bother him, but a potted chrysanthemum or a wrapped present can drive him crazy. He seems to fear anything inefficient, anything that sheds.

"Oh, you've got it," Tim says. "Tell me, do you like the rumba? Does it speak to you?"

He sounds like me. His voice has my cadences, my way of biting off the consonants.

The younger nurse giggles, and a panicky look skates across her eyes. She hasn't had enough practice with the flirtations of the dying. The younger ones are sometimes better prepared for high drama than they are for odd little jokes and non sequiturs. They hadn't expected the gravely ill to be so strange.

"I don't know," she says.

"The rumba," Tim says, "is the dance for you. It'll set your body free and bring your soul right up into your mouth. Trust me on this."

"I think we're all set here," says the older nurse, Florida. She helps the younger one tape the needle to Tim's arm, gives his intravenous bag a little shake. "Mm-hm," she says, and her mouth makes a firm line. Florida has been to Tim's room at least a hundred times, but she always treats him with the same distracted semi-attention, as if he's an illusion that won't coalesce or disappear. Back when he made sense, when some of his old beauty still held, he did a better job of charming nurses.

"Thanks," I say cheerfully. "We appreciate it."

The younger one gives the intravenous bag a shake of her own, and they move off down the hall. I'm alone here, with Tim, in the pale yellow of the room. The hospital has a hum and a steady aquarium light. Wheels turn along the halls.

"The truth of this bed," Tim says, "is the way it adjusts itself. Is it facing north to south?"

"Yes," I tell him.

"Good. Don't let a lot of people come."

"Okay," I say.

There's never a crowd, never much of a crowd. Friends stop by when they can, but I'm the one who's here from hour to hour. I'm the one who watches time pass: This much less, then this much, then this.

I pull the curtain all the way around Tim's bed, stroke his damp hair. He is looking straight ahead, staring at the air in front of him as if blazing letters were forming there, beginning to spell something important but illegible. I inhale, searching for the smell of him threaded in with the smells of medicine and hot machinery and instant mashed potatoes. No one wants him now but me. I run my fingers along his cheekbone, slip my hand down to his shoulder and then under the hospital gown to the hard plates of his chest. He growls, a low sawing sound that lives deep in his throat. I glance toward the door, to make sure no one's coming, and put my lips on his. His breath is sharp and dank. It tastes vaguely like him and it tastes like the bitter medicine that pumps by the quart through his veins. I whisper to him. I say, close to his ear, "Tim? Can you hear me?"

Nothing happens in his face. He looks ahead, murmuring. I hold his hand, feel the sharp smooth surface of the ring that's grown too big for him.

" 'And we are here as on a darkling plain,' " I say, " 'swept with confused alarms of struggle and flight, where ignorant armies clash by night.' "

He laughs. He looks at me, and for a moment he's present.

"Tim?" I say.

"Hey, Mark," he answers. "Hey, baby."

Then he's gone again. His eyes turn inward, and he murmurs, "The truth of this bed is that it doesn't work. It's got nowhere to go."

I hold his hands. We're here, right here, as the future closes up around us. Something will happen next. Something always does. We live with unspeakable losses, and most of us carry on. We find new lovers, change jobs, move to another state. We continue to know animal pleasures; we eat and have sex, buy new clothes. Hardly anyone is destroyed, I mean truly annihilated, by loss. We're designed for endurance.

Still, I'd trade every chance of future happiness if he'd come back one last time. I needed him to look at me, see me, and give me this ring I'm wearing. I didn't want to have to take it off his finger like that.

~ *Randall Kenan* ~

Run,
Mourner,
Run

. . . for there is no place that does not see you.
You must change your life.

—RILKE

Dean Williams sits in the tire. The tire hangs from a high and fat sycamore branch. He swings back and forth, back and forth, so that the air tickles his ears. His legs, now lanky and mannish, drag the ground. Not like the day his father first hung the tire and hoisted a five-year-old Dean up by the waist and pushed him and pushed him and pushed him, higher and higher—"Daddy, don't push so hard!"—until Dean, a little scared, could see beyond the old truck and out over the field, his heart pounding, his eyes wide; and his daddy walked off that day and left Dean swinging and went back to the red truck and continued to tinker under the hood, fixing . . . Dean never knew what.

Eighteen years later Dean sits in the tire. Swinging. Watching the last fingers of the late-October sun scratch at the horizon. Waiting. Looking at an early migration of geese heading south. Swinging. Waiting for his mama to call him to supper—canned peas, rice, Salisbury steak, maybe.

RANDALL KENAN is the author of the novel A Visitation of Spirits *and the story collection* Let the Dead Bury Their Dead, *which was nominated for the National Book Critics Circle Award in 1992. A fabulist of both black history and the history of the South, Kenan sets most of his fiction in the mythical town of Tims Creek, North Carolina. He lives in New York City.*

His daddy always use to say Ernestine wont no good cook, but ah, she's got.

Dean Williams stares off at the wood in the distance, over the soybean fields to the pines' green-bright, the oaks and the sycamores and the maples all burnt and brittle-colored. Looking at the sky, he remembers a rhyme:

A red sky at night is a shepherd's delight;
A red sky in the morning is a shepherd's warning.

Once upon a time—what now seems decades ago rather than ten or fifteen years—Dean had real dreams. In first grade he wanted to be a doctor; in second, a lawyer; in third, an Indian chief. He read the fairy stories and nursery rhymes, those slick shiny oversized books, over and over, and Mother Goose became a Bible of sorts. If pigs could fly and foxes could talk and dragons were for real, then surely he could be anything he wanted to be. Not many years after that he dropped out and learned to dream more mundane dreams. Yet those nuggets from grade school stayed with him.

Dean Williams sits in the tire his daddy made for him. Thinking: For what?

See, there's somebody I want you to . . . to . . . Well, I want you to get him for me. So to speak.

Percy Terrell had picked him up that day, back in March. Percy Terrell, driving his big Dodge truck, his Deere cap perched on his head, his gray hair peeking out, his eyes full of mischief and lies and greed and hate and.

Son, I think I got a job for you.

Sitting in the cab of that truck, groceries in his lap (his Ford Torino had been in need of a carburetor that day), he wondered what Percy was up to.

Now of course this is something strictly between me and you.

On that cemetery-calm day in March, staring into the soybean field and his mama's house, the truck stopped on the dirt road beside the highway, he wondered whether Percy wanted to make a sexual proposition. It wouldn't have been the first time a gray-haired granddaddy had stopped his truck and invited Dean in. Dean had something of a reputation. Maybe Percy had found out that Dean had been sleeping with burly Joe Johnson, the trucker. Maybe somebody had seen him coming out of a bar in Raleigh or in Wilmington or in.

. . . if you dare tell a soul, it'll be your word against mine, boy. And, well . . . you'd just be fucking yourself up then.

How could he have known what he'd be getting himself into? If some fortune-teller had sat him down and explained it to him, detail by detail; if he'd had some warning from a crow or a woodchuck; if he'd had a bad dream the night before that would.

Land.

Land?

They own a parcel of land I want. Over by Chitaqua Pond. In fact they own the land under Chitaqua Pond. I got them surrounded a hundred acres on one side, two hundred acres on one side, one fifty on the other.

How much land is it?

It ain't how much that matters, son. They're blocking me. See? I want—I need that land. Niggers shouldn't own something as pretty as Chitaqua Pond. Got a house on it they call their homeplace. Don't nobody live in it. Say they ain't got no price. We'll see.

When he was only a towheaded twenty-four-year-old with a taste for hunting deer and redheads, Percy Terrell had inherited from his daddy, Malcolm Terrell, about three thousand acres and a general store to which damn near everyone in Tims Creek was indebted. Yet somehow fun-loving Percy became Percy the determined; hell-raising Percy became Percy the cunning, Percy the sly, Percy the conniving, and had manipulated and multiplied his inheritance into a thousand acres more land, two textile mills, a chicken plant, part ownership in a Kentucky Fried Chicken franchise in Crosstown, and God only knew what else. The day he picked Dean up he had been in the middle of negotiating with a big corporation for his third textile mill. Before that day Percy had never said so much as "piss" to Dean. In Percy's eyes Dean was nothing more than poor white trash: a sweet-faced, dark-haired faggot with a broken-down Ford Torino, living with his chain-smoking mama in a damn near condemned house they didn't even own. So it was like an audience with the king for Dean to be picked up by ole Percy on the side of the road, for him to stop the car, to turn to Dean and say: I want you to get to know him. Real good. You get my meaning?

Sir?

You know what I mean. He likes white boys. He'll just drool all over you. Who knows. He probably already does.

That day in March, Dean hardly knew who Raymond Brown was. Only that he was the one colored undertaker in town. How could he have known he was something of a prince, something of a child, something of a little brown boy in a man's gray worsted-wool suit, with skin underneath smooth like silk? So he sat there thinking: This one of them dreams like on TV? Surely he wasn't actually sitting in a truck with the richest white man in Tims Creek, being asked to betray the richest black man in Tims Creek. . . . Shoot! Sure as hell must be a dream.

Sex with a black man. His first one—his only one till Ray—had been Marshall Hinton in the ninth grade, just before Dean dropped out of high school. It had been nothing much—nasty, sweaty, heartbeat-quick—but Dean still remembered the touch of that boy's skin, petal-soft and hard at the same time, and the sensation lingered on his fingertips. With that on his mind, part of the same evil dream, with the shadow of Percy Terrell sitting there next to him in his shadow-truck, Dean had asked: Let's say I decide to go along with this. Let's just say. What do I get out of it?

What do I get?

Had he actually said that? He could easily have said at that point: No a thank you, Mr. Imaginary Percy Terrell. I know this is a test from the Lord and I ain't fool enough to go through with it. I ain't stupid enough. I ain't drunk enough. I ain't.

What do I get?

You know that factory I'm trying to buy from International Spinning Corporation? You work at that plant, don't you?

Yeah.

Well, how would you like a promotion to foreman? And a six-thousand-dollar raise?

More a dream or less a dream? Dean couldn't tell. But the idea: six thousand dollars—how much is that a month?—a promotion. How long does it take most people to get to foreman? John Hyde? Fred Lanier? Rick Batts? Ten, fifteen, seventeen years. And they're still on line. Foremen come in as foremen. That simple. People like Dean never get to be foremen . . . and six thousand dollars.

I don't understand, Mr. Terrell, how . . . ?

You just get him in bed. That's all. I'll worry about the rest.

But how do I . . . ?

Ever heard of a bar called The Jack Rabbit in Raleigh?

Yeah. A colored bar.

He goes there every second Saturday of every month, I'm told.

Dean stared at the dashboard. He admired the electronic displays and the tape deck with a Willie Nelson tape sticking out.—What kind of guarantee I get?

Percy chuckled. A flat, good-ole-boy chuckle, with a snort and a wheeze. For the first time Dean was a little scared. Son, you do my bidding you don't need no guarantee. This—he stuck out his hand—this is your guarantee.

Dean had walked into the kitchen that day and looked down at his mama, who sat at the kitchen table reading the *National Enquirer,* a cigarette hanging out of her mouth, ashes on her tangerine knit blouse, ashes on the table. Water boiling on the stove. The faucet they could never fix dripping. Dripping. The linoleum floor needing mopping—it all seemed like a dream. Terrell.

Just get him in bed.

What Percy Terrell want with you?—She watched him closely as he put the grocery bags on the counter.

Nothing.

She harrumphed as she got up to take the cans out of the brown paper bag and finish supper. He stopped and took a good long look at her. He noticed how thin his mama was getting; how her hair and her skin seemed washed out, all a pale, whitish-yellow color. Is that when he decided to do it? When he took in how the worry about money, worry about her doctor bills, the worry about her job—when she had a job—worry about her health, worry about Dean, had fretted away at her? Piece by piece, gnawing at her, so manless, so perpetually sad.

He remembered how she had been when his daddy was alive. Her hair black. Her eyes childlike and playful. Her body full and supple and eager to please a man. She did her nails a bright red then. Went to the beauty parlor. Now she bit her nails, and her head was a mess of split ends.

Dean sits in a tire. A tire hung off the great limb of a sycamore tree. Swinging. Watching smoke rising off in the distance a ways. Someone burning a field maybe. But it's the wrong time of year. People are still harvesting corn.

No, it wasn't for his mama that he did it. He hated the line. Hated the noise and the dust and the smell. But he hated the monotony and the din even more, those millions of damn millions of fucking strands of thread churning and turning and going on and on and on. What did he have to lose? What else did he have to trade on but his looks? A man once told him: Boy, you got eyes that could give a bull a hard-on. Why not use them?

Oh, Mother, I shall be married to
Mr. Punchinello
Mr. Punch
Mr. Joe
Mr. Nell
Mr. Lo.
To Mr. Punch. Mr. Joe.
To Mr. Punchinello.

That very next day in March at McTarr's Grocery Store he saw him. Dean's mama had asked him to stop on the way back home and pick up a jar of mayonnaise. Phil Jones gave him a lift from the plant, and as he got out and was walking into the store Raymond Brown drove up in his big beige Cadillac.

He'd seen Ray Brown all his life, known who he was by sight and such, but he had never really paid him any mind. Over six foot and in a dark-navy suit. A fire-red tie. A mustache like a pencil line. Skin the color of something whipped, blended, and rich. A deep color. Ray walked with a minister's majesty. Upright. Solemn. His head held up. Almost looking down on folk.

Scuse me, Mr. Brown.

Had he ever really looked into a black man's eyes before then? Dean stood there, fully intending to find some way to seduce this man, and yet the odd mixture of things he sensed coming out of him—a rock solidness, an animal tenderness, a cool wariness—made Dean step back.

Yeah? What can I do for you?—Ray spoke in a slow, round baritone. Very proper. (Does he like me?) He kept his too-small-for-a-black-man's nose in the air. (Does he know I'm interested?) Raised an eyebrow. (He just thinks I'm white trash.)—Can I help you, young man?—Ray started to step away.

W-what year is your car?

My . . . Oh, an '88.

Fleetwood?

No, Eldorado.

Drive good?

Exceedingly.

Huh?

Very.

Dean tried to think of something more to say without being too obvious to the folk going into the store. (What if Percy was tricking me? What if Ray Brown don't go in for men? What if . . . ?)

That it?

Ah . . . yeah, I—

Well, please excuse me. I'm in something of a hurry. Ray nodded and started to walk off.

Mr. Ray—

When Raymond Brown turned around, the puzzled look on his face softened its sternness: Dean saw a boy wanting to play. Ray smiled faintly, as if taking Dean in for the first time. His eyes drifted.—Well, what is it?

Nothing. See you later.—Dean smiled and looked down a bit, feigning shyness.

A grin of recognition passed over Ray's face. His eyes narrowed. At once he was all business again; he turned without a word or a gesture and walked into the store.

> *Lavender blue and rosemary green,*
> *When I am king you shall be queen;*
> *Call up my maids at four o'clock,*
> *Some to the wheel and some to the rock;*
> *Some to make hay and some to shear corn,*
> *And you and I will keep the bed warm.*

Dean Williams gazes down now at the trough in the earth in which his feet have been sliding. For eighteen years. Sliding. The red clay hard and baked after years of sun and rain and little-boy feet. Exposed. His blue canvas high-tops beaten and dirty and frayed but comfortable. His mother says time and again he should get rid of them. A crow *caw-caw-ca-caws* as it glides over his head, as he swings in the old tire. As he thinks. As he wonders what Raymond Brown is doing. Thinking. At this moment.

Some things you just let happen, Ray had said that night. Dean never quite understood what he meant by that. Ray gestured grandly with his hands as he went on and on. He was a little pompous—is that the word? A little stuck-up. A little big on himself and his education. With his poetry and his books and his reading and his plays. But he had such large hands. Well manicured. So clean. And a gold ring with a shiny black stone he called onyx. He said his great-granddaddy took it off the hand of his slavemaster after killing him. Dean had thought an undertaker's hands would be cold as ice; Ray's hands were always warm.

A few days after McTarr's, Dean finally made his play at The Jack Rabbit. A rusty, run-down, dank, dark, sleazy, sticky-floored sort of place, with a smudged wall-length mirror behind the bar, a small dance floor crowded with men and boys, mostly black, jerking or gyrating to this guitar riff, to that satiny saxophone, to this syrupy siren's voice, gritty, nasty, hips, heads, eyes, grinding. Dean found Ray right off, standing at the edge of the bar, slurping a Scotch and soda, jabbering to some straggly-looking, candy-assed blond boy with frog-big blue eyes, who looked on as if Ray were speaking in Japanese or in some number-filled computer language.

Scuse me, Mr. Ray.

Ray Brown's eyes narrowed again the way they had in front of McTarr's. This time Dean did not have to wonder if Ray was interested. The straggly-looking boy drifted away.

You're that Williams boy, aren't you?

Yeah.

Buy you a drink?

Some smoky voice began to sing, some bitter crooning, some heart-tugging melody, some lonely piano. They were playing the game now, old and familiar to Dean, like checkers, like Old Maid; they were dancing cheek to cheek, hip to thigh. Dean knew he could win. Would win.

Ray talked. Ray talked about things Dean had no notion or knowledge of. Ray talked of school (Morehouse—the best years of my life. I should have become an academic. I did a year in Comp Lit at BU. Then my father died and my aunt Helen insisted I go to mortuary school); Ray talked of his family (You know, my mother actually forbade me to marry Gloria. Said she was too poor, backward, and good-for-nothing. Wanted me to marry a Hampton or a Spellman girl); Ray talked of the funeral business (It was actually founded by my great-grandfather, Frederick Brown. What a man. Built it out of nothing. What a man. Loved to hunt. He did); Ray talked of undertaking (I despise formaldehyde; I loathe dead people; I abhor funerals); Ray talked on the President and the Governor and the General Assembly (Crooks! Liars! Godless men!); Ray talked. In soft tones. In icy tones. In preacher-like tones. This moment loud and thundering, his baritone making heads turn; the next moment quiet, head tilted, a little boy in need of a shoulder to lean on. Dean had never heard, except maybe on the radio and on TV, someone who knew so damn much, who carried himself just so, who.

But my wife—Ray would somehow smile and look despairing at the same time—I love her, you know. She could have figured it out by now. She's not a dumb woman, really.

Why hasn't she?

Blinded. Blinded by the Holy Ghost. She's full of the Holy Ghost, see.—Ray went off on a mocking rendition of a sermon, pounding his fists on the bar for emphasis ('cause we're all food for worms, we know not the way to salvation, we must seek—yes, seek—*Him*). He broke off.—Of course there's the money too.

The money?

Yeah, my money.

Oh.

Ray became silent. He stared at Dean. The bartender stood at the opposite end of the bar, wiping glasses with a towel; the smoky air had cleared somewhat but still appeared blue-gray, alight with neon; one lone couple ground their bodies into each other on the dance floor to a smoldering Tina Turner number.

How about you?

What about me?

Whom do you love?

Dean laughed.—Who loves me is the real question. Don't nobody give a shit about me. My mama, maybe.

Ray put his large hand over Dean's: Ray's full and strong, Dean's dry and brittle and rough and small.—Well, I wouldn't put it exactly like that. He kissed Dean's hand as though it were a small and frightened bird.

As simple as breaking bones. Had he thought of Percy and how he was to betray this mesmerizing man? Did he believe he could? Would?

I want to show you something.

Yeah, I'll bet.—Dean smirked.

No, really. A place. Tonight. Come on.

They drove back to Tims Creek, down narrow back roads, through winding paths, alongside fields, into woods, into a meadow Dean had never seen before, near Chitaqua Pond. They arrived at the homeplace around midnight.

Is this where you take your boys?

Where did you think? To the mortuary?

So the house actually exists, Dean thought. This is for real. Part of him genuinely wanted to warn Ray, to protect him. But as Ray gave him a brief tour of the house where he had grown up (Can you believe this place is nearly ninety years old?): the kitchen with the deep enamel sink and the wood stove, the pantry with the neat rows of God-only-knows-how-old preserves and cans and boxes, the living room with the gaping fireplace where Christmas stockings had hung, the surprisingly functional bathroom; as they entered the bedroom where measles had been tended and babies created; as Ray rambled on absently about his aunt Helen and uncle Max (Aunt Helen is my great-granddaddy's youngest sister. She insists nothing change about this house. Nothing. If we sold it, it'd kill her); as he undressed Dean (No, please, allow me); as Dean, naked, stood with his back to Ray, those tender fingers exploring the joints and the hinges of his body; as a wet, warm tongue outlined, ever so lightly, the shape of his gooseflesh-cold body, Ray mumbling trance-like (All flesh is grass, my love, sweet, sweet grass) between bites, between pinches; as they slid into the plump featherbed that *scree-eee-creeked* as they lay there, underneath a quilt made by Ray's great-grandmother, multi-colored, heavy; as they joined at the mouth; as Dean trembled and tingled and clutched—all the while in his ears he heard a noise: faint at first, then loud, louder, then deafening: and he was not sure if the quickening *thu-thump-thump, thu-thump-thump* of his heartbeat came from Ray's bites on his nipples or from fear. Dean felt certain he heard the voices of old black men and old black women screaming for his death, his blood, for him to be strung up on a Judas tree, to die and breathe no more.

Far from home across the sea
To foreign parts I go;
When I am gone, O think of me
And I'll remember you.
Remember me when far away,
Whether asleep or awake.
Remember me on your wedding day
And send me a piece of your cake.

Dean!—His mother calls to him from the door to the house where she stands.—Dean! Did you get me some Bisquick?

Noum, he yells back, not stopping his back-and-forth, the rope on the limb creaking like the door to a coffin opening and closing.

How could you forget? I asked you this morning.

I just did.

You "just did." Shit. Well, we ain't got no bread neither, so you'll just eat with no bread. Boy, where is your mind these days?

Dean says nothing. He just rocks. Remembering. Noting the sky richening and deepening in color. Remembering. Seeing what he thinks might be a deer, way, way out. Remembering.

Remembering how it went on for a month, the meetings at the homeplace. Remembering how good being with Ray felt as spring crept closer and closer. Remembering the daffodils and the crocuses and the blessed jonquils and eating chocolate ice cream from the carton in bed afterward and mockingly calling each other honey and listening to the radio and singing, and Ray quoting some damn poet ("There we are two, content, happy in beauty together, speaking little, / perhaps not a word," as Mr. Whitman would say) and nibbling at his neck and breathing deeply and letting out a little sigh and saying, I've got to get home. Gloria— yeah, yeah, I know, I know. Remembering how he would tell himself: I ain't jealous of no black woman and of no black man; I don't care how much money he got. Remembering how he would drive home and climb into his cold and empty bed with the bad mattress and reach up and pull the metal chain on the light bulb that swung in the middle of the room. Remembering how he would huddle underneath the stiff sheets, thinking of Ray's voice, the feel of his skin, the smell of his aftershave, imagining Ray pulling into the driveway of his ranch-style brick house, dashing through rooms filled with nice things, wall-to-wall-carpeted floors, into the shower, complaining of the dealers and their boring conversations (I'm really sorry, honey; John Simon insisted we go to this barbecue joint in Goldsboro after the meeting and told me all this tedious foolishness about his mother-in-law and)—how he would probably kiss her while drying himself with a thick white towel as she sat reading a Bible commentary, and she would smile and say, Oh, I understand, Ray, and he would ooze his large mahogany body into a king-sized bed with her under soft damask sheets, fresh and clean and warm, and say, Night, honey, and melt away into dreams, perhaps not even of Dean. . . . Hell, I don't give a shit, Dean would think, staring into his bare, night-filled room. So what if he doesn't. So what if he does. Don't make no nevermind to me, do it? I'm in it for the money. Right?

Yet Dean had no earthly idea what Percy had in mind for Ray and, after a few weeks, thought it might have already happened or maybe never would.

But one morning, one Sunday morning in April, when Gloria and the girls had gone to Philadelphia for a weekend to see a sick sister and Ray had decided to spend the night with Dean at the homeplace, the first and only time Dean was to see morning there (through the window that sunrise he could see a mist about the meadow and the pond), while they lolled, intertwined in dreams and limbs, he heard the barking of dogs. Almost imperceptible at first. They came closer. Louder. He heard men's voices. As he turned to jog Ray awake he heard someone kick in the front door. The sound of heavy feet trampling. Hooting. Jeering.

Where is they? Where they at? I know they're here.

The order and the rhyme of what happened next ricocheted in a cacophony in Dean's head even now: Ray blinks awake: Percy: his three sons: the sound *snap-click-whurrr, snap-click-whurrr, snap-click-whurrr*: dogs yapping: tugging at their leashes: Well, well, well, look-a-here, boys, salt-'n'-pepper: a dog growls: the boys grin and grimace: Dean jumping up, naked, to run: Get back in that bed, boy: No, I—: I said get back in that bed: *snap-click-whurrr, snap-click-whurrr*: a Polaroid camera, the prints sliding out like playing cards from a deck: the sound of dogs panting: claws on wooden floors: the boys mumbling under their breath: fucking queers, fucking faggots: damn, out of film.

Like a voice out of the chaos Ray spoke, steely, calm, almost amused.—You know, you *are* trespassing, Terrell.

Land as good as mine now, son. I done caught you in what them college boys call *flagrante delecto,* ain't that what you'd call it, Ray? You one of them college boys. In the goddamn flesh. You got to damn near give me this here piece of property now, boy.

How do you figure that, Percy?

You a smart boy, Ray. I expect you can figure it.

Ray reached toward the nightstand. (A gun?)

A Terrell boy slammed a big stick down on the table in warning. A dog snapped.

Ray shrugged sarcastically.—A cigarette, maybe?

Bewildered, the boy glanced to his father, who warily nodded okay. Ray pulled out a pack of Lucky Strikes—though Dean had never known him to smoke—and deftly thumped out a single one, popped it into his mouth, reached for his matches, lit it, inhaled deeply, and blew smoke into the dog's face. The hound whined.

You got to be kidding, Terrell. You come in here with your boys and your dogs and pull this bullshit TV–movie camera stunt and expect me to whimper like some snot-nosed pickaninny, "Yassuh, Mr. Terrell, suh, I'll give you anything, suh. Take my house. Take my land. Take my wife. I sho is scared of you, suh." Come off it.—He drew on his cigarette.

Percy's face turned a strawberry color. He stood motionless. Dean expected him to go berserk. Slowly he began to nod his head up and down and to smile. He put his hands on his hips and took two steps back.—Now, boys, I want you to look-a-here. I respect this man. I do. I really do. How many men do you know, black or white, could bluff, cool as a cucumber, caught butt-naked in bed with a damn whore? A white boy whore at that. Wheee-hooo, boy! you almost had me fooled. Shonuff did.—Percy curled his lip like one of his dogs.—But you fucked up, boy. May as well admit it.

Ray narrowed his eyes and puffed.

You a big man in this county, Ray. You know it and I know it. Think about it. Think about your ole aunt Helen. Think about what that ole Reverend Barden'll say. A deacon and a trustee of his church. Can't have that. Think of your business. Who'll want you to handle their loved ones, Ray? Think of your *wife. Your girls.* I got me some eyewitnesses here, boy. Let somebody get one whiff of this . . . He turned with self-congratulatory delight to his boys. They all guffawed in unison, a sawing, inhuman sound.

Think on it, Ray. Think on it hard. Like I said, you're a smart boy.

I'll enjoy finally doing some business with you. And it won't be on a cool slab, I guarantee.

Percy walked, head down, feet clomping, over to Dean. He reached over and mussed Dean's hair as though he were some obedient animal. —You did a fine job, son. A mighty fine job. I'll take real good care of you. Just like I promised.

Dean had never seen Ray's face in such a configuration of anger, loathing, coldness, disdain, recognition, as though he suddenly realized he had been in bed with a cottonmouth moccasin or a stinking dog. It made the very air in the room change color. He stubbed out his cigarette and stared out the window.—Get out of my house, Terrell.—He said it quietly but firmly.

Oh, come on, Ray. Don't be sore. How else did you think you could get your hands on such a *fine* piece of white ass? I'm your pimp, boy. I'll send the bill directly.

Get out.

Percy patted Dean's head again.—I'll settle up with you later. Come on, boys. We's done here.—He tipped his hat to Ray, turned, and was gone, out the door, the boys and the dogs and the smell of mud and canine breath and yelping and stomping trailing out behind him like the cloak of some wicked king of darkness. Dean sat numb and naked, curled up in a tight ball like a cat. As if someone had snatched the covers from him and said: Wake up. Stop dreaming.

You get the hell out too.—Ray sat up, swinging his feet to the floor. He reached for another cigarette.

Dean began to shiver; more than anything else he could imagine at that moment, he wanted Ray to hold him, more than six thousand dollars, more than a new car. He felt like crying. He reached out and saw his pale hand against the broad bronze back and sensed the enormity of what he had done, that his hand could never again touch that back, never glide over its ridges and bends and curves, never linger over that mole, pause at this patch of hair, that scar. He looked about the room for some sign of change; but it remained the same: the oil lamp; the warped mirror; the walnut bureau; the cracked windowsill. But it would soon be gone. Percy would see to that.

Ray, I'm s—

I don't want to hear you. Okay? I don't want to see you. I don't want to know you. Or that you even existed. Ever. Get out. Now.

As Dean stood and pulled his clothes on, he wanted desperately to hate Ray, to dredge up every nigger, junglebunny, cocksucking, motherfucking, sambo insult he could muster; he wanted to relearn hate, fiery, blunt, brutal; he wanted to unlearn what he had learned in the very bed on which he was turning his back, to erase it from his memory, to blot it out, scratch over it. Forget. Walking out the door, he paused, listening for the voices of those dark ancestors who had accosted him upon his first entering. They were still. Perhaps appeased.

Little Miss Tuckett
Sat on a bucket,
Eating some peaches and cream.
There came a grasshopper
And tried hard to stop her,
But she said, "Go away, or I'll scream."

Dean looks over at his Ford Torino and worries that it may never run again. It has been in need of so many things, a distributor cap, spark plugs. The wiring about shot. Radiator leaks. He just doesn't have the money. Will he ever? He stands up with the tire around him and walks back, back, back, and jumps up in the air, the limb popping but holding. He swings high. He pushes a little with his legs on the way back. He goes higher. Higher.

Who said money is the root of all evil? Or was it the love of money? Love.

Six thousand dollars. This is my guarantee.

Dean waited six months. Twenty-four weeks. April. May. June. July. August. September. He watched the spring mature into summer and summer begin to ripen into autumn. He waited as his mother went into the hospital twice. First for an ovarian cyst. Next for a hysterectomy. He waited as the bills the insurance company would not take care of piled high. He waited as his mother was laid off again. He waited as the news blared across the York County *Cryer* and the Crosstown papers and the Raleigh papers: TERRELL FAMILY BUYS TEXTILE MILL, INTERNATIONAL SPINNING SOLD TO TERRELL INTERESTS, INTERNATIONAL SPINNING TO BECOME YORK EAST MILL. He waited through work, through the noise and the dust, through the gossip about daughters who ran off with young boys wanting to be country music stars, grandmothers going to the old folks' home, adulterous husbands and unwed mothers. He waited through some one-night stands with nameless truckers in nameless truckstops and bored workers at boring shopping malls. He waited. He waited through the times he ran into Ray, who ignored him. He waited through the times he had only a nickel and a dime in his pocket and had to borrow for a third time from his cousin Jimmy or his uncle Fred, and his mama would have to search and search in the cabinets for something to scare up supper with. He waited. He waited through news of Terrell making a deal with the Brown family for a tiny piece of property over by Chitaqua Pond, and of Raymond Frederick Brown's great-aunt Helen making a big stink and taking to her bed, ill. They said she was close to dead. But Dean waited. And waited. One hundred sixty and eight days. Waiting.

I'm going to Terrell, he finally decided on the last day of September. A late-summer thundercloud lasted all that day. Terrell still worked out of the general store his father had built, in an office at the back of the huge, warehouse-like structure. His boys ran the store. What if he says he ain't gone do nothing? What do I do then? Dean stood outside the store, peering inside, wind and rain pelting his face.

Terrell kept the store old-fashioned: a potbellied stove that blazed red-hot in winter; a glass counter filled with bright candies; a clanging granddaddy National Cash Register. The cabinets and the benches and the dirt all old and dark. Deer heads looked down from the walls. Spiderwebs formed an eerie tent under the ceiling. As Dean entered, he looked back to the antique office door with TERRELL painted on the glass; it seemed a mile from the front door.

What you want? The oldest Terrell boy held a broom.

Come to see your daddy.

What for?

Business.

What kind of business?

Between him and me.

The youngest Terrell walked up to Dean.—Like hell.

Dean saw Percy through the glass, preparing to leave. He jumped between the boys and ran.

Hey, where the hell you going?

Dean's feet pumped against the pine floor. He could hear six feet in pursuit. Terrell tapped on his hat as Dean slid into the wall like a runner into home plate, out of breath.—Mr. Terrell, Mr. Terrell, I got to talk to you. I got—

What you want, son?

Panting, Dean began to speak, the multitude of days piling up in the back of his throat, crowding to get out all at once.—You promised. My mama been in the hospital twice since March. My car's broke down. I just need to know when. When I—

When what, son?

All he had wished to tell Percy seemed to dry up in his head like spit on a hot July sidewalk. His mouth hung open. No words fell out.—You . . . you guaranteed . . .

"Guaranteed"? Boy, what *are* you talking about?—Terrell turned the key in the office door.

Ray Brown. Ray. You know. You promised. You . . .

Son—Terrell picked up his briefcase and turned to go—I don't know what in the Sam Hill you talking about.

Dean grabbed Percy's sleeve. The boys tensed.—Please, Mr. Terrell. Please. I did everything you asked. I . . .

Percy stared at Dean's hand on his sleeve for an uncomfortably long period. He reached down with his free hand and knocked Dean's away as though it were a dead fly.—Don't you ever lay a hand on me again, faggot.

He began to walk away, calling behind him: Don't be too long closing up, boys. You know how your mama gets when you're late.

Dean stood in the shadows watching Percy walk away.—I'll tell, god-damn it. I'll tell.—Dean growled, not recognizing his own voice.

Percy stopped stock-still. With his back to them all, he raised his chin a slight bit.—Tell? Who, pray tell, will you tell?—He pivoted around, a look of disgust smearing his face.—And who the *fuck* would believe you?

Dean felt his breathing come more labored, heavy. He could not keep his mouth closed, though he could force out no words. He felt saliva drooling down his chin.

Look at you.—Percy's head jerked back.—Look-at-you! A pathetic white-trash faggot whore. Who would think any accusation you brought against me, specially one as farfetched as what you got in mind to tell, would have ary one bit of truth to it. Shit.—Percy said under his breath. He walked to the door.—Show him the way out, boys. And don't be late now, you hear?—The wind *wa-banged* the door shut.

They beat him. They taunted him with limp wrists and effeminate whimpers and lisps. They kicked him. Finally they threw him out into the rain and mud. Through it all he said not a mumbling word. He did not weep. He sat in a puddle. In the rain. One eye closed. His bruises stinging. The taste of blood in his mouth. He sat in some strange limbo, some odd place of ghosts and shadows, knowing he must rise, knowing he had been badly beaten, knowing that the boys had stopped on their way out and, snickering, dropped a twenty-dollar bill in front of him (We decided we felt sorry for you. Here's a little something for you. Price of a blow job), knowing he could use the money, knowing he would be late for supper, knowing he could never really explain, never really tell anyone what had happened, knowing he would surely die one day—he hoped it would be now. He could not move.

After a while, though he had no idea how long a while, something stopped the rain from falling on him. An old man's voice spoke to him: You all right, son? You lose something?

Is that you, Lord? he thought. Have you come to take me? With all the energy he could gather, he lifted his head and looked through his one good eye.

An umbrella. An old gray-haired, trampy-looking man Dean did not know. Not the Lord. Dean opened his mouth, and the cut in his lip spurted fresh blood into his mouth. He moaned. No I'll be all right yes yes yes I will be all right yes.

Yes, sir. I did lose something. Something right fine.

Moses supposes his toeses are roses,
But Moses supposes erroneously;
For nobody's toeses are posies of roses
As Moses supposes his toeses to be.

Dean!—His mother calls to him.—Dean! Supper's ready. Better come on.

Dark has gobbled up the world. He can see the light from a house here and there. People are sitting down to suppers of peas and chicken. A bat's *ratta-tatta-tatta* wings dip by. He continues to swing. He continues to wait. He continues to wonder.

Wondering about how two weeks after going to Terrell's office— two weeks after, the wounds and bruises had mostly healed—two weeks after knowing he would not get a raise or a promotion, two weeks of wondering if he should tell someone something, how he was walking down the road toward home with two bags of groceries. How the bag split and how rice, beans, canned tuna, garbage bags, white bread, all came tumbling to the ground (though the milk carton didn't burst, he was happy to see), and how as he knelt down to pick everything up a beige Cadillac drove up, and how he heard the electric *whur* of the power windows going down, and how he heard a soft female voice say—Can I help you out?

He had never actually met Gloria Brown. She sat behind the wheel, her honey skin lightly powdered and smooth, her lips covered in some muted red like pink but not pink, her eyes intelligent and brown. In the back seat perched her two daughters, Ray's two daughters, their hair as shiny black as their patent-leather shoes. Their dresses white and green and neat.

It's all right, ma'am. I'm just down the road a piece.

But it's on my way. And you do seem to be having a little trouble. Hop on in. No trouble.

Dean collected the food and got into the front seat. I've never been in this car, he thought, feeling somehow entitled while knowing he had no right.

An a cappella gospel song in six-part harmony rang out from the stereo. Awful fine car, Dean wanted to say. But didn't.

We're heading to a revival meeting over at the Holiness Church.— She held the wheel gingerly, as if intimidated by the big purring machine. Her fingernails flashed an earthy orange color. Dean could smell her sweet and subtle perfume.

What church do you belong to?

Me? I don't, ma'am.

That's a shame. Well, you know Jesus loves you anyway. Are you saved?

Saved? From what?

Why, from Hell and Damnation, of course.

I guess not.

Well, keep your heart open. He'll speak to you. "For all have sinned and fallen short of the will of God."

Dean felt slightly offended but could think of nothing to say. He groped for words. Finally he said: Some things you just let happen.

Gloria turned to him the way one would turn upon hearing the voice of someone long dead; at first puzzled, then intrigued.—My husband always says that. Now ain't that funny.

Dean forced a chuckle.—Yes, ma'am. I reckon it is.

Gloria dropped him off at his house, her voice lilting after him with concern (Can you get to the house all right? Want the girls to help you?). He thanked her, no, he could manage. The Cadillac drove off into the early evening. This is a road of ghosts, he thought. Spooks just don't like for a soul to know peace. Keep on coming to haunt.

If all the world was apple pie
And all the sea was ink,
And all the trees were bread and cheese,
What would we have to drink?

Dean! Boy, you better bring your butt on in here, now. Food's getting cold.

He doesn't feel hungry. He doesn't feel like sitting at the table with his mama. He doesn't feel like listening to her talk and complain or to the TV or to the radio. He doesn't feel like telling her that he was notified today that as of next Friday he will be laid off "indefinitely." He feels like sitting in the tire. Like swinging. Like waiting.

Waiting for the world to come to an end. Waiting for this cruel dream world to pass away. Waiting for the leopard to lie down with the kid and the goats with the sheep. Waiting for everything to be made all right— 'cause I know it will be all right, it has to be all right—and he will sit like Little Jack Horner in a corner with his Christmas pie and put in a thumb and pull out a plum and say: What a good, what a good, oh what a good boy am I.

~ *Bernard Cooper* ~

Six
Fables

Atlantis

How did the barber pole originate? When did its characteristic stripes become kinetic, turning hypnotically, driven by a hidden motor, giving the impression of red and blue forever twining, never slowing? No matter. No icon or emblem, no symbol or sign, still or revolving, lit from within or lit from without, could in any way have prepared me for that haircut at Nick's Barber Shop, or for Nick himself. His thick Filipino accent obscured meaning, though the sound was mellifluous, and the sense, translated in the late afternoon light, was expressed in the movements of Nick's hands. He flourished a comb he never dropped, a soundless scissors, a razor which revealed, gently, gently, the nape of my neck, now so smooth, attuned to the wind and the wool of my collar.

After our initial exchange of misunderstood courtesies, Nick nudged me toward a wall, museum bright, on which hung a poster depicting the "Official Haircuts for Men and Boys" from 1955. I understood immediately that I was to choose from among the Brush Cut, the Ivy League, the Flat Top with Fenders. To insure sanctity and a sense of privacy, Nick

---

BERNARD COOPER's collection Maps to Anywhere *won the PEN/Hemingway Prize in 1991. Part stories, part essays, part poems, his prose works defy and at the same time expand the traditional parameters of fiction. He has also recently published a novel,* A Year of Rhymes. *He lives in Los Angeles.*

turned off the fan for a moment, lowered his head, and even the dust stopped drifting in abeyance. Above me, in every phase from profile to full front, were heads of hair, luxuriant, graphic, lacquer-black: outmoded curls like scrolls on entablature, sideburns rooted in the past, strands and locks in arrested motion, cresting waves styled into hard edges, like Japanese prints of typhoons.

None of the heads contained a face. One simply interjected his own face. These oval vessels waited to be filled again and again by men's imaginations. For decades, they absorbed the eyes and noses and lips of customers who stood on the checkerboard of old linoleum, or sat in salmon-pink chairs next to wobbling tables stacked with magazines featuring bikinis and ball games.

The haircut was over in no time. (Nick did a stint in the army, where expedience is everything.) I kept my eyes closed. But aware of strange and lovely afterimages—ghostly pay phone, glowing push broom—I seemed to be submerged in the rapture of the deep. The drone of the fan, the minty and intoxicating scent of Barbasol, pressed upon me; phosphene shimmered like minnows in the dark corners of my vision, and I found that this world, cigar stained, sergeant striped, basso profundo, was the lost world of my father, who could not love me. So when Nick kneaded my shoulders and pressed my temples (free scalp manipulation with every visit), I unconsciously grazed him like a cat in Atlantis. His fingers flowed over my forehead like water. I began to smile imperceptibly and see barber poles aslant like sunken columns and voluptuous mermaids in salmon-pink bikinis and bubbles the size of baseballs rising to the surface and bursting with snippets of Filipino small talk.

I can't tell you how odd it was when, restored by a splash of astringent tonic, I finally opened my eyes and saw a clump of my own hair, blown by the fan, skitter across the floor like a cat. For a moment the mirrors were unbearably silver, and the hand-lettered signs, reflected in reverse, seemed inscriptions in a long-forgotten language.

Indeed I looked better, contented. Older too in the ruddy light of sunset. And all of this, this seminal descent to the floor of the sea, this inundation of two paternal hands, this sudden maturation in the mirror, for only four dollars and fifty cents. But my debt of gratitude, beyond the dollar-fifty tip, will be paid here, in the form of Nick's actual telephone number, area code (213) 660-4876. Even his business card, adorned with a faceless haircut holding a phone, says, "Call any time!"

Nick means any time. He means day or night. I've driven by and glimpsed him asleep in the barber chair, his face turned toward the street, his combs soaking in blue medicinal liquid, the barber pole softly aglow like a nightlight, the stripes cascading endlessly down, rivulets running toward a home in the ocean.

Capiche?

In Italy, the dogs say bow-bow instead of bow-wow, and my Italian teacher, Signora Marra, is not quite sure why this should be. When we tell her that here in America the roosters say cock-a-doodle-do, she throws back her head like a hen drinking raindrops and laughs uncontrollably, as if we were fools to believe what our native red rooster says, or ignoramuses not to know that Italian roosters scratch and preen and clear their gullets before reciting Dante to the sun.

In Venice there is a conspicuous absence of dogs and roosters, but all the pigeons on the planet seem to roost there, and their conversations are deafening. When the city finally sinks, only a thick dark cloud of birds will be left to undulate over the ocean, birds kept alive by pure nostalgia and a longing to land. And circulating among them will be stories, reminiscences, anecdotes of all kinds to help pass the interminable days. Even when this voluble cloud dissipates, the old exhausted birds drowning in the sea, the young bereft birds flying away, the sublime and untranslatable tale of the City of Canals will echo off the oily water, the walls of vapor, the nimbus clouds.

There were so many birds in front of Café Florian's, and mosquitoes sang a piercing song as I drank my glass of red wine. Waving them away, I inadvertently beckoned Sandro, a total stranger. With great determination, anxious to know me, he bounded around tables of tourists.

The Piazza San Marco holds many noises within its light-bathed walls, sounds that clash, are superimposed or densely layered like torte. Within that cacophony of words and violins, Sandro and I struggled to communicate. Something unspoken suffered between us. We were, I think, instantly in love, and when he offered me, with his hard brown arms, a blown-glass ashtray shaped like a gondola, all I could say, all I could recall of Signora Marra's incanting and chanting (she believed in saturating students in rhyme), was "No capiche." I tried to inflect into that phrase every modulation of meaning, the way different tonalities of light had changed the meaning of that city.

But suddenly this adventure is over. Everything I have told you is a lie. Almost everything. There is no lithe and handsome Sandro. I've never learned Italian or been to Venice. Signora Marra is a feisty fiction. But lies are filled with modulations of untranslatable truth, and early this morning when I awoke, birds were restless in the olive trees. Dogs tramped through the grass and growled. The local rooster crowed fluently. The Chianti sun was coming up, intoxicating, and I was so moved by the strange, abstract trajectories of sound that I wanted to take you with me somewhere, somewhere old and beautiful, and I honestly wanted to offer you something, something like the prospect of sudden love, or color postcards of chaotic piazzas, and I wanted you to listen to me as if you were hearing a rare recording by Enrico Caruso. All I had was the glass of language to blow into a souvenir.

Sudden Extinction

The vertebrae of dinosaurs, found in countless excavations, are dusted and rinsed and catalogued. We guess and guess at their huge habits as we gaze at the fossils which capture their absence, sprawling three-toed indentations, the shadowy lattice of ribs. Their skulls are a slight embarrassment, snug even for a head full of blunt wants and backward motives. The brachiosaurus's brain, for example, sat atop his tapered neck like a minuscule flame on a mammoth candle.

My favorite is triceratops, his face a hideous Rorschach blot of broad bone and blue hide. The Museum of Natural History owns a replica that doesn't do him justice. One front foot is poised in the air like an elephant sedated for a sideshow. And the nasal horn for shredding aggressors is as dull and mundane as a hook for a hat.

One prominent paleontologist believes that during an instantaneous ice age, glaciers encased these monsters midmeal—stegosaurus, podokesaurus, iguanadon—all trapped forever like spectrums in glass. But suppose extinction was a matter of choice, and they just didn't want to stand up any longer, like drunk guests at a party's end who pass out in the dark den. There are guys at my gym whose latissimus dorsi, having spread like thunderheads, cause them to inch through an ordinary door; might the dinosauria have grown too big of their own volition?

Derek speaks in expletives and swears that one day his back will be as big as a condominium. Mike's muscles, marbled with veins, perspire from ferocious motion, the taut skin about to split. When Bill does a bench press, the barbell bends from fifty-pound plates; his cheeks expand and expel great gusts of spittle and air till his face and eyes are flushed with blood and his elbows quiver, the weight sways, and someone runs over and hovers above him roaring for one more repetition.

Once, I imagined our exercise through X-ray eyes. Our skeletons gaped at their own reflection. Empty eyes, like apertures, opened onto an afterlife. Lightning-bright spines flashed from sacrums. Phalanges of hands were splayed in surprise. Bones were glowing everywhere, years scoured down to marrow, flesh redressed with white.

And I knew our remains were meant to keep like secrets under the earth. And I knew one day we would topple like monuments, stirring up clouds of dust. And I almost heard the dirge of our perishing, thud after thud after thud, our last titanic exhalations loud and labored and low.

Leaving

The statistical family stands in a textbook, graphic and unabashed. The father, tallest, squarest, has impressive shoulders for a stick figure. The mother, slighter, rounder, wears a simple triangle, a skirt she might have sewn herself.

A proud couple of generalizations, their children average 2.5 in number. One boy and one girl, inked in the indelible stance of the parents, hold each other's iconic little hands. But the .5 child is isolated, half a figure, balanced on one leg, one hand extended as if to touch the known world for the last time, leaving probable pounds of bread and gallons of water behind, leaving the norms of income behind, leaving behind the likelihood of marriage (with its orgasms estimated in the thousands), leaving tight margins, long columns, leaving a million particulars, without hesitation, without regret.

The Origin of Roget's Thesaurus

for Brian Miller

When Anne-Marie sidles up and bends slightly forward, her starched uniform crackles like a distant fire, and she discreetly, yet suggestively, offers potatoes with gravy to Dr. Roget. The smell of garlic assails his nose, and then the lilac smell of Anne-Marie, distinct odors fused into something mesmerizing, difficult to name. His nostrils flare. His eyes cloud up. His fork becomes inconceivably heavy. What precisely is this sensation, this suffusion of fragrance, appetite, lust? What rubric or term or adjective could capture it? He thinks *delicious.* No, *delightful.* Then the panorama of *pleasantness* opens in his brain: *pleasing, enchanting, appealing,* a vast and verdant country. But further inland, in the dark heart of Dr. Roget's confusion, lies the antonymous terrain of *unpleasantness,* its odious flora and horrible fauna, and he doesn't know where to turn.

"Peter?" murmurs Mrs. Roget, miles away at the end of the table.

"Daddy?" murmurs Peter junior, beneath a branching candelabrum.

Hush, hush. Doors are opening in Daddy's head, doors that lead to halls of doors that lead to other labyrinthine, musty halls of doors. Door by door, word by word, an entire lexicon will be discovered. A draft will begin to move through portals, the wind to whistle fluently, and someday Daddy will reach a door opening onto the sea.

~ ~ ~

The moment before we make love, I think about the sea at night. I'm clutching the sail of your broad warm back.

What tenuous connections, what tributaries of association brought me from the landscape in Roget's brain to your body beyond the limits of land? What convoluted currents of chance, what chain reaction of history took me drifting from my boyhood on the coast of California and propelled me to you, here in this bed in this vessel on the black undulating ocean, to this very second when I can't stop thinking, synapses flashing like stars, the doors in my head opening, opening, the wind of my words against your back: *supple, tractable, bendable, mutable . . .*

Childless

So I was talking to this guy who's the photo editor of *Scientific American*, and he told me he was having trouble choosing a suitable photograph of coral sperm for an upcoming issue. I was stunned because I'd always thought of coral as inanimate matter, a castle of solidified corpses, though corpses of what I wasn't sure. Of course, I had to find out what coral sperm looks like, and he told me it's round and fuchsia. I could see it perfectly, or so I supposed, as if through an electron microscope, buoyant and livid, pocked like golf balls, floating like dust motes. Still, I couldn't visualize the creature who constitutes female coral, as distinct from male, toward whom one seminal ball went bouncing, like a bouncing ball over lyrics to a song. It was kind of sad to think that, for all its flamboyant fans, osseous reefs, gaudy turrets, coral was one more thing, or species of thing, about which I knew almost nothing, except that it generates sperm, round, fuchsia.

The funny thing about being a man who is childless and intends to stay that way is that you almost never think of yourself as possessing spermatazoa. Semen, yes; but not those discrete entities, tadpoles who frolic in the microcosm of your aging anatomy, future celebrities who enter down a spiral staircase of deoxyribonucleic acid, infinitesimal relay runners who lug your traits, coloration, and surname from points remote and primitive. Certainly you don't believe that the substance you spill when you huff and heave in a warm tantrum of onanism could ever, given a million years and a Petri dish and an infrared lamp, could ever come to resemble you. It would be like applauding wildly at a Broadway play and then worrying that you hurt the mites who inhabit the epidermis of your hands. Death is all around us, and we sometimes assist.

Anyway, there are so many varieties of life, and hardly enough Sunday afternoons to watch all those educational programs that teach you about the reproductive mechanisms of albino mountain goats with antlers that branch off and thin away like thoughts before you fall asleep. And sloths who move so slowly they never dry off from morning dew and so possess emerald coats of mold. And yonic orchids housing pools of perfume in which bees drink and wade and drown.

The first time I was alone in the wilderness, I walked through a field that throbbed with song and wondered whether crickets played their wings or their legs. My footfalls, instead of causing the usual thud, caused spreading pools of solemn silence. Sound stopped wherever I walked. And I walked and walked to hush the world, leaving silence like spoor.

~ *Peter Wells* ~

Perrin
and the Fallen
Angel

Who has not been a slut has not been human.

E ric Westmore did not consider himself either a beauty or a gorgon. People did not run out of rooms gagging: but, on the other hand, not too many were driven to distraction by his glance. This did not preclude great explosions of attraction: yet such was Eric's nature, ironic, self-mocking—or was it merely self-doubting?—that he always put these frissons down to poor eyesight or a case of mistaken identity, which would almost inevitably catch up with him sooner or later.

He sat now in the brackish quiet of the Alexandra Hotel. It was 10 April 1986.

The Alex was a charmingly Edwardian hostelry on the outside, a wedding cake of plaster arranged, tastefully, to snare passersby on two back streets: it looked like the tiara, Eric always thought, of a minor Scottish peeress. It was the last week of it being a gay or, indeed, any kind of pub. It was going to be demolished. All over the city, in a spec-ulative frenzy driven by the stock market, Edwardian and Victorian Auck-land was being reduced to dust.

Even now, as Eric sat in the dullard moments of the quarter hour

---

A native of Auckland, New Zealand, PETER WELLS is the author of the story collection Dangerous Desires. *He also wrote and directed the 1986 film* A Death in the Family.

before noon, demolition drills were attacking the air in nearby streets, a dull repetitive sound, drill to a toothache.

Yet it was a beautiful day, he said to himself, inclined to feel mellow (he was, after all, in the opening stages of, as he himself said, *a romance,* putting just the right ironic emphasis on what some might call a love affair and others might call a fuck). It was a superb day in early autumn: the crispness of winter had begun to lie like an essence over the lingering heat of summer. As if to symbolise his content, just as Eric walked down the street towards the pub, a yacht had serenely passed across the gap between two buildings, tightrope walker on his line of bliss.

Yet.

Eric, on the cusp of thirty-eight, aware that the tidal shifts of time were now beginning to run against him in a way that no amount of gym or artful haircuts could entirely alter, knew there always had to be a *yet,* a determinant in his bliss.

The *yet* he was thinking of now, as he sat in the pub gazing thoughtfully at a block of sun on the carpet—"like winter butter set out on a white porcelain dish," he memorised for his column—was the phone call from Perrin that morning.

The phone had gone off at seven-thirty, aggressive as an alarm.

Matthew was still in the shower, while Eric was standing in front of the stove, staring mindlessly at the milk he was scalding for caffè latte.

Perrin's voice cut through his groggy sleepiness. "Can we meet today?"

"Today?" said Eric, who was still adjusting the sensuality of the night before to the demands of prosaic daylight.

"Yes, today," said Perrin without any of his customary humour. He sounded pissed off—or was it sour?

Did he suspect already, Eric wondered, about Matthew?

Matthew, as if an apparition appearing on cue, walked into the kitchen stark naked. Eric admired his body—which, of course, he was meant to do: his freedom, his flanks, his beautiful tassel-like cock. Matthew did a small coquettish whirl, then sat down, forgetting Eric completely, and, picking up the morning's newspaper, began to study his horoscope.

"As soon as possible," said Perrin's voice, again, in Eric's ear.

Eric had taken his eyes away from Matthew, unwillingly, and cast his mind ahead to his day. He thought of how much more work he had to do to get his daily food column readable. Then there was his guerrilla raid on an unsuspecting new restaurant, the one specialising in New Zealand game products.

"What about after six?" Eric suggested, looking tentatively at Matthew.

Matthew was, instead, investigating his pubic hairs with a monomaniacal scrutiny.

"No. Earlier." Perrin was being relentlessly persistent.

"You could meet me at that new place—Faringays. I've got to *cruelle* it."

Perrin and he always called Eric's reviews "to *cruelle de ville*" it.

A pause.

Perrin's response was definitive. "I don't feel like food."

Silence again as, in the background, Eric heard someone say good morning to Perrin and Perrin, crisply adjusting his tone to genial busy executive, batted back the greeting. Perrin said then, close to the phone: "I want to see you, Eric. *I need to see you baby*," he said in one long breath of confession.

Oh no, sweetheart, you haven't been seeing Sweet Sixteen *again*, Eric was about to whiplash back. Sweet Sixteen was a troublesome, if nubilely splendid, Niue Islander Perrin was being relentlessly pursued by. But something about Perrin's tone told him it was not going to be their usual enjoyable slanging match, in which mutual insult and hilarious parody mounted up until Perrin, almost inevitably, managed to cap Eric off with a flourish of obscene absurdity. Perhaps it was too early in the morning.

Or perhaps, Eric thought more reasonably, Perrin had a hangover. Or was it just that super-melodramatic flu which was casting Perrin into increasingly sombre moods: what Eric lightly dubbed his *"dame aux camellias"* complex.

"*Please*," said Perrin, who was not one to beg.

Eric had quickly succumbed. They would meet at the Alex a few minutes before twelve. They would go on from there to somewhere "quiet."

Just as he put the receiver down, in that second before Perrin clicked off, Eric had an insane urge to put the phone back up to his ear, to listen harder, deeper, more faithfully to the textures of Perrin's silences, the underground music of his tone. But Eric was running late. His deadline for his food column was leering, the phone was already shrilling, and then, of course, he had had hardly any sleep after his night with Matthew. *Matthew.*

It was true, a good seven eighths of his mind was given over to, willingly occupied by, thoughts of this young man who had suddenly, accidentally—impetuously—entered his life. Even as Eric now sat waiting at the Alex, eleven minutes before noon on that April day in 1986, he closed his eyes for a second, to reconnect with that world which still swirled, fragrantly as the scents of sex, through his consciousness.

Obligingly—or was it obediently?—he was wafted up to a serene and great height, as if he were in a glider which could not, would not, ever meet with catastrophe. And far below him he saw the body of Matthew, a vast landscape which stretched from horizon to horizon: a country he was beginning to be familiar with, his favourite destinations—Matthew's mouth, between his legs, his smooth buttocks like peeled grapes. Was it folly for a writer on food to conceptualise his new lover in terms of fruit, of vegetables? (His cock a courgette left on the vine too long and grown tautly too large, the pillows of his chest a perfectly ripe pawpaw he loved to lick and gnaw on, the cleft of his arsehole, well, not to be too ridiculous, moistly pink as perfectly cured Christmas ham. He could go on, his Matthew, his banquet, his feast.)

Perhaps this objectification, Eric lectured himself as he sat there, was simply defensive. It was part of his emotional defensiveness that he tried to picture Matthew in terms of appetite, keeping clear of that minefield, that scarred battleground of the emotions called love. Oh, keep me clear of that, sighed Eric, seasoned trooper of the wars of the heart.

With a conscious effort—but also with a pang of regret that he must leave such a perfumed landscape, one with its own laws, its own hegemony over his unconscious—he tried to focus on the exact present.

He dallied with his glass of tonic, looking for a moment at the bubbles. Then a faint smile of anticipation softened his face. He longed for Perrin to arrive, so he could gently, as if accidentally, spill the treasure of his new romance before Perrin's eyes.

He had been seeing Matthew for over three weeks, and though Perrin and he, old friends, well, *ancient* friends, touched base at least once a week, he had carefully screened the event from Perrin, until the romance, affair, the series of fucks—whatever it was—had some stable *emotional* basis.

Perrin, meanwhile, had noticed nothing: neither Eric's soaring spirits, nor his pleasurable languor, nor even, on the one occasion he had managed to coax Perrin down to the pool, the expressive love bites on the back of Eric's neck.

Perrin was inclined to be myopic anyway. His battles at the Equal Opportunities Commission, where he was a pugnacious lawyer, at times occupied all his fields of vision: when he wasn't, that is, pursuing remarkable pieces of Clarice Cliff, or unusually sensual young men whom he unearthed from unlikely situations, like post offices in small towns or half-empty laundromats—any of those situations which require a selective perception, tempered by endurance and fired by an almost fanatical flare of desire, and desirability. Or was it an unfillable capacity to be approved of, to be loved?

Perhaps that was why Eric wanted to torment Perrin, just slightly, at this moment. Perrin always had such spectacular success sexually (with, of course, its attendant moments of tedium, like courses of penicillin) that Eric felt drab and frowsy beside him. Eric always felt, in this situation, that his own desirability was diminished, a point he was not beyond getting petty about.

So now he carefully, and with a sense of epicurean enjoyment, selected his poisoned shafts. "He (Matthew) is twenty-three (young), a student of architecture (a brain). He plays basketball (good body). And he's cute (rampant sexually)."

Eric toyed with the various ways he could casually, without undue emphasis, introduce this new persona to his and Perrin's life. Eric knew Perrin would want particulars: he would realise, as soon as Eric had introduced Matthew to him verbally, that it was merely a prelude to him meeting Matthew himself. Eric always regarded it as part of his lovers' educational process that they should meet someone as civilised, as exquisitely nuanced, as Perrin. Many a callow youth had learnt a correct table setting in his presence.

Perrin would, perhaps, have him and Matthew round for one of his delightfully casual, perfectly produced Thai meals. Other friends would be there. They would range over politics, personalities, fashion, food. In this way Matthew would enter a mutual zone of friendship, that *terra cognita* Eric had relied on ever since he had discovered it, tremblingly, in a state of hilarious ignorance, in what he now called, with sardonic quotation marks around it, *his youth*.

He looked around appreciatively. It was in a pub like this, Victorian, slightly seedy, scented with all the beers supped by many forgotten drinkers—to drown what sorrows, evoke what dreams, nobody could any longer say—that he and Perrin had first met.

~ ~ ~

It had been Eric's first venture into a gay pub.

In a mood of determination which had about it the air of a suicide mission, Eric had bid farewell to his old self in his bedroom mirror and set out, one Friday night (15 May 1969, his old, deplorable diaries told him—marked with a significant *X*). He had presented himself, white-faced, at the bar. As far as he could see, there were only men there, apart from one extraordinary woman who appeared to be the hostess. She was dressed, head to foot, in a glittering black muumuu, her most pronounced feature a suntan so intense it appeared less her skin than a form of basted flesh on which pieces of gold were placed, ornamentally, to great advantage. This theme was carried into her mouth, where her teeth were bedizened in a similar precious metal. Overall she escaped, by a mere hair's breadth, being spectacularly gaudy.

Eric went straight to the bar and asked for something he took to be a typically sophisticated "gay" drink. "A Negroni, please."

The barman had looked at him, was about to ask how old he was. Then something in Eric's face—his desperation, perhaps—made him hesitate and then, speaking almost *sotto voce,* say, "Wait a sec." He turned to serve two men who hung on each other's shoulders and, both casting conspicuous looks at Eric yet making him feel as if he wasn't quite there, continued to address each other in fluted tones.

Both men wore what Eric took to be a club uniform: white shoes, beige crimplene slacks, and hair which appeared to be both subtly teased and unsubtly lacquered. Their faces, variously wrinkled, were glaucous with moisturiser. "Two double gin and tonics, love," one of them asked the barman, in tones not quite so orchestral.

His companion smiled tentatively at Eric, and Eric felt his face crack a little as he smiled back. His heart was beating so hard he felt sure they could hear it.

The men departed, and the barman casually came back. "Do you know how to make a Negroni," he asked quietly, without any suggestion of aggression or even undue attention in his voice.

Eric flushed. He did. His throat was dry when he started speaking: he coughed up air over sandpaper.

The barman waited. Eric nodded. "Yes," he said, and told him.

While the man proceeded to make it, Eric said to him: "I looked it up." Then he said: "I like reading recipes." As he said this, he felt a swoon overtake him, a flush begin to rise up his face.

The barman had turned to look over his shoulder at him, not so much sharply but as if to check out the ingenuousness of the remark. Seeing Eric's discomfort, he slid the drink towards him and, shaking his head when Eric offered payment, solemnly withdrew.

Eric realised something nice had happened to him.

Safely in possession of something to hold, something to do, Eric slid his tongue into his drink experimentally. As soon as the alcohol hit his tongue, he had to try hard not to let his face react. It did not taste as he imagined the recipe would. Nevertheless, having obtained the drink in such special circumstances, he could hardly go back and ask for something else.

He must enjoy himself: that terrible imperative. He looked around the room to see who was looking at him. No one. It was extraordinary.

He looked around again, in panic. Nobody was taking the slightest bit of notice of him.

It was at this moment—this lacuna in his life—that Perrin McDougal walked in the door.

At this stage, before he had settled sublimely into his looks, wearing them with all the assurance of a bespoke jacket on carefully muscular shoulders, Perrin appeared a diffident, indifferent-looking youth. He was thin, high-nosed, dressed dramatically, head to toe, in black. He paused under a light, as if for dramatic effect, then threw his long amethyst scarf over his shoulder with a defiant emphasis.

This caused a momentary hush—almost of awe at someone contravening "taste" so much. Then at the back a voice was heard to say something—thankfully, Eric thought, indistinct (it sounded like "drama queen")—then there were guffaws or collapsed lungs of laughter.

Perrin, holding his profile in a distinctly Oscar Wilde manner (the young Oscar Wilde), as if he did not hear, obtained a drink and went into speedy exile—a miscalculation of effects?—by a wall.

Inevitably, it seemed, because they were the two people on their own, so spectacularly isolated, their eyes located each other. It was like radar —radar of the dispossessed.

It was Perrin who finally made the move across the room to him. Sidling up, he looked at Eric for a moment, radiant with silence.

Eric, panicking—was this his first pickup?—said, with a dry voice, "There's quite a crowd here tonight, isn't there?"

His new companion turned on him an eye from which satirical emphasis was not entirely absent. "I *hate* crowds," Perrin pronounced.

"Why . . . why do you wear black?" Eric asked, racking his brain for clever, unusual things to say.

"I'm in mourning for the world, of course," Perrin said superbly.

Eric, who was not *au fait* with Edith Sitwell's autobiography, believed he found himself in the presence of acerbic genius. "Are you from out of town?" he asked, looking into Perrin's thin face, pimples just visible by his nose.

Perrin seemed uncomfortable, even nervous. Nevertheless, so convinced was he of his superiority that he looked Eric up and down, then said drily: "The unpleasant fact of the matter is, I come from a Rue Morgue called Hamilton."

Eric's eyes widened. "That has a lake, doesn't it?"

"In which," said Perrin, who spoke as if always between parentheses, "the unhappy citizenry are driven to throw themselves, for their *divertissement.*"

Eric laughed, and Perrin congratulated him on his appreciation of wit, with a surprisingly shy, even tentative, smile. Then he turned to the room, sighing slightly.

"You see before you . . . a refugee. In fact, I clean dishes at the Hungry Horse."

Eric saw that Perrin was by no means as self-assured as the turn of his scarf, the cut of his phrase. With this discovery, he felt himself to have attained a similar, happy refugee status.

A long, not unfriendly silence fell in which both did an inventory of the room, frequently and nervously sipping their drinks.

Eric was soon surprised to find his glass was empty: not a drop could be seduced from its shimmery viscous surface. Perrin's glass was similarly empty.

They both looked down at the diminution of their hopes and, as if in musical concert, sighed heavily together.

It was clear that, having created grand effects, neither had a penny.

"What were you drinking?" Perrin asked.

Eric, tentatively, told him. Perrin was thoughtfully silent (later he would admit he had never heard of the drink). "I only ever drink Fallen Angels," he said, with a high tilt to his nose which Eric read as instant glamour.

From that day on he would always think of Perrin—who later came to detest the drink as oversweet, the epitome of his early lack of sophistication, his suburban pretensions—as synonymous with that first occasion, when they had both tremblingly met and Perrin's mode of identification was, along with Edith Sitwell, a long amethyst scarf, a sense of the early Oscar Wilde, and a drink called Fallen Angel.

~ ~ ~

Later that night they left the pub, as if accidentally, together.

They walked to the bus stop still talking, and each, on the point of saying good-bye, speedily allowed the other to understand that he could be found at the pub the following Friday.

Neither confessed it was his very first visit.

~ ~ ~

Now, sitting in the Alex so many years later, more mature, filled out into his body in a way which made him feel he knew himself, Eric glanced around the bar. The men there all knew they were men: the few women's names bandied about were always used, as it were in quotation marks, knowingly camp. The barman, fleshily muscular, with a tightly trimmed moustache, looked for all the world like a rudimentary Tom of Finland sketch requiring a few master strokes for sublime completion.

This world of the Alex now was light-years away from that hotel, so long ago, in which Eric had nervously awaited his second meeting with Perrin.

That night Eric had allowed himself a small glass of beer. He was determined to keep sober. While he waited, anonymously, the crowd had swiftly grown. It was late summer, and there was that lax, overexcited air of sensuality—of louche possibilities—in the air.

Eric relaxed his body against the wall.

"Everything O.K. here, darlink?" a voice said to the side of him.

Eric turned. Pushing through the crowd towards him, like a beaver, was a small man with waved pale-blue hair and what looked like make-up on his face—or was it simply moisturiser? As he got nearer he closed his pink, slightly unguent lips together, cupid-fashion, and then laughed, revealing teeth which looked older than he was.

"Darlink! hold *onto* your funwig," this man murmured to him, a mite melodramatically. His whole face was animated by a pleasantly puckish charm.

"Oh?" said Eric, not knowing quite how to reply. He broke out laughing.

Now, "Call me Fay," the little man said, pausing as if for breath. "After the late great Fay Wray," he murmured then, looking around the room in small darts and flicks, poisoned pricks of looks. "We call her late," whispered Fay, "because she never comes on time! Famous for it!"

He looked around sharply, no longer smiling. "Excuse me, dear, a dreadful clutch of old hags awaits," declared Fay in a conspiratorial whisper, during which Eric felt his backside pinched, not unpleasurably—as if the man called Fay were a merchant and he was only taking a prudent feel of the fabric. Fay indicated with his head four men standing together, bodies turned, almost on display, to the constituents of the bar: "We call them Boil, Toil, Struggle, and Poke."

"Ciao," he called then, melting back into the throng. Eric imagined the departing remark was a Chinese code-word.

At this point Perrin appeared beside him, unwinding himself out of his long purple scarf, sweating and bad-tempered. He had missed his bus and had to hitch a lift, he said. He intimated it had not been a pleasant adventure. When his lift found out the nature of the pub, he had turned threatening. Perrin had opened the door while the car was still moving and run, he said with superb dramatic emphasis, "for my very life."

But he still had in his hands a gift for Eric: a "borrowed" library copy of Edith Sitwell's autobiography. "The beginning of your *aesthetic* education, my dear," he said expansively.

Eric bought a round of Fallen Angels, nonchalantly, as if this were an everyday drink for both. They drank these perhaps too quickly. Then Perrin bought a round.

By this time the room, as crowded as an audience at a boxing ring, had taken on a certain hectic tone: at any moment, it seemed, the bell would ping, the lights would lower, the main match would start. Obligingly, the bells began to shrill, urgent as the flutter of blood coursing through Eric's wrists.

534 ~ The Penguin Book of Gay Short Stories

Fay suddenly popped up beside him, almost with a suggestion of old-time vaudeville magic (later he found out that Fay had trained in Sydney as a show dancer before breaking his hip and ending up as a waiter). As the tidal swell of men swirled him past, Fay called out, "Do you want to come to a party?"

"Oh," said Eric, thinking.

"*Yes*," said Perrin quickly. "*I* would."

~ ~ ~

Everyone was spectacularly drunk. People were walking about, banging into walls. A middle-aged man, unwatched by most, was doing an im-promptu, slightly wobbly strip on a chair. "Oh, *trust* Fanny," someone was saying acidly. "One *whiff* of alcohol, and *off* come her easies." Another fanatically serious man circulated through the crowd, wearing some-one's mother's best ming-blue bri-nylon suit.

Eric and Perrin stood together in a crowded kitchen. Fay was surrounded by people, as if he were a great courtesan holding court.

"And yes, they put me on the overnight from Wellington," Fay was saying, "*escorted* onto it by two large beasts. *Irish detectives.* They put me on and said, 'Don't be in too much of a hurry to come back.' Just to remind me they punched me. In turns." There was silence. "And then, after that, they said, 'We've got some mates up in Auckland *waiting for you when you get in.* Just to make sure you don't cause any trouble up there, like.'"

Fay left a brief, eloquent pause. "So here I am, a poor helpless wretch," he resumed, raising his eyes heavenward, in roguish imitation of a wilting Mary Pickford. He lisped softly, and with extraordinarily convincing pathos, "just doing the best that I can." A particularly wicked look passed over his face.

Fay then rose with great dignity, the dignity of an Empress Eugenie receiving the news of the fall of the Third Empire, the death of her only son. He turned and, in a spectacular wavering motion, as if tilting to follow the impulse of his feet, he listed towards the door, finding it open almost by accident, so that, faintly surprised, even vaguely nonplussed, the man called Fay disappeared into the halloo-ing night.

~ ~ ~

Eric and Perrin had to walk home, as the buses had long since stopped. They walked through suburbs of spectacular silence. To entertain themselves, each told the other a little about himself.

By the time they had parted—the first car was going to work—they had exchanged the same information: in order to cure them of their homosexuality, Perrin had had shock treatment, Eric aversion therapy.

They looked at each other, slowly smiling, in the diminishing night. It had not worked.

~ ~ ~

Outside, in the street, there was a sudden crumbling sound, as a tidal wave of masonry came crashing down. In a few seconds, all that was left was a cloud, a hideous perfume, a perforation of memory almost.

The entire structure of the Alex had shuddered in that moment, as if in apprehension. Outside the windows, the air became frail with grit.

Pneumatic drills took up their sound again, a drumroll at once curiously undramatic yet relentless.

At that moment, as if blown in by the gust of energy from the latest demolition, a figure arrived, tentatively, and hovered by the door. The light was behind him, yet Eric could see, immediately, the newcomer was not Perrin.

The man moved slowly out of the dust-filled sunlight, feeling his way, almost by toe, towards the bar. Eric felt a quiet claw of shock. The man was dressed with a certain hectic vivacity: his once-tight jeans were now winched in, painfully; over what was clearly a skeletal stomach, a belt with studs glinted with the eyes of a snake which had long ago lost its fury. And the man's face, gauntly handsome, haggard indeed, with deep heavy lines running from nose to chin, was shining with sweat, pale, white: he had not shaved, thus accentuating his dramatic pallor.

For one dreadful moment, Eric imagined he could remember the man: that is, he could recall a finer, fitter, indeed quite handsome man who seemed, now, like a distant, more healthy brother. *That* stranger— not *this* one, surely—had exchanged a few looks with Eric in the bar many years ago. Then *that* man, with his image of health and vigour, of whom this frail, too-old young man was a *doppelgänger*, had disappeared. He was rumoured to be in New York. He was either a waiter, according to one story, or, in the version preferred—because more apocryphal—

he was the lover of someone very rich, very powerful, and, to the public at least, very heterosexual.

Now this man had returned home, and the sum of his voyage was making his way from the door to the bar in the Alex.

The occupants of the pub had grown briefly silent: then a series of falsely animated conversations broke out, like sweat on a forehead.

The newcomer reached a barstool, but suddenly relaxing his body against it, as if he had reached the end of what had become a too long and arduous mission, he misjudged its height so that, like a building collapsing sideways, his whole body began to topple down towards the carpet. At this moment, all pretence was abandoned.

The man beside him, a comfortable pool of flesh who propped up the bar from the minute it opened, getting slowly sozzled as the day went on, reached out an automatic arm, as if he had a spare limb set aside for the safety of drunks and others similarly incapacitated. Holding the falling man arrested for a moment, he got to his feet and, as if the other were a doll now, or a giddy child, plonked him down foursquare on the seat and held him secure.

At this the skeletal brother of the once-handsome man, once so much in command, the accruer of so many ardent looks, let out a wild laugh, its hilarity mocking everyone there in the gay pub, in its last days before being demolished. It was as if this man, so near his own end, clairvoyantly sensed that this place where so much life had gone on—where, indeed, rudimentary yet important transactions of a civilisation, a small branch of culture, had taken place—would be rendered faithlessly, by some dark law of anarchy, into a hole in the ground, an essential nothingness which might become, if it was lucky, the tarmac of a car park.

Eric threw the last drops of his tonic back. Where *was* Perrin, why was he late when he had been so bloody melodramatic on the phone in the morning? And what was so bloody pressing?

Eric's contemplative eye, as if a needle within a compass of anxiety, returned to the man at the bar.

He was talking with an eerie, rambling gusto, telling the story of his travels. Eric could see from the faces of the listeners that they did not know whether to believe what he was saying or believe something more profound, less acceptable.

Eric looked away quickly. He stared longingly out the door. The sun was still there, but it was gauzy with the dust of departing buildings. A huge demolition truck roared along the street, splicing everything abruptly into shadow.

He looked back into the room, quickly. He did not want to think of *that*.

He was prepared, of course, he used condoms, had studied the arcane codes of safe sex. (Come on him not into him, as the explicit ones said.) Yet, to Eric at that moment, the disease was still like a foreign war, happening, thankfully still, *over there,* a distant place from which occasional returned soldiers, like this one, emerged in the locals' midst, gnarled, bearing tales of defeat greater than anyone could possibly imagine. And to a certain extent it was unimaginable: this savage hewing down of men who had just climbed out of the darkness, emerging into light.

What the bloody hell was keeping Perrin? Suddenly Eric had an almost hysterical desire to flee the pub. He wanted to be outside, to be near the harbour or on top of one of the volcanoes, where he could look down at the city, make some sense of his life. What was Matthew but a diversion; he was fooling himself by saying he wasn't falling in love. Of course he fell in love every time. What the fuck do you expect from someone who grew up with the fateful tunes of *South Pacific?* ". . . across a crowded room . . ."

The drills suddenly swerved into closeness. Eric caught his own face in a mirror opposite: he was surprisingly, even insistently, physically *there* for someone who, at that moment, felt a peculiar seesaw of elation dipping down into black depression. He and Perrin had talked in the early days of having tests because, as Perrin had said, "Let's face it, darling, we've both been utter sluts in our time . . . but then," he had added thought-fully, lifting his eyes up and looking towards a far distant point, as if he were delivering the eulogy for a generation, "who has not been a slut has not been human."

Eric had laughed.

Now he tried, with an almost fanatical need, to think of Matthew. He tried to conjure up in his mind those images of their lovemaking which acted, almost, as a way of banishing his anxieties. He began to wish, almost desperately, that Matthew were there with him, so that he might just casually brush by, knocking his body into Matthew's as if to recall what was real—against what could only be feared.

Yet at this moment, when he most needed him, Matthew refused to appear by osmosis.

It was now eight minutes past twelve, on 10 April 1986.

At that moment, as if exactly timed to an acme of pleasurable lateness, Eric saw another figure arrive at the door.

At first, because of the light behind him, Eric couldn't tell whether it was Perrin. It was certainly Perrin's height and approximate weight, but the person's body language was so different: slumped back, not pushing forward, standing there on the mat as if momentarily dazed, as if emerging out of a long black moment of introspection—thought —peregrination—a limning of the harsh white noon light, chalky almost, plashing and pouring down the side of, yes, it was Perrin's face.

He was still at the door, as if breaking off from some thought which possessed him. It was in his eyes as they searched the few people in the room, and the room went momentarily quiet *again* before, in quick shock waves, conversation took up, sealing over the startled apprehension that already, like an almost imperceptible drumroll, the words *again* and *again* and *again* were making themselves heard, explosions from the distant war landing closer and closer to that spot so that it was finally unavoidable that one day soon, or was it even now, a direct hit would be made and the whole culture, if it was not to be wiped out, would have to go underground again—disperse, change its nature—or else *fight*.

As if in the wake of this apprehension—or was it the beginnings of comprehension?—Perrin began to move slowly towards Eric. Each fraction of a centimetre closer he got, it was like a realisation being brought personally, without words, from Perrin to Eric, from Eric to Perrin, from Perrin to Eric.

Eric wanted to rise to his feet, he wanted to open his arms wide and put Perrin within them and hug him forever, till he could recover, get all right. The words were already forming in his mind, angry and furious: we will fight this bloody thing, it can't be allowed to win, *it won't, we won't let it.*

Yet already Perrin had raised his face to Eric's, as if he wished to intimate to him that he could sustain no thought, so deafened was he by the vast explosion which had, the day before, in a quiet doctor's room, blown away everything he believed in and held dear to his life.

So it was, in the pub, in the last weeks before its demolition, before the farewell party which everyone confidently expected to be halcyon, Perrin did what he would never have done, really, or only when completely drunk: he put his hand out, and Eric, as if by accident, caught it.

Together, they began to hold on.

~ *Richard McCann* ~

My Mother's Clothes: The School of Beauty and Shame

He is troubled by any image *of himself, suffers when he is named. He finds the perfection of a human relationship in this vacancy of the image: to abolish—in oneself, between oneself and others—adjectives; a re-lationship which adjectivizes is on the side of the image, on the side of domination, of death.*

—ROLAND BARTHES, *Roland Barthes*

Like every corner house in Carroll Knolls, the corner house on our block was turned backward on its lot, a quirk introduced by the developer of the subdivision, who, having run short of money, sought variety without additional expense. The turned-around houses, as we kids called them, were not popular, perhaps because they seemed too public, their casement bedroom windows cranking open onto sunstruck asphalt streets. In actuality, however, it was the rest of the houses that were public, their picture windows offering dioramic glimpses of early-American sofas and Mediterranean-style pole lamps whose mottled globes hung like iridescent melons from wrought-iron chains. In order not to be seen walking across the living room to the kitchen in our pajamas, we had to close the venetian blinds. The corner house on our block was secretive, as though it had turned its back on all of us, whether in su-periority or in shame, refusing to acknowledge even its own unkempt

From its first publication in The Atlantic, *RICHARD McCANN's "My Mother's Clothes: The School of Beauty and Shame" has commanded attention for its sensitivity and eloquence. He is currently at work on a novel and teaches at American University in Washington, D.C.*

yard of yellowing zoysia grass. After its initial occupants moved away, the corner house remained vacant for months.

The spring I was in sixth grade, it was sold. When I came down the block from school, I saw a moving van parked at its curb. "Careful with that!" a woman was shouting at a mover as he unloaded a tiered end table from the truck. He stared at her in silence. The veneer had already been splintered from the table's edge, as though someone had nervously picked at it while watching TV. Then another mover walked from the truck carrying a child's bicycle, a wire basket bolted over its thick rear tire, brightly colored plastic streamers dangling from its handlebars.

The woman looked at me. "What have you got there? In your hand."

I was holding a scallop shell spray-painted gold, with imitation pearls glued along its edges. Mrs. Eidus, the art teacher who visited our class each Friday, had showed me how to make it.

"A hatpin tray," I said. "It's for my mother."

"It's real pretty." She glanced up the street as though trying to guess which house I belonged to. "I'm Mrs. Tyree," she said, "and I've got a boy about your age. His daddy's bringing him tonight in the new Plymouth. I bet you haven't sat in a new Plymouth."

"We have a Ford." I studied her housedress, tiny blue and purple flowers imprinted on thin cotton, a line of white buttons as large as Necco Wafers marching toward its basted hemline. She was the kind of mother my mother laughed at for cutting recipes out of *Woman's Day*. Staring from our picture window, my mother would sometimes watch the neighborhood mothers drag their folding chairs into a circle on someone's lawn. "There they go," she'd say, "a regular meeting of the Daughters of the Eastern Star!" "They're hardly even *women*," she'd whisper to my father, "and their *clothes*." She'd criticize their appearance—their loud nylon scarves tied beneath their chins, their disintegrating figures stuffed into pedal pushers—until my father, worried that my brother, Davis, and I could hear, although laughing himself, would beg her, "Stop it, Maria, please stop; it isn't funny." But she wouldn't stop, not ever. "Not even thirty, and they look like they belong to the DAR! They wear their pearls inside their bosoms in case the rope should break!" She was the oldest mother on the block, but she was the most glamorous, sitting alone on the front lawn in her sleek kick-pleated skirts and cashmere sweaters, reading her thick paperback novels, whose bindings had split. Her hair was lightly hennaed, so that when I saw her pillowcases piled atop the washer, they seemed dusted with powdery rouge. She had once lived in New York City.

After dinner, when it was dark, I joined the other children congregated beneath the streetlamp across from the turned-around house. Bucky Trueblood, an eighth grader who had once twisted the stems off my brother's eyeglasses, was crouched in the center, describing his mother's naked body to us elementary school children gathered around him, our faces slightly upturned, as though searching for a distant constellation, or for the bats that Bucky said would fly into our hair. I sat at the edge, one half of my body within the circle of light, the other half lost to darkness. When Bucky described his mother's nipples, which he'd glimpsed when she bent to kiss him good night, everyone giggled; but when he described her genitals, which he'd seen by dropping his pencil on the floor and looking up her nightie while her feet were propped on a hassock as she watched TV, everyone huddled nervously together, as though listening to a ghost story that made them fear something dangerous in the nearby dark. "I don't believe you," someone said. "I'm telling you," Bucky said, *"that's what it looks like."*

I slowly moved outside the circle. Across the street a cream-colored Plymouth was parked at the curb. In a lighted bedroom window Mrs. Tyree was hanging café curtains. Behind the chain-link fence, within the low branches of a willow tree, the new child was standing in his yard. I could see his white T-shirt and the pale oval of his face, a face deprived of detail by darkness and distance. Behind him, at the open bedroom window, his mother slowly fiddled with a valance. Behind me the children sat spellbound beneath the light. Then Bucky jumped up and pointed in the new child's direction—"Hey, you, you want to hear something really *good?*"—and even before the others had a chance to spot him, he vanished as suddenly and completely as an imaginary playmate.

The next morning, as we waited at our bus stop, he loitered by the mailbox on the opposite corner, not crossing the street until the yellow school bus pulled up and flung open its door. Then he dashed aboard and sat down beside me. "I'm Denny," he said. Denny: a heavy, unbeautiful child, who, had his parents stayed in their native Kentucky, would have been a farm boy, but who in Carroll Knolls seemed to belong to no particular world at all, walking past the identical ranch houses in his overalls and Keds, his whitish-blond hair close-cropped all around except for the distinguishing, stigmatizing feature of a wave that crested perfectly just above his forehead, a wave that neither rose nor fell, a wave he trained with Hopalong Cassidy hair tonic, a wave he tended fussily, as though it were the only loveliness he allowed himself.

~ ~ ~

What in Carroll Knolls might have been described by someone not native to those parts—a visiting expert, say—as *beautiful,* capable of arousing terror and joy? The brick ramblers strung with multicolored Christmas lights? The occasional front-yard plaster Virgin entrapped within a chicken-wire grotto entwined with plastic roses? The spring Denny moved to Carroll Knolls, I begged my parents to take me to a nightclub, had begged so hard for months, in fact, that by summer they finally agreed to a Sunday matinee. Waiting in the back seat of our Country Squire, a red bow tie clipped to my collar, I watched our house float like a mirage behind the sprinkler's web of water. The front door opened, and a white dress fluttered within the mirage's ascending waves: slipping on her sunglasses, my mother emerged onto the concrete stoop, adjusted her shoulder strap, and teetered across the wet grass in new spectator shoes. Then my father stepped out and cut the sprinkler off. We drove—the warm breeze inside the car sweetened by my mother's Shalimar—past ranch houses tethered to yards by chain-link fences; past the Silver Spring Volunteer Fire Department and Carroll Knolls Elementary School; past the Polar Bear Soft-Serv stand, its white stucco siding shimmery with mirror shards; past a bulldozed red-clay field where a weathered billboard advertised IF YOU LIVED HERE YOU'D BE HOME BY NOW, until we arrived at the border—a line of cinder-block discount liquor stores, a traffic light—of Washington, D.C. The light turned red. We stopped. The breeze died and the Shalimar fell from the air. Exhaust fumes mixed with the smell of hot tar. A drunk man stumbled into the crosswalk, followed by an old woman shielding herself from the sun with an orange umbrella, and two teenaged boys dribbling a basketball back and forth between them. My mother put down her sun visor. "Lock your door," she said.

Then the light changed, releasing us into another country. The station wagon sailed down boulevards of Chinese elms and flowering Bradford pears, through hot, dense streets where black families sat on wooden chairs at curbs, along old streetcar tracks that caused the tires to shimmy and the car to swerve, onto Pennsylvania Avenue, past the White House, encircled by its fence of iron spears, and down Fourteenth Street, past the Treasury Building, until at last we reached the Neptune Room, a cocktail lounge in the basement of shabbily elegant hotel.

Inside, the Neptune Room's walls were painted with garish mermaids reclining seductively on underwater rocks, and human frogmen who stared longingly through their diving helmets' glass masks at a loveliness they could not possess on dry earth. On stage, leaning against the baby grand piano, a *chanteuse* (as my mother called her) was singing of her grief, her wrists weighted with rhinestone bracelets, a single blue spotlight making her seem like one who lived, as did the mermaids, underwater.

I was transfixed. I clutched my Roy Rogers cocktail (the same as a Shirley Temple, but without the cheerful, girlish grenadine) tight in my fist. In the middle of "The Man I Love," I stood and struggled toward the stage.

I strayed into the spotlight's soft-blue underwater world. Close up, from within the light, the singer was a boozy, plump peroxide blonde in a tight black cocktail dress; but these indiscretions made her yet more lovely, for they showed what she had lost, just as her songs seemed to carry her backward into endless regret. When I got close to her, she extended one hand—red nails, a huge glass ring—and seized one of mine.

"Why, what kind of little sailor have we got here?" she asked the audience.

I stared through the border of blue light and into the room, where I saw my parents gesturing, although whether they were telling me to step closer to her microphone or to step father away, I could not tell. The whole club was staring.

"Maybe he knows a song!" a man shouted from the back.

"Sing with me," she whispered. "What can you sing?"

I wanted to lift her microphone from its stand and bow deeply from the waist, as Judy Garland did on her weekly TV show. But I could not. As she began to sing, I stood voiceless, pressed against the protection of her black dress; or, more accurately, I stood beside her, silently lip-synching to myself. I do not recall what she sang, although I do recall a quick, farcical ending in which she falsettoed, like Betty Boop, "Gimme a Little Kiss, Will Ya, Huh?" and brushed my forehead with pursed red lips.

~ ~ ~

That summer, humidity enveloping the landfill subdivision, Denny, "the new kid," stood on the boundaries, while we neighborhood boys played War, a game in which someone stood on Stanley Allen's front porch and machine-gunned the rest of us, who one by one clutched our bellies, coughed as if choking on blood, and rolled in exquisite death throes down the grassy hill. When Stanley's father came up the walk from work, he ducked imaginary bullets. "Hi, Dad," Stanley would call, rising from the dead to greet him. Then we began the game again: whoever died best in the last round got to kill in the next. Later, after dusk, we'd smear the wings of balsa planes with glue, ignite them, and send them flaming through the dark on kamikaze missions. Long after the streets were deserted, we children sprawled beneath the corner streetlamp, praying our mothers would not call us—*"Time to come in!"*—back to our ovenlike houses; and then sometimes Bucky, hoping to scare the elementary school kids, would lead his solemn procession of junior high "hoods" down the block, their penises hanging from their unzipped trousers.

Denny and I began to play together, first in secret, then visiting each other's houses almost daily, and by the end of the summer I imagined him to be my best friend. Our friendship was sealed by our shared dread of junior high school. Davis, who had just finished seventh grade, brought back reports of corridors so long that one could get lost in them, of gangs who fought to control the lunchroom and the bathrooms. The only safe place seemed to be the Health Room, where a pretty nurse let you lie down on a cot behind a folding screen. Denny told me about a movie he'd seen in which the children, all girls, did not have to go to school at all but were taught at home by a beautiful governess, who, upon coming to their rooms each morning, threw open their shutters so that sunlight fell like bolts of satin across their beds, whispered their pet names while kissing them, and combed their long hair with a silver brush. "She never got mad," said Denny, beating his fingers up and down through the air as though striking a keyboard, "except once when some old man told the girls they could never play piano again."

With my father at work in the Pentagon and my mother off driving the two-tone Welcome Wagon Chevy to new subdivisions, Denny and I spent whole days in the gloom of my living room, the picture window's venetian blinds closed against an August sun so fierce that it bleached the design from the carpet. Dreaming of fabulous prizes—sets of matching Samsonite luggage, French Provincial bedroom suites, Corvettes, jet flights to Hawaii—we watched Jan Murray's *Treasure Hunt* and Bob Barker's *Truth or Consequences* (a name that seemed strangely threatening). We watched *The Loretta Young Show*, worshiping yet critiquing her elaborate gowns. When *The Early Show* came on, we watched old Bette Davis, Gene Tierney, and Joan Crawford movies—*Dark Victory, Leave Her to Heaven, A Woman's Face.* Hoping to become their pen pals, we wrote long letters to fading movie stars, who in turn sent us autographed photos we traded between ourselves. We searched the house for secrets, like contraceptives, Kotex, and my mother's hidden supply of Hershey bars. And finally, Denny and I, running to the front window every few minutes to make sure no one was coming unexpectedly up the sidewalk, inspected the secrets of my mother's dresser: her satin nightgowns and padded brassieres, folded atop pink drawer liners and scattered with loose sachet; her black mantilla, pressed inside a shroud of lilac tissue paper; her heart-shaped candy box, a flapper doll strapped to its lid with a ribbon, from which spilled galaxies of cocktail rings and cultured pearls. Small shrines to deeper intentions, private grottoes of yearning: her triangular cloisonné earrings, her brooch of enameled butterfly wings.

Because beauty's source was longing, it was infused with romantic sorrow; because beauty was defined as "feminine," and therefore as "other," it became hopelessly confused with my mother: Mother, who quickly sorted through new batches of photographs, throwing unflattering shots of herself directly into the fire before they could be seen. Mother, who dramatized herself, telling us and our playmates, "My name is Maria Dolores; in Spanish, that means 'Mother of Sorrows.' " Mother who had once wished to be a writer and who said, looking up briefly from whatever she was reading, "Books are my best friends." Mother, who read aloud from Whitman's *Leaves of Grass* and O'Neill's *Long Day's Journey into Night* with a voice so grave I could not tell the difference between them. Mother, who lifted cut-glass vases and antique clocks from her obsessively dusted curio shelves to ask, "If this could talk, what story would it tell?"

And more, always more, for she was the only woman in our house, a "people-watcher," a "talker," a woman whose mysteries and moods seemed endless: Our Mother of the White Silk Gloves; Our Mother of the Veiled Hats; Our Mother of the Paper Lilacs; Our Mother of the Sighs and Heartaches; Our Mother of the Gorgeous Gypsy Earrings; Our Mother of the Late Movies and the Cigarettes; Our Mother whom I adored and whom, in adoring, I ran from, knowing it "wrong" for a son to wish to be like his mother; Our Mother who wished to influence us, passing the best of herself along, yet who held the fear common to that era, the fear that by loving a son too intensely she would render him unfit—"Momma's boy," "tied to apron strings"—and who therefore alternately drew us close and sent us away, believing a son needed "male influence" in large doses, that female influence was pernicious except as a final finishing, like manners; Our Mother of the Mixed Messages; Our Mother of Sudden Attentiveness; Our Mother of Sudden Distances; Our Mother of Anger; Our Mother of Apology. The simplest objects of her life, objects scattered accidentally about the house, became my shrines to beauty, my grottoes of romantic sorrow: her Revlon lipstick tubes, "Cherries in the Snow"; her art nouveau atomizers on the blue mirror top of her vanity; her pastel silk scarves knotted to a wire hanger in her closet; her white handkerchiefs blotted with red mouths. Voiceless objects; silences. The world halved with a cleaver: "masculine," "feminine." In these ways was the plainest ordinary love made complicated and grotesque. And in these ways was beauty, already confused with the "feminine," also confused with shame, for all these longings were secret, and to control me all my brother had to do was to threaten to expose that Denny and I were dressing ourselves in my mother's clothes.

~ ~ ~

Denny chose my mother's drabbest outfits, as though he were ruled by the deepest of modesties, or by his family's austere Methodism: a pink wraparound skirt from which the color had been laundered, its hem almost to his ankles; a sleeveless white cotton blouse with a Peter Pan collar; a small straw summer clutch. But he seemed to challenge his own primness, as though he dared it with his "effects": an undershirt worn over his head to approximate cascading hair; gummed hole-punch reinforcements pasted to his fingernails so that his hands, palms up, might look like a woman's—flimsy crescent moons waxing above his fingertips.

He dressed slowly, hesitantly, but once dressed, he was a manic Proteus metamorphosizing into contradictory, half-realized forms, throwing his "long hair" back and balling it violently into a French twist; tapping his paper nails on the glass-topped vanity as though he were an important woman kept waiting at a cosmetics counter; stabbing his nails into the air as though he were an angry teacher assigning an hour of detention; touching his temple as though he were a shy schoolgirl tucking back a wisp of stray hair; resting his fingertips on the rim of his glass of Kool-Aid as though he were an actress seated over an ornamental cocktail—a Pink Lady, say, or a Silver Slipper. Sometimes, in an orgy of jerky movement, his gestures overtaking him with greater and greater force, a dynamo of theatricality unleashed, he would hurl himself across the room like a mad girl having a fit, or like one possessed; or he would snatch the chenille spread from my parents' bed and drape it over his head to fashion for himself the long train of a bride. "Do you like it?" he'd ask anxiously, making me his mirror. "Does it look *real*?" He wanted, as did I, to become something he'd neither yet seen nor dreamed of, something he'd recognize the moment he saw it: himself. Yet he was constantly confounded, for no matter how much he adorned himself with scarves and jewelry, he could not understand that this was himself, as was also and at the same time the boy in overalls and Keds. He was split in two pieces —as who was not?—the blond wave cresting rigidly above his close-cropped hair.

~ ~ ~

"He makes me nervous," I heard my father tell my mother one night as I lay in bed. They were speaking about me. That morning I'd stood awkwardly on the front lawn—"Maybe you should go help your father," my mother had said—while he propped an extension ladder against the house, climbed up through the power lines he separated with his bare hands, and staggered across the pitched roof he was reshingling. When his hammer slid down the incline, catching on the gutter, I screamed, "You're falling!" Startled, he almost fell.

"He needs to spend more time with you," I heard my mother say.

I couldn't sleep. Out in the distance a mother was calling her child home. A screen door slammed. I heard cicadas, their chorus as steady and loud as the hum of a power line. *He needs to spend more time with you.* Didn't she know? Saturday mornings, when he stood in his rubber hip boots fishing off the shore of Triadelphia Reservoir, I was afraid of the slimy bottom and could not wade after him; for whatever reasons of his own—something as simple as shyness, perhaps—he could not come to get me. I sat in the parking lot drinking Tru-Ade and reading *Betty and Veronica,* wondering if Denny had walked alone to Wheaton Plaza, where the weekend manager of Port-o'-Call allowed us to Windex the illuminated glass shelves that held Lladró figurines, the porcelain ballerina's hands so realistic one could see tiny life and heart lines etched into her palms. *He needs to spend more time with you.* Was she planning to discontinue the long summer afternoons that she and I spent together when there were no new families for her to greet in her Welcome Wagon car? "I don't feel like being alone today," she'd say, inviting me to sit on their chenille bedspread and watch her model new clothes in her mirror. Behind her an oscillating fan fluttered nylons and scarves she'd heaped, discarded, on a chair. "Should I wear the red belt with this dress or the black one?" she'd ask, turning suddenly toward me and cinching her waist with her hands.

Afterward we would sit together at the rattan table on the screened-in porch, holding cocktail napkins around sweaty glasses of iced Russian tea and listening to big-band music on the Zenith.

"You look so pretty," I'd say. Sometimes she wore outfits I'd selected for her from her closet—pastel chiffon dresses, an apricot blouse with real mother-of-pearl buttons.

One afternoon she leaned over suddenly and shut off the radio. "You know you're going to leave me one day," she said. When I put my arms around her, smelling the dry carnation talc she wore in hot weather, she stood up and marched out of the room. When she returned, she was wearing Bermuda shorts and a plain cotton blouse. "Let's wait for your father on the stoop," she said.

Late that summer—the summer before he died—my father took me with him to Fort Benjamin Harrison, near Indianapolis, where, as a colonel in the U.S. Army Reserves, he did his annual tour of duty. On the prop jet he drank bourbon and read newspapers while I made a souvenir packet for Denny: an airsickness bag, into which I placed the Chiclets given me by the stewardess to help pop my ears during takeoff, and the laminated white card that showed the location of emergency exits. Fort Benjamin Harrison looked like Carroll Knolls: hundreds of acres of concrete and sun-scorched shrubbery inside a cyclone fence. Daytimes I waited for my father in the dining mess with the sons of other officers, drinking chocolate milk that came from a silver machine, and desultorily setting fires in ashtrays. When he came to collect me, I walked behind him—gold braid hung from his epaulets—while enlisted men saluted us and opened doors. At night, sitting in our BOQ room, he asked me questions about myself: "Are you looking forward to seventh grade?"

"What do you think you'll want to be?" When these topics faltered—I stammered what I hoped were right answers—we watched TV, trying to preguess lines of dialogue on reruns of his favorite shows, *The Untouchables* and *Rawhide.* "That Della Street," he said as we watched *Perry Mason,* "is almost as pretty as your mother." On the last day, eager to make the trip memorable, he brought me a gift: a glassine envelope filled with punched IBM cards that told me my life story as his secretary had typed it into the office computer. Card One: *You live at 10406 Lillians Mill Court, Silver Spring, Maryland.* Card Two: *You are entering seventh grade.* Card Three: *Last year your teacher was Mrs. Dillard.* Card Four: *Your favorite color is blue.* Card Five: *You love the Kingston Trio.* Card Six: *You love basketball and football.* Card Seven: *Your favorite sport is swimming.*

Whose son did these cards describe? The address was correct, as was the teacher's name and the favorite color; and he'd remembered that one morning during breakfast I'd put a dime in the jukebox and played the Kingston Trio's song about "the man who never returned." But whose fiction was the rest? Had I, who played no sport other than kickball and Kitty-Kitty-Kick-the-Can, lied to him when he asked me about myself? Had he not heard from my mother the outcome of the previous summer's swim lessons? At the swim club a young man in black trunks had taught us, as we held hands, to dunk ourselves in water, surface, and then go down. When he had told her to let go of me, I had thrashed across the surface, violently afraid I'd sink. But perhaps I had not lied to him; per- haps he merely did not wish to see. It was my job, I felt, to reassure him that I was the son he imagined me to be, perhaps because the role of reassurer gave me power. In any case, I thanked him for the computer cards. I thanked him the way a father thanks a child for a well-intentioned gift he'll never use—a set of handkerchiefs, say, on which the embroi- dered swirls construct a monogram of no particular initial, and which thus might be used by anyone.

~ ~ ~

As for me, when I dressed in my mother's clothes, I seldom moved at all: I held myself rigid before the mirror. The kind of beauty I'd seen practiced in movies and in fashion magazines was beauty attained by lac- quered stasis, beauty attained by fixed poses—"ladylike stillness," the still- ness of mannequins, the stillness of models "caught" in mid-gesture, the stillness of the passive moon around which active meteors orbited and burst. My costume was of the greatest solemnity: I dressed like the *chanteuse* in the Neptune Room, carefully shimmying my mother's black slip over my head so as not to stain it with Brylcreem, draping her black mantilla over my bare shoulders, clipping her rhinestone dangles to my ears. Had I at that time already seen the movie in which French women who had fraternized with German soldiers were made to shave their heads and walk through the streets, jeered by their fellow villagers? And if so, did I imagine myself to be one of the collaborators, or one of the villagers, taunting her from the curb? I ask because no matter how elaborate my costume, I made no effort to camouflage my crew cut or my male body.

How did I perceive myself in my mother's triple-mirrored vanity, its endless repetitions? I saw myself as doubled—both an image and he who studied it. I saw myself as beautiful, and guilty: the lipstick made my mouth seem the ripest rose, or a wound; the small rose on the black slip opened like my mother's heart disclosed, or like the Sacred Heart of Mary, aflame and pierced by arrows; the mantilla transformed me into a Mexican penitent or a Latin movie star, like Dolores Del Rio. The mirror was a silvery stream: on the far side, in a clearing, stood the woman who was icily immune from the boy's terror and contempt; on the close side, in the bedroom, stood the boy who feared and yet longed after her inviolability. (Perhaps, it occurs to me now, this doubleness is the source of drag queens' vulnerable ferocity.) Sometimes, when I saw that person in the mirror, I felt as though I had at last been lifted from that dull, locked room, with its mahogany bedroom suite and chalky blue walls. But other times, particularly when I saw Denny and me together, so that his reality shattered my fantasies, we seemed merely ludicrous and sadly comic, as though we were dressed in the garments of another species, like dogs in human clothes. I became aware of my spatulate hands, my scarred knees, my large feet; I became aware of the drooping, unfilled bodice of my slip. Like Denny, I could neither dispense with images nor take their flexibility as pleasure, for the idea of self I had learned and was learning still was that one was constructed by one's images— *"When boys cross their legs, they cross one ankle atop the knee"*—so that one finally sought the protection of believing in one's own image and, in believing in it as reality, condemned oneself to its poverty.

(That locked room. My mother's vanity; my father's highboy. If Denny and I, still in our costumes, had left that bedroom, its floor strewn with my mother's shoes and handbags, and gone through the darkened living room, out onto the sunstruck porch, down the sidewalk, and up the street, how would we have carried ourselves? Would we have walked boldly, chattering extravagantly back and forth between ourselves, like drag queens refusing to acknowledge the stares of contempt that are meant to halt them? Would we have walked humbly, with the calculated, impervious piety of the condemned walking barefoot to the public scaffold? Would we have walked simply, as deeply accustomed to the normalcy of our own strangeness as Siamese twins? Or would we have walked gravely, a solemn procession, like Bucky Trueblood's gang, their manhood hanging from their unzipped trousers?

(We were eleven years old. Why now, more than two decades later, do I wonder for the first time how we would have carried ourselves through a publicness we would have neither sought nor dared? I am six feet two inches tall; I weight 198 pounds. Given my size, the question I am most often asked about my youth is "What football position did you play?" Overseas I am most commonly taken to be a German or a Swede. Right now, as I write this, I am wearing L. L. Bean khaki trousers, a LaCoste shirt, Weejuns: the anonymous American costume, although partaking of certain signs of class and education, and, most recently, partaking also of certain signs of sexual orientation, this costume having become the standard garb of the urban American gay man. Why do I tell you these things? Am I trying—not subtly—to inform us of my "maleness," to reassure us that I have "survived" without noticeable "complexes"? Or is this my urge, my constant urge, to complicate my portrait of myself to both of us, so that I might layer my selves like so many multicolored crinoline slips, each rustling as I walk? When the wind blows, lifting my skirt, I do not know which slip will be revealed.)

～　～　～

Sometimes, while Denny and I were dressing up, Davis would come home unexpectedly from the bowling alley, where he'd been hanging out since entering junior high. At the bowling alley he was courting the protection of Bucky's gang.

"Let me in!" he'd demand, banging fiercely on the bedroom door, behind which Denny and I were scurrying to wipe the make-up off our faces with Kleenex.

"We're not doing anything," I'd protest, buying time.

"Let me in this minute or I'll tell!"

Once in the room, Davis would police the wreckage we'd made, the emptied hatboxes, the scattered jewelry, the piled skirts and blouses. "You'd better clean this up right now," he'd warn. "You two make me *sick.*"

Yet his scorn seemed modified by awe. When he helped us rehang the clothes in the closet and replace the jewelry in the candy box, a sullen accomplice destroying someone else's evidence, he sometimes handled the garments as though they were infused with something of himself, although at the precise moment when he seemed to find them loveliest, holding them close, he would cast them down.

After our dress-up sessions Denny would leave the house without good-byes. I was glad to see him go. We would not see each other for days, unless we met by accident; we never referred to what we'd done the last time we'd been together. We met like those who have murdered are said to meet, each tentatively and warily examining the other for signs of betrayal. But whom had we murdered? The boys who walked into that room? Or the women who briefly came to life within it? Perhaps this metaphor has outlived its meaning. Perhaps our shame derived not from our having killed but from our having created.

~ ~ ~

In early September, as Denny and I entered seventh grade, my father became ill. Over Labor Day weekend he was too tired to go fishing. On Monday his skin had vaguely yellowed; by Thursday he was severely jaundiced. On Friday he entered the hospital, his liver rapidly failing; Sunday he was dead. He died from acute hepatitis, possibly acquired while cleaning up after our sick dog, the doctor said. He was buried at Arlington National Cemetery, down the hill from the Tomb of the Unknown Soldier. After the twenty-one-gun salute, our mother pinned his colonel's insignia to our jacket lapels. I carried the flag from his coffin to the car. For two weeks I stayed home with my mother, helping her write thank-you notes on small white cards with black borders; one afternoon, as I was affixing postage to the square, plain envelopes, she looked at me across the dining room table. "You and Davis are all I have left," she said. She went into the kitchen and came back. "Tomorrow," she said, gathering up the note cards, "you'll have to go to school." Mornings I wandered the long corridors alone, separated from Denny by the fate of our last names, which had cast us into different homerooms and daily schedules. Lunchtimes we sat together in silence in the rear of the cafeteria. Afternoons, just before gym class, I went to the Health Room, where, lying on a cot, I'd imagine the Phys Ed coach calling my name from the class roll, and imagine my name, unclaimed, unanswered to, floating weightlessly away, like a balloon that one jumps to grab hold of but that is already out of reach. Then I'd hear the nurse dial the telephone. "He's sick again," she'd say. "Can you come pick him up?" At home I helped my mother empty my father's highboy. "No, we want to save that," she said when I folded his uniform into a huge brown bag that read GOODWILL INDUSTRIES; I wrapped it in a plastic dry cleaner's bag and hung it in the hall closet.

After my father's death my relationship to my mother's things grew yet more complex, for as she retreated into her grief, she left behind only her mute objects as evidence of her life among us: objects that seemed as lonely and vulnerable as she was, objects that I longed to console, objects with which I longed to console myself—a tangled gold chain, thrown in frustration on the mantel; a wineglass, its rim stained with lipstick, left unwashed in the sink. Sometimes at night Davis and I heard her prop her pillow up against her bedroom wall, lean back heavily, and tune her radio to a call-in show: *"Nightcaps, what are you thinking at this late hour?"* Sunday evenings, in order to help her prepare for the next day's job hunt, I stood over her beneath the bare basement bulb, the same bulb that first illuminated my father's jaundice. I set her hair, slicking each wet strand with gel and rolling it, inventing gossip that seemed to draw us together, a beautician and his customer.

"You have such pretty hair," I'd say.

"At my age, don't you think I should cut it?" She was almost fifty.

"No, never."

~ ~ ~

That fall Denny and I were caught. One evening my mother noticed something out of place in her closet. (Perhaps now that she no longer shared it, she knew where every belt and scarf should have been.)

I was in my bedroom doing my French homework, dreaming of one day visiting Au Printemps, the store my teacher spoke of so excitedly as she played us the Edith Piaf records that she had brought back from France. In the mirror above my desk I saw my mother appear at my door.

"Get into the living room," she said. Her anger made her small, reflected body seem taut and dangerous.

In the living room Davis was watching TV with Uncle Joe, our father's brother, who sometimes came to take us fishing. Uncle Joe was lying in our father's La-Z-Boy recliner.

"There aren't going to be any secrets in this house," she said. "You've been in my closet. What were you doing there?"

"No, we weren't," I said. "We were watching TV all afternoon."

"*We?* Was Denny here with you? Don't you think I've heard about that? Were you and Denny going through my clothes? Were you wearing them?"

"No, Mom," I said.

"Don't lie!" She turned to Uncle Joe, who was staring at us. "Make him stop! He's lying to me!"

She slapped me. Although I was already taller than she, she slapped me over and over, slapped me across the room until I was backed against the TV. Davis was motionless, afraid. But Uncle Joe jumped up and stood between my mother and me, holding her until her rage turned to sobs. "I can't be both a mother and a father," she said to him. "I can't, I can't do it." I could not look at Uncle Joe, who, although he was protecting me, did not know I was lying.

She looked at me. "We'll discuss this later," she said. "Get out of my sight."

We never discussed it. Denny was outlawed. I believe, in fact, that it was I who suggested he never be allowed in our house again. I told my mother I hated him. I do not think I was lying when I said this. I truly hated him—hated him, I mean, for being me.

For two or three weeks Denny tried to speak with me at the bus stop, but whenever he approached, I busied myself with kids I barely knew. After a while Denny found a new best friend, Lee, a child despised by everyone, for Lee was "effeminate." His clothes were too fastidious; he often wore his cardigan over his shoulders, like an old woman feeling a chill. Sometimes, watching the street from our picture window, I'd see Lee walking toward Denny's house. "What a queer," I'd say to whoever might be listening. "He walks like a *girl*." Or sometimes, at the junior high school, I'd see him and Denny walking down the corridor, their shoulders pressed together as if they were telling each other secrets, or as if they were joined in mutual defense. Sometimes when I saw them, I turned quickly away, as though I'd forgotten something important in my locker. But when I felt brave enough to risk rejection, for I belonged to no group, I joined Bucky Trueblood's gang, sitting on the radiator in the main hall, and waited for Lee and Denny to pass us. As Lee and Denny got close, they stiffened and looked straight ahead.

"Faggots," I muttered.

I looked at Bucky, sitting in the middle of the radiator. As Lee and Denny passed, he leaned forward from the wall, accidentally disarranging the practiced severity of his clothes, his jeans puckering benath his tooled belt, the breast pocket of his T-shirt drooping with the weight of a pack of Pall Malls. He whistled. Lee and Denny flinched. He whistled again. Then he leaned back, the hard lines of his body reasserting themselves, his left foot striking a steady beat on the tile floor with the silver V tap of his black loafer.

~ *David Leavitt* ~

A
Place I've
Never Been

I had known Nathan for years—too many years, since we were in college—so when he went to Europe I wasn't sure how I'd survive it; he was my best friend, after all, my constant companion at Sunday afternoon double bills at the Thalia, my ever-present source of consolation and conversation. Still, such a turn can prove to be a blessing in disguise. It threw me off at first, his not being there—I had no one to watch *Jeopardy!* with, or talk to on the phone late at night—but then, gradually, I got over it, and I realized that maybe it was a good thing after all, that maybe now, with Nathan gone, I would be forced to go out into the world more, make new friends, maybe even find a boyfriend. And I had started: I lost weight, I went shopping. I was at Bloomingdale's one day on my lunch hour when a very skinny black woman with a French accent asked me if I'd like to have a makeover. I had always run away from such things, but this time, before I had a chance, this woman put her long hands on my cheeks and looked into my face—not my eyes, my face—and said, "You're really beautiful. You know that?" And I absolutely couldn't answer. After she was through with me I didn't even know what I looked like, but everyone at my office was amazed. "Celia," they said, "you look great. What happened?" I smiled, wondering if I'd be allowed to go back every day for a makeover, if I offered to pay.

DAVID LEAVITT is the author of several novels and story collections, most recently While England Sleeps.

There was even some interest from a man—a guy named Roy who works downstairs, in contracts—and I was feeling pretty good about myself again, when the phone rang, and it was Nathan. At first I thought he must have been calling me from some European capital, but he said no, he was back in New York. "Celia," he said, "I have to see you. Something awful has happened."

Hearing those words, I pitched over—I assumed the worst. (And why not? He had been assuming the worst for over a year.) But he said, "No, no, I'm fine. I'm perfectly healthy. It's my apartment. Oh, Celia, it's awful. Could you come over?"

"Were you broken into?" I asked.

"I might as well have been!"

"Okay," I said. "I'll come over after work."

"I just got back last night. This is too much."

"I'll be there by six, Nathan."

"Thank you," he said, a little breathlessly, and hung up.

I drummed my nails—newly painted by another skinny woman at Bloomingdale's—against the black Formica of my desk, mostly to try out the sound. In truth I was a little happy he was back—I had missed him—and not at all surprised that he'd cut his trip short. Rich people are like that, I've observed; because they don't have to buy bargain-basement tickets on weird charter airlines, they feel free to change their minds. Probably he just got bored tooting around Europe, missed his old life, missed *Jeopardy!*, his friends. Oh, Nathan! How could I tell him the Thalia had closed?

I had to take several buses to get from my office to his neighborhood—a route I had once traversed almost daily, but which, since Nathan's departure, I hadn't had much occasion to take. Sitting on the Madison Avenue bus, I looked out the window at the rows of unaffordable shops, some still exactly what they'd been before, others boarded up, or reopened under new auspices—such a familiar panorama, unfolding, block by block, like a Chinese scroll I'd once been shown on a museum trip in junior high school. It was raining a little, and in the warm bus the long, unvarying progress of my love for Nathan seemed to unscroll as well—all the dinners and lunches and arguments, and all the trips back alone to my apartment, feeling ugly and fat, because Nathan had once again confirmed he could never love me the way he assured me he would someday love a man. How many hundreds of times I received that confirmation! And yet, somehow, it never occurred to me to give up that love I had nurtured for him since our earliest time together, that love which belonged to those days just past the brink of childhood, before I understood about Nathan, or rather, before Nathan understood about himself. So I persisted, and Nathan, in spite of his embarrassment at my occasional outbursts, continued to depend on me. I think he hoped that my feeling for him would one day transform itself into a more maternal kind of affection, that I would one day become the sort of woman who could tend to him without expecting anything in return. And that was, perhaps, a reasonable hope on his part, given my behavior. But: "If only," he said to me once, "you didn't have to act so crazy, Celia—" And that was how I realized I had to get out.

I got off the bus and walked the block and a half to his building— its façade, I noted, like almost every façade in the neighborhood, blemished by a bit of scaffolding—and, standing in that vestibule where I'd stood so often, waited for him to buzz me up. I read for diversion the now familiar list of tenants' names. The only difference today was that there were ragged ends of Scotch tape stuck around Nathan's name; probably his subletter had put his own name over Nathan's, and Nathan, returning, had torn the piece of paper off and left the ends of the tape. This didn't seem like him, and it made me suspicious. He was a scrupulous person about such things.

In due time—though slowly, for him—he let me in, and I walked the three flights of stairs to find him standing in the doorway, unshaven, looking as if he'd just gotten out of bed. He wasn't wearing any shoes, and he'd gained some weight. Almost immediately he fell into me—that is the only way to describe it, his big body limp in my arms. "Oh, God," he murmured into my hair, "am I glad to see you."

"Nathan," I said. "Nathan." And held him there. Usually he wriggled out of physical affection; kisses from him were little nips; hugs were tight, jerky chokeholds. Now he lay absolutely still, his arms slung under mine, and I tried to keep from gasping from the weight of him. But finally— reluctantly—he let go and, putting his hand on his forehead, gestured toward the open door. "Prepare yourself," he said. "It's worse than you can imagine."

He led me into the apartment. I have to admit, I was shocked by what I saw. Nathan, unlike me, is a chronically neat person, everything in its place, all his perfect furniture glowing, polished, every state-of-the-art fountain pen and pencil tip-up in the blue glass jar on his desk. Today, however, the place was in havoc—newspapers and old Entenmann's cookie boxes spread over the floor, records piled on top of each other, inner sleeves crumpled behind the radiator, the blue glass jar overturned. The carpet was covered with dark mottlings, and a stench of old cigarette smoke and sweat and urine inhabited the place. "It gets worse," he said. "Look at the kitchen." A thick, yellowing layer of grease encrusted the stovetop. The bathroom was beyond the pale of my descriptive capacity for filth.

"Those bastards," Nathan was saying, shaking his head.

"Hold on to the security deposit," I suggested. "Make them pay for it."

He sat down on the sofa, the arms of which appeared to have been ground with cigarette butts, and shook his head. "There *is* no security deposit," he moaned. "I didn't take one because supposedly Denny was my friend, and this other guy—Hoop, or whatever his name was—he was Denny's friend. And look at this!" From the coffee table he handed me a thick stack of utility and phone bills, all unopened. "The phone's disconnected," he said. "Two of the rent checks have bounced. The landlord's about to evict me. I'm sure my credit rating has gone to hell. Jesus, why'd I do it?" He stood, marched into the corner, then turned again to face me. "You know what? I'm going to call my father. I'm going to have him sic every one of his bastard lawyers on those assholes until they pay."

"Nathan," I reminded, "they're unemployed actors. They're poor."

"Then let them rot in jail!" Nathan screamed. His voice was loud and sharp in my ears. It had been a long time since I'd had to witness another person's misery, a long time since anyone had asked of me what Nathan was now asking of me: to take care, to resolve, to smooth. Nonetheless I rallied my energies. I stood. "Look," I said. "I'm going to go out and buy sponges, Comet, Spic and Span, Fantastik, Windex. Everything. We're going to clean this place up. We're going to wash the sheets and shampoo the rug, we're going to scrub the toilet until it shines. I promise you, by the time you go to sleep tonight, it'll be what it was."

He stood silent in the corner.

"Okay?" I said.

"Okay."

"So you wait here," I said. "I'll be right back."

"Thank you."

I picked up my purse and closed the door, thus, once again, saving him from disaster.

～ ～ ～

But there were certain things I could not save Nathan from. A year ago, his ex-lover Martin had called him up and told him he had tested positive. This was the secret fact he had to live with every day of his life, the secret fact that had brought him to Xanax and Halcion, Darvon and Valium— all crude efforts to cut the fear firing through his blood, exploding like the tiny viral time bombs he believed were lying in wait, expertly planted. It was the day after he found out that he started talking about clearing out. He had no obligations—he had quit his job a few months before and was just doing free-lance work anyway—and so, he reasoned, what was keeping him in New York? "I need to get away from all this," he said, gesturing frantically at the air. I believe he really thought back then that by running away to somewhere where it was less well known, he might be able to escape the disease. This is something I've noticed: The men act as if they think the power of infection exists in direct proportion to its publicity, that in places far from New York City it can, in effect, be outrun. And who's to say they are wrong, with all this talk about stress and the immune system? In Italy, in the countryside, Nathan seemed to feel he'd feel safer. And probably he was right; he would feel safer. Over there, away from the American cityscape with its streets full of gaunt sufferers, you're able to forget the last ten years, you can remember how old the world is and how there was a time when sex wasn't something likely to kill you.

It should be pointed out that Nathan had no symptoms; he hadn't even had the test for the virus itself. He refused to have it, saying he could think of no reason to give up at least the hope of freedom. Not that this made any difference, of course. The fear itself is a brutal enough enemy.

But he gave up sex. No sex, he said, was safe enough for him. He bought a VCR and began to hoard pornographic videotapes. And I think he was having phone sex too, because once I picked up the phone in his apartment and before I could say hello, a husky-voiced man said, "You stud," and then, when I said "Excuse me?" got flustered-sounding and hung up. Some people would probably count that as sex, but I'm not sure I would.

All the time, meanwhile, he was frenzied. I could never guess what time he'd call—six in the morning, sometimes, he'd drag me from sleep. "I figured you'd still be up," he'd say, which gave me a clue to how he was living. It got so bad that by the time he actually left I felt as if a great burden had been lifted from my shoulders. Not that I didn't miss him, but from that day on my time was, miraculously, my own. Nathan is a terrible correspondent—I don't think he's sent me one postcard or letter in all the time we've known each other—and so for months my only news of him came through the phone. Strangers would call me, Germans, Italians, nervous-sounding young men who spoke bad English, who were staying at the YMCA, who were in New York for the first time and to whom he had given my number. I don't think any of them actually wanted to see me; I think they just wanted me to tell them which bars were good and which subway lines were safe—information I happily dispensed. Of course, there was a time when I would have taken them on the subways, shown them around the bars, but I have thankfully passed out of that phase.

And of course, as sex became more and more a possibility, then a likelihood once again in my life, I began to worry myself about the very things that were torturing Nathan. What should I say, say, to Roy in contracts, when he asked me to sleep with him, which I was fairly sure he was going to do within a lunch or two? Certainly I wanted to sleep with him. But did I dare ask him to use a condom? Did I dare even broach the subject? I was frightened that he might get furious, that he might overreact, and I considered saying nothing, taking my chances. Then again, for me in particular, it was a very big chance to take; I have a pattern of falling in love with men who at some point or other have fallen in love with other men. All trivial, selfish, this line of worry, I recognize now, but at that point Nathan was gone, and I had no one around to remind me of how high the stakes were for other people. I slipped back into a kind of women's-magazine attitude toward the whole thing: for the moment, at least, *I* was safe, and I cherished that safety without even knowing it, I gloried in it. All my speculations were merely matters of prevention; that place where Nathan had been exiled was a place I'd never been. I am ashamed to admit it, but there was even a

moment when I took a kind of vengeful pleasure in the whole matter—
the years I had hardly slept with anyone, for which I had been taught to
feel ashamed and freakish, I now wanted to rub in someone's face: I was
right and you were wrong! I wanted to say. I'm not proud of having had
such thoughts, and I can only say, in my defense, that they passed
quickly—but a strict accounting of all feelings, at this point, seems to me
necessary. We have to be rigorous with ourselves these days.

In any case, Nathan was back, and I didn't dare think about myself.
I went to the grocery store, I bought every cleaner I coud find. And
when I got back to the apartment he was still standing where he'd
been standing, in the corner. "Nate," I said, "here's everything. Let's get
to work."

"Okay," he said glumly, even though he is an ace cleaner, and we
began.

As we cleaned, the truth came out. This Denny to whom he'd sublet
the apartment, Nathan had had a crush on. "To the extent that a crush
is a relevant thing in my life anymore," he said, "since God knows, there's
nothing to be done about it. But there you are. The libido doesn't stop,
the heart doesn't stop, no matter how hard you try to make them."

None of this—especially that last part—was news to me, though Nathan had managed to overlook that aspect of our relationship for years. I
had understood from the beginning about the skipping-over of the security payment, the laxness of the setup, because these were the sorts of
things I would have willingly done for Nathan at a different time. I think
he was privately so excited at the prospect of this virile young man,
Denny, sleeping, and perhaps having sex, between his sheets that he
would have taken any number of risks to assure it. Crush: what an oddly
appropriate word, considering what it makes you do to yourself. His
apartment was, in a sense, the most Nathan could offer, and probably the
most Denny would accept. I understood: You want to get as close as
you can, even if it's only at arm's length. And when you come back,
maybe, you want to breathe in the smell of the person you love loving
someone else.

Europe, he said, had been a failure. He had wandered, having dinner
with old friends of his parents, visiting college acquaintances who were
busy with exotic lives. He'd gone to bars, which was merely frustrating;
there was nothing to be done. "What about safe sex?" I asked, and he
said, "Celia, please. There is no such thing, as far as I'm concerned."

Once again this started a panicked thumping in my chest as I thought about Roy, and Nathan said, "It's really true. Suppose something lands on you—you know what I'm saying—and there's a microscopic cut in your skin. Bingo."

"Nathan, come on," I said. "That sounds crazy to me."

"Yeah?" he said. "Just wait till some ex-lover of yours calls you up with a little piece of news. Then see how you feel."

He returned to his furious scrubbing of the bathroom sink. I returned to my furious scrubbing of the tub. Somehow, even now, I'm always stuck with the worst of it.

Finally we were done. The place looked okay—it didn't smell anymore—though it was hardly what it had been. Some long-preserved pristineness was gone from the apartment, and both of us knew without saying a word that it would never be restored. We breathed in exhausted—no, not exhausted triumph. It was more like relief. We had beaten something back, yet again.

My hands were red from detergents, my stomach and forehead sweaty. I went into the now-bearable bathroom and washed up, and then Nathan said he would take me out to dinner—my choice. And so we ended up, as we had a thousand other nights, sitting by the window at the Empire Szechuan down the block from his apartment, eating cold noodles with sesame sauce, which, when we had finished them, Nathan ordered more of. "God, how I've missed these," he said, as he scooped the brown slimy noodles into his mouth. "You don't know."

In between slurps he looked at me and said, "You look good, Celia. Have you lost weight?"

"Yes, as a matter of fact," I said.

"I thought so."

I looked back at him, trying to re-create the expression on the French woman's face, and didn't say anything, but as it turned out I didn't need to. "I know what you're thinking," he said, "and you're right. Twelve pounds since you last saw me. But I don't care. I mean, you lose weight when you're sick. At least this way, gaining weight, I know I don't have it."

He continued eating. I looked outside. Past the plate-glass window that separated us from the sidewalk, crowds of people walked, young and old, good-looking and bad-looking, healthy and sick, some of them star-ing in at our food and our eating. Suddenly—urgently—I wanted to be out among them, I wanted to be walking in that crowd, pushed along in it, and not sitting here, locked into this tiny two-person table with Nathan. And yet I knew that escape was probably impossible. I looked once again at Nathan, eating happily, resigned, perhaps, to the fate of his apartment, and the knowledge that everything would work out, that this had, in fact, been merely a run-of-the-mill crisis. For the moment he was appeased, his hungry anxiety sated; for the moment. But who could guess what would set him off next? I steadied my chin on my palm, drank some water, watched Nathan eat like a happy child.

~ ~ ~

The next few weeks were thorny with events. Nathan bought a new sofa, had his place recarpeted, threw several small dinners. Then it was time for Lizzie Fischman's birthday party—one of the few annual events in our lives. We had known Lizzie since college—she was a tragic, trying sort of person, the sort who carries with her a constant aura of fatedness, of doom. So many bad things happen to Lizzie you can't help but wonder, after a while, if she doesn't hold out a beacon for disaster. This year alone, she was in a taxi that got hit by a bus; then she was mugged in the subway by a man who called her an "ugly dyke bitch"; then she started feeling sick all the time, and no one could figure out what was wrong, until it was revealed that her building's heating system was leaking small quantities of carbon monoxide into her awful little apartment. The tenants sued, and in the course of the suit, Lizzie, exposed as an illegal subletter, was evicted. She now lived with her father in one half of a two-family house in Plainfield, New Jersey, because she couldn't find another apartment she could afford. (Her job, incidentally, in addition to being wretchedly low-paying, is one of the dreariest I know of: proofreading accounting textbooks in an office on Forty-second Street.)

Anyway, each year Lizzie threw a big birthday party for herself in her father's house in Plainfield, and we all went, her friends, because of course we couldn't bear to disappoint her and add ourselves to her roster of worldwide enemies. It was invariably a miserable party—everyone drunk on bourbon, and Lizzie, eager to re-create the slumber parties of her childhood, dancing around in pink pajamas with feet. We were making s'mores over the gas stove—shoving the chocolate bars and the graham crackers onto fondue forks rather than old sticks—and *Beach Blanket Bingo* was playing on the VCR and no one was having a good time, particularly

Nathan, who was overdressed in a beige Giorgio Armani linen suit he'd bought in Italy, and was standing in the corner idly pressing his neck, feeling for swollen lymph nodes. Lizzie's circle dwindled each year, as her friends moved on or found ways to get out of it. This year eight of us had made it to the party, plus a newcomer from Lizzie's office, a very fat girl with very red nails named Dorrie Friedman, who, in spite of her heaviness, was what my mother would have called dainty. She ate a lot, but unless you were observant, you'd never have noticed it. The image of the fat person stuffing food into her face is mythic: I know from experience, when fat you eat slowly, chew methodically, in order not to draw attention to your mouth. Over the course of an hour I watched Dorrie Friedman put away six of those s'mores with a tidiness worthy of Emily Post, I watched her dab her cheek with her napkin after each bite, and I understood: This was shame, but also, in some peculiar way, this was innocence. A state to envy.

There is a point in Lizzie's parties when she invariably suggests we play Deprivation, a game that had been terribly popular among our crowd in college. The way you play it is you sit in a big circle, and everyone is given ten pennies. (In this case the pennies were unceremoniously taken from a huge bowl that sat on top of Lizzie's mother's refrigerator, and that she had upended on the linoleum floor—no doubt a long-contemplated act of desecration.) You go around the circle, and each person announces something he or she has never done, or a place they've never been—"I've never been to Borneo" is a good example—and then everyone who has been to Borneo is obliged to throw you a penny. Needless to say, especially in college, the game degenerates rather quickly to matters of sex and drugs.

I remembered the first time I ever played Deprivation, my sophomore year, I had been reading Blake's *Songs of Innocence* and *Songs of Experience*. Everything in our lives seemed a question of innocence and experience back then, so this seemed appropriate. There was a tacit assumption among my friends that "experience"—by that term we meant, I think, almost exclusively sex and drugs—was something you strove to get as much of as you could, that innocence, for all the praise it received in literature, was a state so essentially tedious that those of us still stuck in it deserved the childish recompense of shiny new pennies. (None of us, of course, imagining that five years from now the "experiences" we urged on one another might spread a murderous germ, that five years from now some of our friends, still in their youth, would be lost. Youth! You were supposed to sow your wild oats, weren't you? Those of us who didn't— we were the ones who failed, weren't we?)

One problem with Deprivation is that the older you get, the less interesting it becomes; every year, it seemed, my friends had fewer gaps in their lives to confess, and as our embarrassments began to stack up on the positive side, it was what we *had* done that was titillating. Indeed, Nick Walsh, who was to Lizzie what Nathan was to me, complained as the game began, "I can't play this. There's nothing I haven't done." But Lizzie, who has a naive faith in ritual, merely smiled and said, "Oh come on, Nick. No one's done *everything*. For instance, you could say, 'I've never been to Togo,' or, 'I've never been made love to simultaneously by twelve Arab boys in a back alley on Mott Street.' "

"Well, Lizzie," Nick said, "it *is* true that I've never been to Togo." His leering smile surveyed the circle, and of course, there *was* someone there—Gracie Wong, I think—who had, in fact, been to Togo.

The next person in the circle was Nathan. He's never liked this game, but he also plays it more cleverly than anyone. "Hmm," he said, stroking his chin as if there were a beard there, "let's see . . . Ah, I've got it. I've never had sex with anyone in this group." He smiled boldly, and every-one laughed—everyone, that is, except for me and Bill Darlington, and Lizzie herself—all three of us now, for the wretched experiments of our early youth, obliged to throw Nathan a penny.

Next was Dorrie Friedman's turn, which I had been dreading. She sat on the floor, her legs crossed under her, her very fat fingers inter-twined, and said, "Hmm . . . Something I've never done. Well—I've never ridden a bicycle."

An awful silence greeted this confession, and then a tinkling sound, like wind chimes, as the pennies flew. "Gee," Dorrie Friedman said, "I won big that time." I couldn't tell if she was genuinely pleased.

And as the game went on, we settled, all of us, into more or less parallel states of innocence and experience, except for Lizzie and Nick, whose piles had rapidly dwindled, and Dorrie Friedman, who, it seemed, by virtue of lifelong fatness, had done nearly nothing. She had never been to Europe; she had never swum; she had never played tennis; she had never skied; she had never been on a boat. Even someone else's turn

568 ~ The Penguin Book of Gay Short Stories

could be an awful moment for Dorrie, as when Nick said, "I've never had a vaginal orgasm." But fortunately, there, she did throw in her penny. I was relieved; I don't think I could have stood it if she hadn't.

After a while, in an effort not to look at Dorrie and her immense pile of pennies, we all started trying to trip up Lizzie and Nick, whose respective caches of sexual experience seemed limitless. "I've never had sex in my parents' bed," I offered. The pennies flew. "I've never had sex under a dry-docked boat." "I've never had sex with more than one other person." "Two other people." "Three other people." By then Lizzie was out of pennies, and declared the game over.

"I guess I won," Dorrie said rather softly. She had her pennies neatly piled in identically sized stacks.

I wondered if Lizzie was worried. I wondered if she was thinking about the disease, if she was frightened, the way Nathan was, or if she just assumed death was coming anyway, the final blow in her life of unendurable misfortunes. She started to gather the pennies back into their bowl, and I glanced across the room at Nathan, to see if he was ready to go. All through the game, of course, he had been looking pretty miserable—he always looks miserable at parties. Worse, he has a way of turning his misery around, making me responsible for it. Across the circle of our nearest and dearest friends he glared at me angrily, and I knew that by the time we were back in his car and on our way home to Manhattan he would have contrived a way for the evening to be my fault. And yet tonight, his occasional knowing sneers, inviting my complicity in looking down on the party, only enraged me. I was angry at him, in advance, for what I was sure he was going to do in the car, and I was also angry at him for being such a snob, for having no sympathy toward this evening, which, in spite of all its displeasures, was nevertheless an event of some interest, perhaps the very last hurrah of our youth, our own little big chill. And that was something: Up until now I had always assumed Nathan's version of things to be the correct one, and cast my own into the background. Now his perception seemed meager, insufficient: Here was a historic night, after all, and all he seemed to want to think about was his own boredom, his own unhappiness.

Finally, reluctantly, Lizzie let us go, and relinquished from her grip, we got into Nathan's car and headed onto the Garden State Parkway. "Never again," Nathan was saying, "will I allow you to convince me to attend one of Lizzie Fischman's awful parties. This is the last." I didn't even bother answering, it all seemed so predictable. Instead I just settled back into the comfortable velour of the car seat and switched on the radio. Dionne Warwick and Elton John were singing "That's What Friends Are For," and Nathan said, "You know, of course, that that's the song they wrote to raise money for AIDS."

"I'd heard," I said.

"Have you seen the video? It makes me furious. All these famous singers up there, grinning these huge grins, rocking back and forth. Why the hell are they smiling, I'd like to ask."

For a second, I considered answering that question, then decided I'd better not. We were slipping into the Holland Tunnel, and by the time we got through to Manhattan I was ready to call it a night. I wanted to get back to my apartment and see if Roy had left a message on my answering machine. But Nathan said, "It's Saturday night, Celia, it's still early. Won't you have a drink with me or something?"

"I don't want to go to any more gay bars, Nathan, I told you that."

"So we'll go to a straight bar. I don't care. I just can't bear to go back to my apartment at eleven o'clock." We stopped for a red light, and he leaned closer to me. "The truth is, I don't think I can bear to be alone. Please."

"All right," I said. What else could I say?

"Goody," Nathan said.

We parked the car in a garage and walked to a darkish café on Greenwich Avenue, just a few doors down from the huge gay bar Nathan used to frequent and which he jokingly referred to as "the airport." No mention was made of that bar in the café, however, where he ordered latte macchiato for both of us. "Aren't you going to have some dessert?" he said. "I know I am. Baba au rhum, perhaps. Or tiramisù. You know *tirami su* means 'pick me up,' but if you want to offend an Italian waiter, you say 'I'll have the *tiramilo su*,' which means 'pick up my dick.'"

"I'm trying to lose weight, Nathan," I said. "Please don't encourage me to eat desserts."

"Sorry." He coughed. Our latte macchiatos came, and Nathan raised his cup and said, "Here's to us. Here's to Lizzie Fischman. Here's to never playing that dumb game again as long as we live." These days, I noticed, Nathan used the phrase "as long as we live" a bit too frequently for comfort.

Reluctantly I touched my glass to his. "You know," he said, "I think

I've always hated that game. Even in college, when I won, it made me jealous. Everyone else had done so much more than me. Back then I figured I'd have time to explore the sexual world. Guess the joke's on me, huh?"

I shrugged. I wasn't sure.

"What's with you tonight, anyway?" he said. "You're so distant."

"I just have things on my mind, Nathan, that's all."

"You've been acting weird ever since I got back from Europe, Celia. Sometimes I think you don't even want to see me."

Clearly he was expecting reassurances to the contrary. I didn't say anything.

"Well," he said, "is that it? You don't want to see me?"

I twisted my shoulders in confusion. "Nathan—"

"Great," he said, and laughed so that I couldn't tell if he was kidding. "Your best friend for nearly ten years. Jesus."

"Look, Nathan, don't melodramatize," I said. "It's not that simple. It's just that I have to think a little about myself. My own life, my own needs. I mean, I'm going to be thirty soon. You know how long it's been since I've had a boyfriend?"

"I'm not against your having a boyfriend," Nathan said. "Have I ever tried to stop you from having a boyfriend?"

"But, Nathan," I said, "I never get to meet anyone when I'm with you all the time. I love you and I want to be your friend, but you can't expect me to just keep giving and giving and giving my time to you without anything in return. It's not fair."

I was looking away from him as I said this. From the corner of my vision I could see him glancing to the side, his mouth a small, tight line.

"You're all I have," he said quietly.

"That's not true, Nathan," I said.

"Yes it is true, Celia."

"Nathan, you have lots of other friends."

"But none of them count. No one but you counts."

The waitress arrived with his goblet of tiramisù, put it down in front of him. "Go on with your life, you say," he was muttering. "Find a boyfriend. Don't you think I'd do the same thing if I could? But all those options are closed to me, Celia. There's nowhere for me to go, no route that isn't dangerous. I mean, getting on with my life—I just can't talk about that simply anymore, the way you can." He leaned closer, over the table. "Do you want to know something?" he said. "Every time I see someone I'm attracted to I go into a cold sweat. And I imagine that they're dead, that if I touch them, the part of them I touch will die. Don't you see? It's bad enough to be afraid you might get it. But to be afraid you might give it—and to someone you loved—" He shook his head, put his hand to his forehead.

What could I say to that? What possibly was there to say? I took his hand, suddenly, I squeezed his hand until the edges of his fingers were white. I was remembering how Nathan looked the first time I saw him, in line at a college dining hall, his hands on his hips, his head erect, staring worriedly at the old lady dishing out food, as if he feared she might run out, or not give him enough. I have always loved the boyish hungers— for food, for sex—because they are so perpetual, so faithful in their daily revival, and even though I hadn't met Nathan yet, I think, in my mind, I already understood: I wanted to feed him, to fill him up; I wanted to give him everything.

Across from us now, two girls were smoking cigarettes and talking about what art was. A man and a woman, in love, intertwined their fingers. Nathan's hand was getting warm and damp in mine, so I let it go, and eventually he blew his nose and lit a cigarette.

"You know," he said after a while, "It's not the sex, really. That's not what I regret missing. It's just that— Do you realize, Celia, I've never been in love? Never once in my life have I actually been in love?" And he looked at me very earnestly, not knowing, not having the slightest idea, that once again he was counting me for nothing.

"Nathan," I said. "Oh, my Nathan." Still, he didn't seem satisfied, and I knew he had been hoping for something better than my limp consolation. He looked away from me, across the café, listening, I suppose, for that wind-chime peal as all the world's pennies flew his way.

~ *Neil Bartlett* ~

Notes Towards a Performance of Jean Racine's Tragedy *Athalie*

for Simon Mellor

1

Everybody knows that sons don't die before their fathers; that isn't the way things are. That isn't the way things are meant to happen. Fathers die before their sons.

That way there is a time after they're dead when you can live.

After my own father's father died he still used to talk to him. What I want to know is, did he ask him for his advice, ask him about things and then wait for his answers, or did he just tell him about things, keep him informed? Did he tell him things that it was only safe to tell him now that there could be no answer? For myself, I think that after they're dead is the time to say all the things you wanted to say but couldn't, not ever, because he was your father; the time to say all the things you wanted and needed to say out loud, and not just to him but to anyone, to the world, all the things you wanted to say but couldn't, not ever, not to anyone. Talking to a headstone is like calling someone when you know he's not there just so that you can use the sound of the phone ringing in his house or apartment to help you imagine how that place is, exactly, when he's not there. It's like writing him a letter when you have no intention at all of posting it. It's like writing a diary where you put down

---

A playwright and director as well as a fiction writer, NEIL BARTLETT is probably best known for the novel Ready to Catch Him Should He Fall. *He lives in London.*

the things that really matter and then telling him he's not to read it, ever.

Fathers die before their sons so that we can learn from their mistakes. So that we can decide not to be like them if we can possibly help it. And so that we can measure how much the world is changing from generation to generation; if sons died before their fathers, then the world would be going in the wrong direction.

Fathers die before their sons so that you can watch over them as they sicken. That's when you finally realise that you are not a child anymore; when you have the chance to see them small and physically helpless, as you were once. If they get really ill before they die, then you can bathe them and wash them and feed them and decide whether they lie on their back or on their side or whether they're too hot or too cold in the bed. You tell them what is happening to them and what it means, just as they once did for you. You know that you would do anything, anything at all, to protect them from pain—you feel just the same way that they used to feel about you. Sometimes you have inexplicable desires to hurt them, just as people sometimes have with small children, but you stop yourself touching them, you stop yourself touching them because even though he is a father he was once a son, a child. And you realise that fathers die before their sons so that their sons can see them helpless, and that is revenge enough, you don't need to touch them.

Fathers die before their sons. This goes on and on, from father to son, except that some sons are childless (and some sons die first; I've seen it happen), and this makes things different. It means that everything has to be worked out right here and now, in one generation, it means that nothing can be deferred or explained away, it means that you can't just make things tolerable for yourself in the hope that one day things will be better for your son. It means that the whole and unimaginably long history of your family comes to a full, irreversible, and immediate stop with you. It means that everything has to be fought out now with him, and that means that your dreams are bound to be that much more violent. If anyone is going to learn anything from your father's death, it has to be you. If anyone is going to have a life, it has to be you. So you have to confront him. You have to walk right into his room, the room where you know he is, and confront him. You walk in, expecting your father, you know he's in there, except that when you walk into the room and he's there, he turns round, it isn't a father at all, it's a small boy.

2

When you see a small boy it lifts the heart as nothing else can. The beauty of a small boy carried in his father's arms can stop you in your tracks, make you break into an involuntary smile; oh, there is nothing more beautiful than the sight of a small boy carried in his father's arms, the beauty and confidence of a well-dressed small boy carried in his father's arms and knowing he is held, knowing he is loved, knowing he is clean and cherished, a prince, a king, carried in loving arms—he is more beautiful even than a lover. And this small boy being carried also I suppose catches at you because it reminds you of all the pictures and paintings you have seen which have the same subject of a much-loved child, except of course you never see that, do you, you never see the child in his father's arms, you never see that, except of course in those pictures which are pictures of an old man showing you the dead body of his Son.

3

When you wash a dead body, when it's all over and someone has to wash the body, and the someone is you, you're not sure if this is the body of an old person or a young person, if this is a father or a son. What they've been through has made their face haggard; but now that it's over they look calm. They are as wasted as the old, and as light as the very young. The sweat in the folds of the discoloured skin, the hands, the powerless limbs, the smell—they could be those of an intently sleeping newborn child, but they are also those of an old man in the middle of the afternoon. The breathing is the same—and then when it is all over you wash the body; and if you ever have to do this, and you have never washed someone, never given a small boy his bath, if you have no skills as a father to bring to this important task, then I assure you that you will nevertheless find that you know exactly what to do. You will handle the body as a lover would, firmly and carefully. You will bring all your skill in handling a man's body to bear. Lifting him carefully limb by limb, talking gently to him all the while, wiping him clean and then wiping him dry, you will wash him and dress him so that at the end, whatever has happened, he is not torn apart but is again clean and loved; so that even if it is not your father you are laying out now, or if this is not your son's body you are washing, or if this is not your lover but someone you must care for anyway, you are saying to him gently, saying with your hands, You are not an orphan. And this is what I wanted to say, this is what I wanted to hold back my weeping long enough to say, this I think is now the meaning of the last lines of Racine's tragedy *Athalie,* which are: From the terror of this ending, which is no more than we should all expect, we learn what we must not forget: that there is indeed, O King, a judge above us; that innocence has a champion, the orphan a father in heaven.

~ *Gary Glickman* ~

Buried
Treasure

When I first came to New York I had some good luck getting an apartment, a high-sloping garret studio up five narrow flights, full of sun and windows and a long vista of chimneys and rooftops across half the city. Even now, if I'm feeling sorry for myself, certain people insist on reminding me of that time in our lives when everyone was searching and optimistic and envious, but I was already happy in my nest.

I was going to be a writer. Meanwhile, by the time I got home in the evening after my bookstore job I could no more write a full sentence than fly delicately out my big drafty windows and across my romantic-chimneyed rooftops looking for something to write about. Instead, too often, I drank a sweating beer too quickly, collapsed in the old armchair, and stared at a crack in the long blank wall across the room, trying to think up something it resembled. As soon as I could see what it was, I told myself, I would go across to the desk and start to work. Occasionally I remembered the view just behind me out the window and tried to find solace in that. Sometimes a jet passed over the one clear pane of the skylight, and I tried to imagine Europe, and elegant publication parties, and smoky cafés where my life would begin.

One night the door buzzer vibrated long and hard, scaring me from

---

GARY GLICKMAN is the author of Years from Now, *a novel that—along with his stories—challenges the notion that sexual identity necessarily eclipses racial or ethnic identity. He lives in Provincetown, Massachusetts.*

my stupor, spilling my beer but at least getting me on my feet again. I had never heard the buzzer before. When I pressed the button to ask who it was, the answer came not from five flights below but just on the other side of the door.

"It's Ray, your neighbor! Open up!" The man had shouted with only the flimsy door between us. I didn't answer right away, or even touch the door. "From next door!" the voice continued. "Are you just going to stand there?"

My peephole was the old-fashioned kind, a glass lens covered by a metal plate, which you cannot slide open without your visitor hearing and seeing and guessing all your thoughts. So I opened the door—in New York this is always a brave act—and said hello. My neighbor, a man perhaps in his sixties, was leaning straight-armed against the doorjamb like a parody of an advertisement, chin up, head coquettishly half-turned. His plaid shirt was stained and pulling out of loose, dirty jeans. His stomach fell over his belt, and he hadn't shaved for long enough that crumbs were stuck to his gray whiskers. He breathed out of his mouth, snoring on the inhale, but then our two aparments were on the sixth floor, and sometimes I'd be breathing heavy, too, coming up the last flight.

He looked me in the eye only long enough to say, "Hi there!"

"This is very neighborly of you," I said. "Not what I heard about the Big Apple at all."

"This is a friendly building," he said, stumbling past me into the one room of my apartment. "We all know each other. I didn't get on much with the last tenant in here. A nun or something."

I showed him the books she had left behind: *Love and Orgasm, Swedish Massage and You, Wine Wisdom, Divorce and Beyond.*

"Yes," Ray said, flipping through the *Love and Orgasm* book, then tossing it aside. "I hated her, she never said hello, always passed me on the stairs like she didn't really have to live here, and we should all please remember that! But I had the feeling you were one of us."

He looked over to see if I understood him. I did, and smiled.

"So I wanted to welcome you, and show you around, if you know what I mean."

I thanked him. I couldn't imagine what he would show me, but I'd been waiting for a guide to that romantic life I knew must be all around the city, behind doors still closed to me and hidden only by my ignorance.

I had assumed my eventual guide would look different, an erotic angel curling his finger in my direction, a new friend inviting me at last to one of those prestigious parties where I imagined careers and potent intimacies must be spawned. I was wrong about most things, missed out on countless treasures those years might have offered, and have made most mistakes since. At the time, because I knew nothing, I thought it would be a mistake to say no to anything, at least to say no too quickly.

Ray sat down on the sofa, spotted the six-pack on the floor, and asked, "Is there anything to drink?" meanwhile continuing to look for drinks elsewhere—through the window, on the ceiling.

"Ah!" he said, turning again to the six-pack and taking out a bottle. "Something to open with?" I gestured to show him it was the twist-off kind, "Of course," he said. "Of course. I knew that. Well, so what do you?"

He seemed a safe first experiment. With someone like that, someone so peripheral and momentary, I thought you could say anything, the wildest fantasy. "I'm . . . a writer," I said.

He swallowed too much beer in a gulp and spit some of it back up. He wiped his mouth with his sleeve. "What a coincidence! I guess you must have known, asking me in and all, that I'm quite a well-known writer, in a way, myself. I guess you've seen my name around?"

"No," I said. "I'm sorry, but I haven't." I didn't know his last name.

"I happen to have written *Bedtime for Badboys*. That's right, the musical. But also the novelization. It was conceived originally as a movie; I could show you the screenplay." He sat back on my sofa bed and crossed his arms for me to take a good look at him, now that I knew who he was.

"*Bedtime for Badboys?*" I said. "It does sound familiar."

"Of course it sounds familiar. We're talking off Broadway. We're talking international tour, as far as Bucharest, Romania. I went there with them, saw everything. We're talking amateur shows in every high school in America. You must be too young. That was in '65. I was only thirty-five. How do you think I've been living the last fifteen years?"

I shrugged. It did interest me, how writers find the money and time to work. It interested me more to know he was just fifty.

"Well, you're right, it wasn't exactly just from that one. I've written others, obviously; they're all better than *Bedtime,* but no one wants them." He looked down at his bottle. "Actually I've been doing books recently."

"Really!" I said.

"I'll go get them for you." Before I could object to either his leaving for them or his coming back, he had run behind his door, just next to mine—I saw a dark mess in there, stacks of magazines, clothes draped everywhere, a tray of bottles on the floor—and reemerged with two ultra-thin, shiny paperpacks.

"For you, my boy. You can keep them, if you don't have them already." They were stick-figure cartoon books of *Hamlet* and *Wuthering Heights,* and the caption I saw, just flipping through, was "Now Hamlet had this thing for his Mom. . . ."

"Thanks, Ray," I said, following him back into my room, where he sat down again just where I had sat, in the armchair, and was opening another beer.

"And what have you published?" he asked, crossing his legs, with their short black socks, and finally turning away from his scrutiny of walls and ceiling to look at me.

"I'm working on a novel," I said, daring to say it for the first time. I believed it was true. I believed my hours at the bookstore, my staring out my window, my waiting for exciting days to come to me, was all necessary research.

"Very ambitious," he said. "You know, you remind me a lot of myself. Quite a few years ago, I mean—ha ha!" He stared at me, smiling and breathing out of his mouth.

"Not really!" I said, about the comparison. Then I added, "It's not really so ambitious."

"A novel!" he said, dropping the smile and the stare and the wheezing, standing up and shaking his head. "I really don't know if I can help you much there. It's a tough market, you know, catch as catch can. I better be going, don't want to be a pain. Nice talking to you and all. You know, I like what you've done with this place, really do!" He took another beer and was out the door.

I locked my three locks, quietly so as not to offend him, one after another until the bolts just fell into place.

An instant later he locked his own door with three violent twists, a loud push of a dead bolt, and a clumsy, very unsecretive fumble with a chain.

~ ~ ~

After that we passed each other sometimes on the narrow stairs, or on the front stoop, or opening our boxes for the mail. Sometimes I'd hear him through the narrow cracked wall, arguing on the phone or the intercom to the street:

"I don't care if it's for free, I'm not interested. Just go away!"

"Ray, man, gimme a break, just for a minute and I'll be gone."

"I said go away and I mean it!"

Sometimes he would look my way on the street and nod hello, other times when he spotted me he began talking to himself, so that when we passed each other he would be deep in conversation. Once when I noticed him, he turned away as if he hadn't seen. Another time he grabbed the sleeve of my coat and led me around the corner to a dim, empty bar on Fourteenth Street, just behind our building. It was a four o'clock dusk; we were alone with the bartender.

"Here he is, Billy," Ray said, squeezing my shoulder. "The new one."

Billy, who was drying glasses, wiped his hand and then shook mine. "Guess I'll be seeing you around, like ol' Ray here."

"I guess so!" I said, cheerfully.

A few weeks later the cold weather broke, and my sunny garret, cozy all winter, was suddenly a greenhouse, incubating till midnight. Afternoons off, I would sit on the cornice out my window, waiting for love to come, or inspiration, or a breeze. Sometimes while I was reading, a handsome man would pass by below—or rather what appeared, from that height, to be a handsome man—and I would concentrate down toward him a definite message of desire. Sometimes, when that failed, I would drop down a twig of the wisteria just reaching to my window, hoping the man would notice and look up. Or I would call out a common name—John, Jim, Joe—and when the passerby looked up I would wave across the rooftops as if at someone else, and only then pretend to notice the man below and wave down there as well. A few smart pedestrians could count the apartments and figure out which bell to ring. Sometimes I answered; sometimes I ran from the window and crouched until the ringing stopped. It was just long enough ago when it still seemed, for one last moment, that no act was indelible, when the wisteria, now thick as arms, was still only a few scouting tendrils.

One night something crashed just outside on the landing. I opened the door and there was Ray, desperately pulling at the handle of a steamer trunk.

"I don't know why I didn't think of you before," he said. "This stuff is worth a lot of money. I like to help out someone like me. Just like I was, coming to the city, starting out once. You might make it," he said. "I did. I just don't have room for this stuff anymore."

I asked him what it was.

"It's not mine," he answered. "At least, it wasn't originally. The guy before me collected it. I always thought I'd do something with it. But now it's been a long time."

As he stood up he looked at me steadily for the first time and then smiled a brief, private smile before slamming his door, which he locked with all three knobs, then the loud bolt and the fumbling chain. His peephole slid open, and I could see his eye.

Because he was watching, I dragged the trunk inside my door, over to my sofa, and sat down to explore whatever it would be. The catch was rusty and the padlock bent, but I had a screwdriver; before I wrenched open the lid I was ready to quit and chuck the whole thing, all that rust and dust and dead weight. The top creaked open, and a puff of dust flew up like moths escaping. Inside, packed and piled to overflowing and seeming to pose for me alone, were hundreds of sex magazines, gorgeous and guilty as a pirate's booty, some of them dusty and moldering, men's bodies on every cover, dark hairy or baby smooth, looking down tough and threatening, or looking up naked and submissive, all those eyes through the years knowing my desire so long in advance. I was paralyzed, addicted.

The top few I remembered from news racks of recent vintage, bold, explicit, and buoyant with manipulating irony. There were *Torso* and *Honcho, Mandate, Numbers, In Touch, Playguy* and *Blueboy, Inches,* as well as the harder choices, dicier but not so dicey you wouldn't still find them at downtown kiosks: *Drummer, Hunk, Stroke.* The glossier magazines showed naked men in various alluring poses, a booted foot up on a fire hydrant, hairy legs spread provocatively despite their limp offering; or a swimmer relaxing on the beach on his belly, legs spread and dreamy-eyed. My shameless heart pounded for these fantasy men, all together like this, all waiting for the viewer to delight in their bodies and offering, by smile or grim stare, either seduction or delicious subjugation. Still, almost no picture had more than a solitary model in any photo; the naked men were usually alone in the universe: alone, except with me.

Then there were the more obscure magazines that showed penises erect, sometimes glistening, the men attached to them somewhere out of focus in the background, or two men, or three or ten; issues that came plastic-wrapped, with tear-away censors placed at just the most engaging junctures. I knew some of them from the back shelf at the bookstore, where most men eventually wandered over to browse and cast glances, furtive, shameful, hopeful.

But beneath those magazines I knew, the issues grew older and older: lithe, long-haired men-boys from the sixties, staring out to some ambiguous offstage—unaware of observation. They were bold or embarrassed, pale, casually hairy or pastily nude, doing nothing in particular, just standing around naked with friends, or lying on a sofa and reading a magazine. Farther down were "physical culture" magazines from the fifties showing oiled, stiff, muscle-bound men in classical poses, arms above their head against painted backdrops of toppled columns and ruined temples: living sculptures, their private parts just covered by a trailing toga or bit of vine. The oldest issue, near the flaking leather bottom of the trunk, was from the forties, its text typewritten, naked boys diving into a lake.

Long into the night I flipped through photo after photo, story after story, year after year—more than thirty years crammed in of passion and longing, secrets and shame—until the early garbage trucks were grumbling and I seemed to be falling down and down into that cramped, dark trunk along with the copies I'd already looked over and thrown back.

~ ~ ~

At work I was still thinking about those old pictures and stories as I sold their more contemporary replacements. For a week I didn't see Ray and kept stepping around the large trunk in my room, wondering what I was supposed to do with it. Sometimes I'd sort through, looking for stories and photos that in passing I'd thought were sexy but hadn't yet taken out to study. When I came home I would eat my take-out soup and sandwich while flipping through page after page, no longer watching the news, or reading, or even sitting at the desk writing letters, which was at least pretending to be about to begin to write.

Dug up from so much dust and secrecy, packed together like that in the trunk and stranded in the middle of the room, the collection had an enormous gravity. Sometimes it was a force outward toward the world, toward running and swimming and getting healthy like these men and connecting with other people somehow for romance and love and all the lights visible all night from my window. And sometimes it was darker and silent, a suffocating pull down into that solitary, airless trunk. Sometimes I searched out my favorites; sometimes, frightened by all the hours lost, I buried them as deeply as I could.

Finally, after that week, I was having some friends over—my first party—and had to clear out and clean up the room. I tried standing the trunk on its end, a pedestal for a lamp; I tried turning it on its side for a table; camouflaging it with a sheet; pushing it into the closet. But there was no room for a trunk in a studio. So for the first time I knocked on Ray's door; I could tell he was home by the music playing through the wall—old show tunes on scratchy records.

At first no one answered, so I knocked again, and finally found the buzzer, and pushed it for a long time. Ray called out, from what sounded like far away: "All right, all right! Just get the hell out, and I'll meet you in the street!"

I knocked again and called out my name, and eventually I heard him coming toward the door. It opened just enough to show his face, red and furious. Then he saw me.

"Oh—you!" he said. "What a surprise. You can come in. It's sort of a mess today, but—"

"That's okay!" I said. "I'm sure it can't be worse than mine."

The dismal surprise was that his apartment was so like mine and yet so transformed by the dimness, the piles of newspapers and playbills and magazines, shoulder high, the smell of old Chinese food and stale beer.

"Ray," I said, still cheerfully though more nasally, "your place is exactly like mine. The mirror image, in fact."

We looked at each other too long, my grin fading to his grimace, as Gwen Verdon belted "Whatever Lola Wants" as she had many times a day all that week. I couldn't breathe, but because the apartment was like mine but turned around, I had to look for the door.

"Believe me," Ray said, taking me by the arm. "It's exactly the same. Except I have the deck."

He showed me a black metal door where my fourth window would be; he opened it, all five locks, then pointed to an abandoned few feet of terrace filled with old crates and strips of rotting green carpet. The fresh air billowed in.

"Pretty great, huh? You know Anise Nine?"

I assumed it was a kind of drink and shook my head.

"Anise Nine! Anise Nine! You're the big bookworm—don't you know who that is! Famous writer! Wrote all sorts of things. Lived here before I did."

At last I understood he meant Anaïs Nin. I told him I thought she was dead.

He shook his head in disgust. "Of course she's dead. *Now*. Very famous writer, and she lived right here. Had a swing out on this very deck, used to swing right out over the edge and scare all her friends away. Very famous writer, Anise Nine."

"So those were her magazines?" I asked, trying to get back to my purpose.

"No! Of course not, what do you think? They're Jim's, the guy who lived here before me. I lived here with him awhile, when I first came to the city. Like you." He looked at me as before, with that grin-grimace that kept changing, as if he was trying to reflect my mood but couldn't guess it. "I was just a kid then. He was nice to me. Jim died. I stayed."

When he spoke I could look away again, at how much his apartment really was like my own, even though reversed, even transformed by thirty years of haphazard garbage. I was already ambitious for it. If only Ray would leave this place, I was wishing, if only he'd become famous (I was generous in my envy), move to California, and let me knock down the wall, throw out his garbage, and make one large penthouse from our garrets!

Meanwhile there were his records to look at everywhere, tottering piles of them in and out of their sleeves; and Broadway playbills on all the bookshelves. The bed was hidden by a mound of yellowed score paper, much scribbled in, on top of a winter wardrobe of coats and sweaters and felt hats. I couldn't imagine where he slept. The walls were covered with layers of show posters, several of them identical copies of the off-Broadway opening of *Bedtime for Badboys*. Week after week I'd been hearing the songs through the wall. Already I knew the words to "A Hard Man Is Good to Find." Above us was a skylight like my own, but all his big windows faced north, and the shade, and the back of buildings, whereas mine faced south and sun, and the long vista across the whole West Village. His were blocked by a heavy steel grate.

"You keep those closed all the time like that?" I asked, wondering about the safety of my own windows.

"I've had a lot of break-ins," he said. "Boys, mostly, who've seen the place. I don't have much here, though I've lost a couple of stereos. Little whores. They can climb right through a crack."

"Do you think I should get them for myself?"

He looked at me a long time, confused, then laughed and spit saliva across the room. "Oh, you mean the grates! Well, no—for you I don't think so. Not yet anyway. There's never been a break-in over there on your side. I've had lots of boys in here, you know." He was grinning too close to me.

"Anyway, Ray," I said. "About that trunk. What do you want me to do with it?"

"Oh, that. Whatever you want. The collection's a treasure, isn't it? I just don't know where to go with it, and like you saw, I don't have the strength anymore. I thought you might. I just thought you'd like to have a crack at it."

I thanked him and added, before I left—feeling sympathetic to his solitude and grateful for his generosity—that I was having a few people in the next night, and that if he wanted he could come.

"Sure, sure," he said. I was relieved when he waved me off dismissively, as if he hadn't really heard.

The buzzer jolted me out of the shower, and I thought my first guest must be an hour early. But when I was at the door, dripping naked and ready to press the intercom button, I heard Ray's voice. The buzzer had been for my apartment, but his had been pressed also.

"Just get the hell out of here!" he was saying, only a few feet away; privacy was our polite conceit.

"Ah, come on, Ray," said a man's voice from downstairs. "Just let me in for a minute. I've got what you want, you'll see."

"Look!" said Ray. "I don't care what you've got. You pretty damn well better get out, or I'll get the cops. This isn't the first time, you know; there's plenty like you. They'll come for you in a second. You won't even get down the block. Okay, I'm calling right now!"

"Ray, come on, man. Let me in, just a second. Then I'll get out of your hair.

"I said get out now! Just get out!"

When the shouting stopped, I got dressed and dragged the trunk down the five flights—careful not to make a noise—and left it out on

586 ~ The Penguin Book of Gay Short Stories

the sidewalk, next to the bags of trash. It was already dark, and no one saw me except a man going through the bags. I was gone before he opened the trunk.

~ ~ ~

Later, it was Ray who buzzed, when my friends were already in and we were eating and singing songs with a guitar and dancing sometimes in the little space I had cleared in the center of the room. There were about a dozen of us. Candles were stuck in bottles, greasy paper plates were piled high on the table. But though the room was crowded, it wasn't a wild party. People were tired after work and happy for a place to talk awhile before going home to solitary beds.

"I'm with my friend Erroll," Ray said, as I opened the door. "Is it okay if he comes along? I told him there was a party."

I looked out, saw no one.

"Where is he?"

"Right here," he said. His friend climbed up the last few steps, a paunchy man Ray's age, with sparse hair combed low across his forehead. He shook my hand too hard and too long.

"Right glad to meet *you*," Erroll said, in a heavy Texan accent, emphasizing his last word as if I had said it first. He stroked his black beard and stared without blinking into my eyes.

~ ~ ~

The party wasn't a success.

". . . And I told her, 'Pauly, if you publish that, you are gonna be sued, sugar, you can trust ol' Uncle Erroll on that one.' You know I was his publisher? I surely was. And the basket on that one! You can ask me all about it."

Erroll was sitting in the desk chair, commandeering that half of the room with stories of his publishing career. He worked in a large publishing house, editing celebrity memoirs.

"Go ahead," he said to my friend Margot, tapping her knee. "Just go ahead and ask me."

My friend looked away suddenly, as if someone had called her name.

"And you want to know what else I have edited?" he said, turning to no one in particular. One after another, my friends got up and crowded the other side of the room, until Erroll came over too; soon my friends were leaving.

Eventually only Ray and Erroll were left.

"Thanks and all," Ray said, realizing we were alone. He got up and pulled Erroll up with him. "I didn't know your friends were so . . . quiet. I thought you were having a big party. I wouldn't have taken the liberty to ask—"

"That's okay, Ray." I told him I was glad to meet his friend.

"Really?" he asked.

"Really," I said. There seemed no harm in flattering for pity's sake.

After work the next day, Ray buzzed again.

"Can I come in?" he called, before I could get near the door. "It's Ray, your neighbor."

"It's open," I said, turning off the TV and sitting back on the sofa, angry by now, after a day of resenting Ray's uninvited friend of the night before.

"You shouldn't leave your door open like that," he said, looking around the floor.

"There's beer in the fridge," I told him, and he went to get one before falling into the desk chair and wheeling himself over.

"Well," he said, and stopped very close to me. He sat there, staring.

"Well," I answered.

"You certainly did make an impression on Erroll last night. Are you attracted to him?"

"Erroll?" I said, trying to make two syllables sound like nothing at all. "Well, he made an impression on me too."

"Fabulous!" Ray said. "Fab-u-lous!" He spit up some spray and brushed it away with his sleeve. "You see, Erroll's quite taken with you, and you see, he's in a very important position. I told him you were a young writer. He's a very important *editor*! You see what I mean?"

"Not really."

"So it can work out, if you understand what I mean. Don't you get it? Are you for real? Look, he would very much like to have a nice young boy like yourself with him—on weekends, out in Fire Island. You know, he rents a beautiful house out there; I've been there many times myself. With a pool."

"Really!" I said. I always wanted to know how this moment came about, when a person could finally slip from the safe, conventional world of work and lonely evenings into that smoky, intense glamour of sex and money—out there, for example, on that island I'd always heard about. I knew you couldn't get there by car, and the houses were high up on stilts. The woods and the beaches were filled with sex. Now, finally, I saw; until you were famous, this was how to get there.

It was exciting, his mistaking me for someone who did that kind of thing. My own life, I thought, my *real* life, didn't include this. But finally here I was, fully in the world, seamy side and all: something to write about. Saying yes now would entitle me someday afterward to achievement and privilege. Hard-earned and hard-edged, my work would be; and my life.

"He can help your career, no doubt about that," Ray said. He was watching me strangely, letting his offer sink in. "Oh, look, kid, it's not *selling* yourself or anything."

"Oh, no?"

"No; you'd only have to sleep with him once or twice, I'm sure of it. Then you could just be friends, be his date. Nice dinners and things. He's got a pool, remember."

"I don't know, Ray," I said, smiling. I was grateful to him, just for this colorful moment. "It seems pretty close to selling yourself."

He looked at me hard.

"I'd do it, if I were you. In fact, listen, I *was* you. I used to do it— and I'll tell you, it got me where I am today." We both looked across to the opposite wall, the one with a crack, which divided our lives. I thought of his dim room just beyond, and the balcony swing of that dead writer, swinging out over midair.

"Anyway, he asked me to invite you to his apartment for dinner. That's not selling yourself, is it? Then you can decide for yourself."

"True," I said. He had made it sound very simple. Maybe it *was* very simple, all that I had always stumbled over. You just say yes instead of no: a way out of my solitary room, my view of empty rooftops, into that parallel, better world somewhere else in the city, invisible but always rumbling.

He kept his eyes focused on mine. I had nothing more to say and wondered when he would leave, what he was waiting for.

Slowly, in a very low, already despairing voice, he said, "I'd like to get down on my knees and make love to you myself."

We stared at each other awhile.

"But . . . I guess that's my problem, isn't it."

I just hunched my shoulders, sharing the question with him, smiling sympathetically because even then I knew his point of view.

After a while he stood up and left without a word, just a return hunch of the shoulders and a quick retreat.

～ ～ ～

I called up Erroll and let him invite me for dinner. I felt like a hustler and dressed what I thought was the part: tight red T-shirt, tight jeans, thick white socks. Just for the heart-thump on the way over, it was worth it; how often do you get that crashing wave without drugs or calamity? But in the elevator I caved in, timid again in someone else's clothes.

Erroll answered the door, glad to see me but obviously upset. Stiffly he shook my hand, ushered me in. There was another man there, with dark curls and the head of a Roman statue. Stretched out on the sofa, big hands up behind his head, he was tall and muscular, with a thick black mustache cut stiffly above his lips like a broom. I wished Erroll would go away—here was the man I wanted to go away with, away from my old self.

"This is Frank," Erroll said, when Frank had not moved even to nod, had only raised a contemptuous eyebrow in greeting. "Frank just stopped by for a minute—with a friend."

The bathroom door opened, and a very young man appeared, blond and slight and pale, as unoriginal as could be. He came over and shook my hand. "My name is Bobby," he said, smiling far too much for New York. "I'm very glad to meet you."

Frank, who still had said nothing and yet had not taken his dark eyes from mine, finally looked toward the boy named Bobby and smiled.

"Bobby," he said, contemplating the name. "Hey there, sweetheart," he said, and turned back to me, winking like a conspirator.

Erroll looked back and forth from his guests to the little table pushed to the middle of the room and set elegantly for two: candles, crystal globes on long stems, pink linen napkins.

"So, Frank, what are you guys going to do?" he asked.

"I don't know, kiddo," Frank said. "I just thought we could hang out here awhile. Didn't know you'd be home. I want to get to know your friend here."

"Oh," Erroll said. "I guess that's fine."

Bobby and I sat beside each other in stiff chairs, and Frank and Erroll sat across from us on the sofa, murmuring. Frank rolled a joint and passed it to me, smiling but silent. I asked Bobby all about himself, and he answered with his hands in his lap. He was, he said, a "dancer-slash-model," and he had just gotten off a bus that day from Omaha.

"But what will you do?" I asked, already high-voiced and dramatic from the pot. It was hard to believe such a naive story; I'd read about people like him.

"Well," he said, "I've got this appointment with a photographer friend tonight. I just met him; he thinks he can get me some work; he's going to take some free pictures." He turned and stared straight ahead, contemplating his assured success.

On the sofa, Erroll was more and more fidgety, looking at his watch, at Frank, at his forlorn, elegant table for two.

Finally Bobby stood up and asked to use the phone. He had to call his photographer friend. "He wrote his number down for me on the back of my hand here. See?"

When he had gone into the bedroom, Frank, who hadn't yet spoken to me, finally turned to me and spoke in a half-whisper, half-grumble, "Hey, you there. Isn't that kid the prettiest thing you ever saw in your life?"

I smirked, trying to imply that I, too, was confident and worldly enough to judge someone like that; something to look at and play with.

"Frank!" Erroll said, an agitated whisper. "What do you want to do?"

"Sorry, old man."

"Don't call me old man. You're as old as I am."

"Sorry, old guy, I just thought we could come up and use your bedroom. I've just got to get that boy undressed. Get my face between those buns!" He turned to me. "What do *you* think?"

"Yes!" I said, as low and manly as I could, but really I was thinking how lucky that boy was, how much I would like to be swept onto some bed by him, swept ragged by that mustache.

At my answer, he laughed. "Yeah," he said. "I'll bet you would."

Bobby came out and apologized, said he was very sorry but that he didn't really have any more time. It was very nice meeting all of us.

"What! Well, good-bye, sugar," Frank said, standing up before Bobby could get to the door and kissing him good-bye as I had never seen it done before, strong arms enwrapping a whole body. My own mouth must have dropped slack, because after a while Frank looked up, noticed me, and laughed again.

When the boy left, Frank said, "Damn!" and fell down on the chair next to me. "Damn, damn, damn!"

Erroll, watching him a moment, said, "Well, I guess there's enough for three. I'll just go get it ready."

That left Frank and me alone, and we sat some minutes in silence. I didn't dare speak, and Frank didn't bother to. From nervousness I had smoked too much too fast, and I could hardly sit up straight. Frank watched me, grinning occasionally.

Finally, in his deep, contemptuous voice, he said, "You really want me, don't you?"

"What makes you think that?" I said.

With his bare foot—large and with a tuft of black hair on the big toe—he pressed slowly into my crotch. "Oh, I don't know," he said. "I just have that special feeling. You've got that feeling too, now, don't you?"

"I don't know," I answered, eyes closing. I was dropping off the chair, trying not to grab that foot, that leg, that man, every limb, when Erroll came out again, with a tray of smoked salmon and white wine on ice.

"Nice friend you got here," Frank said, standing up abruptly but not moving from in front of me. I stared at his belt, pretending not to notice him. He didn't move till I had looked up. Then he walked over, picked up a long piece of salmon, held it above his head, and lowered it slowly into his mouth.

We ate. Erroll was miserable and quiet, Frank torturingly garrulous. They talked about people I didn't know. I was grateful to be excluded, blinking from the pot and all the wine I drank because Frank kept filling my glass to the brim. When Erroll casually asked me what I'd done with that trunk of magazines buried so long in the mess of Ray's apartment, I told him I threw it out.

"Threw it out!" Frank said, jumping from his chair. "I can't believe he threw it out! What's the matter with him!"

"It was in the way," I said.

"In the way! In the way! Do you know what treasure there was preserved in that trunk! What a record, lost now for all time! All those fingered, sticky pages! The sperm of the ages! I helped Ray collect them, gave him my old ones, found him new ones. All those years, the changing times, the most important generation for faggots in modern history! And you threw them out! Stupid!"

"But—but—" I said.

"Not to mention the price you could have gotten, sugar," Erroll said. "Thousands, probably."

Soon the meal was over. Erroll must have realized the evening was ruined; he asked me to stay but without conviction, and when I shook my head he didn't insist. I was in a hurry to leave at the same time as Frank and offered my abrupt, ungracious thanks.

In the elevator, Frank stood facing me, silent. His eyebrow was raised, his arms crossed. Finally, eloquently, he said, "So?"

I could have jumped over to him, pressed my lips against his, and made the answer very simple. I would have gotten what I wanted and perhaps changed immediately from what I was into someone else, with another place to go than home alone to my desk and my view of rooftops. I would have danced on that crowded resort island, and made love until it became truth as much as fantasy, and found new friends, and discovered, in the last year before the epidemic, just where all the stories came from that I'd always heard, where the men were who were like me, and who I would one day become.

Instead, as we descended, as I imagined giving myself up to those arms and that big chest, too many seconds went by before I answered, cleverly, I thought, "So what?"

"So nothing, then," he said, and the elevator door opened to the lobby. He went out fast and didn't turn around.

On the sidewalk I saw him for an instant in the light of a streetlamp. "Frank!" I called. I started to run. "Frank, wait! I only meant 'what do you mean?' I meant, I mean . . ."

Eventually I stopped, not knowing what it was I meant, or which way to follow.

~ ~ ~

After that I didn't see Ray for a long time. We used to pass each other on the stairs all the time, and then it was not at all. He must have heard about his friend's ruined evening, and his collection lost to my naive impatience. Maybe he knew I was afraid of him, afraid of what I might become. I think when he heard me getting ready to go out he must have hesitated behind his door, waiting until I'd descended the five flights. I think he must have seen me sometimes on the street and walked around the block the other way. Still, I often thought I saw him just ahead, or behind, turning around suddenly.

His records still played, muted through the wall, all the old Broadway songs and most often his own. I still heard arguments over the intercom, and sometimes men and boys would let themselves into his apartment, looking around with suspicious eyes as they closed the door. I kept my peephole always halfway open, and with the lights off I used to watch them. Once Frank came up—I heard his name and his deep voice over the intercom, and he stood in front of my own door a long time, two inches away with just the wood between us, before going into the other apartment. I heard him clear his throat; maybe he raised his hand to knock. I almost called out his name and opened the door; but too soon he was gone.

Eventually a man came into the bookstore and offered me a job, which I took, which led to another job, and then another. My life changed in ways no one could have guessed, and years went by very quickly that had seemed, before they arrived, to be locked into a stately progression, a long parade one didn't have to scrutinize because it would be passing slowly for a long time.

Sometimes I thought about that trunk full of magazines, Ray's whole life, and regretted not having saved it, or given it to someone unafraid to care about it, or sold it outright. I still thought about Ray's apartment sometimes, and wondered if he would ever leave. One year, because I had enough money for some new things but not enough to change apartments, I bought an air conditioner and some furniture, and then installed a mirror along the whole back wall, to catch the light and make the apartment seem bigger. It was the wall separating my place from his. As I look at it now from across the room, the apartments seem to merge, one right into the other, one big apartment as once I wanted; and that's his younger self there, staring at me from far away, and those are his northern windows, stretching out behind him exactly like mine, full of light.

~ *David Wojnarowicz* ~

Self-Portrait
in Twenty-three
Rounds

S o my heritage is a calculated fuck on some faraway sun-filled bed while the curtains are being sucked in and out of an open window by a passing breeze. I'd be lying if I were to tell you I could remember the smell of sweat as I hadn't even been born yet. Conception's just a shot in the dark. I'm supposed to be dead right now but I just woke up this dingo motherfucker having hit me across the head with a slab of marble that instead of splitting my head open laid a neat sliver of eyeglass lens through the bull's-eye center of my left eye. We were coming through this four-and-a-half-day torture of little or no sleep. That's the breaks. We were staying at this one drag queen's house but her man did her wrong by being seen by some other queen with a vicious tongue in a darkened lot on the west side fucking some cute little puerto rican boy in the face and when me and my buddy knocked on the door to try and get a mattress to lay down on she sent a bullet through the door thinking it was her man—after three days of no sleep and maybe a couple of stolen donuts my eyes start separating: one goes left and one goes right and after four days of sitting on some stoop on a side street head cradled in my arms seeing four hours of pairs of legs walking by too much traffic noise and junkies trying to rip us off and the sunlight so hot this is a new york

---

The author of Close to the Knives *and* Memories That Smell like Gasoline, *DAVID WOJNAROWICZ was widely esteemed as a visual and performance artist as well as a writer. He died in 1992 of AIDS.*

summer I feel my brains slowly coming to a boil in whatever red-blue liquid the brains float in and looking down the street or walking around I begin to see large rats the size of shoeboxes; ya see them just outta the corner of your eyes, in the outer sphere of sight and when ya turn sharp to look at them they've just disappeared around the corner or down subway steps and I'm so sick my gums start bleedin' every time I breathe and after the fifth day I start seeing what looks like the limbs of small kids, arms and legs in the mouths of these rats and no screaming mommies or daddies to lend proof to the image, and late last night me and my buddy were walking around with two meat cleavers we stole from Macy's gourmet section stuck in between our belts and dry skin lookin' for some-one to mug and some queer on the upper east side tried to pick us up but my buddy's meat cleaver dropped out the back of his pants just as the guy was opening the door to his building and clang clangalang the guy went apeshit his screams bouncing through the night off half a million windows of surrounding apartments we ran thirty blocks till we felt safe. Some nights we had so much hate for the world and each other all these stupid dreams of finding his foster parents who he tried poisoning with a box of rat poison when they let him out of the attic after keeping him locked in there for a month and a half after all dear it's summer vacation and no one will miss you here's a couple of jugs of springwater and cereal don't eat it all at once we're off on a holiday after all it's better this than we return you to that nasty kids home. His parents had sharp taste buds and my buddy spent eight years in some jail for the criminally insane even though he was just a minor. Somehow though he had this idea to find his folks and scam lots of cash off them so we could start a new life. Some nights we'd walk seven or eight hundred blocks practically the whole island of manhattan crisscrossing east and west north and south each on opposite sides of the streets picking up every wino bottle we found and throwing it ten feet into the air so it crash exploded a couple of inches away from the other's feet—on nights that called for it every pane of glass in every phone booth from here to south street would dissolve in a shower of light. We slept good after a night of this in some abandoned car boiler room rooftop or lonely drag queen's palace.

~ ~ ~

If I were to leave this country and never come back or see it again in films or sleep I would still remember a number of different things that sift back in some kind of tidal motion. I remember when I was eight years old I would crawl out the window of my apartment seven stories above the ground and hold on to the ledge with ten scrawny fingers and lower myself out above the sea of cars burning up eighth avenue and hang there like a stupid motherfucker for five minutes at a time testing my own strength dangling I liked the rough texture of the bricks against the tips of my sneakers and when I got tired I'd haul myself back in for a few minutes rest and then climb back out testing testing testing how do I control this how much control do I have how much strength do I have waking up with a mouthful of soot sleeping on these shitty bird-filled rooftops waking up to hard-assed sunlight burning the tops of my eyes and I ain't had much to eat in three days except for the steak we stole from the A&P and cooked in some bum kitchen down on the lower east side the workers were friendly to us that way and we looked clean compared to the others and really I had dirt scabs behind my ears I hadn't washed in months but once in a while in the men's room of a horn and hardart's on forty-second street in between standing around hustling for some red-eyed bastard with a pink face and a wallet full of singles to come up behind me and pinch my ass murmuring something about good times and good times for me was just one fucking night of solid sleep which was impossible I mean in the boiler room of some high-rise the pipes would start clanking and hissing like machine pistons putting together a tunnel under the river from here to jersey and it's only the morning 6:00 a.m. heat piping in to all those people up above our heads and I'm looking like one of them refugees in the back of life magazine only no care packages for me they give me some tickets up at the salvation army for three meals at a soup kitchen where you get a bowl of mucus water and sip rotten potatoes while some guy down the table is losing his eye into his soup he didn't move fast enough on the line and some fucked-up wino they hired as guard popped him in the eye with a bottle and I'm so lacking in those lovely vitamins they put in wonder bread and real family meals that when I puff one drag off my cigarette blood pours out between my teeth sopping into the nonfilter and that buddy of mine complains that he won't smoke it after me and in the horn and hardart's there's a table full of deaf mutes and they're the loudest people in the joint one of them seventy years old takes me to a nearby hotel once a month when his disability check comes in and he has me lay down on my belly and he dry humps me harder and harder and his dick is soft and banging against my ass and his arm is mashing my little face up as he goes through his routine of pretending to come and starts hollering the way only a deaf mute can holler like donkeys braying when snakes come around but somehow in the midst of all that I love him maybe it's the way he returns to his table of friends in the cafeteria a smile busted across his face and I'm the one with the secret and twenty dollars in my pocket and then there's the fetishist who one time years ago picked me up and told me this story of how he used to be in the one platoon in fort dix where they shoved all the idiots and illiterates and poor bastards that thought kinda slow and the ones with speeth spitch speeeeeeech imped-iments that means you talk funny he said and I nodded one of my silent yeses that I'd give as conversation to anyone with a tongue in those days and every sunday morning this sadistic sonofabitch of a sergeant would come into the barracks and make the guys come out one by one and attempt to publicly read the sunday funnies blondie and dagwood and beetle bailey and dondi with his stupid morals I was glad when some little delinquent punched his face in one sunday and he had a shiner three sundays in a row full color till the strip couldn't get any more mileage out of it and some cop busted the delinquent and put him back in the reform school he escaped from, and all the while those poor slobs are trying to read even one line the sergeant is saying lookit this stupid son-ofabitch how the fuck do you expect to serve this country of yours and you can't even read to save your ass and he'd run around the barracks smacking all the guys in the head one after the other and make them force them to laugh at this guy tryin' to read until it was the next guy's turn, and when we got to this guy's place there was three cats pissing all over the joint crusty brown cans of opened cat food littering the floor window open so they could leave by the fire escape and he had this thing for rubber he'd dress me up in this sergeant's outfit but with a pair of rubber sneakers that they made only during world war two when it was important to do that I guess canvas was a material they needed for the war effort or something and anyway so he would have me put on these pure rubber sneakers and the sergeant's outfit and then a rubber trench-coat and then he'd grease up his dick and he would start fucking another rubber sneaker while on his belly and I'd have to shove my sneaker's sole against his face and tell him to lick the dirt off the bottom of it and all the while cursing at him telling him how stupid he was a fuckin' dingo stupid dog ain't worth catfood where'd you get your fuckin' brains surprised they even let ya past the mp's on the front gate oughta call in the trucks and have you carted off to some idiot farm and where'd you get your brains and where'd you get your brains and when he came into his rubber sneaker he'd roll over all summer sweaty and say oh that was a good load musta ate some eggs today and I'm already removing my uniform and he says he loves the way my skeleton moves underneath my skin when I bend over to retrieve one of my socks.

~ *Peter Cameron* ~

Jump
or
Dive

Jason, my uncle's lover, sat in the dark kitchen, eating what sounded like a bowl of cereal. He had some disease that made him hungry every few hours—something about not enough sugar in his blood. Every night, he got up at about three o'clock and fixed himself a snack. Since I was sleeping on the living room couch, I could hear him.

My parents and I had driven down from Oregon to visit my uncle Walter, who lived in Arizona. He was my father's younger brother. My sister Jackie got to stay home, on account of having just graduated from high school and having a job at the Lob-Steer Restaurant. But there was no way my parents were letting me stay home: I had just finished ninth grade, and I was unemployed.

My parents slept in the guest room. Jason and Uncle Walter slept together in the master bedroom. The first morning, when I went into the bathroom, I saw Jason sitting on the edge of the big unmade bed in his jockey shorts. Jason was very tan, but it was an odd tan: his face and the bottom of three-quarters of his arms were much darker than his chest. It looked as if he was wearing a T-shirt.

The living room couch was made of leather and had little metal nubs stuck all over it. It was almost impossible to sleep on. I lay there listening

PETER CAMERON is the author of the novel Leap Year *and the story collections* One Way or Another *and* Far-flung. *He lives in New York City, where he works for the Lambda Legal Defense Fund.*

to Jason crunch. The only other noise was the air conditioner, which turned itself off and on constantly to maintain the same, ideal temperature. When it went off, you could hear the insects outside. A small square of light from the opened refrigerator appeared on the dining room wall. Jason was putting the milk away. The faucet ran for a second, and then Jason walked through the living room, his white underwear bright against his body. I pretended I was asleep.

After a while, the air conditioner went off, but I didn't hear the insects. At some point in the night—the point that seems closer to morning than to evening—they stopped their drone, as though they were unionized and paid to sing only so long. The house was very quiet. In the master bedroom, I could hear bodies moving, and murmuring, but I couldn't tell if it was people making love or turning over and over, trying to get comfortable. It went on for a few minutes, and then it stopped.

~ ~ ~

We were staying at Uncle Walter's for a week, and every hour of every day was planned. We always had a morning activity and an afternoon activity. Then we had cocktail hour, then dinner, then some card game. Usually hearts, with the teams switching: some nights Jason and Walter versus my parents, some nights the brothers challenging Jason and my mother. I never played. I watched TV or rode Jason's moped around the deserted roads of Gretna Green, which was the name of Uncle Walter's condominium village. The houses in Gretna Green were called villas, and they all had different names—some for gems, some for colors, and some for animals. Uncle Walter and Jason lived in Villa Indigo.

We started each morning on the patio, where we'd eat breakfast and "plan the day." The adults took a long time planning the day so there would be less day to spend. All the other villa inhabitants ate breakfast on their patios too. The patios were separated by lawn and rock gardens and pine trees, but there wasn't much privacy: everyone could see everyone else sitting under uniformly striped umbrellas, but everyone pretended he couldn't. They were mostly old people, retired people. Children were allowed only as guests. Everyone looked at me as if I was a freak.

Wednesday morning, Uncle Walter was inside making coffee in the new coffee machine my parents had brought him. My mother told me that whenever you're invited to someone's house overnight you should

bring something—a hostess gift. Or a host gift, she added. She was helping Uncle Walter make breakfast. Jason was lying on a chaise in the sun,
trying to even out his tan. My father was reading the *Wall Street Journal.*
He got up early every morning and drove into town and bought it, so
he could "stay in touch." My mother made him throw it away right after
he read it so it wouldn't interfere with the rest of the day.

Jason had his eyes closed, but he was talking. He was listing the things
we could do that day. I was sitting on the edge of a big planter filled
with pachysandra and broken statuary that Leonard, my uncle's ex-
boyfriend, had dug up somewhere. Leonard was an archaeologist. He used
to teach paleontology at Northern Arizona University, but he didn't get
tenure, so he took a job with an oil company in South America, making
sure the engineers didn't drill in sacred spots. The day before, I'd seen a
tiny purple-throated lizard in the vines, and I was trying to find him
again. I wanted to catch him and take him back to Oregon.

Jason paused in his list, and my father said, "Uh-huh." That's what
he always says when he's reading the newspaper and you talk to him.

"We could go to the dinosaur museum," Jason said.

"What's that?" I said.

Jason sat up and looked at me. That was the first thing I'd said to
him, I think. I'd been ignoring him.

"Well, I've never been there," he said. Even though it was early in
the morning, his brown forehead was already beaded with sweat. "It has
some reconstructed dinosaurs and footprints and stuff."

"Let's go there," I said. "I like dinosaurs."

"Uh huh," said my father.

My mother came through the sliding glass doors carrying a platter of
scrambled eggs. Uncle Walter followed with the coffee.

"We're going to go to the dinosaur museum this morning,"
Jason said.

"Please, not that pit," Uncle Walter said.

"But Evan wants to go," Jason said. "It's about time we did something
he liked."

Everyone looked at me. "It doesn't matter," I said.

"Oh, no," Uncle Walter said. "Actually, it's fascinating. It just brings
back bad memories."

As it turned out, Uncle Walter and my father stayed home to discuss
their finances. My grandmother had left them her money jointly, and

they're always arguing about how to invest it. Jason drove my mother and me out to the dinosaur museum. I think my mother came just because she didn't want to leave me alone with Jason. She doesn't trust Uncle Walter's friends, but she doesn't let on. My father thinks it's very important we all treat Uncle Walter normally. Once, he hit Jackie because she called Uncle Walter a fag. That's the only time he's ever hit either of us.

The dinosaur museum looked like an airplane hangar in the middle of the desert. Inside, trenches were dug into the earth and bones stuck out of their walls. They were still exhuming some of the skeletons. The sand felt oddly damp. My mother took off her sandals and carried them; Jason looked around quickly and then went outside and sat on the hood of the car, smoking, with his shirt off. At the gift stand, I bought a small bag of dinosaur bone chips. My mother bought a 3-D panoramic postcard. When you held it one way, a dinosaur stood with a creature in its toothy mouth. When you tilted it, the creature disappeared. Swallowed.

On the way home, we stopped at a Safeway to do some grocery shopping. Both Jason and my mother seemed reluctant to push the shopping cart, so I did. In the produce aisle, Jason picked up cantaloupes and shook them next to his ear. A few feet away, my mother folded back the husks to get a good look at the kernels on the corncobs. It seemed as if everyone was pawing at the food. It made me nervous, because once, when I was little, I opened up a box of chocolate Ding Dongs in the grocery store and started eating one, and the manager came over and yelled at me. The only good thing about that was that my mother was forced to buy the Ding Dongs, but every time I ate one I felt sick.

A man in Bermuda shorts and a yellow cardigan sweater started talking to Jason. My mother returned with six apparently decent ears of corn. She dumped them into the cart. "Who's that?" she asked me, meaning the man Jason was talking to.

"I don't know," I said. The man made a practice golf swing, right there in the produce aisle. Jason watched him. Jason was a golf pro at a country club. He used to be part of the golf tour you see on television on weekend afternoons, but he quit. Now he gave lessons at the country club. Uncle Walter had been one of his pupils. That's how they met.

"It's hard to tell," Jason was saying. "I'd try opening up your stance a little more." He put a cantaloupe in our shopping cart.

"Hi," the man said to us.

"Mr. Baird, I'd like you to meet my wife, Ann," Jason said.

Mr. Baird shook my mother's hand. "How come we never see you down the club?"

"Oh . . . ," my mother said.

"Ann hates golf," Jason said.

"And how 'bout you?" The man looked at me. "Do you like golf?"

"Sure," I said.

"Well, we'll have to get you out on the links. Can you beat your dad?"

"Not yet," I said.

"It won't be long," Mr. Baird said. He patted Jason on the shoulder. "Nice to see you, Jason. Nice to meet you, Mrs. Jerome."

He walked down the aisle and disappeared into the bakery section. My mother and I both looked at Jason. Even though it was cold in the produce aisle, he was sweating. No one said anything for a few seconds. Then my mother said, "Evan, why don't you go find some Doritos? And some Gatorade too, if you want."

Back at Villa Indigo, my father and Uncle Walter were playing cribbage. Jason kissed Uncle Walter on the top of his semi-bald head. My father watched and then stood up and kissed my mother. I didn't kiss anyone.

~ ~ ~

Thursday, my mother and I went into Flagstaff to buy new school clothes. Back in Portland, when we go into malls we separate and make plans to meet at a specified time and place, but this was different: it was a strange mall, and since it was school clothes, my mother would pay for them, and therefore she could help pick them out. So we shopped together, which we hadn't done in a while. It was awkward. She pulled things off the rack which I had ignored, and when I started looking at the Right Now for Young Men stuff she entered the Traditional Shoppe. We finally bought some underwear, and some orange and yellow socks, which my mother said were "fun."

Then we went to the shoe store. I hate trying on shoes. I wish the salespeople would just give you the box and let you try them on yourself. There's something about someone else doing it all—especially touching your feet—that embarrasses me. It's as if the person was your servant or something. And in this case the salesperson was a girl about my age, and I could tell she thought I was weird, shopping with my mother. My mother sat in the chair beside me, her pocketbook in her lap. She was wearing sneakers, with little bunny-rabbit tails sticking out the back from her socks.

"Stand up," the girl said.

I stood up.

"How do they feel?" my mother asked.

"Okay," I said.

"Walk around," my mother commanded.

I walked up the aisle, feeling everyone watching me. Then I walked back and sat down. I bent over and unlaced the shoes.

"So what do you think?" my mother asked.

The girl stood there, picking her nails. "They look very nice," she said.

I just wanted to get out of there. "I like them," I said. We bought the shoes.

On the way home, we pulled into a gas station–bar in the desert. "I can't face Villa Indigo without a drink," my mother said.

"What do you mean?" I asked.

"Nothing," she said. "Are you having a good time?"

"Now?"

"No. On this trip. At Uncle Walter's."

"I guess so," I said.

"Do you like Jason?"

"Better than Leonard."

"Leonard was strange," my mother said. "I never warmed to Leonard."

We got out of the car and walked into the bar. It was dark inside, and empty. A fat woman sat behind the bar, making something out of papier-mâché. It looked like one of those statues of the Virgin Mary people have in their front yards. "Hiya," she said. "What can I get you?"

My mother asked for a beer and I asked for some cranberry juice. They didn't have any, so I ordered a Coke. The woman got my mother's beer from a portable cooler like the ones you take to football games. It seemed very unprofessional. Then she sprayed Coke into a glass with one of those showerhead things. My mother and I sat at a table in the sun, but it wasn't hot, it was cold. Above us the air conditioner dripped.

My mother drank her beer from the long-necked green bottle. "What do you think your sister's doing right now?" she asked.

"What time is it?"

"Four."

"Probably getting ready to go to work. Taking a shower."

My mother nodded. "Maybe we'll call her tonight."

I laughed, because my mother called her every night. She would always make Jackie explain all the noises in the background. "It sounds like a party to me," she kept repeating.

My Coke was flat. It tasted weird too. I watched the woman at the bar. She was poking at her statue with a swizzle stick—putting in eyes, I thought.

"How would you like to go see the Petrified Forest?" my mother asked.

"We're going to another national park?" On the way to Uncle Walter's, we had stopped at the Grand Canyon and taken a mule ride down to the river. Halfway down, my mother got hysterical, fell off her mule, and wouldn't get back on. A helicopter had to fly into the canyon and rescue her. It was horrible to see her like that.

"This one's perfectly flat," she said. "And no mules."

"When?" I said.

"We'd go down on Saturday and come back to Walter's on Monday. And leave for home Tuesday."

The bar woman brought us a second round of drinks. We had not asked for them. My Coke glass was still full. My mother drained her beer bottle and looked at the new one. "Oh, dear," she said. "I guess we look like we need it."

~ ~ ~

The next night, at six-thirty, as my parents left for their special anniversary dinner in Flagstaff, the automatic lawn sprinklers went on. They were activated every evening. Jason explained that if the lawns were watered during the day the beads of moisture would magnify the sun's rays and burn the grass. My parents walked through the whirling water, got in their car, and drove away.

Jason and Uncle Walter were making dinner for me—steaks, on their new electric barbecue. I think they thought steak was a good, masculine food. Instead of charcoal, their grill had little lava rocks on the bottom. They reminded me of my dinosaur bone chips.

The steaks came in packs of two, so Uncle Walter was cooking up four. The fourth steak worried me. Who was it for? Would we split it? Was someone else coming to dinner?

"You're being awfully quiet," Uncle Walter said. For a minute, I hoped he was talking to the steaks—they weren't sizzling—so I didn't answer.

Then Uncle Walter looked over at me. "Cat got your tongue?" he asked.

"What cat?" I said.

"The cat," he said. "The proverbial cat. The big cat in the sky."

"No," I said.

"Then talk to me."

"I don't talk on demand," I said.

Uncle Walter smiled down at his steaks, lightly piercing them with his chef's fork. "Are you a freshman?" he asked.

"Well, a sophomore now," I said.

"How do you like being a sophomore?"

My lizard appeared from beneath a crimson leaf and clicked his eyes in all directions, checking out the evening.

"It's not something you like or dislike," I said. "It's something you are."

"Ah," Uncle Walter said. "So you're a fatalist?"

I didn't answer. I slowly reached out my hand toward the lizard, even though I was too far away to touch it. He clicked his eyes toward me but didn't move. I think he recognized me. My arm looked white and disembodied in the evening light.

Jason slid open the terrace doors, and the music from the stereo was suddenly loud. The lizard darted back under the foliage.

"I need a prep chef," Jason said. "Get in here, Evan."

I followed Jason into the kitchen. On the table was a wooden board, and on that was a tomato, an avocado, and an apple. Jason handed me a knife. "Chop those up," he said.

I picked up the avocado. "Should I peel this?" I asked. "Or what?"

Jason took the avocado and sliced it in half. One half held the pit, and the other half held nothing. Then he pulled the warty skin off in two curved pieces and handed the naked globes back to me. "Now chop it."

I started chopping the stuff. Jason took three baked potatoes out of the oven. I could tell they were hot by the way he tossed them onto the counter. He made slits in them and forked the white stuffing into a bowl.

"What are you doing?" I asked.

"Making baked potatoes," he said. He sliced butter into the bowl.

"But why are you taking the potato out of the skin?"

"Because these are stuffed potatoes. You take the potato out and doctor it up and then put it back in. Do you like cheese?"

"Yes," I said.

"Do you like chives?"

"I don't know," I said. "I've never had them."

"You've never had chives?"

"My mother makes normal food," I said. "She leaves the potato in the skin."

"That figures," Jason said.

After dinner, we went to the driving range. Jason bought two large buckets and we followed him upstairs to the second level. I sat on a bench and watched Jason and my uncle hit ball after ball out into the floodlit night. Sometimes the balls arched up into the darkness, then reappeared as they fell.

Uncle Walter wasn't too good. A few times, he topped the ball and it dribbled over the edge and fell on the grass right below us. When that happened, he looked around to see who noticed, and winked at me.

"Do you want to hit some?" he asked me, offering his club.

"Sure," I said. I was on the golf team last fall, but this spring I played baseball. I think golf is an elitist sport. Baseball is more democratic.

I teed up a ball and took a practice swing, because my father, who taught me to play golf, told me always to take a practice swing. Always. My first shot was pretty good. It didn't go too far, but it went straight out and bounced a ways before I lost track of it in the shadows. I hit another.

Jason, who was in the next cubicle, put down his club and watched me. "You have a great natural swing," he said.

His attention bothered me, and I almost missed my next ball. It rolled off the tee. I picked it up and re-teed it.

"Wait," Jason said. He walked over and stood behind me. "You're swinging much too hard." He leaned over me so that he was embracing me from behind, his large tan hands on top of mine, holding the club. "Now just relax," he said, his voice right beside my cheek.

I tried to relax, but I couldn't. I suddenly felt very hot.

"Okay," Jason said, "nice and easy. Keep the left arm straight." He raised his arms, and with them the club. Then we swung through, and he held the club still in the air, pointed out into the night. He let go of the club and ran his hand along my left arm, from my wrist up to my shoulder. "Straight," he said. "Keep it nice and straight." Then he stepped back and told me to try another swing by myself.

I did.

"Looking good," Jason said.

"Why don't you finish the bucket?" my uncle said. "I'm going down to get a beer."

Jason returned to his stall and resumed his practice. I teed up another ball, hit it, then another, and another, till I'd established a rhythm, whacking ball after ball, and all around me clubs were cutting the night, filling the sky with tiny white meteorites.

~ ~ ~

Back at Villa Indigo, the sprinklers had stopped, but the insects were making their strange noise in the trees. Jason and I went for a swim while my uncle watched TV. Jason wore a bathing suit like the swimmers in the Olympics: red-white-and-blue and shaped like underwear. We walked out the terrace doors and across the wet lawn toward the pool, which was deserted and glowed bright blue. Jason dived in and swam some laps. I practiced diving off the board into the deep end, timing my dives so they wouldn't interfere with him. After about ten laps, he started treading water in the deep end and looked up at me. I was bouncing on the diving board.

"Want to play a game?" he said.

"What?"

Jason swam to the side and pulled himself out of the pool "Jump or Dive," he said. "We'll play for money."

"How do you play?"

"Don't you know anything?" Jason said. "What do you do in Ohio?"

"It's Oregon," I said. "Not much."

"I can believe it. This is a very simple game. One person jumps off the diving board—jumps high—and when he's at the very highest, the other person yells either 'Jump' or 'Dive,' and the person has to dive if the other person yells 'Dive' and jump if he yells 'Jump.' If you do the wrong thing, you owe the guy a quarter. Okay?"

"Okay," I said. "You go first."

I stepped off the diving board, and Jason climbed on. "The higher you jump, the more time you have to twist," he said.

"Go," I said. "I'm ready."

Jason took three steps and sprang, and I yelled, "Dive." He did. He got out of the pool, grinning. "Okay," he said. "Your turn."

I sprang off the board and heard Jason yell, "Jump," but I was already falling forward headfirst. I tried to twist backward, but it was still a dive.

"You owe me a quarter," Jason said when I surfaced. He was standing on the diving board, bouncing. I swam to the side. "Here I go," he said.

I waited till he was coming straight down toward the water, feet first, before I yelled, "Dive," but somehow Jason somersaulted forward and dived into the pool.

We played for about fifteen minutes, until I owed Jason two dollars and twenty-five cents and my body was covered with red welts from smacking the water at bad angles. Suddenly the lights in the pool went off.

"It must be ten o'clock," Jason said. "Time for geriatrics to go to bed."

The black water looked cold and scary. I got out and sat in a chair. We hadn't brought towels with us, and I shivered. Jason stayed in the pool.

"It's warmer in the water," he said.

I didn't say anything. With the lights off in the pool, the stars appeared brighter in the sky. I leaned my head back and looked up at them.

Something landed with a splat on the concrete beside me. It was Jason's bathing suit. I could hear him in the pool. He was swimming slowly underwater, coming up for a breath and then disappearing again. I knew that at some point he'd get out of the water and be naked, so I walked across the lawn toward Villa Indigo. Inside, I could see Uncle Walter lying on the couch, watching TV.

~ ~ ~

Later that night, I woke up hearing noises in the kitchen. I assumed it was Jason, but then I heard talking and realized it was my parents, back from their anniversary dinner.

I got up off the couch and went into the kitchen. My mother was leaning against the counter, drinking a glass of seltzer. My father was sitting on one of the barstools, smoking a cigarette. He put it out when I came in. He's not supposed to smoke anymore. We made a deal in our family last year involving his quitting: my mother would lose fifteen pounds, my sister would take Science Honors (and pass), and I was supposed to brush Princess Leia, our dog, every day without having to be told.

"Our little baby," my mother said. "Did we wake you up?"

"Yes," I said.

"This is the first one I've had in months," my father said. "Honest. I just found it lying here."

"I told him he could smoke it," my mother said. "As a special anniversary treat."

"How was dinner?" I asked.

"Okay," my mother said. "The restaurant didn't turn around, though. It was broken."

"That's funny," my father said. "I could have sworn it was revolving."

"You were just drunk," my mother said.

"Oh, no," my father said. "It was the stars in my eyes." He leaned forward and kissed my mother.

She finished her seltzer, rinsed the glass, and put it in the sink. "I'm going to bed," she said. "Good night."

My father and I both said good night, and my mother walked down the hall. My father picked up his cigarette. "It wasn't even very good," he said. He looked at it, then held it under his nose and smelled it. "I think it was stale. Just my luck."

I took the cigarette butt out of his hands and threw it away. When I turned around, he was standing by the terrace doors, looking out at the dark trees. It was windy.

"Have you made up your mind?" he asked.

"About what?"

"The trip."

"What trip?"

My father turned away from the terrace. "Didn't Mom tell you? Uncle Walter said you could stay here while Mom and I went down to see the Petrified Forest. If you want to. You can come with us otherwise."

"Oh," I said.

"I think Uncle Walter would like it if he had some time alone with you. I don't think he feels very close to you anymore. And he feels bad Jackie didn't come."

"Oh," I said. "I don't know."

"Is it because of Jason?"

"No," I said.

"Because I'd understand if it was."

"No," I said, "it's not that. I like Jason. I just don't know if I want to stay here. . . ."

"Well, it's no big deal. Just two days." My father reached up and turned off the light. It was a dual overhead light and fan, and the fan spun around some in the darkness, each spin slower. My father put his hands on my shoulders and half pushed, half guided me back to the couch. "It's late," he said. "See you tomorrow."

I lay on the couch. I couldn't fall asleep, because I knew that in a while Jason would be up for his snack. That kept me awake, and the decision about what to do. For some reason, it did seem like a big deal: going or staying. I could still picture my mother, backed up against the wall of the Grand Canyon, as far from the cliff as possible, crying, her mule braying, the helicopter whirring in the sky above us. It seemed like a choice between that and Jason swimming in the dark water, slowly and nakedly. I didn't want to be there for either.

The thing was, after I sprang off the diving board I did hear Jason shout, but my brain didn't make any sense of it. I could just feel myself hanging there, above the horrible bright-blue water, but I couldn't make my body turn, even though I was dropping dangerously, and much too fast.

~ *Christopher Coe* ~

Gentlemen Can
Wash Their Hands
in the Gents'

The day after I am arrested, my father invites me to lunch. He called this morning, first thing, at ten-thirty. I was in bed and had no plans not to be. This isn't a school day, not that it would matter if it were. I told my father, "Daddy, I don't eat lunch, I never eat lunch, I despise lunch."

He said he doesn't give a good goddamn if I eat or not, just be there at one o'clock sharp. He hung up before I could argue.

~ ~ ~

I was arrested in the library, the public one. Now we are in this private one, the library of my father's club, and my father orders me a Dubonnet. This is the first time I have been to my father's club since I've been old enough to have a drink. I'm not talking legal age, which I have yet to reach. I am talking about my father's laws. According to my father, I am of age for a Dubonnet. This is to be the kind of lunch at which the father will order the son a Dubonnet. This will be the kind of lunch where the son enters languidly forty-five minutes late, blows smoke at the father, and looks sullen.

CHRISTOPHER COE is the author of the remarkable novels I Look Divine *and* Such Times—*one of the fiercest and most powerful literary responses yet made to the AIDS epidemic. He lives in New York City.*

It will be that kind of lunch, because today I am going to be that kind of son. Today I will be the son with the short fuse, who looks sullen and goes as far as he can to be the kind of son no father wants.

As poses go, sullen comes naturally.

My father's pose is not posing. He is a master of the pose that doesn't show. He heard of my arrest from my mother; now he is being unflappable.

My mother could not wait to tell him about it. She is one of those bothersome women who don't know what they're going to say until they say it. She was on the phone to my father, straight from the precinct. She spoke to him before she spoke to me. My mother loves having a reason to call my father. She doesn't need any particular reason, though lately I have given her a few.

To my mother, to my father, the library episode is the worst one yet. It's not the worst at all, really, but it's the one my father will hate; for him it will be the worst. When I stole a horse at the beach and kept it overnight, my father said it was just a natural, boyish thing to do. The man whose horse it was admitted the animal hadn't been abused. To the contrary, I fed that horse not only carrots but raw asparagus; it declined, with quiet, equine disdain, a six-pound Porterhouse.

I burned a deserted beach house, but my father never questioned me about it. No one could prove I'd set the fire, and my father never brought it up. The house did not burn *down*. A few windows gave in to the heat, that was all. Maybe a rug or two were charred, but no one died, because the house was deserted.

Life went on after the deserted house. I'm not sure how it will go on after the library. I haven't told the bad part yet, the part my father will hate. Here it is. Yesterday, when I was in the library, I wasn't arrested in the open stacks. Where I was when I was arrested is what my father calls the "gents'."

I call it the little boys', sometimes the powder room; I seldom call it the men's. My grandfather used to call it the "can," which is what I'd call it, if that didn't have so much the ring of my grandfather.

The "gents'," the "little boys'," the "can," call it what you will—it's where I was when the policeman kicked open the stall. It wasn't as bad as it sounds, but no one is going to believe my version. My mother didn't believe me. Neither will my father. That's why I don't know how life will go on after this lunch.

The "gents'" is the reason for this lunch.

So is the "little boys'."

~   ~   ~

At the table, so far, life goes on. My father doesn't shout. This is his club. He has to come here again, so he doesn't say what the policeman did. My father does not speak of "lewd and disorderly conduct," and he does not use the prissy gerund of the verb "to loiter." For a while the only words my father says are "calves' liver." He says them to the waiter, says his son will have calves' liver, and without consulting me, he tells the waiter I will have it rare.

Actually, I won't have calves' liver, and I will not have it rare. I will blow smoke at my father, I'll look sullen, and I am not going to eat one bite at this lunch.

The truth is it wasn't so lewd. It wasn't even disorderly. In fact, as such things go, it was so damned orderly it was downright impeccable.

My father does not say disorderly conduct, but he does say that there is no need to hold a cigarette so flamboyantly. There is no need whatever, my father tells me, to be flamboyant now. I want another Dubonnet.

As a matter of fact, I'm not being flamboyant. I am being sullen. If my father thinks *this* is flamboyant, he should have seen me yesterday in the gents'.

It wasn't as though the fellow was someone I just picked up at the card catalogue. I'd known Pierre for more than a year. I'd noticed him at a place across the river where, every Friday evening, men and women go to folk-dance. I noticed Pierre in the dance where the men break from a circle of women and form inside it a circle of their own. They bear down with their arms upon each other's shoulders, and when the music cues them to, they all squat quickly on their haunches, touch knees to the floor, and, on cue, rise again in unison.

This dance was new to me, and I watched it with some curiosity, though the only part of it worth watching was Pierre. He was hard-boned handsome, had purposeful loins and the body of what I call a man.

When the dance was repeated, I joined the circle, just opposite Pierre. He looked at me as much as I did at him, which was exactly what I wanted. I managed to be at the bus stop the same time as he, and as we waited together we said a few words. The bus came; no one was on it. We sat together in the back, as though every other seat were taken. Our shoulders pressed together as they would have if we had been the last two men on earth.

I learned quickly that Pierre was from Monterey, California, was twenty-six, and had worked on fishing boats or in the cannery or in gas stations all his life, until he read *On the Road* and decided that drifting was the noble way to live.

He was living in a transient hotel, in a part of town I'd been driven through only to get to the airport. Pierre didn't have the money to live at the Y, though he told me he went there every day to lift weights. He didn't need to tell me he lifted weights. He said he lived on protein, which was another thing he didn't need to tell me. We walked to his hotel. He didn't invite me to his room, and I couldn't tell if I was too young for him or if he was ashamed of living where he did.

The next day I joined the Y. I didn't lift any weights, but I went every day unfailingly, and after swimming thirty laps I'd always detour through the weight room on the way to the showers. I had rehearsed at least five hundred times how surprised I'd be to see him, and in doing this I learned how many different inflections can be affixed to the greeting "Hello."

When I finally saw Pierre, not one of these inflections helped me at all.

We left together that day, but only after Pierre had made a point of not taking a shower. He said he didn't want me to see him naked. What he said was, "I don't want you to see my penis."

It was my reflex to say "Perish the thought." In truth, I could handle the thought. What I'd meant was perish the *word*.

Pierre looked at me in surprise.

What I said was that I didn't want to see anything that goes by that name. As soon as I'd said this, I knew it hadn't made the impression I'd wanted, and for a minute I was afraid this pillar of manly pulchritude would ditch me for being a word snob. He didn't, though. What he did was buy me freshly pressed carrot juice and advise me never to eat raisins or any dried fruit that has been treated with sulfur dioxide. He said that people who eat food with preservatives might just as well be drinking embalming fluid. I liked the carrot juice. I liked that he had bought it for me. It tasted like romance.

This time he did invite me to his room and then went about doing things as I imagined he would if I hadn't been there. He took off his socks but nothing else, tuned in a radio station that played songs from the sixties, and slapped a thick slab of beef liver onto a hot plate. He said that beef liver, cooked just until it's hot, is the best source of protein. He meant, I knew, animal protein. I stopped myself from saying that I'd rather be anemic than eat anything that smelled so alive.

Pierre sat cross-legged on the bed, eating the liver in big chunks, chewing thoroughly as he flipped through a fitness magazine. On the floor by the bed I saw a battered paperback he'd checked out from the library. I picked it up and turned to the index. The book was *Kiss, Kiss, Bang, Bang* by Pauline Kael, and it had just about the best index I had ever seen. There were seven entries for Elizabeth Taylor alone.

Pierre finished the liver and asked me if I wanted to take off my shoes. I did and sat at the foot of the bed.

"Come here," he said.

"Where?" I asked. It scared me how much I wanted to do what he said.

"Here," he said, and pointed to himself. "I didn't want this to happen," and when he said this, I believed him. He hesitated a second or so, as though seeking the clearest word, and then said, "I'm sort of bisexual, and I like you more than I wanted to."

I thought, This is it. I will now either melt or explode.

I'd always thought that when people liked each other the way Pierre was talking about, the first thing they did was pull each other out of their clothes, but I wasn't going to be the one to begin.

I didn't know what we could do without his giving me a look, then I remembered something I'd read about Jewish men cutting holes in sheets in order to have at their wives. This was not, thank God, what Pierre had in mind. Everything we did for the next two hours we did with our clothes on, but Pierre laid down no restrictions as to what we could do with our hands. It was with my hands, then, that I could ascertain that there was nothing whatever inadequate about any part of Pierre. I was certain that I would soon know this with my eyes.

The next day and the day after, Pierre wasn't at the Y. I spent every day that week leaning against parked cars across the street from his hotel. I'd walk around the block, hoping we'd collide. It was two weeks before I learned that Pierre had taken his hot plate and vanished. The man at the hotel told me, without my asking, that Pierre had paid his bill to the end of the week. I was glad he told me that.

The longer I thought about it, the more it struck me that Pierre's disappearance was inevitable. Pierre was a prince in disguise and could not stay long in one place. I did wonder every day, constantly, what it was that he didn't like about his body.

I hate untidy endings. I hate tidy endings. I hate endings.

It was a year later that I saw Pierre upstairs in the library. He was at the other end of the great two-story reading room, sitting at a long table with a stack of atlases. He looked up at the exact instant I saw him, and without any readable expression he rose from his chair and came all the way across the room to me. He seized my hand and pulled me from the room without any discretion whatever. He pulled me down the wide marble stairs, and with my hand in his he led me, all this without a word, into the gents'. No one was in it—the library had just opened—and he pushed me into the stall, locked the door, and grabbed me around my waist. He pressed himself against me, front to front, and forced his tongue into my mouth. I reached between us and grabbed a handful of him. I didn't care about seeing it; I only wanted to contain it.

I thought it was all going to happen there, and I knew then as clearly as I ever will that it is not without reason that so much of the world fears and hates this, opposes it and calls it wrong and worse than wrong, and the reason is that so few people ever get to have it, even for an instant.

Pierre was going to show me, and I was just about to see, when an ugly-sounding voice rose out of hell, accompanied by black ugly boots, and told us the fun was over.

"Beat it, buddy," Pierre said to the outsider.

I didn't want the intruder to see my eyes. "Can't you please just go away for a minute?" I asked.

The policeman's answer was to kick in the door. I knew that all this policeman cared about was his quota. I also knew this was the last time I'd see Pierre.

~ ~ ~

Maybe it was a little lewd, but it was nowhere near as lewd as it could have been. For an instant, there was potential.

What my father says about lewd conduct, a phrase he doesn't use, what he says about loitering, a word he doesn't use, what he says about the gents', instead of anything else, is that nothing needs be uncivilized.

My father says, "You have an allowance. Don't you have an allowance?"

I concede that I have an allowance.

"You can afford a hotel," my father says. "Can't you afford a hotel?"

He's right, of course, in his way. I signal the waiter for another Dubonnet and admit that I could have taken the fellow to a hotel. I call Pierre "the fellow," rather than kill my father more with the fact that Pierre was more to me than a fellow. Pierre was a man who had wanted me enough to take a risk. My father would say something moronic about what a sissy name Pierre is, and I would have to hate him for that. I dislike my father enough. I don't want to hate him.

I knew it would be less than prudent to tell my father that I hadn't wanted to take Pierre to a hotel, that what I'd wanted was to take him in hand. I didn't even get to do that, to take Pierre in hand. We hadn't reached a point where safety would have been an issue.

I'm not sure it would have been one if we had.

"A hotel would have been better," my father says. "Wouldn't a hotel have been better than the gents'?"

Better for *what* is not a question to raise.

"I want to know," my father says, "what would make you do this thing. Why in the library, of all places, why in the gents'."

"What can I tell you, Daddy?" I ask. "Can I tell you that I did it in the library because the library is where I was? Can I tell you that I happened to be in the neighborhood? What do you want to hear?"

My father says quietly that all he wants to hear is my answer.

"Daddy, why would I pay a hotel for what can be done in five minutes in the gents'?"

"Maybe to keep the police out of your hair," my father answers, and I do have to admit this is a sensible reply. "And to be civilized. To be comfortable. In a hotel, you can be a civilized man. You can lie on clean sheets, you can take a shower, you can clean up."

I assume my father means clean up *after,* although he could just as easily mean before. I do not point out to my father that in a hotel you can also get a shirt pressed, order room service, drink too much, make conversation, take a fucking bubble bath, and in no time at all forget what it is you are there for.

You do not forget in the gents', but this is one other thing I do not tell my father today.

"Good God," my father groans. "In a hotel you can excuse yourself. In a hotel, you can wash your hands."

This is not the time to point out to my father that gentlemen can wash their hands in the gents'.

~ ~ ~

This is a place to be sullen, this club. I look around the dining room, at all the fathers and sons. Some of the sons are my father's age.

You don't need to know much to know that every table has a problem. Every table has a reason for lunch. Since when have fathers and sons had lunch because they want to? No one here wants lunch; no one has an appetite here.

I know some of the sons, a few of the fathers. In a corner I see a son, a young man about my age. Half the men in the room must know what this son did a year or so ago, just as a few men here today have probably heard some version of what happened yesterday in the gents', the men's, the little boys'. What the son in the corner did makes lewd and disorderly conduct sound like a prayer meeting, especially lewd and disorderly conduct without so much as a nipple exposed. And the son in the corner isn't the worst. This room is full of more disappointing, more heartbreaking sons, much worse sons than he, worse than I, and my father should know this, should know that some of these sons are worse than any son he could ever have produced.

Most of the time I don't think this way, but today I'm thinking that there is never a time when you could not be worse than you are.

My father tells me again not to hold my cigarette flamboyantly. Where have I learned my gestures, my father wants to know. He thinks he can ask me a question like this. What the hell does he expect, Steve fucking McQueen?

Some things are easy to ignore. All you have to do is ignore them. I wish this lunch were one of them.

Another thing I don't say to my father, although it is what I'm thinking, is that he was the one who wanted this lunch, and I will give it to him.

And now, God help me, here comes the liver. The waiter carries it aloft, through the swinging door. There is no mistaking what it is. It's coming right at me, across the room, and I can tell from here how rare it's going to be.

My father wanted this lunch. He can have it with the kind of son whose disorderly conduct is failed and prim. He can have his lunch with a son who has learned his gestures from where it's none of his business. He can have this lunch with a son who strikes a sullen pose, strikes a flamboyant one, and then offers a pose both sullen and flamboyant at once.

At least *my* poses show. I cut into the liver, only for a look. It's so rare it doesn't even bleed.

My father invited me to this lunch. Now he can have it with the worst son he could have.

~ *Gerry Albarelli* ~

The
Dancing
Lesson

The boys, all nice Italian boys, with dark hair and dark eyes, in their white shirts, ties, and dress pants from the parochial schools they attended during the week, slipped away from the party, all six of them related, brothers and cousins, with Patrick, a younger cousin. They were taking him out to the fort so he could give them the blow jobs he had promised to deliver. They were maybe a little more than he had bargained for (he'd only talked about doing it to two of them) all crowded there in the fort, which was just an oversized wooden box on the ground, some odd-sized boards nailed together between a few trees, with the light like attic light coming in between the slats, a little crowd taking down their zippers, talking, excited, in loud and cautious whispers. Joey, who was sixteen, was smoking a cigarette; he went first, pushing his way to the front with a certain authority since he was the oldest and had arranged it, undoing his belt, pulling out his shirt from his pants as Patrick slid to his knees, opened his mouth and then it began. Joey continued to smoke throughout, putting the cigarette gangster-style in his mouth, turned up, as he leaned back, hands on the fort walls, thrusting forward to give Patrick a mouthful and the others a view. "That's it, Patrick, get it nice

---

A graduate of Sarah Lawrence College, GERRY ALBARELLI has taught at the Harvey Milk High School in New York and currently works for the Gay and Lesbian Oral History Project of Columbia University. He lives in New York City.

and wet," he said to Patrick, down on the floor on his knees, his red Confirmation Day gown spilled out around him. (Up at the house there was a long white sheet cake on the table already half gone, envelopes with money and presents for Patrick.) Next, as Joey moved out of the way, it was Nicholas's turn.

Outside, three younger boys, who had figured out for themselves what was about to happen, were trying to listen, ears pressed to the wood, lying on top of the fort, having crawled up there quietly like animals, like parasites trying to draw out the heat and keep quiet at the same time. Two of the boys on the outside were brothers, twins, and soon one of them accidentally shoved up against the other, making noise. "Shut up!" one twin said. "Shut up! Fuck you, you queer," the other one said.

Tony stood inside the fort with the others but didn't step forward when it was his turn, even though Patrick, his mouth dark and open, his hands wet, reached from his position on the floor for his zipper; the others stood ready to go, and two of his cousins, already zipped up, were pressing him forward, one of them, Joey, his hand hard on his shoulder. "Go on, Tony, what's the matta?" he said. "He's too little," Nicholas said, not looking at him, as though, now that he was with the older boys, he was capable of betraying Tony.

Nicholas and Joey lit cigarettes on the way out, the two of them sharing a match over Joey's cupped hand. It was warm; they walked all together back up to the house. "You all set, Patrick?" Joey said, smirking and raising his eyebrows for the others to see, but putting his arm around Patrick's shoulders because nobody wanted to get caught.

~ ~ ~

"I have no use for those people, whatever you want to call them, I don't give a damn—coloreds, they're still *mullenyans*. I'm sorry. That's it," Aunt Terry, Joey's mother, was saying at the dining room table when the boys all trooped back in, not that time, in the afternoon, but later, when they'd all gone out again. "Hey, they themselves don't know what they wanna be called," Uncle Ralph said, but then he took a piece of pastry and walked out, eating. It was night already. It had been a long day of eating and eating again, and now it was dark outside and time for dessert, which Aunt Roseanne was bringing out from the kitchen to the dining room. They were sitting in the brightly lighted dining room with mirrored walls (more women than men, as if because it was a Confirmation Day party, with religious associations, it had to be more women), gathered around the dining room table, the six bulbs in the chandelier over the table too bright, all of them sitting there, arms, hands folded, as if uneasy under a spotlight or onstage. Aunt Roseanne came out with not one but three trays of dessert, which she had baked the day before, bringing them out one at a time from the kitchen, setting them down on the table, to the delight of her brother-in-law, who said, "Hey," as she turned to go get the third tray, "what'd you do?" And she smiled, complimented, looking at him sideways out of her pointy eyeglasses. They had been having dessert for a long time, the coffee and the anisette were on the table, it was almost over; soon they would be standing up, time to leave, a few at a time, some families making more of a dent than the others in the party, jackets and sweaters coming out of the hall closet. Aunt Terry sat there, having said what she said, with her hair fluffed out like an owl and her arms folded in front of her chest (her face was pasty and puckered, tired, the red lipstick on her mouth a little uncertain), as if challenging anyone to challenge her. Nicholas was standing next to Joey near the back door. "Aunt Terry the bigot," he said, laughing and eating. The boys walked around eating, picking up food off the table, but didn't bother to sit down. They opened the refrigerator door and turned on the faucet without asking anyone's permission, as if they all lived there. "You shut up, you," Aunt Terry said. "You always gotta be opposite anyway." "Why?" Tony asked. "Because they destroy everything," she said, and then everyone was talking at once, though the party was over. "That's right. Look what they did to Mama's house." "That's right," said an out-of-town cousin who wouldn't even have known, turning to Tony and nodding very seriously, her hand on his arm, her eyes on his, as if holding him down, as if by asking the question he had threatened to go away from them, out into the night, the dark American night, which was the opposite or antithesis of all they were and of all this. They were the house brightly lighted, a little white cottage with red shutters in the dark street, a little encampment of Italians in New England; one of two or three houses where the lights were still on late on a Sunday night. They were the flowers growing up all along the fence, bright dashes of color, red, pink, and purple and striped blooms, like wild clothing thrown all over the yard; they were the women with their dark hair, serious expressions, and worried skin, and the boys hovering around them. The sewing machine in the corner from the old house in the city, with the cloth tomato resting on it stabbed through with sewing needles and straight pins; the sacred heart of Jesus on the wall, with his hands holding up the heart on fire. Gathered around the table, which had on it the cake already eaten, the cake knife, resting on a little lace doily under the cake, catching the light on its broad blade. And they were the absence of men: as soon as the conversation had started, three of the men had got up and walked to the living room as though they were so bored or so full they couldn't stand it. "You know what Jules Stein said to me?" Aunt Terry said. "I'll never forget: 'I gotta hand it to the Italian people,' he said. 'They came to this country with nothing.' " "That's right," said the out-of-town cousin. "That's royt," Joey said mimicking her. "Hey, wise guy," his mother said, "don't get fresh!" "I'd like the government to pay *my* way," Aunt Tina said. "Sure. Why not." "Hey, nobody put up signs in Italian when Mom and Pop came here." "That's right." "If you want help, help yourself!" Aunt Terry concluded.

~ ~ ~

"You goddamn lousy son of a *bitch*," Uncle Joe said in his loud, shrill voice, slapping down his cards, as if he really meant it and at the same time didn't, while his brother-in-law Ralph, the winner, got up, half-leaned over the card table, cigar in his mouth, and raked in all the change. There were about ten of them around the table, the men in T-shirts, drinks next to them, and three of the women. (The other women, the ones who didn't play cards, sat talking in the kitchen.)

Nicholas looked at Tony, who puffed out his cheeks and wobbled his head behind Uncle Ralph's chair. Joey stood behind his father with his hands on the back of the chair, watching him, but it was as if he really wanted something else. A new game started. Uncle Joe, with a cigarette in his mouth, was talking while he picked up his cards, the cigarette flapping up and down. He knew his son was behind him, and he let him see his cards but at the same time kept them very tight in his hand, carefully taking one out from behind the other, his shoulders tensed, as if he didn't fully trust him. He handed him his glass. "Get me a refill," he said. It was a Sunday, three Sundays after the Confirmation Day party: every week they went to someone else's house for a poker game, and this time it was Uncle Joe's. The house was small and seemed smaller and more crowded now that the game had started; it filled up with cigarette smoke and renewed vigor once the food was out of the way, as if the game was all they had waited for. "All right, let's get going, let's get a move on it," Aunt Terry had said as soon as they'd finished cleaning off the table. She pulled out the drawer in the kitchen for the two decks of cards, one of them new and not even opened yet.

Tony walked into the living room and sat down on the couch. The top of the big TV set was also crowded: three sets of photographs in gold frames, little lace packets of candied almond tied with purple ribbons left over from a wedding, a ceramic white poodle up on its hind legs. Nicholas sat down next to him; the two of them watched TV for an hour. Where the drapes on the window didn't meet they showed a line of black. Outside, Uncle Ralph's dry cleaner's truck was parked in the driveway with two other cars; everyone else had had to park on the street. Every once in a while shouts erupted from the card table in the next room. Tony looked. Nicholas didn't look. Tony looked at Nicholas, who was smoking a cigarette, which he left when he wasn't smoking on the lip of the ashtray; now he picked it up and slowly brought it to his mouth. He tilted his head and then let the smoke drift around his lips, a little at a time coming out, making a heart at one corner of his mouth.

Then Joey walked in, fresh from the shower: he smelled of cologne, he had on a gold chain, his dark hair was wet and brushed back. "You ready?" he said to Nicholas, not looking at Tony. "Let's go." Nicholas stood up and waited while Joey went to the kitchen for the keys. "You be careful," Aunt Terry said, her voice suddenly rising above the tide of the cardplayer noise. "You hear me? Hey, hey, get over here. I ain't kidding you." "I hear you, I hear you." They were going out in Joey's new car, which had belonged to the grandfather who'd died the year before. Tony wasn't invited. It was eight-thirty. Nicholas stood there waiting because they were going to go out the front door. Tony could feel Nicholas looking at him as he stood there, but he didn't look at Nicholas. "What's the matter, Tony?" Nicholas said. "You bored?" Tony didn't answer him but looked as if to say, Of course. He sat there with his hand on his chin, his arm on the arm of the couch, watching TV. Then Nicholas said, "Hey, Tony," lowering his voice and motioning slightly with his head. "Patrick's here." Tony frowned, and Nicholas laughed. And Patrick, if he had heard, did nothing to show that he had heard, just continued staring at the set. Then before Joey came back from the kitchen, Patrick got up and walked out of the room.

~ ~ ~

"What are you always looking at me like that for, huh, huh, Tony?" Nicholas said, lightly slapping the back of Tony's head. The two of them were sitting close to each other on the couch in the grandmother's house where they were, all the cousins, because it was Saturday. They stayed there every Saturday while their parents worked and then Saturday night when they went out, three of them sleeping in the extra bedroom down-stairs and Nicholas and Tony sharing the bed upstairs on the third floor. Nicholas was sixteen and a half and Tony fourteen. Nicholas, stretching, his arms over his head, said, "I'm only bullshitting you, Tony," the sound of the yawn in his voice as if he'd put it there on purpose. "Don't be so fucking serious all the time." But he looked at him again a minute later as if saying something else. The grandmother was in the kitchen, making soup and setting the table. "You got something on your mind?" Nicholas said, and winked. Then he laughed and got up and turned the channels till he found a baseball game. Tony went and stood on the porch, looked down at the street. After a few minutes his grandmother called him and the others to the kitchen. They sat around the table, the grandchildren and the grandmother, who kept the bread by her plate. She crossed herself before picking up her spoon to eat (then the rest of them did it because she looked out at them over the table, though they did it rather quickly and sloppily, one sort of flinging the sign of the cross there, another looking down and up to see who was not doing it, making it clear it was an obligation; Nicholas didn't do it at all). After the meal, just as soon as they had finished helping her clean up, Nicholas picked up his jacket and said he was going out. The grandmother walked after him to the door and kissed him. "Not too late," she said, her hand on the door, watching him as he went down the stairs.

Tony watched TV until about midnight, then went up to bed.

~ ~ ~

"You still wear pajamas to bed," Nicholas said to Tony as though Tony were ridiculously young for his age, when Tony walked back into the room. It was about two in the morning. Tony had gone downstairs to the bathroom, and Nicholas had come home in the meantime; he hadn't heard him; he was surprised when he saw him standing there in the dark in the bedroom. He, Nicholas, stood there looking at himself in front of the mirror while he got undressed, even though the light wasn't on, taking things out of his pockets and setting them down on top of the bureau, his wallet from the back of his pants, some change from his pocket. He draped his shirt over a chair back and then stood there in just his underwear and socks; he peeled off his socks and jumped into bed.

~ ~ ~

Tony woke up about an hour later. It was dark; he and Nicholas were lying pressed up against each other. Nicholas had taken off his underwear. They had gone to sleep at opposite ends of the bed. Nicholas moved closer and turned, and when he did it fell flat on Tony's hand, thick and hard. Tony's heart was beating fast and hard as if he'd been awake longer than he actually had been. He didn't move, then he moved a little, but Nicholas turned again till it was back on Tony's hand. Tony left his hand there for a second. He could pretend to be asleep; he knew Nicholas was awake, but at the same time he told himself it was an accident, he was asleep. But Nicholas had gone to sleep in his underwear, and now he wasn't wearing any or his underwear was pulled down underneath it; it was dark and big and out of his underwear. Then Nicholas, moving his hand just a little, closed Tony's hand around it. When Tony didn't move his hand away, when he pressed it a little, Nicholas said his girlfriend's name, as if he was talking in his sleep. "Yeah, that's it," he said. "do it." It seemed like a long time and at the same time not a long time. Then Nicholas moved up the bed a little at a time; he leaned into him, getting very close, and pressed it against his mouth; holding it, he forced it, hard, against Tony's lips. He pressed forward a few times. As soon as that happened, Tony turned away, he turned around as if it hadn't happened and faced the opposite wall. But then Nicholas took his hand back, continued to hold Tony's hand against it, rubbing it up and down against it until it was wet.

After about five minutes Nicholas got up and walked out of the room, taking his pillow with him.

In the morning—everyone else had gone to church—Tony walked downstairs into the living room. Nicholas was sleeping under a blanket on the couch. Tony looked around; he stood there in the living room, looking toward the kitchen. "What are you doing, Tony?" Nicholas said in a bored voice. His eyes were dark. Tony walked over to the window, pulled back the curtain, and looked out at the street.

~ ~ ~

One night about a month later, Nicholas and Tony sat in Nicholas's car, waiting for Tony's sister Teresa to come out of dancing school. They were about twenty minutes early. Nicholas turned on the radio, low, and then closed his eyes and pretended to be asleep: he spread his legs. Then Tony touched him as he touched the radio dial. He pressed his hand against Nicholas's leg for a second, and Nicholas returned the pressure. All of a sudden he wasn't pretending to be asleep; he was getting up, moving in the seat, sitting up straight in the dark in the car, pressing Tony down as he moved over to the seat where Tony was. "You touch me? You touch me?" he said, his voice out of breath a little and angry. "What do you want, Tony?" he said, up above him, moving over on his knees, and with one arm holding him down and the other hand unzipping his fly, kneeling on him, he took it out, larger than Tony remembered; he was pointing it at him, close to his face. Tony, low in the seat under him, felt he had to touch it or do something because this was really the same thing that had started a few weeks before. "What do you want? This what you want?" He moved on his knees, digging into Tony, pinning him down, and when Tony sank down more in the seat, he pressed harder. Then, because Tony wasn't doing anything yet, Nicholas reached between Tony's legs and pulled his zipper down, his hand just brushing against Tony's underwear. He thrust forward against Tony's face a few times, pressing him back against the car seat. Nicholas closed his fist around it, jerking it up and down fast, the gold chain around his wrist flapping against his shirt sleeve. It was dark on the street, no one else was around, they were parked alongside a fire hydrant. There was no street-light. Then Nicholas leaned back, and three large drops fell out onto Tony's leg. He sat back behind the steering wheel again, zipped his pants. After a minute he leaned over and opened up the glove compartment. He wiped off Tony's leg, rolled down the window, and threw the napkin, all balled up, out into the gutter. He didn't say anything but turned the radio dial.

A few minutes later the dancing school let out. Teresa came running out to the car.

~ *A. M. Homes* ~

A Real
Doll

I 'm dating Barbie. Three afternoons a week, while my sister is at dance class, I take Barbie away from Ken. I'm practicing for the future.

At first I sat in my sister's room watching Barbie, who lived with Ken on a doily on top of the dresser.

I was looking at her but not really looking. I was looking and all of a sudden realized she was staring at me.

She was sitting next to Ken, his khaki-covered thigh absently rubbing her bare leg. He was rubbing her, but she was staring at me.

"Hi," she said.

"Hello," I said.

"I'm Barbie," she said, and Ken stopped rubbing her leg.

"I know."

"You're Jenny's brother."

I nodded. My head was bobbing up and down like a puppet on a weight.

"I really like your sister. She's sweet," Barbie said. "Such a good little girl. Especially lately, she makes herself so pretty, and she's started doing her nails."

A. M. HOMES is the author of the novels Jack *and* In a Country of Mothers *and the story collection* The Safety of Objects. *Despite her ambiguous moniker and a penchant for writing with great accuracy from the vantage point of adolescent boys, she is in fact not a guy.*

I wondered if Barbie noticed that Miss Wonderful bit her nails and that when she smiled her front teeth were covered with little flecks of purple nail polish. I wondered if she knew Jennifer colored in the chipped chewed spots with purple Magic Marker, and then sometimes sucked on her fingers so that not only did she have purple flecks of polish on her teeth but her tongue was the strangest shade of violet.

"So listen," I said. "Would you like to go out for a while? Grab some fresh air, maybe take a spin around the backyard?"

"Sure," she said.

I picked her up by her feet. It sounds unusual, but I was too petrified to take her by the waist. I grabbed her by the ankles and carried her off like a Popsicle stick.

As soon as we were out back, sitting on the porch of what I used to call my fort but which my sister and parents referred to as the playhouse, I started freaking. I was suddenly and incredibly aware that I was out with Barbie. I didn't know what to say.

"So what kind of a Barbie are you?" I asked.

"Excuse me?"

"Well, from listening to Jennifer I know there's Day to Night Barbie, Magic Moves Barbie, Gift-Giving Barbie, Tropical Barbie, My First Barbie, and more."

"I'm Tropical," she said. I'm Tropical, she said, the same way a person might say I'm Catholic or I'm Jewish. "I came with a one-piece bathing suit, a brush, and a ruffle you can wear so many ways," Barbie squeaked.

She actually squeaked. It turned out that squeaking was Barbie's birth defect. I pretended I didn't hear it.

We were quiet for a minute. A leaf larger than Barbie fell from the maple tree above us, and I caught it just before it would have hit her. I half expected her to squeak, "You saved my life. I'm yours forever." Instead she said, in a perfectly normal voice, "Wow, big leaf."

I looked at her. Barbie's eyes were sparkling blue like the ocean on a good day. I looked and in a moment noticed she had the whole world, the cosmos, drawn in make-up above and below her eyes. An entire galaxy—clouds, stars, a sun, the sea—painted on her face. Yellow, blue, pink, and a million silver sparkles.

We sat looking at each other, looking and talking and then not talking and looking again. It was a stop-and-start thing, with both of us constantly saying the wrong thing, saying anything, and then immediately regretting having said it.

It was obvious Barbie didn't trust me. I asked her if she wanted something to drink.

"Diet Coke," she said. And I wondered why I'd asked.

I went into the house, upstairs into my parents' bathroom, opened the medicine cabinet, and got a couple of Valiums. I immediately swallowed one. I figured if I could be calm and collected, she'd realize I wasn't going to hurt her. I broke another Valium into a million small pieces, dropped some slivers into Barbie's diet Coke, and swished it around so it'd blend. I figured if we could be calm and collected together, she'd be able to trust me even sooner. I was falling in love in a way that had nothing to do with love.

"So what's the deal with you and Ken?" I asked later, after we'd loosened up, after she'd drunk two diet Cokes and I'd made another trip to the medicine cabinet.

She giggled. "Oh, we're just really good friends."

"What's the deal with him really, you can tell me. I mean, is he or isn't he?"

"Ish she or ishn' she," Barbie said, in a slow slurred way, like she was so intoxicated that if they made a Breathalyzer for Valium, she'd melt it.

I regretted having fixed her a third Coke. I mean, if she OD'd and died, Jennifer would tell my mom and dad for sure.

"Is he a faggot or what?"

Barbie laughed, and I almost slapped her. She looked me straight in the eye.

"He lusts after me," she said. "I come home at night and he's standing there, waiting. He doesn't wear underwear, you know. I mean, isn't that strange, Ken doesn't own any underwear. I heard Jennifer tell her friend that they don't even make any for him. Anyway, he's always there waiting, and I'm like, Ken we're friends, okay, that's it. I mean, have you ever noticed, he has molded plastic hair. His head and his hair are all one piece. I can't go out with a guy like that. Besides, I don't think he'd be up for it, if you know what I mean. Ken is not what you'd call well endowed. . . . All he's got is a little plastic bump, more of a hump, really, and what the hell are you supposed to do with that?"

She was telling me things I didn't think I should hear, and all the same, I was leaning into her, like if I moved closer she'd tell me more. I was taking every word and holding it for a minute, holding groups of words in my head like I didn't understand English. She went on and on, but I wasn't listening.

The sun sank behind the playhouse. Barbie shivered, excused herself, and ran around back to throw up. I asked her if she felt okay. She said she was fine, just a little tired, that maybe she was coming down with the flu or something. I gave her a piece of a piece of gum to chew and took her inside.

On the way back to Jennifer's room I did something Barbie almost didn't forgive me for. I did something which not only shattered the moment but nearly wrecked the possibility of our having a future together.

In the hallway between the stairs and Jennifer's room, I popped Barbie's head into my mouth, like lion and tamer, God and Godzilla.

I popped her whole head into my mouth, and Barbie's hair separated into single strands like Christmas tinsel and caught in my throat, nearly choking me. I could taste layer on layer of make-up, Revlon, Max Factor, and Maybelline. I closed my mouth around Barbie and could feel her breath in mine. I could hear her screams in my throat. Her teeth—white, Pearl Drops, Pepsodent, and the whole Osmond family—bit my tongue and the inside of my cheek like I might accidentally bite myself. I closed my mouth around her neck and held her suspended, her feet uselessly kicking the air in front of my face.

Before pulling her out, I pressed my teeth lightly into her neck, leaving marks Barbie described as scars of her assault, but which I imagined as a New Age necklace of love.

"I have never, ever, in my life been treated with such utter disregard," she said as soon as I let her out.

She was lying. I knew Jennifer sometimes did things with Barbie. I didn't mention that once I'd seen Barbie hanging from Jennifer's ceiling fan, spinning around in great wide circles, like some imitation Superman.

"I'm sorry if I scared you."

"Scared me!" she squeaked.

She went on squeaking, a cross between the squeal when you let the air out of a balloon and a smoke alarm with weak batteries. While she was squeaking, the phrase *A head in the mouth is worth two in the bush* started running through my head. I knew it had come from somewhere, started as something else, but I couldn't get it right. *A head in the mouth is worth two in the bush,* again and again, like the punch line to some dirty joke.

"Scared me. Scared me. Scared me!" Barbie squeaked, louder and louder, until finally she had my attention again. "Have you ever been held captive in the dark cavern of someone's body?"

I shook my head. It sounded wonderful.

"Typical," she said. "So incredibly, typically male."

For a moment I was proud.

"Why do you have to do things you know you shouldn't, and worse, you do them with a light in your eye, like you're getting some weird pleasure that only another boy would understand. You're all the same," she said. "You're all Jack Nicholson."

I refused to put her back in Jennifer's room until she forgave me, until she understood that I'd done what I did with only the truest of feeling, no harm intended.

I heard Jennifer's feet clomping up the stairs. I was running out of time.

"You know I'm really interested in you," I said to Barbie.

"Me too," she said, and for a minute I wasn't sure if she meant she was interested in herself or me.

"We should do this again," I said. She nodded.

I leaned down to kiss Barbie. I could have brought her up to my lips, but somehow it felt wrong. I leaned down to kiss her, and the first thing I got was her nose in my mouth. I felt like a Saint Bernard saying hello.

No matter how graceful I tried to be, I could only lick her face. It wasn't a question of putting my tongue in her ear or down her throat, it was simply literally trying not to suffocate her. I kissed Barbie with my back to Ken and then turned around and put her on the doily right next to him. I was tempted to drop her down on Ken, to mash her into him, but I managed to restrain myself.

"That was fun," Barbie said. I heard Jennifer in the hall.

"Later," I said.

Jennifer came into the room and looked at me.

"What?" I said.

"It's my room," she said.

"There was a bee in it. I was killing it for you."

"A bee. I'm allergic to bees. Mom, Mom," she screamed. "There's a bee."

"Mom's not home. I killed it."

"But there might be another one."

"So call me and I'll kill it."

"But if it stings me I might die." I shrugged and walked out. I could feel Barbie watching me leave.

~ ~ ~

I took a Valium about twenty minutes before I picked her up the next Friday. By the time I went into Jennifer's room, everything was easier.

"Hey," I said when I got up to the dresser.

She was there on the doily with Ken; they were back-to-back, resting against each other, legs stretched out in front of them.

Ken didn't look at me. I didn't care.

"You ready to go?" I asked. Barbie nodded. "I thought you might be thirsty." I handed her the diet Coke I'd made for her.

I'd figured Barbie could take a little less than an eighth of a Valium without getting totally senile. Basically, I had to give her Valium crumbs, since there was no way to cut one that small.

She took the Coke and drank it right in front of Ken. I kept waiting for him to give me one of those I-know-what-you're-up-to-and-I-don't-like-it looks, the kind my father gives me when he walks into my room without knocking and I automatically jump twenty feet in the air.

Ken acted like he didn't even know I was there. I hated him.

"I can't do a lot of walking this afternoon," Barbie said.

I nodded. I figured no big deal, since mostly I seemed to be carrying her around anyway.

"My feet are killing me," she said.

I was thinking about Ken.

"Don't you have other shoes?"

My family was very into shoes. No matter what seemed to be wrong, my father always suggested it could be cured by wearing a different pair of shoes. He believed that shoes, like tires, should be rotated.

"It's not the shoes," she said. "It's my toes."

"Did you drop something on them?" My Valium wasn't working. I was having trouble making small talk. I needed another one.

"Jennifer's been chewing on them."

"What?"

"She chews on my toes."

"You let her chew your footies?"

I couldn't make sense out of what she was saying. I was thinking about not being able to talk, needing another or maybe two more Valiums, yellow adult-strength Pez.

"Do you enjoy it?" I asked.

"She literally bites down on them, like I'm flank steak or something," Barbie said. "I wish she'd just bite them off and have it over with. This is taking forever. She's chewing and chewing, more like gnawing at me."

"I'll make her stop. I'll buy her some gum, some tobacco or something, a pencil to chew on."

"Please don't say anything. I wouldn't have told you, except . . . ," Barbie said.

"But she's hurting you."

"It's between Jennifer and me."

"Where's it going to stop?" I asked.

"At the arch, I hope. There's a bone there, and once she realizes she's bitten the soft part off, she'll stop."

"How will you walk?"

"I have very long feet."

I sat on the edge of my sister's bed, my head in my hands. My sister was biting Barbie's feet off, and Barbie didn't seem to care. She didn't hold it against her, and in a way I liked her for that. I liked the fact she understood how we all have little secret habits that seem normal enough to us but which we know better than to mention out loud. I started imagining things I might be able to get away with.

"Get me out of here," Barbie said. I slipped Barbie's shoes off. Sure enough, someone had been gnawing at her. On her left foot the toes were dangling, and on the right, half had been completely taken off. There were tooth marks up to her ankles. "Let's not dwell on this," Barbie said.

I picked Barbie up. Ken fell over backward, and Barbie made me straighten him up before we left. "Just because you know he only has a bump doesn't give you permission to treat him badly," Barbie whispered.

I fixed Ken and carried Barbie down the hall to my room. I held Barbie above me, tilted my head back, and lowered her feet into my mouth. I felt like a young sword swallower practicing for my debut. I lowered Barbie's feet and legs into my mouth and then began sucking on them. They smelled like Jennifer and dirt and plastic. I sucked on her stubs and she told me it felt nice.

"You're better than a hot soak," Barbie said. I left her resting on my pillow and went downstairs to get us each a drink.

We were lying on my bed, curled into and out of each other. Barbie was on a pillow next to me, and I was on my side facing her. She was talking about men, and as she talked I tried to be everything she said. She was saying she didn't like men who were afraid of themselves. I tried to be brave, to look courageous and secure. I held my head a certain way, and it seemed to work. She said she didn't like men who were afraid of femininity, and I got confused.

"Guys always have to prove how boy they really are," Barbie said.

I thought of Jennifer trying to be a girl, wearing dresses, doing her nails, putting make-up on, wearing a bra even though she wouldn't need one for about fifty years.

"You make fun of Ken because he lets himself be everything he is. He doesn't hide anything."

"He doesn't have anything to hide," I said. "He has tan molded plastic hair, and a bump for a dick."

"I never should have told you about the bump."

I lay back on the bed. Barbie rolled over, off the pillow, and rested on my chest. Her body stretched from my nipple to my belly button. Her hands pressed against me, tickling me.

"Barbie," I said.

"Um hum."

"How do you feel about me?"

She didn't say anything for a minute. "Don't worry about it," she said, and slipped her hand into my shirt through the space between the buttons.

Her fingers were like the ends of toothpicks performing some subtle ancient torture, a dance of boy death across my chest. Barbie crawled all over me like an insect who'd run into one too many cans of Raid.

Underneath my clothes, under my skin, I was going crazy. First off, I'd been kidnapped by my underwear, with no way to manually adjust without attracting unnecessary attention.

With Barbie caught in my shirt, I slowly rolled over, like in some space shuttle docking maneuver. I rolled onto my stomach, trapping her under me. As slowly and unobtrusively as possible, I ground myself against the bed, at first hoping it would fix things and then, again and again, caught by a pleasure/pain principle.

"Is this a water bed?" Barbie asked.

My hand was on her breasts, only it wasn't really my hand but more like my index finger. I touched Barbie and she made a little gasp, a squeak in reverse. She squeaked backward, then stopped, and I was stuck there with my hand on her, thinking about how I was forever crossing a line between the haves and the have-nots, between good guys and bad, between men and animals, and there was absolutely nothing I could do to stop myself.

Barbie was sitting on my crotch, her legs flipped back behind her in a position that wasn't human.

At a certain point I had to free myself. If my dick was blue, it was only because it had suffocated. I did the honors, and Richard popped out like an escape from maximum security.

"I've never seen anything so big," Barbie said. It was the sentence I dreamed of, but given the people Barbie normally hung out with, namely the bump boy himself, it didn't come as a big surprise.

She stood at the base of my dick, her bare feet buried in my pubic hair. I was almost as tall as she was. Okay, not almost as tall, but clearly we could be related. She and Richard even had the same vaguely surprised look on their faces.

She was on me, and I couldn't help wanting to get inside her. I turned Barbie over and was on top of her, not caring if I killed her. Her hands pressed so hard into my stomach that it felt like she was performing an appendectomy.

I was on top, trying to get between her legs, almost breaking her in half. But there was nothing there, nothing to fuck except a small thin line that was supposed to be her ass crack.

I rubbed the thin line, the back of her legs and the space between her legs. I turned Barbie's back to me so I could do it without having to look at her face.

Very quickly, I came. I came all over Barbie, all over her and a little bit in her hair. I came on Barbie and it was the most horrifying experience I ever had. It didn't stay on her. It doesn't stick to plastic. I was finished.

I was holding a come-covered Barbie in my hand like I didn't know where she came from.

Barbie said, "Don't stop," or maybe I just think she said that because I read it somewhere. I don't know anymore. I couldn't listen to her. I couldn't even look at her. I wiped myself off with a sock, pulled my clothes on, and then took Barbie into the bathroom.

～ ～ ～

At dinner I noticed Jennifer chewing her cuticles between bites of tuna-noodle casserole. I asked her if she was teething. She coughed and then started choking to death on either a little piece of fingernail, a crushed potato chip from the casserole, or maybe even a little bit of Barbie footie that'd stuck in her teeth. My mother asked her if she was okay.

"I swallowed something sharp," she said between coughs that were clearly influenced by the acting class she'd taken over the summer.

"Do you have a problem?" I asked her.

"Leave your sister alone," my mother said.

"If there are any questions to ask, we'll do the asking," my father said.

"Is everything all right?" my mother asked Jennifer. She nodded. "I think you could use some new jeans," my mother said. "You don't seem to have many play clothes anymore."

"Not to change the subject," I said, trying to think of a way to stop Jennifer from eating Barbie alive.

"I don't wear pants," Jennifer said. "Boys wear pants."

"Your grandma wears pants," my father said.

"She's not a girl."

My father chuckled. He actually fucking chuckled. He's the only person I ever met who could actually fucking chuckle.

"Don't tell her that," he said, chuckling.

"It's not funny," I said.

"Grandma's are pull-ons anyway," Jennifer said. "They don't have a fly. You have to have a penis to have a fly."

"Jennifer," my mother said. "That's enough of that."

I decided to buy Barbie a present. I was at that strange point where I would have done anything for her. I took two buses and walked more than a mile to get to Toys "R" Us.

Barbie row was aisle 14C. I was a wreck. I imagined a million Barbies and having to have them all. I pictured fucking one, discarding it, immediately grabbing a fresh one, doing it, and then throwing it onto a growing pile in the corner of my room. An unending chore. I saw myself becoming a slave to Barbie. I wondered how many Tropical Barbies were made each year. I felt faint.

There were rows and rows of Kens, Barbies, and Skippers. Funtime Barbie, Jewel Secrets Ken, Barbie Rocker with "Hot Rockin' Fun and Real Dancin' Action." I noticed Magic Moves Barbie and found myself looking at her carefully, flirtatiously, wondering if her legs were spreadable. "Push the switch and she moves," her box said. She winked at me while I was reading.

The only Tropical I saw was a black Tropical Ken. From just looking at him you wouldn't have known he was black. I mean, he wasn't black like anyone would be black. Black Tropical Ken was the color of a raisin, a raisin all spread out and unwrinkled. He had a short afro that looked like a wig had been dropped down and fixed on his head, a protective helmet. I wondered if black Ken was really white Ken sprayed over with a thick coating of ironed raisin plastic.

I spread eight black Kens out in a line across the front of a row. Through the plastic window of his box he told me he was hoping to go to dental school. All eight black Kens talked at once. Luckily, they all said the same thing at the same time. They said he really liked teeth. Black Ken smiled. He had the same white Pearl Drops, Pepsodent, Osmond family teeth that Barbie and white Ken had. I thought the entire Mattel family must take really good care of themselves. I figured they might be the only people left in America who actually brushed after every meal and then again before going to sleep.

I didn't know what to get Barbie. Black Ken said I should go for clothing, maybe a fur coat. I wanted something really special. I imagined a wonderful present that would draw us somehow closer.

There was a tropical pool and patio set, but I decided it might make her homesick. There was a complete winter holiday, with an A-frame house, fireplace, snowmobile, and sled. I imagined her inviting Ken away for a weekend without me. The six o'clock news set was nice, but because of her squeak, Barbie's future as an anchorwoman seemed limited. A workout center, a sofa bed and coffee table, a bubbling spa, a bedroom play set. I settled on the grand piano. It was thirteen dollars. I'd always made it a point to never spend more than ten dollars on anyone. This time I figured, What the hell, you don't buy a grand piano every day.

"Wrap it up, would ya," I said at the checkout desk.

~ ~ ~

From my bedroom window I could see Jennifer in the backyard, wearing her tutu and leaping all over the place. It was dangerous as hell to sneak in and get Barbie, but I couldn't keep a grand piano in my closet without telling someone.

"You must really like me," Barbie said when she finally had the piano unwrapped.

I nodded. She was wearing a ski suit and skis. It was the end of August and eighty degrees out. Immediately, she sat down and played "Chopsticks."

I looked out at Jennifer. She was running down the length of the deck, jumping onto the railing and then leaping off, posing like one of those red flying horses you see on old Mobil gas signs. I watched her do it once, and then, the second time, her foot caught on the railing, and she went over the edge the hard way. A minute later she came around the edge of the house, limping, her tutu dented and dirty, pink tights ripped at both knees. I grabbed Barbie from the piano bench and raced her into Jennifer's room.

"I was just getting warmed up," she said. "I can play better than that, really."

I could hear Jennifer crying as she walked up the stairs.

"Jennifer's coming," I said. I put her down on the dresser and realized Ken was missing.

"Where's Ken?" I asked quickly.

"Out with Jennifer," Barbie said.

I met Jennifer at her door. "Are you okay?" I asked. She cried harder. "I saw you fall."

"Why didn't you stop me?" she said.

"From falling?"

She nodded and showed me her knees.

"Once you start to fall, no one can stop you." I noticed Ken was tucked into the waistband of her tutu.

"They catch you," Jennifer said.

I started to tell her it was dangerous to go leaping around with a Ken stuck in your waistband, but you don't tell someone who's already crying that they did something bad.

I walked her into the bathroom, and took out the hydrogen peroxide. I was a first aid expert. I was the kind of guy who walked around waiting for someone to have a heart attack just so I could practice my CPR technique.

"Sit down," I said.

Jennifer sat down on the toilet without putting the lid down. Ken was stabbing her all over the place, and instead of pulling him out, she squirmed around trying to get comfortable like she didn't know what else to do. I took him out for her. She watched as though I was performing surgery or something.

"He's mine," she said.

"Take off your tights," I said.

"No," she said.

"They're ruined," I said. "Take them off."

Jennifer took off her ballet slippers and peeled off her tights. She was wearing my old Underoos with superheroes on them, Spider-Man and Superman and Batman all poking out from under a dirty dented tutu. I decided not to say anything, but it looked funny as hell to see a flat crotch in boys' underwear. I had the feeling they didn't bother making underwear for Ken because they knew it looked too weird on him.

I poured peroxide onto her bloody knees. Jennifer screamed into my ear. She bent down and examined herself, poking her purple fingers into the torn skin; her tutu bunched up and rubbed against her face, scraping it. I worked on her knees, removing little pebbles and pieces of grass from the area.

She started crying again.

"You're okay," I said. "You're not dying." She didn't care. "Do you want anything?" I asked, trying to be nice.

"Barbie," she said.

It was the first time I'd handled Barbie in public. I picked her up like she was a complete stranger and handed her to Jennifer, who grabbed her by the hair. I started to tell her to ease up, but couldn't. Barbie looked at me, and I shrugged. I went downstairs and made Jennifer one of my special diet Cokes.

"Drink this," I said, handing it to her. She took four giant gulps, and immediately I felt guilty about having used a whole Valium.

"Why don't you give a little to your Barbie," I said. "I'm sure she's thirsty too."

Barbie winked at me, and I could have killed her, first off for doing it in front of Jennifer, and second because she didn't know what the hell she was winking about.

I went into my room and put the piano away. I figured as long as I kept it in the original box I'd be safe. If anyone found it, I'd say it was a present for Jennifer.

~ ~ ~

Wednesday, Ken and Barbie had their heads switched. I went to get Barbie, and there on top of the dresser were Barbie and Ken, sort of. Barbie's head was on Ken's body, and Ken's head was on Barbie. At first I thought it was just me.

"Hi," Barbie's head said.

I couldn't respond. She was on Ken's body, and I was looking at Ken in a whole new way.

I picked up the Barbie-head Ken, and immediately Barbie's head rolled off. It rolled across the dresser, across the white doily, past Jennifer's collection of miniature ceramic cats, and *boom* it fell to the floor. I saw Barbie's head rolling and about to fall and then falling, but there was nothing I could do to stop it. I was frozen, paralyzed with Ken's headless body in my left hand.

Barbie's head was on the floor, her hair spread out underneath it like angel wings in the snow, and I expected to see blood, a wide rich pool of blood, or at least a little bit coming out of her ear, her nose, or her mouth. I looked at her head on the floor and saw nothing but Barbie with eyes like the cosmos looking up at me. I thought she was dead.

"Christ, that hurt," she said. "And I already had a headache from these earrings."

There were little red dot-ball earrings jutting out of Barbie's ears.

"They go right through my head, you know. I guess it takes getting used to," Barbie said.

I noticed my mother's pincushion on the dresser next to the other Barbie-Ken, the Barbie body/Ken head. The pincushion was filled with hundreds of pins: pins with flat silver ends and pins with red, yellow, and blue dot-ball ends.

"You have pins in your head," I said to the Barbie head on the floor. "Is that supposed to be a compliment?"

I was starting to hate her. I was being perfectly clear, and she didn't understand me.

I looked at Ken. He was in my left hand, my fist wrapped around his waist. I looked at him and realized my thumb was on his bump. My thumb was pressed against Ken's crotch, and as soon as I noticed I got an automatic hard-on, the kind you don't know you're getting, it's just there. I started rubbing Ken's bump and watching my thumb like it was a large-screen projection of a porno movie.

"What are you doing?" Barbie's head said. "Get me up. Help me." I was rubbing Ken's bump/hump with my finger inside his bathing suit. I was standing in the middle of my sister's room with my pants pulled down.

"Aren't you going to help me?" Barbie kept asking. "Aren't you going to help me?"

In the second before I came, I held Ken's head hole in front of me. I held Ken upside down above my dick and came inside Ken like I never could in Barbie.

I came into Ken's body, and as soon as I was done I wanted to do it again. I wanted to fill Ken and put his head back on, like a perfume bottle. I wanted Ken to be the vessel for my secret supply. I came in Ken, and then I remembered he wasn't mine. He didn't belong to me. I took him into the bathroom and soaked him in warm water and Ivory liquid. I brushed his insides with Jennifer's toothbrush and left him alone in a cold-water rinse.

"Aren't you going to help me—aren't you?" Barbie kept asking.

I started thinking she'd been brain damaged by the accident. I picked her head up from the floor.

"What took you so long?" she asked.

"I had to take care of Ken."

"Is he okay?"

"He'll be fine. He's soaking in the bathroom." I held Barbie's head in my hand.

"What are you going to do?"

"What do you mean?" I said.

Did my little incident, my moment with Ken, mean that right then and there some decision about my future life as queerbait had to be made?

"This afternoon. Where are we going? What are we doing? I miss you when I don't see you," Barbie said.

"You see me every day," I said.

"I don't really see you. I sit on top of the dresser, and if you pass by, I see you. Take me to your room."

"I have to bring Ken's body back."

I went into the bathroom, rinsed Ken out, blew him dry with my mother's blow dryer, then played with him again. It was a boy thing; we were boys together. I thought sometime I might play ball with him, I might take him out instead of Barbie.

"Everything takes you so long," Barbie said when I got back into the room.

I put Ken back up on the dresser, picked up Barbie's body, knocked Ken's head off, and smashed Barbie's head back down on her own damn neck.

"I don't want to fight with you," Barbie said as I carried her into my room. "We don't have enough time together to fight. Fuck me," she said.

I didn't feel like it. I was thinking about fucking Ken and Ken being a boy. I was thinking about Barbie and Barbie being a girl. I was thinking about Jennifer, switching Barbie's and Ken's heads, chewing Barbie's feet off, hanging Barbie from the ceiling fan, and who knows what else.

"Fuck me," Barbie said again.

I ripped Barbie's clothing off. Between Barbie's legs Jennifer had drawn pubic hair in reverse. She'd drawn it upside down so it looked like a fountain spewing up and out in great wide arcs. I spit directly onto Barbie and with my thumb and first finger rubbed the ink lines, erasing them. Barbie moaned.

"Why do you let her do this to you?"

"Jennifer owns me," Barbie moaned.

Jennifer owns me, she said, so easily and with pleasure. I was totally jealous. Jennifer owned Barbie, and it made me crazy. Obviously it was one of those relationships that could only exist between women. Jennifer could own her because it didn't matter that Jennifer owned her. Jennifer didn't want Barbie; she had her.

"You're perfect," I said.

"I'm getting fat," Barbie said.

Barbie was crawling all over me, and I wondered if Jennifer knew she was a nymphomaniac. I wondered if Jennifer knew what a nymphomaniac was.

"You don't belong with little girls," I said.

Barbie ignored me.

There were scratches on Barbie's chest and stomach. She didn't say anything about them, and so at first I pretended not to notice. As I was touching her, I could feel they were deep, like slices. The edges were rough; my finger caught on them, and I couldn't help but wonder.

"Jennifer?" I said, massaging the cuts with my tongue, as though my tongue, like sandpaper, would erase them. Barbie nodded.

In fact, I thought of using sandpaper, but didn't know how I would explain it to Barbie: *You have to lie still and let me rub it really hard with this stuff that's like terry cloth dipped in cement.* I thought she might even like it if I made it into an S&M kind of thing and handcuffed her first.

I ran my tongue back and forth over the slivers, back and forth over the words "copyright 1966 Mattel Inc., Malaysia" tattooed on her back. Tonguing the tattoo drove Barbie crazy. She said it had something to do with scar tissue being extremely sensitive.

Barbie pushed herself hard against me; I could feel her slices rubbing my skin. I was thinking that Jennifer might kill Barbie. Without meaning to, she might just go over the line, and I wondered if Barbie would know what was happening or if she'd try to stop her.

We fucked; that's what I called it, fucking. In the beginning Barbie said she hated the word, which made me like it even more. She hated it because it was so strong and hard, and she said we weren't fucking, we were making love. I told her she had to be kidding.

"Fuck me," she said that afternoon, and I knew the end was coming soon. "Fuck me," she said. I didn't like the sound of the word.

~ ~ ~

Friday when I went into Jennifer's room, there was something in the air. The place smelled like a science lab, a fire, a failed experiment.

Barbie was wearing a strapless yellow evening dress. Her hair was wrapped into a high bun, more like a wedding cake than something Betty Crocker would whip up. There seemed to be layers and layers of angel's hair spinning in a circle above her head. She had yellow pins through her ears and gold fuck-me shoes that matched the belt around her waist. For a second I thought of the belt and imagined tying her up, but more than restraining her arms or legs, I thought of wrapping the belt around her face, tying it across her mouth.

I looked at Barbie and saw something dark and thick like a scar rising up and over the edge of her dress. I grabbed her and pulled the front of the dress down.

"Hey, big boy," Barbie said. "Don't I even get a hello?"

Barbie's breasts had been sawed at with a knife. There were a hundred marks from a blade that might have had five rows of teeth like shark jaws. And as if that wasn't enough, she'd been dissolved by fire; blue and yellow flames had been pressed against her and held there until she melted and eventually became the fire that burned herself. All of it had been somehow stirred with the lead of a pencil, the point of a pen, and left to cool. Molten Barbie flesh had been left to harden, black and pink plastic swirled together, in the crater Jennifer had dug out of her breasts.

I examined her in detail like a scientist, a pathologist, a fucking medical examiner. I studied the burns, the gouged-out area, as if by looking closely I'd find something, an explanation, a way out.

A disgusting taste came up into my mouth, like I'd been sucking on batteries. It came up, then sank back down into my stomach, leaving my mouth puckered with the bitter metallic flavor of sour saliva. I coughed and spit onto my shirt sleeve, then rolled the sleeve over to cover the wet spot.

With my index finger I touched the edge of the burn as lightly as I could. The round rim of her scar broke off under my finger. I almost dropped her.

"It's just a reduction," Barbie said. "Jennifer and I are even now."

Barbie was smiling. She had the same expression on her face as when I first saw her and fell in love. She had the same expression she always had, and I couldn't stand it. She was smiling, and she was burned. She was smiling, and she was ruined. I pulled her dress back up, above the scar line. I put her down carefully on the doily on top of the dresser and started to walk away.

"Hey," Barbie said, "aren't we going to play?"

~ *A. M. Homes* ~

The
Whiz
Kids

I n the big bathtub in my parents' bedroom, he ran his tongue along my side, up into my armpits, tugging the hair with his teeth. "We're like married," he said, licking my nipples.

I spit at him. A foamy blob landed on his bare chest. He smiled, grabbed both my arms, and held them down.

He slid his face down my stomach, dipped it under the water, and put his mouth over my cock.

My mother knocked on the bathroom door. "I have to get ready. Your father and I are leaving in twenty minutes."

Air bubbles crept up to the surface.

"Can you hear me?" she said, fiddling with the knob. "Why is the door locked? You know we don't lock doors in this house."

"It was an accident," I said, through the door.

"Well, hurry," my mother said.

And we did.

Later, in the den, picking his nose, examining the results on his finger, slipping his finger into his mouth with a smack and a pop, he explained that as long as we never slept with anyone else, we could do whatever we wanted. "Sex kills," he said, "but this," he said, "this is the one time, the only time, the chance of a life time." He ground his front teeth on the booger.

We met in science class. "Cocksucker," he hissed. My fingers were in my ears. I didn't hear the word, so much as see it escape his mouth.

The fire alarm was going off. Everyone was grabbing their coats and hurrying for the door. He held me back, pressed his lips close to my ear, and said it again, Cocksucker, his tongue touching my neck. Back and forth, he shook a beaker of a strange potion and threatened to make me drink it. He raised the glass to my mouth. My jaws clamped shut. With his free hand, he pinched my nostrils shut and laughed like a maniac. My mouth fell open. He tilted the beaker toward my throat. The teacher stopped him just in time. "Enough horsing around," she said. "This is a fire drill. Behave accordingly."

"Got ya," he said, pushing me into the hall and toward the steps, his hard-on rubbing against me the whole way down.

My mother came in, stood in front of the television set, her ass in Peter Jennings's face, and asked, "How do I look?"

He curled his lip and spit a pistachio shell onto the coffee table.

"Remember to clean up," my mother said.

"I want you to fuck me," he said, while my father was in the next room, looking for his keys.

"Have you seen them?" my father asked.

"No," I said.

"I want your Oscar Mayer in my bun," he said.

He lived miles away, had gone to a different elementary school, was a different religion, wasn't circumcised.

My father poked his head into the room, jiggled his keys in the air, and said, "Got 'em."

"Great tie," I said.

My father tweaked his bow tie. "Bye, guys."

The front door closed, the lock turned. My father's white Chrysler slid into the street.

"I want you to give it to me good."

"I want to watch *Jeopardy*," I said, going for the remote control.

"Ever tasted a dick infusion?" he asked, sipping from my glass of Dr Pepper.

He unzipped his fly, fished out his dick, and dropped it into the glass. The ice cubes melted, cracking the way they do when you pour in something hot. A minute later, he put his dick away, swirled the soda around, and offered me a sip.

"Maybe later," I said, focusing on the audio daily double. " 'Tie a Yellow Ribbon.' "

"I'm bored," he said.

"Play along," I said. "I've already got nine thousand dollars."

He went to the bookcase and started handling the family photos. "Wonder if he ever sucked a cock," he said, picking up a portrait of my father.

"Don't be a butt plug."

He smiled. "I love you," he said, raising his T-shirt, pulling it off over his head.

Dark hair rose in a fishbone up and out of his jeans.

I turned off the television.

"We need something," he said, as I led him down the hall toward my room.

"Something what?"

"Slippery."

I ducked into the bathroom, opened the cabinet, and grabbed a tube of Neosporin.

"Brilliant," he said. "An antibiotic lube job, fights infection while you're having fun."

Piece by piece I undressed with him, after him. He peeled off his socks, I peeled off mine. He unzipped his jeans and I undid mine. He slipped his fingers into the band of his underwear, snapped the elastic, and grinned. I pulled mine down. He slipped the tube of ointment into my ass, pinched my nipples, and sank his teeth deep into the muscle above my collarbone.

My parents got back just after midnight. "It was so nice of you to spend the evening," my mother said. "I just hate to leave you-know-who home alone. I think he gets depressed."

"Whatever," he said, shrugging, leaving with my father, who was giving him a ride home.

"You don't have to come with us," my father said to me. "It's late. Go to bed."

"See you in school tomorrow," I said.

"Whatever."

A week later he sat in my desk chair, jerking off, with the door open.

"Stop," I said. "Or close the door."

"Danger excites me."

"My mother isn't dangerous," I said, getting up and closing the door myself.

"What we've got here," he said, still jerking, "is virgin sperm. People will pay a load for this shit." He laughed at himself. "Get it—pay a load." Come shot into the air and landed on the glass of my fish tank.

"Very funny," I said. I was working out an algebra problem on my bed. He came over to me, dropped his pants, and put his butt in my face. "Your luck, I haven't used it for anything except a couple of farts all day. Lick it," he said, bending over, holding his cheeks apart. It was smelly and permanently stained. His testicles hung loose and low, and I took them in my hand, rolling them like Bogart's *Caine Mutiny* balls. "Get in," he said. I buried my face there, tickled his asshole with the tip of my tongue and made him laugh.

Saturday, on her way to the grocery store, my mother dropped us off at the park. "Shall I come back for you when I'm finished?" she asked.

"No," he said, flatly.

"No, thanks," I said. "We'll find our way."

"Ever fuck a girl?" he asked, as we cut across the grass, past the playground, past the baseball fields and toward the woods.

"No."

"Ever want to?"

"No."

"Wanna watch?" he said, taking me to a picnic table, where a girl I recognized from school was standing, arms crossed in front of her chest. "It's twelve-thirty, you're late," she said. The girl looked at me and blinked. "Oh, hi. We're in history together, right?"

I nodded and looked at my shoes.

"Miss me?" he asked, kissing the girls neck, hard.

My eyes hyperfocused and zeroed in on his lips, on her skin, on the feathery blond hair at the base of her skull. When he pulled away, the hair was wet, the skin was purple and red. There were teeth marks.

She stood in the clearing, eyes closed. He reached for her hand and led her into the woods. I followed, keeping a certain distance between them and me.

In the trees, he pulled his T-shirt off over his head. She ran her fingernails slowly up and down the fishbone of fur sticking out of his Levi's. He tugged at the top of her jeans.

"Take 'em off," he said, in a familiar and desperate voice.

"Who do you think you're kidding," she said.

"Show me yours," he said, rubbing the front of his Levi's with an open palm, "and I'll show you mine."

"That's okay, thanks," she said, backing away.

He went toward her, she stepped back again. He stuck his leg behind her, tripping her. She fell to the ground. He stepped on her open palms, holding her down with his Nikes.

"This isn't funny," she said.

He laughed.

He unzipped his pants and peed on her. She screamed, and he aimed the river at her mouth. Her lips sealed and her head turned away. Torrent released, he shook it off on her, put it away, and stepped from her hands.

She raised herself. Urine ran down her cheeks, onto her blouse, down her blouse and into her jeans. Arms spread, faces twisted, together she and I ran out of the woods, screaming as though doused in gasoline, as though afire.

Acknowledgments

Grateful acknowledgment is made for permission to reprint the following copyrighted works:

"Arthur Snatchfold" from *The Life to Come and Other Short Stories* by E. M. Forster. Reprinted by permission of W. W. Norton & Company, Inc., King's College, Cambridge and The Society of Authors as the literary representatives of the E. M. Forster Estate. Copyright © 1972 by The Provost and Scholars of King's College, Cambridge.

"Sally Bowles" from *Berlin Stories* by Christopher Isherwood. Copyright 1945 by Christopher Isherwood. Reprinted by permission of Curtis Brown Ltd.

"Me and the Girls" from *Star Quality: The Collected Stories of Noël Coward* by Noël Coward. Copyright 1939, 1951, © 1963, 1964, 1965, 1966, 1967, 1983 by the Estate of Noël Coward. Used by permission of the publisher, Dutton Signet, a division of Penguin Books USA Inc., and Michael Imison Playwrights Ltd.

Selection from *My Father and Myself* by J. R. Ackerley. Copyright © 1968 by J. R. Ackerley. Reprinted by permission of The Putnam Publishing Group and David Higham Associates. Published in Great Britain by The Bodley Head.

"May We Borrow Your Husband?" from *May We Borrow Your Husband?* by Graham Greene. Copyright © 1962 by Graham Greene. Used by permission of Viking Penguin, a division of Penguin Books USA Inc., and David Higham Associates.

by permission of Random House, Inc., and International Creative Management, Inc.

"Good with Words" by Stephen Greco. First appeared in *Advocate Men*. By permission of the author.

"Nothing to Ask For" by Dennis McFarland. First appeared in *The New Yorker*. Copyright © 1989 by Dennis McFarland. Reprinted by permission of Brandt & Brandt Literary Agents, Inc.

"Run, Mourner, Run" from *Let the Dead Bury Their Dead* by Randall Kenan. Copyright © 1992 by Randall Kenan. Reprinted by permission of Harcourt Brace Jovanovich, Inc.

"Atlantis," "Capichee?", "Sudden Extinction," "Leaving," "The Origin of Roget's Thesaurus," and "Childless" (re-titled "Six Fables") from *Maps to Anywhere* by Bernard Cooper. © 1990 by Bernard Cooper. By permission of The University of Georgia Press.

"Perrin and the Fallen Angel" from *Dangerous Desires* by Peter Wells. Copyright © 1991 by Peter Wells. Used by permission of Viking Penguin, a division of Penguin Books USA Inc., Reed Publishing (NZ) Ltd., and Michael Gifkins & Associates.

"My Mother's Clothes: The School of Beauty and Shame" by Richard McCann. © 1986 by Richard McCann. Originally appeared in *The Atlantic Monthly*. Reprinted by permission of Brandt & Brandt Literary Agents, Inc.

"A Place I've Never Been" from *A Place I've Never Been* by David Leavitt. First appeared in *Arete*. Copyright © David Leavitt, 1990. By permission of Viking Penguin, a division of Penguin Books USA Inc., and Penguin Books Ltd.

"Self-Portrait in Twenty-three Rounds" from *Close to the Knives: A Memoir of Disintegration* by David Wojnarowicz (Vintage Books, 1991, U.S.A.; Serpent's Tail, 1992, Great Britain). Reprinted by permission of the Estate of David Wojnarowicz.

"Jump or Dive" by Peter Cameron. Copyright © 1985 by Peter Cameron. Reprinted by permission of Curtis Brown Ltd. First appeared in *The New Yorker*, June 17, 1985.

"A Real Doll" from *The Safety of Objects* by A. M. Homes. Originally published in *Christopher Street* magazine. Copyright 1990 by A. M. Homes. By permission of Donadio & Ashworth, Inc.

"Duck Duck Goose" (retitled "The Whiz Kids") by A. M. Homes. Originally published in *Christopher Street* magazine. Copyright 1992 by A. M. Homes. By permission of Donadio & Ashworth, Inc.